# PRAISE FOR THE RISING DAWN SAGA:

## FOR THE EXODUS GATE:

"This is not for light readers, but for someone who wants to leave reality behind and be swept up into Zimmer's imagination."

**-Bitten By Books**

"I give The Exodus Gate a resounding 8/10 – incredibly imaginative and highly enjoyable, and I really looking forward to Book 2, *The Storm Guardians*."

**-DaveBrendon's Fantasy and Sci-Fi Weblog**

"...a book that Fantasy Book Review recommends for lovers of thoughtful-fantasy."

**-Fantasy Book Review**

"*The Exodus Gate*, Stephen Zimmer's first full length novel, is an enjoyable modern fantasy book and a promising debut."

**-Speculative Book Review**

"Overall, it's a fine start to what promises to be an awesome saga that will keep you reading for days (in between a nap or two, of course)."

**-SpecMusicMuse Review**

## FOR THE STORM GUARDIANS:

"Once again, Zimmer has used his command of cinematic imagery to give us a spectacular vision of war both heavenly and hellish."

**-Pure Reason Book Reviews**

"I love Zimmer's imagination, as each of his creatures play a pivotal role in the bigger picture. Unfortunately, for every auspicious being there is an ominous beast lurking in the shadows. Zimmer's weave of fantasy and religious fables leaves the reader sated"

**-Bitten by Books**

"The expanding conflict first begun in *The Exodus Gate* takes the reader up several notches on the intensity chart in this second book. The only down turn to this whole novel is waiting for the next installment. Zimmer's Rising Dawn Saga has classic written all over it!"

**-Yellow30 SciFi**

# PRAISE FOR THE FIRES IN EDEN SERIES:

## FOR CROWN OF VENGEANCE:

"This reads like a modern day C.S. Lewis and Zimmer manages to pull it all off with great aplomb."

**-Fantasy Book Review**

"I almost never have time to read books anymore, but once I started reading Crown of Vengeance, I found myself squeaking time in whenever possible"

**-Watch Play Read**

"Epic Fantasy at its best, that is what Stephen Zimmer offers us in his riveting series Fires in Eden."

**-Realms and Galaxies**

"Stephen Zimmer is a master of words. He creates intricate people and places that are both wondrous and exciting. Beautiful imagery and amazing characters are found in this book."

**-Bee's Knees Reviews**

"Gear up, for it will leave you breathless and wanting more! Put this one on the top of your Must Read List today."

**-Yellow30 Sci Fi**

## FOR DREAM OF LEGENDS

"Dream of Legends is a solid installment to the Fires in Eden series and left me hanging on to read book three."

**-Bookworm Blues**

"Like Crown of Vengeance, Dream of Legends is definitely a book for people who like character driven stories with gorgeous and detailed descriptions of a fantasy world and their inhabitants."

**-Edi's Book Lighthouse**

"...if you're looking for a rich and florid fantasy this book should meet your needs."

**- Azure Dwarf's Horde of Sci-Fi and Fantasy**

# THE SEVENTH THRONE

# THE
# SEVENTH
# THRONE

## STEPHEN ZIMMER

Editor: Amanda DeBord

Published by Seventh Star Press, LLC.

ISBN Number 9780983740247

Library of Congress Control Number: 2011910829

Seventh Star Press
www.seventhstarpress.com
info@seventhstarpress.com

Publisher's Note:
*The Seventh Throne* is a work of fiction. All names, characters, and places
are the product of the author's imagination, used in fictitious manner.
Any resemblances to actual persons, places, locales, events, etc.
is purely coincidental.

Printed in the United States of America

First Edition

# DEDICATION

To the One Who transcends the limitations of time, gravity, and space…inviting us to infinite realms, containing infinite possibilities.

# ACKNOWLEDGEMENTS

I would like to salute and extend a heartfelt thanks to my reader-friends for continuing with me on this journey. Your support and encouragement really lifts me up on the tougher days, and I will always give you every last bit of effort I have within me.

Despite attempting to get away by moving to the west coast, Matthew Perry, you have not been able to evade me just yet! However, the creation of something truly unique and rare in the realms of speculative fiction continues with the body of artwork crafted for these books. I am tremendously relieved that you have not decided to spend all your time sunning on a beach and drinking margaritas. While I'm sure that would be fun, your artistic talent is far too good to allow it to stay idle. You are an amazing friend. Hang in there, we are building something very exciting here!

I am so glad and honored to have Amanda DeBord as my editor on this series. I hope that these books have been fun for you to work with. Know that I always strive to deliver you the cleanest copy that I can, and catch the things that you have helped me recognize more clearly. You have helped me grow and improve as a writer, and I really thank you for being so fantastic to work with!

To my mother, who continues to demonstrate a toughness that is incredible to witness. You are definitely an inspiration, as you have always been, and I can't express how appreciative I am for your steadfast support and love, even though I've chosen a rather crazy and unconventional path in life.

To Brooke Raby and all of my friends at Joseph-Beth Booksellers in Lexington, Kentucky. You have always made me feel like a million-selling author, and you have always given my work a home on your shelves since *The Exodus Gate* was first released. You have stood with me since the beginning, and will always have a very special place in my heart. It is a real honor and blessing to have a home in Joseph-Beth Booksellers.

"A nation of sheep will beget a government of wolves."
– Edward R. Murrow


"I believe there are more instances of the abridgement of freedom
of the people by gradual and silent encroachments by those in
power than by violent and sudden usurpations."
-James Madison


"Freedom is the right to tell people what they do not want to hear."
-George Orwell


"If you want total security, go to prison. There you're fed, clothed,
given medical care and soon. The only thing lacking...is freedom."
-Dwight D. Eisenhower


"Freedom is not worth having if it does not connote
freedom to err."
-Mohandas Gandhi


"It is well enough that people of the nation do not understand
our banking and monetary system, for if they did, I believe there
would be a revolution before tomorrow morning."
-Henry Ford


"The most important of all revolutions, a revolution in sentiments,
manners and moral opinions."
-Edmund Burke

# SECTION I

# JUAN

"It would seem that these are all disparate groups, from all over the world, with widely different agendas. But in truth, their efforts are focused upon a unified, singular purpose ... something that is called the Convergence, by the ones that know the truth underlying it all," Father Wilson Rader stated, with an air of deep solemnity. "Doesn't matter if it is the Society of the Red Shield, the Order of the Temple, or any of the others involved in this far-reaching cabal. Some of these groups have been around for a great many centuries, and a few are the equivalent of upstarts. All that matters to the ones holding the strings at the top is the Convergence, and achieving what lies at its ultimate end."

Everything that the priest was saying resonated with Juan Delgado, and what he had experienced. Yet it was still difficult to grasp the enormity of everything coming to light in the wake of his defection from Babylon Technologies. He was looking behind many doors that had only recently been opened for him, and the things that were being exposed were frightening to contemplate.

He was eminently grateful for the refuge offered by the two Universalist priests, and had good cause to be. He knew that if he took one step off the church property, he would be entering a dangerous environment.

The threat went far beyond being followed, or placed under surveillance. There was little doubt in his mind that if he were trusted to his own devices and not afforded protection, a perilous shadow would envelop him swiftly.

He had not been able to live with himself in the weeks following his first visit to Saint Bosco, the storied church in downtown Troy, in the wake of the gathering in the Grove River Valley. It was what had compelled him to walk away from the career that he had devoted every ounce of his energy to. But he was savvy enough to recognize the enormity of what was happening at Babylon, and how someone like himself would not be allowed to simply walk away.

There was no longer any doubt in his heart that something terrible had happened to Nathan Morris, the individual from Juan's division who had given the virtual reality device to Benedict Darwin. Nathan's nighttime plunge down the side of his downtown, high-rise apartment building was no suicide.

Juan sank back into the plush, black leather of the high-backed chair. He looked across at Father Rader, and then at Father Brunner, who was sitting in a similar chair to the other priest's right.

The contrasts between the two men were many, more than once providing Juan with a source of personal amusement over the few weeks that he had been harbored at Saint Bosco. On many a winter night, when the snow was falling in abundance all over Troy, and the winds were howling, he had enjoyed lengthy visits with the two men. The differences between the two always surfaced quickly, as they sat together drinking wine or brandy, conversing on a wide range of fascinating topics at the end of a day.

Father Rader spoke in a gentle, softer tone of voice, where Father Brunner's deep timbre was filled with a robust undercurrent of youthful energy. Juan had to stifle grins more than once during Father Brunner's homilies, noting how Father Rader's observations were entirely correct; the younger priest's voice seemed to drop an entire octave during his homilies, taking on a resonant, authoritative hue.

Father Brunner always tried to dismiss the claim, which made Juan determine to record one of the homilies some day, to prove it to him.

Father Rader was a slender man, of average height, who moved with an easy step. His face was angular in the nose, cheekbones, and chin, with darker locks of wavy, gray-flecked hair, parted in the middle of his forehead. He was wearing a yellow cotton shirt, and tan slacks, the kind of attire he wore about half of the time, whenever he was not clad in his black pants, and black shirt, with its distinctive white collar.

Father Brunner was a little shorter, and stocky of build, with a rounded face and dense, short-cropped brown hair. As always, he was garbed in his full-length, black cassock, clothing that hearkened back to much earlier periods in the Church's history.

Their appearances and styles were indeed very different, but both had quickly proven themselves to be true friends to Juan. It always impressed him how clearly they saw both themselves and their work as part of a much greater mission.

Juan glanced up to where Father Brunner's white cat Simeon was perched on the uppermost shelf of a high bookcase. Given the serious matter being discussed, he had to hold back the chortle that threatened to escape as he observed the cat's stoic posture, and serene gaze, as the creature peered down upon the three men. The cat looked as if it was supervising the three humans, and keeping a watch up for any kind of threat or disturbance.

He brought his full attention back to Father Rader, before Simeon had a further chance to elicit a response from him.

"I have heard that exact word from the lips of Dagian Underwood herself, several times before, in fact," Juan said, thinking back to the trip to the Grove River Valley, where the Living ID, and what it could empower, had been revealed to the world's elite.

"Dagian Underwood is at the pinnacle of the Convergence, the innermost circle of this cabal. And she is one of those who, more than most involved, understands just what the Convergence is truly about," Father Rader iterated.

"Don't they all?" Juan asked, his brow furrowing.

Father Brunner shook his head, and leaned forward slightly. There was no sign of the joviality that so often graced the priest's face. "Most who are working towards the aims of the Convergence don't really know what they are pawns of. They are simply men and women of great wealth and power, who share simple, common interests, reflecting nothing more than very prevalent aspects of human nature.

"The consolidation of their power, in bringing about a secure, global order, is a highly attractive thing to them. It makes the variables they face and deal with that much easier to manipulate and control. The levers of power can be worked much more efficiently from a global stage, you see. And this is all that they really believe they are working for ... self-interests, control, market manipulation, and other related issues, on a level that they could only dream about before. They just want to go on their merry way, accumulating ever more power and wealth. They have no interest in, or even awareness of, the Power they are truly serving."

Father Rader chuckled. "It always amuses me that so many of these groups are casually dismissed as the sordid stuff of wild-eyed conspiracy theorists, when they are merely reflections of some of the more basic elements of human experience.

"Like Father Brunner illustrated, they are nothing more than groups of people with shared interests, working together to advance their own security and well-being. You can see the same dynamics working at times in this very church's committees and ministry groups, albeit with a much less sinister edge. Then again, the spats and agendas existing among factions and individuals in a church community are more than enough for me to deal with on most days."

The three men laughed at Father Rader's last comment, a welcome moment of levity given the heaviness of the topic being discussed.

Juan shook his head as the laughter settled, and his grin took on a more rueful tilt. "But if you look at all these groups involved with the Convergence, they represent the heights of worldwide economic and political power. A transnational union, or an unholy alliance, whatever you want to call it, of government and business. They hold everyone's purse strings, and they command all the armies and police forces. What in the world can stop them from reaching their goals?"

"Nothing of the world can stop them. They are serving the One who has authority over the powers of the world," Father Rader replied grimly.

"That sounds very hopeful," retorted Juan, with a thick measure of sarcasm.

Father Rader grinned. "I did not say that nothing can stop them … only that nothing of this world can stop them."

Juan thought back to the profound experience that had occurred when he had first encountered Father Brunner and Father Rader. He could still remember it all vividly enough, when had walked into the church, and had encountered the white-garbed, dark-haired stranger.

Juan had seen the fearsome, towering entities standing to each side of the altar, as well as the sprightly, buoyant, little ones drifting gracefully about the church. All was unseen to everyone but him, as new believers in the church were undergoing an Anointing on their path to becoming full-fledged members of the Universal Church.

The tall, otherworldly figures flanking the altar had exuded an imposing aura, rife with an intimidating sense of power, while the small, delicate-looking beings gliding throughout the nave of the church had radiated a feeling brimming with love and welcoming. Yet Juan had no doubt that both were of the same origin.

Juan had since come to understand that the beings he had witnessed were Avatars, of the kind that he had previously known about only in stories and scriptural writings. He wished that he could gain more answers about what he had observed, knowing in his heart that he had not seen even an inkling of what existed within the realms veiled to the human eye. The profound experience had opened his eyes to the idea of vast, incredible new realities, and it was in this context that he more readily received the somber words of the two priests regarding the Convergence.

Juan sat up a little straighter in his chair.

"But we ... and I mean the three of us here, in this room ... are still a part of the world whose powers are under this other Authority, as you have said," Juan said.

The two priests nodded.

"And?" Father Brunner asked, when Juan hesitated to continue.

"Well, I am as close to certain as I can be that eyes are fixed on this place, at the direct request of Dagian," Juan said. "And we know whose side they are on. That's easy enough to figure out.

"What I want to know, and what I've been meaning to ask you, is whether we have anything helping us, in the shadow of all these numerous groups, organizations, think-tanks, financial institutions, military forces, and everything else that seems to be at the beck and call of the Convergence."

"We've got Athanasius, and so far it looks like he's doing a fair job of keeping Dagian's minions at bay," Father Brunner jested, reaching down to scratch the broad head of the hulking mastiff lying quietly by the side of the chair.

While his question had been entirely serious, Juan smiled, and certainly was not about to dispute the formidable nature of the huge canine.

"Might you be referring to ... the Order?" Father Rader then interjected, with no trace of humor, as he shared a glance with Father Brunner.

"The Order?" Juan queried, looking between the two men.

He did not miss the faint nod that Father Brunner gave to Father Rader, as some sort of agreement passed between them.

"We haven't spoken to you of the Order before," Father Rader said. "But perhaps it is time that you learn of the Order, not the least so that you don't feel like we are completely isolated in this world. There's much more to the story, but we'll start there. John, do you want to begin to address this one?"

"That would be fine," Father Brunner said, nodding to Father Rader, as he turned to look at Juan. "The Order is worldwide, and its roots go back many centuries. Originally, the group of individuals that evolved into the Order ran hospitals in the Holy Lands, during the Holy Wars, in medieval times. Over the course of many years, they developed a military aspect, going so far as becoming an officially recognized monastic order, run by brother knights."

"They fought in a host of battles, and protected pilgrims for year after year, but eventually the last of the Holy Wars came to an end," Father Rader said, taking over from the other priest. "But the work of the Order did not end there, as it had discovered a deeper, more pressing mission during the course of those centuries. It moved forward on this greater task, even as the forces involved in the Convergence gained ever-greater traction. Less public, but no less present, the Order developed a worldwide network to resist the Convergence on many levels, economic, cultural, and otherwise … right up to this day and onward."

"Modern day knights, you mean?" Juan asked incredulously, having heard of nothing like it before. "You mean there's a real Order that has existed continuously since the Holy Wars?"

"I'm sure it is pretty incredible to hear about this for the first time, but all of it is absolutely true," Father Brunner commented, with a huge grin that shined through his close-cropped beard.

"Are they all … still monks?" Juan asked.

"The Knights of the Order are of many backgrounds and professions, bringing a full array of skills and resources to bear in resisting the Convergence," Father Brunner said. "Even if the prophecies we hold to heart say that Diabolos will achieve total, worldwide dominion prior to the Last Battle, nobody ever said that Diabolos would not have to limp into that Last Battle bruised and battered, with a couple of black eyes for good measure."

"Fatalistic, but spirited," Juan said, in a light-hearted tone. "So, are they the only ones out there?"

"No, they are not the only ones. You would probably find the Shield Maidens of the Rising Dawn intriguing as well, among the other groups on our side of the equation, but we'll save that subject for a little later," Father Brunner responded, with a knowing wink towards Father Rader.

"Let's just say, at the very least, we'll make sure that our adversaries don't achieve their aims so easily. I also believe that they won't have time to savor much of anything, before Adonai's Legions issue forth to challenge them in open battle," Father Rader stated, with a flare in his eyes. His voice then took on a yearning lilt. "And how I wish I could witness that timeless moment, when the luminous gate of the White City opens, and the Liberator leads forth the great host for the final battle."

"And I as well," Father Brunner said, "so that all of us can get to the business of true life, beyond all of this wickedness and sorrow that surrounds us here."

"Sounds like we are kind of like exiles," Juan observed. "Exiles who haven't been allowed back home, at least not just yet."

"Wisely said, Juan," Father Rader responded. "As an exile often carries a constant longing deep within, to return to that state of feeling at home once again."

"I'm far from home, in my heart, but I intend to find my way there again," Juan replied, with a wistful smile, thinking of his mother, and his time growing up in a household that was wealthy in love, if poor in material things. "I was there once, so at least I know what I am looking for."

"You are on your way, Juan," Father Brunner said. "But the path there will be far from easy to take. It will be narrow, and require much focus. But we will help you as much as we can."

"We will," Father Rader added.

"And I hope that I will be able to do something for the two of you, given the risks you are taking in helping me," Juan said.

"Whatever may come, first things first," Father Brunner declared. "And that is keeping you out of the clutches of Dagian and her reprehensible kind."

As if offering his own gesture of support, Athanasius got up to his paws, and lumbered slowly over to Juan, setting his great head down on Juan's thigh. The huge dog looked up into Juan's face with its large, soulful eyes, drawing a smile from the church's guest.

"Do you think she'd be brazen enough to come onto the church grounds?" Juan asked, knowing the answer even as he asked the question.

"Without question, and she's got the kind of influence to create a justification," Father Rader said.

"But don't worry, because we've been batting around some ideas, and we've been coming up with some rather unique ones on how to handle this," Father Brunner said, as a smile formed.

Juan wondered what the priests were up to, but they did not volunteer any further information. The conversation soon turned to other, lighter topics, and Father Brunner brought out his favorite brandy, with glasses for Father Rader and Juan.

# FRIEDRICH

The ethereal, rainbow-hued skies had long since showered down an abundance of the hallowed sustenance that was such a grace to all of the souls dwelling in a state of exile within the Middle Lands. A relaxed, timeless feeling pervaded, with not a trace of danger to the air, even within eyesight of the edge of the Abyss.

The reigning serenity was so different from how things had been when the living storm from the Abyss had erupted, blackening the skies and sending a flood of monstrosities and fiery, infernal legions into the Middle Lands. Not a speck of that terrible battle could be seen now, and unless one knew otherwise, it would have been difficult to imagine that such a beautiful sea of tranquility had been wreathed in dark violence so very recently.

Shimmering, golden swathes of high grasses swayed back and forth in a slow rhythm, as if reacting to something beyond the ken of the area's inhabitants. Leaping and bounding through the lustrous grasses, the two-headed Orthun chased vigorously after the diminutive fairy, Asa'an, as she flitted through a swathe of resplendent silver and golden flowers by the edge of a crystalline lake.

Though the creature was huge and brawny, and its two sets of massive jaws displayed prominent sets of fangs, it was hard for Friedrich to call to mind an image of the snarling, fearful beast for whom he had intervened, following the great battle with Beleth's hellish legions.

Eating of the pure white Manna, and drinking of the sacred waters that flowed from their origins beyond the ramparts of the White City, the Orthun had been restored to full vitality. Its tan coat gave off a gleaming sheen, with not a single scar or other sign of injury to be found.

The Orthun had been sorely wounded, and was on the verge of having its awareness expire, when Friedrich had come upon the creature following the horrific battle. It was still not certain to Friedrich how the creatures spawned within the Abyss ultimately functioned in comparison to the things of the natural order, and at the moment that he came upon the Orthun he had no way of knowing whether the creature even possessed an enduring soul.

Regardless, Friedrich's deep impulse was to spare the creature when he was approached by three of Adonai's mighty Avatars; Bahraranges, Zehanpuryu, and the fearsome Katzfiel, bearing the great, lightning-emitting sword.

The High Avatars had appeared ready to allow judgment on the wounded Orthun, to be delivered via Katzfiel's incredible sword. But Friedrich had chosen the path of mercy, seeking to spare the unfortunate beast that had known nothing other than hate and torture throughout its entire existence.

Even so, Katzfiel had appeared to proceed with the judgment, dismaying Friedrich to the core of his spirit. That was when the terrible sword had abruptly plunged into the ground before the Orthun, delivering not even a nick to the creature, as it pierced the surface and brought up a pool of the Waters of Life.

Friedrich had been instructed to give the Waters of Life to the Orthun, which healed the creature's most grievous wounds. The High Avatars had highly commended him for his deep wisdom and the choice of mercy, and the Orthun had been given over to his care and responsibility.

It was a lesson for Friedrich's own existence, a vivid example that the power of mercy transcended even that of justice in the Great Court of Adonai. Friedrich had since realized that Adonai's mercy was what allowed him to survive in Purgatarion following his mortal death, when justice alone would have consigned his own spirit to the Abyss.

That incredible moment of realization had resonated with him often since, as it did then while looking out upon the Orthun bounding happy and free through the tall, golden grasses, pursuing Asa'an.

"Seele, come over here, and stop pestering Asa'an," Friedrich called out, from where he stood a short distance from the lakeshore.

One of the Orthun's heads turned his way, followed by the second, and in a moment the creature was charging rapidly across the ground towards him. It barreled into Friedrich without pause, pinning him to the ground with its broad paws, as each of the massive heads lowered to lick each side of his face.

Friedrich was simply glad that he was in a world not governed firmly by physical laws, and that his spiritual form had no bones to be shaken. As things were, it felt like falling back into a mass of feathered pillows.

"You asked for it," Asa'an called, laughing merrily, as she drifted over on her delicate wings to hover nearby.

"Yes, I suppose I did," Friedrich replied, laughing as he cast a glance towards the Peri. "Maybe I should let him swat you around for a little while longer."

"If he can catch me," Asa'an retorted, with a boastful edge, grinning down at Friedrich.

Friedrich winked up at the Orthun, who stared at him for a moment, as he conveyed a specific image to the creature's mind. It was a method of communication that had grown swiftly between the two, a sharper, more specific version of the kind of rapport that Friedrich had enjoyed with his dog Midnight during his mortal life.

In a flash of movement, the Orthun whirled abruptly, and lightly batted Asa'an with its broad right paw, sending the little Peri tumbling head over heel through the air for a few moments, until she regained control of her flight.

"No fair, he had assistance!" Asa'an huffed, gathering her composure, and casting a pouting expression back at Friedrich.

Friedrich laughed, and to all eyes it looked as if the Orthun was laughing too, as its tongues lolled out from both of its heads. Asa'an flared up at the mirth of the other two, and her entire body brightened.

Friedrich was convinced that Asa'an and her ilk perceived themselves as High Avatars, as there seemed to be nothing that they were not willing to take on. He was highly relieved that she had managed to make it through the terrible fighting against Beleth's legions, especially when the ferocious, bestial Deevs, immortal enemies of the Peris, made their appearance on the battlefield and targeted their hated foes.

That thought brought another chuckle to Friedrich, as he remembered his friend Valaris swatting Deevs with abandon out of the air with a huge grin on his face. It was not entirely unlike the sight of the Orthun batting Asa'an about, though she was admittedly much more comely of appearance than were the savage Deevs. It was hard for Friedrich to accept that the two kinds of spirits had once been on the same side, that of Diabolos.

"Speechless, are you?" Friedrich chided as the little Peri continued to glare at him.

"Why do I continue to be your friend? You human spirits have such hubris," Asa'an snapped back at him.

"And we love having fun with our friends," Friedrich said, rumbling with laughter at Asa'an's continued consternation. "Including teasing and playing jokes on them from time to time."

Asa'an could not brood for overly long, and the gaiety returned to her as she broke into a joyous laughter. "I suppose I have underestimated him."

"I see your new companion has settled in quite well," came a melodious voice, as Friedrich looked up to see the tall form of Enki gliding down, three pairs of wings outstretched, to alight a few paces away.

At first, the Avatar dwarfed him in size, but Enki quickly reduced his stature until he merely towered over Friedrich. With broad, translucent wings, and a body composed of uncountable, minute tongues of fire, the familiar Avatar was always a vision of radiance and majesty. The luminous wings retracted inward, as if folding smoothly into the Avatar's back.

"It is wonderful to see you again, Enki," Friedrich stated, getting back to his feet, and nodding his head in sincere respect towards the high-ranking servant of Adonai.

A hint of mirth played about the dynamic face of the Avatar, as its blazing eyes regarded Friedrich and his two companions. "You have been quite an inspiration to many, and your incident after the battle with your new friend has been spoken of with great regard beyond the gates of the White City," Enki stated.

The Avatar gazed down upon the Orthun. The creature did not cower, but it stayed to the back of Friedrich. Asa'an hovered a little farther back, and Friedrich could sense the Peri's nervousness in the presence of the powerful Avatar.

There were still some vestiges of fear that had not yet worked their way out of the Orthun. Asa'an, like the others of her kind, also carried a deeply ingrained anxiety concerning the greater Avatars, the unease remnants of the days when Enki and the others loyal to Adonai had been her enemies, during the dark age when the Peris had served Diabolos.

"Come, Seele," Enki beckoned to the Orthun, the words having a sweet tone to them that dispelled any fears of threat.

Heads lowering just a little, the big creature padded slowly towards Enki, coming to a halt before the Avatar.

Leaning over, Enki placed a fiery hand upon each of the creature's heads, calling a blessing upon the Orthun from the beneficence of the Great Throne of Adonai. The flames of Enki's body did not burn the creature, though Friedrich sensed that something of power and grace passed through the touch of Enki into the Orthun.

Enki straightened back up, growing quiet and very still for an extended period of time.

Friedrich looked intently at the Avatar, taking note of the entity's change in mood. Radiant and mighty, a creature of purity and light, Enki was still a conscious spirit capable of feeling. Enki was one of the Avatars that Friedrich most often encountered across the expanse of Purgatarion, frequently enough that he had gained a little sense of familiarity with the powerful creature.

He had witnessed Enki growing silent and distant on many occasions, but had never felt comfortable enough to make a personal inquiry of one of Adonai's High Avatars. The current instance proved to be different, even if he was still gripped with considerable anxiety.

"Enki, I have a question that I wish to ask, without giving offense to you, as I do not know whether it is my place to question you," Friedrich ventured, regretting giving voice to the words as soon as he had set them free.

"Did you ever ask questions of Adonai before?" Enki replied, turning his head towards Friedrich.

Friedrich nodded slowly, looking up into the fiery eyes of the Avatar. Inwardly, he was trembling. "Yes."

"Then certainly you can ask questions of a creature, if you can ask questions of that creature's Creator," Enki responded. "Who would I be to accord myself immunity, when Adonai does not forbid any soul's questions before the Great Throne?"

Friedrich girded his resolve, encouraged by the response of Enki.

"I have noticed that you often draw silent, as you have now. I have also witnessed Israfel gazing into the Abyss, with tremendous sorrow, more than once, and I know that Avatars can certainly feel sorrow and pain," Friedrich said, gently. "It sorrows me to see you in moments when you seem greatly saddened yourself. I am just a mere Exile, and I know that I presume much in asking this of you, but what is it that causes you such a terrible sorrow?"

Enki remained quiet for several moments, and Friedrich feared that he had treaded too far with the Avatar. At last, Enki nodded, and answered.

"A separation exists that burns within my own spirit," Enki said. "Erishkegal, who is somewhere deep in that infinite Abyss, is always in my spirit, and in my mind. My very essence, where it attends the Great Throne, sorrows over her fate. Only the Grace of Adonai keeps my spirit from being entirely consumed over the loss of her, so long ago. My only hope is that she is yet out of the reach of Diabolos."

"I have heard something of this. Of how Erishkegal gathered up some of the offspring of the Fallen Avatars and humans, seeking to spare them from the Great Deluge that was loosed upon the world. It is said that she was convinced that the ones with her were outcasts of their kind, who had not done evil in the world, as had their brethren," Friedrich said in a low, sympathetic voice, feeling the pain of Enki like pulsating waves of heat.

"And she was correct. The creatures that she had gathered up had not followed the path of wickedness that their kindred had taken," Enki said. "They were outcasts, hated by their own kind, such that they themselves would have been hunted down, slain to the last by the fell Avatars and their blood-lusted progeny. Erishkegal was very, very dear to me, as we shared a special bond throughout all time. A misunderstood Avatar, whose gentle nature brought her an inviolable strength, she sought only to bring mercy to the outcast, frightened creatures."

The radiance of Enki shifted, and Friedrich was flooded with feelings of deep, burning sorrow that emanated from the Avatar. He felt the tremendous sadness that endured within the eternal creature before him, at an intimate level that could not be conveyed by words. At once, he regretted having evoked the raw feelings by his questions.

Again, as if the Avatar had sensed his thoughts, Enki spoke, "This sorrow is always present, even if dwelling deep inside my spirit. It is nothing for you to feel guilt over. I simply miss Erishkegal, and I cannot hope to find her whereabouts in the Abyss, even when I am certain in the innermost part of my spirit that she could return to the White City, and bring those with her along. I do not know what purpose keeps her hidden within the darkness, and I fear that I may never discover it. Not until time itself is brought to an end. And only Adonai knows when that moment will come."

"Why cannot she be found?" Friedrich asked, perplexed by the thought that an immensely powerful Avatar like Enki could by stymied in such a seemingly minor way.

"The Abyss, even more so than Purgatarion, is part of that which has been separated from the fullness of Adonai," Enki explained. "As a creature in Adonai's Grace, I cannot traverse the Abyss with the same connection that I have with the beings dwelling in the realms beyond the White City.

"The Abyss is a bottomless chasm, with all manner of dangers, even beyond the Adversary's Ten-Fold realm. Unless I have some manner of bearing, a faint sense of her to focus upon, then I cannot hope to find her. It would be a rash and foolhardy path for me to try, searching blindly through infinity."

Friedrich listened to Enki's words carefully, harboring a great degree of sympathy, even as he felt a tighter bond forming with the High Avatar.

"So your very nature, as an Avatar of Adonai, is the greatest barrier in your search for Erishkegal," Friedrich observed.

"It is a terrible irony to think of," Enki said. "That being in full harmony with a realm of the purest love prevents me from finding one whom I love dearly."

The wings of Enki then unfurled from behind his back.

"But alas, I do not wish to burden you with this abiding pain I carry, and I must return to my duties in the service of the Great Throne," Enki stated. The melancholic tone of his layered voice suddenly lightened. "But it was good to see you, that obstinate Peri, and your newest companion. Seele is progressing quite well, and Adonai has granted him further healing, this very day."

Friedrich thought of the blessing that the Avatar had given the Orthun. "And for that, I am grateful to Adonai, and to you for carrying out the blessing. Thank you, Enki."

"It is a joy to carry out such a task," Enki said. "Farewell for now, Precious Soul. I am sure that it will not be long before we meet again."

With silken grace, Enki took to flight, and soared upward, hastening towards the multi-hued firmament. Friedrich watched the form of the Avatar grow smaller in the distance, before disappearing at last within the shimmering, vivid spectrum.

Something like tears welled up, and began to fall down from the eyes of Friedrich, though the shimmering drops were not anything physical in nature. They were the purest substance of emotion, and he could not stop them from emerging as he sorrowed over the bitter plight of his personal friend; for that is what Enki had essentially become to Friedrich, at the moment that the Avatar had confided his individual pain to the Exile.

"Who was I to ask him about such a thing? What can a weakling like me hope to do, when one such as Enki is confounded?" Friedrich bemoaned.

"Do not cry, Friedrich," Asa'an said gently, fluttering at his right shoulder.

He felt the tingle of her little hand, as she wiped at his eyes, a spirit-hand brushing against a spirit-face.

He felt his left hand lifted up by the Orthun, as Seele pushed it upward, and nuzzled its other head gently against him. The creature emitted a low whine, as if echoing the sadness within Friedrich.

Friedrich felt at a severe loss, burning with the desire to do something for his Avatar friend, while knowing that he was just an Exile: an imperfect soul struggling towards the moment that he could approach the White City's unsullied radiance.

"Maybe what you think of as weakness could be something to use on behalf of Enki," Asa'an suggested in a low, soft voice, after a long period had passed.

"Meaning?" asked Friedrich.

"That Enki cannot probe the Abyss, due to the perfect state of his spirit, while you, like me, are still imperfect."

Something within her words tugged at him, and he turned his eyes towards the little being.

"How can being flawed be an advantage?" Friedrich asked the Peri.

"Maybe you can help him, as you might not be obstructed in the same way," Asa'an explained further. "Something within you is still corrupted with the nature of the Abyss, and perhaps that connection can be turned to some manner of use."

The Peri was onto something of significance. That much Friedrich knew, as he turned the notion over and over within his mind.

"Go, and play with Seele," Friedrich asked the Peri. "I need some time to meditate on what you have said."

A look of curiosity formed on the Peri's face, but she did not press him for an explanation. Gliding forward, she looked down at the Orthun.

"Come on, Seele, see if you can catch me now," she called to the creature.

With a burst of energy, the Orthun leaped after her, both of its heads barking excitedly as it gave chase to Asa'an. Friedrich listened to her merry laugh, as she dived and swooped around the Orthun, narrowly avoiding its playful jumps and swipes.

Friedrich smiled at the sight, before turning his thoughts to the plan that was already germinating inside of him.

# SARGOR

Towering over her, Sargor strode alongside Arianna as they gradually wended their way around the edge of one of the two great fish ponds situated on Conrad Rudel's estate.

Nearby, a few other members of his clan, in their human-like forms, were working under Kantel's direction to sort out a considerable number of fish that had been harvested for the evening meal. About half of the catch was a kind of fish called tilapia, taken from one pond, and the rest were catfish, netted within the other.

Winter had passed, but the air had not yet lost that season's cool touch. It would not be very much longer before spring emerged into full flower, though abundant green had already returned to the boughs of the trees.

After the harrowing weeks following the escape through the gateway, departing from their own times and entering a strange new age, Sargor had savored a very peaceful, and restful, few months with the clan on Conrad's spacious property. The tumult of the schism had ebbed, and no other challenges had occurred since, as the most restless of the An-Ki had gone with either Queran or Uria.

With a little guidance, the members of the An-Ki clan learned their tasks quickly enough, as they became active in the upkeep and development of the estate. It was all for their own benefit, as Conrad's property had been developed into a self-sufficient territory, to provide for a sizeable group in a time of need.

Arianna had shown great patience in explaining everything to Sargor, but time was something that they had in abundance over the colder winter months. They had walked together throughout the terrain, as Sargor had come to learn every ridge, creek, and depression in the ground.

On Conrad's property, there were many acres of tilled farmland, herds of cattle and sheep, fish ponds that were well-stocked and tended to, as well as a host of trees that grew all manner of fruit and nuts.

Large cisterns, connected with filtration systems, as Arianna called them, provided a clean, fresh supply of water. The more Sargor learned about Conrad and his refuge, the more he was impressed with the man.

It was hard to fathom that the light of the sun and the power of the wind could be harnessed, yet Arianna had been very clear in her description of the fascinating inventions, called windmills and solar cells. The batches of windmills perched on ridgelines and the array of solar cells covering the roof of Conrad's dwelling more than adequately saw to the power needs of the expansive property.

Sargor knew that the An-Ki missed the thrill of the hunt, save for the occasional herds of deer that moved through the acreage. But the clan had to keep a very low profile during their tenure on Conrad's lands.

The Enemy was well-aware that the An-Ki were in the world once again. If their haven were discovered, there was little doubt that the horrific, brutal Erkorenen would be unleashed in strength to slay the An-Ki at will.

Sargor wondered what the Enemy was doing with the surviving Erkorenen, those that had been saved in the same manner that the An-Ki had been spared the flood waters. In truth, the Gateway had been intended, and crafted, to rescue the Erkorenen. It was only a twist of fate and diligence that brought the device under the control of a man named Benedict Darwin, and the guidance of an Avatar named Calliel.

The Enemy had still been able to gain use of the gate in time to salvage an unknown number of the Erkorenen, the mighty and terrible offspring of fallen Avatars and humans. That much was made clear on the night the Night Hunters had drawn An-Ki blood in the woodlands, the beginnings of a slaughter that was stopped only by the intervention of Calliel and the Watchers.

The Erkorenen had not attempted another hunt, most likely due to caution regarding the Watchers, but Sargor was not about to make assumptions. Neither was Godral, who as vigilant as ever. The dedicated An-Ki warrior was always on his guard, and had instilled great discipline in his patrols.

Some significant changes had occurred in the clan since the time of their arrival. Where the An-Ki rarely took on their human-like forms before, they now sparingly assumed the two types of wolf-forms that they overwhelmingly preferred.

Sargor, with Godral's full agreement, had insisted that the An-Ki restrict themselves from their wolf-forms, unless they were in the midst of the compound's vast expanse. Even then, it was expected that they only do so in small numbers, when underneath some sort of cover where they could not be espied from things in the air.

The An-Ki had grumbled more than a little, but saw the sense in keeping their human forms, as they maintained a lower profile within the boundaries of Conrad's land.

A select few were allowed to remain in their wolf-forms, and these were the fastest of Godral's warriors. They could respond quickly to any alarm, and were capable of disappearing into the brush in an instant.

Godral did not have enough warriors to adequately keep a full watch on the outer perimeter of the haven. But if any human inadvertently came onto Conrad's property, they would encounter what they believed to be humans, rather than enormous wolves.

It took little thinking to recognize that the latter forms would raise quite an alarm in a world that did not believe that creatures such as the An-Ki truly existed.

"Do you like tilapia?" Arianna asked him, as they watched the An-Ki sorting out the fish.

"It is not bad. But I like the catfish better," Sargor said, reflecting his growing ability to speak Arianna's language.

Arianna smiled. "Me too, though I have had enough of it to last a lifetime over the past few months…"

She paused, and Sargor noticed her face brightening as she waved. "Hi Sarangar!"

Sargor looked over to see his son approaching them from across the causeway running between the two ponds. Wearing jeans, and a gray, long-sleeved shirt with a rounded collar, Sarangar looked at ease in the modern human attire.

Arianna had informed Sargor that Sarangar's human appearance would attract considerable attention within human populaces. She had said that women would find him incredibly attractive. His long white locks were neatly combed, flowing down over his shoulders with a lustrous sheen. His bright blue eyes brimmed with merriment, as he gave them a big smile.

Like Sargor's human appearance, Sarangar had strong jaw and forehead lines. Over six and a half feet tall, his body was muscular and well proportioned. Even out of his wolf-forms, Arianna had indicated that few humans would try to cause trouble with Sarangar.

"Hello Arianna. Hello Father. It is good to see you both," Sarangar greeted, giving Sargor a slight bow. His tone was deferential as he addressed his father.

While in human forms, the expressions of clan hierarchy were not as visibly pronounced, but some customs were retained, even if the An-Ki were readying to assimilate into their new world.

"It is good to see you, my son," Sargor said, shifting to the An-Ki tongue. "How are Ossur and Larantyr?"

"Larantyr wants to be faster so Godral will put him on the outer guard. He does not like remaining in this form," Sarangar replied. "Ossur thinks often of Yevia. I believe Yevia and Wenditan will soon be Life Mates."

There was nothing that he could do to help Larantyr gain the speed necessary to be in Godral's outer patrols, but Sargor was pleased to hear the news that another An-Ki family was about to be formed. Yevia and Wenditan had been courting for some time, and they were of the age to become Life Mates. He had no doubts that their cubs would be strong and intelligent, and that the young An-Ki pair would be very happy together.

"And how are you, Sarangar?" Sargor asked his son, watching his expression carefully.

"I am good, father," Sarangar responded, with a relaxed mien.

A smile spread on Sargor's face, as he heard the sincerity in his son's tone. Flesh of his flesh, and blood of his blood, Sarangar was the last of Sargor's lineage. Sargor felt an urge to keep his son protected at all times, but knew that he had to have a chance to grow, and become what he was capable of being.

"Those clothes fit you well, Sarangar," Arianna interjected.

"I like them. Many do not. But I feel good in them," Sarangar replied in the human language.

Sargor could sense the natural attraction that Arianna had to his son, as it was reflected in the subtler aspects of her expression, voice, and eyes. He did not want to think of the problems that might commence if An-Ki males, or females, for that matter, drew such responses from humans unwary of their true nature.

"I do not like these clothes," Sargor said, with a deep chuckle.

Arianna grinned. "I probably wouldn't either, if I could change forms like you can."

"This form is not bad," Sarangar said amiably.

"I had better like it, as it is the only one I have," Arianna joked.

"I would like to speak more with you. About the world we are in," Sarangar said.

21

"I am going to visit my Uncle Benedict shortly. You can come along if you want," Arianna replied.

"I would like that," Sarangar said.

"Go to him now, Arianna," Sargor told her. She had indulged his curiosities long enough, showing not a sign of impatience with his own queries.

"I do not have to go, if you would like to talk more," Arianna said.

"You have been good to me. I need to see some others now," Sargor said.

It was no lie, as there were always things to look into for an An-Ki clan chieftain.

"It was good visiting with you, Sargor," Arianna indicated.

"I will see you soon, Arianna," Sargor said, as she walked off with Sarangar.

It was a shame that the An-Ki and humans were separate creatures, as Arianna was just the type of female that would have made a good Life Mate for Sarangar. The young woman was enduring a terrible trial of her own, ripped away from her own life, and stranded in a storm of uncertainty. She had sacrificed greatly for her choice to aid the An-Ki, something that never left Sargor's mind.

Her spirit and outlook remained strong, despite all of the upheaval. Sargor hoped that she could find her way back to her life, even if he knew in his heart that such a possibility was faint at best.

With a little heaviness of heart, watching Arianna and Sarangar disappear down a trail into the woods beyond the ponds, Sargor turned and started back across the causeway. Sarangar's words had indicated that Larantyr was in need of some encouragement.

Sargor could not fault the stalwart An-Ki warrior for having a restless spirit. He knew how hard it was to abandon forms filled with such an abundance of grace and power, for one that was smaller, and much more limited.

Yet the An-Ki's human form held a purpose, and it was possible that, in time, those strengths would be revealed.

# MANDARIA

Without fanfare, or any visible ceremony, General Guo Jintao and Yuan Pei'an watched from the command center as an array of metallic leviathans departed through the underwater tunnels running beneath the great island naval base. Officers of the Mandarian navy and several high-ranking government officials surrounded them, including the admiral that had issued the formal command to send the undersea titans forth on their momentous journey.

General Jintao was filled with electrifying pride, as the moment for action finally approached. The culmination of years of painstaking preparation was about to be unfurled. The world would know soon enough that the UCAS was not the only superpower willing to project its power in regards to its national interests.

Once outside the base's deeply submerged cave entrances, the huge vessels would not remain together. The cluster of ballistic missile submarines would break apart, with individual vessels journeying onward to destinations all across the world. They would hasten to their locations, where they would all await the appointed signal.

Each one of the vessels carried a fearsome level of martial capability within their lengthy hulls. The oldest models harbored a dozen launching tubes, while another version had sixteen, and the newest, which had mostly existed as an object of speculation to intelligence agencies around the world, had an astounding twenty-four.

Their departure was being screened by the activation of large, land-based lasers that were being used to blind several UCAS surveillance satellites. The use of the lasers was not unprecedented, and would set off a diplomatic row that would involve a great deal of jargon about Mandarian intentions, but in the end it would all be attributed to just another provocative test of systems.

The nuclear-powered, ballistic missile submarines were not the only Mandarian forces being set in motion. A host of attack submarines, ranging from obsolete models, on up to a few that had just progressed beyond a prototype stage of development, had been loosed from a number of naval bases. Most would converge on the area around the Taiyoan Strait, but a few of the most advanced models, with the most experienced submarine crews in all of Mandaria's navy, would head farther into the Southern Sea.

Oceanic tigers loosed to prowl those waters, they would be stalking a very formidable quarry in due time. For the present, it was of the utmost importance to get a full range of military assets into position.

Far above the underground caves and tunnels, in the base's great harbor, a newly-commissioned carrier task force waited in a state of full readiness for the command to issue forth. Missile frigates, destroyers, and support vessels were stocked to the hilt for sea operations, ready to accompany the recently-built aircraft carrier that was a martial juggernaut all by itself.

Squadrons of advanced fighter and bomber aircraft, and teeming multitudes of older models, had been shifted to a number of forward air bases along the southern coastline; where an arsenal of missiles and other military assets were poised just across the strait from the main island of Taiyoan.

Fast amphibious vessels, capable of carrying great numbers of soldiers and armor, were perched on the outer edge of Mandaria, also squarely facing Taiyoan from across the strait. Large numbers of infantry, tanks, self-propelled artillery, and infantry fighting vehicles had been assembled in great numbers, ready to be loaded at a moment's notice.

The island nation of Taiyoan was recognized as a legitimate nation by only a handful of governments in the world, but it was a defiant symbol of self-determination to a great many people, all across the globe. To Mandaria's eyes, it was simply a renegade province to be dealt with at the right moment. It would not be long before the discrepancy was resolved, to Mandaria's full satisfaction. This thought was at the forefront of General Jintao's mind as he monitored the departure of the submarines.

# JOVAN

Bright, blue skies were draped over the enclosed compound, where Dr. Hadar Tricheur and his dedicated research staff delved into what some would deem the darker arts of a modern day sorcery. Pristine laboratories filled the secluded complex, bristling with cutting-edge equipment, along with an array of offices and conference rooms that had seen countless debates, brainstorming sessions, and team meetings.

All of it had been built primarily with funds gleaned from UCAS taxpayers, many of who would soon to be the victims of the virus that had been assiduously crafted there.

Inside the facility, walking along the gleaming, polished floors of a long hallway, a special tour was being conducted. With the time drawing near for Abundant Harvest to be activated, some last worries had to be assuaged.

"Robust, with a more extended incubation period, and easily transferable, this virus will bring the world to a much more manageable level," Samel Malkira stated.

Jovan Avery, Robert Wolfson of the Defense Ministry, Imad al-Dubbay of the Foreign Ministry, and a few other notable individuals listened carefully, as they strode behind him, continuing down one of the main corridors of Eternus Biotechnology Labs. Dr. Tricheur, the genius behind the development of the Abundant Harvest Virus, walked along at Samel's left side. Jovan could sense the excitement and anticipation percolating in the researcher.

Dr. Tricheur was not an impressive-looking man, but it was his mind that was of value, and not his appearance. Pudgy, with scraggly hair that looked as if it had not been washed in days, and pale skin that showed no trace of the sun's touch, he fit the profile of a man who spent innumerable hours indoors, pursuing his research with an iron focus.

One of the biggest, and most controversial, proponents of population reduction within the scientific community, Dr. Tricheur was at the cusp of realizing his grandest dream. Jovan wondered what kind of man had a dream that was centered upon the murder of billions, but there was no question that the brilliant doctor's work would be immensely useful to the Convergence.

"I hope that the risk of mutation is not high with what you have concocted here, especially in regards to the vaccine," Robert Wolfson stated firmly, bringing to the fore his primary concern. It was the same one that he had voiced at the meeting a few months before, where Samel had revealed the existence of the Abundant Harvest project.

"The virus will run its course quickly enough, and we will introduce the vaccine everywhere, when needed," Samel replied.

"Samel is correct," Dr. Tricheur added. "It will do its work, and then we will eliminate it. But it must be allowed to complete its task."

The vaccine, of course, already existed, and would be used to shield the panoply of elites involved in the Convergence, as the human herd was culled across the face of the globe. Even so, Jovan's own nerves were a little jittery at the prospects of loosing such a lethal virus. With a mortality rate exceeding seventy-five percent, and with a longer incubation period before symptoms began manifesting, it would be spread easily enough. The real worry was whether it could be contained after its goals had been met. Once it had decimated the spiraling populations of the world, it had to be stopped quickly.

"We must be absolutely certain that we are capable of halting this virus when the time comes," Imad al-Dubbay said firmly. His dark eyes, normally lively and confident, could not mask his unease.

Out of all the group, only Samel and Dr. Tricheur appeared to be fully convinced that things would go as planned.

"Do not forget that the time you speak of is one when we can get more than one thing accomplished," Samel remarked, looking around at all of them, as if to remind them of the utility that Abundant Harvest would provide to the labors of the Convergence.

Jovan nodded, knowing what a prime opportunity it would be with a massive, world-wide crisis in play, when people would be desperate for the vaccine that only the government agencies would be capable of providing. There would be no need to impose anything distasteful when the government would merely deliver the things that the masses would be clamoring for.

"Are all of the volunteers assembled?" Dr. Tricheur asked, looking towards Samel.

"They are," Samel answered evenly. "I happened to notice that none of your staff here volunteered for the next phase."

Jovan could tell that the researcher was caught off-guard by the statement. He looked unsure for a moment about how to respond, as uncertainty flickered briefly on his face.

"I need every one of my staff here with me," Dr. Tricheur finally replied, his voice a little hesitant.

"I just figured that they would want to take part in the fulfillment of everything you have been working so hard to achieve," Samel said.

"They ... all would ... I am sure of that," Dr. Tricheur replied, though his response was entirely unconvincing.

Jovan could not tell what Samel was seeking to do, but it was clear that his words were prodding Dr. Tricheur in a sensitive spot. Samel must have decided that the man was uncomfortable enough, as his next words shifted in direction.

"Dr. Tricheur, it will not be much longer until you are a world-wide hero, coming swiftly to the rescue. It will be known that you are the one who put a stop to the most dangerous pandemic to ever strike the world," Samel said, and though his lips were drawn up in a grin, the look in his eyes was as ice.

Jovan smiled politely, though Samel admittedly touched upon something unnerving, much deeper inside of him. How he could have been unaware of such a powerful man for so long escaped him. The emergence of Samel, at the unveiling of Dagian Underwood's nanoscale Living ID system, during that magnificent evening within the Grove River Valley, had blindsided so many in the upper echelon of the Society of the Red Shield.

In a world where individuals such as Jovan operated regularly in the shadows, this man had been working within the depths of shadows. Samel was not to be underestimated, and Jovan knew that anyone taking the man lightly would be doing so at his or her own grave peril.

The group continued to an area that culminated in a pair of thick, sliding doors, the facing of which displayed large biohazard warnings. Dr. Tricheur drew to a halt and turned to face the group.

"Mr. Wolfson, let me ease your concerns," Dr. Gellar said. "There is not enough room where we are going for the whole group to proceed, but I can take two in with me. You will have to put on protective bio-suits, and go through a couple of additional safety procedures, but I think that you will rest a little easier when we have returned. Who else would like to go in?"

"I would like to go," Imad stated quickly. He then added, as if it was an afterthought, "That is, if nobody here has objections."

None were forthcoming, and certainly not from Jovan. He was not at all comfortable about the idea of going into a place requiring the donning of bio-suits.

"Are you enjoying the tour, Jovan?" Samel asked politely, after Dr. Tricheur and one of his acolytes had led Robert and Imad through the sliding doors, into the chamber just beyond.

Jovan nodded, and mustered a smile. "Yes, I am, though I must say that much of this is way over my head, as far as the science is concerned."

"We all have our areas of expertise," Samel remarked. "Dr. Tricheur would find himself far out of his element in the world that you inhabit. The Convergence is going to need all of you at your best, with your respective talents, in the days to come."

"Things are just moving so rapidly," Jovan said. "It is going to be quite a challenge."

"Several things are happening at once, but all of it makes the completion of the Convergence possible," Samel said, with another mirthless smile. "It is a grand finale to this great symphony."

The look within Samel's eyes then took on a noticeable glint, like that of firelight reflecting from the edge of a razor-sharp blade. Jovan felt a chill pass over him, leaving a clammy feeling in its wake.

"And it will allow us to deal with the holdouts even more efficiently," Samel declared.

Again, an unpleasant feeling was stirred deep within Jovan, though he kept his expression unchanged, as he nodded back to Samel. He wished that he was in the company of someone with a more soothing air, like Kaira. Samel was an intimidating figure, even if he conducted himself with eloquence and had not yet said one harsh word to Jovan.

"I will do my part, to the best of my abilities. You can rest assured of that," Jovan said firmly, feeling a need to placate the tall man before him.

"I know that you will," Samel responded, with a tone of surety.

"I am glad that I have your confidence," Jovan said, with a deferential air.

"The Society has always done well by the Convergence," Samel commented, glancing down at the ring on Jovan's left hand, with its ruby shaped into the form of a red shield. "It has been a very long road, but the destination is imminent."

For an instant, Jovan sensed that the idea of reaching that destination was something to be desperately avoided, but the troubling feeling passed a moment later. Jovan was not sure why that notion had struck him so abruptly. He was not the kind of man who was afraid of success, and was immediately angry with himself for having that kind of reaction, even if it was so very brief.

"Yes, the goal is within reach, and within sight," Jovan said, bringing up a smile. "Once we get through this final storm."

"A new world awaits, on the other side. Keep walking this road, there is not much farther to go," Samel said.

Without further comment, Samel turned, and walked over to speak with one of the others in the select group, an older man who was on the board of the National Bank Reserve.

Jovan felt a little relieved, as he heard the two men begin talking about money supply, interest rates, and the course of inflation in regards to the two prominent factors. There was no question that he preferred avoiding Samel's direct attention. The man rattled Jovan's nerves in a way few men ever had before, and he wished that he knew exactly why.

With extensive assets, Jovan had not felt the economic fluctuations of recent years as much in his day to day life, but anyone living paycheck to paycheck certainly had felt the impacts. It was one thing to have large numbers shifting on a balance sheet, and another to have to scrape up money to fill a gas tank or grocery cart.

From austerity measures to rising costs, hardship had become the norm for a rising majority of the population. Living ID and a global political order would offer people a way back to better times. Samel was right in that compliance would come willingly from most.

When Dr. Tricheur returned a short while later, with both Robert and Imad in tow, the latter pair appeared to be in a much more confident state than before.

"I say it is time to send the volunteers on their travels," Robert said, with an easy smile, as he looked to the others who had not gone in.

"Send them on their way," Imad added with an air of confidence. "I'm feeling much better about it all now."

While stated as casually as if they were referring to a group of vacationers going aboard a cruise ship, the travels that Robert was referring to would result in the agonizing deaths of millions upon millions. Jovan wondered if the man was cognizant of that fact or not, as he spoke the words.

Despite their show of confidence, Jovan had little doubt that Imad and Robert would be going to the underground refuges, as soon as they heard that the volunteer Initiates were in motion. They might have been reassured by the tour, but they were not reckless men.

Jovan knew that he had to look into his own preparations for an emergency situation, but would have to remain in day to day affairs for as long as he could. As unstable as things might become, it was imperative that a few individuals remained at the controls, as the final elements of the Convergence commenced.

"Then it is time to call for the Abundant Harvest," Samel pronounced. "So that a much more manageable world can be prepared."

Jovan felt more of a sense of relief than elation at the declaration by Samel. He was simply glad that he was counted among the small, elite group that would be looked upon to manage and direct the approaching new global order.

# SETH

After completing his transaction at the self-checkout station, Seth shook his head, as he eyed the CSD kiosk positioned near the entrance area of the huge retail center. The kiosks were for the use of citizens, for anonymously reporting anything that they deemed strange about someone or their behavior. Being that the kiosk was located in a section of the store covered by constant video surveillance, it was hard for Seth to see just how anonymous a person could be when using the terminal.

The only thing good about the sight of the kiosk was the fact that it was sitting idle. The kiosk was nothing more than a call for grown men and women to tattle on each other, as Seth had enough common sense to know that there were no true terrorists anywhere in Madison.

He walked through the theft scanners flanking the main entrance, as the automatic glass doors opened for a mother with three kids in tow, and a cart heaped with bags. He followed the haggard-looking young woman slowly outside, careful not to bump into the small children trundling along, while watching a stream of individuals entering the building just to the right.

As tended to be the norm in public, most everyone looked pensive, and edgy. A good many were focused intently on their handheld devices, whether tapping on the touch screens or talking on them.

Seth's fist closed a little tighter on the plastic bag he carried in his right hand, as he continued out from the front of the retail center. He glanced up at the hydraulic lift towering up from the middle of the parking lot. It supported a four-sided structure at its apex, with dark-tinted windows placed on each facing. Its markings identified it as belonging to the police department.

It was hard to reconcile the foreboding sentinel looming over the privately owned property, casting its unavoidable presence across all who came to the retail center. Even though he had not yet completed his teenage years, Seth could still remember a time when he did not have to go through metal detectors at school, have camera eyes observing and recording his daily life, or encounter police guard towers in store parking lots.

It was not the first time he had seen one, as they had been cropping up with greater frequency over the last couple of years. But his nerves were not nearly as frayed then, as they were now.

The video of the fantastical encounter with the shape-shifting entity in the woodlands was not going to be contained anytime soon. It had gone viral, spreading swiftly across online channels until millions upon millions had witnessed the unbelievable transformations.

It had quickly become of the most watched videos ever on VidShareTerra, logging tens of millions of views alone on the popular online video site. Sea to Shining Sea's host, Zeev Steiner, had brought up the uncut video many times since Seth had called into the late night show, as had many other media outlets, both small and large.

Most commentators attributed the video to the talents of some very savvy digital artists, even going so far as to purport that they could ascertain that the video was not raw, and had definitely been tampered with. But a great many across the nation, and around the world, were spellbound by the fascinating images. The video represented the unassailable proof that so many had been seeking to confirm the existence of shape-shifting creatures, which had so deftly evaded solid documentation over the decades.

The video footage had done wonders for tourism in Venorterra, bringing a torrent of new campers and hikers into the Frontiersman National Forest. It was rumored that a movie project was already in development over the account, and Seth could not help but wonder what actor would be playing his part, as the one who had called in to Sea to Shining Sea.

Any writer of a script would have little to go on, in terms of the broader story behind the video. Seth, Jonathan, Annika, Raymond, Nolan and Randall had managed to keep their pact to lay low and keep quiet. The last thing any of them wanted to do was attract the attention of those who commanded the dark-clad troopers that had admonished the teenagers to stay clear of the woodlands.

"Hurry up, Seth," Jonathan cajoled from up ahead. "Let's get going!"

"Relax," Seth retorted, picking up his pace, as he strode towards Jonathan's car.

"I've got to get back. Annika's coming over sometime around seven," Jonathan said.

Seth rolled his eyes, glad that he did not have to run his schedule around a girlfriend. At the same time, another part of him wished that he did have a girlfriend like Annika to run his schedule around. It was the enduring conundrum that he lived with, but he did not see it changing anytime soon. It was hard enough finding the words to engage in small talk with a girl that he felt attracted to, and even harder to utter them.

Seth got into the passenger seat, as Jonathan took a moment to turn on the engine, and find some suitable music to play. Seth settled in as some heavy-edged riffs came over the speakers, followed by rumbling bass, and the thunder of drums.

"That's the new one from Resistance Horizon, isn't it?" Seth asked.

"Yes, and I never get tired of it," Jonathan said, backing the car up, shifting it into drive, and moving down the lane slowly.

"I still need to download it," Seth replied.

"Get the other three songs they just put out when you do," Jonathan said. "They rock, trust me."

"Mom's got me on a limit, with my online account," Seth said. "Probably just get the one track, as there are a couple more songs I've been wantin' to get for awhile."

As they pulled out of the parking lot, Seth watched in the side mirror as a police cruiser turned from the parking lot and fell in behind them. Turning his head towards Jonathan, he saw that his friend was looking in the rear view, carefully eyeing the law enforcement vehicle.

Seth's chest constricted as the cruiser glided in behind them, following for about a mile before turning off the road into a subdivision. He did not miss the long exhale that Jonathan loosed a moment later.

"We are all drowning in paranoia," Seth said. "This is going to drive us all mental."

"Tell me about it," Jonathan replied, with a dour expression. "I keep expecting those troopers to ambush us, around every corner we turn. They can't be happy about the video."

"I know the feeling," Seth agreed, with a deep breath out.

After reaching Jonathan's house, and parking along the street in front of it, the two made their way inside. They continued up to Jonathan's room, which was in an orderly state, not having the piles of clothes and unmade bed that Seth's typically had.

"Give me a second to check in with the folks, and I'll be back," Jonathan said. "Maybe get those tunes now, while you're thinking of it."

"Sounds like a good idea," Seth replied, as Jonathan exited the room.

On his mobile device, Seth went to straight to his favorite online music site, and logged into his account. After selecting three new tracks, including the one he had just listened to in the car, he went to purchase them and discovered that his order could not be processed. After a little searching, Seth found out that the site belonging to the bank issuing the credit card tied to the account was down, as it had been off and on over the past few weeks.

"Damn. Hackers got the upper hand today," Seth remarked under his breath.

The hackers were flooding sites until they were made inoperable from sheer overload, while government and security elements were looking to block, and hopefully identify and arrest, many of them in the process. It was part of an ongoing cyber war that had escalated into quite a nuisance for casual online users like Seth.

"I'm back," Jonathan announced, coming in with a couple cans of Mountain Mist soft drinks. He handed one over to Seth. "Got the songs?"

"Can't buy any, credit card won't go through right now," Seth said, opening the can and taking a sip.

"They shut it down again?" Jonathan asked.

"As much as it frustrates me when a site's down, I'm rooting for the rebels," Seth said with a grin.

"Just don't say that too loudly, I don't want to go onto any lists," Jonathan responded.

"Hell, half the country is on the no-fly list now," Seth said, his words far less an exaggeration than just a couple of years prior. "They'll probably all get upgraded to enemy combatants, as hysterical as everything is getting right now."

"Land of the free, like you say," Jonathan said, with a distinct edge of sarcasm.

"You are quoting me now," Seth said, chuckling. He set down his mobile device, and turned to face Jonathan.

"My destiny is tied to yours, with that video going up, so I might as well," Jonathan said.

"It will be good for you to change the scenery, when college starts," Seth said.

"What about you? Have you decided on a school yet?" Jonathan asked. "Not a lot of time if you are planning to start right away, after high school's over."

"Still can't figure out what I want to be, or where I want to go. I might even sit out a year. Parents aren't too pleased with that idea," Seth said, growing quiet for a few seconds. He then smirked. "Maybe I should be one of those guys on Sea to Shining Sea … documenting the things of myth and mystery. I've shown a little skill in that department, at least."

"Yes, you certainly have," Jonathan remarked, with a laugh. "Still can't believe we went back in there, after dealing with those soldiers."

"We are insane, aren't we?" Seth responded, laughing himself, as he shook his head. Looking back on it all, he could not believe how reckless they were in going back into the woods.

"Wasn't the sanest thing we've ever done," Jonathan said. "But it was a good thing to do. Like what those guys are defending in shutting down the sites, the information needs to get out there."

"Yeah, and what an effective warning it was. Caused a big upsurge in visitors to the national forest," Seth retorted dryly.

Jonathan grew silent for a moment, staring down at the soda can. "Do you think there's any way they'll figure out it was us?"

"Shouldn't be, unless they've got some kind of amazing voice recognition software that can match my call from Sea to Shining Sea," Seth said.

"It isn't fun having that kind of worry hovering over you," Jonathan said.

"No, it's not, but I definitely don't regret it at all," Seth said, and a little spark came to his eyes. "And I would not hesitate to do it again, no matter how uncomfortable it makes them. Some things shouldn't be hidden from sight."

"I don't think anything those troopers were involved in is good," Jonathan said.

"Let's get real, it's all unraveling," Seth said. "Wars are going on and on, and the economy sucks. Nobody's starting any kind of innovative new businesses, and the ones that are around are scaling down. Half the population is being arrested or cited for something, and a bunch of others just want to lose themselves in sports or gaming ... or stay glued to a bunch of idiotic TV shows. Nobody's making anything, except in Mandaria, or achieving anything of significance anymore. Most of the people I'm seeing when I go in public are total morons. A bunch more just want to get high or drunk, the elections just ping-pong between the two parties that have been there forever, and nothing ever really changes ... we're becoming a nation of losers, I hate to say. And that can't hold up forever. Something is going to give."

"Very nice rant, Seth. I am impressed," Jonathan said, with a rueful chuckle. "But you won't get any argument from me. Makes you wonder what the big folks at the top have in store for all of us."

"Whatever it is, I know it isn't good," Seth replied, in a low voice, as he stared back towards Jonathan. "But when we see it, I'm not going to sit still. That's the only thing I'm certain of."

# XAVIER

Cameras flashed, and a host of video cameras were trained upon the podium, as Ivan Draganovich, head of the CSD, announced that the security systems in place at the airports would be rapidly expanded to public transit systems, stadium events, and several other categories deemed vulnerable to terrorist threats.

Aaliyah and Xavier stood in a conference room deep within the underground labyrinth of the massive Station Central, watching the proceedings on the large, flat-screen monitor anchored to the wall.

"Thank you Aaliyah. This will get much more infrastructure that I need in place when Living ID is introduced," Xavier stated.

"I only hope that we can move quickly enough, with the things that are already in motion," Aaliyah said, casting a sharp glance at Xavier.

The reporters had begun to ask questions of Ivan, though none of the questions were particularly difficult or probing. As Xavier preferred it to be, the major corporate media had long since left the precepts of journalism far behind for the much more lucrative path of supporting the larger agendas of the government.

Lip service was paid to a few uncomfortable topics, such as the blatant conflicts of the burgeoning security procedures with the Grand Charter, but even those issues disappeared quickly enough from the news cycles. Access was everything to the modern journalist, and access was only provided to those who cooperated.

Independent online agencies were a little more problematic, and were currently at the center of a maelstrom, but those outlets would be dealt with soon enough. A killswitch on the entire online world was already in place, enshrined in legislation, and waiting for the proper trigger.

"As long as it is in the process of being put in place, I can work with it," Xavier replied, simply relieved that authority was expanding to allow for the growth of vital security elements.

"You are going to be extremely empowered, very soon," Aaliyah said. "Are you pleased with your new drones?"

Xavier could not be more pleased with the delivery of several Medusa drones for domestic use. They would come in very useful for dealing with the hotbeds of resistance, such as the one involving the obstinate, rural sheriff at Godwinton.

Already used overseas in the conflicts with insurgencies, the new drones had proven their value quickly. They could remain airborne longer than previous surveillance drones, and they could keep watch over a much larger area.

"I am very well pleased," Xavier said.

"Well, you have your Medusa drones, and I have my new weapons," Aaliyah said. "I find press conferences rather dull, so what do you say about a visit with one of my living weapons?"

Xavier nodded. "It would be a welcome diversion from this drudgery."

Aaliyah led him from the room, and they worked their way down gleaming corridors and swift elevators to a highly restricted level, one guarded entirely by Initiates of the Faith. They passed several large chambers, all of which contained various Erkorenen.

Xavier had learned much about the Erkorenen over the past few months, from the ones that resembled immense humans, to others that were undoubtedly the sources of ancient myths and legends.

Aaliyah came to a stop at the far end of the corridor. She proceeded through a handprint and retinal scan that confirmed her authority for access into the chamber beyond.

The large metallic door slid open, revealing an immense space within. A pungent scent filled the air, hitting Xavier the moment that he stepped into the chamber. It was a musty kind of aroma, thick with the smell of sweat and rotted meat. There was not much in the way of furnishings, beyond a gigantic monitor screen on one wall, and a huge pallet, upon which was the living reason for the visit.

A glistening, bloody pile of bones, with sinew and strips of flesh still attached, could be seen against the far wall. Xavier did not have to scrutinize them to know that many of the remains were human.

A loud, rumbling groan sounded in the room as they entered, as an enormous form rolled over on the pallet, and labored to stand up. Xavier found that he was still awestruck at the sight of the giant, the greatest of those brought through the time-transcending gateway.

Things had moved so fast during the time of the rescue that Xavier had not been able to take full account of Helel until long afterwards. He could still remember finding the great giant, and guiding the creature towards the gate.

Trudging through the swelling waters, the giant had carried no less than two of its smaller brethren towards the gate and its promise of safety. No matter what form they possessed, the Erkorenen shared a close bond, and Helel had exhibited that when laboring slowly through the waters, using all of its might to make certain the four-legged, bestial forms it carried over each shoulder would survive as well.

Aaliyah gazed up at the entity as it rose to its full height. Over twenty feet tall, it had a powerful, brawny build. Six-fingered and six-toed, it had some very noticeable differences from the human form, not the least of which was the double-row of large, sharp teeth lining its wide mouth.

It was clad in something like a kilt, or waist-cloth, though the bulging muscularity of its upper body was fully exposed.

"Helel, son of Sahar," Aaliyah greeted the imposing being.

"Satrinah," the creature replied, its low, gravelly tone booming within the enclosed chamber.

Xavier expected Aaliyah to speak in the strange tongue that she used to communicate with the Erkorenen, but what happened next came as a total surprise to him.

"How are you today?" she asked.

"I am well," Helel replied.

"Have you eaten today?"

"Yes," the creature responded. "Many cattle."

"What do you want?" Aaliyah queried.

"Sun and sky," Helel replied, and Xavier noticed a melancholic tone to the creature's response.

"Soon, Helel. Very soon you will walk under the open sky, once again," Aaliyah said, staring up into the giant's face.

Aaliyah looked towards Xavier, and smiled. "He is learning quickly, and it will not be long before the two of you will be able to converse. Think of Helel as a general among his kind."

"Amazing," Xavier said, his eyes fixed towards the looming giant. "He must have been seen as a god in the ancient world."

"Indeed he was, and he will be again," Aaliyah replied, with an air of steely conviction. "I would see all of the Progeny restored to their former glory, and much more."

Xavier looked from Aaliyah back into the broad face of the giant, wondering what kind of world it would be where such menacing creatures were venerated as deities. He also found himself musing over the prospects of using the incredible beings to subdue resistance.

The possibilities were incredible to contemplate, even if they were accompanied with a trace of fear.

# IAN

"So how are you holding up, Chris?" Ian asked.

He slumped down into the chair opposite the weary-looking man seated on the other side of the desk, who was wearing a slightly wrinkled, brown uniform shirt, displaying a distinctive golden badge over the left breast. Ian had decided to check in on his embattled friend during his lunch break, as the church where he was executing his tasks on the latest electrical contract was less than three blocks from the sheriff's headquarters.

Ever since the clash at the Revere home, tensions had been ratcheting up everywhere. National debates had exploded, with a majority of the talking heads decrying the sheriff's intervention on behalf of the Reveres, and the few hardy individuals that had holed up with them during the standoff at the woodland house.

Raw video of the clash strongly corroborated Chris' position that the CSD and WSB agents had fired on the house unprovoked. Most unbiased legal opinions also recognized that, as a sheriff, Chris did indeed have considerable power to exercise, even in the presence of federal agents.

Yet the usual array of pundits, politicians, and government spokespeople kept up a relentless campaign relying on the kind of convoluted logic that would have allowed them to declare with a straight face that the world was square. To them, Chris needed to be declared a domestic enemy or terrorist, the latter being the most promising category. The mere naming of someone as such conveniently swept away any need for even paying lip service to the individual protections recognized within the UCAS' Grand Charter.

The venom spewed in the media was unbelievable, with many openly calling for Chris Howard to be executed. It was hard for Ian to watch the hate and vitriol directed at the small-town sheriff, a man that he had grown up with.

It angered Ian to no end to see his best friend cast in such a terrible light, when, in truth, it had been Chris who had courageously stood up to the real domestic enemies. It was not the terrorists huddled in far-flung caves overseas that had eroded the freedoms enjoyed by UCAS citizens.

"Doin' well as I can, Ian," Chris said, his voice sounding heavy. After a sigh, he added, with a rueful tone. "I'm one man's champion of freedom, and another's terrorist, apparently. I'm an outlaw to one, and upholding the law to another. The final verdict has not been rendered, but I'm not real hopeful."

"You prodded a hornet's nest," Ian responded. "One that's not used to being poked so openly."

"They don't want anyone getting in their way, or ever showing anyone that they can be stood up to. They have to destroy me, or make a big example out of me," Chris said, solemnly. His tone then hardened. "But I'd do it again, believe me. I'm more certain of my decision right now than I ever was before."

Ian took notice of the iron glint embedded in Chris' eyes, and knew that he spoke with unwavering conviction regarding his momentous choice.

"So what's going to happen next?" Ian asked. "You got any idea?"

"The usual round of inquests and investigations, and I wouldn't be surprised if I get dragged into a kangaroo court at some point," Chris answered. "Like I said, they will have to make a big show out of it. They can't conduct themselves without their usual hysteria, and false urgency."

"Nobody around here will stand for that, Chris," Ian said firmly. There was not a person in Godwinton that Ian knew of who did not support Chris at the present moment. In truth, many from the town had stepped forth to be deputized by Chris when the pivotal moment had come during the standoff. Those kind of people would not abandon Chris during his hour of severe persecution.

"Does no good to ignore reality," Chris responded grimly. "We're up against something much larger, Ian … and I think something much more dangerous."

"And they are all focused on you here, with the real violence that is spiking in the cities all across this country," Ian stated with disgust.

"I guess the gangs have hired better public relations folks," Chris muttered, with a slight grin.

Ian was relieved to see that not all the humor had fled from his friend. He could only imagine the weight of the scrutiny being applied to Chris, as he was tried so harshly in the court of public opinion, and illuminated with the blinding light of national attention.

"So how's the new contract going? The Rudel property's kept you busy for so long," Chris said, and Ian could keenly sense his friend's desire to change the subject.

"Going good, so far," Ian replied. "But I keep getting more to do at the Rudel place. That contract keeps growin'."

"Contractor's dream client," Chris observed.

"No doubt he's got a lot going on out there," Ian said. "The guy's all about self-sufficiency. He's got his own food sources, water sources, energy sources … really impressive place, if you ever get the chance to take a tour of the grounds."

"Sounds like a very smart man, especially in these times," Chris said. "They want us all where they can click a button, and shut us down right away."

"Well, if everything falls apart, I think he could survive without much trouble," Ian said.

"If they don't concoct something on him. They want dependency, from everyone," Chris said, ruefully. He shook his head, and smiled, but the expression was not one of joy.

"I must be a lot of fun to be around, as depressing as I'm sounding here," Chris said, looking across at Ian. "Can't even talk about your work without it taking a downturn."

"It's alright Chris. You're under more stress than I can even imagine," Ian said.

"I long for the old days, I'll say that," Chris said heavily.

"Times were a lot simpler," Ian said, thinking back to the days when they had little more to worry about than getting some beer, and deciding where to go fishing or hang out.

There were no piles of bills, putting kids through college, or chronic backaches during those earlier years. The carefree period was hard to envision now, and it seemed like it had occurred ages ago.

"You know, I just want to say something while I'm thinking of it," Chris stated, after a long pause.

"By all means, then say it," Ian said, expecting Chris to vent some more.

"Thank you, Ian, for sticking with me. You've got a whole lot more to lose than I do, with Alena, Peyton, and Allyson," Chris said. "You didn't have to join with me, that day, and you don't have to be here now. I already told you that they're probably keeping detailed notes on who visits me here. You should stay away from here. I know where you stand, don't worry."

Ian sat back in his chair, and thought about his response for a moment. He held Chris' gaze, as he replied in a measured tone. "And what kind of man would I be, and friend would I be, if I deserted you when you are in the deepest trouble? What kind of husband and father would I be, if I abandoned my friends because things get tough? Do you think that would be any kind of example for Allyson or Peyton? Their father running for cover at the first drops of rain? No, that's not the man that their father is, Chris. When I stand by you, I am being a better father, you see."

Chris smiled, though there was a hue of sadness to the sheriff's expression. "I couldn't ask for a better friend. But you don't need to entangle yourself with me. I have a gut feeling that things are closing in on me. And there's not going to be a way out of it."

"Then they are closing in on me too, Chris, and there's not a damn thing you can do to make me go away," Ian replied, without hesitation.

"I can lock you up, for your own good," Chris said, with a chuckle. "I'll let Alena visit you behind bars, don't worry. Wouldn't want your stay in my little hotel here to go too hard."

"Thanks, Chris. Thanks a lot for your consideration there," Ian retorted, laughing. "I'm sure Alena would appreciate that."

A little of the weight appeared to lift from the other man's shoulders. Chris straightened up, and then rose from his chair, taking a moment to adjust his belt.

"So, what do you say we leave the worries behind for a few minutes, and go and grab some brisket? Because I know you gotta eat, before you head back to work," Chris said. "I'm hungry too. And this place is feeling a little too stuffy at the moment."

"Yes it is, and that sounds like a real good idea," Ian said, getting to his feet. He arched his back, which was already stiffening up. "Oh, that feels better. ... Now I'm ready."

"After you then, good sir," Chris declared, gesturing with an air of dramatic, stilted politeness towards the open doorway.

# GREGORY

"Home ... on the range!" Gregory stated, a broad grin on his face, as he squeezed the trigger on the A-15, letting loose a round that left the barrel accompanied by a familiar, loud cracking of the air.

Holding the gun in his left hand, he brought up a pair of binoculars with his right. Looking through them, he felt instant satisfaction, as he eyed the telltale, yellow-rimmed hole in the small black circle positioned over a thousand feet away.

He took a deep breath, drawing in the thick scents of gunpowder flowing on the air currents. They always brought a sense of ease to his spirit, telling him he was in an environment that he understood well, and was highly proficient within.

The sensations of drifting and aimlessness that had pervaded his restless spirit during recent years had come to an end, as a sense of renewed purpose had surged in the wake of the incident at the Revere home.

His inner convictions had been proven to be well-founded, as the CSD that he had always suspected to be malignant turned out to be every bit as vicious as he had imagined. In acting to protect the people holed up within the besieged house, he had upheld his soldier's oath to a greater degree than ever before. It was a realization that brought him a tranquil conscience, and empowering sense of fulfillment.

Gregory was determined to hold onto that cognizance, like a lifeline grasped while caught in the throes of a churning sea. It was good to feel alive once again, and even embrace the tingle of dangerous threats, after his senses had become so increasingly deadened over the past few years.

He had taken a leave of absence from the college library where he had been working at night, as well as a hiatus from tending to the grounds of the St. Martin Universalist Church, in a volunteer capacity. He felt a deep, inner pull to be right where he was at the present, in close proximity to Godwinton.

Gregory rose up to his feet, and handed the semi-automatic rifle over to a younger man standing quietly by him. All around him, in every stall, others were shooting a variety of weapons, continuing a pattern that had arisen not long after the firefight by the Revere house.

Though muffled significantly by the plugs in his ears, a ballistic chorus resonated in the air. Gregory could tell the types of guns being used by the signature sounds of their shots, from the high-powered hunting rifles, to various military-style, semi-automatic rifles, to a variety of handguns.

Gregory increasingly found himself tutoring individuals on their marksmanship whenever he visited the outdoor gun range. He could perceive that something had been ignited by the flagrant abuse of power displayed by the CSD agents and their allies. There was a decidedly more serious feeling to the air that could not be casually dismissed, along with a swell in the number of people making use of the range.

It was true that there was a pervading unease, but underlying it was also a feeling of determination. Gregory did not blame anyone for having anxiety, given the great instability in the country, but he was encouraged by the backbone he was starting to see amongst his fellow citizens.

"Great shot, sir," the young man complimented.

He looked to be around eighteen, with short blond hair, and a thicker southern accent. Gregory liked the alert look to his eyes, and the respectful attitude the young man was showing. At least a few within the younger generations were still being raised well.

"It's decent. But I should be able to do that again and again, when you've had the training I've had. And now it's your turn," Gregory replied, patting him on the shoulder. "Keep the elbow in closer, just like I told you."

"Yessir," the young man responded, with his southern inflection.

Though he had not been in the military, the fellow was a fast learner. He demonstrated improved form, as he took aim and fired off a few rounds at the target. A couple more yellow-lined holes appeared in the black circle.

"Very good. We'll make a marksman out of you yet," Gregory commended the youth. "Just don't go off and join the army on me, not with the jackasses running it right now ... the politicians, or those clowns in the White Pyramid."

The young man beamed at the compliment, and then laughed at Gregory's last remark.

"I'm serious about the advice, and about the fact that the White Pyramid is a circus of fools that gets good young men like you killed," Gregory stated. He was about to make a few more remarks, when a familiar voice interjected.

"There you are!"

Gregory turned at the sound, grinning broadly as he saw his brother striding towards him. Benjamin was carrying a rifle bag with him, along with a smaller case sized for handguns.

"How are you, bro?" Gregory greeted him. "Wasn't expecting you today."

"Thought I would make the drive down here, and get a few shots in myself. Bright day like this beats the indoor range anytime, and it's nice to get away from all the fun going on back home," Benjamin said, covering the last few paces to Gregory. He gazed around, and took in the sight of the young man with the A-15.

"I hope you aren't listening to anything he says," Benjamin told the youth, chuckling.

"That lad is wise, and knows genius when he hears it," Gregory jested. He looked to the youth. "Keep up the good work. I guess I have to go talk to my brother for awhile. Be grateful I'm steering him away, or you would have to suffer his company too."

"He doesn't want you to know which of the two of us is the true genius," Benjamin quipped, as the three of them laughed together. He then added, with a tone of sincerity, "But when it comes to shooting, listen to everything this guy tells you."

"Yessir, I do," the youth replied, steadying his rifle, and sighting for the next round.

Benjamin clapped Gregory on the shoulder, as they strode slowly away from the stall. Three shots from the A-15 burst out behind them.

"Doesn't look like there's any stalls open just yet. Guess we'll have to wait a bit to get a free one," Benjamin stated.

"Busy day down here," Gregory said. "Has been that way lately. Having trouble getting some rounds off here myself. Would give anything to shoot something with some real punch to it."

Gregory ached to shoot his fifty-caliber Burrell rifle again, but was not about to bring the distinctive weapon into such a public place, especially with all of the attention that was focused upon the town. The tales of an unidentified sniper that had wreaked havoc amongst the CSD and WSB agents, and had downed a helicopter, the latter caught clearly on the video that had gone viral, were widespread. Even further, the stories were well on the way to creating a kind of anonymous, heroic symbol of resistance in the greater populace.

It was the kind of celebrity that Gregory could not afford to embrace, as there were a great many in the heights of power that would undoubtedly like to see him eliminated. As confident as he was in his own martial abilities, he knew the kind of capabilities and assets available to the government.

"Would it make you feel a little better if I told you that I brought a rifle chambered for forty-four magnum rounds with me?" Benjamin queried, with a wink.

"Not exactly the same, but it will have to do for now," Gregory said, with a chuckle. "So how's Haley doing? Figured if you were free to get away from work, she'd probably rope you into something."

"I'll likely wish that she did. She's out with a few friends right now, probably blowing through both of our paychecks," Benjamin said, smiling and shaking his head.

"A couple good things about being a lone wolf," Gregory replied, smirking. "I get to hold on to my money, and decide what to do with it."

"Won't argue with you there," Benjamin said, laughing.

"So how are things on the force?" Gregory asked.

"Lots of tension and stress, as usual," Benjamin replied. "Can't imagine how things are in the bigger urban centers right now. Even we are seeing a spike in incidents."

"Doesn't surprise me," Gregory said. "People are desperate, and more every day are feeling like they got nothing to lose."

"And in the midst of it all, we have a new, particular bunch of slime to hunt down. Some people have been getting their doors kicked in during broad daylight. It is definitely the same group perpetrating it. More than one involved, and very organized," Benjamin said. "Doesn't matter if the place has an alarm system, as they know we can't get there in time to stop them from what they are set on doing."

"Got a feeling it is not going to get much better," Gregory said, a little more dourly. "Just gotta hope that whatever scumbags are kicking in the doors run into one of these good old boys or gals, on one of their little adventures."

Gregory looked around at the stalls for emphasis, as the rattle of gunfire continued all around them. In general, the men and women at the range were of the tougher, no-nonsense type that would not be inclined to think about criminal rehabilitation, or leniency, during a violent invasion of their homes.

"Would definitely put a quicker end to it than what we can do," Benjamin acknowledged. He gave a shrug. "But I can't worry about what I hope would happen. We have to deal with things as they are."

"I don't worry about where your efforts are put, but I bet the higher focus isn't on the type that you are talking about. The truth is that they are probably working overtime in that gray monstrosity, watching what people with completely clean records are doing," Gregory said acerbically, thinking of the sprawling federal complex located just a couple of miles from Godwinton. "Bet they are putting every resource to that, while leaving you guys strained and undermanned in the pursuit of the real threats."

The complex was one of a great number of similar edifices across the nation, which served as concentrated surveillance and data processing centers. It was one of the topics that Gregory had followed pretty closely in recent years, watching documentaries, listening to radio interviews, and doing some additional research to corroborate the claims.

"Depends on what you define as a threat," Benjamin replied somberly. "To them, people that want to bring things into alignment with the Grand Charter are the biggest threats."

Gregory had no argument. If anything, it was that kind of spirit that had caused the intervention with the Revere home. The sheriff that had decided to act was simply carrying out his defined role. In that area, he was little different than Gregory opening fire in adherence to his oath.

The sheriff was now being demonized daily in the media for having had the audacity to force the CSD and WSB agents to conform to the same standards as the common citizenry. Powers that were used to operating without oversight or restraint did not react well to being held accountable.

The final verdict was not in just yet, but Gregory had a strong hunch that those holding the levers of power would dig through mountains of legalese, and apply whatever twists of words necessary, to shut down the defiant sheriff.

It was the biggest reason why Gregory had quietly relocated, taking up a small, studio-style apartment closer to the sheriff's town. He felt that his path was aligned with that of the recalcitrant sheriff, even though they had never spoken, or even met.

It had been a long time since Gregory had admired any person to such a high degree, but when a rarer individual like Sheriff Chris Howard emerged, others needed to be willing to stand with him. Something in his gut told him that events were spiraling quickly, and that the sheriff would need others to lift up his banner in the tumultuous days to come.

"Freedom has always been a threat to that type," Gregory growled, as he looked upon his brother, growing silent for an extended pause. His next words were rendered in a lower voice, one woven with concern. "You're looking tired, bro. Your job isn't what's making you tired, is it? Still nothing about your friend, Quinn, or that radio show host?"

"Not a word," Benjamin replied, as a different look came into his eyes. "It's like they just vanished. The trail's ice cold at the moment, I hate to say."

"You'll find them," Gregory said, though in his heart he was not entirely sure. The government had ways of making individuals disappear.

"I won't stop looking for them," Benjamin responded firmly.

"And that's another reason you are down here, am I right?" Gregory said.

Benjamin nodded. "I try to squeeze in as much time around here as I can. I know it's all tied together."

"Anything specific that I can help you with in that department?" Gregory asked him. "You know I'm there for you, if you need me."

"Just need to find the trail again," Benjamin replied, with an edge of weariness. "Then I might need some assistance."

"You just promise to let me know when you do find it, and we'll follow it together," Gregory told him. His eyes then lowered towards the rifle bag, as his timbre lifted up. "Now, how about that rifle? I hope you brought a full box of ammo."

Gregory nodded his head towards a stall where two men were packing up, clearly finished with their shooting for the day. Benjamin turned his head, and glanced at the space that was about to be freed up.

"Sounds like a good enough plan to me," he said, his tone lightening as a grin returned to his face.

Gregory clapped him on the shoulder, and started towards the stall. "Come on then, let's have a little fun before the day's out! We'll have a little competition to see who'll be buying some beers later!"

"Glad I brought some cash, then, as my credit card would probably be declined after Haley's done with it," Benjamin replied, laughing.

# SECTION II

# URIA

Survival was easy enough to maintain, with a group of An-Ki relatively small in numbers. But it had been the task of finding an overall direction for the nascent clan to pursue that had vexed Uria the most, ever since the day that the schism had occurred with Sargor and Queran.

Food had been easy enough to acquire, as Uria's clan was becoming adept at hunting the various creatures populating the surrounding woodlands. Even through the cold winter months, there was no lack of sustenance, and Uria had taken a strong liking to the meat of the larger, brown-furred animals that roved in small herds through the woodlands. The flesh of the creatures had a succulent taste that was very agreeable to his palate, distinctly different from the herd animals he had hunted in their former world.

Though the idea of taking a Life Mate was something to be approached much farther down the line, Uria was finding himself taking on an increasing affinity towards Zeyya. A black-furred, golden-eyed female, she was of greater size and strength than any of the other rugged females that had chosen to break away from Sargor and join his new clan.

Bold, assertive, and possessed of keen initiative, Zeyya had gone on many forays that had taken her deep into human-occupied areas, bringing back a steady stream of insights and observations about their current world. Sharp of wit, she was learning more and more about the main language spoken by the humans dwelling in the surrounding lands, picking up bits and pieces of it in combination with the little they had learned before the schism.

Zeyya was also ferocious in her loyalty to Uria, which was one of the traits he most liked about the stalwart female. In a sense, she was already steadfast at his side, even if she was not his formal Life Mate. No less than three members of the small clan, two males and a female, were still recovering from serious wounds inflicted by her when they had openly raised doubts about Uria's leadership and wisdom.

Uria had not felt the need to discipline them further, once he had seen their shredded flanks and gashed limbs, which had brought one of the males to the brink of death. It was becoming clear that few in the young clan wished to provoke her fury, as Uria could sense the increasing deference being paid to her by the others.

Zeyya's emergence to the fore of the clan was a welcome

development, as there was so much uncertainty swirling around them. For the time being, Uria's clan had taken to residing in some hills not far from a very curious dwelling place of humans. Both Zeyya and Uria found the particular human site to be of great interest, as did several of the other clan members.

The metallic, wheeled carriages known as cars arrived on the grounds of the place with regularity, bringing a variety of humans within them. As the days passed by, a few of the faces became familiar, some arriving and leaving, but never staying for long. Others remained on the site more regularly, apparently residing within a larger, two-level edifice fronting the main area.

It did not take long to ascertain that something of great importance to the humans was being tended to under the surface. Uria wondered if the activity beneath the ground had something to do with the constant, low rumbles emitting from a few devices clustered together, underneath a shelter made of poles supporting a triangular covering. The objects were located adjacent to a high, elongated timber structure set well in back of the main dwelling.

Through the entrance of the wooden structure, the way that the humans went below ground was visible, like a tunnel or passageway descending into the soil. Men and women regularly poured liquid from large containers into the noise-making objects next to the edifice, as if giving them sustenance for whatever task the peculiar devices were carrying out. The liquid carried a very distinctive scent, which drifted on the breezes to Uria from time to time. Zeyya remarked that the scent matched that of the liquid the humans put into the cars.

On more than one occasion Uria, Zeyya, and others of the clan had observed humans emerging with armloads of packs from below the ground. Once on the surface, the humans had loaded the packs onto vehicles that left soon afterwards.

Uria also noted that there were quite a few weapons in evidence among the humans involved with the warded compound. They were weapons of the strange types that were utilized within the new world, capable of striking from a great distance. It was obvious that the humans were very prepared to protect whatever activity was transpiring.

As the days passed, Uria found himself becoming very curious as to the nature of whatever it was that was being conveyed away from the grounds in the cars. It was clearly something of considerable value to the humans, though it could be anything, as there were many various things that were deemed valuable by the humans living in his former world.

Uria began to wonder if the cars could be followed, though he knew that to try trailing one would involve great risk. He also knew that no An-Ki could run as fast as the cars were capable of traveling, as the vehicles could far exceed the speeds attained by the animal-pulled carriages of the old world.

Day after day, Uria began to send scouts farther and farther down the roadway that the cars traveled on, gaining a better idea as to the direction they were taking. Progress was slow, but steady, and knowledge was accumulated with each departure of cars from the grounds.

After an extended period of observation, a place where the cars were making multiple stops was identified. It was a large human dwelling, shrouded by the forest, and well-secluded from other human abodes.

Uria and Zeyya decided to take a closer look at the place together, to see what could be learned about the mysterious contents being brought up from underneath the ground.

Following the routes described to them by the scouts, using many distinctive landmarks, the spacious dwelling was not hard to find. With the benefit of thicker foliage all around it, Uria and Zeyya were able to take up a close watch on the location with little risk of being observed.

# THE ABUNDANT HARVEST VIRUS

No body scanners, explosive material detectors, or metal detectors picked up the greatest weapon to ever pass through the airports of the world. No physical pat down had the slightest hope of detecting it either.

Carried by willing hosts, and invisible to the eye, the microscopic creations of Dr. Tricheur were sent forth. They began to spread out across the world, as the bearers continued towards their predetermined destinations, loosing infection everywhere they went.

Most of the carriers were headed through airports to highly populous regions in underdeveloped parts of the world, but a few were sent into the developed nations as well. The seeds of chaos were being scattered in abundance.

The end game was in full motion, building into an avalanche of momentum as everything sought by the Convergence was drawing into clear sight.

# DAGIAN

Dagian peered up at a sky richly adorned with celestial jewels, a glittering spectacle of lights set into a sprawling canopy of darkness. The unsullied skies spread over Kemet heralded a place of refuge for her troubled spirit.

Her mind was much more at ease than it had been in quite some time. Far removed from Troy, the UCAS, and Aaliyah, the change in location helped to buffer her against the onslaught of fears that had tormented her since she had been made to witness the great Lords of the Abyss, on a night that would otherwise been filled with prestige and triumph.

On that momentous occasion, Living ID, the ingenious, nanoscale implants developed by Babylon Technologies, had been unveiled to some of the most powerful and influential in the world, icons within the spheres of politics, economics, and even religion. Culled from numerous factions, the crowd was firmly united in that its supreme focus and efforts centered upon the Convergence, a vision that all could grasp onto now without difficulty because of what Babylon Technologies had created.

Economic tremors were reverberating powerfully throughout the world. Nations teetering on the verge of financial collapse were threatening to take many others down with them, in what loomed as a cascade of failures that would shake the entire world. Of course, all of this was intended, a comprehensive crisis for which there were ready and available solutions set in place, and laying quietly in wait.

The brilliance of the Convergence was so very simple: conditions could either be created, or reacted to, on each step of the way towards the ultimate global structure envisioned. In the face of the cataclysmic economic tidal waves rushing towards all shores, and with other types of threats looming, Dagian and Babylon Technologies would come forth with the means to protect and secure the economies of the world. People facing the loss of their life savings, benefits, and pensions would stampede headlong towards the offered solutions, not pausing for even an instant to ponder the controls being put in place over everything in their lives.

Things once decided by local communities would now be determined at the apex of global institutions. A new authority would determine the kinds of crops farmers could grow on their land, the type and allotment of energy that a factory could access for production, and the regulations governing the kinds of loans that could be made to businesses.

Most importantly, though, anyone could be denied access to the entire system in an instant, from their financial accounts, to energy and health care. That kind of comprehensive power, executed through the technology developed by Dagian's company, would keep the masses subdued and in their place as the Convergence was completed. Order would be held firmly in place by a pervading fear.

The integral part that Dagian had to play in all of it had been upended by the capture of the final Gateway Device. Everything had almost unraveled, with consequences far too awful to ponder, but even though much had been salvaged, Dagian had still been made to endure a living nightmare.

She knew that she could not afford another major failure, and was driven to rectify things as much as possible. Taking initiative, she was pursuing a significant asset on the long climb back into the favor of beings that were not known for showing mercy.

Not far from where the road coursed through the lands of Kemet were the huge, ancient pyramids that always took Dagian's breath away. The majestic structures hearkened back to a better age, a mythical one filled with a stronger connection between the natural and supernatural, when the great Powers of the Abyss wielded a more open, direct influence upon the face of the world.

Back in that distant age, many humans had been able to make use of powerful, sorcerous arts, including some that were rumored to have become lost as one millennium flowed into the next. Dagian often found herself wondering what mysteries known then were still hidden from those steeped in the Craft during the modern age. A part of her wished that she could have used the gateway devices created under Project Exodus to indulge her curiosities about the times before the Great Deluge, when Lords of the Abyss walked incarnate upon the face of the world, and the Erkorenen were revered as divine.

The only consolation was that a similar age loomed just ahead, when the will of Diabolos would govern all of Terra. The very foundation of the world would be transformed in the Remaking, as the Shining One's light became the guiding luminance for all of creation.

The sedan carrying Dagian, and the other two vehicles escorting them, continued along the roadway for quite some time. There were few distractions, as there was virtually no traffic at the late hour. Many more monuments of the ancient world were passed in the darkness, before the trio of sedans finally slowed down.

Far away from the lights of cities, and provided with only the ambience of moon and stars, the area outside of her window conveyed a secluded, timeless feeling. There was a distinct feeling in the air itself, echoes of a wondrous past, intertwining with the hopes of an even grander future to come.

"Ms. Underwood, I trust that your travel has gone well?" a sharply-dressed Kemetian man asked her politely, in a thick accent, as he held the car door open for her to get out.

Tall and broad-shouldered, with smooth, olive skin, he was a handsome male specimen, one that would have tempted Dagian's carnal appetites if matters were not quite so pressing. He flashed a white smile, displaying a perfect set of teeth.

"Smoothly enough, if not fast enough," Dagian replied evenly. "I have been looking forward to this meeting. I have always had a great interest in the Setian Path, and those who walk upon it."

"As we have a great respect for one so adept at the Craft," the man replied amiably, with the dignified air of an ambassador.

A chilly night breeze swept over them, though the feeling was invigorating to Dagian, as she paused and stared out over the quiet, slumbering landscape. The shadowy form of temple ruins rose in the distance, the entrance into them flanked by two pylons. One of the obelisks still rose intact, while the other had fallen over the ages. A small pyramid loomed a short distance from where the cars had halted, but there was little else to break up the boundless desert terrain.

"Shall we proceed?" she asked the man, who was waiting patiently.

"I will take you to the sanctum, without delay," the man replied, in a deferential manner. He turned to the side, giving her a slight bow, and gestured in the direction behind them. "This way, please. The entrance is not far."

A few well-dressed security personnel from the other dark sedans, all Initiates of the Faith, fell in with Dagian and her new escort as they made their way across the bone-dry, sandy ground. Not a word was spoken, as the atmosphere seemed to compel silence.

They eventually came to the maw of a narrow staircase that descended into the depths of the earth, a few hundred yards from the small pyramid that filled her vision just ahead. At the bottom of the steps, a dusty passage ran ahead for a short distance, to where it opened into a small, rectangular chamber, illuminated by a quartet of braziers.

A stunning array of hieroglyphics covered the stone blocks used to fashion the space, the renderings of figures and objects having a living, breathing appearance within the firelight's embrace. A small group of men and women, in varying colors of long, hooded robes, stood attentively behind a man who cast an aura of commanding authority about his person. Dagian's attention barely took in the others, honing in fully upon the distinctive man just a few paces before her.

A loose-flowing, silken robe of pure white graced the lean man's body. Clean-shaven, of both head and face, many years had been pulled away from his appearance, though Dagian knew the magus was well into his seventies.

A simple golden amulet hung down to the midst of his chest, a fusion of an eye and the open mouth of a serpent. Two slender fangs descended over the watching eye, the two images signifying the wondrous entity that the magus served.

"Welcome, Dagian Underwood. It is an honor to have you here with us. Your presentation of the Living ID was most impressive," he greeted her cordially, in a smooth, elegant tone. "I have greatly enjoyed my other visits to the Grove River Valley, but that particular night was the penultimate occasion, without question."

His dark eyes glittered, as the upturned corners of his lips hinted at a smile. His accent and lighter complexion indicated that he was not a native Kemetian, but rather from the Allied Kingdom. Sharp angles, thick eyebrows and a larger nose conferred an added degree of intensity to his steely gaze.

"I thank you, High Priest of the Setian Path, though pressing matters bring me to you, and required this gathering of the heads of your Pylons," Dagian said.

Like the Order of the Temple, and the Society of the Red Shield, High Priest Gordon Weatherford and those with him represented another piece in the grand mosaic of the Convergence. Steeped in occult arts that were rooted in the ancient world, they were possessed of unique abilities and knowledge, including a few particular areas that Dagian intended to avail herself of.

"It goes without saying that you have been led deep into the mysteries of the Shining One, the great Light Giver," the High Priest said. "You have an understanding of the Arts revealed to us by the Shining One that surpasses any of those gathered here, myself included. … But as you and I have discussed, we have also endeavored to master a few arts that may be of great value to you at this time."

She knew that the High Priest of Set was not being patronizing, or engaging in polite flattery. He knew very well that she possessed an elite mastery of the Craft, at a level attained by only a handful of individuals across the entire world.

Dagian nodded slowly. "An art that can be of considerable help to the ongoing challenges we have been facing, in bringing the Convergence to its successful conclusion."

"All the Pylons of the Setian Path are honored to be asked to assist in your work," the High Priest replied, giving her a slight bow.

"As it is an honor to be welcomed into your sanctum," Dagian said. "But before we go further, I must assure myself of our ability to speak openly."

"We have taken every precaution, Dagian, but please ease any concerns that you might have."

Slowly, she allowed herself to drift into the edge of the trance-like state that allowed her to perceive the things of the unseen world, which ebbed and flowed all around the physical one. The clear outlines of physical objects were blurred, as movements could be seen during the transition.

The narrow forms of several black wraiths, curling and gliding throughout the chamber, gradually came into view. As Dagian allowed her mind to connect with them, and her wishes were conveyed to the dark spirits, more of the entities manifested until the small chamber was thick with their ebon presence. The lingering chill in the air quickly became frigid, such that the breath of those gathered could now be seen, like spectral mists.

Bending the dark shapes to her will, she commanded the wraiths to take to the sides of the chamber, until the walls were a solid black to her enhanced vision. Satisfied that they were warded from uninvited observation, she relaxed her focus, bringing her attention back to Gordon Weatherford and the priests heading the other Pylons.

"We can speak openly now. We shall have no eavesdroppers," she informed the High Priest of the Setian Path.

"Please tell me how the Pylons may be of service to you," he asked her, as she had not yet shared the specific reason for her journey to Kemet to meet with him.

"The Enemy is protecting some that pose a threat to our efforts, and others that have caused us great trouble recently have been hidden from our view," Dagian told him. "Every effort to find them has been frustrated, and I would see an end to this."

"Hidden from the eyes of the Avatars of Diabolos?" the High Priest asked her, a trace of surprise within the tone of his voice.

"As great as the Avatars are, the nature of the material world places restrictions on the power they can exercise within it. You know this well enough," Dagian replied sharply. "The Convergence would have come about much sooner had the Avatars been able to exercise their full power."

"And it is why human servants have some value to the Lords of the Abyss, otherwise they would have no need of us," the High Priest replied, matter-of-factly. "And what value do you seek from the humans who follow the Setian Path?"

"Few who live on the material plane can also take to spirit, through their own conscious efforts," Dagian replied.

The hint of a smile that had been present on the High Priest's face when Dagian had entered the chamber now manifested again, and spread into a knowing grin. He responded, "And for the few who can, the problems that stand in the way of making the art truly effective are many."

"Yes, and they are too many to make the art very useful for my purposes, to address my concerns … at least in the past," Dagian said, letting the last words linger for a moment, as they touched upon the main reason for her trip to Kemet.

Traveling outside of the physical body was not an unknown art, but it was not an area that had previously offered much in the way of concrete results. The practice was more of a triviality, and a topic of intriguing speculation, than it was a dependable technique. Setting the spirit free of its prison of flesh was attainable, but maintaining a focused will, and then retaining what one experienced while in that disembodied state, were tenuous propositions at best.

It was not unlike being within a dream, and for good reason. The dream state was one in which consciousness roamed within, and journeyed across, non-physical realms. It did not matter whether one viewed those places as mental conjurations, or actual places of a non-physical nature. Individuals could reach various states of lucidity within dream states, sometimes governing their dreams and their actions during them to a strong degree.

Yet the details of a dream, even a very lucid one just concluded, were often maddeningly elusive. They were just like the things gained during a willed sojourn out of the body, prior to embedding the spirit into flesh once again. The lack of memory retention following a spirit journey was the one major barrier that had prevented the art from being effective in helping the Convergence progress.

"But you did not encourage me to come here just to reiterate the obstacles of the past," Dagian said.

"No, I have not. I am pleased to inform you that we have one amongst us who has the skill level that you seek," the High Priest announced, a flare of pride within his gaze.

"One who can retain willpower while in the spirit-state, and recall everything upon returning to the body?" Dagian asked him firmly, as everything hinged upon the High Priest's next answer.

The High Priest nodded, and gave her a smile. "Yes, without a question. He is in full command of his travels in spirit. Like no other that has ever followed the Setian Path, during my entire life, or in the accounts of our order that I have studied."

Dagian's expression did not change, but the answer elated her. If it were true that a prodigy had emerged regarding the art of out of body traveling, then she would be able to return to the UCAS with a formidable new asset to deploy.

At a glance from the High Priest, those accompanying him stood aside, as a young man in crimson robes stepped forward from the back. Steely in both the look in his eyes and his expression, he stood quietly, gazing towards Dagian.

He was well groomed, with short-cropped, dark hair, and a neatly trimmed goatee. About the same height as Dagian, his robes hung loosely, indicating a leaner build.

"This is Jibade Mubarak, who is the one that you have been seeking," the High Priest declared. "He is like no other, truly blessed by Set, and he comes from a long line of Walkers of the Setian Path. His lineage is rooted in the legendary ages of Kemet."

"It is a pleasure to meet you, Jibade," Dagian said, inclining her head slightly.

"And it is an honor to meet you," Jibade replied, in a smooth, accented voice. He then pledged, "I shall do all that you ask, to every limit of my ability."

"And much will be asked of you," Dagian said, meeting his gaze with equal intensity. "Are you prepared to depart with me?"

She did not bother to seek approval from the High Priest, in seeking to physically bring the priest of Set back to Troy with her. The question was posed solely for the crimson-robed priest.

"Immediately," he responded.

Dagian turned back to the High Priest. "This is a great revelation, and I understand the need for secrecy. It would not be to our advantage to have the Enemy know that you are sending one with abilities such as Jibade possesses back with me."

"The Enemy may discover his ability, after it is put to use," the High Priest cautioned.

"I know that will happen, but not before much has been achieved," Dagian replied, her mind already thinking of the possibilities involving the rare talents of Jibade Mubarak.

A man like him could be a true, living weapon. She wondered what new frontiers could be explored, involving a man that was in such strong command of his spirit while apart from the shackles of his body.

"I know you wish to depart as soon as you can. But before you leave, let us give obeisance to Set, the one who has revealed His Path to us, and who guides us along it, in the service of the Shining One," the High Priest beseeched her.

Dagian nodded. "It would be my honor, as I wish to show my respects to the great Set."

The High Priest looked around at the heads of the other Pylons.

"Only Dagian, myself, and Jibade shall proceed from here. Await our return."

The others nodded quietly at his directive.

Taking a narrow tunnel, which led from the back of the chamber, they descended farther underground. The trio proceeded in single file, with the High Priest at their lead, Dagian in the middle, and Jibade walking a couple of paces behind. The lengthy passageway finally opened up into a great cavern, the far side of which held a grand altar setting.

A massive sculpture, of a regal figure seated upon a throne, reared up behind a broad, stone altar that consisted of a huge rectangular slab spanning two stout blocks. The head of the figure was that of a long-snouted beast, with erect ears that did not taper, but rather were even at their upper ends. The rest of its body was decidedly human, with arm bands just below its shoulders, similar bands around the ankles, and a semi-circular mantle over a bare, muscular chest. A long garment was wrapped about the entity's waist.

Though it was a sculpture, Dagian had the feeling of being watched as she looked up to the stone eyes of the inhuman figure, a sensation that brought a tingling down the length of her spine. She knew who the statue represented, well-versed in the lore of Kemet and its legacy of symbols.

There was a pair of other well-crafted sculptures flanking the first, set back just slightly, though these were of a more human appearance. Both were figures of regal-looking women, both wearing Kemetian-style headdresses.

Though the female images were each graced with beauty, and possessed of shapely forms, the one to the left had a more comely, softer mien, while the one on the right had a firmly set jaw, and decidedly stern visage. The latter also had a spear gripped in her right hand, lending even further to the figure's warrior air. Dagian guessed at once that the two flanking statures were representations of the legendary consorts of Set: Astarte and Anat.

With blazing torches set in metal brackets around the temple area, smoke wafting up continuously from the flames, the space had a timeless, sacred air about it. Echoes of a mythic age in which the most powerful of the Dark Avatars were revered, and worshipped as gods by humans, were thick in the capacious chamber. The atmosphere compelled reverence from those who stepped before the altar, a place that Dagian knew had been used for rituals and devotions by High Priests of Set ever since the place was built many, many centuries ago.

A fierce pride filled Dagian, as those ancient traditions were being carried onward, even if in a different manner and form, by those such as the High Priest and others steeped in the Setian Path. The religions that had swept across the world could not eradicate the hidden pathways beckoning to the strongest of the human race. Those pathways, gifts of Diabolos, led to knowledge, power, and so much more, often reaching well beyond the mundane world. The gathering of power and mastery of occult arts had, in turn, enabled those who walked on such pathways to infiltrate the hierarchies of popular religions with ease.

Significant degrees of authority within those religions were wielded by individuals who occupied the summits of groups such as the Society of the Red Shield, the Order of the Temple, and the Walkers of the Setian Path.

In fact, she had recognized more than one of the heads of the Pylons, back in the first sanctum. The group had included one man who was a High Vicar in the Universal Church, and another who was a Guided Elder, regularly leading Rashidan prayers in the grandest mosque in all of Kemet.

That their hearts and minds were given wholly to the great Dark Avatar represented by the prominent central sculpture, all the while maintaining exquisite deceptions and subtly working the will of the Shining One from within the world religions, electrified Dagian. It testified to the resilience, strength, and power of the hidden pathways, which enabled those brave enough to embrace them to rise so far above the masses of useless eaters occupying space in the world.

Once they had all entered the expansive chamber, the High Priest walked forward slowly, approaching the great altar. Reaching forward, he carefully retrieved a long wooden scepter lying upon the stone surface. It had a stylized head, which resembled the shape of the figure on the central throne, while the other end of it was carved into a fork. It was undoubtedly old, riddled with cracks, and the painted eye that Dagian could see on the head of it was faded with age.

Holding up the scepter in his right hand, the High Priest began to chant in a low, rhythmic voice, giving utterance to words that Dagian knew were from an ancient Kemetian tongue. He began to sway, and she could tell that he was assuming a trance-like state, as he stood before the towering images of Set, Astarte, and Anat.

A vibrating energy rippled through the air, and Dagian felt the first tugs at her senses, from sight to sound, as the sense of space that she was occupying expanded exponentially. Her perception and awareness were being opened up, guided by the arts of the High Priest, so that the things of the unseen world could be revealed to physical sight and other senses.

Her impressions of the changes taking place in the chamber called to mind the fearsome visions she had witnessed on the night of Living ID's unveiling. She knew in her heart that she was about to stand in the presence of the very being that the priesthood was dedicated to, the ancient god worshipped in Kemet, and Dark Avatar of Diabolos: the exalted Set.

Like wafting tendrils of smoke, plumes of darkness swirled and gathered around the boundaries of the chamber, assiduously enveloping everything, including the grand altar and the statues beyond it. Within a few moments, everything in the chamber was obscured from sight by an impenetrable darkness.

As if it was a sparkling night sky emerging into sight from behind a dense mass of scudding clouds, what looked to be a star-filled firmament of incredible vibrancy manifested. It was a mesmerizing view, like nothing that could ever be witnessed from the surface of Terra. It was a sky like no other that she had ever gazed upon, with no recognizable constellations, and a much greater number of celestial bodies arrayed across the upper darkness.

To the left and right, a vast desert stretched to the far horizons. Undulating dunes rolled outward, unblemished by any other terrain features. A hot, sulfur-laced breeze flowed across Dagian, evocative of scorching desert heat, and things of the infernal. Out over the contours of the sandy dunes, what looked to be swift-moving, sinuous black mists coursed in narrow lengths just above the surface, like so many serpents winding across the desolate scenery.

Soaring up before Dagian and the two priests were a pair of immaculate, golden obelisks. Each would have exceeded the height of the tallest skyscraper in all of Terra. The titanic monoliths flanked the entrance into a pyramidal structure of breathtaking grandeur. Its smooth facings were also of a shimmering, golden hue, mirroring the splendor of the obelisks, and its bewildering size was on a scale that no human undertaking could ever have achieved.

Gathered around the bases of the golden obelisks were at least a few hundred bizarre-looking, humanoid creatures. In form, they looked as if they had stepped right out of sequences of ancient hieroglyphs, of the kind that Dagian had pored over often enough during her studies of the esoteric.

They possessed very tall, broad-shouldered, human-like bodies, exhibiting an impressive musculature of exquisite symmetry. They had long, erect ears that had squared ends, and their faces were anything but human in appearance. Long, down-curving snouts extended from their dark heads, and their eyes were shining orbs of white luminance. If anything, they were smaller reflections of the great central statue back in the altar-chamber, only these figures were sentient, living entities.

They wore a distinctive type of garb, with a wrapping around their waists that descended to their knees. It did not appear to be fashioned of cloth, but rather from some kind of hide. Headdresses, with rectangular extensions running down from each side of their heads to rest atop their breasts, and a broader part that draped down behind to the middle of their backs, were worn by all of the long-snouted beings.

All of them carried a matching kind of staff, forked at the base, and topped by a distinctive form that echoed the shapes of their heads. The staffs also matched the object from the altar-chamber, the scepter now held by the High Priest, only the staffs of the non-human entities showed no sign of age. Dagian gave a slight start as she saw the eyes at the heads of their staffs moving, as if something alive and trapped inhabited the rigid implements.

Accompanying the scepter-carrying beings were a number of peculiar beasts. Supported on four long legs, they were very lean of body, to the point of having a starved, emaciated appearance. Oddly, their heads were of the same type as their humanoid companions, from their curved snouts to their higher, square-ended ears. They were tall in stature, with backs as elevated as the waists of their two-legged comrades. With the latter being at least nine feet tall in comparison to Dagian, the quadrupeds could cast their solid white gazes at a level even with her face, with no effort.

Yet as impressive and striking as the obelisks, pyramid, and array of creatures were, it was the towering Avatar manifesting before the entrance to the grand structure that compelled a sense of unfettered awe within Dagian. Her mind was spinning, as she looked upon the grandeur of the Dark Avatar, feeling insignificant and weak in the great being's presence.

All three of the human witnesses fell down to their knees, as an entity of fearsome countenance and gargantuan size was fully revealed before them by the ebbing blackness.

The soaring being was wreathed in darkness, which rippled over the flaming elements of its six-winged body. The searing gaze from its head peered down upon the diminutive humans before it, and Dagian felt entirely exposed, naked in thought and deed to the piercing scrutiny of the Dark Avatar.

Dagian kept her eyes downcast, in a reverential manner. While she feared the Dark Avatar, the first glimpse of the great being had sent an incredible surge of elation and wonder throughout her.

She had studied ancient texts, and probed the contents of many tales and legends, taking note of every detail that she could, and felt that she knew something of the Dark Avatar towering before her. But all the knowledge in the world was nothing compared to the experience of beholding Set in person.

"Rise up," the ancient being commanded them, in a voice that carried the tones of rumbling thunder. "Do not turn your eyes away. Behold my realm, in this vision that you have been granted, as you bear witness before one of my great temples."

Slowly Dagian got up to her feet, as did Jibade and the High Priest. It was hard to lift her eyes upward, but she forced her gaze higher, though she was careful not to look straight into the burning eyes of the Dark Avatar.

"This one knows what must be done," Set stated, casting his severe gaze towards Dagian. She felt exposed and fragile, as she fell under his direct attention. The unnerving sensation passed a moment later, as Set moved his attention back to the others with her. "You have been given my patronage, High Priest, in order to serve the Shining One. Do not waver in your conviction."

"I will not, my Master," the High Priest responded, and Dagian could hear the tremble in his voice. It was not often that a High Priest held a direct audience with his god, and she could not begin to imagine the emotions stirring within the man.

The regal being then turned his focus upon Jibade.

"Some of your bloodline are in my priesthood, chosen to minister my realm in the Ten-Fold Kingdom," Set stated. "You may one day join their ranks, if you do not fail in my service."

"Praise be to you, my Master," Jibade said, bowing low. Like the High Priest, the younger man's voice was shaking as he spoke openly to Set.

"I have extended many gifts to you, as my priests in the decaying world, who guide others to the deep wisdom of Becoming," Set stated in his resonant, booming voice, addressing both the High Priest and Jibade. "Use your gifts in the great hour to come, and godhead shall be your inheritance."

Both Walkers of the Setian Path bowed low again.

"When the Shining One illuminates your world, you will then be able to shed your rotten humanity, and be transformed into something worthy of the Ten-Fold Kingdom," Set told them.

The mighty being spoke of the same dream that Dagian held, to be given the ultimate gift in the afterworld, of being transformed into a greater creation. The Dark Avatars carried a burning hatred of humanity, the essence of which reflected the very image of Adonai. Dagian knew that human souls left in a human form within the Ten-Fold Kingdom were the truly condemned, made to suffer all the horrors of the dark nether realms.

"But you have not yet been given the blessing of one who has not been revealed to you," Set continued. The Dark Avatar seemed to flare with intensity, as his several wings spread outward. The fires of his body surged, limned by the darkness that was like a layer of clinging, black smoke. Set's voice thundered to the horizons, as he gazed skyward. "I call upon one who is even greater than I … one who binds the darkness to his will, and whose wisdom has guided me to a deeper knowledge of divinity."

Like a rain of stars, a great number of lights within the vast firmament above began to descend. It was a strikingly beautiful vision, as Dagian watched the luminous forms arcing towards them from afar, approaching from every direction as they neared the place where Set had summoned them.

One by one, the lights in the grand cascade began to touch upon the ground before the otherworldly temple. The lights faded, the rays drawing inward, retracting into their sources. Naked, and frightened-looking, a throng of men and women stood in the places where the lights had been.

Understanding came to Dagian in that moment. Set had used the

souls of condemned humans to form the stars of his grand firmament, in the thousands, and the tens of thousands. Using the eternal energy of their spirits, he had rendered them into his own version of celestial bodies. Consigned to the skies over Set's realm, they served his will, a living spectacle arrayed in the depths of darkness to glorify the great Avatar without pause.

It was a terrible fate to endure for the human souls, but Dagian reminded herself, looking upon their naked forms, that these were not spirits who had gained the favor of the Dark Avatars. The beast-headed ones carrying the scepters were the ones that had.

A boundless shadow fell upon the great assembly, the obelisks, and the pyramid itself, as the sky itself was blotted out. An inviolable darkness filled the sky, one that no light could pierce, before it began to coalesce into a form resembling a titanic funnel cloud. A huge Avatar, much larger than the immense Set, was revealed within the towering blackness for just a moment, before the form of a gargantuan serpent took shape and solidified.

Resting upon its enormous coils, the great serpent stared with blazing eyes upon the subdued assembly. Power radiated from the monstrosity, far surpassing the feeling that Dagian had experienced in Set's presence. This was a being to whom even Set directed reverence, worthy of a state of godhead in the infinite depths of the Abyss.

"Great Apep, take these souls into your possession, to be committed to your realm in the Ten-Fold Kingdom," Set stated, addressing the baleful serpent with a lower tone than he had used before.

The hapless souls that had been culled from the starry sky cried out, screaming in brazen terror, as Apep's jaws opened wide. A withering heat emitted from the depths of its great throat, a portal into an even more horrific darkness than the one that the condemned souls had known. With incredible speed, Apep coiled around the entire mass of captive souls, swallowing them into its dark maw a moment later, hundreds upon hundreds at once. A pulsating light rippled down the length of its body as it reared back, and the fires of its eyes surged in intensity.

An ear-splitting shriek ripped through the air, carrying with it an overpowering sense of triumph and rapaciousness. Apep was a being that reveled in its consumption of souls, feeding a hunger that could never be met with full satisfaction.

Dagian did not want to think of the place that those souls had gone, as they plunged down the throat of Apep into a realm of enduring horrors and unimaginable suffering, quite different in nature than the realm that the souls who had become priests of Set experienced. It was a stark reminder that she had to culminate her worldly existence in a state where she held favor when consigned to the Nether Realms, to be as the priests of Set, or others that were put into the service of Diabolos' powerful Avatars. She had to avoid at all costs the unrelenting tortures and terrors that filled the realms of the Dark Avatars, meted out to the millions upon millions of spirits deemed useless; or, even worse, who had gained the ire of Diabolos or one of the greater Dark Avatars.

"You who yet walk the world of flesh, draw forward, to stand before Apep, and receive His blessing," Set commanded the humans.

Dagian stepped forward, as did the High Priest and Jibade. She could think of nothing else but the dark, monstrous serpent looming before her. Perceiving that Set could see into every thought and deed of hers, the feeling that she had in Apep's presence was mind-boggling, far beyond any stretch of understanding that she possessed. Apep's will probed into the underlying depths of her essence, reaching beyond mere thoughts and deeds into the very core of her spirit, and what girded it.

A deafening hiss encompassed her, as Apep's jaws opened wide. A deep, thickly-layered voice boomed over the assemblage. "Receive my blessing, to prepare you for the work to come in the service of the Shining One, Whose light is our guide, and Whose darkness is our sustenance."

Like glistening drips of venom, a viscous liquid formed at the ends of Apep's fangs, and then plummeted down towards Dagian and the two men with her. She stood transfixed as one of the shimmering globules enveloped her.

Yet it was not liquid that touched her skin, but rather a kind of energy that absorbed into her at once. Its touch was like ice, though of a level of cold that was deeper than any physical sensation. It was the caress of death, devoid of even the slightest ember of life. The faint part of her that retained some sliver of what Dagian had been, before she had given herself in mind and soul over to Diabolos, recoiled with a desperate urgency.

Being a creature of the physical world, she knew that she could not have withstood that otherworldly touch for even a fraction of a second longer, and was grateful when the harrowing sensation ended. Without knowing what it was, she knew that something of a profound nature had been introduced within her, at that deep level where Apep's will probed.

It was all she could do to remain standing. She felt as if she was as light as ash in the immediate aftermath of Apep's blessing. It was as if the lightest of breezes could whisk the husk of her spirit away.

Without another word, Apep's body began to change, as the coils lost their solidity, swirling and forming into the great funnel cloud that had preceded the serpentine manifestation. The cyclone then assumed the momentary shape of a six-winged, enormous Avatar, before becoming a formless, vast shadow that cloaked the sky before disappearing from view.

The living constellation was revealed in its fullness once again, looking even brighter to the eye after the sprawling darkness that had shrouded it. Dagian could do nothing more than stand in place, her thoughts without anchor, adrift in an endless sea of consciousness.

"Few of the world of flesh have beheld Apep. Even fewer have received Apep's blessing. You are empowered to do the final work needed, to bring about the will of the Shining One," Set addressed them.

His tone, though like a ripple of deep thunder, now sounded much lighter in comparison to the raging storm of Apep's voice.

Dagian had no response as Set fell silent, and she did not have any idea what to do next. The feeling was very uncomfortable, as the hot breezes brushed over her. She could feel the collective weight of hundreds of stares coming from the priests of Set and the four-legged creatures gathered around them.

Every so often, faint cries came to her ears, laments from the far reaches of the desert. The sorrowful vocalizations were the only thing to break the uneasy stillness. She did not dare to look to Jibade or the High Priest for any kind of cue, as only Set would determine what came next.

From behind Set, another great Avatar emerged from the opening of the enormous pyramid. The advancing Avatar carried a distinctly different, feminine air, and was accorded great reverence by the priests of Set. Upon their knees, they bowed low, as the lofty being strode through their midst.

"Behold Anat, my left hand, who reigns with me over these realms," Set announced, as the second Avatar moved past him, heading straight for the three humans.

Anat's shape changed, the flames of her body drawing in, condensing and becoming like skin, as she walked towards Dagian and the two priests. Though still towering high over the awed trio, the Avatar

assumed a very human-like appearance.

Anat's form was now that of a strongly-built woman, with strikingly beautiful features. She had an intense countenance, one imbued with a marked hint of the feral. Her head, shoulders, and upper back were draped with flowing locks of black hair, and a decidedly savage look coiled within her fiery eyes. Every aspect of her human appearance conveyed an unbowed pride, one that was not diminished in the slightest by the nearby presence of Set himself.

Dagian felt a dizzying sense of wonder, bordering on intoxicating, as she silently beheld Anat's approach. Ferocity was the Dark Avatar's dominion, and any foolish enough to oppose or transgress her would incur Anat's scorching wrath, empowered by the fires of an unyielding cruelty. Standing tall, she held a fiery blade in one hand, and a spear of flames in the other. Severed heads and hands adorned a great sash wound about her body, macabre trophies that Dagian knew at once were not mere accoutrements. She knew their origins, and why they were there, if not their specific identities.

As if to accentuate the terrible plight that they had been subjected to, the mouths and eyes on the faces exhibited movements, though no sound came from the former, and the look in the latter was unfocused, and glazed. They were images of souls receiving a most horrid punishment through the power of Anat.

Opponents of great Baal in earlier ages, these souls had been rejected from the realms of the Enemy, and were forbidden exile in the Middle Lands. Condemned to the Nether Realms, the souls had been claimed by Anat upon their arrival, and she had exacted a terrible retribution upon them. It was a punishment that had not ceased in the ages that followed, a level of suffering that was incomprehensible to Dagian's mind.

"High Priest, and priest of the Path, deliver unto me your devotion," she commanded.

The two men lowered themselves to the sand, getting down to their knees and lowering their heads to the ground, their arms outstretched before them. They remained silent, rendering the Avatar the homage that she had asked.

Dagian hesitated, feeling the need to emulate the two men, though the command had been directed quite specifically towards the two men. Like a cold sweat, a brief swell of fear passed through her, as she did not wish to unintentionally commit an affront to the Dark Avatar.

"Hold, I would speak with you," Anat stated firmly, stopping Dagian before she lowered herself down beside the two men.

Anat's next words were meant for Dagian, and Dagian alone. "You are a warrior of the Shining One in the world of flesh. The mysteries of the Craft have been allowed to you, by the will of the Light Giver. Become everything that you are called to be, so that you can take an exalted place in the Abyss when your work in the world is finished," Anat addressed Dagian, in her melodious, haunting voice. "Eternal thrones await those who transcend the pitiful state of humankind."

"With all my life, and with all my soul," Dagian replied, humbled and overwhelmed by the development. She desired to throw herself down in grateful piety before Anat, but restrained herself.

"You have found disfavor with some in the great court, who attend the Risen Throne. But you must lift yourself up now, and hunt down the enemies of the Shining One … as I have hunted them down," Anat said, her words girded by the grisly trophies displayed so prominently around her waist. Their gruesome forms constituted a clear enough declaration.

"It is within you to regain favor, or remain in disfavor. It is not unlike the Path of Becoming that the Priests here walk upon, in that you must be strong in self-knowledge, self-awareness, and force of will," Anat said. "But you shall not depart here without receiving my sanctification."

Anat then lowered the end of her flaming spear, touching the tip of it upon Dagian's forehead. The Dark Avatar traced something there, though what the precise form was, Dagian could not tell.

A fierce heat flowed through the touch of the spear and into Dagian's body. The energy pouring into her resonated with power, and a sense of resolute self-pride, of the kind that emboldened an Avatar to refuse to bow to Adonai. It was an infusion from Anat's very essence, carrying within it something of her innermost nature.

Though coming into Dagian's body from the outside, the energy coursing through her was in full harmony with her own spirit. Though she did not have a shred of the Dark Avatar's unfathomable level of power, in some aspects they were like sisters, defiant and determined servants of Diabolos.

Without another word, the tall Avatar turned and strode back slowly towards Set, drawing up to his left side. As she moved, her form shifted smoothly back into that of a Dark Avatar, multitudinous flames replacing the image of solid flesh, wreathed with a sinuous edge of darkness.

Dagian, feeling an immense strength coursing throughout her, and brimming with lucidity, lowered her eyes, and bowed low to Set and Anat. She could not withhold a gesture of her gratitude any longer. After all of the piercing horror that she had endured when she had been brought before Azazel, Mammon, and the others, under the spell of Aaliyah, the gifts that she had been given by Apep and Anat were both unexpected and invigorating.

The personal attention from Anat was a boon far beyond her hopes, essentially invited by the great Avatar to claim a place of favor in the eternity that would follow the end of her physical life. It was everything that she desired: a throne of power, and, along with it, the full abandonment and rejection of her frail humanity.

"Rise," Set commanded the three humans. When they were standing once again, he continued. "To honor the favor that has been shown unto you, new lights shall be elevated and placed into the skies of my realm."

Herded from the dark entrance of the pyramidal temple, a mass of men and women were brought forth. Many of the strange-headed priests of Set, and a great number of the four-legged beasts that possessed the same bestial visages, escorted the terror-stricken souls. The loping beasts snarled and snapped aggressively at those unfortunate enough to be on the edges of the huddled, cowering group, while the priests of Set used their golden staffs to prod the doomed souls, eliciting shrieks of agony whenever the ends touched upon the substance of their spirits.

Dagian felt no pity for them, as they were nothing more than slaves in Set's great realm, to be used as the Dark Avatar saw fit. Their lowly state testified that they had done nothing in their lives worthy of favor in the infernal realms.

"You are given leave of your confines below, chosen to be new lights in my sky," Set addressed the trembling, human throng. For a moment the wails, sobs, and cries lessened, as the faintest touch of hope came to the captive mass.

Set paused, and Dagian knew that the Dark Avatar was inflicting the worst kind of pain, in allowing a feeling of hope to manifest, and linger for a moment amongst the captive spirits.

Set stretched his arms and wings wide, his body flaring brightly. It seemed as if the sky itself shook, as rivulets of lightning shot down from all over, concentrating upon the tips of the two obelisks and the great pyramid behind Set. The cascade sent a shimmering wave of energy down the outer facings of the structures, until the three objects were sheathed in the vibrating, bright energy.

The energy rippled outward from the obelisks and pyramid, converging upon the mass of spirits, coming up from underneath them to envelop their forms. A few cries of terror escaped the throng before they were fully encased, as the shred of hope that they had clung onto was proven to be bitterly false.

Like a macabre dance, the men and women began to writhe and contort, as a brilliant light began to emit from within their bodies, surging brighter and brighter. There was no question that the process was incredibly painful for the spirits to endure, as the last faces that Dagian could see before the light fully consumed their images were delirious with an unfathomable level of suffering.

In twos, threes, and then in a flurry, the new lights lifted up from the surface, and raced towards the upper firmament. They expanded in size as they rose, continuing to surge in their radiance. Spreading outward, the ascending stars were sprinkled in among the teeming constellations hovering far above. Watching the captivating process, Dagian looked upon the living lights of the star-scape across Set's realm with a sense of amazement.

"Now go, my priests, and disciple of the mysteries of the Craft, and complete the work of the Shining One," Set commanded.

Dagian knew that the sacred audience was at an end, as she sensed the first vibrations heralding a transformation in her perception. She looked one last time upon Set, with Anat at his left side, two regal Dark Avatars standing before the entrance of the resplendent, golden pyramid. She could feel their penetrating gazes long after the sight of their forms had passed from her sight, and knew that she could hide nothing from them, not even a thought, even though she was leaving their realm and going back to the physical world.

When the smoke-like darkness had formed anew, filling up her vision before again dissipating, to reveal the altar, sculptures, and stone blocks of the temple in Kemet, Dagian was filled with a sense of confidence that had been missing for quite some time. Whether part of the gift of Apep, the sanctification by Anat, or not, the instability that had harried her days recently had been replaced by a feeling of boldness.

She was ready to carry out her tasks with vigor, and Jibade, who was likely basking in the feeling of power bestowed by Apep, would help Dagian put everything to rights. She looked over towards the Kemetian, and her suspicions were confirmed as she beheld the spirited gleam within his eyes, and the knowing grin upon his face. The thrill of what they had experienced was still racing through him, as it was inside her.

Among the wrongs, two matters in particular would bring great personal satisfaction to her, once they had been addressed. Benedict Darwin would be called to account for having stolen the gateway device, and Juan Delgado would be made to answer for his betrayal.

# FRIEDRICH

"You are not going down there without us," declared Maroboduus, his eyes casting a particularly fiery hue, one that matched the volcanic resonance of his tone.

"And know that Maroboduus speaks for all of us on this matter," Valaris added, equally firmly.

"I still do not know how I am going to take this journey, and I have not yet told Enki of my determination to do this either," Friedrich responded, looking about at the somber countenances surrounding him.

"How can you take this journey? Even if Enki were to agree?" pressed Ulrich, looking to his right, where a few short paces were all that remained between the group and the stark edge of the Abyss.

"Can any of us fly?" Friedrich responded, letting the question hover amongst his friends for a moment, before continuing. "No, I think that will have to be addressed after telling Enki of my choice to go."

"Our free choice is to go, Friedrich," Valaris iterated.

Friedrich stared into the determined gazes of his friends, beholding unwavering conviction. He knew that there would be no persuading them onto another course. It was not that long ago that the Abyss had erupted with teeming hordes of Dark Avatars, and a wide array of horrific, infernal entities, as Friedrich and his companions held a position located far up a towering column of rock, gathered upon on a ledge jutting out from it.

From a gigantic, hundred-headed Ladon, to shrieking, swooping Sphingon, their human female visages blended in a macabre fashion with gaping jaws bristling with spiky teeth, the assault from the Abyss had been savage. The Exiles of the Middle Lands who had chosen to stand alongside Adonai's legions had endured it courageously, and often gallantly.

Many had fallen, but Friedrich's companions had acquitted themselves very well, staving off a particularly fierce attack by a group of lion-like Nemeans. All of his comrades had made it through the battle without falling into confinement within the Void, a state that was like dying for spirits.

After staring Beleth's legions in the face, and not flinching, Friedrich's companions were not about to be dissuaded from a foray into the Abyss.

"And the more of us, the better, for whatever Enki is needing that involves a journey into the Abyss," Hans interjected. He spoke in a softer tone than Maroboduus and Valaris, the two oldest souls of the group, who still carried more than a few traces of their barbarian tribal origins.

"I cannot dispute that," Friedrich said, before conceding, "And nor can I persuade any of you, apparently, away from the folly that I am committing myself to."

Without further comment, he turned and walked towards the boundary marking the end of the Middle Lands and the maw of the Abyss. He gazed downward, into the impenetrable murk that had no end. Only the silvery, gossamer threads of the extensive network of webs forged by the Sentinels could be seen closer to the edge, before they too were lost to the black depths.

Friedrich knew that Enki had been repeatedly confounded in his inner probes for the slightest sign or hint of Erishkegal's location. As revealed by Enki, the Abyss frustrated the efforts of a pure creature, one who was in full communion with Adonai, as its depths plunged farther and farther away from the unblemished realms lying beyond the ramparts of the White City.

As with the infinite nature of those realms of enduring light, the Abyss was also of a limitless nature, a bottomless pit that knew no measure in its black depths. Even the expansive worlds within worlds of the great Adversary, Diabolos, could not scratch the surface of the space within the Abyss.

It was terrifying to comprehend, as it meant that Erishkegal could be so deeply ensconced within the lightless expanse that a party could search for countless ages and still not find a trace of her.

The only hope was that Friedrich could somehow become attuned to Erishkegal's spiritual essence, and allow her to draw them to her, like a beacon piercing an endless night. As an Exile, his shortcomings in relation to Adonai's perfected realms were suddenly an asset. An imperfect being who could not withstand for even a moment the places beyond the White City, Friedrich could better endure the nature of the Abyss.

The purest darkness could be approached with no difficulty, while the perfect light remained an impassible barrier. Yet Friedrich was consoled by the fact that his continuing imperfection could be utilized for a compassionate endeavor, to bring an end to the tormenting state of uncertainty that Enki carried.

Friedrich only hoped that the answers, once uncovered, would not cause Enki despair. An Avatar was capable of the most heart-wrenching lamentations, as Friedrich had witnessed with the great Israfel, mourning in great sorrow over the spirits claimed by Diabolos and imprisoned within the Ten-Fold Kingdom. Standing at the edge of the darkness, Friedrich knew that Israfel could see the doomed souls plummeting like a rain of tears into the hellish Vortex.

Friedrich hoped that his own eyes never fell upon that awful, downward cascade. He did not know whether his soul could withstand the terrible sight of spirits on their final descent, journeying to such a horrific destination, one from which they would never return.

He turned his head, and looked back at the seven individuals waiting patiently behind him. A little farther past them, Seele was bounding up, accompanied by Silas. The Orthun padded straight up to Friedrich, showering him with affection, as Silas came to stand next to Hans and Stefan.

"Well, I know that he's not going," Friedrich said, patting the huge creature, laughing as both of the Orthun's heads licked him upon each side of his face.

"But I am," announced Silas, straightening his posture as he made the declaration.

Friedrich looked away from the Orthun, surprised by the pronouncement. "And who will look after Seele?"

"I have already made arrangements. Seele will be well cared for, and diligently watched over," Silas replied. "There are a great many in the Middle Lands who miss their dogs, who are awaiting their arrival in the heavenly realms, so there is no lack of enthusiasm to take care of him. I have a particular individual in mind too."

"Not you too, Silas," Friedrich responded, a little more heavily.

Silas, alone of all the other companions, had not been a warrior during his mortal life. He was from one of the latest generations existing in Germania, having lived in a time untouched by martial conflict, though it was one enveloped in assaults of another kind.

A quest within the Abyss would be entirely unpredictable, and fraught with dangers that would require a warrior's experience and instinctive reactions. The others knew what was involved when they made their free choices, but Friedrich was not sure about Silas. His inclusion would introduce guilt, and perhaps some distraction, if he were to join the others.

It was not just the danger of Silas suffering the fate of the Void. The reality was that it was very possible that all of them, even Enki, would find their souls confined in stasis until the end of time.

"Friedrich, speak plainly, I can see that this bothers you greatly," Silas interjected firmly.

Friedrich looked into the bright, azure eyes of his friend. With his light blonde hair, and youthful luster, Silas carried a somewhat boyish appearance. The form straddling the line of manhood only enhanced Friedrich's worries, as he had seen the light of life departed from far too many such faces during his own mortal years. While Silas had died at a young age back in the material world, the older warrior wished that he had at least taken on a more matured image in the land of exile.

"I fought well enough on the ledge, against the enemy legions, with all of you," Silas pressed. "Why should I hesitate to take my place beside you and the others if you go into the Abyss? I may not be as good of a fighter, but I cannot shield my self from the risks that you would take."

"You showed great courage, Silas," Friedrich said, "As you do now. I do not question your heart. But up on the ledge, we were in a place that we are all familiar with, fighting against an enemy we knew was coming. Not even Enki knows what may dwell in the black depths. The rest of us may well be choosing a grave folly, but all of us understand the foolishness that is often present in a soldier's choice. I would not see you do the same."

"I have cast my lot in with all of you in this place of exile, so clearly I have shown a willingness to embrace folly," Silas said, with a bright chuckle that pierced Friedrich's somberness and evoked a grin. "And I just ask for the honor of continuing in that folly."

Friedrich shook his head, and laughed. "You call keeping company with this sorry bunch honor?"

"As I see it," Silas said, taking on a serious mien. "I have grown more amongst all of you than I did in all the rootless years of my mortal life. I faced the probability of the Void already when I stood with you on the ledge. For me, that was a test, one in which I found that I was willing to stand, despite the great fear I felt in doing so. I can speak with even more surety as I stand before you now, and tell you that I desire to accompany my friends."

Friedrich ruffled one of the Orthun's heads. "And I suppose this one will be the next to ask to join."

"No, he will be staying," Silas said, with another light laugh. "He's seen quite enough of the Abyss."

"Indeed he has," Friedrich declared, as he looked into the sparkling, lively eyes that had once been so dark and angry.

He glanced back towards Silas, and sighed. "I cannot dissuade any of you, but all of you know that I did nothing to try to persuade you. That I want declared openly, and clearly, for whatever account may be kept of this ill-conceived foray of mine."

Silas smiled, and to Friedrich it looked as if the youthful spirit was standing a little straighter, as if he had just received word of promotion.

Friedrich now had several spirits going along with him that he had not intended to be journeying into the Abyss with, but one remained that was necessary for the dangerous expedition. It was, ironically, the one being that would have to be persuaded.

He looked around at his companions. "As much as I enjoy your company, and as much as you have imposed yourselves on my intended journey, I must seek out Enki alone."

"Then we will await the word that you are ready to depart," Maroboduus said, with a broadening grin. "We can afford to be patient. After all, we Exiles have all the time in the world."

# JOVAN

"Looks like there may be some urgent need for the Peace Commission soon enough," Jovan said, swirling the burgundy liquid within his crystal wineglass as he glanced over towards Kaira.

Tensions were mounting swiftly in the Far East. Taiyoan had effectively declared its independence, stoking the fires of Mandaria's long-held ire over the island's resistance to reunification. The Mandarian Prime Minister had demanded that Taiyoan renounce its position, or there would be grave consequences.

"It is such a time for David Sorath to be taken with illness," Kaira responded, her tone sounding full of sympathy.

"Yes, there is that too," Jovan responded.

David Sorath, the appointed head of the World Summit's Peace Commission, had been reported as having come down with a very aggressive illness, right before the tensions had been inflamed in the Far East.

"Do not let Mr. Sorath's absence inhibit you from putting forth your own ideas, Kaira," Jovan encouraged her. "The world cannot be allowed to descend into war. There is too much at stake for everyone."

He thought back to the clandestine meeting that had taken place in the adjacent chamber. High-ranking government and military representatives of the UCAS and Mandaria, and even Taiyoan, had been seated around the room, discussing the very events that were now transpiring. Jovan knew that great violence would occur before things ran their full course, but the upheaval was orchestrated, and with definitive purpose. It was simply a matter of working to identify, and swiftly eliminate, any unintended consequences.

He knew that Lilith would approve of his steadfast assistance to Kaira. The spiritual entity had been very clear about the importance of Jovan's firm and enduring support. He knew that Kaira had some part to play in the grand scheme of the Convergence, and he would do everything he could to be there for her. If he was to be honest with himself, it was now to the point that anything less was unthinkable. Possessing his full loyalty, Kaira had affected him in a way that no other woman had.

"I don't think that I've been shy about voicing my insights," Kaira responded, with a buoyant grin and the energetic sparkle in her eyes that always captivated Jovan.

"That gives me a little relief, as your insights may be needed for more than just the matter in the Far East," Jovan replied.

"As in needed closer to home?" she asked him, her countenance growing more serious.

Jovan nodded. "There will be vital matters of national security to attend to here."

"It sounds as if everything is going to be moving very fast, but I am confident that it can be managed," Kaira replied.

"Many will be taking shelter, in the underground refuges, for the time being," Jovan said. "To ride out the storm."

"Very spacious accommodations, for temporary shelters," Kaira remarked, raising an eyebrow. "Seems like a preparation for a much longer duration."

"For all intents and purposes, they are complete cities," Jovan admitted. "But nobody wants to live like a mole, unless things are too dangerous on the surface. And things may become very unstable for a time."

"All the better reason to bring about the peace that comes with a comprehensive order," Kaira said. "And to do it swiftly, so that they do not have to live like moles for too long."

"It is my hope that it all happens quickly," Jovan said, loosing a sigh. "I would prefer that things are settled and well-ordered myself. The chaos that is looming is not to my liking."

"It can be done swiftly, if the will is there," Kaira said, resolutely.

As was happening with greater frequency, Jovan could sense the rising conviction girding Kaira's words. She was really coming into her own, brimming with confidence now that she was at the Peace Commission. Yet as friendly as she was, he was just glad that the harsher elements of the Convergence lay with others. He knew that Kaira could never stomach the brutality and cold logic inherent in several actions that had to be executed in order to accomplish their ultimate aims.

Blood would flow copiously, carried out by others well-suited for such actions. The loosing of the pandemic was beyond any considerations for mercy, as it was like setting torches to the parched, sun-scorched fields of drought-riddled lands. Young and old alike would be swept up in the inferno, as a wealthy elite was shielded in comfort, having received the vaccine that was ready from the outset.

"I am ready to face whatever may come, Jovan," Kaira stated.

"Much that is very unpleasant will come to pass before a new light breaks through the storm clouds."

He held her eyes for a moment, again amazed at her propensity for being in tune with Jovan's inner thoughts and worries.

"I'm sorry if I seem patronizing at times," Jovan said. "I just find myself wanting to protect you from the worst aspects of the things ahead."

"And such devotion is a quality that I find to my liking, very much so," Kaira said. With a gleaming smile, she brought her legs up onto the couch, and propped her head up, where her hand was braced by her elbow set on the arm of the couch.

Jovan gave her a slight bow. "And my devotion you shall always have, Kaira."

"And I accept it," Kaira said, laughing merrily.

There was no mistaking her intents, though Jovan wished dearly that it could be otherwise. Their relationship was not one that was progressing towards romance, but it was something much more than mere friendship. He felt a bond that transcended even the familial, a sensation that he had never felt before.

He looked down at his near-empty wineglass, and let a sigh out. "Alas, I have drained my cup, and it needs replenishing."

He rose up to his feet, feeling a little light-headed from both the wine and spending time with Kaira.

"Would you mind if I go down to the wine cellar, and select a particularly special vintage?" he asked her.

"By all means," Kaira said. "You have quite the taste for the better things in this world."

"Yes, I do, don't I?" Jovan said, in a jesting manner. "You pause here, and I'll be back in just a couple of minutes. This place, as you know, is big enough that it takes an extra moment or two to get around it."

"I'm just relaxing, and I'll be here when you return," Kaira said.

Jovan grinned, and headed out of the room. He worked his way to the back of the mansion, where a staircase led down to the cellar where his main wine collection was stored.

He eyed the racks that represented a fortune in select and rare vintages. Without hesitation, he went for one of his most prized, from the heartland of Francia and well over a hundred and fifty years old. Jovan whispered into the musty air, "The best vintage, for the best woman that I know."

The hackles on his neck rose, and he felt a deepening of the chill within the air, turning frigid in moments. He did not need to turn to look to know that his otherworldly patron had manifested in the shadows to his right.

"I am pleased to hear those words," Lilith's seductive voice drifted to him.

"I have carried out your wishes, though it is not a chore to do things for her," Jovan said.

A laugh came from the shadows. "Just do not try to cross the boundary."

Jovan knew what she was referring to, and her open voicing of it lanced into him. He responded, more sharply, "I'm well aware of that boundary. I don't need reminding."

"I can feel your hopes well enough," Lilith replied, with an edge.

"What I hope for, and what can be, are separate things," Jovan retorted in irritation. "Why have you come here? I know it is not for idle conversation. That has never been your way."

"Do you not enjoy seeing me?" Lilith replied with another laugh. "No, I come with purpose."

Jovan finally turned to face the area where he felt her presence. A form billowed in the darkness, vaguely feminine, with two shimmering eyes.

As he looked upon her, the outlines of her face solidified, revealing a stunningly beautiful woman.

"Do you prefer this image, Jovan?" Lilith prodded him.

"A little easier to talk to than a shadow, yes," he admitted.

"Then before you go back to rejoin Kaira, let us speak briefly," Lilith said. "It is desired that you convene a meeting of those with influence at the Global Democratic Resource, as well as those of power with the National Bank Reserve and other central banks."

Jovan thought immediately of Kaira and the Peace Commission, which was provided funding by the Global Democratic Resource, another institution of the World Summit.

"And at this desired meeting?" Jovan asked.

"The Peace Commission must receive immediate funding on a level far exceeding where it is now," Lilith replied. "No less than a ten-fold increase in its financing."

"You are expecting quite a surge in need for the Peace Commission,"

Jovan stated. "I must tell you that things are a little awry there with the recent sickness of Mr. Sorath."

"Not a matter to worry about," Lilith replied in dismissive fashion. "You get the funding flowing to the Peace Commission, so that when it is needed, it will have no lack of ability to move with strength and speed."

"Something to do with Kaira?" Jovan asked her.

"She is a leader, Jovan, with wisdom," she answered.

"But she has only recently come aboard the Peace Commission. Are you expecting too much, too soon?" Jovan said, as his protective instincts flared up, even in the face of the spirit-entity.

"We all have our parts to play in the hour to come," Lilith responded. "And I would not guide you wrongly, in any way, regarding Kaira. You will see in time that she is possessed of great gifts."

Jovan did not like the enigmatic answer, but Lilith had never guided him wrongly before, not even once. He took a deep breath in, and let it out slowly. "You have a way, Lilith, but I will do as you have asked. Have I ever not done what you have desired of me?"

"You have served well," she said evenly.

A retort jumped to the tip of his tongue at the notion of serving, but Jovan kept the impulse quiet. Lilith spoke in strange ways at times, and he did not want to end the conversation on a sour note.

He nodded to her. "And is that all?"

"For the present," Lilith said, and her form began to dissipate, quickly becoming indistinct.

Jovan stared at the empty space for a few moments more, as the room returned back to the light chill that had been in the air before her manifestation. Making a mental note to summon an array of bankers and World Summit personnel to his home when the morning came, he took up the wine bottle he had selected, and started back for the cozy den where Kaira was patiently awaiting him.

# JUAN

Juan was sitting in a high-backed, amply padded chair, casually perusing a periodical on an electronic reading device lent to him by Father Rader. After several years of almost daily stress and pressure in the business world, during his tenure at Babylon Technologies, it had been very pleasant to indulge in some idle time. But he was not bothered when he was distracted by the sounds of voices approaching in the hallway, just outside of his room. A break in his recent routine appealed to him.

The sounds drifted into silence at the doorway, as Father Brunner looked in upon him.

"Hey Father Brunner," Juan greeted him amiably, lowering the electronic reader to his lap.

"Sorry to interrupt you, Juan. I need you to come with us, but first, can you change into these?" he asked, while extending a small stack of neatly folded clothes forward in his hands. An underlying tone in the priest's voice told Juan that something serious was afoot.

Getting to his feet, and setting the reader down on the end table by the chair, Juan walked over and took the clothes, wondering. He looked to the priest for some sort of answer, but was offered no immediate explanation. Father Brunner just smiled, pulling the door shut, as he backed into the hallway to allow Juan some privacy.

Juan went through the clothes, finding that he had been given a relaxed-fitting pair of brown pants, a long-sleeved, crème-hued shirt, and an outer coat of three-quarters length.

He donned the new garb, and opened the door to the room when he had folded his other clothes and set them aside. Father Brunner was still standing there, smiling as he looked to Juan.

"I am sure that you found that to be an unusual request, but I promise you it will make much more sense, very shortly," Father Brunner informed him.

There were three individuals standing in the hallway with Father Brunner, and their appearances readily grabbed Juan's attention.

One was a younger man, of about thirty years of age. His short-sleeved shirt exposed the sheath of artwork covering his arms, a mosaic of elaborately rendered tattoos that ran all the way to his wrists. His nose, ears, and lips exhibited an assortment of silver piercings, and his blond hair had many locks dyed in a reddish hue, arrayed in a spiky, haphazard fashion. Despite his tougher physical appearance, he exhibited a friendly smile, and held a warm look within his hazel eyes, as Juan met his gaze.

With him were two women, one who looked to be in her fifties, and the other who Juan gauged to be around her mid-thirties.

The older of the two women had long, thick gray hair, pulled back into a ponytail that ran down the midpoint of her back. Her facial features were more angular, with a sharper nose, and her dark eyes regarded Juan attentively. She had dark brown, flat-soled boots, tan pants, and a loose-fitting, off-white blouse.

The younger woman had her auburn hair fashioned into a style fronted with short, evenly-trimmed bangs. The rest sloped a little longer, as it continued from the shorter hair at the back of her head up towards the front, where the locks framed her rounded face down to the chin. Her bright green eyes carried an electric spark within them, lively and alert.

She wore a dark blue top, with snug-fitting, dark pants, with the ends of flat-heeled black boots emerging below.

"I would like you to meet a few friends of mine," Father Brunner announced. He glanced towards the young man. "First, this fine lad is Kiaran."

"Pleased to meet you, Juan," Kiaran said, shaking Juan's hand with a firm grip. He had a wide grin on his face, with a hint of mischief dancing in his eyes. "Ready for a transformation?"

"And this is Magdalene, a dear friend of mine," Father Brunner said before Juan could ask about Kiaran's last statement, with a nod towards the older of the two women.

"Hello, Juan," she greeted him, with a more formal air, extending him a handshake that also carried a stout grip. He caught her accent, which told him that she was from the Allied Kingdom.

Father Brunner then indicated the younger woman. "And, to round things out, this is Genevieve."

Genevieve flashed Juan a winsome smile that matched the liveliness in her eyes, exchanging handshakes with him. Like Magdalene's, there was a robust nature to her grip.

"Kiaran is with the Order, and you have just met your first two Shield Maidens of the Rising Dawn," Father Brunner announced. "And they are all here specifically to help you tonight."

"Is there anything you need to tell me?" Juan asked him in a half-joking manner, as his curiosity rose. His eyes moved to the faces of the others, hoping to get some sort of clue.

"Just come along with us, and it will make a whole lot of sense very shortly. We have to do something a little unorthodox, but it should be very effective for our purposes," Father Brunner said. He then gave Juan a wink. "We are going to thoroughly confound those eyes that are watching for you."

Juan was ushered down the hall, and on into the main kitchen, where a table had been shifted towards the center of the space. An array of containers, brushes, sponges, and other items lay atop the table's surface, the sight of which put a quizzical expression on Juan's face.

There were a couple more individuals waiting for them in the kitchen. One was a blond-haired man, who was a few inches taller than Juan, while the other might well have been the man's sister, given the similarities of their characteristics.

She was a little shorter than Juan, but had lengthy, bright blonde locks that had an untamed cast about them. Her blue eyes were remarkable, carrying great depth and intensity within their look. She had a strong jawline, and carried herself with her shoulders set broadly, her thumbs hooked into the narrow black leather belt threaded around her dark jeans.

Juan nodded to her, and looked away with a nervous smile, when he realized that his gaze had lingered a little longer than he had intended. Though her full lips did not part, the trace of a grin showed upon them.

"Matthias, of the Order, and Skylar, of the Shield Maidens," Father Brunner stated, in the way of introduction.

"Very nice to meet both of you," Juan said, though he held Skylar's stalwart gaze for only a moment. He looked back to Father Brunner, not quite sure what he was expected to do, or what was happening.

"Many members of both the Order and the Shield Maidens are departing the city tonight, as all signs are pointing to great upheaval occurring very soon. When the turmoil begins, the cities will be all but inescapable," Father Brunner said. "We have a chance to get you out of here, with a protective escort, while we can, but we do not want the eyes watching this place to recognize you when you leave."

"I'm sure that anyone that has been assigned to look for me can pick me out of a crowd in a second," Juan said.

"Which is why you aren't leaving here just yet, until a few precautions are taken," Father Brunner responded. "Kiaran has very useful skills for our needs. He works on the sets of movies and television shows, doing special effects makeup. Fortunately for us, he happens to be very, very good at what he does, and he also happens to be in the Order. Tonight, he is going to help you gain a new identity."

"Have a seat, and we'll get underway," Kiaran said, with another bright grin, as he gestured towards an unoccupied chair by the table. "If we had time to do a full facial cast, it would be just about perfect, but I'll get you suitable at a glance, don't worry."

Juan sat down, still not quite sure where all of this was going. He said little, as Kiaran began to apply the techniques of his trade. Kiaran used adhesives and makeup to secure, and blend in, small latex pieces to his face, at the forehead, chin, nose, and cheeks. The full process took quite some time.

"High time I put my skills to use for something a little more substantial than the vacuous crap I'm usually collecting my paychecks on," Kiaran remarked, chuckling, as he leaned back to admire his handiwork. His brow furrowed, as he stared at something to the side of Juan's face. He leaned in with his vial and brush to touch up some blemish that had attracted his attention.

Kiaran straightened up, peering closely at the spot with a serious mien. He evaluated it for a long moment, and then a smile blossomed on his face. He glanced at the others in the room, "That'll do. Perfect seam, even if it's shown in high-definition. Which should be pretty good for real life as well."

"Outstanding work, Kiaran, as I knew you would do," Father Brunner commended the artist, before giving Juan a wink. "And you, my friend, do indeed have a brand new look."

Father Brunner then gave Juan a pair of shoes that were clearly not designed for comfort, but rather for deception. To outside appearances, the pair of boots looked normal, but inside they were revealed to be a type of stilt, which bestowed him with a few additional inches in height.

His hair was then changed to blond, with the help of a wig that was fitted into place.

"And last, just in case the bastards are smooth enough to take note of some small details," Kiaran remarked, reaching down to his right pocket.

Pulling out a small case, he popped it open, exposing a pair of wells in which rested a set of blue contacts. Kiaran asked, "Do you have anything in right now?"

Juan shook his head.

"These might take a little getting used to, but you only need them on until you are out of the city," Kiaran said. "Hopefully, by then you'll be far removed from those watching for you."

"We can hope," Juan replied.

"Okay, tilt your head back, just a little," Kiaran instructed, as he assisted with the placement of the blue contacts.

"Here, check it out," Kiaran asked him, once the contacts were inserted, offering Juan a mirror. "Stand up too, to get the full effect. This is when all of it will make sense!"

Though the stilt-shoes felt a little awkward, Juan was relieved to find that he could keep a relatively good balance in them, as he rose up out of the chair. Taking the mirror from Kiaran, he stared in astonishment at the reflection, as a sense of awe came over him.

On a casual glance, he bore a strikingly close resemblance to the blond-haired man standing quietly in the kitchen, leaning against the counter by the sink.

"I suppose both of us could go by the name Matthias for the time being," Juan's mirror image stated, in a thicker Germanian accent.

A grin spread on his face, as he continued to appraise Kiaran's handiwork.

"It is not everyday I get to visit with myself, in such a way," he stated, taking a step closer, and looking Juan directly in the eye. The boots were sized perfectly, bringing the men to an even height. Juan could tell that he was not the only one astonished by Kiaran's artistry. "It is strange, but it is also incredible."

"I think that should suffice, for filing out of here, and getting into a car in a relaxed manner," Father Brunner said.

"We shouldn't delay any longer than necessary," Magdalene said firmly, looking to Father Brunner.

"No, we shouldn't," the priest agreed. He turned back to Juan. "Magdalene and the others will be taking you to a safe haven, run by someone with the Order. We are always at risk, but there will be far less risk for you there than here."

"And you? And Father Rader?" Juan asked.

"We have a church congregation to attend to, and many people that are going to need some manner of beacon, when the skies darken across this city," Father Brunner said, with a somber edge. "A starless night is falling, and fear is going to take hold until dawn breaks it."

Big Athanasius padded into the kitchen at that moment, working through the small gathering to Father Brunner's side. The mastiff lifted up Father Brunner's hand with its broad head. The priest rubbed the massive dog affectionately between the ears, and looked back to Juan with a grin.

"And don't worry about me or Father Rader ... we've got this big fellow to keep us company on the church grounds," he said, giving the dog a pat on its muscular flank.

"Thank you for giving me a place to go, and for sheltering me," Juan said, finding that the words were inadequate for how he felt.

"Was there any other viable choice?" Father Brunner asked him. "Keep on your new path, Juan. It may be more difficult to tread, and bring you much more hardship for the time being than the one that you had been on, but the destinations of the two roads could not be more different."

"I will do my best, Father Brunner," Juan said. He stepped forward, and gave the priest a tight embrace.

"And that is all that can be asked," Father Brunner replied.

After Kiaran, Matthias, and Skylar had wished him well, Juan accompanied Magdalene and Genevieve out to their car, a silver, four-door model of recent make. He got into the back seat, sitting in the same spot that Matthias had occupied when the car had first arrived. To any outside observer, it looked as if the recent guests were departing, with every one of them accounted for.

Juan had to admit that it was indeed a very clever, creative ruse, as the car pulled out, and headed down the street, beginning to make its way through downtown Troy.

# GODRAL

A flash of movement, followed by a darting shadow, were all that announced the arrival of Falagen within the moonlit clearing where Godral was patiently awaiting the An-Ki scout. With his great speed, Falagan, and a precious few An-Ki allowed to remain in their wolf-forms, kept up a diligent watch on the outer perimeter of Conrad Rudel's property.

Deeper within the expansive area, the main body of An-Ki belonging to Sargor's clan had settled very well, much to Godral's relief. A cold winter had passed, but the clan had not endured undue hardship. With a steady supply of food, and removed from the immediate specter of the Night Hunt, the refuge provided and maintained by Conrad had been nothing less than a miraculous boon.

The place had helped to lessen the general discomfort when most of the clan had been made to assume human forms, so as not to attract unwanted attention from eyes watching over the woodlands in the skies above. It went without saying that a few hundred giant wolves would have been espied at some point, so Sargor had decided to lessen the chances of the clan's discovery. In time, the decision would also help in acclimating the clan members to a human appearance, and the world that existed around them.

The Celestial Messenger of Adonai, Calliel, had appeared to the An-Ki many times, and aided in the watch for signs of any threats from the Night Hunters. The malevolent entities had not been present in the vicinity since the time they had been so roundly driven off by the strange, formidable creatures called Watchers. The An-Ki's unexpected saviors had not been seen either, after manifesting in the dark hour when a comprehensive slaughter of the An-Ki clan had appeared to be inevitable.

Sargor still spoke with a tone of wonder when speaking of the Watcher that he had encountered, which had fallen upon the Night Hunter that was on the verge of slaying the aging clan chieftain. It was said to have multiple pairs of wings, a human-like upper torso, and a four-legged, extended body, not to mention a glow that emanated from the surface of its skin. It was hard for Godral to picture such an unusual creature in his mind, but he was simply grateful for their existence and intervention, as nothing that he or his warriors could have done would have stopped the carnage.

While the Night Hunters had not been sensed in many paths of the moon, Godral was not about to relax his guard, or allow those with him to do so either. While in his human-like form, and uncomfortably itchy, as he continued to adjust to having his skin covered in textile clothing, Godral still frequented the boundary areas. He wanted to keep appraised of everything observed by the small group of An-Ki warriors assigned to ward the boundary region. It was not entirely unlike the times in the world that they had left behind, when patrols had been maintained on the clan's territory.

"Godral! There is something moving through these woods. But we cannot find a solid trace of it," Falagen announced, having come to a halt a few paces before him.

"What do you mean?" Godral queried, instantly troubled by the other's words.

"Many of those who patrol the boundary can sense something, as if it carried a strong scent, but we cannot gain sight of it," Falagen replied. "Whatever this unseen thing might be."

"What does it seem like?" Godral asked.

"It seems human, to all of our senses," Falagen said. "But no human could evade us so skillfully."

"Where does this presence go?"

"We followed it once to the cabin where Benedict is dwelling," Falagen said. "The place that you asked us to keep a constant watch upon."

"But you saw nothing?"

"No, nothing," Falagen answered.

"And no sign in the ground?" Godral asked.

"Not a single track," Falagen responded.

Godral could see that the An-Ki scout was both confounded and exasperated by the phenomenon. Just as the Night Hunters had not expected the Watchers, it was more than possible that the clan would be faced with something of the Enemy that they did not expect.

Godral wished that he could seek out the Messenger of Adonai, though summoning Calliel was beyond his ability. The Avatar would come and go of his own accord, and Godral could only hope that it was not long before he could consult with the celestial being.

"Can you show me where this presence left these grounds?" Godral asked.

"Yes, I can," Falagen responded.

"Give me a moment," Godral told the scout.

Godral slowly got out of his human clothing, already dreading the pains that came with the transformation. He stacked the clothing, and set it aside, underneath some brush. Turning back towards Falagen, he stood naked in the rays of moonlight filtering down through the trees.

Though it was much more painful to go from a human shape into the four-legged lupine form, than to the two-legged one, Godral underwent a direct transformation into his quadruped form. Bones and muscles shifted, the former realigning significantly, as his jaws extended and his limbs took new angles.

A tingling pain erupted all over his skin, as bristling hairs sprouted and pushed outward, covering him with a layer of coarse, dark fur. His ears lengthened, and slid higher atop his head, and his chest swelled in girth, even as his limbs became leaner and more elongated.

Relief flooded him when he was finished, as he gazed through golden eyes back at Falagen, who was quietly waiting for him to finish the process.

"Let us hope that we can sense this presence soon, and when it departs, we will follow it as long as we can," Godral said to the scout. "Now take me to the place where it left the border of this land."

Falagen turned, and sprang back in the direction he had entered the clearing from. Godral welcomed the feeling that came to him as he leaped after Falagen, breaking into a bounding run through the trees.

He savored the air brushing against his body and the explosions of power as he propelled his body forward, straining to keep pace with Falagen. They wended their way around hills and trees, working towards the boundary.

When they were standing on the edge of Conrad's property, Godral drew silent, thinking carefully. In their non-human forms, the An-Ki would evoke an immediate, and unwelcome, reaction, if they were sighted within the communities of humankind. It would be a great challenge to track an unseen, fast-moving entity, while also avoiding the eyes of humans.

There was also the matter of the nature of the unseen presence. If it could perceive Benedict and the cabin, then it had certainly observed the An-Ki. It would know that it was being tracked, and probably already had a sense that the An-Ki were aware of its presence when it moved amongst them.

"Let us hope the Messenger returns," Godral said, as a gust of chilly wind ruffled his black fur. "I fear we are ill-prepared for what is happening."

# JIBADE

Jibade had only been given a couple of days to settle in, after arriving in Troy with Dagian. The long flight from Kemet had been uneventful, which was a tremendous relief to him. As much as flying far out of his body, sometimes at great heights, felt entirely natural, traveling in planes unnerved him completely.

Dagian had provided him with exquisite accommodations on her sprawling estate, and Jibade regretted that he could not take more time to enjoy them. He had access to all of the wine that he wanted, a heated indoor pool, and many more luxuries that he wished he could indulge in. Still, he was not about to neglect his duties, and set about his preparations for the missions to come.

As a spirit from a living human, Jibade had a special advantage, in that he could evade even Avatars as he traveled about the world. It was not that they were incapable of manifesting on the levels that his spirit occupied when out of his body. Navigating was like being attuned to various kinds of frequencies, in a way of describing it, and any spirit could travel within the astral realms. Rather, Avatars failed to become aware of him until he had already moved onward.

As a precaution, Jibade kept moving, and did not linger for very long in places where some sense of him might be picked up.

Dagian had wasted little time with him, briefing him about his tasks. He was to go after Juan Delgado first, a man who was a former, high-level employee of hers. The next assignment would involve Benedict Darwin, the man who had evidently been the source of so much trouble for her.

The process of leaving his body was simple enough. Lying flat on his back, with no clothes or covers on, Jibade let his body and mind ease, muscle by muscle, and moment by moment. He focused his thoughts upon a single flame, which represented the guiding light of Set to his mind and soul. The deep meditation, combined with the relaxation, brought his body into the state necessary to lift his spirit out.

Nothing about the process brought any anxiety to him, not even the loud roaring that sounded in his ears each time he departed the flesh. He did not worry for even a second when he found himself floating at the level of the bedroom ceiling, his body left below in the bed.

His mind was as lucid as ever when in the astral territory, and he immediately sought out Juan Delgado, heading to the Universalist Church where Dagian said he had taken refuge. The rain-slicked streets outside glistened brightly, as he sped down the avenues and thoroughfares of Troy. People were moving about everywhere, but he paid them no heed, single-minded on the directive he had been given.

There were some distortions to shapes and objects, as he straddled a narrow zone between the worlds, but most things retained their appearances well enough for him to navigate efficiently.

He drew up to the towering façade of the Saint Bosco Universalist Church. It was approached by a set of wide steps from the street level, up to where a heavy pair of bronze doors was set in the entrance. Jibade did not need to activate the electronic door control, and instead passed right through the metal and on into the nave.

There were likely some spirits of Adonai about the grounds of the Church, but they did not appear to perceive him, as he was not interfered with as he drifted throughout the capacious church. He ignored the iconography and statuary within, with its representations of the Holy Liberator and Sacred Mother, as the sights of such things only angered him.

In his mind, only those such as the Shining One, and great Set, deserved to have temples erected to them. He was in a house meant for weaklings, not the strong, and the sooner that they could all be torn down, the better.

Without hesitation, he went right through a stone wall to the left, after satisfying himself that the main church was empty. He found himself in residential quarters, and went more slowly from room to room, and down every hallway, to take account of every living being that he could find.

He kept alert for things of the spirit world. The dark things of the Abyss rarely caused trouble for him, as most recognized the touch of Set upon Jibade. But sometimes there were denizens of the Abyss and native inhabitants of the astral zones that were like wild predators, monstrous things that had to be avoided.

He found three people, a large dog, and a cat within the quarters. None of the three men that he encountered remotely fit the description of Juan Delgado given to him by Dagian.

Two of the men he determined to be the priests who resided at the church, but the third man's identity was a mystery. The only thing that Jibade knew was that he was not Juan Delgado. Tall, with bright blond hair that reached down to his shoulders, the man possessed striking blue eyes. Reclined in a chair, Jibade had come across him idly watching television.

The massive dog had displayed a few signs of agitation, rousing itself up from where it had been lying on the carpet near to the chair. It was not unusual for animals to gain some sense of his presence, but Jibade could tell that it did not perceive him directly.

Jibade returned back to Dagian's estate not long afterwards, waking up within his physical body. He proved his worth quickly enough, rendering a full, detailed report of his excursion to Dagian less than ten minutes later.

She had not been pleased at the news that Juan could not be found, but Jibade could tell that she was very pleased with his skill.

The second major task turned out to be a little more extensive, and, eventually, much more profitable. Intelligence gleaned from within the CSD, and their woodland sweep of the Frontiersman National Forest, narrowed down the area that Jibade journeyed through.

Under the light of a shining moon that was close to full, he suddenly came across a pair of immense wolves. They were far too large to be native to the area. He knew at once they were not supernatural denizens, but instead the creatures that Dagian had briefed him about; and their presence told him that it was very possible that Benedict Darwin was in the vicinity.

Yet one thing bothered him right away, as it seemed as if the two great wolves quickly sensed him. Their eyes did not focus upon his form, so he knew they could not see him, but like a faint trace of scent they were able to trail him at a distance, as he moved through the woods.

The wolves' awareness of his presence rattled him enough to ruin his first foray, causing him to snap back to his body in an instant, but he steeled himself for his next visit.

The following two times that he went into the woods, he did not find any sign of Benedict Darwin. But on his fourth journey, he came across a small, isolated cabin with its lights on.

He broke off that excursion early, as the wolves were coming uncomfortably close to where he was hovering in observation. He was not so sure that they could not draw a direct bead upon his position.

Jibade returned the very next evening. The huge wolves picked up his trace again, and followed him, but he was able to go into the house before they drew close. He saw a man inside quietly reading a book, who closely fit the description of Benedict Darwin.

His rounded face was covered in a short beard, and his thinner hair looked a little disheveled, extending just past the level of his ears. A bottle of scotch, accompanied by a half-empty glass with three cubes of ice in it, rested next to the man on an end table.

Elation coursed through Jibade, as it was a positive identity. He wasted no time, wanting to bring the news back to Dagian without delay. He rushed through the walls, and sped past the wolves that had followed him, causing one of them to whirl about in alarm.

They could perceive him like no other animal ever had before, which bothered him considerably. A part of him wanted to speed back to his body, but a last thought prevented him from doing so.

There was nothing to really stop him, so he decided to take careful note of his direction through the woodlands from the cabin, to be able to give Dagian more detailed information as to where Benedict Darwin had been located. Memorizing several distinctive landmarks, he completed his route, and then allowed himself to return to his prone body.

Dagian had exhibited considerable delight at the news that he delivered to her, which pleased Jibade greatly. After giving her an account of the landmarks that he had memorized, and a thorough description of the cabin, he had turned in for a long, restful sleep.

From what he was told the next morning, Dagian had relayed the information onward to Xavier Gerard of the TTDF. An advanced drone with surveillance capabilities had been dispatched to the skies over the area of the Frontiersman National Forest where the cabin had been located.

Jibade gave the matter little further thought, as he eased into the hot tub set near to the indoor pool. He took a long sip of white wine, and closed his eyes, feeling the soothing massage of the warm waters begin to work on his tired body.

He was just glad that he was not Benedict Darwin, who was not likely to be free of Dagian's grasp for much longer. As for himself, Dagian would seek to use his skills soon enough, and he intended to enjoy his accommodations a little before then.

# GREGORY

"Nice, I'd read about those, but didn't think I'd see one hovering right over Godwinton. This must be what it's like being a bird-watcher, and seeing a newly discovered species," Gregory remarked, with an edge of sarcasm, peering through the long-range binoculars at the elongated craft drifting slowly across the skies.

"What is it?" asked Benjamin, leaning on the railing bordering the walkway on the second level of the apartment building.

Gregory was more than happy to pay for the small studio space on a month-to-month basis, in cash, to be closer to the heart of Godwinton. He had expected to see the kind of sights that he was now viewing through the binoculars.

"A Medusa. Unmanned surveillance. Nine cameras. And with the satellites linked to it, it can take up a constant watch on all the town, instead of focusing on a specific area like most other surveillance drones do," Gregory replied.

"Unless I'm way off the mark on my gut instinct, I think they are going to be paying a visit to Sheriff Howard pretty soon," Gregory commented acidly. "Maybe invoke a few formalities to provide cover, make the right-sounding legalistic declarations to pay lip-service to the things they have no regard for, and then they'll do whatever the hell they want to. It's their mode of operation."

"Sheriff Howard acting like a genuine sheriff turned out to be quite an inconvenience for a group used to playing word games to justify any course of action desired."

"Probably not too happy about all of the folks that joined in to help him out either," Benjamin added, with a pointed glance at Gregory.

Gregory knew that if the CSD or others knew of his identity, he would not be standing right there with Benjamin. His fifty caliber sniper rifle had wreaked considerable havoc amongst the CSD and WSB troopers, even downing a helicopter with one of the better shots that he had ever taken.

Yet it was true that many of those that had taken the stand with Sheriff Howard were identifiable, and known. A few province troopers had been forcibly subdued just prior to Sheriff Howard's intervention, and these had undoubtedly been careful to witness everything that they could. Some of them had spoken out forcefully against Sheriff Howard's decision, in the wake of the incident at the Revere home.

"No, they're probably not happy, and we are going to have to get ready to give them more to be unhappy about, if they want to try and run roughshod again over the people," Gregory declared, holding his brother's gaze.

"That's what I figured you would say," Benjamin replied, with a smirk.

"More than a few of the boys and girls I've been visiting with at the gun range are of a similar mind," Gregory said. "A few marines among the bunch too."

"Don't go off half-cocked, Gregory," Benjamin said firmly. "You know more than anyone what they are capable of, and what they are willing to do."

"I'll keep my discipline, but if what is happening is not confronted, then we only have ourselves to blame for the nightmare they are going to put over all of us," Gregory responded.

Benjamin's communication-link then crackled to life, with a stoic, deep voice summoning all officers in the area to report to duty without delay. Gregory did not have to understand the number codes to know what was going on.

"I think that visit is about to happen, pretty soon, in one form or another," Gregory said.

"A time of reckoning for a lot of us," Benjamin responded, with a grim countenance.

"I have faith in you, Ben. You'll know what to do," Gregory said.

"Thanks, Gregory," Benjamin replied. "But I guess I'd better be on my way, I've got a little bit of a drive ahead of me."

"Well, I'll be stickin' around here. Like I said, I think this is where things are going to heat up again," Gregory said.

"You know what they say about looking for trouble," Benjamin said, with a cautionary tone.

"I intend to find it, and give it the fight of its life," Gregory replied curtly, with a look of steel, before he turned to gaze back up at the drone.

He listened to Benjamin's steps on the walkway, before they echoed in the stairwell down to the ground level.

# DAGIAN

How Juan Delgado had eluded her grasp, Dagian had not an inkling. The area had been watched tightly, around the clock, but somehow Juan had managed to slip out, completely undetected.

After some analysis of the data, looking at all of the comings and goings at the church, it was found that the blond-haired man encountered by Jibade had indeed been observed arriving. But all the surveillance data indicated that he had left the very same day, with the same group that he had come with.

The disappearance of Delgado, and the lack of any observation of the blond-haired man returning to the church grounds pulled strongly at Dagian. She demanded that all camera data be accessed, including the ubiquitous city cameras, to tell her more about where the car with the blond-haired man in it had gone.

Dagian stared out of the tall windows, gazing in thoughtful silence across the buildings and streets of Troy from her lofty vantage. Production was well underway on the Living ID implants, with millions already in storage and awaiting hosts. It would not be much longer before they were brought forth, in a time of terrible crisis, as part of a comprehensive solution that would promise to bring about security and peace across the entire world.

The storms of that crisis were already starting to break out. A few men and women that associated with Dagian had already set out for Northhaven, the sprawling underground city located just outside of Mile

City, to take up a luxurious state of refuge and wait out the inevitable conflict.

Dagian would not be joining them. She had been renewed by Apep and Anat, and would be doing everything she could to lay claim on a throne in the next world. The great hour was arriving, and she could not wait to see what the Shining One would reveal in the days to come.

She sensed something grand and unprecedented, and wanted to be a witness to everything that was about to happen. The Remaking loomed ever closer, that hallowed day when the Light Giver would remake every last thing in His image. Dagian nearly swooned at the thought of what such a world would be like, freed from Adonai's presence forever.

She instilled some sobering caution within herself, as the euphoria ebbed, reminding herself that she could not rest on any laurels. Dagian had made that mistake not that long ago, and the results had nearly been disastrous.

This time, she would pursue everything with a relentless diligence, and that included finding out where Juan Delgado was hiding. He would be called to account for his betrayal, before he could cause any trouble for Dagian. She hoped that Jibade had rested himself, because he was going to be pushed to the limits of his abilities in pursuit of the traitor.

Juan could not hide from her forever, and when she had him within her grasp, what she had done with Nathan Morris would seem like a great mercy. She intended to unleash her fury over everything that had happened, and caused her so much terror and humiliation. Nathan's bone-shattering plummet through the icy heights into concrete would be like floating gently into a soft mattress by comparison.

The touch of death abided within her now, and she had yet to tap its tremendous potential. She was determined to explore the indwelling gifts of Apep and Anat, unlocking new powers, and discovering their capabilities, as Juan was made to face frightful consequences for his treachery.

# SECTION III

# THE OUTBREAK

A couple of weeks had passed when the first definitive cases began to be announced. Only a few confirmed diagnoses were reported initially in the UCAS, but a great many were validated during the same time across Aphrike and the nations of the Far East.

The number spiraled rapidly after another week went by, setting in motion a disturbing trend. Fear spread quickly, blossoming at an exponentially larger rate within the populaces where the deadly virus was making its presence felt. No place of origin for the disease could be determined, and it was quickly named the Thanatos virus in the media, for it seemed as if Death itself was masterminding the erupting worldwide pandemic.

The overwhelming majority of those infected with the virus died in gruesome manners, writhing in the throes of great pain and suffering. All medical efforts to treat the sick failed terribly, and it was not long before the viral menace was regarded as unstoppable. A very small proportion of those who contracted it survived its onslaught, as the scientific community scrambled to assess the characteristics and nature of the microscopic killer.

Once the virus had been identified, the only practical thing to do was to isolate and quarantine wherever possible. In nations that were better equipped and organized, the spread of the disease was gradually slowed. It could not be stopped entirely, as it was soon revealed that a variety of animals could carry the virus, but the swift rate of infections was sharply curbed.

The situation was much different in poorer, overpopulated nations, where the slaughter ensued almost unchecked. In the thousands, then tens of thousands, and finally in the millions, Dr. Tricheur's lethal virus reaped its bitter harvest.

It was exactly what the leaders of the Convergence had desired for many years. The human herd was being culled.

# XAVIER

Twenty high-definition monitors were oriented in a wide semicircle, affixed to the dark wall of the spacious conference room located deep within Station Central. The screens faced a small number of figures sitting in high-backed, black chairs arrayed along the opposite curve of an oblong, glass-surfaced table. The lighting in the chamber was subdued, just adequate enough to illuminate the faces of those who were physically present. The filtered air conducted into the room had a slightly cool, comfortable touch, which was kept at a constant by the temperature control system.

Ivan Draganovich, the head of the CSD, Aaliyah Satrinah, Xavier Gerard, and the others seated around the table were being displayed back to each of the twenty individuals gazing towards them from the wall monitors. The satellite feeds were being conducted with the most advanced encryption available, an absolute necessity given the highly sensitive nature of the meeting.

Ten of the monitors showed the faces of UCAS province governors, while the other ten displayed figures whose identities were much less familiar to the mass public. The province governors and the more enigmatic array of individuals both represented territories comprised of ten different sectors. Each amalgamation of sectors fully comprised the UCAS' territory.

The province governors constituted a special council appointed by the President himself. They were charged with carrying out executive orders, and administering the various regions, in the instance that full martial law was declared.

The President's Council, and its delegated powers, had been created by an executive order several years prior that had gone virtually unnoticed in the populace when it was issued. Several diligent individuals had taken note of it, and broadcast dire warnings about the executive order, which could be read plainly by anyone bothering to take the time to do so. But in a world awash with distractions, spanning all manner of trivialities and amusements, and obligations of family and work, few did so. The reports were quickly pushed to the fringes, and consigned to the territory of wild-eyed conspiracy theories.

The other ten figures were the heads of the ten zones that the country had been divided into by the CSD and the National Emergency

Management Agency. Through the ubiquitous, multi-department intelligence centers already established across the country, known as fusion centers, coordination between various national agencies would be carried out under the leadership of the individuals appointed to preside over each designated region.

The close resemblance of each group's sectors to those of the other was no mistake. Together, they formed an extensive apparatus to assert rapid, comprehensive authority over the country, of a kind that did not have to worry about oversight or the constraints of the UCAS Grand Charter.

"Xavier, are your TTDF forces prepared to support a declaration of martial law?" asked the Governor of the Province of Yorvik, speaking with his slight, characteristic lisp. On the President's Council, he presided over Region Two under the emergency plan, the capital of which was the heavily populated city of Yorvik itself.

"We have our assets in place, I assure you," Xavier responded firmly.

In addition to being one of the world's preeminent financial centers, the city of Yorvik was the most populous in the UCAS, so the governor had good reason to be deeply concerned. Even with improvements in law enforcement, the dense urban jungle harbored a hive of well-armed gangs that could easily sally forth into the open, if things became overly chaotic.

Xavier did not like the man personally. He was another member of the UCAS aristocracy that had essentially bought his way into the governor's mansion over the years. Like many others of the financial elite that Xavier had encountered, the man thought that his deep bank accounts conferred some kind of expertise upon him, in areas where he had already displayed a severe lack of knowledge.

"Even with all federal units activated, we may have a lot of problems in the early phases," the governor replied, with the kind of patronizing air that suggested he was not fully assured that Xavier had thought every possibility through.

"Cities will be easy enough to cordon off, if we have to, especially those such as Yorvik, whose major access points are bridges," Xavier responded, with a noticeable edge, working to keep his irritation constrained. "We will close the city off, if need be, so that nothing can spread outward."

"I sincerely hope it is as achievable as you say," the governor responded, still sounding unconvinced that Xavier had planned for every eventuality regarding Yorvik.

In that moment, Xavier sorely wanted to inform the pompous governor that his wealth and position had not been the result of free markets, or any exceptional talent or ingenuity. The man had simply enjoyed the fruits of a system where more and more regulations and legislation, on local, province, and national levels, had been put in place to entrench people of power such as the governor, and inhibit others from climbing the ladder.

Xavier kept the thoughts to himself, as he had learned to do well in the company of the self-anointed elites.

"So when do you believe that the declaration will be made? What is the most current estimate?" interjected another of the governors, a woman whose home province was that of Tegesta. Region Four, which included Tegesta, was to be administered out of Terminus.

Daley Andrews, the chief of staff for President William Walker, leaned forward in his chair just a few places down from Xavier. "We estimate about two more weeks. Events on the international stage, the resulting impacts on the financial markets, and the first outbreaks of Abundant Harvest will trigger the clear, irrefutable need to impose martial law on the UCAS."

"And what about events such as that which took place in Godwinton? Can you count on the full cooperation of law enforcement assets everywhere?" she asked pointedly.

Though the province of Venorterra was part of Region Four, bringing Godwinton into her sphere of concern, and making the question quite reasonable, the words nonetheless grated on Xavier. He still harbored considerable anger over the ignominious retreat that he had been forced to undertake at the Revere home.

When the small-town sheriff had unexpectedly rallied a large number of police officers and deputies, and then fallen upon the agents ringing the house, after the latter had refused to put down their weapons, a route had ensued. It had come dangerously close to seeing Xavier unceremoniously apprehended, which would have created a media event of epic proportions.

Thankfully, Xavier had taken his position in a fortuitous location, one that had allowed the troopers with him to lay down a thick screen of smoke and fall back, before the motley throng under the sheriff could reach them.

The indignity of the head of the Threat Tactical Defense Force being put under arrest by a rural sheriff would have been intolerable. Xavier intended to pay back the small town sheriff in droves, once unchecked authority was given into his hands. He was not the kind of man to leave a debt unpaid.

"I assure you, Governor, that once martial law has been declared, we will move fast, wherever there is a sign of hesitation on the part of law enforcement assets," Xavier said, keeping the aggravation out of his voice.

"Like my distinguished colleague from Yorvik has indicated, the early stages of this will be the most critical," she replied solemnly, her gray eyes unblinking as she stared towards Xavier.

"And TTDF units across the nation will be ready to respond from the first moment that martial law is declared," Xavier said. "The bases are in place, enclosed communication networks are established, and each unit has been assigned an objective. And there is nothing to worry about regarding the willingness of TTDF units to carry out their operations."

"And online networks?" came the southern drawl of the governor of Texiana, who would administer Region Six out of Sawyerton. "We've learned enough from all the mess in other countries. Mobs can form pretty quick. There was much that wasn't intended to happen in the Central East, with the uprisings in Kemet and other places. Took a lot to rein things back in, and clamp down on the unintended elements. Things proved to be as we wanted them there, but it wasn't done without some difficulty."

"The killswitch will be activated," declared Daley Andrews. "The President will see to that, without delay."

Though Xavier suspected that would be the case, he was highly pleased by the confirmation from Daley. The online networks could create considerable havoc in the early phases, if social networks and the like were not closed off immediately. An effective digital blackout would prevent a great many from getting any thoughts about resistance, as they would not know what the state of affairs were elsewhere in the country.

Independent media, which largely relied on the online environment, would also be taken out of the equation, and the mainline news corporations were easy enough to deal with. They would faithfully put out whatever Xavier, Aaliyah, and the others acting on the part of the government wanted, or their access would be severed without a second thought.

A compliant media, and a government that did not have to answer to the public, were significant components of an ideal environment for Xavier to carry out his tasks.

He eased back into his chair as the meeting continued, as some of his earlier vexation abated. He had received the information that he was hoping to get, so no matter what another arrogant governor might say or imply, Xavier had what he wanted in hand. Any fires of resistance in coming weeks would be scattered, uncoordinated, and stamped out with ruthless impunity.

# MANDARIA

At the boundaries of the world, the first steps of a complex martial dance were inaugurated.

Beams from powerful lasers lanced skyward, spanning vast distances in an instant. The high-powered beams traveled with great precision, guided by intent and purpose, as they struck the sensors of UCAS satellites drifting in low orbits over Mandarian territory.

Intricate electronics and sensors were confounded in a flash of time, as the satellites were blinded in their assigned operations. It was the second time that the invasive act had occurred in less than a month. At first, some intelligence officers within the UCAS perceived the situation to be just another test of Mandarian countermeasures to UCAS surveillance, simply being carried out on an expanded level.

Any such notion was proven wrong within mere seconds, though the satellites were prevented from bearing witness to what followed.

Launched from their tubes in the bodies of the nuclear-powered, ballistic missile submarines, Divine Star missiles ascended the skies from positions all over the world. The missiles were innovative designs, whose existence was being unveiled for the first time. They reflected considerable advancements in propulsion that enabled them to do what no missile launched from a submarine had done before, fully empowered to strike at satellites in deep space orbit.

Once the Divine Star missiles had taken to flight, land-based launchers in Mandaria added their readied missiles to the onslaught soaring towards orbital space. They were not the launchers that had been expected. The four fixed sites that had been so carefully monitored by foreign intelligence were revealed to be the equivalent of giant decoys.

At several other locations, the fruits of long concealed labors far under Terra's surface were harvested at last. Giant metal slabs slid to the sides, as hydraulic lifts raised fully prepped launchers from deep within the earth.

Cloaked by the lasers, only the Mandarians could fully appreciate the incredible success of their preparations. Patient and resourceful, they had masked the digging and assembly of the launchers and missiles.

The fixed-site launchers were not the only kind employed in the operation. All over Mandaria, over forty wheeled mobile launchers contributed to the swiftly-expanding assault, firing shorter-range missiles that targeted foreign satellites in low orbit.

A small number of Mandarian satellites were also committed to the engagement. Their carefully disguised natures were unfurled, as they revealed themselves to be weaponized systems instead of the communication devices that they had been purported to be when first placed into orbit.

Every evasion and countermeasure was employed as rapidly as possible, but the volume of the attack was overwhelming, as foreign satellite after satellite was destroyed or damaged beyond functional use.

The UCAS military was nearly instantaneous in its response, as fighter jets were scrambled, drones launched, and missile volleys fired. Quick adjustments were made, on the spur of the moment, with the mounting loss of satellites, as guidance and targeting systems were increasingly hampered by the progressing attack. The Mandarians had created a more level balance in the greater fight from the outset by taking out the satellites, but the UCAS was far from defeated.

One carrier task force in the area began streaming towards Taiyoan immediately, as it did not take much analysis to determine the purpose for Mandaria's comprehensive attack on the satellites. A second carrier task force, located a little farther off, also began making its way towards the small island nation.

The Mandarians were expecting the firestorm, and set in motion a spectrum of other military assets to address it.

Type-7 class submarines that had recently taken to hibernating deep in the ocean moved towards the incoming carrier task force, like a pack of wolves shadowing a great herd of caribou.

Mandarian air bases were hives of activity, as swarms of fighter jets took to the skies, and sped towards the approaching enemy fleet. It seemed as if every pilot that could keep a plane aloft was being put into action, as old and new models of aircraft alike were committed to the fight. Radar systems on both sides were soon tracking clouds of aircraft, as a metallic storm advanced towards the carrier task forces.

The industrial might of Mandaria had prepared an impressive array of weaponry, one that was designed to counter technological edges with sheer numbers.

Several Dragonfire missiles were then loosed, racing just above the surface of the ocean at subsonic speeds, until they were about ten nautical miles from the nearest UCAS carrier strike force. It was then that the rocket-propelled warheads disengaged from the rest of the missile, accelerating to supersonic speeds as they closed the distance to the enemy vessels.

With the ability to maneuver sharply, the missiles were like darting hornets seeking to get past the broad swipe of a bear. While many capabilities had been reduced or eliminated by the loss of the satellites, the UCAS vessels were still possessed of powerful defensive abilities.

Several of the incoming missiles were brought down by the ship defenses. Walls of projectiles were thrown up by multi-barreled machine guns possessed of incredibly fast rates of fire. Clusters of decoys lured other missiles away, but more than a few missiles made it through to their primary target: the UCASS Deus, the massive nuclear-powered carrier that was the crown jewel of the UCAS fleet.

Explosions thundered as the hull of the gigantic ship began to take hits, rocking the vessel that was like a self-contained city.

Having revealed their positions, the Mandarian submarines stood little chance in the aftermath of their ambush. In the ensuing hours, the majority of the vessels were sent with their doomed crews to the bottom of the ocean in the ferocious retaliations that swiftly followed.

UCAS pilots began to exact a heavy toll on their Mandarian counterparts. Waves of older models of aircraft stood little chance against the sleek, cutting-edge designs used by the UCAS, and it was not long before explosions pockmarked the sky, and metallic debris was raining down upon the ocean below.

Wherever the Mandarians had deployed their own modern jets,

they fared a little better, downing a few UCAS aircraft. But pilot for pilot, the air battle soon tilted heavily in the UCAS' favor, displaying the superior training and experience of the latter's flyers.

Yet the weight of sheer numbers allowed for the Mandarian aircraft to strike powerfully at their desired target; the carrier task force.

Once within range, surviving aircraft loosed their missiles at UCAS vessels, creating a deadly cluster that augmented the missiles and torpedoes launched by the attack submarines.

Many vessels were damaged in the aftermath, and several were sunk, but the heaviest blows fell when the great, nuclear-powered carrier began to submerge. A shock wave was sent throughout the UCAS military as the order was given to abandon the doomed ship, even as it took a few more hits from the last of the air and sea launched missiles.

With the unanticipated loss, the second UCAS carrier task force began to withdraw in an orderly formation, to regroup and reassess.

The assault upon Taiyoan then commenced without hindrance. With the second carrier task force in retreat, the UCAS would not be able to interfere immediately in Mandarian concerns.

Indeed, the first waves of missiles and combat aircraft had already taken to the skies, and amphibious assault ships were beginning the crossing filled with their massive payloads of men, armor, and equipment. Airfields and other targets were pounded relentlessly, as the island was softened up for the imminent landings.

Hordes of helicopter gunships would soon be supporting the advance of tanks and armored vehicles from the beachheads, as bombers and fighters crossed the skies, seeking out new targets.

The fighting would be very bloody in the coming days, and far more Mandarians would fall than soldiers from Taiyoan, but the outcome was never in doubt. The crushing weight of the Mandarian military was too much for the small island to resist, no matter how spirited its defenders were.

As the first shells and missiles descended upon Taiyoan, a dramatic scene was playing out farther in the ocean. As if extending the majestic warship a final salute, the last rays of the sun's dying light reflected off of the hull of the UCASS Deus, as the pride of the UCAS fleet sank slowly beneath the rolling waves.

# SHERIFF HOWARD

Chris Howard slowly looked around at the faces of the deputies gathered within his office, his hand still shaking after setting down the phone receiver. The expletives that he had uttered in response to the declaration just given to him gave little vent to the volcanic emotions churning within. His blood was boiling, in every last vein and artery of his body.

Invoking an Executive Order from the President of the UCAS himself, and declaring the need to address matters of national security, the CSD had been granted the virtually unlimited environment of martial law. The federal agency was effectively taking charge of the entire country. The representative of the zone that Venorterra fell within had not called to consult Chris, but rather to order him to fall into line immediately, or be declared a threat to national security himself.

Without ambiguity, he had made his position very clear to the CSD Director of Region Four. There was no need for any judicial interpretations. By any measure of common sense, the Executive Order usurping the republic was ultimately unlawful.

Chris' elected place as sheriff made it imperative that he uphold and defend the tenets of the Grand Charter, most especially the rights of the people that it described. Those rights could not legitimately be taken away by any Executive Order, or other human-made scheme, as they did not derive from human authority. They were natural rights, which issued from a much higher source, and the brazen violation of them by the new executive order made it very simple for Chris to determine where he needed to stand.

The tension in the crowded office room was thick, and nobody said a word as Chris wrestled with his feelings. He knew that he had to keep a level head, no matter how egregious the situation was.

Loudspeakers suddenly blared outside of the sheriff's office. It was just what he had suspected. Chris did not even need to look out the window to know that the place was already surrounded by a horde possessed of lethal intent.

He knew that the CSD and others involved had planned well. They would not give him any time to organize or respond, knowing what he had done in the case of the Revere home. The door to the office building would be opening soon enough, as the representatives of a government gone rogue tromped through it.

Chris calmly shrugged, with a feeling of resignation and conviction, as he rose to his feet. He straightened his belt buckle, gazing around at the expectant, anxiety-laced faces around him.

His voice was measured, and his demeanor was composed, as he addressed his deputies. "As much as I would like to give these bastards a demonstration of my regard for tyranny, let's all live to fight another day. This isn't the moment. When they come in here, and they are about to, don't do anything rash. Cooperate, and surrender your sidearms without trouble. I'm going to put my confidence in the people we've been serving. They've believed in us, and we need to believe in this community."

"Sheriff, you and I both know that a lot of 'em will just roll over for this," Deputy Lucy Hammond said. He could hear the anger and frustration pulsing in her voice, and see it reflected upon her face.

"Many will, Lucy, and in the big cities many more will see great opportunity in lawlessness ... but the majority of the people of this area are of better fiber. Godwinton isn't Yorvik, thank the Creator. And there are many such communities all throughout this province," Chris responded.

Rapid footsteps in the outer hall preceded the sight of a highly nervous-looking, middle-aged woman, as she burst into the room without announcing herself. With the cramped space, she did not get far, but the deputies nearest to her turned aside to allow her unobstructed sight of the sheriff. Her eyes fixed immediately on Chris, and her voice was trembling as she pronounced, "The building is surrounded. There's a group coming through the front door right now! Soldiers, with guns out!"

"At least they aren't trying to conceal what they are anymore ... enough with the damn pretenses," Chris responded, with a rueful grin, as the sound of heavier footsteps sounded in the hall behind the desk receptionist. She cast a glance over her shoulder as the doorway was filled and shadows fell across her fear-ridden face.

The icy figure that entered the room, shouldering brusquely past her, wasted no time.

"Empowered by Executive Order 2013, the CSD is hereby authorized to assume control under the state of martial law. Your refusal to comply has resulted in your declared status as a threat to national security, Sheriff Howard, and you are now being placed under arrest," the leaden-faced trooper declared, as if he were going through formalities with a common criminal.

"Empowered by a false authority, which is unfounded in the Grand Charter, during a state of martial law, which we all know is an absence of genuine law. Stop with the shenanigans. At least get those parts correct," Chris riposted sharply, his iron gaze leveled at the trooper standing before him. "I'd have much more respect for you."

"I expect you to comply peaceably, the building is fully surrounded," the trooper replied with no change in his stony expression.

Chris was only grateful that his deputies gave the troopers no cause to use their guns in the aftermath of his statement. He and his loyal men and women in the department were then apprehended, and marched out of the building like a band of criminals. Nothing spoke more loudly to the townspeople than the sight of their elected sheriff and his deputies being led forth in handcuffs by unelected, faceless troopers, their identities concealed behind the lowered visors of their helms.

All within sight of the sheriff's department had looks of shock and dismay on their faces, as they watched the travesty playing out. Heavily manned barriers kept them at a distance, but all who observed the incident had no illusions; the UCAS that they loved was no more.

It was not long before a crowd was forming, as people left their places of work and began gathering in the street.

# XAVIER

"A host of systems have been severely crippled. That's very harmful for us, and for the UCAS military," Xavier growled, standing within the command center of Station Central. "That was not supposed to happen. It was not supposed to go that far."

"It appears that a very creative admiral within the Mandarian navy added a significant wrinkle to their operations. He concealed his part of the plan diligently, so as not to have even a hint of it reach the UCAS intelligence agencies," Aaliyah stated.

"And he did a splendid job," Xavier said angrily, though not without a little admiration for the ingenuity of the Mandarian commander. "They could have taken down the aircraft carrier without crippling the entire satellite grid. They have more than enough assets to accomplish that."

"Yes, they could have," Aaliyah agreed. "But it has happened, and now hostilities will have to be brought to a swift conclusion. A broader war cannot be allowed to take place."

"It is not that simple. We've been hit hard along a wide range of weapon and surveillance systems," Xavier replied. He looked over towards an officer standing dutifully at attention. "Do we even know the extent of the damage at the moment?"

"It will take some time to repair the grid, and bring it back to an operational level," the officer said.

"Repair? With each and every one of those destroyed satellites creating the equivalent of a shotgun blast of debris in orbital space?" Xavier retorted incredulously. "Even if we could deploy more satellites, the amount of wreckage now drifting up there has rendered space largely unusable. No, we will have to turn our focus to other systems, resume manned surveillance flights, and take on many more inconveniences."

"What about the remaining civilian sats?" the officer inquired. "There are quite a few that are intact and, as of yet, still undamaged."

"For the meantime, requisition as many of them as are available. We will use them for as long as we can," Xavier responded. "But they will not last in the long run. Make sure we begin a process of conversion to systems and assets that are not dependent on sats."

The officer saluted, turned, and strode away briskly to attend to the orders.

Xavier glanced back towards Aaliyah. "Just make sure the killswitch for the online networks is activated, like we were promised. I don't need any more surprises like this."

"It is going to be done, I assure you," Aaliyah said.

Xavier scowled, as he turned back towards the array of screens dedicated to giving him updates on the rapidly progressing situation. At least there was a small glint of satisfaction to be had, as he had received the report that the rural sheriff had been taken into custody, along with his deputies.

The sheriff would soon find himself herded into one of the many prison camps that were now going to be put to use. It was a fitting place for a mutinous individual to be, but the sheriff would be far from alone.

The CSD, TTDF, and others would not hesitate to apprehend anyone resisting the government mandates. Droves of trucks were at the ready, and the fusion centers were keeping a close, constant eye on the populace.

The TTDF was poised to pounce on the first indication of resistance, if anyone was foolish enough to test the resolve of the security agencies.

# IAN

Ian was stunned as he stared at the flat-screen monitor, listening to the blond-haired woman anchoring the emergency news report.

'As was announced earlier today, the UCAS has been placed under a state of martial law,' the anchor related, in a solemn voice.

Ian could see that she was not merely a talking head at that moment. Anxiety was thick in her voice and expression, and a sense of unease was conveyed strongly through the television screen as she continued.

'President Walker and his council have determined that this is a necessity due to the instability and national unrest caused by the financial markets, the outbreak of the Thanatos Virus, and the conflict with Mandaria.'

Ian registered few details as the anchor continued to describe the national state of affairs, but his attention returned fully when he heard the southern accent of the man who anchored the regional news broadcasts. Like the national anchor, the man had an unmistakably agitated look on his face. The news that he delivered for the immediate area was not favorable either.

'National agencies will be placing cordons around locations where individuals infected with the Thanatos Virus have been confirmed, so as to prevent a full breakout of the virus. In Venorterra, the following areas are being quarantined...'

A series of graphics listing the declared areas was then played across the screen. Ian's only relief was that the locales being placed under quarantine did not include Godwinton. For the moment, Alena and Peyton were safe at home.

Allyson was not, although Ian had already called her, telling her to come home immediately and join the rest of the family. She was well on her way home by now, and Ian was glad to see that the route she was taking did not fall within any of the quarantine zones. His blood pressure was undoubtedly on the rise, as he would not be able to relax until he saw her pulling into the driveway.

He did not want her out of sight with the upheaval spiraling across the nation. The burgeoning war between the UCAS and Mandaria, the viral outbreak, and all of the tremors in the financial markets were the ingredients of a very dangerous tempest, and Ian did not have the first idea as to how everything would shake out.

His other principle worry was for his beleaguered friend, Chris. Knowing how vehemently opposed Chris was to everything transpiring, and how many people in authority bore great animosity towards the sheriff, it did not take much discernment for Ian to know that the climate in Godwinton was extremely volatile.

After telling Peyton and Alena to stay at the house, he tarried only long enough to grab up his keys. In moments, he was barreling down the winding, two-lane road that led into the heart of Godwinton.

With his mind fixated on his worries, he almost went off the edge of one sharp curve. He admonished himself to maintain his focus, as his heart raced in the aftermath of the close call. A little more careful, Ian did not have any other incidents as he proceeded to the outskirts of town.

He did not get very far into Godwinton, as heavily armed troopers clad in helmets, body armor, and fatigues had set up a blockade of the road. He slowed his vehicle down, as a couple of the troopers trudged up towards him, their faces obscured by protective visors. Ian's first inclination was that they were militarized police forces, and not soldiers. He brought the driver-side window down, and assumed as non-confrontational of an expression as he could muster.

The window let in the sounds of loudspeakers in the distance. The words being spoken were clear enough to understand, as they carried to Ian's ears.

'This is an unlawful assembly, and you have refused to disperse in an orderly manner,' a deep, authoritative voice declared. 'Under the authority granted by this state of martial law, you are to be detained by the order of the Citizens Safety Department.'

The sonorous voice sounded so alien and bizarre within the town.

The irony of the words was not lost on Ian, especially the name of the agency invoking such draconian authority. The citizens were anything but safe, having become hapless victims of an oppressive campaign, which ran roughshod over every ideal and virtue that girded the strength of the UCAS in earlier, brighter times.

The first trooper was humorless in manner, and authoritarian in tone, when he reached the window. The second trooper had the barrel of his assault rifle trained upon Ian, the solid black circle at the end of it holding his life in the balance.

He found himself wondering if the faces behind the visors were human or not, as there did not seem to be any shred of individuality or personality about them. They could have been robotic constructs, for all that Ian knew, and he had no illusions that they could be reasoned with.

The troopers did not give him a moment to ask any questions, as he was told, in no uncertain terms, that the area was strictly off limits. Ian was then ordered to turn his vehicle around immediately, or be detained himself. No foothold existed for questions or arguments, and Ian knew he was on fragile ground.

Not wanting to stoke their ire, he did exactly as they commanded. He felt more than a little jittery, unnerved by the sight of so many military trucks and armored personnel carriers clogging the streets of Godwinton, as well as a few helicopters prowling the skies above.

Moving slower, at a higher altitude, was another kind of aircraft, most likely a drone serving as the electric eye over the theater of the security operation. A couple of mobile towers had already been erected in the town streets, giving the heavily cordoned-off area the distinctive look of a prison being watched over by guard towers.

An extensive force had been brought in, and Ian knew that they would not hesitate to employ lethal force to achieve their aims. It was a force comprised of troopers that honored no UCAS oath, and viewed the Grand Charter as useless scribbling on paper.

"They got Sheriff Howard … Ian! … They got the sheriff too!" a voice shouted desperately, from far beyond the blockade, as he worked to turn his pickup truck around.

Only the fact that he had not raised his driver's side window allowed the voice to reach him, and the familiarity of it gave him pause. Glancing over, Ian saw Dan Straley elbowing his way through the crowd, calling out urgently to him.

"They are taking all of us away, Ian!" the older man shouted at the top of his lungs. "They…"

Dan was cut off abruptly, as a pair of troopers seized him roughly. They beat him harshly, and shoved him back into line, prodding him forward with the rest, towards the maw of an eight-wheeled truck's rear.

In orderly columns, administered by a sizeable number of armed troopers, masses of townspeople were being herded into the trucks, though for what ultimate purpose Ian could not say. The sight was chilling to the marrow, as he saw many that were still dressed in the uniforms, or wearing the aprons, of the retail stores and restaurants that they worked for.

Teachers, doctors, teenage cashiers, bank tellers, shopkeepers, firefighters, and city workers alike were being rounded up. They were being treated like so many cattle, to be sent to a fate that none of them deserved. Ian's heart skipped a beat as his eyes fell upon the faces of frightened children. Many of them were crying profusely, as their frantic parents tried to calm them, though Ian knew that the parents were stricken with terror themselves.

Both the sight of the people, many of them very familiar faces, and the words of Dan Straley lanced into his heart, bringing to life one of the greater fears that had been abiding within him ever since the stand at the Revere home had been taken. Deep down, Ian knew that the higher authorities would not long suffer the embarrassment of being resisted without lashing out in retribution.

It was all that he could do not to cry out in the face of the abominations taking place before his eyes. Every part of him screamed at the injustice reigning all around him, but he kept the truck moving.

Most importantly, as he was still under the watchful eye of the troopers, and they still had their assault rifles trained on his vehicle, he kept his reactions subdued. He knew that he could be of far more use to the townspeople from the outside, than he would be if he were to be pushed onto the trucks alongside them. It would do no good to be taken captive.

The drive back to his house took what seemed like hours, as a leaden feeling weighed down his spirit. He pulled slowly into the driveway, shut off the engine, and sat quietly for quite some time.

Though he knew that things were headed in a terrible direction, he realized that he was not prepared for having the world that he knew irreparably torn out from underneath him. Even in the tumult of the standoff at the Revere home, there was still an enduring structure to his world.

The sight of a military occupation of Godwinton, and civilians being rounded up onto trucks, indicated that everything had finally toppled, and was crashing down. A line had been crossed. There was no use in kidding himself about the situation.

There was little consolation to be had either, as whatever rose up in that fallen world's wake was not going to be anything to look forward to. A darkness loomed, and there was nothing that Ian could do to stop it.

A gentle rap on the window brought him out of his stupor. Turning his head, he saw Alena standing at the side of the vehicle with a worried expression spread on her face.

Opening the door, he got out of the pickup truck, the hinges creaking as if they were world-weary too. He reached out and embraced her, saying nothing as he pulled her tight to him. Neither spoke a word as Ian grasped onto the lifeline that kept him from plummeting into the depths of despair.

She was his refuge, an enduring light that held the encroaching darkness at bay. Ian did not want to think about what his state of mind would be without her.

He had a lot to think about, and choices to make, in the wake of what he had witnessed at the edge of Godwinton. A great evil was taking root, and it would have to be opposed, but he knew that he could not bear to see Alena being loaded onto a truck like those he had seen.

He hugged her even more tightly, taking in the welcome scent of her hair, and tried not to think about anything else.

# CONRAD RUDEL'S PROPERTY

With intelligence gathered through one of the most covert means imaginable, a special operations team from the TTDF was deposited by helicopter deep inside Conrad Rudel's property.

Moving with precision and efficiency, the team surrounded the small cabin, entered it, and apprehended Benedict Darwin where he was sleeping in his bed. There was no resistance, as even the An-Ki warding the perimeter of Conrad's land were well away from the immediate vicinity of the cabin when the team was inserted.

Once Benedict had been secured, the helicopter descended, retrieved the team, and raced off into the night.

# ARIANNA

Tears of sorrow and rage streaked down Arianna's face, as she sat enveloped in an atmosphere of disquiet with Quinn, Maureen, Gerald, and Conrad. Their brief period of refuge and serenity was over; the tendrils of the enemy had snaked inside Conrad's haven and snatched her uncle away.

A number of unfamiliar men and women had arrived not long after it was discovered that Benedict had been taken. The An-Ki had also been warned about what had occurred, and Godral's warriors were on full alert.

It was terrible enough that word had arrived that martial law had been declared across the entire UCAS, but the mystery surrounding Benedict's capture was troubling. The captors had been surgical in their extraction, swooping down from the sky upon the small cabin where Benedict had been residing. They had known exactly where he was, and that he was isolated at the time of their operation.

"How could they find him here? How could they know he was alone!" Arianna vented, struggling to contain the emotions pounding within her, and wracking her brain for answers.

"Yes, they did know. And that's what bothers me the most," Conrad said more evenly, though a worrisome expression was etched deep into his face. Arianna could tell that he was rattled by the sudden violation of his land. His next words had an undertone of confession to them. "I just don't know how. I thought you would all be safe enough, and at least get some warning if anyone was coming here. We took every precaution. What possibly could have led them to think that he was anywhere on my land?"

"And who are all these people?" Quinn asked Conrad, with an apparent trace of anxiety.

"All are good friends, to all of us, whether we know them personally or not. They are going to help keep an eye on things for the moment, while we try to figure out what the hell happened," Conrad replied. He glanced to the others. "There is no law right now. Nothing to deter them from swarming over this place. We probably will have to move all of you very soon. If they knew that Benedict was here, it definitely is not safe for any of you."

"Benedict was completely off the grid, Conrad. Not any kind of imprint in the electronic world could have led them here," Maureen stated, her hands clasped tensely between her knees. "Which means that whatever it was that helped them find him is still out there, right now."

"I don't know what it was. Maybe they got some kind of inclination, and trained some surveillance over the area," Conrad said, though he did not sound convinced.

"Maybe it was another kind of surveillance," Arianna said, her mind open to every possibility as of late. "Maybe it was the doing of the enemy Avatars, something less scientific and more supernatural."

"It was not one of the Avatars of the Adversary that found Benedict," a melodious voice suddenly interjected.

As with the others, the sound of the newcomer's voice gave Arianna a start. She looked over to see Calliel in his human-like form, where he had manifested close to the right side of Conrad. The deep blue of the Avatar's eyes conveyed a grave sense of concern for the breach that had occurred.

"How else could anyone have slipped in, with the An-Ki watching the boundaries … and then got out, if it wasn't an Avatar, or something similar?" Arianna asked Calliel.

The Avatar replied calmly, "Avatars are far from being the only creatures of spirit. Never forget that all of you are creatures of spirit too."

"It wasn't an Avatar, and it wasn't physical, then what could it be?" Maureen asked, dourly. "What manner of new opponent do we have out there?"

The faces of the others reflected confusion at Calliel's words, as everyone looked towards the Avatar, and waited for his response.

"They apparently have one that can walk in spirit, with a great degree of control," Calliel stated.

"What do you mean 'one that can walk in spirit?'" Maureen queried him. Arianna could hear the exasperation mounting within her friend's timbre. She was a woman that wanted direct, succinct answers, a reflection of the legalistic profession she had left behind. "One what? If not an Avatar?"

"A human, one no different than yourself," Calliel answered.

"I don't understand at all," Maureen responded, frustration echoing in her voice.

"It is as I have said. You are not a body with a spirit. You are a spirit who inhabits a body, for a short time," Calliel replied, with that imperturbable manner so characteristic of him. "There are many who slip the bonds of the body, and are taken up in spirit, often in the realms of dreams. But this is not a conscious action on the part of most people, something to be controlled by the will. It is something that happens regularly to nearly every individual, without any effort. Any trace of it afterwards within a human's memory is attributed to nothing more than a dream. All of you have done this many times across the years of your lives."

"So what you are getting at is that there are some people who can detach themselves, spiritually, from their own bodies? By their own choice?" Maureen asked, slowly and deliberately, with a slight tone of incredulity, as if she was cross-examining the Avatar.

"Yes, and this ability is nothing to be trifled with. It can be a very dangerous thing to do, and there are many limitations," Calliel answered somberly.

"Such as?" Maureen pressed the Avatar.

"The ability to remember what one experiences while in that state is one limitation. The ability to direct oneself, with access to the conscious memory that an individual possesses when fully awake, is another. These limitations inhibit most from using this method in the way that it obviously has been wielded," Calliel said, sounding as if he were giving a lecture. "You see, for most, the moment the physical body is brought to mind the individual snaps back into the body. In this world, your natural state is to have a raiment of flesh. To go about the world consciously in spirit is not. That is a natural state for another time and place."

"Then how do we defend against someone that doesn't have those kinds of limitations?" Maureen asked, her brow furrowing. "It would seem to me that anyone that can do this would be just about unstoppable."

"We counter the enemy with one of our own who has been especially gifted. There is one such individual, but this person has already been sent forth to discover what has happened to Benedict, and where he has been taken," Calliel answered.

The Avatar's words came as a sudden, tremendous relief to Arianna. There had been nothing to grasp onto, not the least shred of evidence, to point in the direction where Benedict had been taken. Effectively, he had vanished without a trace, with only the dark outlines of a helicopter flying low over the forest, sighted by some of the An-Ki, to give some notion as to who had apprehended him.

The identity of the abductors was not hard to fathom. They might carry any one of a number of well-known combinations of letters, in terms of their affiliation. Those letters would belong to a specific department or bureau, as they were undoubtedly federal agents of some sort. Nobody else would have had the least bit of interest in capturing Benedict, or possess the resources to dart in and abscond with him.

"How long do you think it will be until we know anything more?" Arianna asked Calliel.

There was a different lilt to her voice. A flame of hope had been kindled within her at the knowledge that something was already being done.

"I hope that it will not be long, but who can say? The enemy has revealed a dangerous weapon that has not yet been fully countered," Calliel said.

"Then who knows what they might know about the rest of us here? Or the An-Ki, for that matter," Maureen said.

"They may know much already," Calliel stated. "And they may know far more than I had hoped, about another whose path must now join with yours."

"Another?" Arianna responded quizzically.

Without another word, Calliel turned and strode away.

Arianna followed the Avatar with her gaze and saw that a small group was approaching them, though it was too dark for her to make out many details. Calliel intercepted the others, and looked to be speaking quietly for a few moments with them, before they parted ways. Most in the group headed back the way that they had come, but one of their number accompanied the Avatar as he made his way back towards Arianna and her companions.

"I want all of you to meet Juan Delgado, who has been brought here from Troy, for safekeeping," Calliel stated, introducing the man at his side.

Arianna froze at the name, having heard it from the lips of her uncle. She regarded the man standing quietly by the Avatar with sharply increasing interest.

"This is a man that your uncle knew, Arianna, at Babylon Technologies," Calliel said, staring calmly towards her. "It was from his department that the Gateway Device fell into Benedict's hands."

Juan's eyes widened at the Avatar's pronouncement, and it was clear that he had not been expecting to meet Benedict Darwin's niece. His dark eyes mirrored the interest in Arianna's gaze as he regarded her.

The relationship between Juan and Benedict had been where everything had started. It had initiated the course of events that had led to Nathan Morris lending Benedict the momentous device, which had turned out to be so much more than a reality simulator.

Juan continued to quietly gaze back at her, as the initial spark of surprise ebbed from his expression. She wondered what he was thinking, now that their paths were crossing in such a climate of uncertainty and threat.

"I really liked Benedict. I am so sorry about what has happened to all of you. I never should have authorized anything to leave that building," Juan said regretfully, and Arianna sensed that a great weight was bearing down on his shoulders.

She mustered a smile, despite the heaviness pervading her heart. "And if you hadn't, then all of the An-Ki might have died."

"The … An-ki?" he asked her, looking perplexed. He looked towards Calliel, as if seeking an explanation.

"You will know more soon, Juan, but a great many lives were saved because that device fell into Benedict's hands," Calliel informed him. "The device was turned towards purposes that its makers did not intend."

"It was very fortunate that the device came into Benedict's hands, Juan. You will see for yourself soon enough," Arianna added, seeing more clearly the strong feeling of guilt permeating the man.

He nodded, but did not reply, continuing to look uneasy.

"So you left Babylon Technologies?" Arianna queried.

A rueful grin cracked Juan's somber mien. "I did. But they don't take very kindly to resignations."

"I wouldn't think that they would," Arianna replied, with sympathy.

Juan's predicament was easy to grasp, even if she did not know all the details about his circumstances. She could not imagine that there would be any mercy from a group that had built such an extraordinary device; an object designed for a wicked purpose, intended to bring back living nightmares from a long-lost age.

"Well, Juan, welcome to our little band of exiles," Quinn pronounced amiably, getting up and extending his hand towards the newcomer. His gesture immediately lightened the brooding air shrouding the group.

"Yes, we've forgotten our manners," Maureen said, more lightly in tone, getting up herself.

One by one, the others followed suit, as everyone offered greetings and introductions to Juan.

"Glad to have you with us," Arianna told him warmly when it was her turn, as she clasped his hand. From a close vantage, she saw that he had a kindly look to his eyes, but she could also tell that he was weary. She could only imagine what he had gone through to willingly step away from his job, knowing that to do so would put his very life in danger.

"So glad to be with all of you," Juan replied, with a smile. "And I am sure that we have a whole lot to talk about."

"A lot has happened," Arianna responded.

"But before you two begin talking of past events, it would be best to introduce him to the An-Ki," Calliel interrupted gently.

Juan looked a little confused, eliciting a brief chuckle from Arianna. She thought back to her first encounter with the wolfish creatures, within a desert environment that she had then attributed to an artfully crafted simulation device.

Had she known that they were real at the time, and not a function of a game device, there was little doubt that the fear and awe that had come over her would have been magnified many times over. Even as it was, the vivid memory of her initial encounter with the An-Ki had left a marked impression on her.

"He really does not know of them yet?" she asked Calliel.

"You are the first individuals that he has met here," the Avatar replied.

Arianna looked back to Juan. "Then you are in for an incredible surprise. But I want to assure you that you are completely safe."

"Who are these ... An-Ki?" Juan asked her, with a trace of

apprehension.

"I first met them in that device of yours," she responded.

The look of confusion and anxiety deepened, causing Arianna to laugh a little more brightly. She wanted to put Juan at ease, and told him reassuringly. "It's hard to believe what's happened to me, even now, but the individuals you are about to meet are friends, who I couldn't imagine living without. They are wonderful beings, and their hearts are good, even if their appearances may take you a little by surprise. Don't worry, Juan. You will be fine, but you are about to see something pretty incredible."

"I sense that I need to brace myself for something," Juan replied, looking a little less pensive.

Arianna turned to Calliel. "How about we go with him, to help with the introduction?"

The Avatar smiled. "A very good suggestion."

Quinn stepped up and patted Juan on the back, as the others drew in closer.

"Come with us, Juan," Calliel invited.

# BENEDICT

Benedict's eyes opened slowly, as he looked up into a bank of florescent lights on the ceiling. A heavy grogginess permeated him, making his eyelids feel like they were made of stone, and his limbs cumbrous to move.

Groaning, he took several deep breaths, sensing right away that something was very wrong. Images of black-clad figures with guns jumped into his mind, along with the recollection of a sharp sting. They were the last things that he could recall. He remembered nothing about the room he found himself in, or how he had gotten there.

Ponderously, he brought himself up into a sitting position. His head swam, and he knew that he had been drugged, as he began to examine his immediate surroundings.

He discovered that he was in a small room, which had a highly-sanitized appearance about it. It was sparsely provided, with little more than a sink, metal toilet, cot, and a few shelves, all of which were bolted into the walls and floor. It took little effort to realize that it was some sort of holding cell, though what prison it was within he had no idea.

Bringing his head up, he eyed the black lens of a camera mounted high in one corner. It was trained right on him, and he saw by the bracket and setting that it could be operated remotely. He had no doubt that a report had been given the moment that he had awaken from the drug-induced slumber.

He wondered who the first would be to come through the door to the cell. At the very least, he wanted to learn the identity of his captors.

Benedict did not have to wait long. He heard the sounds of bolts retracting, as the door to the cell was unlocked. The door slid open, and footsteps sounded in the room as a lone figure entered.

"I have to say, what a wonderful prize we have acquired," a silken voice commented. "The very man who has caused us so much trouble. I know that Dagian Underwood would love to have a visit with you."

Benedict looked up into the face of a beautiful woman, most likely Central Eastern in her ethnicity. Her flowing black hair held a luxuriant sheen, and her olive-toned skin was without blemish.

The only thing about her that distracted him was the look resting within her dark eyes. A deep, lancing coldness resided in that stare, and something more that he could not name, as he looked directly into her gaze. Whatever it was, it sparked an element of fear within him.

"Welcome to your new home, at least for a little while," she said, without any trace of hospitality underlying the words.

"Should I even ask where this place is, or why I am here? Or even who you are?" Benedict managed to ask, as he struggled to pierce the extreme daze weighing down his mental faculties.

"My name is Aaliyah Satrinah," she replied evenly. "And there's no harm in telling you that you are in Station Central, far underground, in a place that exceeds the standards of maximum security. The only way you will be leaving is if we decide to take you somewhere."

"Ahhh ... one of those places that officially doesn't exist, am I correct?" Benedict asked her caustically, with a smirk.

"More than a few of the things covered on your radio show said not to exist, do indeed exist. You should know that well enough by now," she replied, showing no reaction to his retort.

"So do I get an attorney, Aaliyah?" Benedict asked, with mocking familiarity, though he already knew the answer.

The question evoked a smile and brief laugh from Aaliyah. "Your inviolable rights given to you by some deity that you've never met, seen, or heard ... is that your concern? Well, that deity must be impotent, because we will violate those rights at will here, and will have no trouble doing so. Not so inviolable, as I see it. And we are going to find out what we want to know from you. If I were you, I would cooperate. I would answer the questions asked of you. It will save you a great deal of pain."

Her penetrating stare conveyed a horrible intent, and Benedict was unnerved for a moment. He knew that he was completely at the woman's mercy, and also that he could not escape this new prison.

"What you want to know?" Benedict asked her.

He had no intention of cooperating with Aaliyah, but he could not help being curious about the knowledge that they were seeking.

"A few things about the incident with the device, as you might well guess," Aaliyah answered pointedly.

"The device?" Benedict asked, with feigned innocence.

Aaliyah's eyes narrowed. "Again, I would suggest that you cooperate, Benedict."

"Oh ... that device," Benedict responded, flippantly. "What do you want to know about it?"

"I want to know everything about how you got it, and who else was involved with you," Aaliyah queried.

Benedict knew at once that even were he to tell her everything, the things she was seeking were not part of his experience. It went without saying that the threats she had hinted at would almost inevitably be visited upon him, and it would not be long until that happened.

"Might as well get started doing what you are going to do," Benedict replied, with an air of defiance, mustering as much resolve as he could into his tone.

Aaliyah's gaze bored into him, and his spirit shivered.

# SETH

With a pandemic breaking out across the world, the flames of war spreading over the continent of Asu, and martial law declared in the UCAS, school was called off indefinitely. Most families in the neighborhood were hunkering down, staying sequestered within their homes, riveted on news broadcasts and hoping for some rays of light to pierce the gloom that had fallen over everything.

Though no local cases had been reported, everyone was terrified of the virus stalking the land. It was a merciless plague of unprecedented scale, recalling long-faded epochs in history when sizeable chunks of the population had died in agonizing fashion.

From the early data collected by scientists, the new virus apparently took its time in manifesting symptoms. With that characteristic, it could take root in a community long before anyone knew it was among them. Even in Seth's own household, the mildest sniffle or cough brought with it a feeling of great unease.

"That's not good at all. They've really shut everything down, haven't they?" Seth queried, staring at the face of his mobile device.

The touch screen displayed the ongoing, troubling message that there was no connection. It had been that way throughout the entire day, and Seth had the feeling that it was not going to change anytime soon.

Annika cradled her tablet computer, already zipped up in its black case, having met with the same unsuccessful results as Seth. For the moment, the devices were largely useless, having been rendered so virtually instantaneously.

"President Walker has shut the entire internet down. The whole thing has been turned off. I never thought I would see this happen," Jonathan commented, shaking his head.

"I suspected something like this would be happening, with all that's going on," Raymond interjected, with a resigned shrug. "Nothing we can do about it. So why worry about it? It will come back, or it won't. Nothing we can do will tilt things either way."

A dismal pall hung in the air over the four teenagers as they continued on their hike through the park on the outskirts of town. The temperature was cooling steadily as the evening approached. Shadows were stretching their arms across the green lawn of the park, like darkness laying claim to the things that thrived in sunlight.

"How long do we have until the damn curfew hits?" Jonathan asked, with a spark of irritation.

"We've got maybe an hour left, before we need to be heading back," Annika replied, checking her watch.

"Curfews … unbelievable," Raymond retorted sullenly.

Seth looked up, and eyed the police cruiser sitting idle at the far edge of the park. At least it was not one of the military vehicles that were now so visible around the town.

"I'm with you, Ray," Seth said. "But what can you do, when almost nobody's complaining."

"It's the virus," Raymond said. "Can't blame them. It's got everyone very afraid."

"I think we're all scared of it, but there's still no sign of it here, and not a lot of new people are coming into town," Jonathan said. "I think interstate travel has been shut down, except for commercial vehicles."

"And don't forget the war, and the talk of nukes. The fighting's getting worse and worse overseas," Seth stated. "Wouldn't be surprised if Mandaria lashes out, even if it has already occupied Taiyoan."

"But they know they'd be hit back just as hard. I don't think they'll do much unless they were invaded, and in danger of losing the war, which isn't going to happen today or tomorrow," Annika interjected.

"Something to be said for mutually assured destruction," Jonathan stated.

"So we just live under this big cloud of fear, with nothing to do, and doing nothing about it, is that it?" Raymond asked the others, with an edge of exasperation to his voice.

"Well, since everything's falling apart, don't you think we should at least try to be witnesses to it?" Seth responded.

"What's there to witness? What's done is done," Jonathan replied morosely. "It's all happened, and nothing really is going to change until they lift martial law, and figure this virus out."

"Not quite," Raymond said, with a lilt to his voice that caused Seth to look over to him. "Seems that there's an awful lot of arrests going on, and I bet I know where they're going."

Annika and Jonathan joined Seth in eyeing Raymond, offering no response as they waited for him to elaborate further.

"That big federal complex outside of town. I've always wondered about it, with all the high, barbed-wire fences. It's set off all by itself, but there's high ground ringing it, at a pretty good distance," Raymond said. "We could take a closer look. I've got a great set of binoculars. Kind of range we can get a view without taking too much of a risk."

"What do you think's happening out there?" Seth asked.

"Don't really know, maybe nothing at all. But we could find out," Raymond said. "What else are we going to do? Sit around and play video games while the world is coming down?"

"A lot of people are right now, but you have a good point," Jonathan said. "I'm finding myself becoming more restless by the hour."

"It would take one helluva hike to even get there, as we can't just go through the checkpoints by car," Seth said. "No way they would allow us to drive anywhere close to something like that."

"And we would be out well beyond curfew," Annika added. "That's a full day of hiking, you all realize. We won't get back in time."

"Nothing ventured, nothing gained, like my dad always said," Raymond remarked, with a shrug.

"What could we possibly gain?" Annika asked. "So, say we find out that something is happening out there. Then what are we going to do about it?"

"I say we just bear witness to whatever it is now, so they can't lie about it later," Raymond said. "You know they'll try to sugarcoat everything, like they've always done."

"But there's no online network to upload it to. At least not right now, with everything shut down," Jonathan said glumly. "Whatever footage we get, we can only show it to ourselves. This isn't like the last time."

"All the better reason to do this," Raymond said. "Build a record, so that when there is a network, we've got something to show to tell the truth. Don't let the sons of bitches off the hook."

"I agree," Seth chimed in, with a determined edge. "Somebody needs to get a record of all this, for the future."

"You really like trouble, don't you, Seth?" Jonathan asked him, shaking his head, as if resigned to whatever course of action was coalescing.

"Well, I found something I'm not too bad at, so why not?" Seth responded, feeling that another adventure was quickly taking form.

# BENEDICT

Benedict had learned far too much for his liking about what the human body was capable of, from the length of time he could go without a breath of air, to the levels of electricity that could be sent throughout his body. His veins had run with more than one payload from a syringe, as many foreign substances were injected into his body.

As he had known, he did not possess the information that his interrogators had hoped to find regarding his possession of the device that had been used to transcend time and space. He did come to grasp a little more about what his captors were searching for.

They had hoped to glean from him insights into whatever network had penetrated Dagian's organization, destroyed the other Gateway Devices, and perhaps caused whatever mistake had occurred which resulted in the final, remaining device being erroneously classified. The torturers could not accept the idea that Benedict had simply fallen into possession of such an important device by sheer happenstance, due to celebrity affinity by a Babylon Technologies employee who was a fan of his radio show.

Exhausting most of their effective techniques, it was finally announced by Aaliyah that Benedict's questioning would have to be taken to another level; one that would encourage him to be more forthcoming with answers.

Her declaration rang in his ears, as his pain-wracked body was conveyed back to his cell, following a particularly intensive interrogation session. It was the last thing on his mind as he was unceremoniously tossed onto his mattress, and slid into the merciful depths of unconsciousness.

Benedict could tell right away that something was different about the mood of the two troopers that came to drag him from his cell for his next session. There was a certain glint to their eyes, as they secured his hands behind his back, and jostled him towards the cell door.

"You are in for quite the field trip today ... really should've cooperated better," one of the troopers said derisively, as they guided him down a well-lighted corridor outside his cell.

Feeling weak and dizzy, he struggled to keep his feet under him. He could not have recalled the direction that they took if his life had depended on it, after proceeding down more corridors and a couple of elevators. The troopers finally halted at a large door with a security panel set to the right side.

When the door slid open, the first impression that Benedict had was of the pungent musk that flooded his nostrils. He gagged momentarily as he was enveloped in the stench, drawing a chuckle from one of his escorts.

"Caught a nice whiff, did you?" the trooper asked. "A little hint of things to come."

They shoved him forward roughly, and he stumbled into an enormous chamber, spreading wide to each side of the door and provided with a towering ceiling. On the other side of the capacious chamber, he saw Aaliyah standing before a recess set in the opposite wall. His eyes quickly went from her to the scaly monstrosity that was curled up within the gaping mouth of the alcove.

The guards kept prodding him forward, towards Aaliyah. His legs complied, but his attention remained fixed on the creature beyond her.

He could see the lengthy talons, folded wings, and elongated jaws bristling with huge, spiky teeth. Each of its breaths resounded within the chamber, as its visible side swelled and settled in a rhythmic fashion.

Aaliyah and the two guards showed no signs of nervousness around the great beast, though Benedict could not help becoming increasingly anxious as each step drew him closer to it.

"She was the only one of her kind that was spared the Deluge, at least amongst those that were not traitors," Aaliyah remarked evenly, as Benedict was brought to her side.

Her eyes remained upon the scaly form in the large alcove. The two guards nodded formally to Aaliyah, their task completed, and withdrew to the far side of the chamber.

The reptilian eyes cast a baleful gaze upon Benedict, and he knew that only Aaliyah's presence prevented the creature from eviscerating him. The lengthy daggers in the creature's mouth glistened, as it emitted a deep snort that carried a hint of agitation towards Benedict's scrutiny.

He could sense a deeper intelligence in the creature, knowing in his heart that this was no brute animal.

"She is a hero to all her kind, as she carried Xavier through the heart of the storm to locate and guide the Erkorenen to refuge," Aaliyah continued, with a trace of pride to her words.

"It would be a true shame if she were the last of her kind," Aaliyah continued, after a moment's pause, and the timbre of her voice spurred a halt in Benedict's breath. "Especially one who was able to contend with Bazazath himself, in open battle, fighting a great Avatar of the Enemy, despite having lived only a modest span of years in this world. Imagine what she will become in time. Her kind continue to grow through the ages."

Aaliyah then looked over towards Benedict, and a cold smile formed on her face. Her dark eyes bored into him, with that strange, surreal quality that always unsettled him to the core. For a moment, her eyes had the same reptilian cast as did the creature looming behind her.

"But it so happened that she was carrying something else within her, when she came through the gate to live in this age," Aaliyah resumed, and Benedict could see that the woman was savoring her imminent pronouncement.

"Obizuth," Aaliyah said, turning to face the huge, black-scaled monster. Her next words were indecipherable to Benedict, but he had heard the language before.

He remembered similar types of words coming from Calliel's lips, and knew that it was the primal language of the Avatars. The utterance of those words from Aaliyah's mouth cause him to stare at her first, in amazement, before he took any notice of what happened in the next few moments.

The look in her eyes, and the strange sense that he always had about her, struck a resonant note in light of the revelation that she could speak the language of the Avatars.

The great creature before him shuffled its bulk, scales and talons scraping on the flooring as it pulled itself forward from the alcove, before rising up within the enormous chamber. It then stepped to the side, exposing the depths of the recess, and what it contained.

Having been shielded behind the dragon, and now revealed to Benedict's eyes, were several reptilian forms. An icy chill came over Benedict as he looked upon them. No less than eight small dragons eyed Benedict hungrily, miniature versions of the juggernaut towering over him.

A couple of the smaller ones scrabbled forward, their talons clacking on the hard surface of the floor. Hissing and snorting, they peered at Benedict with a predator's gaze. He found that he was relieved when their huge mother lowered her head, gave a deep growl, and pushed the foremost ones back with her snout.

"They can ... reproduce," Benedict muttered, astonished, though the statement was more rhetorical in nature than it was any kind of comment to Aaliyah.

"They are possessed of mortal blood, as well as immortal blood," Aaliyah responded. "Did you think such a thing would be impossible for creatures born into a world of flesh and blood?"

Benedict could offer no response as he continued to stare at the scaly offspring, and a cascade of unwelcome implications hit him. Before this terrible revelation, he did not see how the remnants of the Night Hunters that had been salvaged from the Great Flood would have made any significant difference in the modern world. Even a few hundred would have had minimal impact in the greater struggle, beyond assuaging the vanities of the Fallen Avatars that had sired them, and perhaps a few specific, targeted uses.

If they could reproduce, however, especially monstrosities such as the obsidian beasts before him, then it was another matter entirely. Something of increasing danger to all the world was being sheltered, and nurtured, within the depths of the huge federal complex.

Knowing what their origins were, he also doubted that their biology operated on any normal level, commiserate with the natural denizens of the world.

"You are impressed, aren't you?" Aaliyah asked him, with a mocking edge to her voice. "Did you think that we wouldn't want such a grand bloodline to continue, and flourish? Isn't it wonderful to think that living creatures such as this can be fruitful and multiply?"

"Why are you showing me this?" Benedict finally mustered.

"To elucidate you, of course, and to help persuade you to cooperate better with us," she replied. "But before we continue, I need to make sure you will contain yourself. Guards!"

The two guards that had been at the back of the room hurried forward at her summons. Aaliyah ordered them to secure Benedict's legs, such that the shackles fitted about his ankles were connected with a short strand of chain, which prevented him from walking.

Aaliyah raised up a small device that had been clipped to her belt, and clicked a button on it. She said curtly, "Send them in."

Another entrance consisting of two doors, at the far end of the chamber, slid open. A great trepidation rose immediately within Benedict, as he knew that what was about to happen was almost certainly going to be far worse than anything he had been through already.

A column of weary-looking, hollow-eyed men and women were elbowed and shoved forward by several black-clad troopers. Accompanying them were the two main interrogators that had doled out pain in abundance to Benedict over the past few days. He was not surprised to see them, as he had found them to be individuals devoid of even a trace of compassion.

As to who the bound men and women were, he could not tell. Disheveled in appearance, their bodies and clothes were caked in filth, as if they had been living on the streets for quite some time.

"At least here we have a use, for the useless in the world," Aaliyah stated. "And, Benedict, as order is put to the world, these useless eaters will be culled."

"No!" Benedict shouted at her, as he began to suspect her intent for the unfortunate group of people.

Their mouths had been bound, but the muffled sounds of terror, and the tears streaking out of their wide, frightened eyes, thundered into Benedict's raw conscience. His heart beat faster and faster, as he watched their expressions of sheer horror at the huge beast near him.

"You concern yourself with such weaklings?" Aaliyah asked him, in a facsimile of incredulity. "You would have such wonderful, majestic creatures as these offspring of Obizuth go hungry, for the sake of these discarded riff-raff?"

"I would send you to hell if I could!" Benedict roared back at her, flooded with a fire born of something far beyond indignation.

"Familiar enough with such a place," Aaliyah said, with an air of nonchalance. "I can handle that well enough. Come up with something that is more of a threat, and maybe I will listen."

"Damn you!" Benedict thundered.

"Again, redundant," Aaliyah replied calmly, "But I can see fit to spare their miserable lives ... if, and only if, you connect the dots for us."

Benedict then looked into the tearful eyes of a boy that was no older than fifteen or sixteen, beholding a pleading, desperate look in the youth's gaze. In that moment, Benedict would have shared anything that he held within the vaults of his mind, and volunteered himself for any grisly fate, to spare the boy and the others in the room.

The wicked truth was that there was nothing within him that he could offer, and he knew that he was powerless to put a halt to the travesty that was about to occur.

Tears of frustration and a cavernous sorrow welled up inside him, mixed with a few more tears forged out of a pure, tempestuous rage. His voice was choking with emotion, as he looked towards Aaliyah.

"I would give you anything you need to know, if I still held any knowledge you wanted," Benedict said, his tone wavering with the potent feelings flowing over him. "Please, let me take their place. Give me their fate."

Aaliyah stared hard at him for a few seconds, and a distinct flare of anger crossed her face. Her next words were declarative, as if she was confirming aloud what she had just sensed on some deeper level.

Her eyes were steely, and filled with menace, as she stated, "Yes, you would take their place."

Benedict nodded. "I would, and please allow me to."

"I do not make such mistakes," she said, each word a shard of icy resolve.

Benedict's eyes widened at her reply, and a dagger of fear penetrated him. Either his mood was sparking his imagination, or an inhuman growl had sounded from within her, just underneath the words.

"Bring the boy forward," Aaliyah commanded, with a heavy edge.

She gave Benedict a smile, and stared at him quietly for few seconds. He had the clear impression that she was relishing the moment.

Her face then took on an inhuman cast, like that of a snarling beast, before she turned to look up at the black dragon. She spoke several words in the ancient tongue.

Moving with blurring speed, the great head of Obizuth plunged downward, as her jaws spread wide. In an instant, she snapped up the boy, lifting him up, and swallowing his body whole. The youth's legs kicked only for a moment before vanishing, as his body was consumed. Benedict could see the bulge in Obizuth's throat, as she worked the boy's body down into her gullet.

"No! Damn you! Damn you to hell!" Benedict raged at Aaliyah, straining at his bindings, and toppling over to the floor.

"I think I have demonstrated my intent plainly enough. Now, the rest of them are depending on you, Benedict," Aaliyah said, another smile on her face, as she looked upon Benedict's horror. There was an air of unsullied delight in her expression. "But I will accept no substitutions. Only information."

Benedict's silence evoked a sharp response, and Aaliyah's face distorted with anger. For the glimmer of a few seconds, Benedict thought that he saw something bestial underlying her flesh. But the effect passed before he could say it was anything beyond his imagination, or a mirage created by the shadowy ambience and his bleeding emotions.

"Then the rest become sustenance, since you have chosen to refuse," Aaliyah responded coldly, with an edge of accusation.

Benedict voiced adamantly that he knew nothing more than what he had already given them. Finally, in desperation, he fabricated the most plausible story that he could, though he knew it was a lie. There was nothing else that he could do, given the dire circumstances.

Aaliyah knew his story was a lie as well. "Do not conjure up such foolish things in my presence. You cannot deceive me. It seems that we do know what we need to know from you. I believe you have been truthful in that, Benedict, but I am going to give you something to remember for all your years to come."

Knowing what was about to happen, Benedict called out to the huddled group of people, grasping for the only words that would come to his mouth. There was no consolation that he could give, and no possibility of stopping Aaliyah, but he could give them something to hold onto.

"Think of Adonai … put all your thoughts to Adonai!" Benedict exhorted them. "Only Adonai!"

"Shut his mouth! Shut it now!" Aaliyah yelled, with undisguised anger, her expression like that of a rabid beast. One of the troopers hurried forth, and swiftly gagged Benedict, rendering his words into incoherent mumbles.

"That is much better," she stated, in a calmer voice, as the contortions left her face.

She then looked towards the troopers attending to the captive men and women with her former composure. "Feed them, now!"

The terrified, bound men and women were shoved with force towards the ravenous brood of Obizuth. Aaliyah uttered one word to the creatures, which raced forth from the alcove and fell upon the hapless humans at once with a dreadful viciousness.

A terrible stench filled the chamber, as bowels and bladders were voided, and Benedict could only hope that the killings were done swiftly. He could do nothing as he was forced to endure the worst torture of all, entirely helpless to intervene and stop the terrible slaughter. His eyes could be shut, but his ears would not block out the nightmarish sounds that poured into them, rending deep scars into his mind and spirit that no amount of time could fully heal.

At last, only the sound of Aaliyah's laughter filled the chamber, surmounting the morbid sounds of crunching and tearing. For the first time, Benedict heard a trace of genuine gladness pulsing within the frigid resonance of her voice. More than anything, that evidence of undiluted joy within her testified to the elemental nature of the enemies that he, Arianna, and the others were up against.

There was only one path to take against such enemies: that of resistance. Evil was not something to be reasoned with, tolerated, or accommodated. It had to be destroyed. In whatever small way that he could, held in captivity deep within an underground base, Benedict resolved himself to defiance, come whatever may.

The burning fire of determination bolstered his spirit enough to endure the gruesome ordeal he was forced to witness. It did not stop the tears from falling, or the anger pounding inside, but it held him from any thought of surrender.

When he was finally dragged up to his feet by the troopers, and made to face Aaliyah in the aftermath of the brutal feast, he stood tall, and looked her right in the eye. He could say nothing, still being gagged, but even the hideous, triumphant expression on her face did not cause him to lose his poise.

The troopers took him back to his cell, leaving him alone with the acrid stench of the chamber lingering in his nose, and the horrid visions of the things within it flashing throughout his mind.

He did not look forward to going to sleep, knowing that ghastly nightmares were coiled to strike at him the moment that he gave himself over to slumber.

# FRIEDRICH

"Is it certain that this is the course that you choose to take?" Enki questioned Friedrich. His fiery gaze was fixed upon the Exile, as the Avatar peered down intently upon the soul before him.

There was no effort on the part of Enki to influence Friedrich, just a simple question in response to the Exile's insistence that he accompany the Avatar on a descent into the Abyss.

"I know that it is likely that I will be consigned to the long sleep within the Void," Friedrich replied evenly, looking up into the Avatar's blazing features. "But I feel in the depths of my spirit that this is part of my own path towards the White City. And I know that I can be of value to you in the lower places."

"And the others?" Enki asked.

"They will not be dissuaded from going with us," Friedrich said. "They choose to do this, as part of their own road to the gates of the White City."

Enki grew silent for a moment, and appeared to be pondering something.

"Then there is only one more matter, as you cannot fly into the Abyss, and neither can your companions. And I am not going to carry all of you," Enki said, and Friedrich caught a flicker of humor within the Avatar's latter words.

The Avatar grew still, and even the tiny flames comprising his immense form seemed to vibrate less. Though his eyes were open, it was clear that the Avatar was not focusing on anything before him.

The small flames then took on a more dynamic aspect, pulsing and flowing, as the Avatar's head lowered again to regard Friedrich.

"It is done, now let us wait," Enki announced, striding past Friedrich towards his group of companions that had assembled a short distance behind them. Friedrich hurried to catch up, as he looked upon his friends. All were bearing crystal staves, of the type that they had wielded in the recent battle against Beleth's legions.

"And what is this?" Enki asked aloud, as Friedrich and the others turned their heads to regard a small flock of Peris heading rapidly towards them.

Friedrich's countenance was dour as he recognized Asa'an flying at the head of the small band of Peris. As timid as they tended to be around any of Adonai's greater Avatars, Friedrich was amazed, as Asa'an and the other Peris made their way quietly to stand directly before Enki. All of them took to one knee, and lowered their eyes to the ground.

"We have come to pledge ourselves to your journey, Enki, to help you, and those that have chosen to go with you," Asa'an announced, her melodious voice resounding with a strong degree of conviction. "It is our choice, and a part of the penance that we must render for our past transgressions."

"I told you what I felt the last time, but you do not listen again!" Friedrich interjected sharply. His ire rose even more as he counted their number, realizing that there was one Peri for each of the assembled human spirits.

"When do the Peris ever listen to you? Certainly not Asa'an," Enki said, and again the spark of humor was present in his choral voice. He turned back towards the Peris. "Little ones, this is no quest for the likes of your kind. Your penance can be carried out here in the Middle Lands."

"We can be of use to you, when those much greater than us cannot … just as Friedrich and his companions are of use to you within the nether regions," Asa'an responded somberly. "Our fallen state gives us knowledge in some matters regarding the Abyss that surpasses the Exiles."

Friedrich listened to the diminutive being plead her case to Enki, wondering about the kinds of knowledge she was referring to. She had been a creature who had dwelled in the Abyss once, and he imagined that she could indeed be of value, but he did not like the idea of her going into the measureless darkness.

"It is not wise to take a group too great in numbers into the lower regions," Enki responded.

"There is one of us, to accompany each of the human souls," Asa'an replied. "No more than that, great Enki. To be of help to you, and to be of help to each of the others."

"Do you mean to carry us forward?" Friedrich asked her, still incredulous at her proposition and boldness. "And I suppose that you have already chosen to attach yourself to me, if there is one intended for each in this group."

Asa'an finally looked away from Enki, and brought her attention towards Friedrich. She nodded, her face exhibiting a grim countenance, entirely devoid of the gaiety normally present there. "We will not carry you, but with our size we will not make the group any more noticeable than it is now. And yes, Friedrich, I would accompany you into the Abyss."

Her voice then lowered in tone, and there was an unmistakable contriteness woven into her next words, as she turned back towards Enki. "We know much more of the Abyss, and the Nether Kingdom, than do any of you. I do not say this out of pride. Perhaps the folly my kind embraced so many ages ago may be turned to your benefit in the coming journey."

Friedrich felt the deep sorrow emanating from all of the little beings, as Asa'an gave voice to the time of their service to the Shining One, in the early stages of the Great War. It was a statement filled with shame and regret. Yet having served Diabolos and dwelt in the Ten-Fold Kingdom, the Peris would indeed hold some unique knowledge that was far beyond that of the humans, and likely even Enki.

"I cannot deny what you say, little Asa'an," Enki said gently, the multi-layered, harmonious tones of his voice brimming with compassion. "Nor can I find it within me to forbid you and the other Peris from continuing forth on this journey."

Asa'an and the others slowly rose up to their feet, their delicate-looking wings shimmering as they stood as tall as their diminutive statures would allow. As a group, they kept their eyes lowered, in a continuing display of their respect in the presence of the powerful Avatar.

"Thank you, Enki," Asa'an said, with an air of solemnity. "May we be of service to you in the journey to come."

Irritation welled up swiftly within Friedrich, as he watched Asa'an lead the small group of Peris over to stand near to his side. He cast a sharp look in her direction, but Asa'an did not turn her eyes away, or even flinch, when her gaze met his.

"I was worried that I would be a little late, as I had to find a few of the warriors now here with me, but we are ready to go forth with you and your companions," Asa'an declared, a steely glint carried within her gold-flecked, blue eyes. "I knew of your intentions, and was awaiting the call for departure. I knew you would not be flying out of here by yourselves."

"Are my intentions conveyed to all across the Middle Lands?" Friedrich asked her.

"No, this is my doing," interjected Silas, gently.

"And what did you think this will accomplish, where we are going?" Friedrich replied incredulously, turning towards the youngest human soul in the group.

"A smaller being can sometimes succeed, where a much larger one cannot, as Asa'an just said," Dietrich stated matter-of-factly, standing to Silas' right.

"Are all of you allying against me now?" Friedrich responded, with exasperation.

He shook his head as they continued to wait with Enki. The great Avatar made no comment on the verbal exchange, although Friedrich guessed the fiery entity was amused with his agitation at the fairy creature's persistence.

The tenacity of Asa'an was something to behold, more than a match for beings far larger in form, and vastly more powerful, than a Peri. It was plain enough that Enki had not been able to refuse the little creature's abundant determination.

"Well, I couldn't get rid of you up on the ledge, my pesky, foolhardy friend. And it appears that I can't get rid of you now," Friedrich stated, conceding the issue. His mood was split evenly between great frustration and good humor.

"No, you can't," Asa'an replied adamantly, before adding, in a considerably gentler tone, "as I am not going to leave the side of my friend, when he chooses to go into a place of great peril."

"Then that is that," Friedrich responded with a shrug, and the beginnings of a smile. "I guess you are going."

A calm settled over the group. There was no further discussion amongst the Exiles, or the Peris, as they patiently awaited whatever it was that Enki was expecting to arrive. Friedrich savored the tranquility, knowing it was a feeling that was going to be in short supply all too soon.

"And here come your true steeds for this journey, Friedrich," Enki announced at last, gazing intently eastward.

Another group of winged creatures soared through the uppermost skies of the Middle Lands. Their forms were clearly outlined against the shimmering, rainbow-hued firmament. Figures of elegant grace, they glided down in a loose cluster, alighting smoothly upon the surface a short distance away from the assembled Exiles.

With tall, robust bodies exhibiting the forequarters of an eagle, and the heavily-muscled hindquarters of a lion, they were formidable creatures in appearance. Their broad, golden-hued wings were tucked close into their sides, as they gazed upon the Exiles with luminous eyes. As with the band of Peris, the new arrivals' number was precisely equivalent to that of Friedrich and his human companions.

"They come here upon no order of mine, and no order from Higher. Their own choice brings them here, to carry you onward," Enki announced.

The Gryphons stepped forward slowly, their talons gleaming in the resplendent light from above. Once near to the human souls, they lowered themselves, so that the Exiles would have an easier time of mounting the tall creatures. As if they had selected their riders in advance, Friedrich saw that there was one Gryphon positioned before each of the Exiles.

Mustering his resolve, he swung his leg over the back of the Gryphon that had drawn up to him. With a little maneuvering, he got into a sitting position just beyond the base of its thick neck, forward of the majestic wings now folded into the sides of its body.

Once Friedrich was comfortably astride it, the creature rose up to its full height, effortlessly. The experience was already much different in nature than being in the saddle of a horse.

Friedrich was elevated much higher from the ground than he had been on any horse he had ever mounted in his mortal life. His legs were also spread considerably wider apart, due to the significantly greater girth of the Gryphon.

He was glad that his form was not of a physical nature, even if it mimicked several properties of a material body. A physical form would have accumulated soreness in abundance, in a short amount of time.

He looked around at his companions. As he expected, looks of wonder had sprouted on every one of their faces. Maroboduus and Valaris looked especially enthralled, with big, lively grins spread across their visages.

"I would wager that the Red Beard never had one of these fine steeds in his stables," Friedrich remarked to Heinrich, who had been a bonded knight in the time of a famous Germanian king.

"No, none like this," his friend replied with a tone of awe, his eyes gleaming with excitement as he looked back to Friedrich. A joyous laugh escaped the former knight, as the Gryphon under him shifted about to face Friedrich and his steed directly. Heinrich then exclaimed, "I never thought I would ride upon a steed of such grace!"

For just a moment, the daunting nature of the impending quest was forgotten. Friedrich felt a surging thrill at the thought of his group embarking upon an adventure, mounted on the backs of such incredible steeds. He had not expected anything like this, and was deeply humbled at the thought that the Gryphons had come entirely of their own fee will to assist the human souls.

"And I never had a steed, not even for a day," jested Maroboduus, a giddy expression breaking out as his Gryphon trotted forward, carrying him a little farther out from the others. He chuckled, as he quickly added, calling back over his shoulder, "Then again, I didn't need one in those days. Probably do need one now, as the Abyss is going to be a little different than the woodlands."

"Silas, how are you faring?" Friedrich asked the newest of the Exiles, the only member of the group that had not had a martial background in his mortal life.

"Simply incredible … just amazing," Silas exclaimed, a broad smile shining on his face. The air about the younger soul was not altogether different from Maroboduus, even if their mortal lives could not have been more different.

"I think it is now time for us to get settled," Asa'an then announced, from where she and the other Peris were standing on the ground.

Lithely, the Peris took to flight. Like the Gryphons, they separated apart, such that one Peri was allocated to each of the Exiles. Asa'an eased into place just behind Friedrich, moving so smoothly that he did not even feel her landing upon the Gryphon's back.

"No matter what I do, I just can't get rid of you, you vexing little spirit," Friedrich teased her, though he knew that the words rang with truth.

"When one is as small as we are, perseverance is not a bad quality to develop," Asa'an responded amiably.

"Despite all my misgivings, I do enjoy your company," Friedrich conceded.

"So you are glad that I chose to go with you now?" Asa'an asked, with a flare of her usual gaiety.

"Don't presume too much, little Peri," Friedrich retorted, a bit more sharply. He raised up his crystal staff. "I still have this to swat you with."

"And I have this to dart in and poke you with, if you dare to try such a thing," Asa'an replied, gently pushing the end of the spear-like crystal that she carried into Friedrich's side.

The two shared a laugh together, and the feeling helped ease a little of the anxiety underlying his anticipation of the forthcoming journey down into the Abyss.

"Acclimate yourselves to your steeds. The final companions for this journey now arrive," Enki stated, pulling Friedrich's attention away from the Peri.

Friedrich looked about in curiosity, wondering what the Avatar could possibly be referring to. Only the small, bright flickers of movement, set against a relatively still backdrop, indicated the location of Enki's announced additions to their group.

The figures moved with great swiftness, miniature lights racing towards the assemblage with tremendous speed. They slowed to a gliding drift close to the Exiles, making their way directly towards Enki. It was only then that Friedrich could finally take account of their peculiar forms.

The entities were much smaller than even the Peris. Quite strange of appearance, the winged creatures were like nothing Friedrich had ever seen during his lengthy tenure within the Middle Lands.

The bizarre pair had faces that were close to human-like, placed at the forefront of elongated bodies that had more of a resemblance to insects than to anything mammalian or reptilian. Multi-legged, and segmented in structure, they looked capable of having an incredible degree of flexibility and dexterity. The surface of their bodies was something to behold, containing a shifting, kaleidoscopic effect that displayed the gamut of the color spectrum. The changes were not limited to hue, but also richness and luster, periodically taking on spectacular appearances mirroring that of resplendent jewels or precious metals.

The creatures alighted upon Enki at the level of his shoulders, one per side. Their hues brightened and reddened, shifting to match that of the Avatar, as if attaching themselves to the fiery being. Friedrich wanted to question Enki about the astounding entities, but sensed that it was not a propitious time for explanations.

"All are gathered now for the journey," Enki pronounced, turning towards the craggy edge where the Middle Lands broke off into the beckoning maw of unending darkness.

As if taking a cue, the Gryphons followed in the Avatar's wake, needing no commands from their riders. Their movement showed clearly enough where the authority in the group resided. Friedrich hugged the sides of his own steed with his legs, wondering what he should do with his hands in the absence of reins.

"Grasp onto the feathers, and do not fear, Precious Soul … you will not cause injury or harm to me," an unfamiliar, deeply masculine voice sounded within his interior mind.

It took Friedrich only a moment to realize that the words had come to him in a telepathic manner, from the very creature that he was astride. He was astonished at the development, even though he knew that he should not have been surprised.

With some hesitation, Friedrich reached down and grabbed lightly onto the golden feathers of the creature. He felt a great strength in them, and he knew instantly that they did not have the same properties as the winged creatures of Terra. Even so, he was reluctant to hold on to them overly tightly.

"Hold fast to them, without worry," the interior voice came again, conveying a strong sense of insistence.

The ginger nature of his grip became more robust, as the creature trotted towards the boundary. Asa'an sat quietly behind him, dwelling in her own thoughts as they approached the onset of the great journey.

Just ahead, Enki's pairs of great wings fanned outward, starkly limning his blazing form with the darkness of the Abyss. Tilting forward, the fiery being launched outward from the edge of the Middle Lands, and glided forward.

Like a living beacon, the beaming form of Enki went before the others, cleaving into the darkness. One after the other, the Gryphons behind spread their wings, and sprang forth from the rocky lip.

An intense, dizzying sensation came over Friedrich as his Gryphon left the edge of the Middle Lands, and entered the fathomless expanse of the Abyss. The considerable light emanating from Enki's spirit illuminated the front facade of the boundary, revealing jagged, rocky heights, akin to enormous cliff facings. They were of a staggering measure, descending far below the reaches of the Avatar's light.

In addition to the rock facing, the light revealed the spectacular creations of the Sentinels spread abundantly all throughout the area. From his new perspective, Friedrich could appreciate for the first time just how intricately woven the vast webs were. Seeing their profound beauty, he felt that it was a bitter shame they were cloaked within the darkness.

Farther below, a dense zone of silvery webbing sloped down and outward, extending away from the rock facing. Friedrich wondered what anchored the webbing away from the support of the cliff-like edge, allowing it to stretch so far out. He had an inkling he would soon be learning the answer.

Losing all sense of distance, Friedrich kept his mind steeled as the group headed deeper into the unknown. All of the webbing disappeared from sight, as they became shrouded in the lightless expanse of the Abyss. There was nothing at all to see, not a single reference as to whether there was anything above, below, or to either side. For all that he knew, any number of things could be concealed in the darkness, a fraction beyond the reach of Enki's light.

Friedrich felt increasingly unnerved as they pushed through the featureless blackness, not entirely certain whether they were moving through a vast emptiness. It was a place devoid of sounds, to such a degree that the very silence was oppressive. Troubling thoughts danced about his consciousness, and he wondered if some manner of hideous denizen from below might be lurking close by, or perhaps even stalking them.

Friedrich took some strength and reassurance from the presence of Enki at their lead, as well as the fact that he could sense that both his Gryphon steed and Asa'an were unruffled. He was not alone, and knew that his companions were a tremendous blessing, as he could not otherwise have retained his sanity.

The passage was nonetheless challenging to endure. A short while later, if time could have been measured with any accuracy, it was made apparent that Asa'an perceived his rising agitation.

"Friedrich, do not let the darkness of this place conjure unnecessary fears," Asa'an said to him. Her soft voice sounded loudly within the weighty stillness.

"I will get used to it," he replied.

"The Outer Darkness can never feel welcoming to beings whose hearts burn with a longing for the White City," Asa'an responded. "Even I feel a great unease, though I spent ages within its depths."

"So you are saying that I should be encouraged by the fact that I am highly unsettled?" Friedrich queried, with a half-hearted chuckle.

"In a way, yes," Asa'an replied.

"Maybe you are right," Friedrich said, staring towards Enki farther ahead.

The Avatar's huge form shone like a column of flame, as he guided the others through the darkness. Friedrich grew quiet and focused upon the fiery light, allowing it to consume his focus, to the exclusion of everything else.

It helped make the travel more bearable, even if it seemed like they were tethered to an endless path, as the distance from the Middle Lands accumulated steadily.

# URIA

As silent as evening shadows, and swift as gusts of storm winds, Uria and Zeyya bounded around the side of the expansive dwelling. Staying close to the trees, and well clear of the reach of the lights, they easily remained concealed, wending their way around to the rear of the large property.

Uria and Zeyya padded forward quietly to the treeline, carefully eyeing the sprawling grounds before turning their gaze upon the prominent structure within them. Their noses instantly picked up the thick, musty scents of canines, even as they took notice of a number of brawny dogs sequestered in separated confines. The quarters that the creatures were kept in were bounded by web-like arrangements of metal, arranged into four tall, enclosing sides.

Almost at once, Uria could sense the anxiety and tension within the dogs, most of which were of a thick-jawed, very muscular type. Muffled, rhythmic sounds came from within the main structure, undeniably the strange music that humans now indulged in. It was far different than the kind that they had in the former world.

The hackles rose up all over Uria's neck, and his eyes narrowed at the end of his long muzzle. A couple of human males lugged a dog into an open part of the yard, to the side of the cages. The dog yelped and whined pitifully, and was undeniably in terrible pain.

The mood of the humans was very casual. The nonchalant demeanor was reflected in their voices, as they spoke to one another. Uria could understand very few of the words exchanged, but he could tell that they were not concerned about the dog's condition at all. If anything, he sensed that they intended it harm.

The wounded dog abruptly snarled, as if mustering some resolve, and snapped violently at one of the men.

The man reacted angrily, and pulled out a long staff of some kind, jamming one end of it into the dog's side. The crackling impact caused the dog to jerk violently, and Uria could see that the poor creature had lost control of its movements. He wondered what sort of weapon could produce such an effect, and emblazoned the image of it into his mind, lest he unwittingly fall victim to such a device.

The other man took up a club, and proceeded to bludgeon the dog relentlessly. Uria was stunned at the raw violence, having thought that they were going to mete out some kind of discipline to the dog. He could see that the man enjoyed the brutality, even laughing at the end, long after life had fled the dog. Hot bile rose up in Uria's throat, as anger swelled quickly within him.

"Destroy them. Tear them apart," Zeyya rumbled at his side, in a low, menacing voice. Uria could hear the distinctive pops and cracks as her body began shifting into its two-legged form.

Uria could feel a terrible rage emanating from her, and the two of them were in harmony, as he was burning with malice towards the two humans.

Reason fled him as the wrath took over his faculties, and he did not worry for a moment about consequences, as a primal, elemental nature took full hold of him. Transforming into his two-legged form, he joined Zeyya as she stalked through the shadows, closing the distance towards the two humans. The men were still laughing together, staring down at the bloody, misshapen carcass of the dog, and had no idea of the peril they were in.

The two men had not an instant of warning of the fury that descended upon them with a rush out of the night. Zeyya drove her talons deep into the guts of the first man, the one that had used the strange, buzzing weapon. The air fled his lungs swiftly, and he could only gasp meekly, his eyes widening in shock and a staggering degree of pain.

With one arm, she lifted him off the ground. Her jaws opened wide, as she drew the man in towards her, clamping down on his throat and ripping it out in one motion. His body thumped against the earth as she tossed it several paces aside. Turning about, her muzzle gleamed with fresh blood, and her eyes danced with a fiery, crazed desire.

When Zeyya had impaled the first man with her claws, Uria snapped his jaws down on the forearm of the man holding the wooden club. The human shrieked in agony as bone-crushing power was delivered mercilessly to his arm. With a violent wrench, Uria tore through the flesh and muscle. A bloody stump was all that was left behind. The man would not wield a single blow with that arm against any other hapless creature.

The man's hand was still enclosed on the handle of the elongated club, as Uria grabbed onto it, raised it high, and brought it down with tremendous force. The blow far exceeded anything a human could deliver, and the man's head exploded apart in a mass of bone fragments, blood, and pulped flesh at contact.

Uria looked around, and took in the sights of the caged dogs. Some of them barked, and others were cowering down, though all were attentively watching the two huge An-Ki that had just pulverized their human tormentors.

Uria could smell the fear from the dogs, all of whom were terrified. Effectively trapped, they did not know whether they were the next to be attacked.

"Free them," Uria growled to Zeyya, blood dripping from his fangs.

One by one, the dogs were freed, as the gates to their cages were torn off their hinges by the An-Ki. The dogs backed up in their confines as far as they could, unsure of what was happening.

Uria threw a gate far to the side, and backed away from the opening, locking eyes with the robust dog snarling in the rear of the space.

"Get out," Uria said, though he knew that the dog had no way of understanding the An-Ki language.

Although its movements were a little hesitant at first, and its eyes never left Uria, the dog carefully worked its way out of the cage, and then bounded fast across the yard, sprinting towards the trees.

The scene was repeated several more times, and only one dog was so consumed by fear that it lunged at Uria. The An-Ki swatted the creature aside, eliciting a sharp yelp from the dog. While annoyed, Uria withheld his urge to lash out.

"Go!" Uria thundered at it.

The dog wanted no part of challenging Uria, having felt the An-Ki's power, and sped after its freed brethren across the grounds.

A loud, startled voice sounded behind Uria, as he approached one of the final cages.

Uria whirled about at the voice, and saw that another human was standing outside, looking around at the burgeoning chaos. He was joined by another man, a moment later. Both of the men reached down to their waists, and raised their hands with the modern-type of human weapon grasped in them.

They had not seen Uria, but they did see Zeyya very clearly, who was facing them squarely, with her fangs bared. A heated growl sounded from the depths of her throat.

Uria did not hesitate, storming towards the humans from the side. He badly mauled one, and tore out the back of the other's neck with his jaws, before they even knew what was upon them.

The one who had been mauled did not die at first. Uria grabbed onto the man and heaved him far out into the open yard. A couple of the newly-freed dogs, given a prime chance to exact revenge on their tormentors, did not hesitate at the opportunity. With furious snaps and growls, they hurled themselves upon the man, and began rending him apart with great savagery.

"Such evil as this will be ended," Uria declared to Zeyya, as more fresh blood dripped from his soaked muzzle.

The winds ruffled the two An-Ki's fur, the rhythmic music continuing from the house as the barks of the elated dogs echoed into the night. Uria turned towards the entrance that the men had just emerged from.

"Kill them all," Zeyya said icily, a murderous glare reflecting in her eyes as the two An-Ki strode into the edifice.

Numerous scents bombarded Uria, many unfamiliar, but he caught the distinct odors of several other humans, even as his ears took in their raucous cheers from somewhere lower within the dwelling. He paused at first, looking around at the unusual interior, but his purpose drove him forward.

With Zeyya just behind him, he had to duck more than once as he went through the entryways into other spaces. He honed in on the sounds of the humans, until he found a stairway that led downward.

The purpose of the dogs was soon made clear, deeper within the house, as Uria continued to the right from the bottom of the stairs. His eyes fell upon a deep, circular pit. He could smell the blood of dogs within the air of the terrible place, and could see that two more canines were about to be set into the pit.

Men and women were talking and laughing, and there was an atmosphere of amusement and revelry within the large chamber. Several were drinking out of vessels, and a few were holding short, narrow objects that were lit on one end, which they raised to their mouths, and appeared to suck on, before blowing out smoke.

A young woman espied Uria, looking up a few moments after he had peered into the room. A guttural scream fled her, as she dropped her drinking vessel, spilling its contents on the floor.

The blood-rage filled Uria once more, as he and Zeyya waded swiftly into the small group of humans. A deathly tempest, they shredded flesh and crushed bone, and the humans did little to defend themselves, as most were stunned with fright at the mere sight of the lupine monstrosities besetting them.

The pungent scents of human blood, urine, and feces filled the room, as the slaughter was brought to a grisly conclusion. Only the dogs remained alive out of the room's original occupants. They whined nervously on the opposite sides of the pit, where the gates into it had still not been raised to initiate their combat.

The muzzles of Uria and Zeyya snapped around, drenched in blood, as they riveted their attention upon a lone individual. Having just entered the room, the man's hands were held outward, in a placating fashion. Oddly, Uria did not sense any fear within the man, which was perhaps the only thing that prevented him from immediately launching himself at the human.

After a moment, Uria's inner rage came to the fore again. He readied to assault the human, the lips of his muzzle curling back in a vicious snarl, intending to tear the man apart.

"I am not with them in this. I just sell them what they want," the last survivor stated, speaking calmly in the An-Ki tongue.

The words of their own language being spoken by a human stopped Uria from charging across the chamber and ripping into him. Even more strangely, the man continued to be surprisingly placid, in stark contrast to the paralyzing fear and hysteria that had been exhibited from all of the others.

"Why are you here?" Zeyya questioned him in a low, threatening rumble. She took a couple of slow strides towards the man, sloshing through a swathe of gore that was the remains of three people.

Uria could sense that she had not abandoned the idea of attacking the human, and could feel that she was about to spring forward. He said nothing to stop her, though he was intrigued by the odd behavior of the man.

"Like I said, I only sell them what they want. I have no part in this," the man said. He looked around at the carnage in the room, showing no sign of concern over the fates of the slain. "And I have no regard for them. I could care less what has happened to them, but I find the two of you far more interesting."

"And how do you know our words?" Uria asked him.

The sustained lack of fear in the man instilled some caution in Uria. There was something about the man that was very different than most humans. Uria sensed it like a distinctive smell.

"I am not what I seem," the man said in reply, a cool look resting within his gray eyes.

"Are you a Messenger then?" Zeyya asked. She had come to a stop, evidently becoming wary herself.

"Of a kind, you could say," the man replied evenly.

"You are a creature of flesh," Uria stated.

The Messenger of Adonai that had guided the clan under Sargor had taken the form of a human man, but he was not of a body of flesh and bone. Neither was the Watcher that they had recently encountered. The two were composed of a substance that was like nothing that Uria sensed anywhere within the world that he lived in.

Interestingly, the distinctive element that Uria sensed on the man before him was very akin to what he recognized in the essence of the Messenger and the Watcher. There was something unique about it that he could not yet identify, but the non-physical nature of it was unmistakable.

Even so, Uria could not be for certain. The man's body was made of flesh, without a shred of doubt. He was not the image of a human, like the Messenger of Adonai, but made of flesh, blood, and bone.

As if perceiving Uria's thoughts and puzzlement, the man held his arms outstretched, and closed his eyes. He looked to be concentrating intently for a few moments.

Uria's and Zeyya's eyes widened, as the man's body lifted suddenly off the ground. He floated upward, ascending several feet into the air. He hovered aloft for several moments, before alighting gently back onto the floor.

He opened his eyes, and a smile came to his face. "Have you

161

witnessed any who are just human do such a thing?"

"I have not," Uria responded, marveling at the impressive display.

"There are many like me, who occupy bodies of flesh, more within this age than ever before," the man replied in an even tone.

It was not inconceivable that Messengers took different forms. Uria could accept that idea, especially in the wake of meeting the Watcher. It was simply that the man represented something entirely new to Uria, embodied clearly in flesh and blood, but still carrying the traces of a Messenger.

"Why should you walk from this place?" Uria asked, as an underlying element of threat returned to his words. Whether he was just a man or not, it was not certain that the human figure was of no danger to the An-Ki.

"I can be of great help to you," the man replied. "I can guide you in this world."

"Guide us to servitude, under Sargor," Uria snapped, thinking of the Watcher. "I know what you would counsel us. I have heard such already. I will not go back."

The man shook his head. "No, you have great strength in you. You have no need of anyone else. You are a clan leader, and this is your time."

The declaration filled Uria with a bolstering sense of pride. It was all that he had ever hoped to hear from one of the celestial Messengers, as it was what he embraced deep within his heart.

The clear rejection of Uria's choice by the Watcher had grated bitterly upon him, evoking a sustained anger within his spirit. The words of the possible Messenger before him extinguished that fire in an instant, as vindication healed his sorely wounded pride.

Yet it was also true that the man had been encountered in a group that Uria would never have expected to find a Messenger of Adonai amongst. The humans that he and Zeyya had slaughtered were of the vilest type, fully deserving of the violence that had befallen them. The thought tugged forcefully at his conscience, straining to contend with the satisfaction that Uria felt at being recognized as a capable clan leader. He could not reconcile the man's words with the surroundings.

"Why are you with such humans?" Uria challenged the man, casting a glance around at the dead, mutilated bodies.

"A time of judgment nears," the man answered. "And I walk among those who will be condemned in the time to come."

As keenly perceptive as the An-Ki were, Uria could sense no trace of falsehood within the words. The man spoke with a firm conviction.

"These have been judged," Uria replied curtly.

"And received what they had earned," the man responded, without hesitation. "I do not dispute that. They have only begun to receive their reward."

There was a troubling air to the man's last words, but Uria could not pinpoint what it was that bothered him. He could tell that the man was still not lying, but that realization nonetheless brought him little comfort.

"Help me in my work," the man said. "And you will be rewarded in a time that is soon coming. I will help you find your place in this world … not as a servant, but as a master."

"By what name are you called?" Uria asked him.

"Carlton Tephros," he replied.

"And what is your first counsel to us, if you seek to guide us?" Uria queried, curious to know what the man would say.

"To move easily through the world of humans, and to speed up the time it will take for you to be comfortable in it, you will have to embrace your third form," Carlton Tephros stated evenly.

The words fell heavily upon Uria. He despised the third form of the An-Ki, shunning it all of his life. Weaker, slower, and smaller than the other two forms, he often wondered why the An-Ki ever had the ability in the first place. It had allowed the An-Ki to move among human settlements, without causing the fear that their other forms did, but it had little other use.

Yet once again, the man had spoken truthfully. Though he wanted to avoid the issue, deep within his heart Uria knew that the third form would likely have to be embraced to survive in the new world. The presence of humans in the new age far exceeded that of the former, and Carlton was simply stating what should have been obvious to Uria.

"Remain here, and you will meet the ones who live at the first place that you came upon," Carlton said.

Uria was caught off guard by the statement, realizing that the man was well-aware of the first location that Uria's clan had been observing. His words also indicated that he was very knowledgeable about Uria and his clan.

"How do you know of us?" Uria asked.

"How do I lift myself into the air?" the man responded, with a noncommittal shrug.

Uria knew that it was probably not wise to probe the powers of such an individual, and he remained silent. He decided then to explore Carlton Tephros' offer to be their guide. Glancing towards Zeyya, he could tell that she was in agreement.

"Show us the ways of this world," Uria told the man.

# FRIEDRICH

Friedrich could not say how far they had come, or how long they had traveled, but he knew that they had put a substantial distance between themselves and the outer perimeter of the Middle Lands. He would have guessed that they had been on their journey for a very considerable amount of time, though there was no sign of fatigue in the Gryphon. The endurance of the creature was astounding, seemingly boundless.

At long last, faint, shadowy lines could be seen far ahead, manifesting out of the sheer blackness. A glittering network of webbing then came into view just beneath the small company. Silver strands converged from many directions, concentrating together, as their endings massed upon a narrower swathe of rock facing immediately ahead.

Friedrich took everything in carefully, as they encountered the first new visible elements since the group had departed the Middle Lands. He felt a sense of relief as he looked around, simply elated to be out of the unsullied nothingness.

A significant number of forms could be seen moving along the webbing, from the more concentrated areas to individual strands. Other shapes climbed about the nooks and crevices of the rock facing.

The same kind of entities moved along the surface of the lands coming slowly into view. Eight-legged, Friedrich knew immediately that all the creatures within sight were Edge Dwellers, or Sentinels, like those found within the Middle Lands.

Other than marking an end to the mind-numbing, comprehensive nothingness, the vision of the landmass emerging steadily out of the darkness did little else to raise Friedrich's heavy spirits. It was a thoroughly dismal environment.

A dreary vista lay before him, cloaked in ash gray, a desolate-looking landscape that spread far beyond the reaches of his sight. As in the Middle Lands, he could swiftly make out the changes within the general terrain. What looked to be a series of towering cliffs were arrayed far to the right, while a cluster of vertical rises soared upwards just to the left. The latter were not unlike the soaring rock columns where Friedrich and his companions had fought so vigorously against Beleth's legions.

The drab skies were a gaunt perversion of the vivid, rainbow hues that graced the heights of the Middle Lands. Varying shades of gray, some dancing on the edge of deepest black, mocked the shimmering brilliance of their counterparts reigning across the skies of Purgatarion.

Like the Middle Lands, the skies had a dynamic quality to them, shifting and dissolving through the gray spectrum. Yet even the lightest gray put forth little ambience, casting all of the terrain in a subdued, shadowy hue.

Enki swooped downward, heading for the land surface, and the Gryphons fell in close behind. The Sentinels did not react to their approach, as Friedrich continued to look upon the massive, spidery creatures going about their tasks.

As they drew near to the boundary, he saw several niches in the rock facing where the still forms of winged Gulagar could be seen. Their fearsome visages were motionless, as their stony bodies maintained silent vigils.

The group passed well beyond the edge, and finally touched down upon the landmass. Where the Middle Lands had a bountiful appearance, rich in flora, the landscape before Friedrich was desiccated, with barren stretches broken up by sickly-looking brush and frail wisps of grasses.

It did not take long for the new arrivals to attract some attention. Several forms began to approach them from the distance ahead, like moths being drawn towards a beckoning flame. The light from Enki then began to ebb, as if the luminance from the multitudes of flames was being drawn back into his body. It continued to concentrate within him, dimming the area around the group until Enki had a form not unlike the Exiles.

Friedrich stared at the Avatar in astonishment, having never before witnessed Enki in anything other than his fiery, multi-winged form. He was now a tall, broad-shouldered figure, dressed in robe-like garments that hung loosely about his body. A dark beard rested on a face that contained piercing, solid blue eyes.

Friedrich did not have to look to know that his companions were likewise staring at the Avatar, following the unexpected transformation.

"What is this? Why have you changed?" Friedrich inquired of the Avatar, unable to contain his curiosity any longer.

"You will see," Enki answered. "I desire for you and the others to understand the nature of this place, before we move onward. I want you to see what disease flourishes within this corrupted realm. It may bring you wisdom for your own paths."

"This place? The Grey Lands?" Friedrich ventured, with a sense of wonderment, knowing the answer before the Avatar replied.

The Middle Lands were said to have once been a continuous land, without any jagged boundary, and much larger in size than they were now. Sometime before Friedrich's entrance into it, and before the beginning of Maroboduus' tenure, a large swathe of the Middle Lands had been broken away. The sundering of the Middle lands had been attributed to the arts of Diabolos, and those in league with the great Adversary.

The breaking of the Middle Lands had opened them up to assault from the Abyss, in a profound display of power signifying that the Adversary had grown mightily in strength since being cast down from Adonai's realms. In time, it became clear that the violent act had another, and much more ominous, purpose.

The Exiles that could not yet be claimed permanently by Diabolos, but were moving farther away from their path towards the White City, were said to dwell within the desolate Grey Lands. As their spirits grew heavier, diminishing in growth towards Adonai, they were drawn to the Grey Lands; no longer able to withstand the brighter environments of the Middle Lands.

It was also the place where the Abyss' minions took any individuals that they could capture on their raids of the Middle Lands, if they could get back into the Abyss unscathed. While most souls were returned soon enough back to the Middle Lands, aided by the guardians, some chose to remain. These were the souls that would have found their way sooner or later to the Grey Lands, finding them to be more comfortable to endure.

Like the ones that had come entirely by choice, they dwelled in what was formerly a part of the Middle Lands. In the Grey Lands, the things of darkness were capable of gaining more of an influence over the souls dwelling within them. The diabolical spirits of the deeper Abyss could then harbor their hungry, insatiable desires, that such Exiles would eventually reject the path to the White City in full, upon which time they could be claimed for irrevocable bondage to the Nether Kingdom.

For an Exile to be claimed in such a way, conscious, free choice had to be exercised. It was the most critical element of the corrupting process that the dwellers of the Grey Lands were subjected to, as seductive whispers and other subtle manipulations were worked out of the shadows.

"It is a place of sadness and resentment, but all hope has not fled those who remain here. Their fates hang by a thread, but those who dwell here have not fully turned their faces from Adonai's Light," Enki replied.

"Are those ... Exiles?" Friedrich asked, regarding the figures in the distance.

"Yes, but they are ones who are falling farther and farther away from the White City," Enki said. "But they do so by their own choice, as even in a place provided in mercy, and for purification, a spirit can choose to turn away from Adonai, towards the darkness."

Friedrich shuddered to think how any spirit spared condemnation to the Abyss could willingly turn away from a path to the White City. The idea was incomprehensible to him, as his very essence longed to approach the radiant, majestic gates.

"Adonai does not coerce a soul, while the Adversary has forged a realm of slavery," Enki said, as if perceiving Friedrich's bewilderment. As he spoke, sets of wings manifested from the Avatar's back, like highly translucent membranes of light. "But let us not tarry here further. There is more that I would have you understand about this place."

Enki then led the group on a short flight, taking them towards the tower-like rock formations. As they drew nearer, Friedrich espied a small number of beings moving near the base of one of the prominent vertical structures. They looked to be walking through some tendrils of dark mist, which wafted steadily through their midst. Enki guided the Exiles with him towards the figures, leading the Gryphons down to a spot located a short distance from the others.

The group within the rivulets of black fog took quick notice of the newcomers, and walked slowly towards them. They were sluggish of movement, as if a considerable weight was bearing down upon them.

They were men and women, whose bodies were shrouded in

featureless, robe-like garments of a deep, grayish hue. Friedrich had seen pallid skin tones that matched theirs many times before, during his mortal life. It was a look that he sorely wished he could forget, the pallor of a dead body. Their eyes were uniformly dull, and their countenances sullen.

The narrow wisps of black mist seemed to follow them as they moved, until Friedrich realized, with horror, that the black, gliding elements were not mist at all. Rather, each of the tendrils was a formless, sentient entity whose mere presence caused something deep within Friedrich to recoil. The dark wraiths were not natural denizens of the Grey Lands, but instead things that had come up from the bottomless pit.

"Who comes to these lands? You are not alike to us?" queried one of the approaching figures, a tall, thin-faced man at their forefront. His voice was hollow, sounding as if it took an effort simply to speak the words.

"Passing through, on a journey of our own concern," Enki responded evenly.

"Then pass through, and do not disturb us," the tall man replied. Other than the weariness that seemed to pervade the man, Friedrich noted a conspicuous lack of variation in the speaker's leaden tone.

There was simply no spark of life or enthusiasm in him, or any of the others gathering around.

"May your path bring you to the White City then, and all the glories that lie beyond its gates," Enki addressed the denizens of the Grey Lands, the words sounding like a blessing.

"We do not seek after illusions, or follow the mirage of empty hopes. We only concern ourselves with what is," the man replied cheerlessly.

"Is that what is whispered into your ears? Is that what the shadows tell you?" Enki queried, and Friedrich caught the slight edge in the Avatar's voice, the hint of a challenge. "Do you so easily take heed of leeches who only seek to take all hope from you? Do you dwell on thoughts that can only offer you a path to ruin?"

Friedrich looked more closely upon the drifting, shadowy forms that remained clustered around the strange, robed party. Their movements were a little quicker, as if they were becoming agitated by Enki's words.

"Whispered in our ears? There is only us here," the man replied. "Do not speak to me of things that you cannot prove, of things you say are unseen, but which are imaginary."

Friedrich could not understand how the other group could fail to see the dark, vaporous shapes gliding so thickly amongst them. The wraiths were so plain and evident to his eyes, but it seemed like the others took no notice of them.

"Just because you do not have the eyes to see what plagues you, does not mean that they are not there," Enki replied firmly. "The first step towards a greater world for all of you is to accept that it is possible that there is more than what you can perceive. There is much more than what you understand, and know. The vision you have does not reveal all things to you. Nor do your minds possess all understanding."

Friedrich glanced towards the human-looking Enki, and found it curious that the Avatar spoke merely of possibility, and not in absolutes. Looking back, he saw that the cluster of wraiths seemed to be swirling and moving about the other figures more quickly, as if becoming increasingly irritated by Enki's words.

"The gibberish of faith, I have heard it all before," the man replied. This time, his voice took on a slightly mocking edge, and Friedrich noticed that a number of the wraiths were gathering closer to him. "Do not trouble me with word games. You speak to me of things you cannot show me. There is nothing in this place beyond you trespassers, and us."

Without warning, a blinding light filled the area, as a wave of heat engulfed the space containing the two groups. Ghastly, inhuman cries and piercing shrieks filled the air an instant later, as the horde of shadowy, wraith-like forms darted away from Enki's presence. Friedrich could feel the naked terror from the formless things that had just been swirling around the gray-hued exiles, as Enki revealed his own form, in all of its radiance and glory.

After glancing towards Enki, Friedrich looked back towards the other group, and could see by their widened eyes that they had finally perceived the throng of caliginous shadows, as the latter had been driven away by Enki's display of celestial power.

"And if you had eyes to see, you would witness such corruption all across the face of this decaying world that you have chosen to inhabit," Enki declared, now returned to his glorious, multi-winged form.

The gray people shrank back several paces, their faces looking anxious, and not a few of them cowering in fear. It was the most lively that Friedrich had seen them since they had approached.

"Go from us! Go from us now!" the tall man cried out, in a desperate, pleading tone of voice.

Others amongst them now took up the same cry, as they began to edge farther away. Their words were fearful and raving, and Friedrich knew that their very foundations had been unearthed and shaken to the core.

"The things that plague you will return to beset you," Enki addressed them firmly. "It is in your power to reject them, and allow yourselves to perceive other possibilities once again. You desire to take a path to knowledge? Then take that path, and discover the essence of knowledge. Only the worst of fools claims to know all things."

"Leave us!" the man shrieked, trembling as he continued to back up towards the high rock columns.

Enki quietly watched the others retreat, as Friedrich stood at his side. The Avatar made no move to threaten the ones from the Grey Lands, but they acted as if they were being harried.

"Hope is not yet lost with them," the Avatar observed. "Adonai's spark still lies deep within them. But they are of a mind that even if they are shown proof of higher things, they will yet strain to deny what has been given to their perception."

"But it seemed before as if they just needed proof," Friedrich replied, a little confused. "I thought their anger was because of that. What is there to deny anymore, with what you have just shown them to be true? Those things that they denied existed were brought to light. Surely they can see things differently now, even if it frightens them at first. They know that you did not deceive them."

"Such is the irrationality of those who claim to live by reason," Enki responded. "They struggle to deny anything that does not find harmony with their perception. They are not really open to revelation. They merely seek out what conforms to the vision that they hold fast to. Let us go, and continue forward with our journey."

Taking to flight upon their steeds again, Friedrich and the others followed Enki's lead, as they continued across the Grey Lands. Many more times, Friedrich espied movements within the bleak, sprawling terrain below, though whether they were more Exiles, or some other manner of being, he could not tell.

He was greatly dismayed to witness several more instances of the dark, formless entities, moving in vast clusters like low, drifting clouds across the landscape below. Anything dwelling within the Grey Lands was vulnerable to contact with the wraiths. As far as he could see, the black shapes were nearly unavoidable.

After passing over incredible distances, and many variations in terrain, from mountainous formations to flat plains, they finally descended, landing near the edge of the Abyss. It was at a place where the ends of a vast multitude of webbing strands culminated in a concentrated mass, creating a distinctive formation that looked like a great fan-shape from a higher vantage.

Friedrich could see immediately that the area was heavily guarded, even more so than the place where they had first entered the Grey lands. Numerous Sentinels, of many kinds, could be seen both on the ground and out along the silvery webbing.

Like a forest of finely-carved statues, an array of Gulagar hibernated in a dense, semicircular zone, positioned just beyond the place where the converging mass of threads touched the substance of the Grey Lands. Friedrich was encouraged to see their inert forms, as any movement from the creatures was a signal that danger was imminent.

A large flock of Wyvverns drifted smoothly along the upper heights a little farther away. Their forms were almost obscured against the deep gray skies, as they kept a high-altitude vigil for any abyssal creature foolish enough to stray near to the heavily-protected tract.

Enki stood silent and motionless after they had landed. After a few moments, one of the great eight-legged guardians strode towards them from the edge.

Friedrich was struck profoundly by the grace of its strides. The details of its movement were hard to observe in the spiders of his mortal life, with their darting, scuttling tendencies. Of course, no spider of that world towered over him as this one did, with its multiple eyes intently regarding the group of wayfarers.

The huge Sentinel was one of the Lycosae, with an elongated body that was covered in coarse hairs. Its kind was capable of attaining great speeds, as Friedrich had witnessed during the battle with Beleth's legions. He still vividly remembered the Sentinels hurrying across the plains, just before the enemy legions burst upon the Middle Lands like a volcanic eruption.

"Zolos," Enki greeted the giant creature, as it drew up close and loomed over them.

"Enki, honored High Avatar, Adonai's Grace be upon you," came the reply, in a strange, oddly melodious voice. The tone was one that Friedrich had not expected to hear coming from such a creature.

"We must pass through, on a journey of great importance. I know that the enemy often tries your mettle along the boundary, with the exception of the more strongly-warded places such as here, where the strands woven by your kind anchor to the Grey Lands. Have there been many disturbances along the borders recently?" Enki asked.

"Few, and those have quickly been beaten back, though it seems that the dark ones grow thicker in number within the Grey Lands," Zolos replied solemnly.

"And they will increase, with more and more Exiles dwelling in this grim place," Enki stated, just as gravely.

"The dark ones, and the ones from below, do not challenge the anchoring places for the webs," Zolos said. "But I do not think it will be long before they do."

"And it will not be long before they challenge many other places," Enki said. "I do not wish to distract you from watching over these lands. I have come here because I wish to journey farther below, with as little risk as possible of disturbing the Sentinels as we proceed into the deeper regions."

There was a noticeable pause in Zolos, and though it was nearly impossible to read any expressions on the creature, Friedrich had the distinct sense that it was taken aback at the pronouncement by Enki. It seemed for a moment that the creature did have a clear sense of how to respond.

"You are going into the deeper Abyss?" the Sentinel queried, tension emanating from its voice.

"Yes, to find one that was lost to us, many ages ago, who may yet remain free of the Nether Kingdom," Enki responded.

"Then there is such a passage close to here, formed for such times as the Avatars deem necessary," Zolos said. "If you will follow me."

Zolos turned about, and headed back towards the jagged boundary of the Grey Lands. Enki and the Gryphons fell in behind the Sentinel, forming a loose, staggered file.

The Sentinel followed a path running parallel to the edge for the equivalent of a couple of miles, or perhaps more, continuing alongside the webbing that was so dense that it looked like a solid surface to

Friedrich's eyes. He could only begin to imagine how many strands were involved in that concentrated mass, reaching across the bottomless pit in an extensive lattice-work, which eventually culminated in the Middle Lands at the other end.

Zolos had a swift stride, but the Gryphons trotted along at the ground level, keeping pace easily. Friedrich took the time to continue marveling at the silvery network, wondering at the sheer immensity of the undertaking in fashioning all of it. Other Sentinels, of several types, were going to and fro along the webbing, and Friedrich found himself curious about the tasks that each individual Sentinel was about.

He turned his attention forward as Zolos slowed down, and came to a halt. The mouth of an enormous funnel within the concentrated expanse of webbing could be seen just beyond the edge. It beckoned to the darkness of the infinite pit, a portal descending into impenetrable black.

"Through this gateway to the Abyss, we will not mistakenly disturb any Sentinels with our passage into the deeper regions," Enki remarked to Friedrich and the others. The Avatar turned back towards the Sentinel. "Thank you for guiding us here, Zolos."

"It is the least I can do for an Avatar of Adonai," Zolos replied. "May Adonai guide and protect you on your journey."

"And may Adonai guide and protect you in all your labors," Enki replied.

The Sentinel stepped aside, watching quietly as Enki led the group towards the mouth of the funnel. Its circumference was great enough that the group could launch off the brim and swoop down into its cavernous midst as a loose throng, with no worry of striking the sides.

The webbing of the funnel was a blur within moments, as they raced down the throat towards the beckoning darkness. The Gryphon's wings were brought in tightly as they dived, and Friedrich leaned forward to align himself with the neck of the creature. He felt a fast-rising apprehension build within him as they hurtled towards the lightless ocean, already knowing many of the horrors that its fathomless depths harbored.

There were no guarantees of returning from this journey, not even with a High Avatar like Enki at their side. As powerful as Enki was, Friedrich knew that there were entities even stronger within that menacing darkness. It was a dangerous wilderness, abounding in creatures that would be ravenous at the prospects of tearing into souls from the Middle Lands and, most certainly, one of Adonai's High Avatars.

The thought was disheartening, and left Friedrich anxious as the group finally shot out from the bottom of the funnel, entering a dimension that was staggering to comprehend. Friedrich and his companions were now in the full embrace of the infinite Abyss, and he had the distinct sense of that embrace tightening swiftly, as they plunged downward at tremendous speeds.

# SECTION IV

# SKYLAR

Easing herself into a relaxed state, breathing in a slow, controlled manner, Skylar let her eyes drift shut. Her method of detachment was different than that of her counterpart with the Enemy, but it was no less effective in its results.

Her intention was focused upon the Will of Adonai, rather than the path of Becoming that the Walkers of the Setian Path took. She was not trying to elevate herself to godhead, but merely embracing an unusual gift that had been granted to her, and had been with her ever since she could remember.

She was just lucky that her father had taken her to a Universalist church where there was a Sister who had possessed the kind of knowledge and foresight to guide her properly. The Sister had engaged in a long talk with her father, which had resulted in Skylar taking her first steps on the path that had led to her eventual initiation as a Shield Maiden of the Rising Dawn. The Sister's keen understanding had been quite fortuitous, as Skylar was one of the only individuals that could effectively counter the formidable weapon recently revealed by the Enemy.

After several moments of calm, deliberate breathing, it felt as if she was sinking inwardly, falling ever deeper within herself. As the sense of motion took hold, her ears were filled with a sound that was like the rushing of air. It built to a crescendo, and then ceased, at the moment that she regained her vision once again.

The bedroom around her was still, but she did not need to look down to know that her physical body was just beneath her. The ceiling appeared a few feet closer, its textured surface filling her sight at first. Orienting her thoughts, she willed herself to move, and drifted smoothly through the window next to the bed.

The woodlands sprawling outside Conrad's house were draped in shadows, with that strange, slightly offset look that everything had in the frequency situated closest to the physical world.

There were many other frequencies that she had experienced, but she had always refrained from indulging in exploration. Being a Shield Maiden of the Rising Dawn required firm discipline, and having a dangerous gift like the one that she possessed demanded the highest level of personal restraint.

She never forgot for a moment that she was in a wilderness. It was not the realms of Adonai or those of the Adversary that she was experiencing when in the first stage of her disembodied state. The environments that comprised the potentially infinite frequencies were their own states of existence, with denizens of a variety of types. Some were huge monstrosities, and others were small, harmless-looking entities, but she did not take any of them lightly.

She had often wondered what the creatures that she periodically encountered were ultimately capable of, in regards to her roving spirit, but she was not about to put anything to the test. The present was no exception, as she took note of a large, scuttling form, with glittering eyes, that moved amongst the shadows just ahead of her.

Whatever it was, it seemed hesitant, and perhaps a little afraid of her, but she did not wait around as she took to the skies over the hilly woodlands. She glanced back to make sure that she was not being followed, as some of the creatures occupying the various frequencies had exhibited an ability to fly. Thankfully, nothing pursued her, and she could not see anything in the air around her.

The scenery from high above was magnificent to behold, a moon-bathed forest graced with a surreal touch. The silvery light gleamed off the surfaces of creeks and ponds in the landscape, as well as outlining the expanse of trees.

While she wished that she could take time to appreciate the spectacular vision, Skylar had a pressing task to attend to. She put all of her thoughts towards Benedict Darwin, summoning up everything that she knew about him within her mind.

As if picking up the wisp of a scent on the air, she felt a faint pull towards the west. Orienting upon the slight tug, the feeling grew a little stronger, though she knew at once that it would not be an easy one to follow.

Setting off through the skies, she began to drift westward, picking up speed as she traveled. She kept her wits about her, knowing that the Enemy's servant had traveled through the very area that she was navigating.

She had never encountered an out-of-body traveler with a hostile intent. If she was wary of the creatures seen within the astral realms, then she had to be just as diligent with a being that shared her own nature and origins.

Moving farther to the west, she did everything that she could to grasp onto the trace of Benedict that she had sensed. It was a difficult ordeal, as she had to keep her thoughts trained upon him, with little distraction.

A thick-bodied, multi-limbed creature launched into the air, heading directly towards her. Its brisk approach broke her concentration, causing her to instantly lose her hold on the slim hint of Benedict that she had been following.

The creature stood no chance of catching her, as she turned her thoughts towards her body, where it lay in the silent bedroom. In a flash, her vision became blurred as she was snapped back into her body.

The powerful effect was always a little disorienting, but she was glad that things worked the way that they did when roaming the frequencies beyond the physical plane. She had trained herself not to think of her body when she wanted to stay within the other frequencies, but it was the first thing that she brought to her mind when she needed an emergency escape.

Opening her eyes, Skylar slowly brought herself up into a sitting position, and then stood up. Something about the stillness bothered her, eliciting caution as she turned around carefully.

A flash of light occurred just at the edge of her peripheral vision, off to the right. Whirling around, Skylar beheld the form of a tall, dark-haired man, with eyes of solid, light blue. She knew at once that he was not another like herself, a human spirit detached from the shell of the physical body.

"For whom have you been searching?" he asked her calmly, in the layered, harmonic tones that indicated that he was indeed an Avatar.

A deep sense of unease came over Skylar, as she had no way of knowing whether the Avatar before her was aligned with the Adversary, or with Adonai. Either way, an Avatar held great power, and if hostile, the being before her represented a grave danger. The nature of the physical world limited the powers that an Avatar could wield within it, but Skylar was in no frame of mind to discover just what those boundaries were.

When she did not reply immediately, the other figure continued. "Perhaps I know of the one who you are seeking. Benedict Darwin is the one you are searching for. Am I correct?"

A smile spread across the other's face, showing that Skylar's manifesting expression had confirmed the other's suspicions.

"As I thought," he continued. "It was another with an ability such as yours that found him."

"What do you know of this … other?" Skylar asked, with a scrupulous reservation.

"A Walker of the Setian Path, I believe. I did not think it would be long before one aligned with Adonai would be searching Benedict out," the other responded.

The Avatar's words deeply unsettled her, as it was apparent that he was well aware of the one that had found Benedict. It was also abundantly clear that he had been expecting some manner of counter response.

Yet there was little use in trying to mask the obvious.

"And if I am seeking Benedict Darwin, and you know of this Walker of the Setian Path, what do you want with me?" she asked, trying to force as much resolve as she could into her voice.

"Benedict does not have much time. You can continue to search for him, and hope that you discover his location soon, or you can allow me to guide you right to him," the Avatar replied.

Skylar mustered up every last bit of conviction that she could. An important bit of information needed to be gained. "Show me your Avatar form."

A blinding light filled the room, and then diminished, as the appearance of flesh took on the image of flames. A fiery, winged form towered over her, but Skylar shrank back from the vision at once, jolted by an unwelcome revelation.

A conspicuous, dark, misty layer lined the teeming flames. The Avatar's blazing form, sheathed in the shadows of the Abyss, declared the being's alignment.

Skylar had never seen a Dark Avatar before, and a mixture of fear and amazement rippled through her. The creature was wondrous to behold, a balance of elegance and power that knew few rivals. Even though she was a Shield Maiden, pledged to Adonai, she was not so foolish as to take the infernal creature lightly.

It was possessed of a level of intelligence and power far beyond that of humans, and it had existed since before the world was even formed. She knew that she had to proceed carefully, and offer no provocation.

There was also no denying that her curiosity had been awakened. It was not often that a chance to speak with a supernatural being presented itself.

Skylar knew that the temptation to engage in dialogue with the abyssal creature had to be resisted, lest she find herself treading on fragile ground with a cunning adversary that sought the ruin of her very soul.

"You have not set your eyes upon our kind often," the Dark Avatar stated, breaking the extended silence.

"No, I have not," Skylar replied in a leaden fashion.

"You have nothing to fear. The nature of the material plane limits our kind."

"I have chosen Adonai, with my heart and soul," she responded sharply. Voicing the words brought her a little more confidence in the presence of the flaming entity. "We have nothing to discuss."

"You can wait, and risk being far too late, or I can show you now where Benedict has been taken," the Dark Avatar said.

"And why would you do that?" Skylar challenged the being, perplexed by the offer.

"We all have our reasons, for the choices that we make, and my purpose is my own concern," the Dark Avatar replied evenly.

"You serve a liar, and you chose your false path long ago," Skylar shot back, surprised at the strength resonating in her timbre. She raised her voice, "Get away from me! I have no cause with your kind."

The Dark Avatar nodded towards her, showing no intention of disputing her claims, or trying to convince her of anything. The form of the fallen celestial being collapsed into a small orb of light, before speeding from the room. Left alone in the shadowy room, she found that she was breathing fast, and that a light sweat had broken out across her forehead.

Skylar was as confused as she was awed. A visit from one of Diabolos' minions was the last thing that she had expected at the outset of her given mission, and certainly not one that had offered to assist her in finding Benedict Darwin.

# SETH

"The GPS still isn't working," Raymond said with clear frustration, looking down at his navigation unit. "Don't know why I even brought this damn thing. Should have known, with the entire internet still shut down."

The others peered apprehensively down the ridge overlooking the sprawling compound, with its double line of outer fencing. Pensive expressions were exhibited on all their faces, and a heavy tension gripped the air.

"GPS shouldn't be working, Ray, if Mandaria has been blowing up satellites left and right," Seth replied, matter-of-factly. "What we've gotten on TV says that they've knocked quite a few satellites out with their missiles."

At the moment, it was not hard for Seth to speak so casually about a war that could easily degenerate into a nuclear exchange. The thought of the UCAS' martial conflict with Mandaria compared to what he saw spread out below was like an early spring breeze to an arctic wind; at least in terms of the feeling that encompassed him.

Icy shards of fear lanced into him, as he took in the unnerving vision of the compound. The worst of his speculations regarding the place had been confirmed.

He still retained enough presence of mind to quickly bring up the small video camera from the case hanging at his side, and began recording footage. The zoom lens allowed him to get a closer, much more detailed look at the layout and contents of the sizeable compound.

What was transpiring in Mandaria was thousands of miles away, while the things happening below were right on the edge of his home. The things he was seeing went far beyond the inconveniences of a curfew and closed-down internet. They were images that shook the very foundations of the life that he had known, heralding the dire tidings that his day to day life, and that of everyone around him, would never be the same again.

A lengthy train had pulled to a stop on the rails that ran along one side of the huge compound. Throngs of people were being offloaded brusquely from several of the cars by armed guards.

It was not the sight that Seth had expected to discover at the end of the half-day-long hike through the woodlands. His legs felt like they were made of jelly after the lengthy trek across highly uneven terrain. His depleted condition made him feel even more nervous. Trying to run away, if the presence of the teenagers was discovered, would be an onerous burden given his severely exhausted state.

"We'd better keep down, because we don't want anyone taking notice. Especially by anyone who's leaving there," Annika said, pointing towards a small airfield set adjacent to the compound.

A twin-engine plane was trundling to the end of one of its two runways as she spoke, and a few other smaller aircraft were resting out in the sunlight. There were also a few helicopters in view, all but one being military in nature.

Guard towers were set at intervals along the perimeter, which was outlined by a twin set of high, barbwire fences. It was notable that the barbwire was facing inward, arranged not to keep anything from getting into the compound, but rather to prevent anyone inside from leaving it.

The most chilling sight that caught Seth's eyes was a large playground filled with children. It was set within the midst of the rectangular, barracks-like structures populating the compound. It looked like any other playground found within a city park, with all manner of swings, slides, little bridges and towers, and other things suited for the amusements of children.

It was not the objects themselves, or the children currently playing about them, that bothered Seth. Rather, it was the idea that the large playground had been constructed within the facility well in advance; anticipating the arrival of numerous families with children.

Seth knew that it was not a prison constructed for criminals, dedicated political dissidents, terrorists, or any other usual category of detainee. This was a facility that had been built for harboring civilians in great numbers, and the realization of that sickened him to the core.

"You okay, man?" Raymond asked him gently.

Seth nodded his head, and replied evenly, "I'll be fine Ray. Just not expecting all of this. That's all."

"Me neither," Raymond answered glumly. "Thought at first it might be a place where they put bunches of protesters. But those kids weren't protesters. They're rounding up people in droves, evidently, kids and all."

He brought up his binoculars again, and stared quietly for a few moments.

"And I'm pretty sure that the folks being taken off that train aren't diehard protestors either," Raymond said.

Seth brought the camera around to view the area adjacent to the train, dreading what the small color monitor would reveal to his eyes.

He saw a mother cradling a little, bundled-up infant. She was walking slowly, as two other children clutched tightly onto her pants. Seth could see the fear evident on her face, as she continued forward under the watchful eye of a pair of troopers, whose rifles were trained on the mass of arrivals.

Near to her, an elderly man was shouting at other troopers. Seth could not read lips, and had no idea what the man was saying, but he could see the arrogant smirks on a couple of the guards' faces, as another trooper yelled back at the old man. Seth was afraid for the old man, who kept moving along with the others, even as he continued to shout back at the guards.

Seth winced as a couple of the guards suddenly tromped forward, heading in the direction of the rancorous old man. The crowd moved quickly out of their way, clearly afraid of the armed men.

The guards proceeded to employ shock devices on the unfortunate old man. He fell heavily to the ground, and his limbs jerked as the electric currents coursed all throughout him.

Seth felt hot tears of anger and frustration well up in his eyes, as he took notice of the hat that the old man was wearing. It had tumbled off the man's head during the violent spasms induced by the shocks.

Seth knew what the hat meant, as one of his grandfathers possessed one. It signified that the man was a military veteran, and the hat was a personal display of pride in his service to the country.

Seth looked on in horror as his attention was drawn from the old man towards some conspicuous movements within the crowd. Another man from farther away in the dense throng was shouldering and jostling through the masses of people to come to the aid of the old veteran.

The newcomer reached the area too late to help the old man. Even worse, he received shocks and several heavy blows for his efforts, as a number of guards surged into the fray to maintain order in the crowd. Though his heart ached at the sight, Seth brought the zoom lens in closer to the tragic sequence, in order to gain the identities of the figures involved.

Seeing the faces of the old man and the younger one who had tried to intercede, there was little doubting the similarities of their features. Seth was all but certain that the pair was a father and son, caught within a grievous nightmare.

A terrible anger surged within him as he recorded the travesty, and continued to observe the incoming throngs from the train. He took footage of the compound itself, including the barracks and the chilling playground. It was one of the more difficult things that he had ever done, but he was determined to document as much as he could of the horrid place.

Recording the shape-shifting creature had been done in an atmosphere of fear, but the scene before him was at the extremes of injustice. It was a debilitating feeling that came over him, and sapped his spirits, as he felt helpless in the face of a power that could deploy a compound such as the one below. But he knew that he had to continue capturing the footage, no matter what egregious acts transpired in the sphere of the lens.

Next to Seth, Raymond passed the binoculars onward. Annika and Jonathan became very subdued as the details of the compound and its ill-fated detainees were revealed to their eyes.

"Let's get the hell out of here," Raymond finally said in a low voice, the first words that were spoken amongst them in quite some time. Raymond's voice was sorrowful and laden with weariness.

Set had seen more than enough to scar his memories, and offered no argument, as he quietly shut the camera off, packing it up within its case.

The quartet silently filed away from the ridgeline, and Seth had no doubts that the others' hearts were just as heavy as his. The thrill of adventure was completely absent, as the gravity of what he had witnessed brought him a pervasive feeling of emptiness and sadness. He had documented the compound, but hope evaded him, as he could not see how such a malevolent power could be opposed. The image of a playground within a prison kept returning to the forefront of Seth's thoughts.

He had proof of what was going on in the compound, but there was nowhere to send it. A defeated pall hovered over Seth as he called up his last reserves of energy to move his legs.

A light rain began to fall about midway back during the return hike, as if the heavens themselves had begun to weep.

# GREGORY

"A line's been crossed. No doubt about it, and those of us that served know damn well the oath we took," Gregory said, sweeping his gaze across the stoic faces around him. "And for those that weren't in the service, you know damn well that everything we value is now under open assault."

Most of the men were from Godwinton and the surrounding areas, individuals that Gregory had come to know over the previous weeks. They had agreed in advance on a meeting place should any major upheaval occur. Only about half the number that he expected had shown up to the rendezvous location, and he had a good notion regarding what had happened to the rest.

"I watched them rounding everyone up, and it took every amount of skill I had to get out of town," Gregory related to the group. "I knew it the moment the crowd began to assemble to protest Sheriff Howard's arrest."

The mention of the sheriff's arrest brought scowls and darkened expressions on the others' faces. Several of those gathered in the room had been among the group deputized when Sheriff Howard had intervened at the Revere property. Like Gregory, they had come to see the sheriff as a living symbol of resistance to the authoritarianism that now shadowed their country.

"Well, we sure can't go off half-cocked, Greg," a burly, bearded man said, in a thick southern drawl. His name was Jacob Wethington, and he was one of the more reclusive types that lived deeper in the hills. "Never does any good."

"I don't intend to, but we've got to have some organization right from the beginning," Greg said. "That's why we're here now."

"They'll have jets, tanks, all that kinda stuff," said a young, blond-haired man in his early twenties. He had been one of Gregory's most eager students at the gun range, assiduous in practicing everything he was taught.

"Sean, I don't think everyone in the service will be fully cooperative," Greg stated. "I know I wouldn't be, if I was told to open fire on my friends and neighbors."

"But the TTDF? They seem pretty committed," Consuela Gonzalez interjected. "And we know their hardware is as good as anything the military has."

Consuela was one of the individuals present who had significant, previous military experience. Gregory had been relieved to see her arrive at the rural house they had designated as the meeting place, as she had been working in the heart of Godwinton when the town had been cordoned off. Having done a couple of tours overseas, she knew what the military was capable of, and also knew what it was like to be in a firefight.

"They will be something we have to deal with, and there will be some who don't have the qualms that I do," Gregory acknowledged.

"Unless we submit, things are going to get heavy really quick," Consuela replied.

"Do I look like I feel like submitting?" Gregory replied, a glint in his eye, as a slight grin came to his face.

A few of the others chuckled at his words, breaking some of the tension in the room.

"We're gonna have to take account of the guns that we have available, and the ammo, and really make sure we are careful about anyone that can load their own shells," Gregory said. "All the guns in the world aren't gonna help unless there's something to shoot out of them."

The topic was perhaps one of the greatest challenges facing them, as any resistance force would have to work with a polyglot of weaponry. From bolt-action hunting rifles, to shotguns, to semi-automatic, military-style weapons, there was quite a range of guns owned by the group, utilizing a fairly broad spectrum of ammunition. The only silver lining was that if they came across any ammunition in the future, they likely had a gun somewhere in their possession that could fire it.

"We'll get started on an inventory right away," Consuela replied.

"And it won't be long until they start sweeping houses for weapons and ammo, so we'd better conceal what we've got," Gregory added.

"I got a few places for ya," Jacob said.

If anyone had some ideas regarding advantageous places to squirrel away some caches of weapons, Jacob was the kind of man that Gregory expected to offer some of the better suggestions.

"Beyond that, we need to designate some groups, kind of like fire teams, that will work close together," Gregory said.

"What about some snipers? There's some real good shots in this bunch," a tall, lean man named Ollie Pryor asked. "You can harass the hell out of 'em if you want to."

"And that's where you come in," Gregory said, turning his head, and grinning at Corey Holt. "We are going to need your skills."

Corey was a competition shooter, and a heavily decorated one, having won more than one title at the national level for rifle marksmanship. Gregory had been ecstatic to learn of her skills during the days he had spent at the outdoor range, and knew that she would be invaluable in the struggle to come.

She was about five and a half feet tall, and slender in build, but the determined look in her hazel eyes more than balanced her smaller stature. She had a composed, warrior's look about her, even though she did not have a military background.

"I'm your woman," Corey replied, with an icy, composed tone. "I'll be more than glad to take a few of those bastards out."

Her brother had been one of those rounded up in Godwinton. Gregory could not imagine how furious he would have been if Benjamin had been seized. Underneath her cool demeanor was a heart that was almost certainly hungering for vengeance.

Gregory nodded to her. "In time. We just have to do things real carefully."

He then took a quick appraisal of the others in the room. Two others were nominated to join him and Cory, to form a nascent sniper unit. His eyes then fell upon Sean.

"And I want you with me. We'll have to train some more, and you've shown great promise in the time I've been around you," Gregory said. "As long as you keep listening to me like you have."

The young man positively beamed as Gregory addressed him.

"Can you do that?" Gregory asked.

"Yessir, I can," Sean replied, nodding his head, in that hesitant, deferential way that told Gregory that the lad was devoid of an attitude problem. The youth's challenges would lay more with being decisive and assertive in his actions.

"Then I'll make you something they are going to really fear," Gregory replied, patting Sean on the shoulder with a smile. He brought his gaze back up to the others. "Alright, we'll finish declaring a few of our new fire teams, and we'll get underway on inventory. Sound good?"

Nods and verbal affirmations met his query.

"Good, then let's get started," Gregory replied.

# FRIEDRICH

A luminous vortex churned far below, its swirling form shining brightly within the gloom of the Abyss. Spirals within spirals, there were ten primary rings that could be seen within the enormous, funnel-like expanse.

The sheer vision of the dynamic Vortex, as it steadily took shape from the initial speck of light that had appeared out of the blackness, sparked a feeling of terror within Friedrich. The lancing fear passed quickly enough, but its sharp edge raised his apprehension. He felt Asa'an tense up considerably behind him, to the extent that her little hands grasped onto his back, in a kind of reflexive action.

"The Ten-Fold Kingdom," Enki remarked. "And our path has brought us within sight of its infernal coils."

Even though he had known what the Vortex was, within his spirit Friedrich was dismayed at the Avatar's grave pronouncement. He had hoped never to see the sight of Diabolos' realms in person. It was the place that had come perilously close to becoming his eternal destination.

"Will any from there see us, or be able to sense us?" asked Hans, with a nervous lilt to his tone.

"That place is farther away than you can begin to imagine. It is not likely," Enki replied. "Yet like all of the Abyss, we must proceed with great caution. Let us continue forward."

The group started forth, as Friedrich followed the inner pull that was guiding him to a place that was not in harmony with the vile, demonic realms he could now see immediately below. After a little while, his anxieties began to rise further, as he realized that their path was taking them even closer to the massive Vortex. It was undeniably growing in size as they crossed over its faraway rings. A sense of despair began to take root in him.

Asa'an remained very quiet behind him, though Friedrich suspected a number of thoughts were contending within her. The realms below had been the home of the Peris, before their prodigal ascent to the Middle Lands. It still was the home of the Deevs, the bestial spirits who were their dedicated enemies. More than anyone in the group, even Enki, Asa'an knew precisely what lay within that twisting, flowing vortex.

"Are we really far away?" Friedrich asked her, needing some reassurance himself, as the Gryphon carried them dutifully forward.

191

"What you see below are worlds upon worlds," Asa'an replied curtly.

Friedrich could sense an extreme level of tension within her, echoing powerfully in her voice. While he had not wanted to lay his eyes upon the swirling Vortex, it was evidently nothing compared to what the Peri was struggling against.

"I apologize for asking you about it," Friedrich offered. "The mere sight of that place disheartens my spirit."

"Who else can guide you around that cursed place? Who else knows its nature better than one who has resided there, and crossed through many of its realms?" she asked him. "It is not easy to see the Ten-Fold Kingdom again, but it is why I came, Friedrich."

"I had hoped we would have found Erishkegal's domain before then," Friedrich said, regretfully.

"She is not within those realms, but wherever she abides is not far from it," Asa'an said.

"Why would she dwell near to those realms?" Friedrich asked, with an air of disbelief that any creature opposed to Diabolos would reside anywhere close to the ominous Vortex.

"It may be easier to conceal oneself closer to the realms of the Adversary that would hunt you," Asa'an replied. "I do not know for certain."

"I do not desire to see that place, much less reside near to it," Friedrich responded.

"I feel as you do," Asa'an said.

The group continued through the silence of the Abyss for a long while. Though both Asa'an and Enki had indicated that the distance to the Ten-Fold Kingdom was enormous, it still felt much better when he noticed that the rings were no longer growing in size. Their course had leveled out, at least in relation to the radiant Vortex.

Though he loathed the fact that he was seeing the Ten-Fold Kingdom, he could not help but keep staring upon it. The brightest part of the Vortex was at its farthest point, deep within its core.

The longer that Friedrich gazed upon the Ten-Fold Kingdom, especially the dazzling luminescence at its focus, the more that he felt something calling to him across the vast space.

Growing stronger with every moment, and beckoning to every part of his spirit, the feeling enticed him to abandon his journey, offering him a promise of swift fulfillment in the place of struggle. It whispered vows to him, to bring his suffering and longings to an end, if only he give himself over to the resplendent light within the Vortex's midst. It seemed such an easy thing to do, only a mere thought away.

"Do not look upon it for long," Asa'an interjected sharply. "The light will work its seductions upon you, and probe your every weakness."

Her voice startled Friedrich, severing the trance that was falling over him. He broke his eyes away from the sight of the Vortex.

"It has a strange effect on me," Friedrich replied a moment later, in a low voice. A trace of shame echoed in his tone, as he knew he had been allowing the beguiling feelings to gain a foothold within him.

"It is the purest essence of temptation, cloaked in a radiant light," Asa'an responded. "It will invite you to seek it out, until you desire it with all of your spirit, more than anything else. All the while, it is drawing you closer to its snares. It will only show its true face when you are held captive by it. As long as you have a choice, it will sing with a melodious voice, and display a comely visage to you."

"I am no match for it," Friedrich confessed, perceiving the great weakness within him. On his own power, he knew that he could not oppose the enticing pull of that brilliant light.

"No imperfect being is," Asa'an said. "Not even myself. Only by a light of greater radiance can you find a path away from it. It is of the greatest fortune that you and I are working our way along that path."

"But if I gaze into that light again, and you are not here to stop me from my folly? What then?" Friedrich asked her, fearful of the power that had been exercised on him by the Vortex.

"Think of the destination of the path that we travel on, that which takes us to the gates of the White City and beyond. Think of the light that shines from its high ramparts, and the source of that light. Let that light enter your mind and spirit. The light below cannot co-exist with it."

Using all of his will, Friedrich kept his eyes fixed ahead, resisting the still-compelling urge to look below. The feeling ebbed slowly, as he quieted his mind, and kept nothing but the darkness in his field of vision.

He called to mind another image, thinking of the resplendence of the light radiating from the White City. He centered his inner focus upon that light, and where that light came from.

He could not envision the Great Throne, or anything beyond the White City, for that matter. Yet the turning of his thoughts was like fire to a leech. They recoiled as if singed, jarring Friedrich for a brief instant.

Yet just when he thought that he might be able to endure the rest of the journey to Erishkegal's location, a tingling sensation encompassed Friedrich's spirit. It was a feeling entirely different from the seductions that he had been contending with, causing him to cast his gaze about. He could not help but glance below, as the prickling energy rippling through him carried a sense of alarm.

For just a moment, something like a sprawling flock of birds crossed the light coming from the outermost edge of the Vortex. Limned by the brilliance from the distant coils, the formation was revealed to be approaching Friedrich and the others at a tremendous rate of speed.

A shrill chorus of shrieks and cries, all of which were of a decidedly inhuman nature, cleaved the heavy silence of the Abyss. There was a ravenous hunger within the sounds, like that of starved predators descending upon a fattened herd.

"Galla!" Asa'an cried out from behind him. "Move quickly!"

The Gryphon did not need any prompting, surging forward just as the dark, screeching entities closed in around them. Within moments, the black, winged shapes flowed all about the group, filling the space with their piercing cries.

Without warning, a brilliant light exploded out of the darkness, causing many of the winged entities to scatter as Enki's great, flaming sword appeared. The light in the area swelled, as it was bolstered a moment later by the shining crystal staffs of the riders, as the weapons burst into life with the energy of their spirits.

A few of the inhuman cries took on tones of pain and rage, as Enki and the others set to defending themselves. Friedrich could not easily see the attackers until they were close in proximity. Their forms were as black as the Abyss that they flew within.

A savage face with gaping jaws, and long, jagged teeth, came into the light emitting from his crystal staff. Friedrich did not hesitate for a moment, swinging the weapon with all his might, and crashing it into the side of the depraved creature's head. He caught a glimpse of its elongated, multi-legged body, as it screeched pitifully and plummeted downward.

"Behind, Friedrich!" Asa'an called urgently to him.

The Gryphon whirled about, as if it had keenly understood Asa'an's warning. It swiped another of the attackers out of the darkness with one of its front claws, before Friedrich could lash out with his own weapon.

Another high-pitched cry rang out in the darkness, as the Galla tumbled away.

With Asa'an watching his back, and the Gryphon and Friedrich working in close concert, they were able to dispatch three more of the horrid entities. The space around them was filled with the Galla's presence, as if a huge cloud had encompassed his companions.

Enki's fiery blade flashed farther off, and Friedrich could see a swathe of burning forms dropping away, leaving short contrails that dwindled off into the blackness. The passage of the fiery blade revealed a swarm of Galla around the huge Avatar. Friedrich did not want to think about how things would have been otherwise, had Enki not been with them.

As the fighting continued, Friedrich's band of Exiles gradually splintered apart. He became more isolated, and he found himself being harried by a larger number of the frenzied assailants.

At one juncture, two of the Galla attacked at once. The Gryphon shrieked out in agony, as talons raked its right flank. Only the fast reaction of Asa'an, darting forward and thrusting her crystal spear right into the face of the malicious entity, saved Friedrich's steed from incurring further wounds.

Friedrich twisted about and delivered a clubbing blow to the other Galla, which had come in from another side. He stunned the assailant just long enough that the Gryphon was able to bring its body about, and vent its pain and fury in the form of a powerful snapping of its great beak onto the creature's head. The Galla fell headless towards the Vortex, light gushing out and its form beginning to fade as the Void claimed a new resident.

A faded light leaked from the gashes on the Gryphon's form, sparking great alarm in Friedrich, as he did not know what would happen if his steed were cut out from under him. He knew that he could not fly willfully, but did not know exactly what would become of his spirit if it were flung into the darkness of the Abyss.

"They are driving us away from the others!" Friedrich shouted, seeing what was happening. "We cannot stay in place here, or we will be overwhelmed."

"Fly away then, and do not stop, or we will find ourselves in the Void," Asa'an called back to him.

The Gryphon sped away, banking to the right. But a sizeable cluster of the attackers followed immediately, keeping just behind them. Their shrieks carried a triumphant edge, like baying hounds closing in upon their quarry.

The sounds of pursuit grew louder as the Gryphon raced through the darkness. Friedrich's hopes sank precipitously, just before another group of shrieks emitted from directly ahead of them.

"They are herding us into a trap!" Friedrich yelled.

In an instant, the Gryphon dived downward, but the cries behind and ahead mirrored the steed's evasive maneuver. The jaws of the enemy were closing fast. There was no way to avoid the inevitable collision with the much more numerous Galla.

"Maybe we should use the Void!" Friedrich shouted back to Asa'an, thinking as fast as he could.

He knew that the Void existed behind a thin veil separating the realms that he now dwelled within and the material plane. Conceivably, it could be accessed anywhere, as a spirit consigned to the Void, falling in battle, could be anywhere within the Abyss or Middle Lands. Perchance Friedrich, Asa'an, and the Gryphon could go into the Void for a moment, and then reenter the spiritual planes.

"The danger is far too great, Friedrich! It is warded by powerful guardians," Asa'an replied, speaking quickly, fear resonating in her voice. "Even the Avatars take a great risk in crossing the Veil! It is a forbidden place, and we dare not tread there!"

Friedrich did not know what else to do, as he, Asa'an, and the Gryphon were being driven farther and farther away from the others. The raucous shrieks of the Galla were building into a manic state, drawing closer and closer, and he knew that help would not arrive in time. There was no other choice.

"Do it! Get us into the Void, Asa'an!" Friedrich commanded her, adamantly.

"No, Friedrich, it is too dangerous!" Asa'an pleaded.

"Now, Asa'an!" he snapped, with an air of desperation. "Or we will be going there anyway, and permanently!"

Before he had spoken his last words, something shimmered before Friedrich's eyes, blurring the form of the Gryphon's head. It was as if something was bending the light from his crystal staff.

The phenomenon abruptly ceased, and he saw the back of his steed's head distinctly once again. Though darkness like that of the Abyss met his forward vision, he knew at once that he was in a very different place. A quick glance down confirmed his suspicion, as there was no trace of the Vortex. The pursuing shrieks were gone entirely, and he was shrouded in a thick silence, but he could not feel any sense of relief.

A terror clutched at him. The brooding atmosphere was something entirely alien to his spirit, and the essence of the place repelled him.

"Is this ... the Void?" he asked, his voice sounding thin and hollow.

"It is," Asa'an answered in a harsh whisper, almost like a hiss, before adding, "And keep silent! In a place of nothingness, the slightest disturbance may attract attention. And dim that light!"

Friedrich focused upon the crystal staff, and withdrew the connection to his spirit. The light ebbed from it, and they were left within a sightless, formless realm. The Gryphon drifted slowly through the vast emptiness, as Friedrich tried to collect his rattled thoughts.

Somewhere within the measureless space around him were the spirits contained in stasis until the end of time, from both sides in the great conflict. There were no realms to be found within the nothingness. It was an austere place, to be crossed swiftly for any creature daring to go between the planes of existence.

Friedrich knew that they could not remain for long. Something was already working upon his very essence, the repellent feeling transforming into a compulsion to depart the Void. It was not unlike being in air that grew steadily thicker, and harder to breathe.

"Friedrich! A Djinn comes! We are found!" Asa'an suddenly cried out, brazen terror permeating her words.

Friedrich hurriedly cast his vision about, and saw that there was no value any longer in keeping silence. Like a distant speck, but swelling rapidly in size with each passing instant, something fiery and colossal sped towards them. Friedrich could make out nothing about the blazing form's details, but knew that they stood no chance against the thing rushing towards them. He knew without asking Asa'an that the entity could not be parlayed with, or resisted.

A feeling of heat encompassed Friedrich, the temperature rising quickly to an uncomfortable level. He sensed a terrible rage coming from the onrushing mass of fire.

He understood then that he and Asa'an were nothing more than trespassers to it. Whatever was coming at them was primal and elemental, but it was also possessed of intelligence, and self-awareness, like a violent, massive storm imbued with a degree of sentience.

Friedrich's spirit had begun to burn when the strange, shimmering effect occurred once again. The pain vanished a moment later.

All around Friedrich, Asa'an, and the Gryphon, a great brightness flowed, rushing about them with considerable force. It was like being on the surface of an ocean, caught within the power of an irresistible current.

It did not take long to fathom what had happened. With a sickening feeling, Friedrich realized a terrible lot had befallen them. They had emerged from the Void at the very edge of the Ten-Fold Kingdom. They were not above it anymore; they were within its very perimeter.

He clutched tighter to the Gryphon, even as he felt Asa'an hugging closer to him from behind. Her little body was shaking, undoubtedly riddled with fear.

Looking upward, Friedrich was stunned momentarily, as he watched a steady trickle of lights falling down from the darkness above. The lights descended rapidly, as if being pulled downward, bearing a considerable weight.

As the bright shapes came to a level more even with his position, he saw that vaguely human forms were contained within the midst of the ghostly lights. The source of the luminance was then revealed, to Friedrich's stark horror. It came from flames, fed by the forms of the descending figures.

He could hear cries coming from the beings as they plummeted on past him, some forlorn and sorrowful, and others filled with anger and madness. They were all requiems of despair, and Friedrich wished that he could shut out the dismal sounds.

"I cannot bear this, Asa'an," Friedrich forced outward, his spirit trembling with a deep, burdensome sadness. He knew what the cascade of lights was, and what the figures within them were.

He understood the Avatar Israfel much more clearly in that moment, as to what caused the mighty celestial creature to weep so terribly upon gazing into the Abyss. The vision of the disheartening spectacle, a waterfall of lost souls, struck him profoundly, driving to the deepest core of his being.

He wished that he could help the poor souls, but they were beyond his power to assist. They had chosen the path that had brought them to the Ten-Fold Kingdom, something that Friedrich understood much more clearly after his long tenure in exile.

Even if were an impossible thought, he wished that he could spare them from the grasp of Diabolos. Friedrich understood then that it was the claim of the Adversary that infused the power pulling the souls downward, into the heart of the Ten-Fold Kingdom.

At the very least, it would be a small consolation to deny the Adversary any satisfaction gleaned from claiming a lost soul. The glaring truth was that such a thing was not within his ability.

He could only help those that had not made a final decision. Having witnessed the falling of lost souls with his own sight, he made a resolute promise to himself to redouble his efforts at Invocation if he made it back safely to the Middle Lands.

"Do not dwell upon them, Friedrich," Asa'an said gently. "Not now, at least."

He could hear the great sorrow in her own voice, and knew that she was not immune from the feelings reaching into the innermost part of his spirit. "How can I not?" he replied, his tone thick with emotion. "It is the worst sight that has ever met my eyes."

"Do as best as you can," she responded.

"Where are we, then, Asa'an? What lies here?"

"We are on the very boundary of the Ten-Fold Kingdom, at the cusp of its outermost realm."

Friedrich noticed a conspicuous gravity to her voice.

"And what is that realm?" Friedrich asked, feeling certain that he was going to find no comfort in the answer.

"The outermost realm is the very ramparts of the Ten-Fold Kingdom," Asa'an responded. "The strongest of Diabolos' forces dwell there, ever-growing in strength. Power flows into this realm more than any other, save the Risen Throne itself. If the White City could be threatened, the one who would lead Diabolos' forces in such an assault governs this realm."

"And who is that?" Friedrich asked, with growing trepidation.

"Ares," Asa'an replied solemnly. "Lord of War, and Diabolos' greatest general … and we are going to have to enter that realm."

Even as she spoke, he felt the light around them pulling them downward, with an increasing force that he knew they could not long resist.

# SKYLAR

Deep in the night, as most of the An-Ki and humans alike were slumbering within the boundaries of Conrad's property, Skylar settled into place once again. Lying on her back, she eased herself into the familiar, relaxed state of being, and contemplated the Will of Adonai.

Once again, she slipped the bonds of the flesh, and made her way outside of the house by passing directly through the closed window. There was no scuttling entity in the area around the house this time, but she stayed alert as she rose higher into the sky.

She decided to take up a hovering position, one that provided a prime vantage for surveillance of the vicinity as she contemplated her challenge of locating the path to Benedict. His trace was faint, but it was not long before she honed in upon it.

Skylar readied herself to follow it, when something moving abruptly caught her attention. Instantly on guard, she focused her sight on the motion.

Gliding just above the trees, far below, was a decidedly human shape. The silvery light from the moon elicited a spectral glow from the being. The being was wholly unaware of Skylar. Whoever it was, the traveler was not aligned with the Order, or any other group pledged to Adonai.

Perhaps it was a solitary explorer, some adventurer treading the dangerous ground of the mystical. Yet Skylar could not discount the idea that it was the individual that had discovered Benedict's location. If so, then the being was firmly in the service of the Adversary.

She knew that she had to follow the other astral traveler, and try to discern its purpose. Lowering down from the heights, she carefully shadowed the figure as it made its way across the woods, heading towards one of the cabins placed around the expansive property.

Skylar noted that it was the cabin where the newcomer had been taken, the man that had assumed her own brother's appearance in order to evade those watching for him back in Troy. The approach of the out-of-body traveler made much more sense in that light, if the absence of the man from the church in Troy had been uncovered by their adversaries.

The traveler dissolved into the side of the cabin as it invaded the edifice. Skylar descended in full, bringing herself to an even plane with the unsuspecting searcher.

She glided forward, passing through the walls of the cabin at the place where the other had entered. Her sight was momentarily obstructed, but cleared again within the room on the other side.

The man from Troy, Juan Delgado, was turning about restlessly in his bed, as the searcher hovered almost directly over him. Though it was dark in the room, the traveler's body gave off a subtle light, revealing the details of its features.

Whirling about, the being had the face of a man in about his thirties, oval in shape with a larger nose. His eyes widened in abject surprise upon seeing Skylar in the room with him, but the expression changed quickly, becoming a mask permeated with hostile intent.

Skylar braced herself, expecting some manner of attack, but despite the display of animosity the man clearly had other ideas. He shot out of the room, his movement occurring so fast that it looked as if he simply vanished.

She knew he was snapping himself back into his physical body, taking the information that he had gained back to whoever had sent him on the foray. Focusing in on the place where he had been, she picked up a very faint trace of the traveler.

It was the hint of whatever it was that tethered the man to his physical body, the element that reached across the frequencies of the non-physical planes to connect matter with spirit. Some called it a silver cord, and there were a few who claimed to be able to see it, but Skylar had never perceived anything of the sort. Yet it made perfect sense that there was an unbroken connection in place for a being of the physical world that left the natural confines of the body.

With a quick glance at the sleeping form of Juan Delgado, who looked to be resting easier in the absence of the intruder, Skylar honed in on the trail of the traveler, following it back out of the cabin. Upward she drifted, until the trees were just beneath her, and then the path leveled out as it led her westward.

There were no creatures to disturb her pursuit this time, but she had not counted on the trail fading. Her hopes of following the traveler back to his origins took a sharp downturn as the trail slowly dissipated, becoming harder and harder to detect.

Finally, she lost all sense of the pathway, and slowed to a halt, frustration welling up inside of her. She gazed to the west, wishing bitterly that she could get an idea of the man's physical location, and perhaps see the identity of those around him.

Then she remembered that the man had found Juan Delgado, and had avoided conflict with her in his hurry to depart with the discovery. It could only mean one thing; the scout had succeeded in his given task, and whoever had dispatched the scout would be close behind.

Having a strong notion of what would be coming in the wake of the traveler's visit, Skylar knew that she had to disseminate an urgent warning to everyone harbored on the grounds of the refuge. Lifting her mental inhibition on contemplating her physical body, she swiftly found herself back inside of it.

After taking a moment to gather her composure, she hurried out of her bedroom to begin spreading the alarm. Nothing less than an evacuation was in order.

# GODRAL

Godral watched the van trundling down the gravel road, taking in the anxious faces gazing back at him through the rear window of the vehicle. The clan was being dispersed, but it was the result of absolute necessity, as Conrad's property was no longer a haven.

Instead of being a refuge, it was now a target, and had been from the moment that the unseen scout of the Adversary had come across the man named Juan. There was no way of knowing exactly when the enemy would strike, but Godral knew that an attack on Conrad's land was assured. It would come swiftly, and it would arrive bearing great force.

The humans working to help the An-Ki had acted quickly in the aftermath of the discovery. Though Sargor and Godral both had tremendous reservations about the plan and the temporary breakup of the clan, there was little other choice.

There was no doubt that the enemy would be swarming through Conrad's land very soon. Whether the interlopers were human, a large group of Night Hunters, or a combination of both remained to be seen, but there was no question that the An-Ki could not stay on the property. To remain would be the same as condemning the clan to total destruction.

From what Conrad and others in the group of humans called the Order had explained to Godral, there were several refuges maintained throughout the region. None were as sizeable, or as effectively prepared, as Conrad's property was, but they would have to suffice for the near future.

"Are you ready, Godral?" a friendly voice asked him.

Turning at the sound, he looked down into the face of Arianna. Her jade eyes were lively, and brimming with determination. The young human female harbored a strong spirit, and despite all the ordeals they had been put through, she had not wavered.

He knew that she was suffering inside over the loss of Benedict, whose fate was still unknown. The departure from the haven without any answers regarding a man that shared her blood had to be very difficult to endure, yet she was plainly working to bolster the morale of the An-Ki.

At her side was Sarangar, who lowered his eyes in respect to the An-Ki warrior who ranked second only to Sargor himself. Sargor's son would be going forward with Godral, at his direct request, instead of continuing with Ossur and Larantyr.

The two had faithfully assisted Sargor in guiding and caring for Sarangar throughout the years, ever since the youth's brother, sister, and mother had died violently, slain by the Night Hunters. Yet Sargor had agreed that it was time for Sarangar to take another step in his life, after Godral expressed his desire to mentor the youth more closely.

It was not all about Sarangar, though. Truth to be told, a part of the reason for Godral's proposition to Sargor was that he wanted to maintain some kind of direct, significant connection to the An-Ki leader that he deeply respected and, in so many ways, revered.

While Sarangar was not the primal force that his brother Gerec had been, or the abundance of charisma that was his sister, Ziranta, the youth was coming into his own with every passing day. All signs boded well, as he reflected much of his father, and Godral looked forward to seeing Sarangar take his full place within the clan.

"No," Godral replied, with full honesty.

"I can't blame you," Arianna replied, with a tone of sympathy.

"We must go," Godral said. "It is no choice. It is survival."

She nodded, and glanced towards Sarangar. "It won't take very long to get where we are going, and Conrad said that we've got a nice place to stay in for awhile."

Godral did not reply, as he watched another pair of vans lurching into motion, carrying another small group of An-Ki with them.

"I know this is a difficult time, Godral," Arianna said, her voice full of sympathy.

Godral looked back down to her. "The clan is no longer together."

"In time, it will be again."

"If a group is attacked, I cannot be there to fight."

"But to stay would mean that all the clan is in terrible danger."

"I know."

She reached forward and put her hand on his arm. Sympathy filled her voice. "The clan will be brought together again soon. The storm will pass, Godral."

He fixed her with a somber gaze. In the time and place that the An-Ki had left behind, the storm that had fallen upon the world had not ceased until everything had been destroyed. It had horrified him to learn of that fact in the days that had followed the escape of the An-Ki through the gate.

He could only hope that the An-Ki would survive again, in the face of the new threats looming. He nodded slowly to Arianna.

"We will survive, Arianna," he declared.

A smile came to her face, and she squeezed his arm firmly where she was still resting her hand. "Yes, Godral, we will."

"Alright, it's time to load up the vans and head out," one of the men from the Order called over to Arianna.

"Time to get your group onto those two vans," Arianna stated, turning towards Godral.

He dreaded the moment, as there was a sense of finality to it. He could not shake the fears and worries that clawed at him, as he strode slowly with Arianna and Sarangar towards the two idle vans.

He hesitated for a moment before entering the elongated vehicle. Leaning over, he got into it gingerly, brushing his head against the top. Rotating about, he hunched over as he took his seat by a window. The interior was cramped, as even in human form, his stature was well-above average for their kind.

His breathing quickened rapidly as Sarangar, Vailia, her Life Mate Rayzal, Arianna, Quinn, and then Maureen got into the dark van and took their seats. There was no room at all for any others, human or An-Ki. Arianna sat next to him, and was pressed snugly against his side in the tight confines, with Sarangar on her other side. Godral felt entirely trapped as the side door to the vehicle slid shut, emitting a distinctive click.

Behind them, the other van was loaded with the humans Gerald Darwin, the newcomer Juan Delgado, and the An-Ki Kantel, Dedran, and Godral's own Life Mate, Mariassa.

Having Mariassa with him was the only consolation in the dark, foreboding hour. He knew that he would have been tormented with worry over her if she had been separated from him. She would keep his spirits from falling too far, as she had always done in the past.

Godral hated being parted from Sargor, but knew that the old chieftain was accompanied by many that would give him comfort and counsel in the uncertain days to come. Berenthia was one of those who had gone with Sargor, and Godral knew that she understood the clan chieftain as well as any of the An-Ki. In many areas, she could relate to Sargor much better than Godral.

She had lost her own Life Mate, a powerful An-Ki warrior named Trommaon. Berenthia had also lived through many more years with Sargor than Godral had, entailing some of the most harrowing times that the clan had experienced. The thought that she was with Sargor gave Godral a needed sliver of encouragement.

His heart rate accelerated rapidly as the man from the Order seated in the front of the vehicle turned a small, thin piece of metal, which was inserted just beyond a circle that he grasped onto. A rumble emitted from ahead of the man, and Godral felt vibrations running throughout the vehicle.

The prevailing mood was pensive, and none of the An-Ki or humans said a word, as the van started into motion. Godral had watched cars, vans, and other vehicles often during the time spent at Conrad's estate, but nothing had prepared him for the strange sensation of being carried forward within one.

He peered out the side window, as the van accelerated. He knew that the van was not the result of supernatural powers, but rather an invention of human ingenuity. Godral was in awe of their abilities, which had flowered abundantly since his former age, to the point that they could reach the sky, and, if Arianna and the other humans could be believed, even the stars beyond.

The ride became smoother as they traveled down the road. Godral felt both a sharp thrill and a deep unease at the velocity they were able to attain. The land around them raced by, and he knew that they were journeying at speeds that far exceeded the swiftest of the An-Ki.

More than once, Godral had to close his eyes, and remind himself that traveling in such a way was entirely normal for humans. He turned his attention as much as possible to the scenery around him, taking in all manner of buildings, other cars, and changes in the landscape as they burst out from a wooded stretch into an open, cleared area. Passing through the space, they entered another zone where the trees closed in around them, hemming in the roadway.

Godral quietly stared out the window as they proceeded past many other sights, and he could not help but marvel at the presence that humans had established in the world. It far exceeded their place in the world during the ancient time. Humans truly were creatures driven to progress, invent, and create, and he knew that such characteristics were related in some intimate way to the spark of the Creator dwelling within each of them.

A part of him did want to explore the world, and learn all that he could of the wonders within it. But he could only do so when the clan was in a state of safety and stability, qualities that appeared to be drifting further and further away.

Godral became lost in his thoughts during the last stretch of their journey, only coming back into focus as the van slowed down and finally turned off the road. The vehicle shook and rattled as it traveled slowly down an uneven path covered in gravel. The narrow roadway meandered around a couple of low hills, until a broad clearing opened up before them.

Godral knew at once that they had reached their next place of refuge. He only wondered how long their stay would last.

# ARIANNA

Looking towards the left, Arianna saw a large barn, the open doors of which revealed the presence of a tractor inside. To the right was a two-story, timber cabin with a high-pitched roof and sheltered porch. A short distance beyond the cabin was a sizeable pond, which had been provided with a wooden dock that extended a good length from the shore.

The place had a very tranquil feel about it, but Arianna knew that she would never be able to put her mind at ease. No place was safe, as had been soundly demonstrated when they had been forced to evacuate Conrad's land.

The van pulled up before the cabin, while the other one following them halted just behind. Maureen opened the sliding side door to let the vehicle's occupants out.

Arianna could feel the relief in the air as the An-Ki began to get out of the van. She could not imagine that the travel had been very comfortable for any of them.

Godral and Sarangar had not said a word throughout the drive, both of their eyes riveted on the sights passing outside the windows. Arianna had to remind herself that even though they had made long strides in acclimating, and had been learning a new language very quickly, there was still so much remaining that was entirely foreign to them.

She watched Godral's Life Mate, Mariassa, walk up to him from the other van. Arianna was happy that Godral had her there with him, as her presence undoubtedly was a comfort to the heavily burdened An-Ki warrior.

In her human form, Mariassa was simply beautiful. Like the other An-Ki, she was tall, at least six feet, four inches in height, and long-limbed, with flowing locks of light-brown hair that graced her athletic-looking set of shoulders.

Her face carried high-cheekbones, and a sharper jaw-line that carried an echo of her lupine visage. Only her bright yellow eyes gave away her non-human nature, but in the modern age, that could be explained away easily enough by claiming that she was wearing a set of specialty contacts.

Arianna watched Mariassa stroke Godral on the arm tenderly, as they spoke quietly together. The sight evoked a smile on her face, though deeper inside she found herself wishing that she had someone with her as well.

The treacherous road from the apartment she had shared with Maureen had been a very lonely one. She had discovered levels of inner strength that she never would have thought she possessed, and knew that she could face the coming days on her own feet. Yet she still found herself being visited with a melancholy feeling whenever she was around the likes of Quinn and Maureen, or one of the closely-bonded An-Ki Life Mates such as Godral and Mariassa.

With a wistful sigh, Arianna pushed the heavier feelings back and turned her attention away from the An-Ki couple. She took in a few cleansing breaths. The scent of the air was fresh, a welcome aspect after enduring the musty, stuffy confines of the van.

"Holding up well?" Maureen asked Arianna, having come over to her side as she looked around. "I already know those golf carts will come in handy."

Maureen directed Arianna's attention over to where a pair of battery-powered carts rested underneath an awning set to the right side of the cabin.

"This must be a pretty big property," Arianna replied.

"You can see a few trail heads from here," Maureen said, pointing away from the cabin.

Arianna looked towards the edge of the woods, and saw at least three narrow dirt paths running into the trees.

"A good five hundred acres, with ponds, a couple of creeks, and a lot of woods," interjected Quinn, who had ridden up front with the man from the Order. "I learned that much on the way down."

"You were about the only one that did any talking," Maureen replied.

"Well, I wanted to get some idea about the place we will be staying at," Quinn replied, grinning. "Makes a little sense, doesn't it?"

"At least it sounds like it's big enough to do some exploring in. I'm glad we aren't gonna be too cooped up," Maureen answered. "I came to like having a little space at our last site."

"Ooooohh…," groaned Gerald Darwin, as he strode slowly up to them, wincing, and stretching his arms out to his sides. "These old bones stiffen up quick."

Arianna grinned. "Stop your whining, Uncle. That wasn't even a forty-minute drive."

"You'll see what I mean one day … and I don't wish that day upon you, my dear niece, believe me," Gerald replied, chuckling.

Juan walked up slowly behind Gerald, looking a little hesitant. His dark eyes were downcast, and he refrained from meeting anyone's gaze.

"Come over here, Juan," Arianna invited him amiably, with a welcoming smile.

"I'm so sorry. This is because of me," he replied in a low voice.

"They would have come after us sooner or later, whether you were with us or not," Arianna replied, and her words were not without truth. With martial law declared, no property or person in the UCAS was safe, and the enemies of the An-Ki could do whatever they wanted with impunity.

"Still, to be uprooted like that," Juan said. "I didn't think they'd be able to follow my trail."

"Seems they resorted to extraordinary measures," Arianna replied. "Not much we can do about that."

"And it was good to learn what they are capable of," Gerald interjected.

Juan nodded slowly, though the glum expression remained.

"And this place looks pretty good for a next stop," Quinn pronounced, looking out in the direction of the pond. "On a warmer day, I'm going to be making use of that water, believe me. Get a little running start down the dock, and then a good jump, and…"

"You'll land right on top of a big snapping turtle," Maureen jested, interrupting him with a laugh.

A lone figure strode out from the house at that moment, an elderly man with narrow features and a wide-brimmed beige hat. A symbol of the Rising Dawn gleamed from where it was exhibited in the open collar of an off-white, button-down shirt. A pair of faded blue jeans and leather cowboy boots rounded out his attire, lending him an appearance that resonated well with the cabin and rustic surroundings.

"Are these my new guests?" he called out to one of the drivers, with a heavy southern accent.

"Yes, Benton, they sure are," the driver called back, with a broad grin. "And they're all ready to check in."

Benton looked towards the small group milling about in front of the cabin. "You look like a healthy bunch. May have you earn some of your keep while you're staying here!"

Chuckling, he stepped down from the wide, covered porch, and made his way towards them. He had a mild limp to his gait, favoring his right leg, and it took him a few moments to reach Arianna and the others.

"I'm Benton Crandell," he announced, with a smile. His gray eyes held a look of youthful merriment, which shone through his deeply-creased face. "Will be glad to have some company around here. Too much hunkerin' down with the virus rampaging out there, and all the unrest in the big cities. Good time to be rural, you know. Now who might you all be? Let's start with you, young lady."

His eyes fell on Maureen, who smiled back, and introduced herself, starting a process that continued through the humans and An-Ki.

"Been wantin' to see what you guys are capable of," he said to Godral, who stood with Mariassa close by his side. They were flanked by Kantel, Vailia, Rayzal, Dedran, and, about a step back from the others, Sarangar. The frailer-looking human standing before the strongly-built, comely figures towering over him made quite a sight. "I hear you all can do some impressive things."

Godral looked a little reticent to respond, and he cast a brief glance towards Arianna, as if looking for some sort of assistance. He finally said, "Thank you for giving us a home."

"That's no trouble at all," Benton replied in a friendly manner. "But there's too many of you for this little cabin, so we're gonna need to make use of the barn, or it was suggested that some of you could take to one of your other forms."

He looked back to Godral and the other An-Ki. Arianna could see the eagerness surging in their eyes. As with virtually all the An-Ki, they longed to be in their wolf-like forms. The assumption of human forms had been done with great reluctance, and more than once An-Ki had expressed their hopes to Arianna that they could take their favored shapes once again.

Godral nodded, and looked to the An-Ki with him. "You can choose to take the first and second forms."

The faces of most of the An-Ki exhibited obvious relief, and a swell of excitement, to the extent that Arianna was surprised they did not begin transforming right there and then. Yet one of their number held a markedly different reaction from the rest.

"Can we stay in this form?" Sarangar asked, from the back of the small group of An-Ki.

"Yes," Godral said, turning to gaze upon Sarangar. "And I will be staying in this form."

"If it is just the two of you that will be keeping human, then we've got enough room in the cabin, if we work on some makeshift bedding in the front room," Benton said. He turned to look at the humans among the arrivals. "Well, what do you say we show you your new quarters?"

Nobody objected, as Benton turned and slowly made his way back towards the cabin.

# CONRAD RUDEL'S PROPERTY

Not even Conrad was present when a substantial convoy of armored vehicles roared down the main road onto his land. Helicopters simultaneously deposited special operations teams at several points around the perimeter, as well as at the cabins identified. Every sector of the property was violated by heavily-armed teams, all of which were ready for combat the first moment that any threat emerged.

Completing the encirclement, no less than twenty-four Erkorenen were conveyed to positions evenly spaced around the property. They were divided into groups of threes, but no less, based on what they had gleaned from the unwelcome encounter with the Watchers.

Their number included Jeqonadin, and a couple of the others that had gained some painful experience with the newer breed of Watchers.

Jeqonadin, and another Erkorenen with a similar form to his, kept to the ground, accompanied by Obizuth. The dragon flew low, keeping just over the trees, and shadowing the advance of the Erkorenen while keeping a sharp lookout for the presence of Watchers.

Obizuth had contended with an Avatar before, and was now even larger and stronger than the time of that storied battle. If the Watchers manifested, the dragon was ready for a fight.

Though they were braced for conflict, the Erkorenen and human troopers encountered no resistance, or obstructions of any kind. All intelligence had pointed to a large number of people occupying the property very recently, as well as residents of a non-human variety.

It was as if everyone had abruptly vanished, and the absence of humans and An-Ki came as a rude surprise. More than one of the Erkorenen vented their fury at being thwarted, loosing chilling cries into the night.

211

Conrad's main home was searched, as were the cabins, but nothing was turned up. It was clear that the place had not been abandoned for long, making the leaders of the operation begin to wonder if those on the property had been warned. If that was the case, they could not fathom how anyone could have determined that a raid was imminent.

As frustrating as it was, only the person reporting back to Dagian Underwood dreaded giving the news that nobody had been apprehended in the operation. The name of a specific, former employee of high rank at Babylon Technologies was among those designated to be sought out among the property's inhabitants. Like the others, he had managed to evade the grasp of the TTDF, though how he and everyone else had done so was a mystery to the units swarming Conrad Rudel's land.

# FATHER BRUNNER

It was difficult to keep a smile on his face, and a friendly tone in his voice, as Father Brunner was waved through yet another checkpoint. He was relieved that they had gotten Juan out of Troy when they had. As he had feared, the larger urban centers of the country were becoming a living nightmare for anyone with a sense of justice.

On one hand, the streets were swiftly becoming much more dangerous. With the fraying of law and order, even in the aftermath of martial law being imposed, armed gangs had become emboldened. Chaos rippled throughout the city on a regular basis, with riots and demonstrations breaking out routinely. Criminal elements navigated the ebb and flow of upheaval with great skill, preying with abandon upon the more vulnerable elements of society.

On the other side of the equation was the heavy police and military presence that had descended upon the city. Soldiers bearing assault rifles, armored vehicles, and military helicopters were a regular sight in Troy now, reminding Father Brunner at every turn that the world was transforming rapidly.

The military and police forces had flexed their brute strength more than once since martial law had been declared. Suppressions of many public demonstrations, several being entirely peaceable assemblies, of the kind specifically protected in the Grand Charter, were harsh. Citing martial law, large public gatherings were expressly forbidden by the new authorities. Hi-tech means were employed in the rapid crackdowns, such as sonic blasts emitted from truck-mounted devices, as well as older tried and true methods, like tear gas, rubber bullets, and water cannons.

Military checkpoints were everywhere, and Father Brunner always felt that he was walking on very fragile ground when he made a foray out from St. Bosco. Fortunately, his priest's collar still carried a little currency, insofar as the police or soldiers he encountered did not regard him as much of a threat.

The Order was being stretched to the limit, as were the Shield Maidens of the Rising Dawn and other groups pledged to Adonai in the greater struggle. A great many had already departed the city, such as the ones that had escorted Juan Delgado to the rural haven.

In addition to preparing for resistance, the members of the consecrated groups were doing everything that they possibly could to protect and aid those most at risk in the populace. Those that remained in Troy were working around the clock, with scant respite. There were already shortages of goods, and prices were inflating in the stores, raising the pressure on families, the elderly, and others trying to recover from the shock of having their worlds being turned upside down.

Suicide was a regular occurrence, as were instances of individuals snapping, and becoming detached from reality in dramatic fashion. Some of the latter lashed out in violence, but were gunned down without hesitation.

Father Brunner knew that the unseen world was alive with activity, and that the darker spirits were feasting on the misery, suffering, and anger rife within the city. It was their hour, an ascendancy of wickedness, and he could only hope to endure until the nightmare drew to an end.

An onerous number of worries weighed on Father Brunner's mind, as he continued beyond the checkpoint towards Paladin's Light, on the outskirts of Troy. The night had a brisk chill to it, but was thankfully devoid of rain. A voice on the radio kept droning on with news reports, though Father Brunner did not know what to believe anymore when it came to the media allowed to function in the martial law climate.

There were stories of insurrection coming in from all around the country, ranging from the acts of lone wolf types, to militias that had evidently been waiting for precisely a moment such as this. Father Brunner knew that the resistance was an uncoordinated effort, though, which stood little chance against the high technology and overwhelming firepower enjoyed by the federal authorities.

Still, a part of him felt good and encouraged that not everyone was acquiescing to the gross violation of everything that the UCAS had once stood for. Tyranny was a manifestation of evil, and evil had to be opposed with every last ounce of strength that an individual could muster.

There were more reports on what the government was doing to contain the viral outbreak. Other than trucks, Father Brunner imagined that interstate travel was now down to a trickle, if not on the verge of being forbidden, and that confirmed cases of infected individuals were hastily addressed. It was the one favorable aspect of living in an industrialized nation under martial law, as the spread of the deadly virus would at least be slowed.

In the developing nations it was another matter entirely, and the figures of death being bandied about were beyond catastrophic. Millions had already perished, and millions more would inevitably succumb to the ravages of the disease.

Father Brunner could only imagine the Sisters, priests, and others of the Church laboring in the midst of so much death and squalor, knowing that they would most likely share the same terrible fate as those they tended to. That required a level of courage that was hard for Father Brunner to imagine, and he wondered if he could measure up to such a test.

Slowing down, Father Brunner turned to the right, as his headlights illuminated a closed gateway. A high, chain-link fence had been erected around the boundary of the makeshift compound known as Paladin's Light. Though they carried no weapons, a few men and women wearing security uniforms stood around the entrance, eyeing Father Brunner's car warily as he edged up towards them.

Beyond the security guards was a sight that had become all too common across the UCAS in recent years.

There were recreational vehicles, as well as school buses, whose interiors had been gutted and converted for domestic dwelling. Camping tents, lean-tos, and a wide range of other constructs, using all manner of styles and building materials, dotted the grid of pathways throughout Paladin's Light. At the center of the compound was a large, rectangular community building, which was the result of a joint effort between the Universalists and other denominations of the Savioran faith.

As tent cities went, Paladin's Light was one of the better ones. There was no train track running right next to the grounds, to constantly rattle the nerves of already stressed residents. Winters were admittedly rough, but at least the summers in Troy did not have a sun beating down with an insufferable heat that rendered sleep all but unattainable.

With the involvement of the churches, the tent city also carried an official status, and even in the climate of martial law it was doubtful that the place would be interfered with. As long as the population residing there was calm and orderly, and posed no challenge to the prevailing system, the authorities would pay Paladin's Light scant attention.

Some tent cities that Father Brunner had visited in the past had little more than a couple garden hoses as the main source of water, and a few portable sanitary units for waste. Paladin's Light had true showers and bathrooms, items that were luxuries to people that had found themselves with nowhere to turn as they lost their jobs and homes.

"Welcome back, Father Brunner," one of the security guards greeted him, a tall, broad-shouldered man with an amiable smile.

"Hi Jason," Father Brunner replied. "And how are things here lately?"

"Good as they can be," the guard said. "We have more arriving here every day. It's a big challenge keeping them organized until the doctors can test them for the virus."

"Screenings are a necessary thing, though, where so many are living together," Father Brunner said.

"Without a doubt," the guard said, nodding in agreement. A little fear flickered in the guard's eyes, and Father Brunner knew that he was uneasy about being on the frontline in dealing with new arrivals.

"Well, I don't want to distract you, and I'd better get going with what I came here for," Father Brunner stated.

"I suppose we'll let you through, Father … this time," the guard replied with mock sternness, emphasizing the last two words before loosing a chuckle and waving for the gates to be opened.

Once through the entrance, Father Brunner pulled off to the right, parking his car in one of the few open spaces remaining amongst a cluster of vehicles. Getting out of the car and locking the doors with his key remote, he looked up at the sky for a moment, watching a few clouds drifting across the face of a bright moon.

Some faint music carried to his ears from one direction, and an outburst of laughter from another, but the overall atmosphere within Paladin's Light was more subdued than normal. His footsteps crunching on the gravel of the parking area, Father Brunner walked away from the cars and headed into the core of the residences.

Proceeding through the dwellings, Father Brunner was greeted warmly by many of the occupants. He was a recognizable figure to many living on the grounds, as it had long been one of the charitable projects that he lent his time and efforts to.

All manner of people lived within Paladin's Light, but the old stereotypes of the homeless were the exception, and not the rule, in the struggling populace. Professionals of many trades and career paths, a great many college educated, were rife within the beleaguered masses.

Families were the hardest for him to lay his eyes upon. Father Brunner's heart had broken more than once when he had looked into the eyes of newly-arrived families within Paladin's Light. The hollow, weary gazes of mothers and fathers were among the worst things by far that he encountered there, expressions full of resignation and battered self-confidence. He had to walk off by himself more than once, so the residents could not see the glisten of sorrow welling up in his own eyes.

He finally came to a halt by a structure whose fashioning had involved a number of varying materials. A blue tarp had been spread over the roof, while all manner of vinyl siding, drywall panels, and timber boards had been utilized in the construction of the dwelling.

To one side of the makeshift edifice was a small garden plot, warded by a cobbled-together perimeter that included some chicken wire, a segment of chain link fence, and random scraps of wood.

"Hank, are you around?" Father Brunner called out, his voice sounding loudly in the subdued atmosphere.

A man emerged a moment later from the dwelling, pulling aside a large sheet of plastic hanging down over the entrance. His jeans and long-sleeved flannel shirt hung loosely on his lean frame.

Hank's past was very typical in nature for a single resident of Paladin's Light. He was a military veteran, and had worked for many years as a crane operator, in addition to doing any job that he could find during the economic downturn. He possessed a great work ethic, and was skilled in a number of areas. Father Brunner had seen Hank's abilities on display several times, as he helped others in Paladin's Light to erect their own living quarters.

There was nothing wrong with Hank that had prevented him from getting work. He had simply hit the impassible barrier of no available jobs.

Hank's face exhibited a deep weariness, and Father Brunner knew that he endured many sorrows during moments of solitude, but the man still carried his head high. The spark in his eye had not been dulled by all of the hardship and disappointments, and Father Brunner could see the kind of fiber embodied in Hank that had made the UCAS a great nation in the past.

"I'm here, Father Brunner, and I'm still standing," Hank said, with a grin. He then chuckled, with a rueful edge. "But not much success in my job hunts today."

"I would think it is a little dangerous to do job searches these days," Father Brunner replied.

"There is that," Hank replied, nodding. "You're just about taking your life into your hands if you venture into some areas of the city. Knocked on the head by a thug, or given a nice electric jolt by a police officer, for no good reason … take your pick. So what brings you out here?"

"I wanted to get an idea how things stand at the moment," Father Brunner replied, holding Hank's eyes with a knowing gaze.

Hank nodded. "Let's go see. Let me grab a jacket first. It's a little brisk tonight."

He disappeared for a moment before rejoining Father Brunner, and was clad in a dark jacket half-zipped in the front.

They walked down the pathway, before turning to the right. The two men came to a halt at a dome-shaped tent, large enough for at least four to go camping together. The tent was now being used as a permanent residence, and its sole occupant came out of the tent at their call.

"Hank … Father Brunner," Zhang greeted, glancing between the pair of visitors.

Zhang's dark eyes were alert and lively, and like Hank he had not entirely lost his zest for life, despite his circumstances. To Father Brunner, Zhang was an embodiment of what had made the UCAS a great success.

Zhang was a first-generation citizen of the UCAS, whose parents had come from Mandaria. He had once been an employer, and had lived through the debilitating ordeal of a slow national decline.

He had endured many cutbacks and trims, as costs rose everywhere, and revenues shrank. Every effort had been made to turn things around, and eighty-hour workweeks had become commonplace, but it was all to no avail. He finally had to shut his doors, unable to sustain operations in a climate that made it impossible to compete.

To Father Brunner, Zhang's story was illustrative of what was fundamentally wrong with the UCAS at the present, and what had caused its lamentable demise. A quiet, relentless war on individual initiative had been going on for decades, and it had been won by powers with a malefic agenda, filling places like Paladin's Light to capacity as it achieved its greatest victories.

Father Brunner had felt like screaming whenever he heard pundits or others blathering about creating jobs or improving the economy. They knew nothing about what it took to actually grow wealth or build opportunity. Every action and decision made during the downturn simply made it harder and harder for the type of individual that genuinely created wealth and jobs.

Zhang was one such individual, and he was now dwelling in a tent, without any viable prospects. Zhang's presence in Paladin's Light said all that needed to be said about the state of the nation.

"I don't know what we are facing, entirely," Father Brunner said. "And I don't want the people at St. Bosco to be trapped, if everything collapses, or something worse arises…"

"What do you mean, worse?" Hank asked him, his eyes narrowing. "It's getting about as bad as it could get."

"There's something following all of this. I know it in my heart," Father Brunner replied, somberly. In his mind, he thought of two words, 'Living ID,' and the technology that they represented. Its ultimate purpose had been explained by Juan Delgado, and the current climate was perfectly suited for its implementation. "The imposition of martial law is just a predecessor to something else … something that is much, much worse."

"So what do you mean to do?" Zhang asked.

"I need to start getting more people out of Troy, and into the countryside, where at least they'll have a fighting chance," Father Brunner replied.

"There are checkpoints on all the routes in and out of Troy," Zhang said. "No way to move a large number of people out of there, except through the police and military. I doubt they will permit a large exodus. I'm not even sure interstate travel is allowed anymore. I haven't talked to anyone that's tried it outside of commercial vehicles."

"Then we'll have to figure out how to enact a breakout," Father Brunner stated, his eyes taking on a steely, determined edge as he gazed into the eyes of the other two men.

"We're the only two members of the Order in here, and we don't have a lot of interaction lately with the others," Zhang replied.

"I do have some contact, as does Father Rader," Father Brunner said.

"What can we possibly do?" Hank asked him.

"I'm looking to you to get the people in Paladin's Light far from here," Father Brunner said.

His words lingered in the stillness for several moments, as Father Brunner's intentions dawned upon the other two men.

"Get the people of Paladin's Light out of here?" Hank asked, his countenance filled with incredulity. He looked at Father Brunner as if the priest had just lost his mind.

"Yes, because I don't want to see these people corralled when what is coming is unveiled," Father Brunner said.

"You really think something big is imminent, don't you?" Hank asked him.

"I know something's coming," Father Brunner responded succinctly, without hesitation.

"Do you think it is the time of the Saints?" Zhang asked him, with a cautious timbre.

"Just about," Father Brunner answered, thinking of everything that Juan Delgado had revealed to him. "Everything happening points right to it."

"Then we need to see what we can do here," Zhang responded, initiating a discussion that would last deep into the night.

# GREGORY

The first target to be struck was a convoy bringing in supplies and equipment to the forces deployed in Godwinton.

Gregory had watched its sinuous approach from far away, atop the summit of a hill that provided an advantageous view of the road snaking through the wooded hills.

There were several of the older multi-purpose wheeled vehicles in the convoy. Most had been fitted with kits making them suitable for the transport of supplies and medicine. A few two-and-a-half ton trucks and eight-wheeled, ten ton trucks rounded out the lengthy formation.

Among the latter, there were some variants. A couple of them were tankers, one was a recovery vehicle, fitted with a winch, and another pair was designed purely for cargo, provided with cranes mounted at the rear. The off-road capable vehicles would be very valuable to the occupation force in Godwinton.

The convoy was a little lax in its travel, as the distance between vehicles and speed maintained was highly inconsistent. Gregory chuckled, as he contemplated the rude awakening that they were about to receive, before he got on a motorized bike to hurry down the pathway to join the others gathered to greet the convoy.

Minutes later, as the trucks made their way around an extensive curve, the ones in the lead were met with a massive barricade manned by an array of armed individuals. Through loudspeakers, the drivers of the convoy were informed of their precarious situation.

With a long drop to their right, and a steep hillside to the left, the convoy was not in any kind of position to attempt a breakout, and the drivers were in no mood to fling their lives away. Abandoning the vehicles, and surrendering to the armed fighters, they were led away from the road as the contents of the trucks and trailers were searched.

Cases of ammo, additional assault rifles, some machine guns, explosive materials, and all manner of highly useful items were uncovered. Laboring diligently, the members of Gregory's band whisked off the crates, cases, and boxes. Small, highly camouflaged depots were being established all throughout the woodlands, and the supplies gleaned from the convoy would bolster the holdings of many of them.

When the pillaging was finished, explosives were placed on the vehicles in swift fashion. Booms echoed over the hills, and the vehicles were soon ablaze, and left burning in the road. Columns of acrid, black smoke reached towards the sky, visible from miles around, heralding the onset of a hardened, determined resistance.

# JOVAN

Yorvik had become the nightmare that many had feared, at least for the time being, and Jovan had been forced to relocate to his countryside estate. Things were simply too dangerous within the city's confines for him to conduct business affairs at his downtown office.

Juliana Pullman had also come back to the estate with him, bringing a few assistants along, and establishing a temporary office herself. Having her residing on his grounds was certainly a silver lining in the dark cloud enveloping everything. She kept a diligent watch on everything that Jovan was involved with, allowing him to focus on the major tasks. She was simply invaluable, and he was not about to have her risking life and limb back in Yorvik.

Despite having some of the most severe laws in the country related to the ownership of guns, the city was now teeming with armed gangs that each possessed an arsenal of firepower. There had been several bloody gun battles already, and the reigning atmosphere in the streets was chaotic at best.

With the ongoing breakdowns in government services, a great majority of the city's occupants had effectively gone haywire. With a population of over ten million, it was impossible to sustain any degree of calm when the distribution of food stamps and other forms of public welfare abruptly ceased. Instead of turning to each other, large segments of the populace began to turn aggressively on each other.

Looting was rampant, and violence was at epidemic proportions. Large mobs were forcing their way into stores, and absconding with anything that could be carried out. The stores that somehow managed to remain unscathed were experiencing terrible difficulties in getting restocked with even the most basic of items. The conflict with Mandaria was causing tremendous problems in that regard, and delivery systems were running anything but smoothly. Quite a few trucks had been visited with the same treatment that so many retailers were experiencing, as throngs beset them and pillaged their contents.

Homes were no longer places of refuge, but instead attractive targets for indulgent robbers and the desperate alike, as everyone knew that the police were completely overwhelmed with the avalanche of crime. Brazen home invasions were now commonplace occurrences, bringing along a great degree of brutality in their wake. Here and there, some apartment complexes and neighborhoods were spared the terrible onslaught, wherever elements of the community cooperated together for the sake of mutual protection.

Yorvik had truly become a wilderness, a concrete and asphalt jungle where the timeless saga of predator and prey was playing out ubiquitously, as the stronger asserted themselves upon the weaker. Jovan had heard the crackle of gunfire coming from more than one direction as his helicopter had departed downtown Yorvik, and carried him out to his rural estate. He had felt a great sense of relief as the skyline of Yorvik faded into the distance behind him.

With the city fully cordoned off by the TTDF, military, and police, and a methodical campaign to established full control over the city, it would be safe enough to return in coming weeks; but now was not that time.

He was still deeply worried about Kaira, who had elected to remain in the offices of the Peace Commission, but he knew that the World Summit buildings were being heavily guarded. At least one call a day had been made to check up on her situation. From what she had told him, things were very stable in her sector, though her workload had become very substantial with the ongoing illness afflicting David Sorath.

Thoughts of Kaira never left his mind entirely, as Jovan swirled the red wine in his glass and took another sip. He looked around at the faces seated at the table, from the venerable Gendry Resinger, to Abner Nithael, Head of the World Interfaith Council, and the other elite individuals that had gathered for the impromptu meeting.

"There is certainly no turning back," Jovan remarked.

The conflict between the UCAS and Mandaria was still ongoing, and threatened to worsen at any moment. The plague was spreading rampantly, the markets were in complete disarray, currencies were unstable, and society was breaking down. To say that the situation was tenuous was an understatement.

"The end game is well underway," Gendry stated in his deep, authoritative voice. "Living ID will be the solution for the UCAS, and then the entire world."

"And the unrest? There's resistance cropping up everywhere in the UCAS, well beyond the gangs in the cities," Jovan replied.

"With martial law active, use all means necessary to subdue it," Gendry replied calmly.

"We need to unveil the vaccine, and pair it with the Living ID, to get things back under control," Jovan stated.

"As we are about to do, Jovan," Samel Malkira said, from where he sat next to Abner Nithael.

Jovan regarded Samel and Abner, both of whom left him with an unsettling feeling deep inside. Neither man showed the slightest sign of being ruffled by anything transpiring, from the volatile financial markets, to the warfare in the Far East and the viral outbreak rampaging across the world. To Jovan, they possessed a degree of composure that was virtually inhuman.

"The churches of the Saviorans, Temples of the Rashidans, and Synagogues of the Davidians will factor in nicely during the days to come," Abner said, in the cool, collected fashion that was so characteristic of him. "They will be of great value in getting people to comply smoothly, and efficiently, with the implementation of Living ID."

"And the resistance that's breaking out? What if that takes a deeper root in the countryside?" Jovan asked.

"If they receive Living ID, they can be tracked," Gendry responded. "If they do not, they cannot buy anything, get medical treatment from any licensed health center, go through a checkpoint, receive electricity or gas, or any number of indispensable needs for the world we have today. I think they will be brought into compliance soon enough. And if not, then they can be hunted down and eliminated."

"Most will rush to Living ID, to receive the vaccine, and regain a sense of stability," Samel said. "They will be unable to live without it, and in due time there will be mandatory incarceration for anyone refusing to take Living ID."

"And with Living ID established in the UCAS, it will be demonstrated to be a great model for a globe in turmoil," Gendry said.

"And the central banks? Are they truly ready for the next phase?"

Jovan asked, knowing what would follow the implementation of Living ID on a worldwide scale.

"The day could not come fast enough for them," Andrew Greenwell interjected. He smiled broadly. "The Nuumus represents the realizations of all of their ambitions. No more of the inefficiency and instabilities that come with having this ongoing, ungainly hodgepodge of national currencies."

Jovan settled back into his chair and listened quietly, as Andrew Greenwell initiated a discussion regarding the implementation of the forthcoming global currency. The new horizon was now within sight, the first light of a nascent dawn beckoning across centuries of disorder.

There was not much longer to go, before everything was in place. All of the tumult would be over. The wars would be ended, the virus would be stamped out, markets would be stable, and Jovan could enjoy the delights of a world crafted for the strong.

The thought of it sent an exhilarating thrill racing through him. That day could not come a second too soon.

# GREGORY

"It's not going to be so easy next time, boys and girls. Now that they know there's an organized resistance, they'll be much more wary. And we won't be able to be so generous ourselves," Gregory stated, his last words carrying great solemnity.

The first incident had been bloodless, and very bountiful, but the next encounters would be decidedly more difficult.

"I say we take out assets wherever we can … hardware, supplies, fuel, anything they're making use of," Consuela said.

"But always softer targets," Gregory cautioned her firmly. "They've got the skies, and there's nothing we can do about that. So we have to hit fast, and we can't stick around to admire our work. A pitched fight would be a disaster. Believe me, when I was overseas, I saw what happened to insurgents foolish enough to stick around and engage in a firefight."

The front door to the small home opened at that moment, and

Jacob trudged in. Behind him walked a shorter, nervous-looking man with a slouched posture. He was wearing glasses, and had a round face covered in a graying beard. Though not long, his wavy hair was decidedly unkempt. To Gregory's eyes, he was probably in his late forties.

"Chuck's not too happy I dragged him here, but he knows we need him," Jacob announced, looking to Gregory. "He's got some skills we can use, that's for sure."

Chuck's eyes shifted about the room, taking in the hardened-looking individuals staring back at him. Gregory nodded to the anxious man and smiled, knowing that Jacob would never have gone out of his way for something unimportant. Whatever it was that Chuck was capable of, Jacob had deemed it necessary to bring him into the epicenter of the growing band of rebels.

"Welcome to our little club here, Chuck," Gregory said, affably. "So what have you done to get Jacob to bring you here?"

"Always thought he just kept building up piles of junk, storing some of it at his buddy's cabin not too far from my place," Jacob said. "But it turns out what he's got is pretty valuable too. Not just his skills. Tell him about it all, Chuck. I can't explain it good. It's not my area."

Chuck hesitated for a moment, and when he talked, Gregory noticed that he had a bit of a nervous tic, wiggling the fingers on his right hand as he spoke. His voice was low, and soft. "Jacob felt my radio equipment can help you out. Now that they've shut the internet down, and the power grids are not predictable anymore."

"And what kind of radio equipment is that?" Gregory asked him.

"He's a ham radio operator, it turns out," Jacob interrupted.

"Yes ... I am," Chuck added, continuing to fidget. "It's a better word for amateur radio, which is a term we don't really like. Are we really amateurs, when those of us in the field know a whole lot more about radios than commercial broadcasters do?"

A smile spread on Gregory's face. Ham radio always had a diehard legion of enthusiasts, but few people in the mainstream ever appreciated the underlying value in the pursuit.

To most, it was just a pastime, a haven for anti-social types that liked to squirrel away gadgets. Now that the world was crumbling, Gregory had more than an inkling that his group was about to discover that the field was far more than a mere hobby.

"And you've got gear?" Gregory asked him.

"Does he have gear?" Jacob interjected again, rumbling with laughter. "He's got more piles of junk than anyone I've ever known. Even has old working eight-track tape players. Good lord, he's got gear!"

Gregory did not remind Jacob that the totality of the people he knew was probably not overly substantial. But he looked towards Chuck with a sharply rising interest.

"Got enough for you to make use of, for what you all are doing," Chuck said. "And my gear can be powered by portable solar panels. I took units out to many field days before everything broke down. They work good. No need for the power grid."

"That is music to my ears, Chuck," Gregory said. He looked over towards Jacob. "And thank you for bringing him here. This will be of great help to us."

"Wasn't too hard," Jacob admitted. "He's inclined towards our way of thinking anyway. No love lost for the tyrants, that's for sure."

"I knew it was all coming. Used to listen to Sea to Shining Sea every night. I've seen this all heading our way for years," Chuck declared, speaking faster, with a much firmer voice. A little gleam of excitement danced in his eyes. "They used to brush me off, but I was right about it. Just like I told them it would be."

Gregory could imagine that Chuck was regarded as more than a little eccentric by those around him. From Jacob's description, he was undoubtedly a packrat when it came to technology. Gregory had seen the type before, and it did not take much discernment to sense that Chuck was feeling more than a little vindication, now that things were unfolding just as he had predicted.

"And I'm telling you, they've got more coming. They're going to announce some kind of implants next, this is all orchestrated," Chuck continued, with a frenetic edge, as if a lid had been removed on his previous reticence. "There won't be countries anymore, it will be one big, worldwide system. And they might even bring out something that they'll call aliens, but it will be something much worse, and I'm guessing that it'll be creatures called Nephilim. They really exist, you know …"

"Settle down there, Chucky," Jacob interrupted, cutting him off. "Don't want you to work yourself into a stroke before you can get your radios working."

"Oh … okay," Chuck replied, returning instantaneously to his more subdued level, though his fingers continued to wiggle for several more moments.

Gregory could not help but laugh. "It's okay, Chuck. I want to hear what you think is going to happen later. With everything unraveling, I'm open to just about anything right now, and a couple of the things you said aren't far off from what I'm thinking."

Chuck straightened up a little, appearing encouraged by Gregory's response.

"But for right now, let's keep focused on the ham radios," Gregory said. "Can we go assess the gear right after the meeting?"

Chuck nodded. "Sure."

"Good, then just hang out with us here for a little while, and I'll go with you when we're finished," Gregory said.

Chuck worked his way to the back wall, as Gregory resumed the meeting.

"Now where were we, before Jacob and Chuck arrived?" Gregory asked, before answering the question himself. "Yes, hitting soft targets, quickly. And we can use a tried and true method of guerrilla warfare everywhere."

"Things that go boom?" queried a robust man close to Gregory's right.

Dante Johnson was another major asset to the group, a former soldier who had experience in one of the key skills needed by an effective insurgency. He was thoroughly schooled in the area of explosives, having taken on the unwelcome task of defusing many improvised explosives during his multiple deployments in the wars overseas.

He had a great understanding of the methods by which bombs were constructed, what materials could be used, and, even better, what were the most effective ways to mask explosive devices when they were set in place.

Dwelling in a rural area populated with farmers, Gregory and some of the others had been able to round up a considerable amount of material that could be applied towards the creation of explosives. Dante was the man that knew how to build them, and then put them in place.

They had also gained a modest supply of military grade explosives from the looting of the convoy. The highly potent material required less improvisation in its application, and Dante was well-familiar with its nature.

"Yes, things that go boom," Gregory said, with a slight grin.

"Just turn me loose, we'll make a mess of their entire operation," Dante replied, exhibiting his toothy smile. "They'll have rattled nerves the second they take one step off their little bases."

"Let's pick our spots with this carefully," Gregory said.

"If I could pick a spot, it would be their damn concentration camp," Dante said angrily. "Blow the gates right off their hinges, and get all the townsfolk out of there."

"You and me both," Gregory said, his countenance darkening at the mention of the detainment center.

Thought they had not scouted it out yet, Gregory knew that the big federal facility located a little ways outside of Godwinton was being put to use. He also knew that a fusion center was close by, and likely being utilized to coordinate all of the federal and provincial activity in the area.

"Then let's mess that place up real good," Dante said, his eyes narrowing, as a determined expression surged onto his face. Murmurs of agreement rippled throughout the room.

"There are a couple places I've marked for our attention, and that's definitely one of them," Gregory assured Dante and the others, letting his gaze drift slowly past the faces around him.

"That is good to hear," Consuela replied, "I was hoping we could pay that place a little visit."

Another round of affirmations met Consuela's remarks, and it was clear that the group's disposition was favorable towards undertaking a high-impact mission.

The challenges looming before all of them were immense in scope, but Gregory could see the initial signs of a solid chemistry forming amongst the group. They all knew what was at stake, as well as how important it was to coordinate their efforts and delegate tasks.

The surface they were all walking upon together was fragile, not unlike crossing the ice of a pond feeling the first touches of spring. The group could be wiped out in an instant, as the enemy held the ability to deploy overwhelming force with great speed.

It was up to Gregory, and a few of the others with military experience, to inculcate a healthy caution within the group towards the capabilities of the enemy. Yet they had to do it without making it seem as if the budding resistance had no chance at all. The art of balancing morale and wariness would have to be mastered in a short time, but Gregory felt that things were definitely on the right track.

Of course, the most important element of a successful resistance was the support of the surrounding populace. That was one area that had yet to be gauged fully, though Gregory could not see how anyone with any good sense could possibly support the outright tyranny that was transpiring across the country.

Fear would be a powerful ally to an enemy that held the reins to an individual's personal economics, medical care, and so much more. Gregory knew that a great many would not actively help the resistance due to the threat of being cut off from access to the things that the government controlled. But he did harbor hope that a significant proportion would be inclined to simply look away, and not actively assist the government either.

Ultimately, there was no way of knowing for sure which way the population would tilt until the resistance began making its presence felt more prominently. As far as Gregory was concerned, the enemy would find the next manifestations of the resistance to be like receiving a solid fist to the jaw. At the very least, the populace would see that the resistance stood a serious chance of causing significant disruption, or perhaps something more, if it was given leniency by the masses.

Gregory knew in his heart that the more that it seemed as if the resistance could sustain, or even prevail, the more unlikely it would be that the people of the surrounding community would betray them. With that in the forefront of his mind, he steered the meeting towards deciding upon the next targets, and what it would take to achieve a successful engagement.


# FRIEDRICH


"Keep within the heights, Friedrich," Asa'an urged, as they glided swiftly along the hot currents, in the midst of a billowing, sulfuric mass comprised of something like volcanic ash.

Through small breaks in the scudding, dark-hued substance, Friedrich could see an enormous plain stretched out beneath them. It was a parched, desiccated landscape that he laid his eyes upon, bereft of any signs of growth or vitality.

The barren plain led towards a semi-circle of towering, obsidian mountains, a granite diadem of gargantuan scale. It was so great in height that the tips of its peaks pierced the tempestuous skies, like great lances cutting into a soft underbelly.

Yet there was one feature in the scene below that drew Friedrich's attention. It was a spectrum of lights that rained down from the dark skies, onto some manner of structure that was much too far away to identify.

Deep red hues intertwined with greens and violets. The luminous cascade might otherwise have been a thing of beauty, within another context. Placed within the desolate vista, it invoked a deep unease within Friedrich. It was a poisonous luminance, and nothing about it boded favorably.

Asa'an guided them clear of the area with the lights and structure, taking a course that led farther into the barren desert-scape spreading out from the semicircular formation of black mountains.

In the distance, a white object caught Friedrich's eyes as it broke up the featureless terrain. It stood out starkly from the surroundings, as they sped towards the area.

"Down, now!" Asa'an said, just as the Gryphon went into a steep decline.

The object grew larger with every moment. It had the look of a temple that had been constructed on a natural dais. It was built on a scale suited for beings that dwarfed Friedrich and his companions.

The Gryphon landed a short distance before the gargantuan building, as Friedrich's gaze drank in the impressive sight. His steed broke into a trot as soon as ground was underfoot, heading directly for the structure.

Whatever material had been used for the construction of the edifice had a hue that was akin to sun-bleached bone. Steps that were at least a mile in width led up towards the grand structure. Enormous columns, each over a thousand feet in height, supported a massive roof. It was a temple building suited for giants, or, more likely, Dark Avatars of incredible power.

It was an edifice reminiscent of ancient structures found on Terra, though the truth of it was horrifying to contemplate, as Friedrich drew close enough to examine its surfaces.

Human skulls, of numbers far beyond count, had been used to fashion the abhorrent temple. Every last part of the roof, columns, surfaces, and steps had been formed with the skulls, oriented such that thousands upon thousands of sightless eye sockets faced the observer. It was a colossal monument to death, and Friedrich felt his spirit flinch in the presence of the dreadful construct.

The Gryphon slowed down as they approached the bottom of the steps.

"This is the temple to Ares that Kyknos wished to have built in your former world," Asa'an stated grimly, gazing upon the gruesome structure. "Here, there is nothing to stop the building of such an abomination. Ares commanded it done, when my kind yet dwelled in these realms."

"Kyknos?" Friedrich asked.

"Ares was among those who took flesh, before the flood that washed the world clean. Kyknos was one of his two sons, born of mortal and celestial blood," Asa'an answered. "Kyknos and his other son, Ismenios, who was in the form of a great dragon, were slain in the Deluge. Ares' rage was terrible in the aftermath, when his spirit returned to the Abyss. His wrath was felt across all realms in the Ten-Fold Kingdom. It was that rage that had this temple built. You do not wish to know how the skulls were gathered."

Friedrich did not press her for an explanation. It was all that he could do to keep his composure. His eyes roved the facing of one of the steps, taking in the teeming hordes of dark sockets casting their unseeing gazes back towards him.

"Why is there no one here?" Friedrich asked her, listening to the hot winds blowing through the columns.

"Some who dwell in the Abyss conduct rituals, and the realm of Ares is one such place," Asa'an answered. "It is fortunate that this temple is not being used at the moment."

There was nowhere to hide, as the huge temple, and the rock dais that it was set upon, rose up out of the barren, empty plain.

"What kind of ... rituals ... are done here?" Friedrich asked, apprehensively.

"Power formed from war and violence flows into Ares' realm, from all sides, in any conflict, whether a fight between individuals or a clash of armies," Asa'an explained. "All conflict ultimately increases the power of Ares. An unbroken stream comes from your world, empowering Ares

231

without pause, which expands the power of the Shining One.

"Those powers are channeled to serve the will of the Shining One. And the harnessing of that power at a higher level is expressed through ceremonial rituals that take place here."

Asa'an suddenly brought her head upwards, and looked back, peering into the distance, to where the eerie, shimmering lights showered down before the lofty, obsidian summits. The alarm on her face was unmistakable.

"What is happening?" Friedrich pressed her.

Whatever troubled the Peri was also bothering the Gryphon. The creature shifted about with a nervous edge, pawing at the dry ground. Its golden eyes stared fixedly in the same direction as Asa'an.

"A ceremony is about to take place," she replied. "Here. They are coming."

"Who is coming?" Friedrich asked.

"We have no time left, we must hide ourselves in the temple," Asa'an said.

Looking around, Friedrich could see that there were no other options. Everything was flat and exposed for leagues around.

"They will use the temple as a place of ceremony, but it is not likely that they will enter it. Hurry, quickly, to the columns! There is nowhere else we can go!" Asa'an exclaimed urgently, taking to flight and speeding up the front of the broad stairs.

Without prompting from Friedrich, the Gryphon followed the Peri, as she guided them past the first of the columns. She alighted at a position behind a column in the next line.

The massive column of skulls soared above him, to the underbelly of the roof. The uneven surface formed by the skull facings allowed him to peer through the column while keeping his body well concealed. Though he felt anything but safe, it was a favorable hiding place. One question still remained.

"Should we go into the inner part of the temple?" he asked, glancing back at the dark entryway leading to the temple's interior.

The Peri shook her head emphatically. "The Sanctum is warded ceaselessly. The eyes that watch over it would raise an alarm the instant that we crossed into it."

Friedrich gazed back into the shadowy entrance, wondering what was contained in the Sanctum, and what kind of spirit watched over such a place. The knowledge that they could go no further, but were unable to go back, caused his anxiety to rise.

He got down from the Gryphon, and lowered into a crouch, as if he could make himself even more diminutive amongst the huge columns. Looking over, he saw Asa'an's eyes widen in surprise. She was peering outward, towards the open plain in front of the temple.

He brought his eyes back around just in time to see what looked to be an onrushing mass of storm clouds. The dark, roiling formation was quickly revealed to be a horde of creatures converging fast upon the temple area. Friedrich remained frozen in place, not wanting to let an inkling of movement reveal his position to whatever it was that was racing towards the structure.

The extensive flock of winged nightmares rushed over the great temple, stirring up a tempest in their wake. A pungent stench engulfed the temple, as the flying creatures disappeared from view, taking up roosts all about the roof of the enormous building. Their high-pitched screeches were deafening, piercing the air around Friedrich and rattling his composure. He was assaulted by a barrage of sound and scent, and did the best that he could to maintain his focus.

"The Birds of Ares," Asa'an said in a low voice, glancing upward with an anxious expression. "They are like no birds of your former world. Even their feathers are weapons, like lethal darts."

The thought of thousands of the hideous creatures atop the roof was disconcerting, but Friedrich did not have long to think about his precarious position located just beneath them. Only moments later, his gaze was drawn towards the sprawling plains, focusing on an approaching light that at first had the appearance of a pillar of flame.

Details emerged slowly, as Friedrich perceived that it was not just one being that was advancing across the arid landscape. The fiery light came from a single figure, whose luminous form shone starkly against the much larger creature trudging immediately behind.

When they drew up to the temple, Friedrich marveled at the contrasting pair of beings. One was as graceful as the other was dreadful, the former a vision of elegance, and the latter an embodiment of brute strength.

Striding towards the base of the steps was an unusual, captivating figure, whose liquid-like surface carried a molten appearance. The contours of the entity's body were decidedly female, shapely and proportionate in form. Her face was beautiful, and lengthy, fiery extensions, like locks of hair, undulated and flowed as if buoyed by a steady breeze.

Friedrich wanted nothing more than to shrink back deeper into the temple, as he looked upon the figure's radiant, white eyes. They looked to be capable of piercing through any gloom or obstruction. He wished that he were anywhere but where he was at that moment, helpless to do anything about his predicament.

"Enyo, one of the greatest Avatars that serves in Ares' realm. Bloodshed and violence is her dominion. Enyo will convene this ritual," Asa'an observed in a hushed tone.

Enyo was gigantic, able to ascend the great steps with ease as she made her way up to the top. The moment she was standing by the columns, she turned towards the barren plain. The relief that Friedrich felt when she faced away from the temple did not last for long, as the Dark Avatar emitted a soul-wrenching cry, which sounded like an abundance of grating shrieks.

It was then that Friedrich turned his full attention to the gargantuan entity that had followed Enyo. It had come to a stop at the base of the temple steps. The creature was a living juggernaut, with stout legs ending in huge claws that tore the surface of the plains with every step that it took.

The skin covering its heavily muscled body had the look of iron, and its cavernous maw held several rows of blade-like teeth, of a similar dark, metallic hue. It had several eyes, each one a fiery orb that radiated malice. Curving, wickedly sharp horns of great length and girth sprouted along the top of its wide head, looking like some kind of natural diadem.

Out of all the creatures that Friedrich had witnessed that came from the Abyss, only the multi-headed Ladon at the most recent battle in the Middle Lands, and the mightiest of the Dark Avatars, rivaled the menacing, titanic beast.

"Kydoimos... " whispered Asa'an, her awe unmistakable as she gazed, transfixed, upon the creature.

The beast did not ascend the steps, but at the cries from Enyo it slowly turned around to face the open plains. The desolate land and temple then shook in the force of its deafening bellow. The intertwining tones conjured up images of grisly violence and bloodlust, blending together every sword clash, gun shot, and cannon fusillade that Friedrich had ever experienced during the wars of his mortal life, and rendering them into one terrible, sustained chorus.

He was shaken to the core when the overwhelming din ceased. Staring sullenly outward, he showed no visible reaction when the horizon was spanned with a reddish light. It was like a sun cresting the boundary between sky and land.

The light swelled in intensity, as legions of Avatars and Dark Aishim flowed en masse towards the great temple. Rank upon rank swept across the plains, filling the land before the skull-fashioned edifice, with the exception of a considerable swathe of ground left open before the first step. Numerous sigils, far too many to count, could be seen among the Dark Aishim and Avatars, signifying the identity of those in command of the various contingents.

Friedrich had seen enough Dark Avatars to distinguish between those of lower and higher ranks, and he noted that there was more than one legion comprised of immensely powerful Avatars. If he were to venture a guess, the huge, fiery creatures were only one rank below that of the elite Seraphim.

The great sea of fire then parted, forming a wide channel that cleaved through the midst of the assembled legions. At the far end, the brightest light of them all appeared, and began moving towards the temple.

Friedrich knew at once that he was beholding Ares. The winged Avatar's body blazed ferociously, emanating waves of pride and power as the being was conveyed in grand fashion towards the temple.

A massive platform, wreathed in billowing flames, carried the titanic figure. It was pulled forward by four black monstrosities. Six-legged, they vaguely resembled brawny stallions, but when they opened their muzzles, bellowing roars issued forth across an arsenal of huge, jagged teeth. The hellish steeds' eyes were portals into blazing infernos.

To either side of Ares were two other massive Avatars, each grasping tall, flaming lances. The great sigil of Ares was displayed above the majestic trio, a resplendent battle standard comprised of infernal light.

Behind the chariot-like platform of fire was a broad, deep column of warriors that stretched as far as the eye could see. There were many thousands in the shadowy column, keeping a perfect order as they advanced.

No sign of fire showed anywhere on their bodies, which had a single pair of wings folded against their backs. Each of the entities in the dense file was shrouded with a swirling darkness, which extended to the lances that they carried.

"Phobos … and Deimos," Asa'an said, and Friedrich could feel the fear pouring from her. "And behind them, the Makhai, dark spirits born of the wickedness given life in each and every battle fought in the mortal world."

Friedrich was terrified, feeling miniscule and fragile in the face of the dizzying might on display before the temple. Even one of the figures marshaled on the plains was a deadly adversary, and to contemplate thousands upon thousands of them at once was staggering.

Ares descended smoothly from the chariot-like platform, and made his way up to join Enyo. His movements were devoid of haste: each step was purposeful and calm, as the mighty being cast a commanding air over the entire area.

Ares was followed by Phobos and Deimos, who kept to a fixed distance, several paces behind the High Avatar. The huge creatures harnessed to the blazing chariot then churned up the ground, as they pulled it towards the farther side of the temple from where Friedrich and his companions were hidden.

The dusky ranks of Makhai proceeded to split into two contingents, some following the chariot, and the others taking to the opposite side, as they took up positions flanking the temple. It took a long while for the lengthy column to march forward and divide, and when they were finished a great multitude was assembled on both sides of the temple.

The fiery ranks drew completely silent, and Friedrich had the sense that even a whisper would have shattered the stillness. The full attention of the massed legions and Makhai was given towards their commander, who faced outward with Enyo by his right side.

"The line of my son, drowned in the waters sent by the Accursed One, shall not end with his confinement to the Void," the fiery being proclaimed. A rippling anger could be felt in the multi-layered tones of the great Avatar's voice. His words shook the airspace when he continued, causing Friedrich to sway where he cowered behind the inner column. "You are gathered before the temple envisioned by Kyknos, whose life was also stolen from him by the Accursed One's waters. You are to witness a great triumph over our Enemy. … From the teeth of my son Ismenios, a great vengeance is born."

The High Avatar then descended the steps slowly, coming to a halt at the last, as a great silence fell over the gathered hosts.

Ares' right hand then cast forth the teeth of his dragon-son. The sharp, jagged objects crossed the air in wide arcs, and clattered onto the desiccated surface a moment later.

At first, nothing happened, but signs of movement transpired gradually wherever the teeth had fallen. One by one, as if seeds casting forth roots, tendrils extended from Ismenios' remains and burrowed into the ground.

A low rumble expanded into an earthquake of enormous magnitude that shook the temple. The skies over the hosts were seared by streaks of lightning that lanced through its underbelly, as thunderous booms resounded over the arid plains.

The lightning held the colors of the lights raining down before the gigantic mountains in the distance. The incoming forks and rivulets of energy amalgamated within the upper skies, forming an expanding pool of rippling, pulsating light that stood out in dazzling fashion against the deep grays and blacks of the cloud-like cover. Like a cyclone of incredible scope, the energy swirled and reached towards the ground in a massive, churning funnel.

The shaking grew in force as the energy rushed into the ground. It was all that Friedrich could do to prevent himself from tumbling away from the side of the column. He endured as best as he could, clutching onto a pair of skulls for support.

The lofty pool of light gradually emptied in the descending passage into the ground, until the last of it disappeared from sight. The furor unleashed in the storm of light abated, as the tremors slowed to faint vibrations, and then stilled entirely.

A cold blue light then emanated from the expanse where the teeth had fallen, shimmering dynamically and sending immense waves of power across the vast assemblage. Friedrich could feel the energy coursing through him as it flowed over the temple structure. He knew that he was witnessing a tremendous exercise of power, and found himself becoming increasingly apprehensive.

Slowly, dark forms began to take shape and grow where the teeth had taken root. Rising, spreading, and condensing, distinct bodies emerged into view, as heads, limbs, and torsos began to manifest.

As if vines were running beneath the surface, and propagating a wicked fruit, the spaces in between the growing figures also began to fill up with other similar, enlarging shapes. Ultimately, there were far more of the nascent entities than the number of Ismenios' teeth could account for.

The hellish figures could easily have been deemed giant skeletons, were it not for the thinnest of membranes stretched across their bony structures. It was like decayed, parched skin, and the creatures' forms bore the essence of a severe famine, as bones and joints jutted outward. The tightly-drawn skin exhibited a mottled appearance, as if riddled with a horrid disease.

If pestilence, decay, disease, and violence could take on a living, sentient form, then the creatures emerging before Friedrich's eyes were the physical embodiment of those afflictions.

The eye sockets of the entities retained a fully skeletal essence, and nothing but sheer blackness resided within the hollow recesses. Leathery wings grew and spread outward from their backs, the membranes stretched thin across bony frames.

The icy-blue light waves then surged in intensity, and each of the demonic figures began to move, as if awakening from a deep slumber. Their wings flexed, their limbs moved, and it was clear that they possessed sight, as they looked down at their bodies.

"Behold the one who has called you into life," Ares thundered.

Hundreds upon hundreds of heads turned in Ares' direction, followed by many more, as others completed their genesis. Before long, several thousand of the newly-born creatures were staring attentively towards the High Avatar.

"As war gives life to war, and bloodshed to bloodshed, the weapons that you bear must take their power from a world that you will soon tread," Areas continued.

He extended his right hand outward, in the direction of the descending lights in the cradle of the towering black mountains. Pulling his arm back in against his blazing form, he summoned another torrent of energy from the distance.

As before, the light gathered in the upper skies, but this time it did not transform into a huge funnel. Without any warning, bolts of energy shot down toward the newborn entities. Splitting and branching outward, single segments of light fell upon each of the beings, as if the lake of power was being used to anoint the supernaturally-generated multitude.

Reflexively, the entities reached out with blurring speed and grasped the shards of energy, which formed into something like long,

double-ended lances in their clutches. It took scant moments for the entire throng to be armed with the weapons formed from the light, as the pool of energy above was drained to the last once again.

"Let only the strong be called the Sons of Ares," the High Avatar boomed, as the latest element of the progression came to an end.

Friedrich wondered what was going to happen next, as there was no movement out on the plains for an extended period of time. A ponderous silence gripped the air tightly, throwing a weighty pall over the entire scene.

He then saw a great many of the new entities begin turning their dark gazes skyward. Their movements brought his eyes up from the plains, and he saw immediately what had drawn their attention.

Descending out of the whirling, surging masses draped across the skies of Ares' realm, a force that was an army in itself sped towards the forefront of the temple area. Brandishing the flaming weapons characteristic of the Avatars, the hordes of Dark Aishim were rapidly drawing closer to the space where the arisen multitude had sprouted from the ground.

As if they knew what was expected, the spawn of the dragon's teeth launched themselves into the sky. Though sorely outnumbered by the incoming force, the newborns showed no hesitation as they raced to engage the Dark Aishim. The entities rent the air with multi-toned screams, loosing them at a volume that would have shattered any human ear.

A ferocious battle then ensued in the skies over the temple, as the entities and Dark Aishim came together. Friedrich already knew that the Dark Aishim were daunting opponents, warriors of the Abyss that were larger, faster, and much stronger than the best of the Exiles within the Middle Lands.

The beings that had come from Ismenios' teeth proved to be something far more lethal. Fiery blades slashed, and flaming spears stabbed, while the light-weapons of the entities were wielded with astounding speed.

Bodies of many Dark Aishim began drifting and plunging towards the ground, trailing ethereal light from the gashes and wounds torn into their forms. The force of Dark Aishim enjoyed a great advantage in numbers at the outset, but was soon whittled down, until they were hemmed in and pressed from every side by their relentless opponents.

A few of the Sons of Ares fell in the rain of casualties, but the overwhelming number of beings dropping were Dark Aishim. Nevertheless, the lesser Avatars, once mortal beings who were given favor and transformed in the afterworld, acquitted themselves well enough.

They showed no sign of submission or fear, even when it was clear that they were being cut down to the last, and had no hope of escaping. They were consigned to the Void in the battle frenzy until not one of the thousands that had descended from the upper skies remained.

When the fighting was over, the victorious entities glided back towards the swathe of ground that they had occupied before. When they had alighted, it looked to Friedrich as if they had not lost any of their number, so few were the casualties that they had incurred.

"You that remain are worthy to be called Sons of Ares," the High Avatar exclaimed. "The ground before this temple has been consecrated, and will become fertile. As others come into being, they too will be tested, and your host will grow in this final age.

"Though Kyknos and Ismenios were claimed by the Void, in the waters sent by the Accursed One, they will bear witness at the dawn of the Remaking. The temple that Kyknos desired ages ago stands unassailable under the skies of my realm, and Ismenios' line proceeds forward in abundance and strength. Vengeance will be claimed, when all of the Accursed One's realms are torn asunder. War is my grace and dominion, and it shall be loosed upon all who are not of the Ten-Fold Kingdom."

Ares drew silent, and as if it was some manner of cue, the four huge steeds pulled the fiery carriage around to the front of the temple. Phobos and Deimos walked down the steps, and the three surmounted the platform.

The Sons of Ares drew to the sides, opening up the channel running through the ranks of Avatars and Aishim. The carriage passed down the midst of the gathered hosts, as the Sons of Ares formed into a broad column and marched behind. After them came the Makhai, and it took quite some time before the last of the dark horde of warriors strode past the farthest ranks of Avatars and Aishim.

The sprawling hosts then departed with their dynamic array of sigils, becoming an indistinct, bright line on the horizon before vanishing from sight.

With a cacophonous outburst, the Birds of Ares took to the air, forming into a dense, dark flock that hastened onward. The last to go were Enyo and the hulking Kydoimos, whose massive form blocked the sight of the Avatar as the demonic creature followed her into the distance.

It was a long while before either of the intruders spoke. Friedrich could not believe that they had not been discovered with the tens of thousands of beings that had been arrayed around the temple.

With a sigh of relief, he glanced over to Asa'an, and froze in place. She looked unusually thin, and had a hollow look to her eyes. She slumped down to a knee before his eyes, before falling over to the ground.

Friedrich hurried over to her, as did the Gryphon.

"Asa'an! What is happening?" Friedrich exclaimed, rife with worry.

Her little form looked so fragile, and her eyes had a dull cast to them. The lively spark in her was nowhere to be found, and she looked very diminished from her prior state.

"I did not ... wish to tell ... you," she whispered, laboriously.

"Tell me what?" Friedrich asked, wondering what possibly could have happened to her.

"I had ... to shield ... you," Asa'an managed to get out, with obvious difficulty.

"What can I do?" Friedrich pressed, fear spiraling inside of him. He gently pulled her to him, and cradled the Peri close.

Her face was severely drawn, wracked with exhaustion. She abruptly shuddered, as her expression contorted into a reflection of deep pain.

In his heart, Friedrich appealed directly to Adonai, seeking a grace in the form of sparing Asa'an from whatever it was that was afflicting her. In one of the most powerful realms of the Adversary, Friedrich put all of his mind and spirit into Invocation.

He directed all of his thoughts toward the Great Throne, holding fast to the idea that not even the Shining One's realms could impede a genuine Invocation.

A meek smile came to Asa'an's face a few moments later. Her words emerged lightly. "I can feel what you are doing."

The smile ebbed, and she fell back into silence. To Friedrich's great dismay, nothing happened in response to his Invocation. The Peri looked to be teetering on the edge of the Void.

"I do not know what has fallen over her," Friedrich said to the Gryphon, which was quietly watching over the other two. A feeling of desperation was welling up within him.

243

'She used her strength to hide us. Ares would have known of us if she had not used her power,' the Gryphon's voice sounded within his mind. 'She did not tell you, for she knew that you would not want her to risk herself.'

He could not bring himself to say the words aloud, but his next question was conveyed to the mind of the Gryphon.

'This place will weaken her,' the Gryphon's voice came again. 'She may go to the long sleep in the Void.'

Friedrich looked out towards the empty plain, and then peered up at the cloud masses. There was only one action that he could take, even if the outcome was entirely uncertain.

"I have to get you free from here," he told Asa'an in a low voice, standing up with great care. She did not respond, looking far too weakened to speak, as her eyelids fluttered. Friedrich looked towards the Gryphon. "We need to fly out of this place, with as much speed as you can muster."

'Climb to my back,' the Gryphon directed, lowering its body down to the ground.

Despite carrying Asa'an, Friedrich was able to mount the Gryphon smoothly. He clutched onto the Gryphon using one arm, and kept Asa'an tight to him with the other.

With their spirits so close together, he could sense the great strain she endured in retaining her sentience. A slender, delicate thread of awareness kept her from succumbing to the Void, and he knew even that was fraying.

The Gryphon rose back up to its full height, and carried Friedrich and the Peri forward, striding to the edge of the top step.

Friedrich looked down at the Peri. He urged her, "Stay with us, Asa'an. Your place is with me. And your road is to the gates of the White City, not the Void."

Spreading its wings and leaping forward, the Gryphon launched into flight. It ascended at a sharp angle, heading for the underbelly of the great masses of ash-hued vapors crossing swiftly above.

Nothing moved to intercept them, and in moments Friedrich could see nothing, his vision obscured as they passed through the dense, billowing formations.

# SECTION V

# JOVAN

Away from the eyes of the media, and absent from the official dockets of the World Summit, a small gathering of tremendous importance was taking place. Inside the main World Summit building, two clusters of individuals represented the two giants engaged at the heart of the conflict straining the world's tensions near the breaking point. A world war loomed, chafing at the brink of a nuclear holocaust.

There were other representatives attending the convocation, familiar individuals to all the others, hailing from a few of the larger powers in the east and west. There was also a brand new face within the midst of the throng of dignitaries and ambassadors, one that many of them had not expected to see. It was impossible to avoid her, as she was at the epicenter of the prominent assemblage.

"With the severe illness affecting Mr. Sorath, and the unavoidable demands on some of the others at the Peace Commission who possess more experience than myself, I have been sent to be the Commission's representative at this meeting," Kaira stated, with an air of confidence and authority.

Jovan leaned back in his chair, gazing proudly at the younger woman. Kaira was really coming into her own, right before his eyes. She cast a commanding presence over the gathering, standing tall, and not exhibiting even the slightest hint of being out of place as she served as the Peace Commission's representative.

With the financial markets swirling and heaving, and Living ID on the cusp of being asserted on the UCAS populace, the need for the fires of war in the east to be doused was paramount. The Mandarians had not yet invoked one of their most dangerous weapons, the financial strings that they held to the massive UCAS debt load.

Jovan worried that the shooting war would trigger the ultimate financial one at any moment, but the Mandarians were not a reckless people. They knew that they would suffer great economic harm themselves, even as they pulled the financial rug out from under the UCAS. The suspension of trade between the two countries was already sending seismic waves throughout all markets, and goring both of the nations' huge economies.

"The conflict between the UCAS and Mandaria must be brought to an immediate halt," Kaira continued firmly, casting a stern look about the chamber that brooked no arguments. "The instability that it has caused in the world is far too great, and the consequences of this continuing could not be more dire."

All eyes were fixed upon her, and not all of the attendees were pleased with her words. Jovan's eyes shifted to a member of the Mandarian contingent who had risen to his feet.

"We will not allow the UCAS to act in the way that it … and its partners … have acted in the Central East for years," the representative stated icily, his dark eyes thrusting daggers at the UCAS contingent seated across from him. "We are merely conducting a matter of national sovereignty. It is one that has been long overdue. We will not be interfered with … as the UCAS has interfered with so many, for so long."

"We support Mandaria's position in this. We have observed the Western Powers use every word game, every twist of interpretation, to provide its fig leaves for doing whatever it wants to do," a woman from the Muscovy delegation chimed in, standing up in a show of solidarity with her Mandarian counterpart. "Protecting humanitarian aid swiftly becomes a license for ground invasion and occupation, and shielding civilians becomes a license to take a side in a nation's internal conflict. We have seen the ways of the Western Powers often enough. We will not be the fool, and we are in support of Mandaria's right to pursue a longstanding matter of sovereignty … without interference."

Jovan could feel the coiling ire and tensions within the room. The delegates were certainly forgoing the fine art of saying little to nothing, in the game otherwise known as diplomacy. Their candor was refreshing to witness, as Jovan was always annoyed with the dancing and obfuscation that took place between nations in the public eye.

Having the industrial titan Mandaria and the energy rich Muscovy appearing so united in common cause was not a surprise. The policies pursued by the UCAS and its allies had fomented nothing but suspicion and resentment in the east.

Further, those prevailing sentiments fueled quiet support from a host of smaller nations for stripping the veneer of invincibility from the UCAS. For those desiring to come out from the shadow of western nations, the embrace of Mandaria would be an easy step to take, and the Mandarian delegation had undoubtedly taken that mood into their calculations.

"Mandaria has known of our security agreements with Taiyoan, ever since it was established," interjected a narrow-faced woman from the UCAS delegation. Her flinty eyes were trained rigidly upon the Mandarian and Muscovy representatives. "You knew what our position was, when you decided to move on the island. You chose the path of war, and now you have the temerity to make such claims?"

"And is Taiyoan a nation in your eyes? Have you recognized Taiyoan at the World Summit?" the Mandarian delegate shot back acidly, his words snapping as he glared towards his UCAS counterpart.

"You should know very well why we have always had that diplomatic position, and it does nothing to take away the fact that you knew we had security agreements with Taiyoan," the UCAS delegate responded firmly. "But that matters little, as the moment you attacked our satellites, you declared war on the UCAS."

"You are not above the use of preemptive strikes when it serves your interests," growled the Mandarian delegate, with an edge of accusation.

"We are getting nowhere," Kaira interjected firmly, holding her hands up, palms facing towards the two irritated delegates. She had the air of a parent calling a halt to a spat between children. "We are here to reach a consensus."

"How can we possibly reach a consensus when we have lost thousands in the fighting already? The UCAS populace will never accept a cessation," the UCAS delegate replied, looking towards Kaira.

The caustic edge was gone from the delegate's voice, even if it was clear that she was not backing away from her position. It was as if she was trying to get Kaira to see the rationale of her position.

"The populace of the UCAS has seen martial law declared, in every province. The people have been watching energy and food prices soar, and now they fear a complete collapse," Kaira responded. "The war with Mandaria has caused tremendous upheaval in the UCAS economy, as the shipping of products, and supplies produced in Mandaria, have ceased. So many companies have discovered just how dependent they were on Mandaria for raw materials and manufacturing. I do not think that they will mind the end of hostilities between Mandaria and the UCAS, not when trade resumes between the two countries."

Jovan agreed with Kaira's position, but he could not stop from reflecting on the major worry bothering him about the entire conflict. Teetering on the edge of all the issues spoken of by Kaira were the vast financial holdings that Mandaria possessed, in regard to the UCAS' massive debt. That card had yet to be played, but as warfare broke out between the two nations, every veteran economist feared the damage Mandaria could do in that sector much more than missiles and bullets.

The rationale presented by Kaira was settling into the minds of the UCAS delegates. Their faces were still hardened, but he could not detect an air of resistance towards Kaira.

She turned her attention towards the Mandarian delegation. "The dispute regarding your territorial claim has been resolved, and nothing short of total, global war could be attempted to undue it. That is in nobody's interest. Not yours. Not Muscovy's. Not any one of the nations you have friendly relations with.

"The cessation of hostilities, and the resumption of limited trade, will do much to stabilize world markets. You will benefit from that, as much as anyone. Let us speak plainly tonight. The demands of food and energy required by your populace and industries can ill afford a sustained period of war."

As with the UCAS delegates, the Mandarian group showed no argumentative posture towards Kaira's words. Jovan kept his face solemn, but inwardly he was beaming with pride. She had asserted herself as a person of authority over two of the largest nations, militaries, and economies on the face of the world. What he was witnessing was truly incredible to behold, and he suspected that it was a moment that was unprecedented in the annals of the world.

"I know that both sides will need to hold some positions and sanctions to save face with their populaces, and this I understand," Kaira said. "But the conflict must be pulled back from where it is now, and put on a course that will see the resumption of trade, and the cessation of military hostilities."

"How can we possibly sell the resumption of trade to the people of the UCAS?" a man from the UCAS delegation asked Kaira.

"You underestimate their desire to feel solid ground beneath them again," Kaira replied. "It is why the majority will not only accept the forthcoming Living ID, they will welcome it."

The man nodded, appearing to be satisfied with the answer.

"A conciliatory tone will serve you well," came the deep, accented voice of Gendry Resinger, from where he was seated in a place approximately midway between the representatives of the warring nations. "Admit that there was an overreach in this matter."

252

"When so much blood has been drawn?" the female UCAS delegate queried.

"Make them understand that they have much more to lose. Not just economic reasons. Tell them that you are working to avoid a nuclear conflict," Gendry said.

Jovan saw the logic in the argument. There would undoubtedly be sore feelings everywhere towards Mandaria when thousands had died, and many thousands more had been wounded.

Yet everyone feared an exchange of nuclear missiles, as there were no illusions that Mandaria was incapable of delivering a massive strike to the UCAS. Having demonstrated their ability to take out a host of satellites, the Mandarians could send a nuclear volley racing over the ocean and into UCAS territory.

"I thank you Gendry, for your wisdom," Kaira said, acknowledging the older, patriarchal figure with a smile. "As Gendry said, make it clear to the people that so much hangs in the balance, and that it is in the best interest of the world to see this conflict brought to an end."

The room fell quiet, as Kaira swept her gaze across the faces of all the attendees, no matter what nation or organization they represented. The fires in the Mandarian and UCAS delegations had clearly been put out. The two contingents had subdued expressions on their faces as they digested her words.

Kaira stepped around from where the Peace Commission's designated place was, and made her way to the center of the circular chamber. It was a move that broke with all protocol, and conveyed a degree of boldness that came as a mild surprise to Jovan.

She strode right up to the Mandaria delegation, and leveled her gaze at the member that had been the most vocal during the deliberations. "We need to leave this meeting in consensus. The details will be followed up on by the Security Council and a meeting of the world body, but this conflict must be ended."

Turning, she made her way across towards the UCAS delegation. Not a word was spoken in the room, and all eyes tracked her every step. She cast her attention upon the woman who had protested the most.

"Do what you must to sell this to your populace. But this warring must cease. We must show the world that stability is of the highest priority. What happens to one large nation affects the rest, and too much damage has been suffered already by those that are not party to this conflict."

Turning around, her gaze took in the rest of the chamber, and her next words were for all ears.

"Global institutions will serve to resolve this conflict. The people of every nation will see the possibilities of a strong world body ... if it can bring the two greatest economies and militaries to the table for a peaceful resolution. Let this moment be a beacon to a greater unity."

Jovan smiled as he looked upon Kaira. In just one night, she had emerged to become a world leader of a sort. He knew that the media would soon be announcing the end of the Mandarian conflict with the UCAS.

As Kaira indicated, there would be discussions and minor details to be worked out, at the Security Council level as well as in the Main Assembly of the World Summit. Trade would have to be eased back in after so much blood-letting, but the process would be initiated.

The importance of the Peace Commission had undoubtedly taken a major step forward, fulfilling the vision that Kaira had for it as being able to bring a great war to an end. If it could broker an accord between the two strongest nations in the world, then it could be called upon to assist with the array of petty conflicts that were always taking place across the globe.

Privately, Jovan was relieved that the conflict would simmer down. It had threatened to go much farther beyond the boundaries discussed in the chamber on his estate, due to the maverick Mandarian general that had implemented the well-concealed plan to gore the UCAS satellite network.

Overall, the climate was not looking quite as disconcerting as before, in regards to the final steps of the Convergence. The vaccine was about to be released, Living ID was on the verge of being mandated, and the war was not going to slide into chaos. Further, the utility of global institutions was being given a large boost. What had just happened before Jovan's eyes could be used to win the minds of so many people towards a world order.

The smile spread a little wider on his face. Good moments had to be savored when they happened, and he basked in the current one as he continued to observe Kaira's ascension before the eyes of the world.

# SETH

Seth finished making the foot-long submarine sandwich, squirting some ranch dressing down its length and closing the top half of the bread. Wrapping it in paper, he slipped the sandwich into a plastic bag along with some napkins.

Handing it over to a middle-aged woman on the other side of the counter, he rang up her total on the cash register, and took the payment for it. He gave back her change with a smile, and politely wished her a good day. The woman thanked him amiably, and walked away.

It was a transaction that he had made countless times before, enough to appreciate just how much things had changed in such a relatively short amount of time. The price of everything had risen so much higher, an unwelcome cascade set in motion by gas prices and an economic malaise that had seen upward mobility grow increasingly out of reach. Inflation and dampened incomes had slowed business considerably, but there was little room to maneuver when the price of ingredients and everything else was non-negotiable. Seth only hoped he could hang on to his job, as meager as the pay ultimately was.

Nobody was waiting in line, and there were only a couple of tables occupied within the sandwich shop. He loosed a long breath, and looked towards the storefront where his last customer was just then exiting.

It was a gray, rainy day outside, and there was not much traffic on the street. Likely, the rest of the day would proceed uneventfully, with only scattered customers, making things easy enough to handle for the two individuals now on the clock: Seth, and his manager, Guillermo.

In some ways, it simply felt good to be doing something completely mundane, the process of which was largely the same as it had been prior to the terrible upheaval and martial law. Yet at its core, work was still work. Seth had successfully managed to keep his eyes away from the wall clock, as watching its face always made time slow to a ponderous crawl. He knew that it was the afternoon, but did not have an exact idea until an accented voice called out from behind him.

"You're about finished for the day, Seth. Soon as Marcie gets here, you can go."

Seth turned around, and saw Guillermo emerging from the back room. He had likely been cutting vegetables, and attending to other preparatory work to restock the depleted bins holding the various toppings for the sub sandwiches.

Shorter of stature, and paunchy of build, Guillermo was not an imposing figure, but he was a firm manager. He was also fair-minded, which was the element that Seth liked most about him. As long as Seth performed his given tasks, everything went very smoothly, and he was spoken to respectfully; something that he had not always experienced in the jobs he had done before.

An honest mistake was not met harshly, but unprofessional conduct was addressed swiftly, and staunchly. That was the way of things under Guillermo Lopez, and Seth knew what was expected of him, which was all he really ever wanted out of a boss.

"Thanks, Guillermo, I didn't think it was so close," Seth said, with a grin.

Guillermo smiled. "They say, time flies when you are having fun."

"Don't get me wrong, I like my job, but I wouldn't go that far," Seth replied, with a laugh. Fun was the last word that he would associate with a work shift.

A few minutes later, Marcie Jenkins strode through the front door, dressed for her upcoming shift that would extend to the store's closing time in the late evening. She was a college student, a couple of years older than Seth, but that did not stop him from aspiring to catch her interest. It never hurt to hope.

"Hey Marcie," Seth greeted, as she came behind the counter.

"How's the day been going Seth? Have we been busy?" she asked, her smile bringing forth the dimples that looked so cute on her cherubic face.

"Not too bad today. A little bit of a lunch rush, and that was about it," he replied, unable to hold her eyes for very long without starting to feel the edge of his nerves.

He was already feeling self-conscious, wondering if he had anything on his face, whether his hair was sticking out, and a plethora of other issues. It was the burden invoked by the presence of an attractive young woman, something that he had never been able to shake.

"Sounds like the same as it's been lately. Well, go have yourself a great Saturday night, unlike some of us!" she exclaimed, with a merry laugh. She started down the back of the counter. "Let me clock in here, so you can be freed up."

Seth walked after her. "I guess I should clock out then."

"Lucky … lucky you," she responded, laughing, as she swiped her time card.

"Hope you have a good night, Marcie. I'll see you tomorrow," Seth said. He caught a hint of the flowery scents from her brunette hair, as he edged around her to clock out for the day.

"Don't get in too much trouble," Marcie said as she started back, to take up the well-familiar position behind the counter.

"I'll try my best not to," Seth replied, with a grin. "Then again, trouble sounds fun."

"You think so now!" she chided, laughing again.

It felt great inside every time he made Marcie laugh. The small victories had to be held onto, since the big ones were so frustratingly elusive.

After wishing Guillermo a good evening, Seth made his way out of the back room, and walked down the midst of the shop's main seating area. A couple of very enticing young ladies, of approximately Seth's age, were sitting idly at one of the tables located near the front windows. Wearing tight-fitting shorts, which compelled his eyes to track the lengths of their shapely, immaculately smooth legs, the young ladies spurred the onset of a quickening heartbeat within Seth's chest. The feelings of self-consciousness rushed back as well, making him worry that he was about to trip over his own legs.

He wished he were the kind of guy who could feel comfortable walking up cold and introducing himself. But in his sandwich shop garb, he feared the ladies would only derive amusement from any attempt to meet them. He could not see how in the world they would possibly be inclined to take him seriously, and thought it best to just save face and keep going.

He looked away from them, but still went ahead and took the visor off, running his hand through his disheveled locks of hair as he opened the door, and walked outside. He could hear them breaking out together in laughter behind him, and, as always, a small part of him wondered if it was somehow at his expense.

Where the interior of the sandwich shop still held an air of familiarity, the surroundings outside did not. The streets and buildings were the same, but everything felt markedly different in the hold of the strange, new age. A tension clung to the air, and the streets were gripped in a hushed silence as a light drizzle fell.

STEPHEN ZIMMER

A couple of police squad cars were in a parking lot across the street, oriented with one vehicle facing in each direction, side by side, so that their drivers could easily converse. Seth glanced up at the light poles nearby, where a few newly-installed surveillance cameras were perched, their unblinking, tireless eyes gazing upon all who walked in the vicinity.

The cameras were like those that had been used extensively in the bigger cities, prior to the imposition of martial law. After taking control of Madison, the security forces had wasted little time in putting up a thorough network of cameras, all throughout the town.

A deepening scowl crept onto Seth's face, as he turned away and headed down the sidewalk, towards another parking lot set adjacent to the sandwich shop. As he had expected, nobody was waiting for him. It was yet another stark reminder of how much better things would be if he had his own car.

He strolled over to the brick side wall of the sandwich shop, leaned up against it, crossed his arms, and waited. Little came into his thoughts as the minutes passed, the lip of the roof sheltering him from the light rain. Only one individual parked in the lot, an elderly man that paid him little heed as he went about his business. Raymond's car finally turned into the parking lot, with a high-pitched squeak of the brakes.

"You better get those worked on," Seth remarked, getting into the passenger side.

"So says the guy not allowed to have a car," Raymond retorted, with a rumbling chuckle.

"You have a point," Seth conceded, settling in as Raymond worked to turn the car around. "And thanks for the ride. I sincerely appreciate it."

"Not a problem. It's a long walk," Raymond said, bobbing his head to the pulsing riffs of a heavy metal song playing on the radio. Alongside the thick guitar sound, the chugging bass guitar was accompanied by the potent thumps of the kick-drum.

"At least they haven't banned that yet," Seth commented, getting into the groove of the song himself.

"Oh, sooner or later they will. Anything that gives people a pulse," Raymond said, with a laconic chuckle. "They want us to be good zombies … drones … You know, we the sheeple of the UCAS! You know that Seth!"

"Unfortunately, I do," he agreed.

"Well, we're not counted in those groups yet, my friend," Raymond said, with a grin.

"So what's goin' on tonight?" Seth asked, shifting the subject. "Don't want to waste my Saturday night completely."

Raymond glanced over briefly. "Let's go see Jonathan, and find out. What do you say?"

Seth nodded. "I don't have any better suggestions."

"And neither do I," Raymond said, an undercurrent of regret sounding in his voice. "I wish it were like the old days, plotting with Nolan and Randall about where we were going to get beer, what parties were happening, and what girls we were going after. Man, I miss those days a lot."

"Things were simpler, I'll say that," Seth said. He gazed out the passenger side window, as the soft drizzle began to fall more quickly on the windshield. The little flecks of water accumulated steadily. "Not a night to be outdoors."

"Nothing much to do anyway, even if the weather was good," Raymond said.

"Well, if we aren't going to throw a party, and we're tired of the same video games, what do you think we should do?" asked Seth.

"Maybe we can talk about what to do with the video," Raymond said, clicking on a faster rate of speed for the windshield wipers.

Seth looked back over to Raymond. "Makes me nervous, Ray, thinking we're the only ones with it."

"Me too, because its proof they can't deny," Raymond said, his face looking somber. "I have a couple of friends whose parents were arrested, and they can't even see them, or even know where they've been taken. Bet they're right there in that camp, and the ones that put them in it want to keep a lid on the place."

"Let's blow the lid off, then," Seth replied without hesitation, with a spirited edge.

"Now you're talkin'," Raymond said, with a widening grin. "Bold is the only way to go."

Raymond pulled next to the curb in front of Jonathan's house a few minutes later. A white van cruised slowly down the street, passing them as Raymond clicked the engine off. Though unmarked, Seth had little doubt that it was a part of the large security presence choking the town.

After being greeted by Jonathan's mother at the front door, Seth and Raymond were allowed through, to go on up to Jonathan's bedroom.

They tromped up the steps and made their way to his door.

"Surprise!" Raymond announced boisterously, walking straight into the room.

"Figured you would be by," Jonathan said casually, where he was seated in the office-style chair next to his computer desk.

"Hey guys," Annika greeted. She was sitting cross-legged on Jonathan's bed, where she had been tapping away on the touch screen of a tablet computer.

"Playing that game with the birds and slingshots again?" Raymond asked her.

Annika raised her right eyebrow. "So you think that's all I do on this?"

"What else is there to do these days?" Raymond asked, with a grin.

Annika broke out into a laugh. "Okay, you got me this time. Yes, I was."

Raymond looked towards the others. "See, I'm always right, aren't I?"

"So how are you doing Seth? Good to be off work, I bet," Jonathan said, ignoring Raymond's boast.

"The one moment I look forward to ... when I'm clocking out," Seth said, with a chuckle, though he was not speaking untruthfully. In fact, the act of swiping his time card at the end of a shift felt so much better than anything else he experienced at the sandwich shop, save perhaps for talking with young ladies like Marcie.

"Well, that's done and over with, so we can turn our minds to other things," Jonathan said.

"Was thinking we could talk about the video footage," Raymond said. "I mentioned that to Seth on the way over here."

Jonathan shrugged. "Sounds as good of an idea as any. We need to figure out what to do with it anyway. Doesn't do anyone good just sitting idle."

"Yes, we do need to figure out what to do," Annika said, her face growing serious. "That footage is too much to keep contained. People need to know. No different than the wolf-things you caught on camera, and maybe even more important."

"We all know that, Annika," Raymond said. "Just where do we take it, though? And what are we risking? A whole lot's changed, you know."

"Oh, that's news to me," Annika said, with a mild tone of

sarcasm. "Of course we are taking a risk. I don't think they're wanting documentaries made of that camp site."

"So where do we even begin?" Seth asked.

"We don't have online access. That hasn't been reinstated yet. And even if it was, I bet there'll be some pretty major changes in what can be accessed or done. There isn't much left but the main television and radio stations," Jonathan said.

"We should take our chances with the local media then," Seth said, looking at the faces of the others. "It's just a local station. Come on, how crazy can that get?"

"They're being allowed to broadcast. With martial law in place. Think about it," Annika remarked, pointedly.

"Then the worst they'll do is not play it at all. But we should give them the choice, at least," Seth argued. "Because nobody has answers around here."

"No, it's too dangerous," Jonathan said firmly. "They don't play the copy, and then we get our copies confiscated. And maybe worse. 'Matters of national security' is a nice catch-all to let them do anything, you know."

"Then what? We just sit here, when we know what's happening with everyone that's been taken away?" Seth said, with an air of incredulity.

"Jonathan, I've got friends that have had parents, or uncles, or aunts, taken away, and they don't know a damn thing about what's happened to them," Raymond said. "However you look at things, that's not right at all."

"So what do you all suggest?" Jonathan said.

"So we don't have online access ... okay, that's closed to us. But I bet we can get a bunch of drives and discs pulled together," Annika interjected, with a slight grin and a spark in her eyes.

Seth, Raymond, and Jonathan looked towards her.

"We just take this straight to the people. Get every thumb drive and digital disc we can find, and then we just go door to door," Annika said. "A little old school, but it'll pull the cover off what they've done."

Seth saw the potential in her idea right away, and smiled.

"I like that," Raymond said, grinning, and shaking his index finger towards Annika. "I like that idea a hell of a lot, Annika."

"Puts lots of copies out there, in formats that can be copied themselves. It breaks the news, gets a lot of word of mouth going ... I really think that's the best option right now," Annika replied.

"Then we've got some work to do," Jonathan said. "We need to get a master file made, and then we should bring our systems together for making a big batch of copies."

"I'm not doing anything tonight, are you all?" Raymond asked, looking between the others.

"Can you run me by my house? I can pack my computer up quick," Seth said.

"And we can go by my house too, I'll scoop mine up," Raymond said.

"And while you two are busy doing that, I'll go and get mine," Annika said.

"Looks like we have a new project attend to," Jonathan said.

"I like to stay busy," Raymond said, with a wink towards Seth.

"And like I told my hot co-worker just a little while ago, trouble sounds fun," Seth replied, laughing.

# UCAS

Multitudes of military families all across the UCAS greeted the news of the cease-fire joyfully, and with great relief; though for so many there was a bittersweet edge to the announcement.

While deployments of any kind carried an element of danger, it had been several decades since the UCAS had suffered so many casualties in a single conflict. The tally of fallen in the fighting between Mandaria and the UCAS far exceeded anything the country had experienced in the simmering, lengthy conflicts involving UCAS deployments in the sands of the Central East.

The majority of the UCAS populace had been shocked when the first casualty reports had come in following the outbreak of hostilities between the two huge countries. The five or ten reported killed in a significant day of fighting in the Central East was dwarfed immediately, as over a thousand had fallen on the first day of the war with Mandaria alone.

Mandaria had the size and technology to resist the UCAS, and prosecute an extended war. Its possession of nuclear warheads held the UCAS back from using its own weapons of the type. In light of the economic and civil upheaval, the undertaking necessary to prosecute a successful war against Mandaria was incomprehensible. Even the most simple-minded could see that a full-scale war, followed to its ultimate end, would end up destroying the UCAS, whether or not a military victory was achieved.

While it was a terrible thing to swallow for a great many, there was little denying that the closure of the fighting was in the best interests of the UCAS. Of course, everything could not go back to the way things had been before; at least not right away. Sanctions were implemented on both sides, and much still remained to be worked out, to extract from the entanglements of the conflict, but the war had been brought to a halt.

Rumors swirled in the media that the World Summit's Peace Commission had been instrumental in bringing an end to the conflict. An announcement had been made that a young woman standing in for David Sorath had brokered the key understanding that had led to the unexpected peace accord. The two titans had stopped trading blows, and were backing away from each other; it was lost on no one that the world would be spared in the process.

While both Mandaria and the UCAS were stained with the blood of each other, the Peace Commission emerged with an unprecedented respect and affinity. It was seen as the bearer of a pure, radiant light; the light of world peace itself.

# IAN

Ian stared morosely at the beer bottle he had been drinking out of, while sitting quietly at the kitchen table. Lately, he had not felt motivated to do much of anything during his time off. Even that sphere of his life was growing increasingly more difficult, as the simple act of leaving his house brought him nothing but anger, and a sick feeling inside, as he went about his way within a hometown under a smothering occupation.

From camera eyes everywhere, to manned checkpoints and questioning that had the tinge of interrogation, it was like walking on thin ice at all times. Everyone that had not been detained during the impromptu demonstration following Chris Howard's arrest were at the whim of militarized police and TTDF elements; both of which were deployed in force within Godwinton.

Ian was realistic, and his sober acceptance of things kept his discipline honed, despite the regular, bitter affronts to his sensibilities. One cross word, or a failure to follow an instruction quickly enough, could result in an incarceration. It was a terrible way to live, and, as the days passed, the strain of enduring the new way of things was accumulating.

The only beacon of light was that there was some kind of resistance movement manifesting within the forested hills surrounding Godwinton. Word of mouth had spread rapidly about the presence of a rebellion fomenting in the rural countryside, even if the approved media channels shunned talking about resistance, casting all defiance to the federal onslaught in a bad light.

Ian could sense that the demoralized people of Godwinton were rooting in their hearts for the budding insurgency, and he could not help but feel a growing fondness for the latter himself. He hoped that they kicked the authorities right in the teeth.

In Ian's view, the ones that were taking a stand were the individuals that embodied the principles that the nation once stood for. They were not human cattle to be herded and fattened in a malaise of apathy and amusements. Rather, they tread the road of risk and responsibility, with all of its uncertainties and possibilities, the only path that gave a man or woman the wings allowing their souls to fly.

"Ian, come in here … quick!" Alena called out suddenly from the living room. He could hear the television, and knew without asking that she wanted him to see something taking place.

He looked up from the beer bottle, but was slow to get up from the chair. The news was a stream of almost constant negativity, whether it involved the terrible viral outbreak, foreign wars, or the latest financial tremors.

Only the recent announcement that the fighting with Mandaria had ended brought any trace of gladness to Ian's heart. That had promised to be a horrific war that nobody could win.

"Dad!" Allyson shouted, with a hit of urgency in her voice. "Hurry up! Get in here!"

Ian roused himself with a little more energy, and headed into the living room. Alena and Allyson were focused intently on the television screen, where a news anchor was announcing that a vaccine for the deadly Thanatos virus ravaging the world had been found.

"This is great news! I just can't believe it!" Allyson exclaimed, speaking rapidly. Her mood was buoyant, as she turned to look at her father. "And so quickly! There's so many diseases that they've been researching for years, and they still haven't found a cure. It really is a miracle that we've all been praying for!"

Allyson's words struck at the very core of Ian's first impressions. But in the pit of his stomach, something did not feel right.

Ian quietly watched the broadcast, standing at the side of his wife and daughter. A man named Dr. Hadar Tricheur was being credited with the brilliant, stunning discovery. It had evidently taken place within the facilities at the company Dr. Tricheur headed, Eternus Biotechnology Labs. The anchor proclaimed, with a gleaming smile, that science had come to the rescue of a terrified worldwide populace. The anchor's tone had a boastful edge that did not sit well with Ian.

Dr. Tricheur was being hailed as a savior. A well-recognized expert in viruses imbued with hemorrhaging effects, such as the deadly Ebola virus, Dr. Tricheur was said to have followed his instincts assiduously, pursuing them with a tireless focus following his first analysis of the lethal new virus. Yet even the news report could not fail to admit the extreme rarity of discovering a solution in such a brief amount of time.

Ian doubted that there would be much questioning. Everything would be swept up in the public euphoria that a vaccine had been found, drowning out any reservations.

According to the reports, full production of the vaccine was already well underway, and was being accelerated with the active, comprehensive involvement of the federal government. According to the anchor, every available resource was being committed in the effort to generate enough vaccine to bring a swift halt to the virus' spread. The mass distribution of the vaccine would be expedited, and the means of doing so were to be addressed very soon.

The report was followed by the announcement that a major initiative would be unveiled later that evening by the UCAS government. No less than the president himself would be making the revelation, in a direct address to the entire nation.

"And there's the punch line," Ian muttered sardonically, his face darkening with a scowl as he gazed at the screen.

"What?" Allyson asked, a puzzled look on her face.

"There's just something really weird about all this. And I sure wouldn't bet that the announcement they're talking about is going to be anything good for most of us," Ian replied. He shook his head, and let out a bitter-laced chuckle. "But I guarantee you, it'll be good for more than a few of the upper crust. You can count on that, like you can the sun rising in the morning."

"Just be glad there's a cure, at the least," Allyson replied, though her voice now carried a hint of doubt.

Ian glanced over at his daughter. She had so much of her mother reflected within her features: the same eyes, slope of her nose, and hair color.

She was a little taller than Alena, and perhaps longer-limbed, but there was no disputing the strong likeness to her mother. The similarity pleased him greatly, as Allyson, like Peyton, was the highest expression of the love Ian held for his wife. He knew that he would go to all ends to protect and support all three of them, no matter what the cost might be to himself.

"Allyson, I'm just glad you are here," he said more gently, a lighter smile breaking through his thunder-clouded face. "At least we're all together, right here at home, during all of this going on now."

"But you aren't happy about the cure?" Allyson pressed, still looking caught off guard by his subdued reaction.

"What's bothering you about it?" Alena asked.

"Well, it happened pretty damn fast, don't you two think?" Ian responded firmly. "And isn't it interesting that they're making a big announcement, on a new government initiative, right when they are declaring that a cure has been found? Timing is pretty curious, isn't it?"

"We'll just have to see what the initiative is," Alena replied. "No use getting stressed out about it yet, Ian. It may be nothing serious."

"Everything happening now is serious," Ian said ruefully. "And they sure as hell wouldn't be having the president make the statement otherwise."

"We'll just have to see," Alena replied in a low voice, though Ian could see weightier concerns forming in her expression. "No sense getting ourselves worked up about it, until we know just what it is."

He knew at a glance that she was merely trying to lighten the tension. The look in her eyes showed that she harbored deep suspicions herself. It was simply that she was less inclined to lay her own concerns bare in front of their daughter.

"Well, the two of you can tell me what this great, visionary initiative is all about, later. I'm sure it will be just wonderful for everyone," Ian said with thick sarcasm, turning away, and starting back towards the kitchen. His next words carried a sense of the inner weariness that he felt. "I've had enough of the media circus for now. I think I'll have another beer. At least I know that's something I'll enjoy a little."

Alena and Allyson said nothing in reply as they watched him walk slowly, with a brooding expression, from the living room.

# THE UCAS

The momentous declaration was made during a direct address given by President Walker to the people of the UCAS. It was carried on all major media channels, from television to radio. The tone of the president's speech was decidedly positive, the pronouncement of good news for each and every citizen of the UCAS.

Called Living ID, the newly-unveiled technological marvel was presented as a crucial step on the path back to national stability. From matters of personal identity to economic security, Living ID would be the means by which order would be brought out of the chaos pervading the country.

The President summoned the power of national pride, hailing Living ID as a device born of UCAS ingenuity. He explained how it had been developed by a team of innovative minds within Babylon Technologies, located in Troy, right in the heart of the country. He lauded the CEO, Dagian Underwood, as a living, modern example of the UCAS spirit, a woman who had led her company with resolve and vision.

An unnoticeable, nanoscale implant, the new technology would safeguard a person's identity, as well as consolidate a range of issues regarding health care, commerce, finances, and so much more, simplifying everything into one universal system. It was an instrument of tremendous efficiency and convenience, a comprehensive answer to a plethora of challenges that had begun appearing to be insurmountable. Living ID was a thunderbolt at a decisive hour, bringing renewed hope and promise when all had seemed lost.

Due to the unique, encompassing problems facing the UCAS, Living ID would be mandatory for all citizens. President Walker explained that the requirement was a matter of national security, and added that the implementation of Living ID would serve to provide an unprecedented degree of personal safety for everyone.

The implant would be obligatory in order for citizens to participate in commerce and the health care system, in addition to all other government-related activities. Without it, citizens would not be able to conduct financial transactions, vote in future elections, see a doctor, travel, pay taxes, or any number of activities that a person normally took for granted. It would replace the Citizen Identification Cards, which had been a big step beyond the older identification methods, but were still limited in scope, and could be counterfeited.

For the sake of convenience and efficiency, President Walker announced that Living ID would be administered right alongside the distribution of the new vaccine introduced earlier in the day. Some specifics had to be ironed out, but the new system would be rolled out immediately.

The use of cash would be brought to an end, with an adequate transition period that would see cash turned in to the government, and exchanged for digital dollars tied securely to an individual's Living ID implant. After the allotted period of time for the changeover, cash would no longer be acceptable currency.

As President Walker explained more than once during the address, Living ID was being implemented for the comprehensive safety and security of the UCAS citizens. The plague of identity theft would be brought to a halt, and finally eradicated. Everyday life would be made simpler, and much more efficient. Living ID was the road back to a brighter, successful future, both for the country as a whole, as well as the individual. Within moments of the conclusion of the president's address, pundits, celebrities, and political leaders, of all types and parties, were hailing the announcement with feverish enthusiasm; and championing the embrace of Living ID.

# FATHER BRUNNER

So many things were weighing down upon Father Brunner's mind that he forgot how fast he was traveling, and how quickly he stopped, until he saw the startled looks registered on the faces of the security guards outside the gates of Paladin's Light. Skidding to a halt, he took a deep breath, and admonished himself to retain his focus.

His mind had always been prone to distractions, and things were now flying at him from every possible angle. From the day to day needs of the congregation at St. Bosco, to the activities of the Order, a flurry of activity was underway. It was getting increasingly harder to remain attuned to the most mundane of activities, such as driving a vehicle.

"Father Brunner!" one of the guards called out. "I hope you weren't planning to run us down, and bust through the gates."

Though a smile was on the guard's face, the look in his eyes made it clear that the statement had not entirely been rendered in humor.

"No, not quite," Father Brunner replied, a regretful expression forming on his face. "I just let myself get a little distracted. I've always been a little bad about that, and these days it's gotten worse."

"Well, thanks for regrouping in time to avoid rolling over us," the guard replied with a light chuckle, though underneath the facetiousness, Father Brunner could detect a little annoyance with his far-too-quick approach.

"I'm really sorry," Father Brunner said, with an air of genuine contrition.

"Okay, we'll let you off easy this time, Father," the guard replied, nodding to his comrades, who proceeded to open the gates into the grounds of Paladin's Light.

Father Brunner drove inside slowly, and found a parking place inside of the entrance. A touch of chill was in the air, under the overcast skies, and he surmised that it would soon be raining.

Quickening his stride, Father Brunner set off to find Hank and Zhang. Neither could be found at their dwelling spaces. After asking around, he tracked the two down at the main community building.

The large structure serving as the hub for the community had managed to continue with the regular serving of meals and provision of showers. Bolstered with the influx of new arrivals to the compound, it was more crowded than ever, and it took Father Brunner a little time to

269

work his way through the crowded interior. He smiled and returned a few greetings from individuals that knew him, or recognized his priest's collar, but most of the faces that he saw were leaden. He took the latter expressions in stride, knowing that extreme hardship was not a good facilitator of politeness.

He paused for a moment, as a young girl of no more than six or seven years of age walked in front of him, cradling a small bowl of soup as if it were the most precious possession in all the world. She looked up and gave Father Brunner a beaming smile, and giggled as he grinned back at her. It was yet another testimony of how young children could carry light within the depths of shadows, though he wished that he could bring the hardship surrounding the little girl to an end.

Zhang was found seated at one of the long bench tables eating from his own bowl of soup, while Father Brunner discovered Hank toweling off in a small room designated as a dressing area for those that had finished with their showers. Not comfortable discussing the matters at hand amid such a congested crowd, Father Brunner guided the two men outside of the building.

As they strolled down one of the lanes lined by the makeshift abodes of the residents, Father Brunner initiated the discussion.

"We are going to have to speed up our plans," he said bluntly, glancing between the two others. "And add a few more things to the list."

Both of the other men turned their heads immediately at his words, looking to Father Brunner with expressions of incredulity. He was not surprised by their reactions, as getting the populace of Paladin's Light moved away to safer harbors was not a light undertaking. Hastening the schedule, and adding even more to the list of tasks facing them, was not something they were likely inclined to enjoy hearing.

"Oh, just great ... and we're not even sure we can pull the rest off yet," Hank grumbled.

"More? And bumping up the schedule?" Zhang asked, disbelief written all across his face. "How many people do you think we have involved here? Let's just say we're short-staffed already, as it is."

"Living ID has been announced, and trust me, it's not something you want forced on anyone living in here," Father Brunner responded, thinking upon the conversations that he had engaged in with Juan Delgado. The concept of Living ID always brought a chill to his soul, as he understood its extensive utility in the hands of those serving a

270

relentless Enemy.

"Everyone around here's been talking about it. I don't doubt you that it's real bad news. I suspected as much," Hank replied, somberly. "Nothing coming from the feds can be any good these days. Pretty damn convenient they have martial law in place too, don't you think?"

"It's all part of it," Father Brunner said. "Out of the chaos they've crafted carefully over a long, long time, a new order rises."

"Hardly new, I'd be willing to bet," Zhang replied, with a stony countenance. "Same Enemy that people have always had. Just one more visage out of a thousand faces."

"Again, correct," Father Brunner said. "And this is why we have two things to do."

"Get the people the hell out of here, before they're forced to take those damnable implants," Hank said. "I know that's one."

Father Brunner nodded. "Without question."

"So, what's the other?" Zhang asked. "Does this involve the new additions to the list?"

Father Brunner nodded. "Warn everyone else about Living ID."

"And how in the world are we gonna do that, exactly?" Hank queried, looking at the priest as if he was slipping his bearings.

"A short time ago, we provided a refuge at St. Bosco for one of the top people at Babylon Technologies," Father Brunner answered. "The Order and the Shield Maidens worked together to get him out of here. Call him a defector, but what he learned about Living ID really shook him up.

"Well, we need to bring him back inside Troy. And we are intending to commandeer one of the broadcast facilities here, so he can share what he knows. We've found that one of the stations here still has functioning satellite access. It has viable, working uplinks, for whatever is transmitted from the facility. You both know how valuable that is, these days. And it may not last forever, as the debris from all the damage caused by the Mandarians takes a toll every day on the satellites still up there."

Both of the others nodded, the two men looking at him intently as they digested his words.

Father Brunner continued. "The broadcasts from it can be spread a little more extensively ... with a little help from others in the Order, the Shield Maidens, and the like, positioned all across the country, in places that can receive the feeds."

"Sounds pretty complicated," Hank stated flatly.

"It is, to an extent, but we'll get word to the right people, if we can just get Juan down to the station in Troy," Father Brunner said.

"So, you want to break one guy into the city, while we break hundreds out of here," Zhang summarized, speaking more slowly.

Father Brunner nodded again. "Exactly, and I know it would be best if we do the two things at once. One operation. Two big objectives."

"We're not going to get many chances, Father," Hank said dourly, and Father Brunner could tell that the man was not pleased at all with the news. "This really complicates things a whole lot."

"We are going to have to rally everyone that we can," Father Brunner said. "Just need to open a channel for Juan and those with him to get inside."

"And that's going to make a big difference? Broadcast from Troy? And a few other stations?" Hank asked. "You know they'll close it off as quick as they can."

"Won't even last one news cycle," Zhang added.

"We just need to get him into this particular network affiliate, and we will have several in place across the country who will take the signal from Troy," Father Brunner said. "It is the best chance we have to get a mass warning out there."

"I can't argue with that. Options are limited nowadays," Hank said. "But one station's really gonna do it? Even if you hit the other affiliates, you think a lot of people are gonna see it?"

"No longer have the big mess of satellite stations that you had before. It's a little more like the old days," Zhang chuckled. "Just a few networks to choose from. And by default, each one has a huge audience now."

"And that's where our big advantage lies," Father Brunner piped in.

"Which is why the channel needs to be made, so your guy can reach the station," Hank stated.

"That's exactly it," Father Brunner said.

Hank looked pensive, but after a moment he nodded back to Father Brunner. A determined look was anchored within his eyes. "We'll make it happen."

"It is going to be a little tricky, but we can make it work," Zhang agreed.

"I just thought it would be best to consolidate everything, because

272

we'll have our largest numbers, from all the groups involved," Father Brunner said.

"Better hope we have enough manpower," Hank declared. He then added, after a moment, with a slight grin, "And woman power too ... can't forget the Shield Maidens."

"No, we can't," Father Brunner concurred, with a laugh.

"Those are some tough gals," Hank commented, smirking.

"Are the locations designated as refuges ready to receive the people of Paladin's Light?" Zhang queried, bringing the focus back to the topic at hand. "I hope this isn't being rushed too much. I want to at least have a chance to accomplish our primary goal."

"No, those places are ready, today, if need be. Don't worry about that for a single minute," Father Brunner said emphatically. "I assure you, not a thing is going to be compromised, in terms of the refuge sites for the people here."

"I know that this thing with the guy from Babylon Technologies is important, and don't get me wrong, but the people living here in Paladin's Light are my biggest concern," Zhang said.

"And mine too," Hank said. "We can't save the world, but we sure as hell can help spare a few from the nightmare that's coming."

"Well, just keep in mind that getting them out of here faster will save them from Living ID. Living under government protection and authority, these people won't be given a choice when they begin implanting Living ID," Father Brunner said. "And if they receive the implants, believe me, it will be too late. They'll be able to track every single man, woman, or child down, wherever they are taken to."

"And the sick thing about it is the president and all the political scum will still be prattling on about our freedoms, all the while this is happenin'," Hank growled.

"Sad to say, but you're probably right," Father Brunner replied. "Their rhetoric has rarely matched the reality."

"Well, then Hank and I need to get busy. We need to coordinate the members of the Order involved with the breakout, and meet with our liaison with the Shield Maidens," Zhang said. "We'll have to alter a few things to help with clearing a channel to get someone into the city, but we'll find a way."

"Coordinate with everyone as soon as you can, and be careful," Father Brunner urged him.

"We're always careful, with everything we do," Zhang answered.

"And what about the people from your church? If things are speeding up, are the ones that will be coming with us gonna get here in time?" Hank asked.

"Let me handle that. Those that choose to go will be here," Father Brunner said.

"And you are staying?" Zhang asked, bringing to light the one lingering aspect of it all that clearly bothered both Hank and Zhang.

"If even one member of the congregation stays in Troy, I will be staying with them," Father Brunner said. "That congregation is the family I was given, and I will not abandon even one of them. I'm aware I seem like a complete fool, but Father Rader and I would betray everything we profess if we bailed out on the people that were given to us."

"Let's hope they all decide to go, then," Zhang replied.

"I will look into getting you some more help. I've gotten some word that there is a recent inflow of some very capable individuals, who are being quartered at a few places owned by Knights of the Order," Father Brunner informed them. "I've been told they could be very useful in an operation like the one we're about to do."

Hank's eyebrows rose. "Reinforcements? Now that was something I didn't expect."

"It's only from bits and pieces of what I've heard. I'm looking into it. But they're said to be in the place where Juan is," Father Brunner replied.

"It would help to have a few more boots on the ground, as they say," Zhang remarked.

Father Brunner could hear the eagerness in Zhang's voice, reflecting the strains they were facing in terms of the numbers that could be called into such an extensive operation. He hoped that the reports given to him were accurate, regarding a considerable number of able-bodied individuals residing on property owned by individuals in the Order.

Everything had to be hurled at the impending operation, both for freeing the people of Paladin's Light, as well as inserting Juan Delgado into the television station. Time was perilously short, as the net of Living ID was already descending.

He hoped that the entirety of the congregation at St. Bosco chose to go to Paladin's Light, and join with the impending exodus. Left unsaid to Zhang and Hank was the fact that if he were to remain at St. Bosco, one of his tasks would be to counsel the remaining congregation to refuse Living ID, as he would be doing himself.

Understanding what it was, there was no way that he could ever allow it to be implanted on his own body. Yet at the same time, he knew that he would be calling others to a path of hardship, and transgression of the law itself.

He had little doubt that were he to remain in Troy, his path would lead to imprisonment, as it would for any others that heeded his warning about Living ID. It was a terrible burden to take upon himself, but he knew that as a priest of the Universal Church, it was the only thing that he could do.

# SETH

Heading out in broad daylight, Seth, Annika, Raymond, and Jonathan carried several boxes filled with mini-drives, thumb-sized drives, and DVDs. They loaded them into Raymond's and Jonathan's cars, and drove out a few blocks, before parking the vehicles on the street.

Sticking to pairs, with Annika and Jonathan forming up one team, and Seth and Raymond as the other, they walked the lengths of the neighborhood streets. Knocking on every door, and approaching anyone they came across, they disseminated the video footage to every person they could reach.

It was a tedious process, certainly much more difficult than uploading a video file that could go viral to millions within hours. As his legs grew rubbery later in the afternoon, Seth wished it were as streamlined as the click of a button. Yet the current endeavor was one that Seth felt was entirely necessary, given that it was very likely few people realized what was taking place just outside of the town's boundaries.

There was not a shred of doubt within him about the situation. The detention camp that Seth and his friends had witnessed was anathema to every sense of justice that he possessed. It was a vile thing, one that had no place in a free land.

With the rhetoric about the UCAS being so far askew of the reality, it was hard to imagine that even the most close-minded of individuals could deny the state of things any longer. The video footage would undoubtedly meet with a receptive audience, and the only way to get it out there was by the old-fashioned method of pounding the pavement.

Seth knew that time was of the essence. The Living ID announcement that everyone was talking about had come very unexpectedly. He knew in his heart that something was very wrong with the new mandates and technology, slated to affect every single person no matter what their status or age. While missing the initial announcement, Seth had learned everything he could about it since.

The topic had dominated conversations at his home. His father and mother, like most individuals Seth had spoken with, were resigned to accepting the implant, since it was a non-negotiable decree from the federal government. For him, the matter was not so cut and dry.

He did not want a life that required anything to be implanted within his flesh. A person's body was the last bastion of self-determination, and to have that violated by government edict was a boundary that Seth refused to cross. The fact that the same group making the implants mandatory was the very same one holding authority over the detainment camps was not lost on Seth either.

A malignant end to the implementation of Living ID was clear to Seth's eyes, even if his parents, and friends of theirs, dismissed the worries he voiced to them as the stuff of conspiracy theories. While not feeling entirely easy about Living ID, they embraced the things being used to sell it to the public. To their eyes, Living ID would protect them.

In Seth's unblinking gaze, Living ID was both a collar and chain. The entire nation was on the verge of becoming an enormous prison camp, some incarcerated behind high, barbed-wire fences, and the rest shackled with the miniscule devices. There would be nowhere for anyone to escape to.

For Seth and the others, the preparations for their distribution effort had taken hours, making use of all of their personal computers and laptops. He went through eight cans of Mountain Mist just to get through the night, as the duplication process, creating one drive or disc at a time, became a monotonous affair very quickly. He would much rather have been engaged in a lengthy gaming session, but he understood the dire importance of what he was doing.

When morning had arrived, he felt a little dizzy, and was quite sapped of energy, but a prodigious pile of discs and mini-drives had been readied for the day's mission. As large as the volume had initially seemed to Seth, he and his friends managed to distribute every single copy before the end of the afternoon.

The final stop of their day-long foray was a television station in the midst of town, an affiliate of the UCAS Broadcast Company's network. With the footage already distributed directly to so many people, Seth felt a little better inside, as they walked up towards the front doors of the broadcast facility.

His group had circumvented the station, in terms of allowing the place to assume any gatekeeper role in regards to the town. The hope riding on the visit to the station was a larger one, one that Seth's group could not address without help.

Seth stared at the flock of large satellite dishes set just to the side of the station's main building. They looked like so many flowers oriented towards the sun, with their metallic round faces all pointed in the same direction.

He wondered how many of them were still being used, or even operable, after the great damage suffered during the fighting with the Mandarians. He surmised that most of the dishes were now little more than fancy decorations.

The station was probably getting much more use out of the giant tower, which soared upwards just beyond the fenced-in area. Numerous devices, in an assortment of shapes, were attached along the considerable length of its metal trussing. They likely served a wide array of functions and purposes, and, unlike most of the satellite dishes, they could carry out their given tasks.

Also visible was a stout-looking metal-support of modest height, which propped up an oddly-shaped, white object at the apex. Seth guessed that it was the main element in the station's weather radar system.

Passing under the sheltered entryway, Raymond held the main door of the facility open for the others to go in. Seth nodded to him as he walked by.

"Here we go," Seth remarked, with a deep breath and a smile.

"Here's hoping," Raymond responded.

Inside, a young, attractive woman wearing a thin headset greeted them amiably, from where she was seated behind a low counter spanning the left side of the room. "Hello ... how can I help you?"

"Hi! We're here because we have what we think is some very newsworthy video we recorded recently. We'd like to turn it in to your station, but we'd like to talk to someone about what it is too," Jonathan replied to her politely, smiling warmly as he stepped up to the counter. He held up the small, padded package he was carrying for her to see, which contained both a thumb-size drive and a disc.

"Give me just a minute, and I'll have someone come up to talk with all of you. You can have a seat over there," the woman replied, indicating the cluster of well-padded chairs occupying the more open space to the right side of the room.

The area was arranged as a mini-lounge. A large, flat-screen monitor was affixed to the wall, facing the chairs, tuned into the station's current broadcast.

Seth and the others settled into the chairs and waited, casting a few nervous glances between each other. His eyes went to the screen a few times, but with his mind occupied with the task at hand he registered little taking place on the airing program. The hard clack of footsteps on the tile flooring sounded a few minutes later, approaching the chairs.

Looking away from the monitor, Seth beheld a tall, comely woman in a gray pant suit, with dark, short-cropped hair, and an impeccable, opal smile. He recognized her face immediately, having seen it many times before on television, billboards, and in other media.

"Hi, I'm Nancy Wiley, reporter with Eyewitness News. I am told that you have some video for us, in regards to a news submission," she said, in her smooth, velvety tone, which was well-suited for live television.

Seth and the others nodded, as Jonathan spoke up. "Yes, we do … and it's something that you're going to want to see, and get out there, right away."

"What format did you bring the video on?" she asked, her eyes lowering to the package cradled in Jonathan's lap.

"We've brought it here on disc, and on a thumb drive," Jonathan replied.

"That won't be a problem at all then. Both will work. Come with me, and we'll take a look at it right now," she replied with a polite smile.

She beckoned for the group to follow her, leading them out of the waiting room, and down a narrow hallway. After proceeding midway, they turned into another hall to the right.

They continued up to where Nancy guided them into a conference room that held seating for about a dozen, in high-backed black office chairs situated around an oblong table. A flat-screen monitor was mounted on the wall at one end, and a projection screen was rolled up in a bracket set just above it.

The side of the conference room running along the hallway was largely floor-to-ceiling glass, with raised blinds that exposed the interior for all passing eyes to see. A few curious looks were cast towards the visitors from station personnel going about their tasks.

"Well, let's take a look at what you've got to show," she invited, glancing towards the package in Jonathan's hands. "A DVD will be just fine for our purposes here."

Jonathan reached into the open end, and took out a small, square case of clear plastic. Opening it, he carefully took hold of the video disc resting inside by the outer edges, popped it out, and handed it over to her.

After picking up a small remote lying on the table surface at the end near the screen, she put the disc into the holding tray of a drive located underneath the flat screen monitor. Everyone waited for a few moments as the disc loaded up. When the menu screen finally displayed on the monitor, Nancy wasted no time, and clicked the play button on her remote.

She watched the raw footage intently. Though she exhibited a somber expression all throughout, Seth could tell that she had a very profound interest in the troubling images playing out across the screen.

"So how did you come across this?" she asked, several minutes into the video, keeping her eyes affixed towards the screen. There was a noticeably different tone to her voice than before. It was no longer the congenial timbre of a station representative, but rather a heavily concerned individual.

"Just had a hunch, and we acted on it, and got it on video," Seth replied.

"How did you avoid getting in trouble? I'm sure they didn't just let you start taking video of this place," Nancy said, casting them a sideways glance. "This is a federal facility, right outside of town. The security there looks heavy."

"We kept at a good distance," Jonathan said. "Believe me, we didn't want to go any closer than we had to."

"I thought so, with the shaking of the camera it looks like it has been zoomed in pretty tightly," Nancy remarked, continuing to absorb the footage.

"And you see why we wanted to turn this in to you," Annika said. "There's been so many people arrested, and nobody knows where they've been taken. I'd bet it was right there, to that camp. All this time, they've probably been detained right outside of town."

"That place can hold thousands," Raymond added bluntly.

"Looks like it," Nancy said grimly.

Seth did not miss the anxiety that had risen in her voice. Though she still conveyed a professional, composed air, there was no doubt that she was becoming increasingly disturbed by what she was seeing.

Though he had watched it more than once since recording the video, Seth was still aghast at the sequence involving the older man, and his son. There was nothing to dispute. The video footage was damning.

The look rooted in Nancy's eyes was markedly different when she clicked the disc off with the remote, and turned to face the quartet that had brought it to her. Even then, she presented a composed demeanor overall, but there was no doubt in Seth's mind that the footage had rattled her greatly inside.

"Thank you for bringing this to me," she said. "You are right. It is newsworthy, definitely. No question about it. And you risked more than you might think in getting it."

The others nodded their agreement. She pursed her lips, and stared down at the conference table for a few seconds. The tension heightened in the lengthening silence.

"You know things are very different nowadays," she said in an even tone, looking back up. There was no mistaking the concern that she held towards the teenagers. "It's all changed from how it was before. Everything is so much different. You have to be careful."

"Believe me, we know," Jonathan said, as the others nodded their agreement.

"Our broadcast depends on the whim of the ones put in charge of this area," Nancy stated. "They are, as much as I hate to say it, both judge and jury."

"But that video still needs to get out. I have a friend who doesn't know what's happened to his own father," Raymond said irritably. "It can't be kept quiet. People at least need to know where everyone's being held."

"I sympathize with that, and I really think that this does need to get out there. I will see what I can do, I promise you," she stated with conviction, looking to Raymond.

Seth knew it was the best answer they were going to get, and her response to the video carried a strong ring of sincerity within it. Even so, he did not feel any sense of relief when Nancy ushered them from the conference room, and back out to the front of the building.

He wished that he could somehow get to Troy, and get the footage in the hands of Zeev Steiner, the host of Sea to Shining Sea. Even with the online networks shut down for the moment, he did not doubt that Zeev would talk extensively about the footage on the air, and describe everything depicted in it, regardless of the hovering threats from those in authority.

It was clear that Nancy did not have the ability to put the footage on the air of her own accord. She answered to her own bosses at the station, who were undoubtedly afraid of the individuals holding jurisdiction over the town, under the authority of martial law.

It was a very long shot that the footage would be aired in any capacity, but it had been worth a try. At the very least, Seth knew that he and his friends had done everything they could to get the information out to the public.

Yet despite the thorough distribution of the video in the neighborhoods, Seth could not shake the melancholy feeling that gripped him as they drove back home. The world had simply changed so much, in such a short amount of time.

Things had strayed far beyond the days when his biggest concerns were fretting over not having a girlfriend, and worrying about whether he would go to college. An impenetrable murk lay over the future, and a growling thunder rumbled within it.

# FUSION CENTER 4-12

Deep within the belly of the fusion center, inside one of its many operations rooms, a surveillance officer was riveted to the live images onscreen. Speculations forming already in his mind, he watched the car pulling down the street with the four teenagers that had just delivered a small package to the UBC news station.

Patrol cars had earlier noted the youths going door to door, throughout more than one neighborhood. Going house to house was an activity that had become an anomaly in the aftermath of martial law. Only religious proselytizers were venturing out with the regularity of before, and the four teens were clearly not engaged in such an activity.

With the new camera system set in place, it was easy enough to follow their path. Several of the cameras had directional microphones that could be tapped for audio surveillance, and the officer gleaned enough from what he heard to ascertain that the teenagers were handing out some kind of media.

He had heard references to remaining numbers of both drives and discs, and wondered what it was all about. They were not selling anything. Rather, the four youths were giving away the media to the houses that they visited. They wanted something to be spread, though the specific nature of it was a mystery to the officer.

Whether on purpose or not, the teenagers refrained from discussing the specific content on the media they were carrying. There was a noticeable tension observable in their expressions, and they looked around often, as if they were on edge about being watched or followed. Every instinct in the officer told him that the discs and drives being distributed were not related to a hobby or school project.

When their path led them to the news station, the interest of the surveillance officer was piqued considerably. He had already made notes to detail each and every location in the neighborhoods the teenagers had visited, as well as send someone to the station to discover what had transpired there during the visit by the youths.

He knew that whatever the four were up to, it was not a trivial matter. Routing to the available agents on the ground, he requested that focused surveillance be placed on all of the youths involved with the station visit, and apparent canvassing of the neighborhoods. Answers needed to be obtained, as swiftly as possible.

If any threats to government authority were being fomented, they would have to be shut down quickly. The officer could pull the trigger on an extensive operation, as assets were in place for activation on the spur of a moment.

A decision would have to be made, and it all hinged on the nature of the media that the youths had been giving out.

# IAN

Night had fallen, but Ian could not sleep. He had tossed and turned repeatedly, unable to settle. Finally, he had conceded to the restlessness, so as not to disturb Alena where she lay in peaceful slumber next to him. Now sitting in the ponderous silence of his living room, he brooded over everything happening around him.

Under other circumstances, a couple days off from work would have been extremely welcome. As things stood, he found himself becoming increasingly agitated. He was doing everything he could not to be irritable around his family, but it was admittedly getting harder all the time.

He felt awful about every instance where he was less than amiable to his loved ones. His responses to them were increasingly curt, and he found the fuse of his temper growing shorter as his patience declined. He kept to himself as much as possible, as while he was not physically abusive, he knew that it took little to engage in verbal mistreatment.

In just a few more days, the first batch of the vaccine would arrive in Godwinton, along with the treacherous Living ID. Ian knew what was coming, and could not shake the creeping dread he felt regarding the recently mandated identification system.

From the television reports, it would seem that the majority of people all across the country were jubilant, not only about the vaccine, but also about the comprehensive identification system. Time and time again, Ian had watched all kinds of people being interviewed, lauding the merits of the Living ID System. He had never held a greater feeling of disgust for his fellow human beings than he did watching the parade of men and women talking excitedly about receiving an implant that would corral every aspect of their life, and tether it to government authority.

There were many instances where snide, patronizing comments were made about those who objected to the new measures; assigning fear of change, and even technology itself, as the main reasons for reticence. Substantive discussions were nipped in the bud, as the hosts of the various shows were careful to project the idea that there was no rational argument for objecting to the new system, given the emergencies, threats, and instabilities facing the country.

Even the most reasonable concerns were rapidly consigned to the territory of wild-eyed conspiracy theorists, as the media marched lockstep with the government mouthpieces to promote the virtues of Living ID. For all intents and purposes, it was being hailed as a miraculous technology, promising a comprehensive solution to seemingly insurmountable problems.

Also conveniently, in Ian's eyes, the markets, after taking a terrible beating during recent weeks, had shown a sharp upturn in the wake of the Living ID announcement. From stocks, to energy sectors, and even with the national currency itself, the financial reports were all glowing and hopeful.

"Idiots," he growled to himself, addressing the screen as he watched yet another person on the street babbling on with praise about the supposed merits of Living ID. "You'll sell your souls for the promise of safety, won't you? Freedom scares you too much, doesn't it? Even with your big fancy degrees, you all can't figure this thing out, can ya? Jackasses!"

His blood beginning to simmer, he picked the remote up from the end table and clicked the television off, unable to bear watching the naked display of stupidity any longer. If he continued, he knew he would do nothing more than risk working himself up into an immensely distraught state where he would likely suffer a heart attack.

He knew where he stood, without question, and what loomed before him. Another time of decision was approaching fast, but Ian already knew that he could not accept any implant on his body.

None of his family wanted it either, but to refuse Living ID would ultimately be the same thing as renouncing citizenship. There were not going to be any waivers issued, like there had been for various other government initiatives in the past.

Rich and poor alike were going to be required to accept Living ID, perhaps the first time in Ian's entire life that economic status would make no distinctions in how people were treated. The wealthiest billionaire and the most destitute street beggar would both be tied into the new system.

The situation facing Ian was no different than having a gun put to the head, he mused darkly, as he continued to glower in the shadows of the living room. A country that purported to uphold the ideas of freedom was engaged in the most insidious coercion, on a mass scale.

A soft rapping on his front door snapped Ian out of his reflections. His brow furrowing, and blood rushing, as defensive instincts sprung to the fore, Ian got up and slowly approached the door. In his socks, his step was soft as he moved noiselessly across the carpet.

Keeping as quiet as he possibly could, he picked up the shotgun leaning against the wall, just inside the front door, where he had recently begun keeping it. It had eight rounds loaded, and the feel of the weapon in his hands was instantly reassuring.

He edged towards the door with the barrel leveled straight ahead. His index finger alighted on the surface of the trigger, ready to squeeze in an instant.

"Who is it?" he asked brusquely, through the closed door, wondering who in the world would come to his house during the middle of the night. Hospitality was an afterthought, and protection of his household was first and foremost in his mind. He was poised to act in a flash, should there be any hint of threat. With the world spinning awry, Ian was not going to take any chances at all when it came to his loved ones.

"It's me, Sam Thornton," came the reply from the other side of the door, in a deep, familiar voice that was unmistakable. The tone of it was firm, but entirely devoid of tension, containing no urgency or sense of alarm.

The response came as a complete surprise to Ian. Sam Thornton was the proprietor of the burger stand in town where he and Chris Howard had gotten lunch together so often. The last time had occurred when the media had been swarming all over Godwinton, just prior to the momentous day at the Revere household where brazen tyranny had been soundly rejected by the will of the people.

"Anyone with you?" Ian queried sharply, not ready to open the door just yet. He raised the barrel of the shotgun upward, but did not set the weapon down.

"Just Ollie Pryor," Sam replied, calmly. "That's all there is out here. Just me and Ollie, Ian. Nobody else at all, I promise you, on my word."

Ian leaned the shotgun back against the wall, in the corner behind the door. He unlocked the deadbolt, and pulled the door open. Beyond the screen door, Sam and Ollie stood on the front porch, somber expressions displayed on both of their faces.

Looking past them, he saw that they were indeed alone. He had never deemed Sam to be a liar, but the unprecedented was increasingly becoming the norm. Like a wise saying he had once heard counseled, trusting someone did not omit the need for verification.

"An odd time to be visiting," Ian commented evenly, wanting to know what the two men were about. He knew it was no casual social call.

"Odd times we're in, Ian," Sam stated flatly. "You don't need me to tell you that. You gonna come out and talk with us, or can we come in and talk with you? It's pretty important, why we're here, and I think you'll want to hear about it."

Ian did not smile, or say a word in immediate response, but he pushed the screen door open, pulled the front door shut behind him, and stepped out onto the porch. He looked to the two men, eyeing them with both caution and curiosity.

"Everyone else's asleep inside, and I don't want to wake them. We can talk here just fine."

Sam nodded. "Don't blame you, Ian. And it's nice to know that some folks can get rest these days."

"Tell me about it. I've forgotten what rest is like," Ian said. "So, what brings you two fellas out here, in the middle of the night? I know it isn't to have a beer with me."

"No, it isn't, as much as I wish it were," Sam replied grimly. "You probably know all about Living ID. I know you know half the town was rounded up when they protested the arrest of Sheriff Howard."

"Well aware of all that," Ian responded bluntly. "More than pissed me off, but I managed to keep out of the roundup. And don't get me started on the Living ID."

"Probably don't think you've got many options, now that they're forcing the vaccine and implant on everyone. They're gonna chain everyone into their shiny, new, fancy system," Sam stated, his last few words thickening with sarcasm. An iron glint sparked in his eyes.

"Funny you bring that up. It was what I was thinking about, right before you two showed up," Ian replied. "I sure as hell don't want that implant on me, but I also don't want my family homeless and poor. Kind of a big problem, don't you think?"

"Well, hear us out, then. There's another option, and I don't think you'd be too opposed to it," Sam said.

The words piqued Ian's interest immediately, and he looked between the two men. There was nothing particularly unusual about them. Sam had run the burger stand, while Ollie was an insurance broker. They had never been associated with anything remotely controversial. They were just two men with rather straightforward lives, like Ian, making a living and raising families in a small town in the heart of the UCAS.

"And I bet what you've got to tell me doesn't have anything to do with burgers or insurance policies," Ian replied.

"I sure wish it did, as that would mean everything was back to normal again," Ollie interjected.

"No, we're here because there's resistance to all of this, and it's growing," Sam declared, with a sudden edge to his voice.

"You mean the resistance around here?" Ian said.

The news had been filled with reports of increasing violence wracking the major cities of the country, and there were sporadic reports of rural militias sprouting up and becoming active. The resistance around Godwinton, spoken of in hushed tones by the townspeople who remained after the mass arrests, had not asserted itself much further beyond the stories of a convoy ambush that had recently taken place just outside of the town, in which a great bit of material had been looted.

"Do you really think they'd talk about resistance movements on the rise, now that they've got a full clamp down on the media, and the internet?" Ollie asked him. "Or tell you what is really happening out there?"

"No," Ian replied, having no illusions anymore about the media.

"We've got a very capable leader spearheading this. An ex-marine, real tough fellow, who's a pretty damn good shot with a rifle. Turns out he was the one who downed that 'copter at the Revere house," Sam informed Ian.

Ian was at once intrigued, as the story of the downed Skyhawk helicopter had become something of a legend in the aftermath of the clash. He had often wondered who the unseen benefactor was, and it came as no surprise that such an individual would be involved in the genesis of resistance.

"You're the kind of guy we really need with us, Ian," Ollie said. "We're going to be making a lot of use of generators, solar and otherwise. Your knowledge and skills would be very useful to what we're doing."

"But the Living ID ... I'm sure there's a lot more built into that implant than they're letting on," Ian responded. "Will anyone be able to lay low, or hide, with those implants in them? You know what I mean."

"I know what you mean, Ian. No doubt it's got some way to track a person ... would be simple enough with a little RFID technology added to the mix," Sam observed. "And that kind of technology's been around for awhile."

"Then you'd either have to stay unattached, and completely off the grid, as I see it, or you could all just be tracked down at their convenience," Ian observed.

"And that's where it gets a little tricky, but we've thought of how we're gonna handle it," Sam replied. "There's a few that will have to take the implant, and we'll have to be real careful how we use those folks in the resistance. But most of the fighters will not take the implant."

"We'll be taking to the hills, so to speak," Ollie added.

Ian did not know what to say in response. There was no question he was in full support of any resistance to what the federal government was doing, but the fate of his wife and children were paramount in his concerns.

The choice spread before him was far from an easy one, yet there was one path that beckoned strongly to him. His wife, son, and daughter could go onto the government's new grid, while he joined the resistance, and remained outside of the digital net. Otherwise, he would be pulling his loved ones out of their very home, and onto a path of unrelenting hardship and danger.

"We'll figure out a way to remove the implant, once we know a little more about it," Sam said. "We've got some real tech-savvy fellows aboard. Your wife and kids can stay on the grid for the time being. My wife is gonna take the implant. I don't want her thrown out of her home either. I know what you're worried about, Ian."

"Same here," Ollie said. "My family is going to keep a roof over their heads. But if we can get a full blown revolution going, we'll get those implants removed as soon as possible. It's just that things are going to be very rough in the early going. And there's no guarantees about any of it."

Ian gave a rueful chuckle. "Believe me, I know that well enough."

He then thought of all the townspeople, wondering where they had been taken. They had been incarcerated, as had Sheriff Howard, and were probably confined together, at a mass detainment facility.

He suspected that the new throngs of prisoners would not be given a choice when it came to the Living ID. If it was a non-negotiable mandate for citizens, it would inevitably be forced upon the detainees.

"Count me in," Ian stated firmly, locking a steely gaze for a moment with each of the men. "And I'm speaking only for myself. I'll get things arranged so that Alena has it a little better, but I'll give you every ounce of effort and skill I have in me. You need generators worked on, connections established, wiring tended to ... well, you got your man."

Smiles came to the faces of Sam and Ollie, as they nodded their approval of his decision. They had an air of relief about them as well.

"Welcome aboard, Ian. It's the right thing to do," Sam exclaimed, shaking his hand firmly. "I don't have a single doubt about it."

"It's the only thing I can do, if I want to live with myself," Ian replied.

"Great to have you with us, Ian," Ollie said, his grin broadening as he patted Ian on the shoulder.

The hint of tension that had been in the air prior to his choice dissipated completely. Ian could tell they had harbored uncertainty regarding his response to their invitation.

"Not gonna stand by and watch the bastards run amok ... not if I can do something about it," Ian said.

Though he smiled, there was a sharp, defiant edge to his words. A sense of determination and conviction pervaded him, even as the listlessness plaguing him during recent days fled. Just like the day he had stood with Sheriff Howard at the Revere home, he knew that his choice was the right one.

It felt so good not to be alone, and to know that he would stand in opposition to the loathsome affliction besieging his community. The disquiet that had shadowed him in recent days vanished entirely, as the declaration unburdened him in the passing of a moment.

He had chosen a harder, narrower path, but it was a free one. That alone made it far better than the wide, gleaming road that beckoned with empty promises; and eventual bondage.

# MADISON

There were no warnings before the storm broke with full fury on the unsuspecting streets of Madison. The operation commenced with both precision and speed as the surveillance officer at Station 4-12 pulled the trigger.

Several black SUVs with dark-tinted windows pulled swiftly onto the street running in front of Seth's house, coming to stops in a line of vehicles facing the house. The rubber of tires screeched as others pulled to halts on several other streets, including the next street over, in back of Seth's house.

TTDF troopers, clad in helmets and body armor, and armed with short-barreled submachine guns, glided through the back yards of the surrounding houses, taking up positions that cut off all points of escape. They peered through high-grade night vision goggles, seeing everything around them in clarity. The security cordon took only moments to set in place, and nothing would get through it without being seen and confronted first.

The troopers were just the vanguard of a much larger firestorm. Sweeping up behind them, and converging from all around, was a wide net of military and police units. Well over a couple thousand in number, they were armed and well-coordinated, rapidly setting to their tasks with a determined focus.

Soldiers and police alike were swiftly engaged in brazen searches of the houses visited by the four teenagers. Wherever computer equipment, drives, and discs were not handed over voluntarily, they were confiscated by force.

The few individuals who protested the naked violations of home and hearth were met with curt, unsympathetic responses. They were brusquely informed that the searches were being done as a matter of national security. Knowing they were consigned to the whim of heavily armed thugs, most stifled their anger and resentment, enduring the crude violations of their homes without further objection.

Even with full cooperation on the part of the people in the houses being searched, little regard was given to property or person. The occupants of the homes were shoved aside, valuables damaged, and rooms ransacked with reckless abandon. There was no disputing the will of the security forces, as they collected the drives and discs with the video footage captured by Seth's group.

Many were left in tears, and others shaking in helpless rage, as home after home was left in shambles in the wake of the troopers' departure. Several others were apprehended wherever firearms were uncovered, or anything else that ran afoul of the mandates that had been put in place under martial law.

A good number of those who were detained had an idea as to where they were going to be taken, having already viewed the video footage that the youths left at their houses. The dread of uncertainty clung to them with a malicious fervor, as they were loaded onto vehicles for transportation to the prison camp.

# GREGORY

"First of all, we're going to shut that damn thing down, and put it out of business for good," Gregory growled hotly, staring at the shiny facing of the stout, innocuous-looking building complex. "And we're gonna do it before the sun sets."

Station 4-12's main function was, until recently, more focused on intelligence gathering, though to Gregory that was enough of a cause for full condemnation. The relentless, invasive collection of data on regular UCAS citizens was an unforgivable transgression of the Grand Charter.

It did not matter if the High Court had done absolutely nothing to stop the egregious activity. In Gregory's eyes, that branch of the government had long since become little more than a cluster of functionaries in black gowns, rubber stamping the initiatives of the regime. They had no more credibility than the president's press secretary when it came to being impartial.

Gregory did not need a law degree to interpret the words of the Grand Charter. The document was written in plain enough language, and if nine justices were in grievous dereliction of their charge, Gregory was not. He had taken his own oath, in the military, and he was living up to that vow to the fullest degree in the endeavor he was currently engaged in.

The place standing before his eyes had taken on a much more sinister function than intelligence gathering. It was now the veritable command center for the CSD and other apparatus imposing outright tyranny across the UCAS. The implementation of Living ID would greatly expand the power wielded out of that facility. In some ways, it would become the spider at the center of a regional web, and its bite would be loaded with venom.

For a place as sizeable as it was, and with the considerable number of people that Gregory knew were inside, the stillness encompassing the sprawling property was disquieting. The atmosphere was like a held breath, restrained and tensed.

Gregory had incurred that feeling several times before, while deployed in combat zones. It was more than a little disconcerting that the feeling of an enemy presence was taking place in the heart of the country that Gregory had fought for, and called his own.

The day also marked the first large display of force for the budding resistance. The operation underway involved over a hundred and eighty armed fighters. There were also several others serving in technical areas of support, such as the ham radio operator situated close to Gregory, who would help coordinate the groups positioned on the far side of the federal complex. Chuck and two more operators were handling the radios on those ends, and a couple more were deployed farther away, accompanying lookouts keeping a close watch on the skies and approaching roads.

The time for entreaty had ended, and the time for action had arrived. Many outreaches had been made to those inside Station 4-12, using every means of communication possible.

The occupants of the buildings had stubbornly refused to come out and surrender to the force ringing the compound. In Gregory's eyes, they had embraced the consequences of their choice, and he had no qualms about leading an attack.

He looked over towards the flat-bed tow truck and one-ton pickup positioned close by, both of which had been converted to a specialized use. They were now what he called technicals, regular vehicles that had been modified and assigned to the service of the resistance. Mounted on the vehicles were recently-constructed rocket launchers, each one fitted with eight tubes. The barrels of the sixteen tubes were all oriented squarely towards the buildings below.

Though they were not precision weapon systems, and did not have tremendous range, the systems could do damage, and they would come as a great surprise to an enemy thinking that it was facing only rifles. The psychological value alone, when the enemy realized that it could not make any assumptions about the resistance, was worth it. An opponent insecure in its balance was one that could be toppled to the ground.

"Well, they're sure not gonna open their doors, so let's form an entrance for ourselves!" Gregory commanded, giving the crews on the bed of the trucks a nod. "We don't have much longer. They're hunkered down in there for one reason ... they're expecting some help to come."

Near to him, the ham radio operator gave the signal to one of the groups located on the far side of the building complex. A third rocket system was positioned there, on another pickup that had been converted into a technical.

A bevy of rockets were loosed at the complex a few moments later, sixteen streaking from one side, and eight from the other. The roars of their flights were followed with loud, reverberating booms as the missiles impacted with blunt force. The teams on the three technicals wasted no time, immediately beginning to reload the rocket tubes.

Another twenty-four rocket volley was loosed, and the air was again riddled with the sounds of explosions, sending a cascade of echoes through the surrounding hills. Black columns of smoke wafted from the stricken buildings, and a swathe of debris littered the areas in front of the targeted points.

Gregory peered up into the sunny skies, knowing that drones or helicopters would be making their presence felt soon. For the moment, thankfully, there was no sign of enemy aircraft. The lookouts positioned farther outward would send warning the first instant anything other than a bird was sighted. The weather was favorable, as the skies were relatively free of cloud cover.

"Cover those up, get them back, and do it fast!" Gregory shouted, as groups of men and women scrambled to pull large camouflage nets over the technicals with their rocket launchers. "We're done using those, because we'll definitely lose them if we continue. Roll them out of here! As quick as you can!"

The vehicles were pushed from their positions with the netting over them. Gregory was going to take no chances with the heat signatures from running engines, and had been adamant that they be kept off all throughout the operation.

The technicals were guided deeper into the trees, providing further cover from optical sensors. Gregory knew from experience that the exact places that the rockets had been fired from could be calculated with precision, but hopefully any targeted strikes from the enemy would churn up only dirt and trees.

"Let's get the rest of this over," he said, satisfied that the technicals stood a chance of surviving the combat. "Begin the second phase."

The radio operator relayed his wishes down to where other units were positioned for the next stage of the operation. A few seconds later, a quartet of vehicles, one SUV and three pickup trucks, raced into sight, heading directly towards the building complex.

Fighters armed with rifles were tightly packed together in the beds of the pickup trucks, and inside the SUV. They swept out from the vehicles when they came to a halt before the heavily damaged parts of Station 4-12.

The force had scraped together as much as possible in the way of protection, and most of the group sent to penetrate the buildings were clad in a range of bulletproof vests, helmets, and tactical accessories. It was a hodge-podge of styles, ranging from police to military issue, but it was far better than nothing.

There was nothing in the way of an official uniform, but all of the fighters, like those in the hills, wore small emblems of silver, in the distinctive image of a sword wreathed in flames. As an Avatar bearing a flaming sword was said to have warded the gates of a sacred realm many ages ago, those who had joined the resistance saw themselves as the wards of a free land.

The idea of the emblem had been put forth by a jeweler who had recently joined the ranks, and it was quickly embraced, resulting in the design and casting of the pins the resistance fighters now wore as they charged the federal building. Those that had taken up the Silver Sword now found themselves on the threshold of igniting something of great magnitude, a strike that would be felt from coast to coast.

Looking through binoculars fitted with high-grade optics, Gregory watched the fighters disappear into the haze and smoke. The muffled sounds of gunfire came from within the building seconds later. Flurries of staccato bursts overlapped, and Gregory knew that the enemy was exchanging fire with the fighters penetrating the breaches in the structures.

"Commander Andreas," the ham radio operator called out to

Gregory, a worrisome expression spread across his face.

"What is it?" Gregory responded.

"Birds sighted," the operator responded firmly. "From the north."

"As I expected," Gregory said. "We don't have long. Send word to everyone in the hills to spread out, and take cover."

Whether helicopters or drones, Gregory knew that the resistance was helpless to counter the enemy in the skies. They did not have anything capable of bringing down enemy aircraft.

Gregory had pulled off an incredible shot when he had downed the Skyhawk helicopter hovering over the Revere property, but the looming situation would be very different.

The radio equipment and other gear were hastily gathered up, as Gregory and the others in the resistance fragmented, just as discussed prior to the operation. They would not give the enemy any easy concentration of troops to fire upon.

Farther below, the vehicles that had transported the fighters to the buildings raced away, hurrying to get out of the open ground. Anything foolish enough to remain in the areas surrounding the buildings was as good as destroyed, with the advanced targeting systems possessed by the drones and helicopters.

Gregory and a couple of others ran a few hundred yards across the uneven ground through the trees, and got into a small earthen dugout that had been prepared just the previous day. A large explosion shook the trees around him, just as he got inside the cramped confines.

For the time being, they would have to maintain a tight radio silence. Any signal created a dangerous vulnerability, as the electromagnetic waves could be intercepted and traced, providing coordinates for the weapon systems aboard the federal aircraft. Gregory could only hope that the mission was executed according to the plan.

# STATION 4-12

A pair of Sky Dragon combat drones roved the skies above Station 4-12, their operators selecting targets and engaging the formidable weaponry of the unmanned aircraft, from the safety of air-conditioned rooms located many miles away. The whooshes of incoming missiles were followed with robust explosions, as the besieging rebel fighters were attacked from the heights.

The supply of missiles was not unlimited, and it was not very long before the drones were whittling down their payloads. With the extensive damage to the satellite network, the two *Sky Dragons* had each been armed with full complements of fourteen Lightning Bolt missiles.

Fire-and-forget munitions, they were fitted with wave radar seeker technology. The missiles were designed to take out enemy armor, and were more than enough to blast an SUV or pickup truck to bits.

Cruising at altitudes unreachable by anything possessed by the rebels, the nearly seventy-foot wingspan *Sky Dragons* enjoyed an unchallenged supremacy.

# OUTSIDE STATION 4-12

Convoys moving to the aid of Station 4-12 were brought to an abrupt halt, coming under a ferocious, unexpected attack. Resistance units concealed in strategic positions along the two main roads approaching the building complex unleashed a firestorm on the military vehicles.

Radio silence finally had to be broken on the part of the rebels, as warnings were sent to the fighters who had made it into the building complex. The federal forces rushing to the defense of Station 4-12 could be stymied a little, and slowed, but they could not be stopped.

The resistance did not have enough strength or assets to engage in a sustained firefight, and had been strictly ordered to evacuate once the convoys had been engaged. In truth, they could inflict little overall damage, other than the massive explosion from a bomb embedded in the roadway to take out the lead vehicle.

Yet damage was not the principle goal of the ambush. Buying time was the sole object of the rebels' efforts, and this they accomplished as the convoys pulled to a halt, regrouped, and began to push forward with vehicle-mounted weapons primed, and sensors scanning for targets.

It was not long before the officers determined that the rebels had vacated the area, and the convoys were able to pick up speed. But the small window of time was exactly what the rebels had hoped for.

# STATION 4-12

Chaos ensued outside the building complex as resistance fighters and federal agents alike were loosed in all directions. The remaining drone overhead had to refrain from firing into the crowds, as rebel and government loyalist alike were interspersed in the throngs evacuating the buildings.

It was all part of the plan devised by Gregory and the others. There were not enough fighters to take even a fraction of the federal agents into custody, though a few had been selected and secured when the building was taken.

Enemy aircraft could not fire indiscriminately without killing droves of their own. Gregory was bitterly aware of the fact that officers were not averse to risking casualties to friendly fire, but he knew that they would not chance the deaths of many intelligence officers, technicians, administrators, and others from the horde of federals loosed from the fusion center designated as Station 4-12.

His calculation was correct, and no further missiles were launched from above as the crowds scattered outward.

Huge explosions rattled the forest moments later, as the charges put in place by Dante and the others who had entered the building were set off. Portions of the buildings collapsed, as if a partial demolition of the complex had been executed.

Having the buildings rendered unusable was an added bonus, as the primary targets were the array of servers and equipment utilized at Station 4-12. The bombs and fires that followed annihilated vast amounts of data, and destroyed an extensive amount of highly valuable assets.

The empty buildings were husks of smoke and ruin when the first soldiers from the incoming convoys finally reached the area.

# FRIEDRICH

Breaking free of Ares' realm, the swirling light of the Vortex's outermost ring filled Friedrich's vision, blinding him for a moment. As soon as they were immersed within the churning, spectral luminance, he could feel the downward pull on his spirit. The essence of the Ten-Fold Kingdom endeavored hungrily to claim him, as well his companions, working tirelessly on both Asa'an and the Gryphon.

Their rate of climb slowed precipitously, and soon it was as if they were slogging through a viscous substance. Friedrich's inner senses perceived the incredible strain that the Gryphon was enduring just to move forward.

"We must take the path through the Void again!" Asa'an called out, a trace of anguish in her weary voice. "Or we will not escape this."

"Then do it!" Friedrich called back emphatically, knowing that they could easily find themselves in the clutches of demonic entities, if they sank back into one of the nether realms.

The ghostly light flashed into blackness, and the Gryphon's exertions eased, as they drifted in a slow glide through the timeless stasis of the Void. This time, it was not absolute nothingness that met Friedrich's gaze. Instead, translucent figures appearing to be suspended in space, as far as his sight reached, were visible in every direction. Their numbers were uncountable, and Friedrich looked upon the multitudes in awe, beginning to discern the tremendous range of shapes, sizes, and types of beings.

They all had a spectral hue to their forms, emitting the lightest of glows, but no sign of consciousness could be found on them. Immersed within an ethereal hibernation, they were like pallid statues, inert and unresponsive to the three intruders that had suddenly manifested amongst them.

"I ... have never ... seen this," Asa'an said, in a delicate tone that was no more than a light whisper.

"The souls..." Friedrich replied, his voice trailing off as he stared upon one incredible sight after another.

He eyed creatures that were different than anything he had ever seen before, reaching far beyond his foundations of myth and imagination. Some were humanoid, while others held a more prominent relation to the worlds of amphibians, insects, and reptiles. There were still others that had strange, amorphous appearances; entities which had no identifiable structures like heads, arms, or legs.

The differences in sizes were vast, with some entities being very diminutive, almost unnoticeable within the incorporeal array. A few were enormous in scale, and would have been measured in the hundreds of feet, either in height or body length, back on a world such as Terra.

Some of the beings appeared suited for flight, and others more for the depths of seas, like one great leviathan that Friedrich looked upon in stunned amazement, as the Gryphon passed over its broad back.

"No spirit … that I have known … has been to this place," Asa'an commented.

Friedrich could tell that the Peri was as overwhelmed by their surroundings as he was. Multitudes upon multitudes of apparitions in slumber radiated out from them, as they continued farther on through the black, infinite realm. So overwhelming were the sights that even thoughts of the great Djinn warding the Void were subdued in his mind.

"There are beings here … like nothing in my world," Friedrich remarked, taking in the sight of a multi-legged, multi-winged creature that was at least three times as large as the Gryphon. It had an elongated head with sharper features, and Friedrich wondered what realm it came from.

"Or the places I have known," Asa'an said.

A tingling feeling swelled in Friedrich's spirit, at about the same time Asa'an declared promptly, "The Djinn are coming."

Turning his gaze, Friedrich saw the reddish light in the distance, streaking directly towards them. From ahead came another, and, from below, still one more.

The Djinn were not inhibited by the masses of creatures within the silent equilibrium. They passed right through the spirit-forms, bearing down on Friedrich, Asa'an, and the Gryphon with no obstruction to their approach.

"Now, Asa'an," Friedrich urged. "Take us back!"

The shift between Void and Abyss transpired once again, and to Friedrich's relief, the great Vortex of the Ten-Fold kingdom was now a speck in the far distance. The Gryphon moved easily, and Friedrich did not feel the slightest trace of force acting upon his being.

Without question, they were safely beyond the tow of the swirling Vortex. They had evaded Ares' realm and the Djinn, and even though they were still separated from Enki and the others, Friedrich was flooded with a deep, soothing sense of relief.

Faint, high-pitched cries erupted out of the darkness.

"Galla!" cried Asa'an, shattering Friedrich's flicker of well-being.

The cries mounted, joined by a flurry of others coming from all around. They still sounded distant, but Friedrich knew that the pursuit had begun.

They could take their chances within the Void again, but Friedrich was not about to be cavalier about their luck. They had manifested in emptiness the first time, and among the spirit-forms the second, but they could just as easily find themselves directly on top of a Djinn the third.

For the moment, Friedrich worked to orient his thoughts back to the original purpose that brought the group out from the Middle Lands, behind Enki, and into the Abyss. Shutting out the faraway shrieks, he thought about Erishkegal, calling to mind that delicate, inner tug that they had been following prior to being swarmed by the Galla.

It was still there, and, surprisingly, beckoned stronger than it ever had before. A spark of hope flared within Friedrich.

"She is not far!" he exclaimed, as the Gryphon banked in the direction to which Friedrich had tethered his inner senses.

Lurching forward, the Gryphon accelerated to a great speed, as Friedrich maintained his full concentration on the desire to locate Erishkegal.

The initial surge of hope ebbed gradually, as they raced onward through the darkness. The unseen beacon was growing stronger in its pull, without question, but the shrieks were growing louder, and at a much faster rate.

A flash of brightness at the edge of his vision told Friedrich that Asa'an was readying her lance. Though he knew she was exhausted, he could feel her alarm, like a surging heat at his back, but she kept quiet, allowing Friedrich to keep his entire focus on the inner beacon.

He knew they were very close to the destination they were seeking. A perilous gamble lay before them, continuing and hoping that they could cross the last remaining distance before the Galla reached them, or risking the Void once again.

As much as he wanted to reach their destination, he knew that the fates of the Gryphon and Asa'an would stand a better chance if they were to brave the Void one more time. The shrieks of the Galla filled his ears, and he knew without looking that a great multitude of them were just behind them.

"The Void! Asa'an! The Void once more!" Friedrich called out to the Peri.

He looked forward, feeling the robust sense of Erishkegal closer than ever. It felt as if they were very near to their goal, and he was cloaked in bitterness as he braced for the disconcerting, stark shift into the Void. The screeches and guttural cries of the Galla swelled even louder, and did not cease in their intensity.

"The Void! Chance it, Asa'an!" Friedrich cried out urgently.

"I cannot! Something prevents me!" Asa'an called back, sounding both surprised and frantic.

Every part of Friedrich was chilled with fear at her pronouncement, as the Gryphon sped forward with every bit of strength that it had, to the uppermost limits of its attainable velocity.

"Keep trying! Asa'an!" Friedrich called out to her, at a loss for what to do.

The dense cloud of Galla drew ever closer, their outcries raucous and savage. Friedrich could feel the pull that had guided them through the darkness more strongly, but still nothing but a lightless gloom met his eyes.

"I cannot do it, Friedrich!" Asa'an lamented in a wail. The sorrow in her voice was cavernous, and he knew that she had called upon every last mote of power within her to try. "I am too weakened."

He gripped his crystal staff, and it erupted with a dazzling light. If he was going to be consigned to the Void, then he was going to fall in battle.

He turned his gaze about, and looked upon a constellation of glittering eyes looming just behind them. He could see the hideous countenances of the nearest ones, macabre, multi-fanged visages contorted in madness and violence.

A deafening chorus of shrieks and cries emitted from the diabolical horde behind them, and suddenly they broke off their pursuit. Scattering in all directions, the Galla darted and banked away with a desperate urgency.

Friedrich abruptly felt the presence of something enormous within the darkness just as a thick column of flame shot overhead. The fiery jet cleaved into the black cloud of demonic entities, brilliantly illuminating

# STEPHEN ZIMMER

them and eliciting a wave of screeches and howls.

The Gryphon then angled sharply downward, and everything became an impenetrable gray. Lights then came into view, swarming and swirling all about him. Friedrich's eyes could focus on nothing in particular, as if light itself was bending and warping, distorting his entire perception.

Everything then turned into a featureless, ash-gray once again. Then, as if passing through a dense cloud-mass, a startling vision was suddenly revealed.

A barren, gray vista that echoed the hue of the layer he had just passed through led up to obsidian walls of an unfathomable height. A darker, vertical line revealed the location of an immense gateway, and it was toward the great portal that the Gryphon oriented its flight.

Wings outstretched, the Gryphon slowed into a glide, and alighted on the surface before the soaring black gates. Friedrich stared upwards, unable to see the top of the wall, where it cut into the rolling gray skies far overhead.

Behind them, a featureless, empty landscape spread as far as he could see.

Exploding out of the darkness, a vast, shadowy form hurtled downward. Its immense wings flared outward as it slowed, before finally landing upon the ground. Wings unfurled, and head raised high, the black colossus was incredible to behold, as it glared down at the trio before the gate.

Starting at a place set just above its golden, reptilian eyes, a high, grand crest ran along the center over the top of its head and continued down its broad neck. Four long, thick limbs supported its huge body, as its red-hued, mesmerizing gaze, cast forth by eyes like great smoldering embers, engulfed Friedrich, Asa'an, and the Gryphon.

It was a creature both majestic and terrifying. Nothing could be done, and Friedrich felt grim resignation come over him. There was nowhere to run, and they were trapped against the gateway and towering wall.

The extended muzzle of the great dragon harbored giant, unsullied fangs, like glistening stalagmites and stalactites of pure opal. Rich beauty and deadly capability were interwoven all about the juggernaut's incredible form.

Its black scales shimmered with an unusual quality, as if both

302

reflecting light from without and enhanced by some manner of luminance from within. It was a creature of power and grace, as awe-inspiring as it was fearsome.

From behind, Friedrich heard Asa'an utter a single word.

"Kur."

The name sent a charge racing through his spirit-form, as he looked upon the greatest of the Nephilim to cross the Veil and enter the Abyss with Erishkegal. The dragon was truly gargantuan, and Friedrich knew that even a great horde of Galla would be no match for it.

One by one, farther behind Kur, other winged shapes burst through the shrouding, gray masses, and landed upon the barren ground. Though none approached the sheer grandeur of the one at their head, they were all formidable creatures in their own right.

All were dragons, and a few closely resembled Kur in their features. Some had countenances that evoked a comparison to lions or serpents, but all were four-legged, and flight capable, possessed of a pair of wings.

"The boundaries of this place are indeed well-guarded," Friedrich muttered to Asa'an, pensively, as he stared out at the bevy of dragons. "What are we to do now?"

"The gate, Friedrich," Asa'an said. "It is opening."

Casting a glance over his shoulder, not wanting to take his eyes off Kur and the other dragons, he saw that the great black gates were swinging slowly inward. Before he could concentrate on what was beyond, movement within it demanded his attention.

Padding out of the gateway was a massive creature, one that was very different in nature than the dragons gathered before it. Like them, it was winged, but the similarity ended there.

Its robust body was akin to that of a lion, though its head was that of a human. A dark brown, braided beard hung down from the creature's oval face. Green-flecked, golden eyes, with pupils like those of a cat, were oriented squarely on Friedrich and his companions.

The look within the creature's eyes was stern, but not entirely unkind, giving Friedrich a sliver of consolation. He had no illusions that he, Asa'an, and even the Gryphon were anything other than at the mercy of the guardian creatures looming both behind and before him.

It was an uneasy predicament, like being caught between jaws that could clench at any moment. Friedrich girded himself, as the creature from within the gateway came to a halt before them. It stared down at his group for several tense moments, with not a flicker of change to its solemn, stony expression.

Friedrich had the unwelcome feeling of being weighed in some manner, though what was being measured was hidden from his awareness. He knew without looking that all of the dragons were still in place behind him, and that everything hinged on the verdict of the giant ward of the gateway.

"Who comes to the gates of Erishkegal's dominion?" the strange creature asked them. Though the tone of the creature was even, its voice boomed in the encompassing stillness.

Friedrich was simply relieved to hear speech, though he did not miss the lengthy fangs exposed when the creature opened its huge mouth.

"Just three who were lost, who were put to chase by the things of the Abyss," Asa'an replied. "It is this realm that we have sought."

Friedrich was glad that she took the initiative to answer, as he found that he had no response.

"Do you serve the Lord of the Ten-Fold Kingdom?" the creature asked them, as its gaze narrowed. There was an undercurrent of threat to the air surrounding them, which felt as if a highly-charged energy was being held back with the slimmest of restraints.

"No, we seek Erishkegal, coming with others from the higher places. An Avatar of Adonai, great Enki, led us on this journey," Asa'an replied.

At the mention of Enki, the creature's face softened in its intensity. The feeling of coiled tension diffused swiftly.

"Then know that Enki came through these very gates, with others such as you," the creature announced.

Friedrich was filled with gladness and relief at the welcome pronouncement.

"Manzazu is warded by seven gates, through which you must pass," the creature announced. "If but one guardian denies you passage, you shall not enter."

"We understand," Asa'an replied.

Turning, the creature led them through the gateway, leaving Kur and the throng of other dragons behind. Once inside, the two halves of the gate swung slowly back into place.

Where the outside of the gateway was featureless, blending in closely with the rest of the immense wall, the side on the interior was magnificent in its adornment. Lustrous jewels were embedded within the surfaces of the gate's two halves, a mixture of sapphire, emerald, diamond, and ruby sparkling to the uppermost heights. Thick golden bands spanned the width of the gateway at several points along its prodigious height, as if girding the realm's first point of entry.

The surfaces of the bands were inlaid with what looked to be some manner of glyphs, along which subtle tracings of light trekked along the contours. Though he could not decipher them, they resembled the sigils that hovered above formations of Avatars arrayed for battle. Friedrich knew the markings were not merely ornamental, but another part of the layers of protection set in place to fend off threats to Erishkegal's realm.

"Go forward, to the next gatekeeper," the ward of the first gate instructed them, as Friedrich continued to gawk at the interior side of the gateway.

Under the watchful eyes of the guardian creature, Friedrich and his companions started across another stretch of barren ground. Looking to the left and right, Friedrich could see nothing within the space between the first and second gates.

The next five gates proved to be very similar in nature to the first. Set within obsidian walls whose heights were indecipherable where their summits were engulfed by the cloud-like masses overhead, the gates swung inward and featured resplendent arrays of jewels on the inside, as well as more of the glyph-inlaid, golden bands.

Each of the guardians they encountered at the gates had appearances that were as startling as they were intimidating.

Friedrich found the ward of the second gate to be particularly bizarre. Its four-legged body was covered in snake scales, and its lengthy neck ended in a head like that of a serpent. A prominent, single horn jutted out from the creature's forehead, and its front legs ended in the claws of a lion, while the rear legs culminated in eagle's talons.

Like the first guardian, the second questioned them sharply on their purpose and allegiance, before finally allowing them through to the third gate.

The skies above them had rippled with violence for a moment, as a sonorous boom of thunder shook the space they were crossing. Friedrich had found himself wondering what Erishkegal's realm looked like, once they had passed through all the gates. He could only hope that they were allowed all the way into the realm, a matter that would remain uncertain until all seven gates had been accessed.

He doubted that it would be a place of calm and radiance, given what he had already experienced. Hers was an abyssal dominion, and he knew that he had to be very cautious in everything that he said or did once inside of it. The only consolation was that it was abundantly clear that her realm was not in alignment with the Ten-Fold Kingdom, but even that was of little comfort.

When the third gate swung open, a towering, brawny creature had emerged from within. At first, seeing its four circular hooves and dark, muscular body, Friedrich thought it was an enormous bull. It had a broad, sharp set of horns, as well as the ears of a bull, but the comparison ended there. Its face was fully human; that of a broad-faced man, with a large nose and thick beard.

A beast with the body of an enormous lion, and the tail of a scorpion met them at the fourth gate. Friedrich thought they were going to be rejected, as it took the creature a considerable amount of time to render its judgement. Its golden, feline eyes stared unblinking at them the entire time, and Friedrich felt highly alleviated when the guardian had finally released them to proceed onward to the fifth gateway.

The fifth gate had opened to reveal a serpentine creature of tremendous length. The head of the scaly being contained an extended set of jaws lined with spiky teeth. It had two upper appendages, like long arms, that it used to prop itself up when it addressed Friedrich and his companions.

None of the guardians could have been described as amiable, but the fifth one came the closest to having a pleasant tone as it interacted with them. It spoke to both Friedrich and Asa'an about their purpose, and the journey they had taken through the Abyss. Finally, it gave its approval for them to move onward to the sixth gate.

A dragon-like beast, larger than any of the ones outside the first gate, save for Kur, attended the sixth gate. It was more mammalian than reptilian, with a head like that of a male lion. Of the first six guardians, it came to the quickest decision, curtly informing them to continue.

"We have now seen Kur, and six of the mightiest of the Nephilim to go with Erishkegal," Asa'an remarked, as they walked across the arid, flat stretch of ground spanning the distance between the sixth and seventh walls. To Friedrich's relief, the Peri clearly looked to be recovering more of her vitality and strength. "I wonder who will meet us at the seventh gate."

Friedrich looked upwards as a blinding flash of lightning emanated from the swirling cloud masses.

"We are about to find out," he replied, a little nervous and anxious now that they were on the brink of entering Erishkegal's mystery-laden realm.

# GODRAL

With a soaring leap, Godral cleared the fallen tree. He landed smoothly, keeping his gait steady, and bounded across the forest floor. It had been some time since he had been in his four-legged form, and the fluid motion of running felt wonderful.

Air rushed in and out of his lungs as he pumped his legs vigorously. His broad paws gripped the ground, propelling him forward with abundant force. Godral's body was stretched to the limit, as he reached with his forelegs for the next stride, maintaining an even rhythm.

He slowed as he neared the edge of the trees. Beyond was the small lake nestled close to the abode where most of the humans dwelled. The surface of the water glittered in the moonlight, stirred by the night air brushing against the surface.

A lone figure stood in the silvery luminance, staring intently toward the trees. A gust of wind lifted her hair, blowing several strands across her face.

Godral padded out from the trees, heading towards Arianna. She turned her head in his direction, fixing him with her gaze.

"I've been waiting for you," Arianna called to him. "I have news that I have to give you, before you go any farther."

Godral drew to a halt a few paces from her, and saw the concern reflected in her face. Often jovial in demeanor when they had taken walks together, it was clear that Arianna was deeply bothered by something.

"They are going to need you, Godral, and several other An-Ki," Arianna said.

He could sense the young woman's apprehension, hanging thickly in the air about her. Her tone was subdued, and carried considerable tension within it. She was plainly unhappy with the news she was bringing him.

"What do they wish?" Godral asked her.

"To help with an attack. They need to get into the city of Troy," Arianna said.

"An attack? On humans?" Godral asked, feeling uneasy, and understanding Arianna's great reticence.

The last attack on the group of human soldiers had been born of necessity, as the An-Ki were moving through the woods on their way to their first refuge. This attack would be much different in nature.

Arianna nodded gravely. "They need to take control of a bridge, and it is heavily guarded. They think your special abilities will allow you to get among them. They want you to shift forms and surprise the guards of the bridge."

"We will attack humans?" Godral asked, still in mild disbelief that something like this was being asked of him.

"Yes," Arianna replied evenly. "I wanted to tell you myself. Before they do. They want me to bring you to the cabin."

"Who wishes this?"

"The Knights of the Order, and the Shield Maidens," Arianna replied.

"The human warriors?" Godral queried, thinking of the men and women that had been appearing with more frequency at the refuge. He still understood little about them, other than knowing that they were on the same side as the Celestial Messenger.

Arianna nodded. "Yes, the warriors."

"What numbers ... of An-Ki?" Godral asked.

"Enough to fill the back of a truck trailer," Arianna replied. "Maybe twenty or more?"

"Word must be taken ... to other places," Godral said, after pausing a moment to envision the number described by Arianna.

Numbers were one of the things in the human language that he was still having some trouble with, but he knew that twenty would require the addition of many more An-Ki than he had available at the refuge.

They were scattered in many locations, presenting a significant challenge. The act of finding the warriors he wanted, and then bringing them together, could not be done by himself.

"The Knights and Shield Maidens will help you with the An-Ki in the other refuges. I have no doubt they have a great need to take the bridge," Arianna said. "There is something of tremendous importance that they must get into the city. As far as I can understand."

"If we attack, I need best warriors," Godral said.

"And you should have them all with you," Arianna said.

Looking up, Godral saw three figures heading towards them. One was a woman, the other an older man, and standing over a head taller than both of them was the white-haired, highly recognizable form of Sarangar.

The younger An-Ki looked to Godral with a dour expression, and the expressions on the two humans with him were austere.

"Help me gather An-Ki. We will fight for you," Godral announced, before any of the others said so much as a single word.

Godral did not miss the flicker of relief in the eyes of the two humans. They had evidently not anticipated a quick assent.

There was little other choice, as Godral saw the situation. The humans and An-Ki were up against a common enemy, one that had already demonstrated the ability to strike at them without warning. Perhaps it was time to deliver the enemy a surprise blow. The mere thought made his blood run a little hotter in his veins.

# GREGORY

Late in the night, Gregory and a few others that had taken cover in the aftermath of the assault on Station 4-12 moved out from their dugouts, and hastened to a rendezvous point designated well in advance. Arms at the ready, they could assume nothing, and two wore lower grade night-vision goggles, gleaned much earlier from the precious, small batch that had been gathered together for the insurgency's use.

A smile broke out from Gregory's face as he beheld the unmistakable forms of Dante and Consuela, standing amongst the group waiting for them. Dante flashed a gleaming white smile, while Consuela's lips stretched into a grin, as they looked to Gregory.

Giving them each a short embrace, Gregory exclaimed, "I'm still not forgiving you for forcing me to stay in the damned hills. I should have been down there with you, right in the thick of it."

"Not gonna lose our best commander in the first big fight," Dante replied, grinning. "Besides, I wanted you to hear my handiwork. Did you like the music we made in that little venue called Station 4-12?"

Gregory thought back to the enormous booms that had sounded later in the afternoon. The timbre of the explosions was unmistakable, as were the tremors that ran through the ground. Gregory had known then that the operation was a success, as had the two others in the dugout with him.

Packs of high explosives had been carried into the building with Dante and the group penetrating the building complex. Their task had been to gain a few captives, uncover whatever they possibly could, and then destroy as much as was feasible in the short time available.

"I loved the music. It had my kind of beat. It told me you were in the dance," Gregory replied, mirroring the other man's grin.

"You have that little faith in us?" Dante replied, in mock-disbelief. He chuckled. "We subdued those bastards pretty quick. They weren't expectin' us to break down their walls."

"A few fought back," Consuela interjected, a glint in her eyes. "But we silenced them pretty fast."

Gregory looked between Dante and Consuela, and they did not need any words to understand the cheerless question conveyed in his eyes.

"Two with light injuries, one serious, and two were killed," Dante said, his expression losing every last speck of good humor.

"And we got the one in serious condition to the doc?" Gregory asked.

"As soon as we could," Dante said. "He'll survive, but won't be able to fight for awhile."

Gregory nodded, absorbing the news of their first casualties with grim resignation. It was a fact of war that some would fall, and others would be maimed.

"We took out at least a dozen of them in return," Consuela interjected, as if eager to shift the melancholy subject. "After that, everyone in the building was throwing up their hands."

"Made it easy to herd them out when it was time to detonate," Dante said.

"And the mess outside kept the birds from attacking," Gregory stated.

Dante and Consuela both nodded.

"Then it all worked pretty well, if not perfect," Gregory said.

"Maybe better than you think," Dante said, as another grin rose upon his face.

"Better?" Gregory said, intrigued.

Dante turned to his right, calling out, "Hey Marcus, bring the case over here."

"Case?" Gregory asked.

"You said to uncover what we could ... and we did," Consuela said.

"Yeah we did!" Dante said, with enthusiasm. "Check out what we brought back."

"And this isn't all. There's more, but this is definitely a prize worth celebrating," Consuela said.

Marcus, a tall, wiry fellow, who had been one of the men in the fire teams sent into the building complex, lugged a large black case over, and set it down on the ground before Gregory. He looked up to Dante, who nodded back to him. Unlatching it, he opened the case up, exposing its inner contents.

Inside were an array of identical vials, each set within their own round slot, in orderly rows.

"Could that be what I think it is?" Gregory asked, his hopes rising.

"Oh yeah. No need to have to get Living ID to get a vaccine," Dante said, rumbling with laughter. "We got us a big case of vaccine now."

"And no need to attack an administration center to get a supply of the vaccine right away," Gregory said, welcoming the news wholeheartedly, as it spared him a dedicated mission in the near future.

"Might be that we can find someone to take some of this, and work on making some more of it," Dante said.

"Let's hope," Gregory said. "But at least we can vaccinate the fighters who are staying off their damned grid."

"Makes me feel a little better, I gotta say," Dante said.

"Me too," added Consuela.

"Well, I'd say we've sent a shock wave through the ranks of the bastards," Gregory said. "And we've helped our cause greatly in the process."

"Kinda my thoughts on it all too," Dante said.

"I'm ready to hit them again," Consuela said.

Gregory saw the flare in her eyes, and was impressed with her resolve. She was the kind of warrior that he loved to have at his side, but he also understood the dangers inherent in zeal.

"In good time, Consuela," he said. "We'll pick our time and place, and believe me, we're gonna hit them really, really hard."

A steely edge came into his voice on the last words, as he thought of the next target. It was as horrid of a place as Station 4-12, and similarly needed to be overcome and destroyed.

"What are you thinking of next? If you don't mind me askin', that is," Dante said.

Gregory smiled. "Let's celebrate the good fortune, remember the ones that have fallen, and take things in the moment. Tomorrow will come, and we'll get to the next step right away. One thing at a time, Dante."

"I just hope whatever we hit next will leave them with a black eye," Consuela said, and Gregory had no doubts that she would have marched straightaway to another battle if there was one to be had.

"If we pull it off, it will leave them with two black eyes, and a broken nose," Gregory said, and behind the grin on his face there was an icy glint in his eyes.

"That's what I wanna hear. Can't wait for tomorrow to get here," Consuela said, smiling back to Gregory, with a raw eagerness reflecting in her gaze.

"It will be a long day, so just try and get a little rest," Gregory replied, knowing that he would have just as much trouble gaining sleep as Consuela.

# FRIEDRICH

Friedrich instinctively withdrew a few paces as the black gates swiveled open, revealing a titan whose immense form filled the great portal. He craned his head back, staring up in amazement into the broad, unsmiling face peering down upon their group.

A giant warded the seventh gate, a mountain of a creature with a stone-gray hue to its skin. Very human-like in structure, it had six digits on each of its hands and feet, and wore a simple, tunic-style garment of deep black, and loose-fitting trews of a matching color.

"The others passed through the Seven Gates," its voice boomed, as if it had been expecting them. As its mouth opened, Friedrich caught glimpses of the huge, jagged teeth spanning its upper and lower jaws. A prominent pair of teeth on the bottom, and another on the top, resembled great swords, tapering from wider bases to wicked-looking points. "None enter the dominion of Erishkegal through any other way."

"I only seek my companions," Friedrich called upward, in as humble of a tone as possible. "We do not mean to trespass, or cause offense."

Asa'an then glided forward. "Great Neti, please allow us access to join our companions. There is nowhere else that we can go. Do not leave us at the mercy of the Abyss."

The giant grew silent for a few moments, its expression solemn. Having passed through the other six gates, Friedrich would have thought that the seventh would have been a matter of course, but as he stared at the giant, it became clear that the massive gatekeeper looming before them was the most important of all.

Friedrich wondered how Asa'an had known the name of the giant, but that was a question which would have to be put aside until a later time.

"Do you serve the Shining One?" Neti asked them.

"No, great Neti. The Shining One is our Enemy, as He is yours," Asa'an replied.

"I serve only Adonai, Most High," Friedrich called up.

The giant grew quiet for a few more moments. As had happened six times before, Friedrich had the feeling of being weighed in some invisible balance.

"Have your steed bear you in flight to the summit of Egalkurzagin, where her holy Sanctum abides," Neti stated, with all the decorum of a figure possessing considerable authority. "Your journey will be swift, and you will find my Queen there. Your fates, and the fates of those that arrived before you, are held within her hands."

Stepping back, and giving them a slight nod, Neti cleared the gateway, allowing the trio access to proceed into the dusky, foreboding realm of Erishkegal. Friedrich was dazed for a few moments as he took in his first sight of the sprawling vista, coming to a halt a few paces inside the final gateway.

Murky gullies and deep gorges cleaved through the vast landscape. The terrain was brilliantly illuminated with grand bursts of lightning, periodically rippling through the dark, overcast skies. Rocky hills and mountains dotted the shadow-strewn region, though their haphazard arrangement revealed plainly that they were not the result of any natural processes.

The glassy surfaces of expansive pools and lakes shimmered in the lightning, as did a few lengthier waterways coursing through the stark lands. The place had echoes of the natural world, but also reflected something else, which to Friedrich seemed like an expression of enduring suffering.

There was nothing joyful about the dominion that had been established as a haven for the Nephilim outcasts. It was not a hell, to be sure, but it was nothing short of harsh and brooding in its general character. Suspended in unceasing twilight, the realm's appearance also reflected the astronomical storms on Terra that in a far gone age had necessitated its origins, in the bold act of mercy undertaken by its founder, Erishkegal.

In the distance, rising up in the midst of everything, was a broad mesa, of staggering proportions. It rose higher in elevation than any of the surrounding hills or mountains. It was the pinnacle, dominant object in the breathtaking scene, taking up a commanding presence within the rugged landscape.

Atop the mesa was a great black edifice, which looked conspicuously like an ancient temple. Rectangular pylons flanked a façade marked by a line of stout columns, but little else could be made out regarding the structure from where Friedrich and the others stood. Pathways could be seen leading up the sides of the mesa, the tracks cut into the rock as they zigzagged towards the summit.

"I say we go, lest the gatekeeper changes his mind," Asa'an interjected impatiently, as Friedrich continued to soak in the incredible sights.

Friedrich cast a glance over his shoulder, and saw that Neti was indeed staring at them with a somber countenance. "A good suggestion," he agreed.

The Gryphon lowered down for him, before he had even turned towards the creature. Once mounted, Friedrich settled in as the Gryphon launched itself from the ground and took to the air.

Taking a sharp incline, they rose quickly in altitude as they began their approach towards the giant mesa. For a few moments, Friedrich stared up at the underbelly of the lightning-riddled cloud masses choking the skies. The sooty clouds were comprehensive in their scope, as not a single thing could be seen of whatever was beyond the churning, rolling vapors.

From a higher vantage, Friedrich's initial impressions of the abyssal realm were unchanged, as he looked out over the inhospitable landscape. He did not want to think what it would be like to spend every moment within such a dismal environment.

They drew closer to the mesa as they gained an altitude that brought them even with the temple structure. Friedrich could see that it extended far back, like a great complex of buildings, though what lay beyond it was obscured from his view.

A large open space was spread before the columns and pylons of the main edifice, and the Gryphon angled their path of flight downward. Flapping its wings powerfully, it kept fairly steady as it slowed down and neared the surface.

A trio of human-looking individuals, clad in flowing, robe-like garments of black, stood attentively within the open ground, as if they had been awaiting the new arrivals. They rendered low bows to Friedrich and his companions, as the Gryphon alighted just beyond the jagged lip of the mesa. One had female characteristics, and the others were masculine in appearance, though all had pale skin, and were devoid of any hair on their exposed heads.

They had a disciplined look about them, and were very proper in their manner, as if they were some kind of monastic ascetics. Though not hostile, their unsmiling visages were far from welcoming.

"Welcome to the Sanctum at Egalkurzagin," the figure in the middle addressed them solemnly, with an air of formality, as the Gryphon lowered itself, conveying to Friedrich the idea to dismount.

Friedrich stood on the flat rock surface a moment later, while Asa'an took to hovering steadily at the level of his right shoulder. He looked towards the robed figures, not knowing exactly how to respond.

"Thank you," he replied, with a respectful nod of his head. "I have

come here to speak with Erishkegal, and to find my companions, who came here before me."

"Follow me," the central figure replied stoically, turning quietly, and starting back towards the temple-structure.

Friedrich glanced towards Asa'an, who had a nervous expression on her face, and then followed after the three spirits that had greeted their arrival. The Peri glided along at his side, her eyes unable to hide her rising apprehension.

The two pylons were like gigantic, rectangular slabs of granite, evoking a sense of determined strength where they abutted the wide span of columns. Friedrich had only a moment to gaze upon the pylons from close proximity before they passed beneath the roof supported by the columns.

Visible on the pylon facings at close range were a series of carvings, looking to Friedrich's eyes like the script of an ancient tongue. They were intermingled with other markings like those on the golden bands seen on the inner side of the gates. He wished he knew what they meant.

Friedrich and the others passed through a few ranks of wide, obsidian columns, which each had a number of thin, crystalline veins winding their way from the bases to the tops. Deep inside of the columns were two enormous doors, each displaying several resplendent bands of gold, the surfaces of which were inlaid with intricate symbols. The towering doors parted slowly as the party approached, swinging inward at a smooth, controlled pace.

Another human-looking figure, much taller than the three who had greeted the visitors, strode forward. Friedrich's head did not even reach the stately being's midsection.

Dark-skinned, with gleaming, silver eyes, the figure was clad in ceremonious-looking golden robes that flowed all the way to the ground. Its head was bare, making its pair of large ears, each culminating in sharp points at the apex, stand out prominently where they framed its long face.

A single, circular earring of gold adorned each ear, while a thick torque of the same lustrous material ringed its neck. The surface of the torque had some sort of markings worked into it, though Friedrich could not make out the details.

Though broad of shoulder, the figure was of a modest build, neither lean, nor particularly brawny. It moved with a regal air, with its head carried high and its posture firm and erect.

The three robed figures escorting them were immediately deferential to the newcomer, bowing their heads low, and keeping their eyes fixed rigidly towards the ground. Friedrich did not have to wait long to learn the being's identity, or what it was.

"Welcome to Egalkurzagin, travelers from the realms above. I am Namtar, Vizier of Queen Erishkegal, and one of the Nephilim who crossed the Veil with her before the foundation of Manzazu," the being addressed them in a low, velvety tone that conveyed both elegance and authority.

Taking a cue from the others native to the realm, Friedrich gave a low bow to the figure in return, and replied, "I am Friedrich, a dweller of the Middle Lands, and this is Asa'an, of the Peris. The Gryphon bore us through the Abyss, in search of this place. We only seek audience with Erishkegal, and to find the others who set forth with us on the journey."

"I will take you to our Queen without delay. She is expecting you, as word was sent ahead of your arrival from the gates," Namtar responded.

Led by the robed trio, and Namtar at their head, Friedrich, Asa'an, and the Gryphon proceeded through the entrance to the structure. They strode into the midst of a grand chamber lying just beyond.

A great, circular dais rose from the floor in the center of the capacious room. Large braziers set on pedestals were placed at even distances all around the outskirts of the chamber. The burnished vessels all cast forth a light blue illumination, which was of a spectral, shimmering essence, rather than a more elemental source such as flame.

Striding towards them, from the bottom of the dais, was a tall woman of exquisite beauty. Her aquiline nose harmonized with a comely face, balanced perfectly in its features. Her olive-toned skin was unmarked by scar or any other imperfection, and held a youthful vitality and sheen. Dark, lustrous hair cascaded gracefully over her shoulders. She was clad in a simple, elegant garment, which like a silken tunic of the purest white. Her eyes were of a brilliant blue, those of an Avatar, and Friedrich knew her identity at once.

Despite her incredible beauty, Erishkegal's expression was severe, without even a trace of good humor or welcome. Her layered, melodious voice did nothing to lighten the tense air about her, as she addressed them.

"First Inanna, then Enki, with many human souls, Peris, and

Gryphons, and now the three of you. It seems that many have suddenly gained interest in my domain, after these long ages where we were left to ourselves," Erishkegal stated. "Well, you have found your way to my realm, Manzazu, and now stand in the heart of Egalkurzagin, before me … and you will be given the chance to get used to this domain."

While not cold, her tone was anything but friendly, and Friedrich could feel her gaze boring hotly into him. There was a strange intensity to the gaze, as if she was searching for answers to some long-vexing question.

His spirit was nonetheless buoyed by the mention of Enki and the others, though he was very surprised to hear the name of one who had not been with them; the one Erishkegal had called Inanna.

His curiosity about Inanna was secondary, though. As with the giant Neti, warding the Seventh Gate, he wanted to find out just how many human souls had arrived with the group. A part of him feared the answer, as he had been parted from the others during the violent storm of Galla. It was more than possible that one or more of his friends had fallen to the Void. Yet as much as he did not want to learn of fallen comrades, the lingering uncertainty about the matter was just as tormenting.

"What foolishness to enter the Abyss, and leave the Middle Lands and realms of Adonai behind," Erishkegal commented, with a sharp tone of admonishment, glowering at Friedrich and Asa'an. "What recklessness came over you, to embrace such witless folly."

Friedrich wanted no part of an argument with Erishkegal, but he felt the duty to respond, in the face of her unmistakable tone of accusation. At the very least, he wanted to uphold his part in the journey.

"As for myself, and the other humans and Peris, we only came to assist Enki on the journey," Friedrich said, careful to maintain a subdued, deferential manner. "Being from the Middle Lands, and imperfect, we had abilities that Enki did not, as a being of the Pure Light."

"Abilities in the nether regions, where an Avatar from above is obstructed in many ways," Erishkegal replied evenly, as if understanding Friedrich's claim. "Though not all, evidently."

Her last comment eluded Friedrich's understanding at first, and he wondered at her meaning.

"Inanna was able to find my realm," Erishkegal said, as if responding to his unvoiced question. "Though she paid a great and terrible price to do so. No Avatar is safe when treading the Abyss. Things you cannot imagine dwell in the deep dark. Not even Mikael, Metaraon, or any of the greatest of Adonai would be assured safe passage through the abyssal regions."

The mention of Inanna once again grabbed powerfully at Friedrich. He had thought that the search within the Abyss was strictly a personal undertaking of Enki's.

He could hear echoes of cavernous sorrows and biting anger within Erishkegal's voice, as she spoke of Inanna. A flicker of something gentler then broke through her storm-ridden countenance, if only for the brevity of an instant.

It was then that Friedrich remembered Enki's references to another individual, when they had spoken together back in the Middle Lands regarding the desire to find Erishkegal. He had little doubt that Inanna was that very being, and that the Avatar had taken it upon herself to find Erishkegal, and spare Enki from his abiding pain and longing.

Perhaps she too had a bond similar to Enki's, in relation to Erishkegal. It did not take long for Erishkegal to confirm his speculations.

"She meant to find me, and return back to the realms above, knowing that Enki had finally determined to search the Abyss. She had her own reasons as well," Erishkegal continued, somberly. "For this ill-fated choice, she now finds herself on the cusp of the Void. An Avatar took the path of a fool, dweller of the Middle Lands."

Friedrich perceived a harsher anger within the Avatar before him, directed towards everyone involved in the quest to find her domain. He gained the distinct sense that Erishkegal was entirely content dwelling within her shadowy domain, and was not at all pleased by the recent intrusions.

"We mean no offense to you, great Erishkegal," Asa'an said in a placating fashion, speaking for the first time. Her voice sounded tiny in the wake of Erishkegal's regal, multi-layered tones, but the Peri's timbre did not waver as she spoke to the great Avatar. Knowing how timid the Peri usually was when it came to Avatars, Friedrich recognized the great courage Asa'an was displaying at the moment. "Friedrich speaks truly, we only desired to aid great Enki in his search for your realm. We had no other purpose, and to my eyes, it was love of you that drove Enki into the dark depths. Of great Inanna, I cannot speak, as I have not been in her company."

"Little Peri, has the path of your kind led beyond the gates of the White City?" Erishkegal asked, her eyes seeming to flare brighter, as she focused her full attention upon Asa'an.

There was a caustic edge to the Avatar's voice, as she laid bare the most sensitive matter possible for one of the Peris. Friedrich could not help but feel a little resentment towards the Avatar, as he had no doubts that Erishkegal already knew the answer, and was simply throwing the past transgressions of Asa'an in the little creature's face. Asa'an did not cower under the withering gaze and lancing question, but Friedrich could see the strain escalating in the little one's face.

"Not yet, great Erishkegal. Our offense was great, so long ago, and not a single one of us deserves forgiveness. It is only by Adonai's Mercy that we have been allowed the Grace of the Middle Lands," Asa'an replied softly, her expression contrite. Friedrich's heart ached as he saw the deep pain coming over Asa'an, as she addressed the past that had brought so much shame and burden to her, and all her kind.

"And a Mercy it was, given your service to the Adversary," Erishkegal responded, more severely. "You, who rejected the Great Throne, and threw in your lot with the Miscreant who would usurp the One who had given life to all of us. You, who willingly served the will of the First of Liars, who erected a throne of wickedness, and relishes the torment of all who love Adonai."

Asa'an said nothing in reply to the brutal chastisement, merely nodding quickly, and bowing her head towards the floor. Friedrich could see her little form begin to tremble, and heard the light patter as her tears fell upon the smooth floor beneath, pooling and glistening.

The Peri suddenly pitched over, bracing herself on her hands as she collapsed and her knees hit the floor. Her shoulders shook with her heaves and sobs, and her delicate wings drooped over her sides. Never before had Friedrich seen Asa'an so utterly miserable and weary, as her inner pain was laid bare.

He wished with all his spirit that he could do something to bring comfort to her. Yet he knew that until the day Asa'an stepped through the gates of the White City, the inner torment she unceasingly struggled with could not be eliminated.

"We are very sorry, great Erishkegal, for any disturbance or offence we may have caused, for none was intended," Friedrich then interjected, gently, adopting a little of Asa'an's custom. He hoped only that he could bring an end to Erishkegal's interrogation of the Peri, as he knew the little being was at her breaking point and could withstand no more. "And we thank you for allowing us to enter your realm, and have this audience with you."

Erishkegal stared at the Peri for a moment longer, and Friedrich did not miss the disgust in the Avatar's expression. As shrouded and menacing as Erishkegal's dominion may have appeared, the Exile understood clearly there was no place within it for even a trace of the Adversary. It was obvious that she bore a fierce, unceasing animosity towards Diabolos, and any that would bend knee to the Shining One. In the Avatar's eyes, Asa'an was merely one of the latter, no matter how contrite she professed to be now.

"You will come to regret the moment you descended into the Abyss," Erishkegal countered sharply, her gaze shifting to Friedrich. "Ages ago, I came here out of a desperate necessity, but have never forgotten the nature of the Abyss. Do not forget, for even a moment, that you are in a pit that consumes all light."

"I would have regretted it far more to abandon Enki in his time of need and pain," Friedrich replied, relieved that Asa'an was spared from further assault. The Peri was still crying, but her body was not shaking as intensely as before. "I will accept whatever comes in this place, but I do not regret my choice to help Enki on this journey. If it leads to the Void, I will trust to Adonai when the End of Days comes."

Erishkegal's blazing eyes remained solely fixed upon Friedrich for a few moments, as she silently regarded him, before slowly nodding.

"You have wisdom, Exile," she replied. "But it does not dismiss the foolishness of Enki or the quest that you followed him into."

Erishkegal swerved her gaze back towards the Peri, and Friedrich tensed, fearing a renewed onslaught. Asa'an could not see the Avatar, as her head was still down, and her face hidden under tangles of hair.

"Help your friend," Erishkegal directed. "But know that the weight that bore her down is one that she brought upon herself at the dawn of time."

Friedrich moved to the side of the Peri, stooping down.

"I cannot … rise," Asa'an said, stammering. "I … am … too weak."

"Then I will bear you," Friedrich said, gently lifting the Peri up to where he could carry the small being cradled in his arms.

"To the Gryphon," Asa'an said, in a whisper.

Friedrich walked over slowly to the Gryphon, and lifted Asa'an up to its back. He tenderly assisted the Peri, helping her into a sitting position.

"I ... will ... be fine," Asa'an replied, looking at him with eyes glimmering with heart-wrenching sadness.

Friedrich turned back towards Erishkegal, knowing they had not yet been dismissed from her presence. She was staring at him with an unreadable expression, and he wondered what thoughts occupied her mind.

"Go now, to Enki," she said in a commanding tone. "Soon, you will all be summoned before my Anunnaki Tribunal, my judges of the Seven Thrones. Your fates will be determined then. Namtar, we are finished."

At her words, Namtar strode forward, bowed low to Erishkegal, and then beckoned for Friedrich and his companions to follow him. Friedrich walked behind Namtar, with the Gryphon keeping pace just behind. Erishkegal remained in place, and her gaze remained on the visitors until they had departed her audience chamber.

Namtar led them around the huge dais, on the right side of the chamber, and continued forward to where a doorway was set into the back wall. An extended passage stretched beyond the portal, lighted by periodic sconces set into the side walls.

Proceeding through several long passageways, and passing many closed doorways, Friedrich and his companions were guided to the far reaches of the Sanctum.

Namtar slowed when their forward path was blocked by a large set of double doors. With a single gesture from the Vizier, the doors swung outward. Their opening revealed the sight of a drifting, unbroken mass of storm clouds, as an icy tendril of wind lanced down the passageway. The Vizier guided them through the portal, and, at last, they were in the open air once again.

A wide platform was spread before them, which came to an abrupt end a short distance ahead. There was no kind of railing or barrier to protect someone from walking right off the edge. A brisk gust of wind whipped about the platform for a few moments, and then ebbed, leaving a subdued, pensive atmosphere in its wake.

Two massive, winged creatures turned at their emergence. Their dark-feathered bodies were those of great eagles, while their heads were akin to lions, down to the thick manes that framed their feline visages. Gleaming talons, each of which looked as if they had been honed to maximum sharpness on a whetstone, clacked on the stony surface, as the

323

creatures oriented themselves squarely towards the group.

A fierce look blazed in their cat-like eyes as they regarded the newcomers escorted by Namtar, but they showed no sign of hostility towards Friedrich, Asa'an, or the Gryphon. Friedrich had no doubts that such creatures could eviscerate a spirit-body in little time, using their wicked-looking talons to send an enemy into the timeless sleep within the Void.

"The Anzu will take you from here to Enki, who is not far," Namtar said, while indicating the two winged creatures gazing back at them. "Ningishzida will find you, when Eriskhegal summons the Anunnaki Tribunal to the Great Mount."

"The Anunnaki Tribunal?" Friedrich asked.

"The Seven she has empowered to judge all matters concerning Manzazu," Namtar answered evenly. "Go and avail yourself of the time you have been given by her, as I cannot say when the summons will come."

The idea of being summoned before a judgement council sparked a feeling of unease that spread fast throughout Friedrich's spirit. He nodded quietly to Erishkegal's Vizier, and walked over to the Gryphon, getting onto its back and sitting tall as he prepared himself for the impending flight.

Asa'an shifted and settled in just behind Friedrich a moment later, pulling herself closer to him. A quick backward glance showed him that Namtar had already departed their company, heading back through the doorway into the Sanctum. The double doors finished closing as he watched, shutting tight without a sound.

The pair of Anzu stretched their wings, giving the prodigious, feathery appendages a couple of flaps before lifting off from the surface. The Gryphon followed the Anzu, as the group flew outward from the mesa.

Friedrich was given his first look at what lay beyond the far side, opposite the one with the pylon-flanked entrance to the Sanctum. His eyes were drawn immediately towards an incredible, and unexpected, sight, taking in the horizon now fully exposed to his vision after it had been obscured from his vantage back at the seventh gate.

Hugged by a low, roiling mist, a choppy, undulating sea lashed powerfully at an extensive, rocky beachfront. Two towering mountains, like grand pylons of an ancient temple, flanked the far ends of the lengthy beach.

Propelled rapidly through the skies with rhythmic flaps of their broad wings, the Anzu led them directly towards the beach area. After taking in the spectacular nature of the view, Friedrich began to hone his attention upon the smaller details within the scene. It did not take long for his gaze to be drawn towards a singular, bright element within an environment consisting predominantly of ash-gray rocks, darker mists, and ubiquitous shadows.

Standing near the edge of the sea, where the waves crashed thunderously into the shore, was the multi-winged form of Enki. His blazing celestial body contrasted starkly with the darker, angry surroundings. The Avatar was clarity amongst cacophony, his image a luminous beacon in the midst of the shadowy murk.

The Gryphon angled downward, towards Enki, descending from the heights. The Anzu remained behind them, turning away finally and flapping speedily back towards Egalkurzagin, apparently recognizing that their task was finished. The Gryphon alighted on an open patch of ground, not far from the Avatar.

Friedrich dismounted the Gryphon, and turned to look at Asa'an, concerned about her condition. She looked much better, having rallied significantly during the flight. Friedrich imagined that being removed from Erishkegal's presence was more than a little helpful in that regard.

"I can fly again," Asa'an said as he looked up to her, giving him a smile that brought gladness to his heart. Her eyes still carried sadness, but some of her liveliness had returned.

Friedrich returned the smile, turned, and started towards Enki as Asa'an flitted behind him. The Gryphon followed a few paces after them in silence. The Avatar turned away from the frothing sea, and looked upon the three with his blazing eyes as they approached.

"Enki, I am so glad to see you!" Friedrich exclaimed, casting formalities aside, and flooding with relief and euphoria at his reunion with the familiar Avatar. Drifting within the spectral boundaries of the Ten-Fold Kingdom, the moment that he was now experiencing had seemed impossible to attain.

"As am I, great Enki," Asa'an added, though her words were not spoken as casually as Friedrich's, as she maintained the deferential tone she used when addressing the greater Avatars.

"And it fills me with joy to see the three of you here, unharmed," Enki responded, the brightness of his form surging a little in intensity.

"None have been lost. We are all here now … secure in her realm."

"It is only by Adonai's Grace that we made it here," Friedrich responded, relief flooding him at the news that all had survived, and thinking of the perilous route they had somehow managed to navigate. Looking back on the harrowing experiences, Friedrich thought the fact that he was standing before Enki a miracle in itself.

"As with all of us," Enki replied, with a stoic edge.

"We have been through much," Friedrich said. "And there are some things we came across that I think you would like to know."

"And I would hear of it, every detail," Enki said, looking between the Exile and Peri, as if he sensed something of their incredible foray.

"This is a dark place," Friedrich commented, looking out upon the turbulent sea, with the shadowy mists clinging so close to the surface. He wondered what existed farther out in the waters, as nothing could be seen beyond a short distance from the shore.

"Yet it is not an evil one, though there are many great mysteries about this realm," Enki stated. "And many unwelcome revelations."

There was a curious lilt to the Avatar's last words, and Friedrich did not miss the sorrow that coursed through them.

"What did you find here, Enki?" Friedrich asked, in a low, hesitant tone.

"Things about this place that I would not have thought possible, and a burden that is mine own to bear," Enki replied. The brightness of his form ebbed, mirroring the melancholic atmosphere that had come over the conversation.

"We are not the only ones that undertook this quest, are we?" Friedrich asked, having a strong intimation as to what Enki was getting at.

Enki said nothing at first, but Friedrich could feel the swirling, powerful emotions that his words had sparked in the Avatar.

"Inanna sought this place too," Friedrich stated, in a cautious voice, hoping that he did not unintentionally provoke Enki to anger. "We heard of this from Erishkegal."

"Inanna," Enki repeated heavily, and the utterance of her name carried a deep sense of sorrow.

"I am sorry for mentioning her," Friedrich said, regretting that he had brought the matter up.

"She is here, and Erishkegal holds me to blame for her presence,"

Enki said. "Erishkegal has Inanna confined, and I fear that something is terribly wrong. She will not allow me to go to her."

"Confined? Another Avatar of Adonai?" Friedrich questioned, with a hint of disbelief that an Avatar of Adonai could do such a thing to another.

"I do not sense that it is a confinement like one who is imprisoned," Enki said. "It is more like she has hidden Inanna from me, and I feel in my spirit that something has gone terribly wrong."

"How can you find out?" Friedrich queried.

"We will be called before the Seven Thrones soon enough," Enki said. "I believe we will gain the answers we seek then."

"We were told that this ... tribunal ... holds authority over the entire realm," Friedrich said. "Were these the seven great ones that were said to have aided Kur in gathering the Nephilim who rejected the ways of their progenitors?"

"Aside from Kur, the seven strongest of the Nephilim to cross the Veil ward the seven gates. The seven who were given thrones on the Anunnaki Tribunal were deemed by Erishkegal to have the greatest wisdom and forbearance, well-suited to be judges to administer her new dominion."

"And their judgement can be enforced on one such as you?" Friedrich asked, incredulous.

"Many of the Nephilim here are stronger than I am. Do not forget their heritage, Friedrich, as they have the power of Avatars within them," Enki said. "And the long ages have seen Erishkegal increase in her own strength. This realm surrounding you is testament to just how powerful she has become. I am at the mercy of her judgement, and that of her tribunal, as much as any of you are."

Friedrich could not think of any argument to Enki's words. While austere, Erishkegal's realm was something to behold, and he reminded himself that it was her exercise of power, and hers alone, that had brought it into existence.

She had called her dominion into being out of the substance of the Abyss, molding and shaping it into the vivid landscapes that he had witnessed. She had forged a refuge and haven for the motley throng of outcasts facing a storm-generated doom, and the undertaking involved was far beyond monumental.

As dismal as its appearance was, Friedrich also had to remind himself that everything he saw was an expression of mercy. It was a place that testified to compassion, and ultimately he had to trust that those kinds of things still coursed underneath the daunting exteriors.

"Then I will have to place trust in the wisdom of these judges, and the wisdom of the one who empowered them," Friedrich said.

"As will I," Enki said. The Avatar turned his gaze back out towards the frothing sea.

"What brings you to this place, in particular?" questioned Friedrich. "What is beyond that ocean?"

Enki made no reply, continuing to stare outward. Friedrich did not press the Avatar, sensing that he had touched upon one of the mysteries concerning Erishkegal's realm.

A freezing gust blasted in from the ocean, enveloping Friedrich and the others. It bore no resemblance to a natural phenomenon, like the things surrounding him. It could even be seen rushing towards them, as a faint, shimmering light outlined its prodigious mass.

He shivered violently in its frigid embrace, feeling as if the spectral wind speared right through the essence of his spirit. It was a horrid, invasive feeling, and he was greatly relieved when the lurid sensation passed quickly.

"That chill is the lightest touch of a far, far worse place," Enki commented. "A faint wisp escapes a maelstrom … but for now, keep your eyes upon the waters."

They fell into an extended silence, watching the waves continue to thunder into the rocks. After some time had passed, a strange sight occurred. Soaked and lethargic, a lone figure was carried along one of the incoming waves, and flopped heavily onto the gritty shoreline.

The figure was emaciated, with a cadaverous pall to the surface of its clammy skin. It had a human backside, and was entirely naked, exhibiting a gruesome array of scars, gouges, and sores all over.

Slowly, the figure began scrabbling weakly at the harsh surface, trying without success to get up. It gasped as it raised its head to peer around the beach. The being had a man's countenance, with a long, bearded face, haggard and gaunt.

The signs of violence were visible all over the spirit's face as well. Friedrich knew that the ocean had not produced the awful markings. The man had endured something terrible, of a nature unimaginable. His eyes were dull and glassy, very much like the eyes of the dead that Friedrich had seen far too often in his physical life.

"Do not dwell upon darker thoughts," Enki admonished in a low voice, as if Friedrich's inner thoughts had been words voiced in the open.

"Should we go to him?" Friedrich asked.

"Keep up your observance. Aid will come to that soul. It is important that you bear witness to this," Enki instructed him.

As if emerging from places of concealment, several others came into view, hastening down the beach towards the new arrival. All were human spirits, with the bald-headed, dark-robed appearances of the ones that Friedrich had encountered atop the mesa, at the entrance to the Sanctum. They gathered all around the prone man, lowering down and helping him with great care up to his feet.

The man's balance was shaky, and he would have fallen in an instant without assistance, but with the help of the other figures he was able to move away from the shoreline. The attending beings were patient and gentle. Initially, it seemed strange that they did not just carry him, but Friedrich gradually got the impression that it was important that the man walk on his own, as much as possible.

"What is that?" Friedrich asked, deeply perplexed by the strange scene that had transpired.

"Something that I did not expect when we set out on this journey," Enki answered firmly.

"The man on the shore was a spirit like me?" Friedrich inquired. "A human spirit? And the ones in the Sanctum and out there helping him?"

"Yes," Enki confirmed. "All of them are human spirits."

"But I thought that Erishkegal left the world with only the Nephilim that had rejected the ways of their brethren," Friedrich countered. "Nothing was said of any others going across the Veil with her."

"She did cross with only Nephilim," Enki said. "The human souls that you see were not part of that exodus so long ago."

"Then where did they come from?" Friedrich asked, growing ever more confused.

"The realms of Diabolos," Enki stated rigidly.

The implications hung thickly in the air between the Avatar and human soul, and Friedrich recognized quickly why Enki sounded so pensive about the matter. Souls claimed by Diabolos, and confined to the hellish worlds of the Ten-Fold kingdom, were understood to be irreparably doomed. It was common knowledge that there was no escape for a condemned soul claimed by the Shining One.

Yet if the human souls that he saw were from the infernal regions, then something very unusual involving Erishkegal's realm was transpiring. He saw at once why Enki had referred earlier to great mysteries.

The event on the beach was plainly as confounding to the Avatar as it was to Friedrich. The idea that something could thoroughly mystify an Avatar was both surprising and dispiriting to the Exile.

"There are many thousands of them dwelling within her domain," Enki commented.

"But ... how did they get free?" Friedrich queried.

"A tremendous mystery, as of now. But it is plain that they wash up on her shores, and are given refuge," Enki responded. "Who am I to question this? A thing such as this could not happen outside of Adonai's Will."

"Mercy," Friedrich stated suddenly.

Enki turned, and quietly regarded Friedrich for a moment, staring down at him intently, with his fiery, celestial eyes.

"As with Seele, mercy is being shown, even if we do not understand the individual instances of it," Friedrich said. "Erishkegal showed mercy to the Nephilim who were not supposed to survive, according to the understanding of others. Is it not fitting that souls believed to be irretrievable find their way to a place of sanctuary here? Is this not a vision of hope?"

"Wisdom has grown strong within you," Enki responded. "And there would be a rapturous joy all across Adonai's realm over even one soul salvaged from the grip of Diabolos. But this was hidden from me, and likely all of the Avatars.

"I do not comprehend it, but if Adonai has provided a path for even those that the wisdom of Avatars perceives to be ill-fated to eternal ruin, then I am filled with thanksgiving and celebration."

"Once, reading the Sacred Writings, I wondered at the original language that spoke of a sentence of eons for those forbidden Adonai's realms, turned over to the Jailer, or cast into perdition. An eon is a measurement of time, and is not the same as eternity," Friedrich said. "I never got an answer, when I asked a few priests about it, but are not all things possible with Adonai?"

"You are full of many surprises, Precious Soul," Enki remarked.

Enki then started forward, his lengthy strides carrying him away from the beach swiftly.

"Come, there is important work to be done here, or we will not be leaving this place," Enki called back to Friedrich, who had remained in place.

At that moment, the two little creatures that had been the very last to join their group at the edge of the Middle Lands darted into view. As before, they alighted on Enki's shoulder area, and appeared to fuse with his fiery body.

"Why would we not leave this place?" Friedrich asked, hurrying to catch up to the Avatar. "You mean ever?"

"As I have told you, we will not leave if Erishkegal will not allow us. The moment you saw human souls in her Sanctum was the moment your confinement here began," Enki replied solemnly. "Not even I have the power to break out of here. Not with the strength she has gathered and built since the founding of this place."

The pronouncement doused the budding feelings of levity that had arisen after learning of his companions' survival and the acts of mercy along the shoreline.

He looked around at the dismal surroundings, his spirit quailing at the notion of being effectively incarcerated within Erishkegal's shadowy domain. As if accentuating his spike of fear, a dazzling wave of lightning raced through the cloud masses far above.

"Confined? Here? In this awful place?" Asa'an whispered at his side, where she was gliding alongside.

"Not the news I was hoping to hear, after what we have been through," Friedrich replied grimly to the Peri.

"I don't want to stay here until the End of Days," Asa'an said, and he could hear the trace of panic rising in her tone.

"I certainly don't either. Let's just hope Enki has some ideas about getting out of here," Friedrich said, as they followed the Avatar.

# MADISON

Behind the converging TTDF agents, another set of beings advanced. At first, they trotted upon furry legs, and their approach drew no attention.

One was one a Golden Retriever, bounding across the front lawns of the homes lining the streets. Another was a brown and white tabby mix, padding through the shadows, as it kept to the contours of the houses themselves. A third was a trundling basset hound, lengthy ears flopping as it carried its low-profile, stocky body down the sidewalk.

The troopers paid the creatures little heed. To them, they were just simple pets from the neighborhood, drawn in by the beacon of activity. Barely a glance was cast in their direction, as the government forces kept their focus upon the operation that was well-underway.

None of them took notice that the animals, coming from different directions, were heading towards one house in particular.

# SETH

At the epicenter of the comprehensive operation, troopers of the TTDF swarmed Seth's house from all sides. There were no military or police personnel involved, as the teenager's house had been designated for special assignment by the CSD authorities.

Seth, Jonathan, Raymond, and Annika heard the distinctive rotors of a helicopter chopping the air, low over the house. The sounds erupted just before a host of light rays filtered through the ground-level windows opening into the den, where they were gathered together. The four were hanging out on the semi-circular arrangement of couches, idly watching a movie on Seth's parents' home theater system. Seth grabbed the remote control and clicked the television off, as the lights swept across the carpet and furniture.

Seth's heart caught in his throat and he felt a chill as he heard the front door being pounded on forcefully, and the startled voices of his parents as they moved to respond. Sharp voices of authority barked at his parents from the outside, and in seconds the tromping of booted feet filled his ears, as his home was invaded.

"Seth, and everyone else downstairs, come up here," his mother's shaky voice called. Something terrible was happening, and there was no escaping it.

Seth looked over to his friends. All of them had fear in their eyes as they got to their feet. His legs felt unsteady, as he started across the carpet towards the short staircase leading up to the main, ground level of the house.

"We're coming up," he called out.

"Come up slowly, and with your hands raised up!" ordered an unseen, masculine voice.

Seth stepped out from the top stair and found himself before the barrels of several submachine guns, looking into the expressionless face visors of several troopers. His mother and father were a few feet away, standing close together, unspoken questions perched on their faces as they gazed towards their son. His friends came up from behind. All of them had their hands high in the air as they had been instructed.

"Seth Engel ... Annika Schoen ... Raymond Danner ... Jonathan St. George," one of the TTDF troopers addressed them. "You have been engaged in activities that are in violation of martial law governing this region. You have been declared threats to national security, and we are here to apprehend you. Do not resist."

Everything was a dizzying blur as black-booted troopers stomped forward and Seth was forced down to the floor along with his companions. His hands were yanked down and cuffed behind his back, before he was hauled roughly back up to his feet.

"What has my son done?" Seth heard his father question, his tone filled with incredulity and shock.

"He and his companions have been engaged in illegal activity," was the curt reply from the trooper.

"Where are you taking him?" Seth's mother pressed.

"That information is not to be disclosed," the trooper said.

"You can't just do that! He has not been convicted of anything!" Seth's father challenged. Seth could hear the rising anger in his dad's voice, and knew that if he did not stop his father it would end badly.

"Dad, don't argue with them, I'll be fine. Just cooperate. Please don't make it any worse," Seth urged his father as he was spun around and shoved towards the front door.

"Keep your hands off my son!" Seth's mother snapped.

"Shut your mouths, or you will go with them!" riposted the trooper that was the apparent spokesperson for the others.

"Mom, dad, don't get in their way!" Seth called emphatically over his shoulder.

"You bastards!" his father's voice shouted, and Seth heard his mother cry out as the sounds of a scuffle broke out behind him.

His heart sank, as he knew that his dad had abandoned all reason. A mild-mannered man, his father was the type of person that exploded with anger whenever he was finally pushed past a certain edge. Seth knew that his father had rolled right over that boundary, and had done something ill-advised.

Seth heard the frenzied shouts of the troopers as they subdued his parents. The noise of scuffling and thumps made him livid, as he knew the thuggish troopers were being unnecessarily rough with his mother and father.

Seth and his friends were unceremoniously herded into the front yard, which was ringed by troopers and several military vehicles. A helicopter roved the skies overhead, a blinding searchlight trained on the doomed property, illuminating the entire front yard.

The sight of his parents being pushed forward, handcuffed, from the front door of their own house, was an appalling vision, which both enraged and saddened him to a great degree. They had no criminal record whatsoever and neither had spent so much as a single night in jail.

His father cast him a plaintive glance, as his mother sobbed heavily, still dressed in her pajamas, robe, and slippers. He could see the confusion written on both of their faces, and guilt nagged at him, as he knew that it was his own actions that had brought terrible misfortune upon his own parents.

Before they took another step, a brilliant light flooded the area. It was not from the TTDF, as the cries, shouts of surprise, and the ensuing rattle of gunfire attested. Seth winced at the explosion of radiance. Spots danced before his eyes, his vision struggling to regain clarity.

He could barely follow the events that followed. Bodies of TTDF troopers flew through the air, several at a time. More than one entity of immense size blazed through the forces surrounding the house. The huge shapes, outlined by light from within, were very hard to focus on. They moved with incredible speed. Their strength was stunning to behold as they barreled into the TTDF ranks and ran down fleeing troopers with ease.

Seth caught a few glimpses of the attackers as they ripped through vehicles and soldiers alike. Thuds, screams, and gunfire were mixed with deafening roars and bellows that cleaved through to the depths of Seth's spirit. The latter sounds were otherworldly, sounding like hundreds of creatures in each terrifying intonation, and certainly like no animal that naturally tread the surface of Terra.

He realized that the attacking creatures were winged, and that their basic shapes were like nothing he had ever seen before. They had large, four-legged lower bodies, with human-like torsos flowing up in a smooth continuum.

At any other time, Seth would have guessed that such creatures would move awkwardly, but these entities moved with exquisite balance and grace as they tore through the TTDF troops. They were quite simply fearsome sights to witness, storms of power unleashed under the starry night skies.

The hackles rose on Seth's neck as he watched one that had a broad, bull's head run down three troopers. It caught them in just a few strides and trampled them brutally. The sounds of bones being snapped and crushed as the troopers were pulverized with the creature's massive hooves was like nothing that Seth had ever heard before. Nauseous and jittery in the aftermath, he wished that he could do something to block the awful noises out.

Vehicles were uplifted, and thrown over, as if they weighed nothing, and all sense of order broke down as TTDF troopers, en masse, ceased resistance and began running for their lives. It was a futile effort, as the enormous assailants raced about, catching each and every one of the government troops before they could get very far from the security perimeter they had established.

The ones that tried to hide were uprooted from their places of concealment, as terror-stricken screams pierced the night. To Seth, it appeared that there were about four main attackers involved in the growing carnage, though he could not keep his eyes trained on any of them for very long, with the extreme alacrity of their movements.

His eyes lifted upward, as he saw one of the shapes take to flight, multiple pairs of luminous wings spread outward as it streaked towards the helicopter overhead. A few moments later, the helicopter's rotors went from rhythmic, confident beats to a tinny, unstable whine, just before the aircraft tumbled haphazardly out of the sky. A loud explosion shook the ground, as the helicopter crashed far out of Seth's view, a fiery flash of light filling the air above the impact area.

Seth looked back, and saw two of the rampaging creatures entering the house. The screen door and front door were both ripped off their hinges and discarded, and somehow the huge pair managed to force their large bodies through the entryway.

The sudden eruption of gunfire from within the house told him that a few TTDF troops had taken refuge there during the struggle. The guns fell silent seconds later, and Seth did not even want to imagine the fates of the troopers that had been holding them. As much as he bore a smoldering hatred in his heart towards them for what they had done, especially in regard to his parents, he could not help but feel a little pity.

A ponderous silence settled over the scene, as Seth began to look around, and take hold of his own faculties. He, his friends, and his parents were the only humans left alive. The bodies of TTDF troopers were scattered all around them, and not all of them were intact, as Seth's eyes fell upon one sickening sight after another.

The troopers, with all of their weapons and technology, had fared poorly, standing no chance against their bizarre assailants; a couple of which now stood out in the open, staring down at the bound, huddled survivors. One of them was very close to Seth, and with his hands secured behind his back, he felt completely helpless. If dozens of TTDF troopers in body armor with submachine guns were torn and broken in moments, Seth and the others were fully at the mercy of the strange beasts.

Seth gasped in shock as he took in the sight of the huge, multi-winged creature, a monstrosity with a multitude of eyes. He stood in place, stupefied, as he peered into the lion-like face of the deadly entity looming just paces before him. A freezing terror raced through his veins, stifling his breath, as panic and anxiety swelled inside.

"If you remain here, you will die, or be taken to be imprisoned and tortured," the creature announced suddenly, with an incredible vocal quality, like many individual voices harmonized together. The creature's choral voice was melodious and soothing to Seth's ears, and he found the worst of his fears ebbing.

The last thing that Seth had expected was for the creature to speak in his own language. It took him a moment to regain his composure, following the initial shock.

"What … are you?" Seth mustered, with great effort. Though he was no longer in the throes of panic and fear, he was far from comfortable in the presence of the lethal monstrosity.

"A Watcher, of an Order in service to Adonai Most High," the creature replied. "My name is Talthannor."

Seth did not like his options, as he effectively did not have any, other than to discover the intent of the winged beasts. But he had no doubts regarding the intentions of the troopers with their black visors and body armor.

They had come to his home in a spirit of hostility, and the creatures had intervened with deadly force. Were it not for the entity before him, and its comrades, Seth and everyone else in his home would have been whisked off to incarceration; probably confined in the very same place he had acquired video of.

At that moment, the other creature remaining outside the house stepped up to the side of Talthannor. It was taller and larger in girth, the great bull-like one that Seth had seen stomping TTDF troopers into the ground with its immense hooves. Its broad horns and hooves glistened, and Seth had no doubts as to what the viscous substance coating them was.

"I am called Utahor," the second creature announced, its voice much lower in tone than Talthannor's.

"Heed my words," Talthannor addressed the humans. "You cannot remain here. The enemy will come here with even greater force. We are here to carry you far from this place. Take with you the objects that brought the enemy to your home."

"My parents," Seth protested, "I cannot leave … "

"They will be taken to a refuge," Talthannor interrupted him. "They can remain here no longer. The danger to them, as to you, is too great."

"What … objects?" Jonathan interjected, shuffling over to Seth's side.

"The testimony that you gained of the evil they are doing to those who are innocent," Talthannor answered. "This is why the soldiers were here, to wipe away the testimony from all who had received it. Evil seeks to do its work in darkness. The testimony you acquired brought their wickedness into the light for all to see."

"The testimony?" Seth asked, still perplexed.

"He means the video," Annika spoke up from just behind him.

Seth nodded, finally understanding. "It's in the house. We have several copies."

"Do not waste time. Go and get the testimony, and return without delay," Talthannor commanded.

"I can't ... there's another problem." Seth said. He hesitated, and then turned sideways, so that Talthannor could see his hands bound tightly behind his back.

Talthannor simply stared towards the handcuffs, bringing a multitude of eyes focusing upon Seth's bindings. He heard the clicks of the locking mechanism, even though no key had been inserted. The handcuffs fell free of his wrists, landing in the grass of his front lawn.

Seth rubbed his wrists vigorously where the metal had bit into his skin, and brought his arms back around to the front. Spasms rippled through his shoulders, released suddenly from their taut position.

One by one, the others were freed in a similar manner.

"Now go, and get the testimony," Talthannor implored Seth.

He headed back towards the house, keeping a little berth between him and the final two Watchers, who had just emerged from the inside. One had eagle-like features, and the other reminded him of the centaurs of myth, though no such creature from those legends possessed so many eyes. He nervously eyed the Watchers looming over him as he reached the porch.

The doorframe had been shattered to bits. Seth's shoes crunched on broken glass, shards of wood, and other debris as he walked through the crudely widened entrance.

He had to step over the remains of the TTDF troopers that had taken cover inside, as he worked his way to his room to get a few of the video discs and mini-drives. His shoes squished with a couple of his steps, and he kept his eyes fixed forward, determined not to look down.

Rooting for a moment in a drawer on his computer desk, he quickly found what he had come for. He put the discs and mini-drives into a small backpack, and slipped his arms through the straps, pulling the buckles snug to secure it.

Starting back down the hallway from his room, he came to an abrupt halt. There was one more matter that he could not forget to attend to.

"Niles," he muttered.

He imagined that the cat had taken cover during all the chaos and tumult. Seth breathed a sigh of relief that he had not been too overwhelmed by the surreal events to forget the final member of his family. There was no way that he could leave the cat to an uncertain fate.

"Niles!" he called out, a little louder. "Where are you Niles? I don't have much time. Help me and come on out."

He moved into his parents' room, and eyed the king-sized bed, knowing that one of the cat's favorite hiding places was beneath it.

"Niles, come on out from there. It's just us here now," Seth said gently. "Nobody else … just me and you."

A soft, plaintive meow came to his ears a moment later, as the bottom of the bed covering rustled, just before the pointy ears and rounded head of Niles came into view. The cat wriggled the rest of the way out, and then arched the back half of his body, as he extended his front paws out, stretching for a couple of seconds. Once limbered up, Niles stepped up to Seth, as his ears rotated and twitched, alert for any sounds of danger.

"I don't blame you for being afraid. I sure was," Seth said, kneeling down and stroking Niles' back a couple of times, before lifting the cat gently into his arms.

Cradling the cat, he turned and found the carrying case they used to transport Niles to the veterinarian. "You would bolt, if you saw what's standing outside," Seth remarked, as he worked to maneuver the cat into the carrying case. Niles meowed with a hint of irritation, and resisted lightly, but Seth managed to get the cat into the case without too much difficulty. He zipped the open end shut. "And I wouldn't blame you. Part of me feels like bolting right now."

Talking to the cat helped ease his raw nerves a little more, and he stood up with a firm grip on the carrying case. He paused to take a couple of deep breaths before he left his parents' bedroom, and continued through the house on his way back to the front lawn.

The quartet of Watchers, his parents, and his friends stared at him as he emerged. More than one eye went to the carrying case, from both humans and Watchers.

"I'm not leaving Niles behind. He's family too," Seth declared, surprised at the resolve in his voice as he looked to the massive creatures. His last words were directed squarely towards them. "He's coming along."

"Give him over to your father and mother, Seth," Talthannor directed, as matter-of-factly as such a layered voice could sound.

Seth was a little surprised, having expected more of an objection from the Watcher, as it was hard enough getting other people to understand how a cat could be considered a family member. He strode over to his father, and handed the carrying case over to him. Inside, Niles mewled nervously and shuffled about, ears splayed and flattened as he peered through the mesh with saucer-wide eyes towards the Watchers.

"It's gonna be alright, Niles," Seth said gently. "Take good care of him, Dad."

"I will, Seth," his father replied.

Seth shared a glance with his mother and father, right before they hugged each other. He could see the fear brimming in his parents' eyes, but felt an emotional sense of pride as he looked to them.

He recognized the courage they were both displaying in keeping up a semblance of composure. The experience they had all just endured involved a tremendous amount to digest, especially so quickly, and Seth's parents were handling it all quite admirably.

"Let us hurry. More of the enemy will arrive soon," Talthannor called from behind.

Under Talthannor's instructions, Seth, his companions, and his parents mounted up on the backs of the four Watchers. Jonathan was assigned to the human-like one, which Seth learned was named Arundinel, and Annika was directed to ride Jakiel, the one with eagle features. The biggest of the four, Utahor would carry both of his parents, Niles, and Raymond.

Though the faces of his parents registered extreme disbelief towards the things that were transpiring, they continued to cooperate fully, as the hard reality of everything could not be denied either. Seth managed to get over to them and embrace them tightly once more, before they got up onto Utahor's wide back.

He watched for a moment as his dad situated the carrying case with Niles in front of him. The cat made a sound that was almost like a human moan, and Seth could not fault his unease.

When all of the humans were mounted up, the Watchers did not tarry a moment longer, as they left the empty house and sprawling scene of carnage behind. Not a soul had emerged from any of the surrounding houses the entire time, and an eerie pall had descended over the ravaged neighborhood.

# TALTHANNOR

Talthannor bounded away, charging into the night. In mere moments he took Seth away from his neighborhood, and it was not long before they were beyond the edge of the town itself.

The two were a blur as they passed, startling animals and humans alike. Dogs loosed startled barks in their wake while humans paused, questioning the reality of the indistinct flash of movement that they witnessed. After enduring the invasion of the security forces into their homes, most of the people consigned the strange vision to their rattled nerves, hoping that the nightmare evening would just come to an end.

Once in the depths of the hilly woods surrounding the town, Talthannor slowed down, but it was only a few moments before his sense of alarm skyrocketed. Every instinct in the Watcher cried out at once, heralding the imminent presence of danger.

A huge shadow flowed along the ground, and over Talthannor's body, followed by several others.

Peering through the branches above, Talthannor espied many distinctive forms outlined by the moon's silvery light. The Enemy was not as unprepared as he had previously thought.

Several winged Nephilim circled in the air above the trees, clearly honing in upon Talthannor's position. Within their midst was one of the greater of their kind, in the unmistakable form of a massive dragon. It glided on its broad, leathery wings, as its elongated neck arched to keep its head oriented towards Talthannor.

The creatures were flying low in altitude, and there was no question that they were shadowing Talthannor's movements through the woodlands. Even as powerful as he was, he knew that there were far too many of the Adversary's beasts, and the dragon alone would have been a very formidable opponent to contend with. A flash of deeper recognition informed him that the particular dragon above had been the one to challenge an Avatar outright, in distant ages, before the Flood had washed the world clean of the Nephilim's unholy presence.

There was only one possible route of escape, as the skies filled with roars and guttural cries, both bestial intonations carrying potent undercurrents of bloodlust and eagerness. Only the harmony within his heart assured the Watcher that the bold notion he grasped onto was not in conflict with Adonai's Will.

Without delaying a moment more, Talthannor built up speed, and concentrated his will on a singular purpose.

# SETH

Fear thrashed Seth's nerves to the point of delirium, as his ears filled with the raucous cries of the winged entities above the trees. They were not allies of the strange creature that now carried him. The Watcher seemed to be taken aback at the emergence of the dark shapes in the sky, and only a couple of moments later had sprung forward with urgency, breaking into a dizzyingly-fast run through the trees.

Despite the tremendous speed, Seth could not fathom how they could evade the flying cluster hunting them. He could hear the salivating anticipation in their shrieks as the monstrosities in the air gave chase, and he dared not look above, clinging to the Watcher as tightly as he could.

Abruptly, he found himself within a total, consuming darkness. The only luminance was from a reddish glow emanating from the very skin of the Watcher.

To his further bewilderment, Seth realized that they were no longer on solid ground. Talthannor's three pairs of wings were outstretched fully just behind him, as if they were gliding through the air of an impenetrable night.

He had the distinct sense that they were moving forward, and gained the unnerving impression that they were suspended over something vast and incomprehensible. Trying as hard as he could, he could see nothing beyond the edge where the blackness swallowed the subtle radiance limning the Watcher.

An oppressive silence reigned everywhere, and the darkness was simply inviolable, a dreadful murk like nothing he had ever experienced. Seth's heart thundered as naked panic spiraled within, and then his eyes were filled with a blinding flash of light.

His focus returned swiftly, bringing him instant relief, as he gazed into a world of staggering wonder. His senses were bombarded to the cusp of being overwhelmed by the bounteous display. An otherworldly, effulgent sky was spread above them, resplendent with all manner of colors, which continuously shifted and changed in intensity and hue.

Below was a landscape filled with gold and blue, cloaked with an abundance of flora whose vividness and nature were far beyond anything to be found on Terra. Like the Watcher, the unusual flowers gave off a light from within, faint, but unmistakable. They swayed slowly, though Seth felt no breezes as they glided over the lavishly-adorned ground.

The Watcher angled downward, heading towards the shore of a lake whose waters were so clear and radiant that the liquid itself seemed to contain the properties of crystal. Several figures were gathered near the water's edge, and as Seth drew closer he saw the other Watchers, along with his three friends. Of his parents, there was no sign, bringing him the only feelings of discordance and anxiety among the flurry of sensations he experienced while absorbing the encompassing splendor.

Annika, Jonathan, and Raymond looked entirely spellbound, as Talthannor glided down and alighted a few paces in front of the group. The touch of the Watcher's huge paws upon the ground was impeccably smooth and graceful, making Seth feel a little silly that he had cringed at the last moment, bracing for some sort of jarring impact.

Talthannor lowered to the ground, and Seth got down from the Watcher's back. His feet met a surface with very unusual properties, feeling completely stable, while conveying a buoyant lightness to his every step.

Annika stepped forward right away and hugged him fervently, as he took a place with his friends. The other two moved in closer, as Raymond hooked an arm around his shoulders for a moment, and Jonathan patted his back.

"I'm so glad to see you guys. Where are my folks?" he asked, impatiently, feeling a spike of nervousness as he openly voiced the question.

"They're okay," Jonathan answered reassuringly.

"Where are they?" Seth asked.

"They were left with some men and women that will look after them. I don't know exactly where, but Utahor, the bull-one, said that they would be safe for now," Raymond added.

Seth's worries eased a little at the news, though he wished that he knew more about the people they had been left in the care of. He understood that his parents could not have been left at the house, and was glad that they had been taken away to a safer haven.

"So … what is this place?" Seth whispered to them, his eyes roving across the magnificent sights.

He looked out over the lake, the shoreline, and the swaying golden and cerulean fields around them. Seth was amazed at how everything seemed to possess a faint glow, with sustained light that was coming from within.

"Is this … Heaven?" Seth asked hesitantly, knowing that he was in a place far removed from the only world he had inhabited before.

"This is Purgatarion, known also as the Middle Lands," Talthannor interjected, causing Seth to flinch.

Seth turned to regard the Watcher that had carried him into the incredible realm. Its three companions were also present, and all were significantly larger in size than before. The bodies of the Watchers had also taken on a more surreal, transcendental quality within the remarkable surroundings, the glow limning their forms now much more prominent.

"What is Purgatarion?" Annika asked deferentially.

Seth had heard the word before, though the placement was lost within the depths of his memories.

"A Mercy granted by Adonai," Utahor responded, its layered voice deep and resonant. "A place where those who cannot approach the gates of the White City may dwell until they are ready to bear the Pure Light."

"The White City? You mean the gates into Heaven itself?" Annika responded, her voice brimming with excitement and wonder.

Seth felt a thrill race through him at her words, thinking immediately of his grandparents and several others who had died during his life. He wondered if they were somehow within reach, full of life and consciousness in a world that was not governed by time and space.

All the pain and sadness he had suffered in the trials of their passings would wash away in an instant if the stories were indeed true about an eternal realm. A hunger surged within his soul, as the desire for some sort of confirmation from the Watcher leaped to the fore.

Though the creature did not smile, Seth thought he saw a joyous sparkle dancing within the eyes of Talthannor, as the teenager looked to the Watcher that had carried him across worlds. Something both comforting and exhilarating was conveyed in the Watcher's expression, and Seth felt his heart leap.

"In time, Precious Soul," Talthannor responded with a gentle timbre.

Seth flinched, recognizing at once that the Watcher had responded to him as if he had openly ventured a question.

"The ramparts of the White City are the boundary to the Middle Lands. The Great Gates do indeed open into the infinite realms of Adonai, from which the Waters of Life flow, and in which the Tree of Life flourishes," Arundinel stated, in reply to Annika's question.

The distinct sounds of sobbing from behind took Seth's attention away from the Watchers. To his considerable surprise, Raymond was openly crying, his body shaking as tears streamed down his cheeks.

All of the bravado and swagger that Raymond normally carried was gone. In its place was the image of a young man surrendering to an eruption of emotions that had been held deep within, for far too long. The sight was troubling. Seth had never seen Raymond in such a despondent state.

"My ... mother?" he asked the Watchers, choking up heavily with the words. There was a desperate look to Raymond's face, as he searched the countenances of the four Watchers. He begged them passionately, "Please ... please tell me. Help me ... please."

Seth knew that Raymond had lost his mother to a long, arduous bout with cancer, when he had been just ten years of age. He rarely spoke of her, and his father had remarried since, but it was now plain to Seth's eyes that his friend had been carrying around a terrible, abiding pain deep inside.

"Precious Soul, we cannot take you to her," Jakiel responded in a chorus of gentle, soft tones.

Like an abrupt change in temperature, Seth could feel the intentions of the Watcher within the melody of its words. It was a profound, powerful thing to experience, a way of communication very different in nature than the methods people used to interact with each other. At its core was a pure, interior connection, which needed no language to translate, or physical sense to perceive.

There was a deep undercurrent of sympathy and compassion flowing within the permeating feeling, as well as a regretful sadness. Seth knew at once that the Watcher would have liked nothing more than to take Raymond, right at that moment, to reunite with his mother.

"But ... she is ... there?" Raymond stammered out through his tears, his eyes blinking rapidly, as he struggled to hold his gaze upon the celestial creatures.

A strange thing ensued as the Watchers grew silent and still for several moments, and Seth had the distinct impression that they were waiting for something. It was as if they were engaging in some manner of interior communion, seeking some type of response. Their multitudinous eyes all held a faraway look during the extended pause, but the focus soon returned, and they all became more animated in their expressions as they regarded Raymond.

"A soul is eternal, and your mother's place is not in these lands, or the regions below," the eagle-like Watcher stated. Where the powerful senses of compassion, sympathy, and sadness had coursed, a new feeling emerged, and took precedence over the others. It was one of pure gladness. "Precious Soul, know that she thrives in lands where death has no dominion, and disease has no place, forevermore."

For a few seconds, it was as if Raymond was suspended in time. He just stared towards the Watchers, speechless, the glisten of tears continuing down his face in narrow rivulets.

He suddenly ran forward, and spread his arms out, grasping onto the broad chest of Jakiel, as it was much too large for him to wrap his arms around. He buried his face into the body of the huge creature, immersing into its otherworldly glow. Tears continued from his eyes, but they were now those of abundant joy, no longer the overflow of sorrows.

Jakiel seemed a little surprised by the action, but made no move to shrug Raymond off, or discourage him from his emotive gesture. A little awkwardly, the Watcher finally lowered its human-like arms, and cradled Raymond with its large hands.

"Thank you … thank you so much for telling me," Raymond managed get out, with his face pressed tightly against the feathered chest of the Watcher. "It's all … I ever wanted … to know. Just that …" His voice trailed off as he shook with another cascade of emotions, empowering tears of happiness, and bursts of joyous laughter.

"The answer to Raymond was a special Grace allowed by Adonai," Utahor then announced, looking to the other three humans. His voice held a sense of compassion, but was notably firmer than Jakiel's as he addressed them. "We cannot indulge your other curiosities. You have been allowed a temporary refuge here, but this is not your place, and soon you must return back to your world."

Seth had been on the verge of inquiring about his own loved ones who had passed from Terra. He imagined that both Annika and Jonathan were about to make their own queries as well.

Despite having his nascent hopes stymied by Utahor's words, Seth took comfort in the response given to Raymond. There was no envy in him regarding the special grace bestowed upon his friend. It was undeniable that Raymond had quietly been enduring a horrible pain, and now the burden had been taken away from him.

Seth discovered that he had been given his own grace in the process. A new, wonderful optimism had been kindled within him, regarding all those he had lost in his life.

Something deeper within pulled his gaze towards the east, and a whisper of joy sounded within the core of his spirit as he peered towards the far horizons. An unseen promise beckoned to him from that direction, a mysterious, powerful invitation that spoke to every last speck of his being.

"In time, Precious Soul. ... In time. ... But now a task lies before you," Talthannor said.

Seth turned back towards the lion-like Watcher, and grinned. "I'm sorry, this is just a lot for me to take in so quickly. Not used to this kind of thing at all."

"I imagine that it is not easy," Talthannor replied, with traces of mirth in both his eyes and voice. "Walk with me, and let us speak together for a moment."

Talthannor turned and padded away from the group. Seth saw that the other Watchers were guiding the ones they had carried into Purgatarion to go off together in a similar fashion. Raymond walked alongside the massive Utahor, as Annika kept pace with Jakiel, and Jonathan with Arundinel, all heading in separate directions. To Seth, it felt like the Watchers had become like some kind of individual mentors.

Seth's heart gave a sudden start, as he realized that he was still standing in place. He hastened towards Talthannor, quickening his stride to catch up to the Watcher ahead of him. When they had proceeded a short distance away from the others, Talthannor came to a halt, and turned to face Seth.

"Circumstances created by the Adversary forced me to bring you here, as they did with your companions," the Watcher said. "But you must not forget your work back in the world of time and space, during the allotment of time that has been given to you there."

"I would be lying if I said I wanted to go back, except for my parents," Seth replied, his sweeping gaze indicating the spectacular environment encircling them.

"And this is nothing ... a mere shadow ... a faint echo ... a dim reflection of even the lowliest of realms in the Infinity beyond," Talthannor stated, his words accompanied by an overpowering sensation of awe and reverence.

Taking in the incredible beauty that far surpassed anything he had ever encountered in his life, it was hard for Seth to get his mind wrapped around the idea that what he now witnessed paled in comparison to something much grander. He could only accept the words of the Watcher, as he could not envision their meaning in any significant way.

Yet there was no chance of misinterpreting the powerful interior communication that had passed to Seth with the open words. The idea was both sobering and mind-blowing to him, to such an extent that he felt a little fearful towards the realms beyond spoken of by the Watcher.

"But what task could I possibly do? I can't go back to my house, without being arrested. I really can't ever go back home," Seth finally responded, jolted by the frank admission.

It was as if a gulf opened within him as he said the words. There was no turning back to the life that he had known, in any fashion, and the realization daunted him.

"The testimony that you carry now, on your back, is your next task," Talthannor said.

In the overwhelming experience with the revelation of Purgatarion, Seth had all but forgotten the small backpack he carried, containing the video footage.

"What can I possibly do with it?" Seth asked.

"It is valuable to others, who are being guided on their own path by Calliel."

"Who?" Seth asked.

"An Avatar of Adonai, of a different Order than mine own," answered the Watcher.

Seth shook his head, feeling another wave of disbelief at the enormity of everything being unveiled to him. "Avatars ... Purgatarion ... and even a heaven? This is all just incredible."

"To think that some considered to be the most gifted in their wisdom and intelligence amongst human kind cannot even fathom the possibility of what you are experiencing," Talthannor said.

"Some people think they know everything," Seth replied, with a chuckle. In his own life there had been many candidates that would suit his statement, including older adults and peers alike.

"And such is their greatest weakness, a foolishness that clouds their eyes, minds, and even their hearts," Talthannor said, with a strong conveyance of regret and pity.

"Maybe they just need to see what I'm seeing now," Seth said.

"It is likely that they would deny the vision of their own eyes. To accept even the possibility of this would be to humble themselves in a way that their pride cannot allow," Talthannor responded.

Seth shrugged. "I can only do what I can do. So how do we get the video I have to this ... Calliel? If that is what must be done."

"I will take you there, and your friends will be carried by the others."

"I wish we could stay longer," Seth said wistfully, looking up into the leonine face of the Watcher. It was not easy getting used to seeing so many eyes peering back at him, all of them directed by the will of only one being.

"Time is only a concern for those in your plane of existence," Talthannor replied. "Only a few properties of time exist here, and it has no authority in the realms beyond."

Seth wondered what a place existing outside the grip of time would be like to experience. It was difficult to imagine, and he did not have any inkling where to start. Yet there was something magical in the concept, as with time things came to an end, whereas a place where time had no presence could not.

Aging, death, and decay all depended on the passage of time, and Seth conjectured that those things would be barred from such a place as well. The thought was invigorating, and encouraging.

"So when do we go?"

"I must see Calliel, and then you will be taken to him, and the ones that he guides," Talthannor informed Seth.

"Then I will enjoy as much as I can of this place, while I am here," Seth said, gazing around.

"As you should on Terra," Talthannor retorted, with a light trace of admonishment that was not lost on Seth.

He felt no shame, taking the hint of chastisement in stride, knowing he had often wished he could hurdle the awkward years of his youth, and go straight into adulthood. Seeing things from a different perspective, he realized that Talthannor was right. He had to savor the good moments and beauty in life, and not be in a headlong rush to race past the positive things that even his world had to offer.

"Point taken," Seth replied, with a grin.

"Think upon that, and share this experience of Purgatarion with your friends. I shall return soon to you," Talthannor said.

Seth nodded, as the great Watcher turned, spreading out his large, translucent wings. With fluid, lithe movements, the creature bounded forward and took to the air, soaring rapidly toward the rainbow-hued heights.

In moments, Talthannor disappeared in mid-air, in what Seth perceived to be a flash of light. He turned back towards his friends, who he saw were alone, gathered by themselves at the edge of the lake. There was no sign of the other Watchers, and he surmised that they had departed the same way as Talthannor.

He strode towards Annika, Jonathan, and Raymond, and grinned broadly.

"Let's take a little walk, and check out a few things ... what do you all say?" he asked.

"Sounds great to me," Annika replied with a smile, as the other two added their assent.

They walked away from the lake and entered the lustrous fields. Seth felt the knee-high, ethereal grasses brushing against him, the touch as soft as silk. He savored the feeling, as he stared up into the enchanting sky, watching the shimmering, shifting cascade of brilliant hues.

While nothing on Terra rivaled what he was seeing now, he promised to himself that he would work to stop and appreciate the magnificence that could be found in the world. The things of Terra might be to a lesser degree than what lay within Purgatarion, but then Talthannor had made it clear that the things of Purgatarion paled next to the sights in endless worlds beyond.

Ultimately, Seth reasoned that the things of beauty and inspiration in both Terra and Purgatarion were like signposts towards the realms of infinity. The thought brought a warm smile to his face, as leveled his gaze toward the eastern horizons.

# SECTION VI

# JOVAN

Jovan had to hurry to keep up with Kaira's strides as they made their way down the gleaming hallway of the downtown hospital. One of Yorvik's finest facilities, it was located close to the World Summit within a heavily secured zone, where it could meet the medical needs of international delegates and WS personnel.

Everything had happened so fast. One minute he was having an enjoyable dinner with Kaira in one of Yorvik's finest five-star restaurants, and the next they had raced to the hospital at her firm insistence.

David Sorath was dying. Jovan knew that most everyone had seen that approaching on the horizon, but the imminence of it caught him by surprise.

The implications were just beginning to dawn on Jovan, as they neared the hospital room where David was being attended. The dying man had made his wishes very clear when it came to the Peace Commission, and the prime beneficiary of those last requests walked slowly into the room, moving past a few others who had already gathered there.

The successor to David Sorath's position had not been declared, but it was clear that Kaira would be assuming a role of greater importance. Her deft handling of the Mandarian-UCAS conflict had assured that.

Jovan entered the room behind her and held back, as Kaira stepped towards the hospital bed. David looked incredibly frail, and his sunken eyes had a dull glaze across them as he looked up sluggishly to Kaira.

"I am so happy you came," he uttered, in a low, scratchy voice.

"I received your message," she replied.

"Then I want you to know I have made ... official arrangements," he paused, and a pained expression formed on his face as he coughed violently. After a few moments, he resumed, "I have arranged for you to succeed me at the Commission."

Jovan was surprised at the extent of the declaration. Kaira had not been at the Peace Commission for long, and there were several others that had been viewed as capable successors to David.

All the same, he could think of nobody better for the position. It was clear that David viewed the situation in the same light, and had taken the leap to install her in his place before he departed the world.

"No one could have handled the Mandarian and UCAS conflict like you did," David said. His chest heaved again, as he shook with coughs, and he took a moment to clear his throat.

"Thank you," Kaira answered gently. "And know that I will advance the work of the Peace Commission, with every ounce of strength I have in me."

"I know you will," David replied.

"I will take your vision forward, to resounding success," she said, giving him a gentle smile.

"You are the one person who can," David said, and to Jovan the man's voice had an almost reverent timbre.

The air within the room grew considerably colder. Flickers of movement drew Jovan's eyes to the corner of the room, to his left. Though faint, the form of a spectral woman had taken shape, a ghostly entity with a very familiar countenance.

Jovan's eyes widened as he recognized Lilith, wondering why she had manifested at this place and time. She gave him a smile and slight nod, as Jovan blinked in amazement. Her eyes glittered, and her form had a slow, undulating motion to it, as if the air around her was like water.

Jovan's attention was yanked from Lilith as a sustained monotone sounded from a monitor at David's bedside. A flashing red light pulsed, as an alarm sounded out in the hallway. In moments, three nurses raced into the room, and the other visitors backed up to make way for them.

Kaira stepped aside, as a doctor entered and joined the nurses around the bed. A curious sight then transpired. Like a cloak of shadow, a misty darkness lifted out from David's body. The amorphous mass drifted away from the bed, before dissolving, and finally vanishing from sight.

Applying defibrillators, and sending powerful voltages through David's body, the medical personnel were able to resuscitate him, and get a heartbeat back. They worked diligently to stabilize him.

The look on David's face was markedly different than before when he opened his eyes again. He looked around the room with an air of bewilderment, as if he did not know where he was.

His eyes fluttered for a moment and then stared upwards, as the flat-line tone sounded in the room once again. The doctor and nurses reacted quickly, but this time the defibrillators failed to bring his heartbeat back.

After a few moments, and a couple more attempts, the doctor turned and looked to Jovan, Kaira, and the others who were standing around the bed. "I am sorry."

All heads then snapped back towards the bed, and Jovan's heart leaped, as a guttural scream cleaved the room. David bolted upright in the hospital bed, his face a mask of terror.

The fear emblazoned on the man's face shook Jovan to the core. He pressed up against the back wall, as the medical team, recovering from its own shock at the eruption, moved in to help.

The monitors still registered absolutely nothing in the way of heartbeats, contributing to the bizarre nature of the scene.

David's body slumped heavily back into the mattress, though his face was still frozen in a contortion that conveyed unmistakable horror. Jovan did not want to try, even for a moment, to imagine what could possibly bring forth such a dreadful look.

Jovan looked over to Kaira, who had managed to hold her composure intact as she observed the stunning proceedings. Where he had thought to comfort her, the calm strength she was displaying bolstered him.

"Are you alright?" he still asked, amazed at her fortitude.

She nodded, and said nothing at first, continuing to stare silently towards the bed and the corpse on it. Jovan glanced over to where he had seen Lilith. The ghostly apparition had vanished, and he noted that the room now felt much warmer.

"We can go now. There is nothing more we can do here," Kaira said evenly.

Taking the lead, she stepped past Jovan, and he followed her out of the room and on down the hallway. He was immensely relieved to be out of the hospital room, as echoes of the dead man's final visage played repeatedly within his mind's eye. Shaken by the experience, Jovan could only listen to the steady rhythm of Kaira's footsteps on the tile floor, as he commanded his own legs to carry him away from the terrible scene.

# FRIEDRICH

Flying across the rolling skies of Erishkegal's realm, the Gryphon carried Friedrich a short distance behind Enki. The Avatar shone brightly against the churning backdrop of dark, vaporous masses, as he blazed forward.

Enki was heading for a sprawling, mountainous region, filled with immense rises capped with sharp, jagged-looking summits. The rocky slopes were steep, riddled with crevices and ledges all along the lengthy inclines.

Darting and gliding about the air in the vicinity of the great slopes were an abundance of winged shapes. A portion of them were reptilian, many mammalian, and still others more avian in their features. Friedrich recognized several that were like the pair of lion-headed, eagle-bodied Anzu that had guided him to Enki from the Sanctum at Egalkurzagin.

Many creatures were resting idly on the ledges, or were tucked farther back in the shadowy recesses of the nooks and crevices. Screeches and cries echoed all about the incoming visitors, but there were no threats forthcoming, or any move to intercept the newcomers.

There was a curious atmosphere about the place, which grabbed strongly at Friedrich, as he stared at the flying forms plunging and ascending all around them.

His eyes fell upon one of the Anzu flying near to them. It swooped close to the Gryphon, giving Friedrich a good sense of its bodily scale.

It was decidedly smaller than the Gryphon, where the two at the Sanctum had been much larger creatures. It also had the look of an adolescent, and a momentous realization began to dawn upon Friedrich.

He looked around at the ledges, as everything came to him in a spiraling rush. The area that Enki had led him to was a kind of nesting ground, not simply abodes for long-living creatures that had escaped the doom of the Great Flood.

Enki guided them lower as Friedrich contemplated the disturbing implications. As big as Erishkegal's dominion was, Friedrich wondered how large the Nephilim population might have grown with so many ages transpired since the Great Flood had occurred.

After the Gryphon had landed upon the ground, Friedrich dismounted. He gazed upwards at the winged shapes swirling in the air high above as a surge of lightning rippled through the cloud masses, his mind still wrestling with the ramifications of the new revelation.

Enki had grown very quiet as well, standing a few paces away, and peering upward. Friedrich wondered what thoughts were foremost in the Avatar's mind.

"Many have been born in this place," Friedrich remarked, after a little time had passed.

"A great many," Enki replied firmly.

"Incredible," Friedrich said. "That so much of their physical state carried into the dominion that Erishkegal founded for them."

"Another discovery, and another great mystery about this place," Enki said.

"They have likely been breeding here ever since they arrived," Friedrich said. "Their numbers could be enormous by now."

"Who knows how many now dwell in this realm?" Enki asked solemnly. "I have only begun to get a sense of how large this place is, but it is vast, and multitudes could dwell easily enough within its boundaries."

Friedrich could tell that the Avatar was deeply troubled at the notion that the Nephilim were actively reproducing within the depths of the Abyss. It did not entirely surprise Friedrich that the Nephilim could multiply. They were creatures of flesh and blood, and had crossed the Veil in their entirety when Erishkegal had intervened to spare them. They had been born of a natural process, even if the ones that had sired them had committed a serious offense against the order Adonai intended for the physical world.

"Then it is much more than a mere refuge here," Friedrich observed, after a long, uncomfortable silence. "They are thriving here, and increasing."

"And could only do so with Erishkegal's conscious assent," Enki stated.

"What purpose could she have? Other than perhaps strengthening the ability of this realm to defend against attacks," Friedrich said.

"I do not know," Enki responded.

Friedrich thought back to the huge guardians warding the seven gates into the realm. If a force of creatures like those titans had been established, then Erishkegal could resist all but the strongest attacks out of the Abyss.

"I would not think her consent would be given for a reason other than defense, given what this place is close to in the Abyss," Friedrich said, recalling the terrible Vortex that had almost ensnared his group.

"It is my hope that is the only reason," Enki said. "Erishkegal treads upon dangerous ground."

Friedrich knew what Enki feared. The Avatar's greatest worry was that Erishkegal had severed the bond that her soul held with Adonai. A deliberate choice to go against the Will of Adonai would be enough to break that state of grace, making her little different than any of the Fallen Avatars that had joined with Diabolos, in the prime rebellion that had shaken the heavens.

Looking around at the stormy horizons, and up towards the airborne shapes, Friedrich knew that Erishkegal had made many, many choices in establishing and administering the shadowy refuge. It was no wonder that Enki harbored an abiding tension regarding the Avatar he cared so deeply for.

Friedrich knew that, despite finding Erishkegal, there remained the very real possibility that she could not return to the heavenly realms, even if she were willing to do so. A being in disharmony with Adonai could not withstand the very essence of the infinite realms. He was painfully aware of his own inability to approach the White City.

"I believe we are about to be summoned into her presence," Enki declared, breaking Friedrich's line of thought. The Avatar turned about slowly, and gazed skyward. "Perhaps we will gain some insights into the mysteries that thrive in this hidden place."

Friedrich turned about with the Avatar, following the other's stare. He beheld a group of figures descending from the skies, speeding directly towards them. Around a dozen in number, they had not come from the mountains, but rather from the general direction that Enki and Friedrich had taken to reach the expanse of high, craggy summits.

Some of the incoming figures were carried on the strength of their own wings, while others were mounted upon flying steeds. As the group alighted, the identity of their leader quickly became apparent. All of the others exhibited considerable deference to one particular individual, who dismounted a violet-scaled, narrow-bodied dragon, which peered towards the Avatar and Exile with resplendent, emerald-green eyes.

Save for two, most of the others held back as their leader approached Enki and Friedrich. The prominent figure walked towards them with a proud bearing, and the look entrenched within its eyes held an intense, unyielding glint.

In the physical world, the being would have been deemed a giant, rising to about twelve feet in height. Yet this was no crude, brutish creature of the legends and stories bandied about in Friedrich's mortal period.

The being had beautiful skin, of an ivory hue, matching the lengthy tresses falling down over its broad shoulders. It had no facial hair or eyebrows, and there were no scars or other surface markings to be found anywhere on its impeccable skin.

The face of the being was elongated, with sharper lines that culminated in a narrow chin, and it had an elevated hairline that exposed a smooth forehead. Its ears were larger in proportion than the average human form, tapering into slight points.

Further differentiating the entity from a common human appearance was the fact that it had six fingers on each hand, and six toes on each foot.

While the appearance of the being was unusual, it was the solid, blood-red pupils that drew Friedrich's eyes the most. The contrast with the unblemished white surrounding them, not just within its eyes, but also in its skin and hair, caused the crimson pupils to stand out strikingly.

The being was clothed in a long, tunic-like garment that had been fashioned out of a black, silken material, which carried a lustrous sheen to its surface. On its feet, the being wore a type of sandal-boot, crafted out of what looked to be strips of dark leather.

Friedrich knew at once that the being was a veteran warrior, even if it carried no visible weapons. The perception reflected something that he had developed a strong sense for, after a lifetime spent among soldiers during the storms of war. It was one of his abilities that had remained intact between states of existence, carried over with him from the material world and into the afterworld realms.

Two winged, humanoid creatures in coarser black garb, also of a tunic-style, flanked the leader. They also moved with the well-balanced step and posture inherent in those possessed of martial ability. It was hard to read their expressions, as one was eagle-headed, and the other lion-headed, but both had the stern air of dutiful warriors attending to their commander.

Enki stood patiently, saying nothing as they drew nearer. When they were a few paces away, the trio came to a stop, as the leader's eyes fell squarely upon Enki.

"I am Ningishzida," the tall figure announced to them. While the being gave Enki a slight bow, the deeper tone of its voice was authoritative. "I have been sent to you at Her command, to summon you to appear before the Tribunal."

Enki gave a slight nod of acknowledgement in return, but said nothing. Ningishzida nodded back in response, turned, and started back towards the dragon-steed he had flown in upon.

After surmounting the Gryphon, Friedrich kept close to Enki as they took to flight, following Ningishzida at a high altitude over the murky lands of Erishkegal's realm. Many of those with Ningishzida fanned out to the sides, as if they were hemming in the ones they were charged to escort.

After passing across great distances, a single rise dominated the horizon, rising out of an expanse of low, rolling hills. The promontory reminded Friedrich of Egalkurzagin, in that nothing within view around the conical mount came close to approaching its preeminence.

The look of the immense rise radiated a sense of power, enhanced by the lightning pulsing in the distance within the shrouded skies. It was an awe-inspiring vista to look upon, and Friedrich knew that the mount was their destination.

Though they were already flying at a great height, Ningishzida had to lead them even higher in altitude to approach the lofty summit. As they drew closer, Friedrich saw that the immense rise was crowned by a great, gaping caldera.

Passing over its lip, Friedrich peered far down to where a grand obsidian structure was cradled at the center of the circular expanse. Crystalline veins ran along its surface in abundance, just like the Sanctum at Egalkurzagin.

Glancing about, Friedrich could see that winged forms occupied many of the nooks and ledges along the rocky walls ringing the huge caldera. Unlike the mountain range that Friedrich and Enki had just come from, all of the winged creatures here had an attentive, alert demeanor, and every single one that Friedrich beheld had their focus trained intently on the incoming group. Their nature echoed the seven guardians of the gates to Manzazu.

After landing, Friedrich saw that the structure ensconced within the caldera was of a towering height. It had an extended, rectangular shape, which had two soaring, square-topped pylons flanking a broad entryway set into the facade.

A pair of the lion-bodied, human-headed creatures with eagle wings stood to each side of the entrance. The quartet of robust creatures lowered their eyes at Ningishzida's approach, making no move to stop anyone within the group from passing into the entrance.

Friedrich stared up at the guardians as he walked by them. Their long-bearded faces looked entirely human, though the winged, muscular, four-legged forms that the countenances were a part of shattered any illusions of human origins.

Ningishzida came to a halt within a large chamber inside the entrance, just as Friedrich's eyes fell upon the others from his group. Joy and relief reflected on the faces of Valaris, Maroboduus, and all of the other Exiles as they recognized Friedrich.

Friedrich was elated at being reunited with his companions, wanting to rejoin them immediately, but Ningishzida began to speak, with a tone of solemnity that kept the Exile rooted in place.

"You have all been summoned before the Anunnaki Judges, the Seven Wise Ones chosen by Erishkegal to form the Tribunal in which all matters concerning Manzazu are weighed," Ningishzida stated. "Do not think to challenge the authority of the Tribunal. The judgement of the Seven will be enforced."

His words carried a thick undercurrent of warning to Enki and the others. Having seen the multitude of creatures in the walls ringing the caldera, and the four huge wards of the entrance, Friedrich had no doubts that Ningishzida could quickly call upon great strength.

"We are not here to challenge anyone," Enki replied. "But do not think there are no consequences for doing harm to servants of Adonai."

The warning inherent in Enki's words more than matched that of Ningishzida, and Friedrich had the distinct impression that some sort of understanding passed between the two beings. Ningishzida's red pupils had a steely look to them as he held Enki's fiery gaze, unblinking. After a few moments, he gave Enki a low bow.

"Treachery has no place here, be assured of that, Enki," Ningishzida said. "But the judgement of the Tribunal, which is given the full authority of Erishkegal, will stand. Wait here, and I will announce your arrival."

Without waiting for reply, Ningishzida strode forward, and disappeared through a broad portal ahead of them.

With Ningishzida gone, Friedrich walked briskly over to his fellow Exiles, embracing them fervently, one by one. Near to him, the other Peris flocked about Asa'an, and their forms visibly brightened as they merrily greeted their fellow creature.

"Decided to take a different path?" Silas asked.

"A more scenic route, I suppose," Friedrich replied with a chuckle.

"We will have to share tales soon, then, as our path was far from easy," Heinrich stated.

"Those accursed Galla. Droves of them, everywhere you turned in the darkness," Maroboduus stated, shaking his head. "We had to use the Void to evade them."

"As did we," Friedrich said. "But our path took us into the realm of Ares, at the edge of the Ten-Fold Kingdom."

Maroboduus' eyes widened at his pronouncement, and a hush came over the others, as they regarded Friedrich with looks of curiosity and a little apprehension.

"Obviously, we got free of the place," Friedrich said with a grin. "Nothing to be nervous about, my friends. I'm here, am I not?"

"A great relief to all of us, and maybe it was best that we did not know where your path led," Heinrich said. "Speaking for my part, I would not have been able to endure the uncertainty, knowing where you were. It seems we have much to talk about."

"Indeed we do," Friedrich replied, not wanting to go into his unsettling discovery that Ares had called into being a fearsome mass of warriors, one that could swiftly devastate a much larger force of Aishim. He looked around at all of the familiar faces of his friends, feeling a sense of thanksgiving that he had made it back to them. "But it is just good to see that we are all here, no matter what paths we took."

A chorus of assent and broad smiles met his words, and Friedrich perceived the abiding sense of relief amongst his companions. He could tell that they had been deeply worried about him, and recognized they had not had it easy, either.

The cheerful reunion was short-lived, though, as Ningishzida returned from the chamber beyond, and beckoned for everyone to follow him. Enki was the first in the group to step forward, then the Exiles and Peris, and finally the cluster of Gryphons, who had so dutifully, and courageously, carried their riders through the terrors of the Abyss.

The tall entity led them through the rectangular portal at the rear of the chamber. Friedrich steadied his thoughts, knowing that they were about to see Erishkegal again, within the weighty atmosphere of a judgement council.

He could only hope that the verdict rendered was in their favor, an outcome that was far from certain.

# SKYLAR

Skylar returned from yet another fruitless search, blinking her eyes as she felt her mind gain authority over her physical body. She had gone far and wide, but had been unable to pick up any traces of Benedict or the enemy traveler.

Nothing had interrupted her foray, as the shadowy denizens of the astral plane had either kept to themselves, or not taken notice of her as she sped through the skies. It was one of her longest stints out of body, and to return empty handed made her want to pound her fist into the mattress as she sat up in the dim bedroom.

"I can take you to your enemy's man," a soft, layered voice intoned, coming like a whisper from the corner of the room.

Skylar gave a start, and whirled about, setting her eyes on the otherworldly figure that had begun appearing to her with regularity.

"I have nothing to discuss with you, Fallen Avatar," Skylar replied curtly.

"What harm can it do to let me guide you to the one that you actively seek?" the entity questioned her. "This offer will not remain for long, as a time approaches where I can be of help to Benedict Darwin. I may not be able to return to you after those moments pass."

"Help Benedict Darwin? When your side has him firmly in their control?" Skylar asked, laughing with no trace of humor within her timbre.

"I have no side, not anymore," the Fallen Avatar replied. "Banned from Adonai's realm, and a traitor to the ultimate traitor. Indeed, I am alone, Skylar, of the Shield Maidens."

The response stilled the caustic retort that came to her lips, and she stared at the human-looking figure with the solid, radiant eyes. She was still wrestling with the idea that such a spiritual entity could be remorseful, and seek redemption, after serving the greatest demonic power to ever exist for so many ages.

The nature of Diabolos was control, and it was known that every creature held within the realms of the Ten-Fold Kingdom lived in a kind of slavery. Even the greatest Fallen Avatars, including some mighty entities who were close to being peers to Diabolos, did not possess freedom. Even they were shackled to the Risen Throne.

Diabolos sought to subjugate and conform the will of every living

365

spirit. It was dictatorship in the purest sense, which was why, in Skylar's mind, human tyrannies always coursed with the essence of the demonic.

The Lord of the Abyss was not one who could be placated, or pleaded with. The insatiable desire for control that emanated from the Risen Throne had existed from the moment that Diabolos had rejected Adonai and instigated the Great War.

Those that had abandoned Adonai in the rebellion soon found their fates tied to the most pitiless Master of all. In Skylar's view, they got what they deserved, after knowing Adonai in fullness, and consciously rejecting Him in the light of that knowledge.

The more she thought about it, the angrier she got, and her lips grew taut as she glared towards the Fallen Avatar.

"Get out," she commanded, sharply.

"I deserve the Outer Darkness," the entity replied, in a melancholic voice. "It does not mean that I have no will of my own. In claiming it back from the Shining One, some would say that I doom myself in the Ten-Fold Kingdom."

"Every last one of you bastards is doomed," Skylar shot back, surprised at her aggression. "You wield your influence to harden hearts, deceive, and bring something of hell into the world. One day you will be locked away forever."

The Fallen Avatar nodded. "Perhaps in the delirium of madness Diabolos believes victory can be achieved, but the Shining One would consider dragging the majority of immortal souls into the Abyss to be a triumph in itself. I do not know the designs that are forming in the core of darkness, but I do know that I am ashamed of my own path, and merely wish to serve Adonai's cause before the key is set to the lock of the eternal prison."

"And you would turn over one of the greatest weapons in the hands of the Shining One's worldly servants?" Skylar asked, still in disbelief.

"I will not only locate the enemy's scout, but I will give you a way to destroy him in the astral plane," the Fallen Avatar replied.

Skylar stared at him for a moment, not quite sure if she had heard him correctly. "Destroy him in the astral plane?"

"I believe I know a way," the Fallen Avatar stated.

"So it would not be a matter of tracing this son of a bitch back to wherever his body lurks, and then fomenting a plan to get him," Skylar ventured.

"You could sever his line to the mortal plane, right after you are brought to him," the Fallen Avatar said.

"Impossible," Skylar retorted.

"Impossible because the method has not been used before?" the entity asked her.

"Do you know how dangerous that would be if those who are taken up in spirit, or walk the planes out of their bodies, could kill while in spirit form?" Skylar countered. The possibility frightened her with its implications, as much as it fascinated her.

"Very dangerous, and you will be courting terrible danger, if the capability is made known," the Fallen Avater replied.

"I would think so," Skylar agreed.

"You can choose to bring an end to the walker of the planes. Or you can continue to allow him to run rampant, unchallenged as he searches out new targets for the ones that sent him forth," the Fallen Avatar said bluntly. "The choice is yours to make. But you will not have the choice available for long, as I go soon to the aid of Benedict Darwin."

Skylar did not know what to say. Consorting with infernal beings was not something that she could afford to dabble with, but if the entity spoke truly, and was engaged in its own rebellion, then she might have a way of halting the enemy's astral traveler.

Benedict's location was unknown, and not a thing was known about the whereabouts of the enemy traveler. To her knowledge, she was the only Shield Maiden capable of walking the spirit realms as she did. The burden of finding the Walker of the Setian Path rested squarely on her shoulders.

No matter what way she looked at it, she did not see how stopping her counterpart would be of any benefit to the Enemy. If anything, a terrible loss, of a very rare asset, would be suffered by Skylar's adversaries.

"So what is your theory, as to how I could bring an end to the enemy walker when he is disembodied?" Skylar finally asked the Fallen Avatar.

"You must wield a weapon of the spirit realms that can channel the force of your soul. It is a weapon that only I can help you with, as it is not something that can be brought into this physical plane," the Fallen Avatar explained.

"What is this weapon like?" Skylar asked.

The Fallen Avatar answered her, in great detail, and no matter how uneasy she felt about the concept of accepting help from a fallen spirit, she could not see a single flaw in the logic presented to her.

She was in a position that she did not wish on anyone. A grave risk loomed on one side, and on the other was the desperate need to stop the enemy scout.

The only thing that she could do beyond all else was to petition Adonai, and hope for some kind of answer on the matter. No deception could endure when put before the Pure Light of the Great Throne.

Before the Fallen Avatar left her that night, she resolved to make her determination after engaging in lengthy benediction. If one tiny splinter of discord could be found in her heart following such a period of focused devotion and supplication, then she would not act.

# FRIEDRICH

Ningishzida led Friedrich and the others into the midst of an enormous, black-walled chamber. A series of sconces and braziers arrayed all about the chamber cast forth a cool blue light, enough to reveal the details of both the capacious chamber and its intimidating occupants. A somber quiet met the entrance of the arrivals, lending an immediate air of formality to the proceedings.

The inner curve of a semicircular dais faced the entrance to the chamber. Seven figures stood at even distances along its considerable length, the top of which was well above Friedrich's head. All were staring intently towards Enki and the others as the group filed in.

There were a couple of prominent figures on the ground level. One was Namtar, Erishkegal's vizier that Friedrich had encountered back at the Sanctum.

A little farther back on the lower level was Erishkegal herself, and there was nothing amiable about the countenance she bore. Behind her was a short ramp that led up to the center of the curving dais.

Friedrich looked around at the tall figures looming above them on the dais. Like the seven gatekeepers, they were all strange of form, each one demanding a brief portion of his curiosity.

Nearest to him, at the end of the dais just to his left, was a humanoid being structured like a bird, though its head, torso, and legs were entirely human-like. The face of the being was that of a comely woman, with long, dark hair that gave off a glimmering sheen in the blue light. Like a bird, the lower part of its body sloped back from the neck and breast; only it was the segmented, barbed tail of a scorpion that extended to the rear, instead of feathers or wings.

Next to the scorpion woman was a powerfully built figure with thick hooves supporting its two bull-like legs. Its upper torso was that of an amply muscled human male, and the face of the entity was decidedly human, save for the horns and ears of a bull that sprouted from its head.

The third judge had the lower legs and talons of a great bird of prey, the brawny, heavily muscled body of a man, and the thick-maned head of a lion.

The fourth had the wings and head of a bird of prey, and the body of a man.

The fifth being would have resembled nothing more than a tall, human female, were it not for the coating of fish-like scales that ran over her entire body. The reflective surface shimmered in the light within the chamber, but her eyes were like orbs of onyx.

The sixth was somewhat like the lion-headed, third figure, in that it had the talons and lower legs of an eagle, the body of a man, and the head of something else. Instead of a lion's mien, it had a monstrous, inhuman countenance, with a short muzzle, deep-set eyes, and triangular ears.

The final, seventh figure was perhaps the strangest and most mysterious of all the seven. Draped in a hooded robe, the details of its bodily shape were concealed. But the loose folds of its attire did not mask the snake-visage peering out of the dark recess, and its forked tongue flicked outward as Friedrich gazed towards the being.

Ningishzida bowed low, and addressed Erishkegal directly, despite the presence of Namtar before him. His voice was low and obeisant, nothing like the tone he had used to address Enki and Friedrich. "Great Erishkegal, Queen of all who live in Manzazu, here are the ones you have summoned to appear before the Tribunal of the Anunnaki."

She gave him a slight nod in return. Eyes lowered, Ningishzida bowed low again, and stepped off to the side, fully exposing the group behind him to Erishkegal, as well as the seven Anunnaki judges of her underworld realm.

Namtar then addressed the group in a resonant, formal tone. "You stand in the presence of the Seven Wise Ones, who hold authority given to them by Great Erishkegal. All within Manzazu will enforce the judgements of this tribunal. Speak when questioned, remain silent when not."

The instructions were unnecessary. Friedrich wanted to do nothing more than stand behind Enki, and remain silent. He felt a bothersome nervousness continuing to rise within, as he had no idea what the tribunal was weighing when it came to his companions. He knew that everything hinged on the decision of the seven judges, as far as his group's ability to depart Erishkegal's dominion.

"Enki, I have called you before this tribunal of my wisest as your presence here, and that of the ones with you, represent a danger to all of us, if you should depart," Erishkegal stated, with a tone of deep solemnity. "Why have you sought out this refuge, a haven created for the ones spared from a doom that they had no part in causing?"

As she spoke, the look in her eyes became increasingly severe, and as her last words passed her lips, it was withering. In Friedrich's estimation, no one could have surpassed the sense of conviction being displayed by the other Avatar. There was an extended pause, as she waited for Enki to respond.

"Erishkegal, my spirit has longed to find you, ever since the rains fell in abundance upon the world," Enki said. "I have carried this burden for ages. I could bear the uncertainty no longer, and had to seek you out."

The Avatar sounded almost deferential. The atmosphere within the chamber grew heavier, bringing a tension to the air that was palpable. The two Avatars, separated from each other's presence for so many long ages, regarded each other in a deep, extended silence.

"I chose to cross the Veil, and I founded a place of refuge for those that I brought with me," Erishkegal stated, breaking the uncomfortable impasse. "I felt no disharmony within me when I led them from the world. I do not feel any disharmony now, after these many ages."

"You have created a place for many others, ones that were not there when the rains fell, and who did not walk across the Veil with you," Enki replied evenly, with a trace of accusation that did not escape Friedrich.

"A matter of gathering strength, to protect this realm," she replied in stolid fashion, exhibiting no sign of irritation with Enki's words.

"The things of the mortal world were not intended for the Abyss,"

371

Enki said. "The Abyss is the abode intended for everything separated from Adonai's Grace, though your realm has left me with many questions that find no answer."

"Those whom I was moved to spare were never intended for the mortal world," Erishkegal responded. "So it was no surprise to me when it was revealed that they could multiply in this realm."

Friedrich found that he had increasing sympathy for the outcast Nephilim, as they were exiles to an even greater extent than he was. Their very survival was precarious, under threat at all moments, as hordes of Galla and other denizens of the bottomless pit hunted in the abyssal regions surrounding Erishkegal's realm.

It was no wonder why Erishkegal was so protective of her dominion, and Friedrich knew that he could not begrudge her if the judgement of the Anunnaki Tribunal went against his group. She carried a terrible burden of responsibility, encompassing an entire population of beings.

Friedrich had been a commander in his mortal life, and had felt the ponderous kind of weight that came with making decisions that impacted the fates of large numbers of individuals. He had never taken the lives of his soldiers lightly, and could not begin to imagine what it was like for Erishkegal, having multitudes of living beings to consider in all of her decisions.

"I did not bid you to trespass, Enki," Erishkegal replied, with a sharper edge to her voice. "Nor did I bid Inanna to undertake her ill-fated journey into the Abyss. Those were choices that the two of you made, of your own free accord."

"You did not ask us to take the journey, Erishkegal, and our choices were our own. Now that I have found a few of the answers that I sought, and have the peace of knowing that you are here, in this well-guarded place, I seek only to offer you a gift, Erishkegal, and to petition you for the release of Inanna. We will return to the realms above, and trouble you no further," Enki said, his voice conciliatory.

"Your departure would bring a great danger with it," Erishkegal stated. "The Galla swarming in the darkness are simple enough to confound and defend against, but the more powerful servants of the Adversary would seek to destroy this realm if it were brought to their attention.

"No dominion is spared in the Abyss, if it is not governed by the will of Diabolos. The Shining One's will to dominate is insatiable, and ever hungry to consume. We endure under that threat with every moment that passes in these lands.

"The comings and goings of an Avatar of Adonai within the endless depths may very well attract notice from the Ten-Fold Kingdom. The arts that I have used to veil this realm from roving multitudes of Galla will not be enough to confound the ones who attend the Risen Throne of Diabolos." Manzazu's queen paused for a few moments, letting the words settle upon Enki and the others.

"And Inanna? What of her now?" Erishkegal resumed, an undercurrent of indictment within her words. "She was nearly overcome in the darkness, and only Kur's arrival spared her from destruction. Only a moment more and the Void would have been her dwelling until the end of all things. She would never have entered the depths of the pit were it not for you, Enki. Her ill-conceived folly was born out of your own foolish desire."

Enki continued to say nothing in response, but Friedrich could see the sense of alarm that came over the Avatar. His body blazed brighter, and his fiery eyes cast a piercing gaze into those of Erishkegal. The two celestial beings were locked in a mounting confrontation that set every part of Friedrich on edge. Something unspoken passed between the two Avatars, bordering on the cusp of hostility.

"Did you think that I imprisoned her, Enki? Do you think that is why I have not allowed you to see her? No, I have spared you further pain, but cannot do so any longer. I have confined her in a place where I can attend to her, to the fullest of my abilities, Enki, but she is soon going to fall into the Void." While her gaze was steady, Erishkegal's voice had lowered.

"If your abilities cannot stop her from declining, she is certain to fall into the Void's embrace," Enki replied, in a melancholic tone.

"I am well aware of that, Enki!" Erishkegal shot back, with an abrupt flare of anger. "I have done everything that I can to keep her from the timeless sleep. I have used powers that I can little afford to spare."

"I may be able to help her, Erishkegal," Enki replied simply, and humbly, without a speck of pride or boastfulness in his reply. "Though what I speak of does not concern my own abilities, but gifts that I had intended for you."

Erishkegal's eyes were riveted on Enki, and her stern countenance went unchanged as she pondered his words.

"I have with me something from above, that can spare Inanna the timeless sleep," Enki finally ventured, when it seemed the latest standstill would never come to an end.

"Then do not delay, Enki, not a moment longer," Erishkegal said, without hesitation. "Yet know that even if Inanna is brought back from the edge of the Void, the two of you together are not strong enough to contend with my judgement, or the judgement of the Tribunal."

"I do not seek to contend with you," Enki responded.

"You cannot leave this place unless it is allowed by the Tribunal. Do not test my will in this matter," Erishkegal replied, with an edge of warning.

"Come with me, and let us speak together, Erishkegal, so I can reveal to you the things of above that can bring healing to Inanna," Enki said.

Erishkegal turned, and regarded the seven Anunnaki judges on the curving dais above her.

"I will go with Enki, to see to the needs of Inanna, as any help that Enki may have for her must not be delayed," she stated. "But the matter of these visitors is not decided, and we shall reconvene this tribunal, when Inanna's healing has been seen to … if it is possible."

She cast a piercing glance back towards Enki, and Friedrich knew that another shrouded communication passed between the two Avatars.

"Enki shall go with Erishkegal, and the others must return to the outer chamber," Namtar declared.

Ningishzida stepped in from the side, and looked toward Friedrich and his companions. "Follow me."

Friedrich looked back, as he and his companions were led out of the chamber. Enki stepped forward, walking at Erishkegal's side as they made their way up the ramp to a broad doorway leading to another part of the grand structure.

# ENKI

"And who are these two, who you have concealed from all eyes? Elegist and myrmidon, come to soothe my anguished spirit?" Erishkegal questioned Enki, with a trace of bemusement.

The little winged creatures hovered in the air between the two Avatars. They waited obediently for a cue from Enki, as Erishkegal gazed upon their delicate forms.

"Consolations from Adonai's Kingdom, for the sufferings you have endured these long ages, in your labors and burdens," Enki answered her gently.

He recalled the moment before Erishkegal led the outcast Nephilim from the face of the world. Defiant and resolute, she had blazed with a resplendent luminance as she guided the creatures she had spared across the Veil. Like a pillar of flame, she had served as a beacon for an exodus born of mercy, and in doing so Erishkegal had embodied Adonai's Light.

"I was blind in that moment, when the storms fell on the world, as were my companions. We did not see the path that Adonai ordained. You trusted to Adonai, and founded a realm that now calls to some of those fallen into deepest darkness."

He stared into her eyes as he openly broached the mystery that confounded him the most. How souls were coming to her realm, escaping the claws of the Ten-Fold Kingdom, was far beyond his understanding. He hoped that she would give him some insight into how the incomprehensible was happening in her dominion with apparent regularity.

"I know not the mystery of how one comes to my shores. I only know that they do, and that I must await all who can find their way to refuge," Erishkegal said. Every layer of her voice sounded heavy, weighed down with an unfathomable weariness. "I can see that my realm is serving a purpose that I never conceived of when I led the outcasts through the Veil. I do not question this purpose, as my path has led to it. I sense the workings of Adonai deeper within the arrival of each and every human spirit that the waves carry into Manzazu."

Enki was deeply saddened as he recognized the depths of suffering that Erishkegal had endured, governing a realm existing in a place utterly alien to an Avatar of the Great Throne. He did not fault her for her severity, or for her intractable defiance in protection of the mission she had undertaken. It was clear that she was being guided by an inner faith, as apparently she did not fully understand the profound things taking place in her realm.

He loved her with a tempestuous fire, and the ache that he felt at the thought of her long suffering was cavernous. He wept tears of flame that floated down from his face, dissipating as they neared the ground.

"Do not weep for me, Enki, for this is the path I chose," Erishkegal said, more softly. "It is true that my heart has longed to be amongst you, dear Enki, and the other Avatars, my brothers and sisters, once again. Sometimes it is hard to remember the eternal Light in these shrouded lands, but I cannot turn from this path."

"Then before we go to Inanna, allow me to bring you a measure of comfort from above," Enki said.

He conveyed his will to the pair of little beings he had brought with him, filled with a burning love for Erishkegal. He regretted that he could not assume her pain, and take it into his own being.

The first of the celestial creatures approached her, drawing forth a thin, delicate-looking object it had carried protectively all the way from Adonai's limitless realms. It was a single blade of grass, taken from the hill that the eternal Tree of Life surmounted. It glowed with a soft light that could never be dimmed. The little creature laid it gently into the palm of Erishkegal's right hand.

# ERISHKEGAL

A comforting heat radiated from the touch of the celestial blade of grass, spreading throughout her spirit. She basked for a moment in the relief that the heavenly object brought to her.

Memories flashed through her mind's eye, as she recalled with perfect clarity the day that she had embraced a lonely, sorrow-filled path. After being amongst her kind since before even time existed, that day had been the last she had set her eyes on an Avatar, until Inanna had arrived at the gates of her abyssal dominion.

Every last shred of her power had been employed in the guidance of the outcast Nephilim across the Veil, through the Abyss, and into the realm she had been compelled to call out of the darkness.

In a tainted atmosphere, far removed from Adonai's radiance, the shadowy forms that had begun to take shape did not even contain the echoes of the heavenly realms that the Middle Lands possessed. Crafting the darkness into vast landscapes was an agonizing strain, as Erishkegal willed the essence of the Abyss into something that would not be entirely unfamiliar in nature to the world the outcasts had left behind.

An arid, rocky land, creased with undulations, dotted with mountains and hills, and carved with deep gorges began to take form. The tears of the pain she endured had been the genesis for the lakes and rivers of the new land, every single drop expanding into an increasing flow.

The clouded skies that soon billowed over the embryonic lands took on the essence of her righteous anger. Rippling with surges of lightning, and always churning, the vaporous masses had never ceased in their stormy, brooding appearance.

The Nephilim had entered the new lands as Erishkegal turned her efforts to the final elements of the nascent dwelling place. The ground had shaken as towering obsidian walls were called up from within them. One after another, seven tremendous barriers arose, of immense heights that reached the clouds themselves.

She had chosen seven as a tribute to Adonai, in honoring the seven High Avatars given the honor of attending the Great Throne. The names of the sacred Avatars had flowed through her mind as she established the ramparts to ward her new dominion; Uriel, Raphael, Raguel, Mikael, Zerachiel, Gabriel, and Remiel.

Each of the seven Avatars signified certain qualities, but it was the seventh, Remiel, that struck her profoundly as she contemplated the nature of her budding realm. It was known that Remiel was the Avatar tasked with bringing forth all souls at the conclusion of time. It was Remiel's voice that would pierce the darkness with the sweetest of melodies, the song of life itself.

Through Remiel, Adonai would call all back into the fullness of consciousness, including the vast multitudes held within the deep slumber of the Void. The Avatar would have the tremendous honor of presiding over the last gasps of death, which would be banished to the Outer Darkness forever.

The throne of Remiel represented so much to Erishkegal, beckoning with eternal light across the ages. The Nephilim she had taken into her care trod upon a long, arduous path, one she had chosen to walk with them.

If she could guide them to a destination where death held no dominion, and they too could partake of the final triumph, she knew all the pain and agony involved would be justified. The vision of the outcast creatures hearing Remiel's voice, calling to them from the Seventh Throne into Adonai's Light, had girded Erishkegal through every trial.

Above everything, including the seven great ramparts, Erishkegal had then instilled a layer that distorted light itself, an impenetrable shield that had served her capably ever since. It was a thin draping that had taken almost every last shred of her energy to create, but it had effectively thwarted the denizens of the Abyss in the long ages to follow.

Confounding things like the swarms of Galla endlessly hunting in the darkness, it left any potential adversaries in a state of disarray. In later times, that disorientation had left the things of the Abyss highly vulnerable in the presence of Kur, and the other Nephilim that had taken to guarding the boundaries of her dominion.

Egalkurzagin, her mountain palace, and the majestic Sanctum that crowned it, were forged in the last gasps of her strength.

She remembered collapsing within the newly fashioned abode, and falling into a kind of hibernation, as she slowly began to recover and regain her strength.

When she had eventually set forth to create the gates in the seven walls, the grand chamber where the seven judges of the Anunnaki Tribunal would hold court, and other places within the gloomy, storm-ridden realm, she had known that things would be very different in her new existence. While her strength had returned, a great heaviness of spirit had taken hold.

That ponderous feeling had dwelled within her all throughout the extensive ages that followed. It had even grown, enlarging as the mysterious ocean formed that lapped at the edges of her realm.

Her spirit had suffered much by the time the first of the human souls washed up on her shores. Only the faintest recognition of an inner resonance with Adonai saved her from absolute despair.

She ached for the touch of heavenly light, but knew that she had to forge ahead with the enigmatic path she had chosen to take. Each step was more laborious than the last, living in a realm shrouded with shadow and uncertainty.

Peril crouched at every turn, and she could find no succor, or respite from the mounting burdens. Her spirit cried out fervently to Adonai, full of longing, but she could no longer hear His voice. Despite being surrounded by many thousands of living beings, the Avatar had felt entirely alone for ages.

Only now, as she gently cradled the blade of grass in the palm of her hand, did she feel a lightness of spirit returning once again. She savored the joyous sensation, as the essence of laughter coursed within her.

A radiant smile came to Erishkegal's face, and the appearance of her body began to shimmer, as small flames manifested in the place of skin. Wings flourished outward from her back, translucent and graceful, as her primary appearance manifested before Enki's eyes. It was the first time she had taken her original form since she had assumed it within the realms beyond the White City.

She reveled in the invigorating feeling, spreading her pairs of wings outward, and desiring with a burning passion to soar all the way up to the heavenly realms. It took all of her willpower not to give leave to the powerful desires within, anchored as she was to the path and responsibilities she had accepted.

The sensations gradually ebbed, but did not disappear entirely, as she regained the fullness of the human form she had maintained since the foundation of her realm.

The second creature left the side of its companion and drifted slowly forward, bearing another gift from Enki to Erishkegal. Without a word passing between them, Erishkegal knew that the little being wanted her to open her mouth, and extend her tongue. She did so, as she noted the tiny pouch of translucent skin on the creature's breast, holding a sparkling liquid, the twinkling elements of which were like motes of effulgent light.

The creature came as close as it possibly could without alighting on her tongue. With great care, it deposited a little of the contents within the pouch. Erishkegal knew the nature of the precious liquid from the moment that it touched the essence of her being.

A single drop of the Waters of Life rested upon her tongue, as she closed her eyes. Rejuvenation flooded her, washing away all of the weariness and sorrows she had endured throughout the ages. An abounding sense of delight danced throughout her spirit, as memories of wondrous sights and exquisite harmonies flowed throughout her.

Behind all of the powerful images and rapturous feelings of elation, the softest of whispers sounded within the depths of her soul. The Voice that she had despaired of ever hearing again graced her for only a moment, but each of the words spoken were treasures inestimable. For the first time since she had left the higher realms behind, holding fast to an inner conviction that she could not shed, a peaceful smile spread across her face, as a spectacular light emitted from within her.

She looked to Enki, and felt the abundant joy in him at her revival.

"You heard His Voice," Enki said, simply.

"I despaired of ever hearing Him again," she confessed.

"Then know with confidence the path you are on is still in harmony with Him," Enki stated.

"I can endure everything that may come knowing that," Erishkegal replied, with humility.

The oppressive weight had been taken from her, and she knew she could continue forward with a fresh vigor. She felt completely revitalized, surpassing even the day she had stepped across the Veil. In all of her existence, she had never felt stronger than she did that moment.

"I thank you, Enki, for these unexpected gifts, though I would rather that you and Inanna had remained in the dominions above," Erishkegal said, as her mind returned to the matters at hand. "Let us go to her, and perhaps these gifts will save her from the grasp of the Void."

# SETH

Seth craned his neck back, peering into the shifting, colorful hues spread high above him. It was a magical vision, vivid and surreal, and he would have thought he was dreaming were it not for the intensity of the reality.

The walk to the top of the cobalt rock column had been a lengthy one. A narrow path ascended the pillar, winding around its circumference with a modest slope of incline.

Despite the considerable distance, Seth did not feel tired at all. If anything, he was increasingly invigorated. He doubted he could ever grow weary in such a spectacular atmosphere.

"Unbelievable," Raymond commented, from Seth's side.

"Not your everyday view," Seth replied, continuing to gaze skyward.

"And I thought encountering the wolf things was pretty incredible," Raymond stated. "This ... well, I can't find the words to describe the feeling."

"It keeps getting more and more amazing, doesn't it?" Seth asked, finally bringing his eyes down.

He looked out over the sprawling vista. To either side, and to the back, were ranks of other columns such as the one he had surmounted. They stretched as far as his eyes could see, like a great forest of stone monoliths.

If the gates to the heavenly realms lay to the east, he wondered what was beyond the western horizon. Some instinct within conveyed a feeling of apprehension, as he contemplated the boundary of Purgatarion opposite the one bordering the infinite realms.

"There's another one of those statue things," Annika remarked, pointing downward to a niche in the side of one of the other columns.

Seth followed her gesture, and saw the stone-carved creature that was just like one they had passed on their way up to the top of the column. Winged, with long claws, an arsenal of sharp teeth, and well over ten feet tall, the sculpture was incredible in its detail.

It was a rather fearsome-looking statue to place in such exquisitely beautiful environs, but he was aware he knew very little of the ethereal world surrounding him. He wished they had some time to roam farther, but the Watcher had been clear that they did not have long until they returned to their own world.

"Wow, now you definitely don't see that every day!" Annika said excitedly, now pointing outward, over the plains stretching westward.

A pair of Gryphons was flying by the columns. Seth could barely believe his eyes, even if he recognized what they were immediately.

Movies and games had portrayed the creatures often enough, but seeing living ones was an incomparable experience. They flew with an easy grace, their eagle-heads fixed forward, and their forelegs tucked into the undersides of their bodies.

One of the creatures glanced briefly in the direction of Seth and the others, but did not slow, as it continued forward with its companion. Seth, astounded with what he was experiencing, watched them grow smaller in the distance.

"There, again," Jonathan said, looking in yet another direction.

"You're seeing things, Jonathan," Annika teased him, with a grin.

Seth laughed, again seeing nothing, despite Jonathan's adamant insistence that some kind of fairy had been trailing them.

"I'm telling you, something's following us," Jonathan said. "Small, with wings."

"And if it is, it won't harm us. I don't think the Watchers would leave us alone where we could be in danger," Seth replied.

"I'm not afraid of it," Jonathan said, keeping his eyes fixed to where he had claimed to see the fairy creature. "I just want to know what it is."

"They're coming in," Raymond said, drawing Seth's attention back up the skies.

Seth looked upward, and saw four winged shapes approaching the column they stood on. The airborne quartet became more distinct as they neared, and Seth saw that Talthannor was in the lead of the others. Jakiel and Arundinel flew together behind the lion-maned entity, with Utahor bringing up the rear.

After a few moments, Talthannor alighted on the broad surface. The others landed smoothly, in good order, as Talthannor paced up to Seth. "You traveled a fair distance," the Watcher said to him.

"Wanted to explore a little," Seth said. "I'm sure not many from my world have had a chance to see this."

"Very few. And it is far past the time to return to your own world," Talthannor replied, looking over toward the other three Watchers that had carried them into Purgatarion. The other creatures were speaking with Seth's friends, though he could not hear their conversations.

Talthannor's words were not what Seth wanted to hear, but he was not in a position to take issue. He said nothing, as the Watcher crouched down, allowing Seth easy access to the entity's back.

Seth felt a deep pang of regret when they leaped from the edge, and flew away from the rock columns. His eyes voraciously drank in all the sights that he could, as they passed over the undulating, shimmering plain below.

He wanted to stay with all his heart, and found that he harbored a longing that surged when he looked towards the east. It was an unexpected recognition, but there was no denying it.

Something pulled at him from that distant horizon, a welcoming feeling, as if he were being called home. It invoked a range of powerful emotions within him, most melancholic in nature. He had to wrench his gaze back forward, unable to bear the wistful feeling flooding over him for very much longer.

As before, they passed into the strange, lightless dominion, which seemed to consume all light and sound, before emerging into the chill of a night sky. Seth felt air invading his lungs, and realized then that he had not noticed the sensation of breathing during his brief tenure in Purgatarion. It had been like being in a dream. He had felt no impetus to draw breath.

He could feel the weight of his body, and the flex of his muscles where he gripped onto Talthannor's back. The world around him had a decidedly duller cast, after having experienced a world where everything gave off a luminance from within it.

The land below sped by in a blur, clusters of lights marking small towns in the rural area. The moonlight showering on the terrain outlined the forms of wooded hills, while a few tiny moving lights indicated where lone cars wended their way around the rises on the curving roadways.

Talthannor angled downward, taking a sharp descent towards an open swathe of ground. Landing within the clearing, Seth beheld a small group of men and women coming out from the trees. One of them, a taller, bearded man, had solid blue, radiant eyes that shone brightly from the dusky shadows. He needed no confirmation from Talthannor to know that this was Calliel, the Avatar the Watcher had mentioned earlier.

"They will help you, and they have need of what you acquired," Talthannor said, lowering to the ground so that Seth could dismount.

Seth took his backpack off, holding it at his side from the loop at the top.

"I hope they can make good use of it," Seth said, feeling a little nervous as he watched the blue-eyed figure and others approaching across the grass.

"They will," Talthannor said.

Close by, his companions had dismounted and were walking towards him. They all cast glances towards the others striding towards them.

"I am Calliel, Avatar of Adonai Most High," the blue-eyed figure announced, drawing close and displaying a kindly smile towards Seth and his companions. "Talthannor says you have something that we can make use of."

Seth extended the bag containing the copies of the footage. While not entirely comfortable as he looked into the Avatar's deep, cerulean gaze, his voice resonated with confidence. "We do … and it's all right here."

# ERISHKEGAL

An unseen force suspended Inanna's form in the midst of the dark, circular chamber. Rolling gray cloud masses could be seen through an opening high above, and the interior was lit up brightly with the bursts of lightning within the thick sky cover. Between the intermittent flashes, blue light emanated from niches in the wall, where small braziers of a burnished, metallic appearance had been set.

When she had arrived at the Seven Gates, Inanna had taken on a human-like appearance comparable with the one that Erishkegal assumed within her realm. Were they human, the two could have passed for sisters.

Inanna had the same tone of skin, ebony locks of hair, and height. She was a little leaner of body, and had some minor differences in her facial characteristics, but like Erishkegal she was a stunning beauty to any who looked upon her.

Her face was now contorted into an expression of great pain, looking as if she was frozen in an agonizing moment of time. Eyes closed, and unmoving, she showed no sign of consciousness as she floated mid-air.

The semblance of flesh had faded from her appearance, taking on a worrisome translucency. Despite her anger towards Inanna's foolishness in journeying alone into the Abyss, Erishkegal had nonetheless employed every last bit of power that she could muster to keep the Avatar's form from dissipating entirely.

Erishkegal's mystical arts had stemmed the rate of the fading, but had not stopped it. A terrible danger loomed, and Inanna teetered on the edge of a precipice. If her form vanished, then she would be lost to the Void until the End of Days.

Erishkegal strode quietly towards Inanna, as the two little winged creatures brought by Enki drifted along silently behind her. The anger that the sight of the inert, dimming Avatar normally evoked in Erishkegal was not present this time. She felt a purity of compassion towards Inanna, desiring only the full restoration of the other's vitality.

"Kurgaru and Kalaturro, bring succor to Inanna, a beloved Avatar of Adonai, as you have done for myself," she instructed the two creatures in a low voice, coming to a halt a couple of paces away from the hovering form of the other Avatar.

The two shimmering beings fluttered slowly to Inanna's side. They took up positions close to her soft lips, as one of them had done so very recently with Erishkegal.

Erishkegal watched with hope and expectation, having experienced the sheer power of the gifts that the two creatures had graced her with. She did not see how the forces eroding Inanna's vitality could withstand the celestial benefactions, hearkening from the undying realms themselves.

The one that had given Erishkegal the Waters of Life made its way to the lips of Inanna, and bestowed another drop of the sacred liquid. Erishkegal could see the visible effects of the power radiating across Inanna's body as the liquid was absorbed into her, bringing her form back from the brink of dissipation, and infusing an appearance of solidity.

The second creature then moved forward, and Erishkegal expected to see it withdraw another of the grass blades sheltered before the Tree of Life. What happened then astonished the Avatar.

Instead of a blade of grass, the creature brought forth a crimson drop of liquid it had been cradling in a pouch of skin on the middle of its underside. Erishkegal sensed at once that the drop was blood, but its nature both mystified and awed her.

The tiny drop emanated tremendous power. Her perception was that it was a human drop of blood, but there was also the presence of something greater, the essence of divinity. Though the notion confounded her, the idea that the drop possessed a wholeness of both humanity and divinity resonated strongly with every sense of truth and insight that she held.

She wondered whom the mysterious blood belonged to, as there had been no such being in the flood-doomed world she had left behind so many ages ago. Her gaze then fixed to Inanna, to see what the blood was capable of.

The look of pain fled Inanna's face, and the Avatar stirred into consciousness the moment the drop of blood was placed gently upon her forehead, as if she were being anointed. Her spirit-body filled the chamber with a brilliant surge of light coming from within.

Wings of fire flared outward as Inanna rose into an upright position. Her eyes burned with a fierce intensity as she turned her head and looked towards Erishkegal.

Erishkegal could say nothing, amazed at the swiftness of Inanna's revival. The power contained in the tiny drop of blood was incredible, as if it encapsulated the essence of Adonai.

"Erishkegal, beloved friend, and Avatar of the Great Throne, you have suffered much to spare me the timeless sleep," Inanna addressed her, speaking with a melodious strength that provided yet another testament that she had been restored to fullness.

"I would have taken your place, if I could have," Erishkegal replied. Her countenance then hardened. "But it was not I that beckoned you to this place. Your own choice brought you here."

"I am accountable for my own actions, as is the way of all creatures of Adonai," Inanna stated.

"It brings me great joy to see your strength returned," Erishkegal said. "I could not stop the decline that had come over you. The wounds you suffered to your spirit were too great for the power allowed me."

"There is nothing that the Blood cannot heal," Inanna said.

"Who carried that Blood in the world?" Erishkegal asked, unable to restrain the one question pulsing inside her.

The intensity of the light in the chamber lessened then, as Inanna assumed her previous, human-like form. A serene, kindly smile rested upon her face when the transformation was complete.

"One who walked the world in the ages that followed the Great Flood," Inanna answered. "There is much to tell you of the things that have happened in the world since you stepped across the Veil."

"And I would like to hear all of it," Erishkegal said, thirsting for knowledge of the enigmatic figure alluded to by Inanna.

"I will tell you all that you wish to know, but you must return with us to the higher realms," Inanna responded, her tone becoming more somber.

"I cannot abandon the task I have accepted here," Erishkegal replied, her timbre matching the gravity of the other Avatar.

Her conviction was unbending, and nothing that Inanna could say would convince her to abandon her abyssal dominion. The stream of souls washing up on her shores had to be attended to. Erishkegal knew that truth within the core of her spirit; even if the manifestation of the turbulent, mist-shrouded sea, and the souls carried into Manzazu by it, remained deep mysteries.

Though they had now lived for the equivalence of ages, the Nephilim in her realm also needed her continuing guidance. The Anunnaki Tribunal had grown substantially in wisdom, but the power and knowledge of a full Avatar was necessary to address the threats of their common Adversary.

Still capable of bringing forth new life within the otherworldly domain, the Nephilim had expanded greatly in number inside the boundaries of Erishkegal's underworld realm. She knew that she served as their only connection to the highest of realms, and was the only creature remaining with them of the kind that had brought about their genesis.

Though their origins had been the result of a wicked transgression of Adonai's will, they nonetheless shared a sort of kinship with Erishkegal. She could not, in any tiny fragment of her conscience, even consider abandoning them.

Inanna stared at Erishkegal without reply for a few moments, before nodding. "Your purpose and your calling bond you closely to the fate of those you harbor within this place."

"I cannot leave those whom I have been given to care for," Erishkegal stated.

"It saddens me that we will be separated for a while longer, as I must return to the dominions above," Inanna said.

"If the Anunnaki Tribunal deems it permissable," Erishkegal responded firmly.

She could feel the sudden surprise emanating from Inanna, as the other Avatar realized the implications. It was still not decided whether the departures of Inanna, Enki, and the others that had come with them, were too great of risks to take.

The Anunnaki Tribunal had to reach consensus on that issue, as the matter at hand involved them, and all of their kind. Erishkegal could not make a unilateral declaration on her own, and then see that decision result in the gaze of the Shining One fixing upon her realm. If Diabolos' attention focused in their direction, they would face almost certain destruction and bondage.

No single Avatar of Adonai possessed the power to overcome the Lord of the Abyss, as the Risen Throne had voraciously accumulated strength ever since the Great War began. Only Adonai surpassed the might of Diabolos, a being that had seized the crown of death, and who wielded powers born of the Outer Darkness; that fearsome dominion separated fully from Adonai's Grace.

None would dispute Erishkegal's authority, were she to command the release of the visitors. The Nephilim had long ago acclaimed her as Queen of Manzazu, even when she had given them the Tribunal. She had accepted the title, as queens were figures of authority that existed in the world they had left behind, and her assumption of such a role helped to guide the exiled Nephilim in the early ages of Manzazu.

Yet it had always been vitally important to her that the occupants of Manzazu exercised their own free will, and ultimately governed their own affairs. To bypass the Tribunal entirely, in a scenario that could affect every last one of the Nephilim and human souls within Manzazu, would not just be reckless; it would represent a grave betrayal on her part.

Erishkegal left the chamber, unshakably resolved to seeing the will of the Tribunal adhered to. She would accept nothing less.

# GREGORY

A long, loose column of men and women marched through the trees, as the damp touch of pre-dawn mists wafted over the nearly one hundred resistance fighters in their polyglot garb. At their head, Gregory strode with the confident gait of a determined warrior.

His mind was collected, and his resolve was set firmly. A great gamble was about to be risked; one that could inject lightning into the resistance, or watch it disintegrate in moments.

Either way, Gregory could accept his fate when the sun set. If the course of the coming battle went favorably, he would be fighting onward, seeking to take the resistance to greater heights. If it did not, he figured he would not survive to see the next day.

Should the resistance fall, dying was not the worst of outcomes. He already knew he could not live under the technology-driven subjugation of the human spirit that the enemy intended for everyone.

Benjamin was leading another similar force through the wooded hills, from the other side of their objective. Very soon, the two groups would be fanning out, and placing their intended target under siege.

The looming assault was so close to the last one, rolling in on its heels. Gregory knew that the enemy would not capitulate after the destruction of the fusion center. Rather, the enemy would call in greater strength, and counter operations would be launched, but the full assembly of additional troops, equipment, and resources would take a little time.

Nothing was for certain in the maelstrom of war, but Gregory believed that the resistance had a small window of time to take advantage of. With the resistance forces virtually unscathed following the strike on the fusion center, an attack could be concentrated upon a target of significance. The coming day would see the resistance ratcheting up their boldness even further.

Dante and a small contingent would sweep into the airfield next to the prison compound, and disable any military assets that could be found. The runway would then be rendered unusable for fixed-wing aircraft.

The rest of the fighters would ring the encampment as best as they could. Given the significant size of the place, and their lower overall numbers, it was not certain that the resistance could keep a tight encirclement maintained, but they would try.

Word was being spread, even as the two columns marched. The surrounding populace was being informed with leaflets and broadcasts about the nature of the operation, and the reasons for undertaking it.

The broadcasts were being made through the efforts of the team overseen by Chuck. The frequencies the reports were being carried on had been disseminated carefully over the past few days, with no hint of what was to be broadcast on them.

Ultimately, it was a mission of liberation, launched to free hundreds of unjustly incarcerated people caught in the claws of a malignant tyranny. Gregory had no doubt that the sympathies of the surrounding populace would be heavily in the resistance's favor, even if many would refuse open support out of fear.

The technicals were not being utilized at the epicenter of the mission this time. The main road to the federal compound was being watched assiduously, with armed checkpoints, and there was no other sensible way to bring the vehicles close enough.

Gregory had decided to deploy the technicals in carefully concealed positions, where they would be sacrificed in the act of delaying enemy relief forces. A barrage of rockets into a column of vehicles was a sure way to cause an enemy to hesitate, and the stakes were high enough that Gregory and the other resistance leaders were willing to concede the technicals.

The crews operating them had been strictly commanded to vacate the vehicles as soon as the first volley was loosed. There would be no time to reload for a second round, and to stay in the vicinity meant almost certain death or capture.

Gregory and Consuela climbed the slope to the top of an extended ridgeline. Both brought their binoculars up to their eyes, and stared out towards the day's prize.

The mere sight of the massive prison compound stoked his ire. The inward-facing barbed wire and watchtowers betrayed its purpose immediately. The airfield and rail line outside of it confirmed the great importance of the federal facility.

Gregory could see throngs of people milling about. All were detainees that had been snatched away from families and productive lives, who did not warrant even a minute imprisoned in such a terrible place.

"We're taking that abomination out today," Gregory said in a tight, low voice, which resonated with the burning anger he was feeling inside.

"I'm with you, come whatever may," Consuela declared, putting the binoculars back into the case attached to her belt.

She brought her rifle around from where it had been slung over her shoulder. She sighted through the scope, slowly moving the barrel as she examined a few potential targets.

"I've got a few options already, especially on the guard towers," she remarked icily.

"Be sure to save a few for me," Gregory replied, equally cold in tone.

He brought up his fifty-caliber sniper rifle, and gently stroked the barrel. "Didn't get to use her in the last fighting. Felt a little guilty about keeping her cooped up."

Consuela grinned. "Well then, be more of a gentleman this time."

"I'm bringing her to this dance, that's for certain," Gregory said, with a grin.

Some rustling behind him indicated that the radio operator was coming up with his gear. This time, Chuck had been assigned to attend Gregory.

"Hello Chuck, ready for a busy day?" Gregory asked, with an echo of sarcasm. "Things are about to get really exciting."

A mixture of nervousness and excitement was exhibited on the other man's face. He stammered in his response. "Yes … I'm ready … sir!"

"Get me connected to Benjamin, as soon as you can," Gregory instructed.

"Yes sir!" Chuck responded quickly, opening the cases he was carrying, and laboring to set everything up.

Gregory scanned the compound again, and looked out towards the airfield with its primary runway. A pair of Skyhawk helicopters, just like the one he had downed at the Revere home, could be seen near one hangar. A few smaller, civilian-model aircraft were scattered about the grounds, a couple situated close to the runway.

Gregory knew that Dante and his group were closing in on that area, and hoped that they took the Skyhawks out swiftly. The two helicopters in the air could pose a huge dilemma during the early stages of the attack.

"Got him … sir!" Chuck called out, his right hand displaying the nervous tic that Gregory was beginning to get used to.

Gregory turned, and walked over to where Chuck had set up the equipment. He put on the headset he offered, which was fitted with a microphone.

Benjamin had walked away from the police force, no longer able to stomach continued participation following the mass arrests in the recent days and weeks. It had not taken long for Gregory to recruit his brother, and install him in command of a contingent of fighters.

"So you are set up already, Ben?" Gregory asked, chuckling. "You are taking to your new role quickly."

"We're all in place for the big day," Ben replied, sounding buoyant.

"Everything's looking pretty quiet around here."

"Then let's make a little noise, and see if we can't get these clowns to clock in early today," Gregory said.

"That would be nice, wouldn't it?" Benjamin responded. His voice lowered, growing more somber. "But my gut tells me they won't."

"Then we'll just have to give them a little old-fashioned encouragement," Gregory posited, a steely edge coming into his voice.

"So are your troops ready to spread out, and help mine to get this place a little more enclosed?" Benjamin asked.

"We're ready," Gregory said.

"Good luck," Benjamin responded, a solemn undertone to his words.

"You too, Ben," Gregory said, matching his brother's timbre.

Gregory took the headset off, and handed it over to Chuck.

"Keep a connection going with Ben's radio man, and keep an ear out for incoming reports," he instructed Chuck, who nodded, looking back to Gregory with his widened eyes, still glimmering with excitement. "We need to know right away if anything is approaching us from behind our lines. Immediately. You got that?"

Chuck nodded quickly. "Yes, sir!"

"Benjamin's in place?" Consuela called over to him.

Gregory nodded, as he walked back to where she stood. The morning had a calm demeanor, unveiling a day that promised to be clear and sunny. Light breezes ruffled the leaves of the trees around them. The tranquility was about to be shattered irrevocably.

"Send the command to secure the perimeter," Gregory ordered Chuck in a stout voice, staring down at the federal compound.

"Yes ... sir!" Chuck replied, acknowledging the command, as he clicked his communication channel open.

# SKYLAR

Though extremely uneasy about the situation facing her, Skylar called upon every ounce of willpower within, compelling herself to trail the Fallen Avatar through the air. Across hills and valleys, and soaring over roads, towns, and cities, the unlikely pair covered a vast distance in the passing of a handful of moments.

The astral landscape rushed by in a blur far beneath her, and it was all that she could do to keep up with the spirit-entity before her. Though the Fallen Avatar retained a human-like form, it did not lessen her apprehension in the slightest.

She kept reminding herself that this was an entity that had willingly joined the ranks of Diabolos at the beginning of time, and had served the Shining One ever since. That fact could only be disregarded at her mortal peril.

"He is there, below," the Fallen Avatar informed her, after drawing up into a steady hover.

Sure enough, the figure of a man limned by a faint, spectral glow was visible farther below. The Fallen Avatar had been able to hone right in on the astral traveler, like a hound tracking the scent of its quarry. As the Fallen Avatar had explained, the things of the dark Abyss were well-attuned to their own kind, sharing a bond attached with the Risen Throne of Diabolos.

She looked back to the Fallen Avatar. "This is the one that found Benedict?"

The infernal being nodded in confirmation, and replied dispassionately. "He is the one. Do not dismiss caution, for as you can harm him, so he can harm you. You are both of the same substance."

Skylar nodded in response, though she had intended to keep her guard up. Wariness and caution had served her well, all throughout her life.

She glanced down at the slender object grasped in her hand. It looked conspicuously like a short blade, formed out of a black, crystal-like material. It had a reflective surface, but did not appear particularly remarkable.

It was not a physical object. She had only been able to receive it once she was in the astral, disembodied state. Before she had allowed herself to be taken up in spirit, the Fallen Avatar had invited her to grasp it. Her flesh had passed right through it, as if it were just an illusion.

When she had lifted free from the shell of flesh, bone, and blood, the object suddenly had physical properties. The Fallen Avatar had not been very forthcoming in regards to where the object had come from, other than to say that it was a conduit for an imperfect spirit of mortal origins.

"Remember, that weapon is nothing without the empowerment of your spirit," the Fallen Avatar instructed her.

"I know," she replied.

"Then go, and see that my desire for redemption is no ruse, as I help you to overcome a spirit of great importance to those serving the Shining One," the Fallen Avatar said.

"It all remains to be seen," Skylar responded dourly, before starting towards the drifting, glowing figure.

Taking a circuitous route, she came in behind the astral body of the man. On closer inspection, there was no doubt that this was the same individual that she had encountered searching for Juan Delgado.

She concentrated intensively on the space behind the astral form, finally identifying the narrow, shining thread of light that she knew was the ethereal tether back to his physical body. What she was contemplating was unprecedented, and went beyond anything that she had learned, or been trained for.

A part of her was still suspicious, wondering whether the Fallen Avatar was manipulating her into doing something deeply abominable. Yet at the same time she knew that she had made little headway concerning the Walker of the Setian Path.

He was a terrible weapon in the hands of the enemy, and allowing him to continue was to imperil so many that were depending on her. The Fallen Avatar claimed that he would be working to save Benedict, so the least that she could do was put an end to the Setian.

Most importantly, she had spent an entire night in supplication to Adonai, and had emerged with peace in her heart, and a conviction to follow through with the proposed mission. She grasped feverishly onto that resolve as she moved to do something that was entirely unprecedented, and deemed in concept to be impossible.

She glided up smoothly behind the other traveler, who was so intent on his task that he failed to notice her approach. He was busy observing a small group of people sitting on the porch of a cabin.

Two were young women, one was an attractive man of about the same age, and the other was an older gentleman, perhaps in his upper fifties. They all looked relaxed, simply enjoying each other's company under the early evening's moonlight.

Eyeing them, Skylar realized suddenly just who they were. She had seen them back on the property where Benedict had been taken.

No matter what the Fallen Avatar's underlying agenda was, she knew that to leave the premises would be to consign the men and women to an ill-fated path. The astral rogue in front of Skylar was not there for voyeuristic purposes.

She concentrated intensively on the black blade in her spirit-hand, and felt a pulsating energy begin to course through her. The permeating sensation was very different from anything that she had experienced. A heat enveloped her body, right as the surface of the weapon began to change in appearance.

A surging flame steadily replaced the black surface until she was gripping onto a pure blade of fire. The weapon did not burn her, though robust flames licked the surface of her wrist and hands many times over.

With the weapon fully formed, Skylar did not hesitate for a moment. With a downward slash, she cut with deadly intent through the faint, silver line. A feeling similar to a light shock jolted her briefly, but passed without incident. No sign of the faintly-gleaming strand remained to be seen.

The traveler twisted about, and his face displayed livid anger as he beheld Skylar. His eyes widened as he took in the sight of the blazing weapon in her hands, and it was then that he realized what had happened. His gaze darted about, and panic was reflected in his face.

What followed seemed to crawl before Skylar's eyes. An intense, blinding light flooded over the man, and for an instant, he disappeared from sight.

When he came back into view, a horrendous scream poured from within him. It was the sound of elemental terror, and frenzied desperation.

A fire broke out over his body. Unlike the blade that she had held, the flames emerging from the man's surface clearly wracked him with tremendous pain. He shrieked over and over again, as he jerked and twisted about violently, as if trying to shake the fire off. His efforts were futile, as the flames lapped at him with a cavernous hunger.

The man began to descend, and it looked as if a gulf of impenetrable blackness opened up just underneath. The man was powerless to resist, building up speed as if he was being sucked downward with great force.

His forlorn cries faded, until he was gone from sight and the rift closed itself. Skylar shuddered, and glanced down at the blade she had used to sever the man from the mortal coil.

The fires were ebbing before her eyes, lowering and sinking back into the blade until it displayed a shiny, obsidian surface once again. She lingered in place, staring at the weapon for several moments as she pondered the magnitude of what had just taken place.

Skylar glanced up at the four people sitting on the porch, entirely oblivious to the deadly incident that had just transpired. Her act had spared them from whatever dark purpose the Setian represented. She had no regrets about what she had done, though the aftermath of the cord's severance had been a terrible thing to witness.

A part of her wondered about who had sent the man, and their reaction to his death. Whether they could determine how he was killed remained to be seen, but if they did fathom the nature of his death, Skylar was certain they would muster a response.

The only thing working in her favor was the incredible rarity of those who could be taken up in spirit, whether a Shield Maiden like herself, or a Walker of the Setian Path like the man she had slain. Having discovered the deadly ability, she was glad for that fact. If there were numbers of astral assassins roving the non-physical planes, the havoc that would be wreaked was inestimable in scope.

Of course, she had had an accomplice in the action, having been given the weapon that served as a conduit for her spiritual energy. The slaying had not been entirely achieved by herself, and to do it again would require the use of the strange weapon. She would have to procure the blade from the Fallen Avatar, as it was not something she could take back with her into the physical world.

Then again, the Fallen Avatar, or perhaps any Avatar, whether in league with Diabolos or serving Adonai, could bestow such a weapon on any traveler of the astral planes. The thought was highly troubling, and she knew that she would have to render an extensive report on the matter to the greater authorities amongst the Shield Maidens.

They would need to be warned that such an assassination was possible. Informing them would also require a confession that she had cooperated with a Fallen Avatar, presenting a dilemma that she did not want to begin to broach.

As the vexing thoughts began to swirl in her mind, Skylar soared up to where the Fallen Avatar had remained hovering in place. The expression on the Avatar's face was ambiguous.

"It is done," Skylar informed him impassively, though she doubted that the powerful entity had missed a single thing that had transpired.

"And he has gone to the destination he chose," the Fallen Avatar replied sternly.

She extended the black blade towards the demonic being, the hilt-end first. For the most part, she was glad to be rid of it, and was not sure that she wanted to know anything concerning its origins.

The Fallen Avatar accepted it from her calmly, and looked into her eyes. "A killing in the spirit world by a mortal being is no small thing."

"It had to be done," Skylar said.

"Do you feel exultation?" the Avatar asked her.

Skylar shook her head. "None. None whatsoever. I did what I had to do, but I felt no joy in the act, and I do not celebrate the killing."

The Fallen Avatar nodded, and she sensed that the being was pleased with her answer. She knew in her heart that she had spoken truthfully. The only emotion that she had felt was in being shaken by the horror displayed on the condemned Setian.

"Then what you did was not tainted by the touch of the Risen Throne," the Avatar informed her. "Did you see a light that blinded you?"

"Yes, just after I cut the cord," she answered.

"The man faced Adonai, and all his works were laid bare, before he was sent to the place he chose with his free will," the Fallen Avatar stated.

Her curiosity begged a further question. "Why did he not go straight to the nether regions, if that is what he chose?"

"Adonai is the source of the man's spirit, and an account was demanded of him, as it would be of any creature whose life was ordained from the beginning, even before my kind existed," the Fallen Avatar said. "Adonai is merciful, which is the only desperate hope that I cling to, but He is also just. The man chose his path, as did I, and we both received what we elected.

"I understand that I may never return to add my voice to the chorus before the Great Throne. If that is so, then I will accept an eternity of remorse and contrition, and the punishment of being bound to a Liar's Throne in the Outer Darkness is the least I deserve.

"I know that every act I do to aid you, and the others serving Adonai, makes my plight increasingly worse, as the Shining One will inevitably uncover what I have done. No mercy will be shown me, and the wrath of the Risen Throne will be unleashed on me forever. I will be reviled throughout the nether realms as a traitor to Diabolos. Yet I do not care, as I see more clearly now, than I ever have before.

"Never forget that to be the least before the Great Throne is far better than being the greatest in the Outer Darkness. What a fool I am, and have been."

Skylar was moved by the outpouring of sadness and regret that she heard within the other's words, and pitied the supernatural creature. To all understanding, the Fallen Avatar was irrevocably condemned, having fully known Adonai, and rejected the Great Throne when joining the ranks of Diabolos.

That the Fallen Avatar was so full of penitence, and cognizant of the futility of seeking to return to the heavenly realms, conferred the purest essences of tragedy and nobility to the creature's hapless path. In her heart, she had no doubts that the Fallen Avatar's claims were genuine.

The infernal spirit was willing to dream an impossible dream. Skylar could not stop a few crystalline tears from falling after she returned to her physical body, and awoke to full consciousness within an empty bedroom.

# TROY

"You said you had a truck full of them. You weren't kidding. Some big fellows and gals too," one of the TTDF troopers remarked, eyeing the cluster of tall, robust-looking men and women inside the trailer of the semi.

"This is the only vehicle we could get to bring them all in," the woman replied, in an amiable, polite tone.

Sensors indicated that there was nothing to worry about in the back compartment of the truck. There was no sign of weapons, or anything else, other than the group of people riding in the trailer.

"A group of factory laborers. Just bringing them in, to get the vaccine and the Living ID," the woman replied to the guard, with a smile. "Good thing they found a cure so fast."

"Might as well get it over with. Everyone's gotta have it," the guard replied evenly, his eyes still trained on the figures looming in the shadows of the cargo space. He took note of the bright, golden eyes of one of the females, before noting a reddish hue in the eyes of a powerfully-built male just to his right.

"All of them wearing colored contacts?" the guard asked, finding the sight to be a little unusual.

"Artistic types," the woman replied, with a grin. "You know how they can be."

"Not my thing," the guard grunted.

With the long hair and thick beards on the men, and casual attire on all of them, her words nonetheless resonated with the guard. Even so, he had not seen many artists with the considerable statures of the individuals in the truck.

"Still, we gotta do some further checks. Pull this vehicle off the road," the guard indicated firmly, pointing away to the right. "And keep them all in there, doors shut, for now."

"No problem," the woman replied cooperatively, still smiling. She shut the two doors and slammed the bolt in place, placing all of the occupants inside locked in darkness. "It's done."

She gave three solid raps on the door, nodded to the guard, and moved back towards the cab of the semi. The guard's eyes roved along her tight-fitting jeans, as the sight of her shapely contours aroused his desire.

He heard a lot of movement and shuffling inside the locked trailer, as the woman put the truck in gear and pulled it off to the side of the checkpoint. He imagined that the occupants of the trailer had been jostled quite a bit during their travel, and thought nothing of it.

Using the com-link on his shoulder, he requested more troopers to come and assist with the search of the vehicle. With so many passengers, he was not going to take any chances, should things take a turn for the worst.

Several submachine guns trained on the group would be more than enough to keep any disruptions in check. A display of force worked well enough for all the other gatherings and assemblies in Troy, as everyone knew by now that the federal authorities were not reluctant to employ as much force as was deemed necessary.

# GODRAL

Shedding his clothes quickly, Godral listened to the first pops and cracks as the others in the cramped space began to change within the darkness. He willed his own transformation to proceed, feeling the painful onset of the metamorphosis as his bones shifted, and muscles and skin began to realign.

His skin tingled as coarse hairs began to bristle all over his body. His upper and lower jaws then extended, which always proved to be one of the more agonizing changes he had to endure. Human teeth retracted into his thick gums, as deadly fangs descended, accompanied by the formidable array of teeth suited for a lupine muzzle.

Once the conversion was complete, Godral stood with his muzzle facing the doors. Lowering into a crouch, he prepared to spring. All around him, other An-Ki got into position, poised for attack.

There were no misgivings regarding what he was about to do. It had only taken a few moments to detect the subtle, yet distinct, trace of the thing that bonded the men outside with the Night Hunters.

The black-clad men with their weapons were dedicated servants of the enemy. They were no different than the contingent marching through the woods that the An-Ki had destroyed prior to reaching their first refuge.

The doors opened again, swinging wide and revealing a large number of the black-clad human fighters. Godral was the first to leap outward, spearheading a crashing wave of An-Ki. The armed humans standing around looked frozen in fear, as they beheld the massive, wolfish beings falling upon them.

A few got off bursts from their weapons, the air cracking as a few painful yelps and cries emitted from stricken An-Ki. Yet most hesitated for a fraction of a second, stunned by what they saw. For them, it proved to be a fateful delay.

Godral tore into the first enemy that he could reach, his jaws finding vulnerable flesh on the man's neck. Blood sprayed as the An-Ki warrior tore his jaws free, and the doomed man toppled over to the ground, twitching as his life poured out of him.

In the swirling chaos and terror, the human fighters that the An-Ki were allied with started rushing up, as had been described to Godral. He did not stop to regard the incoming fighters, as he knew that the An-Ki had to bring down as many of the enemy humans as possible.

He stayed his right claw from mauling a terrified-looking woman who had gotten out of her vehicle and was running by Godral. Only those in the black garb, carrying weapons, were to be harmed.

The woman stared into his face and screamed hysterically, tripping and falling in her haste to get away. Godral ignored her, and continued forward.

Nearby, Sarangar roared, and threw one of the enemy soldiers high through the air. The man sailed over the edge of the bridge, his screams dwindling as he plummeted down to the river far below.

"Come! Sarangar!" Godral commanded, through blood-caked teeth.

Looking to the right, he saw An-Ki leaping over vehicles, hurling themselves at enemy soldiers with fury, and racing towards others that were farther back. Fear swept over the humans, and they appeared far more interested in fleeing than with fighting back.

Godral sprung atop the hood of a vehicle, and caught a glimpse of the terror-stricken occupants inside of it, just as he saw another trooper cowering beneath him. He dived forward, barreling into the man and pounding him into the ground. The unconscious man was mercifully spared the crushing bite on his throat that followed.

Snapping his head up at a loud thump, Godral saw another trooper on the front of the vehicle before him. Godral dodged left just as the trooper's weapon flashed, and several shots tore into the ground right behind the An-Ki.

The weapon then made a clicking sound, and a look of horror sprouted on the trooper's face as Godral rushed at him. He grasped the man about the ankles, swung him by both legs over the top of his head, and slammed him down into the road face-first, breaking the man's body in an instant.

A stream of vehicles thundered by Godral and the others, racing across the bridge. The allied fighters, with their conspicuous metallic emblems, flowed all around.

"We've got it from here!" shouted one of the incoming men, looking to Godral. He could see the brazen fear dwelling in the man's eyes.

"Cease!" Godral called out to the An-Ki nearby.

His orders were passed onward, and the An-Ki storm abated swiftly. Godral and the others of his kind gathered together, as the humans began

attending to the people that remained huddled in their vehicles.

It was not long before enough vehicles were moved out of the way that the big one the An-Ki had been carried in could be backed up. Proceeding slowly, it finally reached a space before the bridge where it could be turned around. Godral, Sarangar, and the others climbed up into the dark hold of the trailer, under the watchful, widened eyes of several allied human warriors.

# JUAN DELGADO

A Knight of the Order or a Shield Maiden occupied every exit, and all of the fighters were armed and resolute in purpose. Fingers graced the triggers of their weapons, primed to fire the instant an enemy threat emerged.

The operation was going very smoothly. The checkpoints on the bridge had been overcome rapidly, opening a channel for the incoming force to speed to the television station, and take it unawares.

"You've cooperated nicely with your masters, but don't feel like you are betraying them now, because you aren't being given a choice in this," Genevieve growled, stomping down the hallway, as she herded the frightened-looking station manager ahead of her.

Juan's heart was beating fast as Matthias accompanied him just behind.

"Keep the broadcast going as normal … for now!" Genevieve ordered, when they were in the station's control room.

One glance at the weapons carried by the intruders was enough to convince all involved with the station to cooperate fully. They did everything that they were instructed to do, though a few of the station personnel trembled with the fear gripping them.

"Get set up, and I want someone on standby for the switcher," Genevieve stridently commanded the station manager, a dark-haired woman who could only nod meekly in response.

The footage given to the Order by the teenagers was then loaded into the system, under the watchful eye of a Knight who was familiar with the operations of television stations. It was cued up, primed and awaiting the moment that was fast approaching.

"It's about showtime," Astrid, a brown-haired Shield Maiden, told Juan, as he stood by one of the studio cameras, mounted on a servo-controlled base that could be operated remotely from the control room.

"Are you ready?" she asked him, when he did not respond immediately.

"I am, don't worry," he replied, seeing an echo of relief cross her face.

"We should have all the links up about now, so this message will carry far," Astrid said.

"Juan, go ahead and stand in there, in front of the cameras," Genevieve called from the door that led to the control room.

Feeling tightness in his chest, and lightness in his belly, Juan walked forward to an area just a few feet in front of the semi-circular anchors' desk, utilized for the station's newscasts. He turned around to face the cameras, and compelled himself to take a few deeper breaths.

He took little notice of the unnerved-looking station employee that came up to him, and affixed a small lapel microphone to his shirt. The man struggled a little to clip it to the fabric, as his hands were shaking.

"Give it a quick test," Genevieve called. "Say anything."

"Testing … one, two, three … testing," Juan said.

"That's good!" Genevieve replied.

Juan looked around the room, his vision obstructed somewhat by the bright studio lights. Only Astrid, Matthias, and Genevieve were in view, though he knew that the control room was crowded.

Technicians were at their stations, being watched over by armed Knights and Shield Maidens. He could only begin to imagine the tensions beyond the broad window looking out from the control room and into the main studio area.

"Okay, Juan, follow my countdown," Genevieve called out.

There was no time to work his anxiety up any more.

"Five … four … three … two … one … you're on," Genevieve called, pointing towards him at the last words.

He paused for a second, and collected his first thoughts.

"My name is Juan Delgado, and I headed up a division at Babylon Technologies charged with new product developments. I was also present at the time that Living ID was unveiled for the first time," Juan said, staring into the black eye of the camera lens.

The camera eye leered at him, a cold, black hole appearing to consume everything in his world. Juan tried as best as he could not to think of what lay beyond the lens, in terms of the multitudes that were watching him now. His voice remained steady, even if his nerves were close to fraying.

"There is much that you have not been told, and I am here to warn you," Juan stated. "Listen to me carefully, as this may be the only chance you have to hear somebody speaking the truth."

Juan proceeded to describe everything he had witnessed at the unveiling of Living ID. He did not hesitate to name many names, and their affiliations.

Fame, money, and political power did nothing to spare a great many from being identified. Juan did not spare Dagian Underwood in the least, speaking at length of her connections in government and industry.

It was a damning indictment, filled with detail about what Living ID was, who had guided it, and what it was to be used for. The clarion danger to everyone watching the broadcast could not have been made more clear.

At the end of his address, Juan spoke about the detention camps, and the video footage that had been acquired. The transmission finished with the broadcast of the raw, uncut footage of the prison camp.

"We're done here, it's time to get out," Genevieve declared, from where she was now standing to the side of the central studio camera. Her tone softened, as she looked to Juan. "And you did wonderfully. Let us hope there are some out there with eyes to see, and a few with ears to hear."

"Thank you, Genevieve," Juan said.

In his mind the speech was a blur, and he hoped that Genevieve was not just being polite. Based on what he knew of her, he did not think she was the type to cushion a poor display.

He jerked his head to the left, as the muffled sounds of gunfire suddenly broke out.

"Get out of here! Now!" Matthias yelled at Genevieve and Astrid, as Magdalene appeared at one of the exits leading out of the studio.

She had a rifle securely in hand, and a grim look on her face. She yelled out, "They're coming at us from every side. Get to the roof!"

Juan, Astrid, Matthias, and Genevieve hurried after her, as she led them down a hallway and then slammed open a stairwell.

"Up, up! All the way!" she yelled, holding the door open, and keeping her eyes on the hallway.

Juan almost tripped twice as they ascended several floors. His legs felt heavy, out of condition for ascending many stories worth of stairs rapidly. He was out of breath by the time that they reached the top.

"Let me go first!" Genevieve shouted, kicking the bar that opened the door.

Her gun was leveled as she moved out onto the roof, scanning about for any threats. Matthias went out behind her, keeping a similar posture, followed by the others.

Ahead of them, on a circular landing pad, was the station's private helicopter. Someone was piloting it, and the engine was already engaged.

The commandeered news station's helicopter was revving up, the rotors chopping the air, as the revolutions of the blades increased in speed. The air was whipped around with great power, beating relentlessly against Juan as he hesitated a few paces outside of the door.

He felt a firm grip just above his elbow.

"We were assigned to get you out of here, and I intend to see to it," Genevieve said rigidly. She yanked him into motion, as she started towards the helicopter.

Gunfire rattled everywhere, as police and other security elements battled with both Knights and Shield Maidens farther below. Off to the right, two men stood by a pair of cables.

"The escape route for everyone else," Genevieve remarked, as they closed the distance to the helicopter.

Juan wondered what she meant, but there was no time for questions as they hurried forward.

"I'm coming, but a few of them are rushing up behind me quick," Magdalene called out, as she burst from the doorway and started across the roof at a full run.

Juan glanced over his shoulder, and saw a trooper in body-armor coming through the doorway and onto the roof, his rifle lowered. Magdalene's back was fully exposed, and there was only time to act.

But he could not possibly get there in time to help her. Despair filled him as the trooper steadied his gun and took aim.

A blond-haired figure lurched into view, just as the barrel of the trooper's gun erupted with fire. Matthias took several shots intended for Magdalene, his body jerking about as he absorbed the deadly projectiles and fell backwards.

Juan knew that Matthias was dead on impact, and the shock of the moment prevented the wellspring of emotion that would otherwise have surged to the fore from within him. He had only a split-second to take it all in, as the trooper was still facing them, assault rifle at the ready, from across the roof.

Matthias' sacrificial interference allowed just enough time for Genevieve, who had just boarded the helicopter through its side door, to fire back. Her aim was steady and true, at least two shots catching the trooper in the neck and downing him instantly.

"Hurry! Get up here now!" Genevieve shouted, as she kept her eyes trained past Magdalene and Juan for other enemy fighters.

The last two scrambled aboard, joining Genevieve and Astrid in the main compartment, and the helicopter lifted off from the pad a moment later. Juan glanced down through the window at his side, and saw the cables running at a downward slant from the roof of the station building to a building across the street.

More figures ran out onto the roof, and his heart nearly stopped, until he realized that they were Knights and Shield Maidens. Without delay, two at a time, they hooked themselves to the tethers spanning the buildings, and streaked down the length of the cables.

He was gladdened by the sight of several fighters escaping the building, but he was not spared the sight of a few falling in a hail of gunfire, as police and federal troopers gushed from the doorway.

Rising higher, the helicopter rotated and set off across the jungle of concrete and steel, following a course for the countryside. The staccato sounds of bullets being exchanged lowered in volume as they gained distance.

Juan's heart pounded as they flew over the city streets. He listened to Genevieve talking to the pilot. "There may be drones, or other helicopters nearby. They've had far enough time to scramble something in the air," she said, in a grave tone.

"There have been a few decoys set off," the pilot replied, a deep-voiced man. "There's a good chance we'll have a window to get out of here."

"Let's hope so," Genevieve added somberly. "This doesn't stand a chance if we get intercepted by something military grade."

"No, it definitely doesn't," the pilot agreed.

The words were anything but reassuring to Juan as he peered out the large windows. To escape the firefight and then get blasted out of the sky was not the end that he wanted, but he also knew that he was not in control.

Every nerve in his body was rattled as they pressed forward, the pilot pushing as rapidly as the helicopter was capable of flying. Traffic crawled on the streets below, as it was still daylight, and the curfew was hours away, but the flow was nothing compared to the days when Juan worked in the downtown building of Babylon Technologies.

His stomach felt queasy as he looked out to the skies, expecting to see a threat hurtling towards them at any second.

At the edge of the city, Juan could see a flurry of flashing lights and other activity at the bridge they had crossed to go into Troy. The place was swarming with federals, and many armored vehicles were parked along the bridge and in the area beyond it. All traffic into the city was blocked, and Juan could see where cars were being rerouted and turned back. He imagined more than a few faces were looking skyward as they passed overhead. The helicopter left the bridge behind without incident.

Juan turned and peered at the skyline of Troy. A few columns of smoke were rising deeper within the city, likely the 'decoys' mentioned earlier by the pilot. It was hard to believe how much things had changed in such a short time. The irresistible march of history was speeding up, as fundamental changes occurred across the globe.

Juan knew that they were in uncharted waters, with nothing to study or cite from the past to assist in making the best decisions for the future. He wondered where everything was heading towards, but was at peace in his heart. Win or lose, he was on the right side of the conflict, Juan knew he would never turn back, even if he knew his side would fall, and he was given a choice in the matter.

"Are you okay, Juan?" Astrid asked him gently.

He looked back to her and smiled. "I'm more than okay."

Beyond suburbs to the south of Troy, the helicopter raced into the countryside. To everyone's relief, no sign of pursuit manifested as it headed for safer harbors.

# SECTION VII

# URIA

All the An-Ki within the house were rife with signs of discomfort and suspicion. None would openly challenge Uria, but the air was thick with aversion towards what they had been compelled to do.

From the wilderness into a human dwelling place, the experience was difficult to absorb. Uria understood that well, as it had only been his blood rage that had propelled him into the house on the night its previous occupants were slain in a storm of fury.

Yet, as Carlton Tephros had indicated, the house was a safe zone for the An-Ki clan. It would also allow them to acclimate to the typical things of the modern world, and shelter them from many risks.

There was a daunting range of human tools and inventions to get used to. Uria remembered how three of his strongest warriors had leaped back, and taken up fighting postures, when vivid images had manifested on a dark, flat surface that Carlton called a television. It was like the object burst into life, flooding with colors and sharp images.

Since then, the rectangular object on the wall had become a target of tremendous fascination, rather than fear. Uria already saw its usefulness for learning the language of humans, and getting some idea of the unfamiliar customs they embraced.

With each day that passed, Uria understood more clearly the logic in Carlton's insistence that they quarter within the house. But he still needed to run free in the winds, and under the boughs of the trees, from time to time.

Piercing looks were cast down lengthy muzzles towards Carlton Tephros, who looked as if he were appraising each member of Uria's clan with scrutiny. From six and a half feet tall, to well over seven feet in height, they loomed high over Carlton, though Uria could see nothing in the man's posture or expression to indicate unease. Carlton radiated confidence, not showing even a flicker of anxiety as he addressed the An-Ki clan leader.

"I could use your aid. And I can help you gain some greater safety for your kind. I also want to help you learn the ways of this world very quickly, and all I ask in return is a little aid with my plans," he said firmly, staring directly into Uria's eyes. As he was not of the An-Ki, Uria did not interpret the direct look as a challenge.

"What help?" Uria asked, warily.

413

"Let me explain. It is like the humans I am around are of many clans. I seek to stop the fighting between these clans. I do not want to harm the clans. I just want us to work together," Carlton explained.

Uria could not sense any deception in Carlton's words. Whether a very unique kind of man, or a Messenger, Carlton had not misled the An-Ki so far.

"What if a larger clan of humans attacks you? We would be their enemies," Zeyya interjected sharply, and Uria could hear the reservation in her voice. She was very loath to helping humans in any way, and Uria did not fault her mistrust.

Uria remembered well the wars that humans had fought in the times before they had crossed the gateway. There was always an outpouring of blood in the aftermath of a conquest. The clan leader did not want to see his young clan affiliated with the losing side in a war.

"None will find profit in being my enemy, and that is what you will help me achieve," Carlton replied firmly, with a level gaze towards Zeyya. "I seek a position where no clan wants to even attempt war with me."

"Only if you succeed," Zeyya countered quickly, with a thick air of defiance. "If you do not, An-Ki blood will flow."

"You will all have to take on your human forms, very regularly," Carlton said, turning his head, and fixing Uria with a tight gaze.

"You wish us to take our third forms for long amounts of time?" Uria asked him, surprised by the revelation. He knew Carlton wanted them to use the third form, but he had not anticipated being asked to assume it for extensive periods.

"Yes, often, as it is the only one you can use to walk through the world of humans, and you must become comfortable in it," Carlton said. "But your other forms will come in very handy, in any potential conflict."

"It is the weakest form, when An-Ki are most vulnerable," Zeyya cut in. Incredulity was abounding in her words as she asked, "You would ask us to be vulnerable often?"

"It is the form that will best conceal your natures," Carlton replied, continuing to show no sign of irritation with Zeyya's confrontational tone. "Do not worry, you will have plenty of opportunities to take on your other forms, but you will know when it is best to do so. You will always have an advantage over others."

"Do not think I will not take my stronger forms if there is a threat," Zeyya replied, her voice almost a growl.

As she spoke, as if to accentuate her point, she raked her right claws down the table's surface. The talons cut shallow channels into the wood, with little effort. The room grew quiet, until the only sound was that of her claws digging five long furrows.

"Flesh is softer," Zeyya added, her eyes a feral blaze as she peered towards Carlton.

"I am only seeking to help you learn how to move through this world," Carlton said calmly, when she had finally stopped. "I am not asking you to risk any more danger than you have been doing by yourselves in the woods."

"The wilderness is where I roam. The human dwellings are not for us," Zeyya countered, and Uria could hear the anger rumbling just underneath the surface of her voice. "Our ways are not human ways."

"I know the An-Ki have their own ways, but it is dangerous for you to stay in the woods. It may be hard for you to believe me now, but it is best for the An-Ki to go into the human cities," Carlton said, in a patient tone. "The ones that seek to harm you are not there, and you all know that your enemies have begun to hunt your kind."

A strange thing transpired, as Carlton's gaze seemed to expand, and encompass Uria. Vivid images flashed within Uria's mind of the Night Hunters, whirring tempests of talon and fang that no An-Ki could hope to outrun. Uria knew very well that their hated enemies were in the new world, as he had been personally warned about them by the strange, bestial-looking Watcher back in the hills.

As precarious as his clan's situation was, he had no desire to risk encountering the Night Hunters, if there was another viable path. Yet one lingering fact troubled him deeply, as he recalled his former world.

"They were in the great places where humans dwelled," Uria said. "Night Hunters and humans lived together."

"Yes, that is true. Half of their origin is human, Uria. And they were worshipped by humans as gods in those days," Carlton said. "But this is a different age. They are not in the human cities now, and are not being worshipped as gods today. Most humans know nothing of them, and the ones that do keep them in very special, hidden places."

"How do you know about the Night Hunters? If they do not live in the … human cities … as you call them," Zeyya pressed, her eyes narrowing. Deep suspicion hovered in her lupine gaze.

"I have shown you that I am not just a human, though I have a physical human body to command," Carlton said, evenly. "You have had beings such as I guide the clan you were a part of before. Others of my brethren, who stood with me at the dawn of time itself. I wish to guide you to a place of strength, where you will be able to live in the world of humans. If I lead you to such a place, and help you avoid destruction, am I a friend or a foe?"

Uria suspected that Carlton Tephros was wholly a Messenger, even if he were a different kind he had never encountered before, possessed of a genuine physical body. The An-Ki chieftain knew there was little to no chance that Carlton was one of the malevolent kind of Avatar that sired the Night Hunters. If Carlton were, he would surely be with those creatures now, rather than guiding and aiding the An-Ki the Night Hunters preyed upon.

"Then guide us further, and we will give help to you in your purposes," Uria stated, making his choice for the clan.

Carlton nodded, and smiled. "Unlike others who have made similar claims, you will find my burdens light. Your clan will rise in the world of humankind, to greater heights than any clan in the legacy of your kind. You will not be relentlessly hunted, as will the ones you broke away from. It will be shown in the days to come that they are poorly led."

Uria wondered for a moment how Carlton would know that the other An-Ki would be hunted without abatement, but the concern passed quickly, as he noted the withering look from Zeyya. He knew she was greatly angered with his decision, but she was not the leader of the clan. The choice was his alone, and the opportunity to immerse into the new human world was far too great for him to pass up.

If his clan rose to prominence and dwelled beyond the reach of the Night Hunters, while the other An-Ki clans were pursued and hunted down, then there was no dispute that Uria had led his clan wisely. Zeyya could not deny that either, and he would just have to endure her unceasing suspicion of the human world until that time arrived.

Another thought struck him, as he gazed into her eyes, dancing with a ferocity that always excited him. Perhaps the time when the wisdom of his leadership was indisputable, and lauded by all in his clan, would also bring a favorable moment to ask her to become his Life Mate. There had never been a female he had been more attracted to, or deemed to be more worthy of standing at his side.

Now was not that time, though, as much remained to be concluded before any thoughts could be turned towards gaining a Life Mate. He looked around at the other members of his clan. While not showing the hostility towards his decision that Zeyya was, he could tell that they were extremely displeased about the prospects of being tangled in the affairs of humans.

What they did not understand was that the human world, in the new age, was unavoidable. The only choice was between sooner or later, and a Messenger had stepped forward to assist them with the former option.

"You shall have your help, Carlton Tephros," Uria said curtly, turning away and striding through the An-Ki gathered around.

He made his way to the back of the house, and inhaled the essence of night, as he gazed towards the trees lining the property. A bright, full moon was beaming down through a virtually cloudless sky. Soft breezes were flowing through the trees, as the swaying leaves whispered invitations to him.

He felt Zeyya stepping up to his side.

"Enough of humans," she said bluntly.

Uria said nothing, knowing that no words of his would placate her ire. The only concern he held was that her furor would cause her to transgress his authority as chieftain of the clan. He could only hope the fierce loyalty she had always demonstrated towards him worked to counter any rash impulses.

His ears took in the pops and cracks as Zeyya shifted into a four-legged form. She stepped down into the open swathe of grass stretching onward to the treeline.

"Forget humans. Let us run together," Zeyya exclaimed, with a little less edge to her voice, as she swung her head back towards Uria.

Uria needed little encouragement, beginning his own transformation. In moments he was padding across the soft grass towards her.

"If you can catch me," Zeyya said with a hint of mischief, as he neared.

With a great leap, she burst into a run, a vision of grace and power as she raced for the trees. Uria bounded after her, feeling the night's cool touch against his flanks as he built up speed, with the air rushing across his thick fur.

In moments, the two were hurdling over fallen trees, and streaking through the pooling shadows under the woodland canopy. It was all he could do to keep up with Zeyya, who was as agile and fleet as any in his clan.

After being penned up in the human dwelling, it felt wonderful to exercise his muscles. A part of him felt melancholy, though, as he knew the more they proceeded into the world of humankind, the rarer moments such as this would be.

He was not going to allow anxiety about the future to ruin the present, and he blocked the thoughts from his mind as he spurred himself to run faster. Just when he closed the distance with Zeyya, she would make a sharp cut to one side, and open up more ground between them.

She did not even break stride when they neared a wide creek, catching the lip of the near bank and vaulting across it. Her forepaws touched down on the opposite side, and she bounded forward without a hitch in her form.

Uria sprung across after her, admiring Zeyya's exceptional smoothness. It was little wonder that she was such a good hunter, as any prey she got a favorable jump on stood no chance of evading her.

At last, she raced up the slope of a hill that was not too far from the human dwelling, a place that had become a favorite spot of theirs due to the overlook it provided. Uria joined her at the top, and the two An-Ki panted heavily as they caught their breaths.

Zeyya looked out over the woodlands, broken here and there by the fire-less lights of the humans. Far overhead, in the mid-air, other lights were visible, embedded in one of the flying objects used by the humans. Uria listened to the rumbling noise coming from the incredible human invention, swelling as it neared, and then fading, as it continued towards the far horizons.

"They are everywhere," she said, staring outward.

"Yes, they are," Uria said, gently, knowing what she was referring to.

"I wish we had a place to go where there were no humans," Zeyya said.

"As do many of us," Uria said.

"What I wish will not change what is," Zeyya said, somberly, glancing towards Uria.

"We must do what we can, to survive," Uria said.

"It will not be easy for me," Zeyya said.

"Do not misunderstand my choice. It is not easy for me," Uria said.

Zeyya stared at him for an extended moment.

"No, I know it is not easy for you," Zeyya said, with a conciliatory edge.

"Know that I care nothing for humans. I only seek the best path for the An-Ki," Uria said.

"If humans get in the way of the best path … kill them all," Zeyya said, with a low growl, fires sparking in her eyes. Moonlight glinted off her lengthy fangs, exposed by her snarling visage.

"We will slay them together, if they come against us … or if they stand in our path," Uria replied, with a determined rumble.

"Your words bring me comfort," she responded. "And what if we come across others, like those we first found at the dwelling? I could not restrain my rage that night."

"We must control our anger," Uria told her, knowing that Zeyya was not the only one who had lost discipline, as he had been blinded with rage the night they fell upon the humans at the dwelling. "But we will not let any such human escape us. As we hunt prey in the dark … stalking … and then striking … so we will be among the world of humans. We will hunt them, when we choose to."

The look in her eyes was very intense, but it reflected great satisfaction with his words. The An-Ki were not going to skulk in the shadows. They would be a terror in the darkness to any human that threatened them, or provoked them, such as the ones they had slaughtered at the dwelling.

The mere thought of becoming an active hunter of humans sent an invigorating thrill through Uria. It also opened territory that no An-Ki clan had ever crossed into before.

Those such as Sargor strictly forbade any aggression against humans. Defending one's own life against a human attacker was the only tolerable violence between the two races.

Uria and Zeyya had shattered that admonishment when the two had been driven to extreme anger by the sight of the humans brutalizing the dogs. Yet that had been an eruption of emotion, and such things had been known to happen periodically over the course of generations amongst the An-Ki.

What Uria conceived of was something much different. Bringing the superior qualities of the An-Ki to bear upon anyone they deemed to be an adversary, or deserving of death, Uria's clan would break through the stringent confinements of the past.

When they came down from the slope a while later, Uria had a much clearer vision of how the An-Ki would conduct themselves on their new path. They would go forward with pride, and with cunning and strength.

Uria remembered the hot taste of human blood, thick on his muzzle, the night they had torn through the human occupants of the dwelling. It had been a rapturous experience shredding the humans, who were under the illusion they were the superior race in the world.

He had avoided admitting the unequivocal truth to himself, perhaps due to some lingering reticence caused by years of being led by weaker An-Ki. His clan would not be one guided by feebleness, but rather by initiative and boldness.

The more that Uria looked back on how Sargor had been so tentative and careful when it came to humans, the hotter the blood flowed through his veins. It was as if Sargor feared humans, when none of the lesser race could come close to the strength, speed, and sheer power possessed by an An-Ki warrior.

Humans were locked into one form, when the An-Ki had three. The An-Ki had the third form to use for moving undetected in the human world, and two allowing them to become living, frenzied weapons that could cleave through a throng of humans in scant moments.

The An-Ki possessed every single capability that humans had, and so much more. That was irrefutable truth, not hopeful thinking. There was simply no viable reason why the An-Ki had to live as if they were secondary to the human race.

Uria would accept Carlton Tephros' guidance, but he would find ways to lift up the An-Ki whenever, and wherever, he could. If a human blocked that path, then they would be torn asunder without hesitation.

# FRIEDRICH

Friedrich stared up into the somber visages of the seven Anunnaki judges. Not one, but two Avatars stood a few paces in front of him, as both Enki and the restored Inanna had been brought before Erishkegal and the Anunnaki Tribunal.

Inanna looked like a sister to Erishkegal, a dark-haired beauty of exceptional grace and noble bearing. Standing to the right of Inanna, Enki had taken a human form, mirroring the two feminine Avatars in assuming a corporeal shape.

Tall, broad-shouldered, and exhibiting a strong chin line, he was an impressive figure. The shade of his skin and darkness of hair matched the other two Avatars, and he could easily have passed as a brother to them in the human world.

Erishkegal faced all of them, Avatars, human spirits, Peris, and Gryphons, and though her countenance was undeniably stern, the look in her eyes was no longer confrontational. Her sheer beauty struck Friedrich profoundly in that moment, as she turned slowly away from his companions, and looked towards the seven Anunnaki judges.

Whether a figment of his imagination or not, he thought he saw a slight echo of regret within her expression. Something had undeniably changed since he had last stood before the Tribunal. A tint of melancholy had replaced roused anger, though the air of authority she emanated had not waned in the slightest bit.

"Tribunal of the Anunnaki, the choice is yours, and yours alone. All of you know the risk that must be weighed in this consequential deliberation," the Queen of the shadowy realm intoned, with formal solemnity. "I leave you to your careful judgement, and trust to your wisdom."

Erishkegal walked slowly up the ramp, striding to the top of the black, curving dais. Tendrils of something that looked to be dark smoke or mist reached up from the surface of the dais, intertwining, bending, and forming into a majestic, black throne.

Erishkegal sat down upon it, and rested her hands upon the ends of armrests that had been among the last elements to take form. The murky substance flowed and coursed throughout the shape of the throne, but it had all the properties of full solidity.

Smaller thrones rose behind the seven judges, with a great variance of shapes and sizes, to account for the widely differing forms and statures of the figures. The Anunnaki made no move to use the thrones, and the intensive looks in their eyes continued to bore into Enki, Inanna, Friedrich, and all his companions.

A blend of shadows, black surfaces, and spectral blue light, the environment within the huge chamber felt surreal, and unsettling. He knew that his chances of departing Erishkegal's realm now lay entirely with the seven strange, austere judges. She would not override their verdict, even if her sympathies may have tilted towards the group from the higher realms.

"The maw of Diabolos ever seeks to consume us," proclaimed the third Anunnaki judge from the left, the lion-headed entity possessed of a particularly withering gaze. The creature glanced to each of its companions. "It would be great folly to allow them to leave. To draw the eyes of the Shining One is to invite our destruction. We cannot thwart the eyes of one such as Diabolos. We have survived so many ages because we have not been reckless."

"If the Shining One's eyes perceive, that is," interjected the sixth of the judges, with its bestial head atop a brawny human torso. "It is possible that they might slip out as they arrived, undetected."

"And why take a risk when it is not necessary?" countered the fifth Anunnaki sharply, the female figure with the coating of fish scales. Her form shimmered in the chamber's cerulean light, and the black pools of her eyes were fixed rigidly upon Enki and Inanna.

"My brothers and sisters, the risks are great, I do not deny that. But do we not hope our own path leads to the White City?" stated the seventh of the judges, the hooded one with the serpentine visage protruding out from the cloth folds. The judge's head turned slowly, as he swept his slitted gaze across the others of the tribunal. "Have they not brought succor to our great Queen? Have they not braved their own destruction for her sake alone? They did not come to our realm for their own benefit."

None of the other judges spoke, as they stared back towards the reptilian speaker. Friedrich wished deeply that he could gain an inkling of what they were all thinking, but their expressions confounded him, hardened and unchanging.

"Shield them with the help of Kur, and all of the mighty ones that ward our boundaries. The Galla will scatter like flies, and these spirits can get far from here, before they begin to ascend," the seventh judge continued.

"And the Shining One will not notice a great force scattering the Galla, all across the Abyss? The Shining One will not notice a combined effort pushing in one direction, involving those such as Kur?" asked the bird-headed fourth judge, with the kind of dubious tone that indicated the seventh judge's position to be entirely preposterous.

"There are two Avatars of the higher realms in this group. They will not be mistaken for creatures of the Abyss," declared the first judge, the rather bizarre looking one with the face and attributes of a human woman, the body shape of a bird, and a barbed scorpion's tail.

"Then what have you to say to this, Great Enki, and Great Inanna?" the seventh judge calmly asked the two Avatars, turning its head towards them, and showing no irritation with the critical words of its peers.

"It is true that we may draw the eyes of the Ten-Fold Kingdom towards your realm, as the presence of beings from the higher realms is a rarity in these light-abandoned depths," Enki responded. "I cannot give you absolute assurance that would not happen. But Inanna and I will use every last spark of the strength given to us by Adonai, Most High, to confuse and evade the eyes that gaze from the infernal Vortex."

"This realm has remained unmolested since the beginning of its formation," the third judge countered pointedly. "What good is there to take any risk?"

"This realm is a beacon of refuge to many who have found their way to our shores," added the first judge. "How this happens, and why, remains a mystery to us all, but we must not endanger the mercy that has been granted to tormented souls."

"But does that justify us to imprison these souls? Do you think to gain favor with Adonai by holding two of His Avatars against their will?" the seventh judge challenged the others.

His words brought an extended silence over the other six judges. All looked to be consumed in states of private contemplation, their eyes focusing on nothing in particular.

"It would seem that six judgement thrones of this Tribunal are against their departure, and the seventh advocates their cause," rumbled the second judge, its form a balanced fusion of bull and man. Its bull-like ears twitched, as a deep scowl crept onto the human features of its face. The creature's voice took on a sharper, almost accusing edge, as it continued. "And what is it that keeps you from bringing this Tribunal to consensus?"

"We have never given a judgement lightly, and when we have, all held the conviction of the decision in their hearts," the seventh judge replied. "I do not feel as the rest of you. I feel a terrible unease about this, if we were to prevent Great Inanna, and Great Enki, from returning with their companions to the higher realms."

"Do you not feel unease about exposing our dominion to the notice of the Shining One?" the fifth judge queried, with conspicuous incredulity. "A risk we do not have to take, that might lead to our entire realm being put to ruin?"

"We would put all we have built to ruin by allowing fear to overcome justice," the seventh judge said. His voice then lowered in pitch, taking on the resolute air of a challenge as he continued speaking to the other six judges. "And are not this realm and our lives, no matter how long both have endured, passing in nature? What will you say when we are called to account at the End of Days? Will it matter if you lived a thousand ages, or one day, if you allowed fear to destroy justice?

"We have taken pride in our rejection of the path sought for us by those that sired, or gave birth, to our kind. The risk of destruction was far greater then, as we were hated and hunted by all, due to our choice. Only the mercy shown to us by Great Erishkegal spared us the doom that fell upon the world. Every one of us would have drowned in a pitiless storm were it not for that mercy. Are you so secure in these borders that you can toss mercy aside in matters such as this?"

Friedrich looked around at the other judges, and took in the sheer concentration reflected in their eyes, as they assiduously pondered the words of the seventh judge. His arguments had undeniably touched upon something profound within every one of them, as there were no caustic remarks, or immediate objections voiced, in the wake of his address.

After a lengthy, cumbersome silence, the third judge looked towards Erishkegal, sitting quietly upon her dark throne.

"We must seek your guidance, Great Erishkegal, as if we do as Emqu counsels us, we could undo everything you have gained for us," the third judge said, in a deferential timbre.

A gentle smile came to Erishkegal's face. The expression surprised Friedrich greatly, under the indeterminate circumstances.

"Nothing can be undone, good Parzillu, of the mercies that have been shown in one's life. Those acts of the will are timeless, and everlasting," Erishkegal said, in a serene, harmonious voice. "Emqu gives you wise counsel. The Seventh of the Avatars attending the Great Throne, Remiel, will be sent forth from his own throne at the End of Days, to call the souls harbored in the Void, and all across creation, to awaken once more. The mercies one has shown in life will stand in testimony before the Great Throne, when all trappings of wealth and power have fled.

"Do not forget that you are not creatures of the realms of spirit, but living beings of flesh, blood, and souls. Your mortal life continues in this refuge, long-lived though you have all proven to be.

"Even were all in this realm to perish, and the dominion itself to vanish forevermore into the darkness of the Abyss, there would not be a speck or blemish on the acts of mercy shown. They are inviolate treasures, outlasting all the gold hoarded by humankind across all generations in the mortal realms.

Friedrich could sense great discomfort in several of the judges, and most of them purposely looked away from her. She had given them a stern admonishment, and it was clear that the essence of her message was not lost on any of them.

The Anunnaki were not immortal beings, and their lives had not yet been measured. The choices they made, even in a non-material level of existence, came with serious ramifications.

"Queen Erishkegal, your counsel would lead us to risking the entire realm that you shaped out of the darkness," the third judge said, its leonine eyes looking plaintively towards her.

"Only in the path to Diabolos is there no risk. That is the safe, wide road ... easy to trod upon, and smooth to the step. You will have many companions on that path, as it is one that feeds on popular acclaim. You will find far less danger to yourself on that path ... at least until it reaches its destination," Erishkegal replied, looking to the beings arrayed on each side of her. "The path to the endless realms often involves great risk to oneself. It is narrow, and the footing very uncomfortable at times, even painful. It does not always look inviting, and is difficult to travel on. Often, you will walk alone, when all others regard you as foolish, simply because you do not align with the majority.

"I see now that my own choice long ago, to guide all of you across the Veil, was one such instance on that harder path. I could have gone back with Enki, and the others that had pursued me to the edge of the boundary between the worlds. Instead, I chose to shoulder a heavy burden, and paid a great price, but in doing so I walked farther along Adonai's path."

The chamber fell into a lengthy silence, as each individual pondered the words of the great Avatar. Friedrich took her words into his own heart, as they were filled with timeless wisdom.

The path of Diabolos was one where everything was relative, while Adonai's held an absolute quality. The highest path taken by an individual was of an immutable nature, not subject to whim, popular consensus, or compromise. As Adonai was unchanging, so was the ultimate path of a soul.

The lower paths, which conjoined into the broad road leading to Diabolos, could shift like the sands, whispering promises of greater comfort and safety, when they guided souls to a place of devastation, personal ruin, and unceasing peril. It was like the material world itself, where nothing lasted, all things changed, and every life was sliding towards death, whether the journey took one year or an eon to get there.

The seven Anunnaki could make whatever choice they wished, but Erishkegal had made it abundantly clear that there was only one that resonated with the less-traveled road; the rightful path to the undying realms.

Friedrich looked over to the seventh judge, whose serpentine face was almost hidden within the voluminous folds of its hood. Erishkegal had only offered her counsel when asked, and the other judges had only sought it when they could not sway the seventh into full consensus.

There was sacred merit in being willing to stand alone before concerted opposition. The strong conviction of the seventh Anunnaki judge had given all the others pause, enough that they had asked for Erishkegal's guidance.

The others had not been seeking a wrongful path, but the steadfastness exhibited by the seventh judge led to them putting deeper scrutiny to their own reasoning. The choice that had seemed so obvious to the other six was not so certain anymore.

A road that had seemed immaculately paved, and girded by solid ground, now looked much more like a crumbling, rickety bridge, spanning a gaping abyss. Many of the judges now had the sobered looks of one who had been halted just shy of reaching the central area of that bridge; where a point of certain collapse lay in diabolic ambush.

# URIA

Uria gazed out over the ranks of men and women gathered within the lengthy, enclosed space Carlton Tephros had guided them to. The An-Ki's head was still swimming with strange images, sounds, and scents, which had swarmed his senses during the extended ride into the human city.

Tantalizing news had greeted them upon their arrival at the building, delivered by a man waiting outside for Carlton. Word had come of heavy fighting in the city, involving both humans and beasts, and Uria chafed for answers regarding the latter.

Carlton had said nothing after hearing the news, and had not even looked towards Uria, but the An-Ki clan leader knew there was much more to the incident being described. He did not doubt that the ones deemed as beasts were An-Ki, as the man rendering the news had talked of them as looking like huge 'wolf-men.'

The only mystery regarded whether they were from Sargor's clan, or if they were from Queran's, the third major faction involved in the schism of the original clan to cross through the gateway. The idea that one of the other two clans was becoming boldly active in human affairs, enough to engage in such brazen violence, was bothersome to Uria. He wondered whether the development would affect the course he had chosen for his clan, under Carlton's guidance.

The lack of satisfying answers and the exceedingly unfamiliar environment were not the only discomforts to be endured. Uria wore a short-sleeved shirt that was very tight-fitting on his body, and already he sorely despised human clothing. It was confining, and smothering, not to mention the rampant itches it caused everywhere on his skin. He felt encased in a false skin, and the constant awareness of the clothing deepened the scowl on his face.

Zeyya looked highly uncomfortable as well, wearing an upper, black garment called a 't-shirt,' and lower, blue ones called 'jeans.' Like him, she wore black, leather footwear, 'work boots,' which Carlton said would be appropriate for a tougher-looking appearance in their third form. Like the other An-Ki of his clan, both he and Zeyya had their long locks pulled back, secured with circular ties behind their heads.

In his third form, Uria had jet-black hair, deep-set eyes, and a robust, muscular neck. His chin was broad, covered in a dense beard that touched upon his brawny chest. His biceps were carved orbs where they bulged substantially, stretching the sleeves of his shirt. Likewise, his ample pectoral muscles pressed his snug clothing forward.

Zeyya had a narrow waist, and though she did not have the bulk of Uria, she had a strong-looking body in her third form. Her face was more oval in shape, with light blue eyes that held an icy sheen. Her hair was of a lustrous silver hue, a color that Uria had not seen on any human female.

It was obvious that humans regarded her as highly attractive. Many lingering glances had betrayed the lusts harbored within the men that looked her way. Whenever Uria caught such a hungry look, he found himself feeling an instant, hostile defensiveness. He desired to gouge his talons into the flesh of the salacious men.

He was a little surprised when he took notice of such prurient looks coming from a couple of the women amongst the humans. Uria did not know what to make of that development, but he regarded the human females no better than he did the males, and had no qualms about tearing them limb from limb.

There was a wary look within Zeyya's eyes, and Uria knew that she was not comfortable standing before such a large gathering of humans. Uria could not blame her for having deep misgivings, as the humans filling the room were a motley assortment.

Attuned as he was to eyes and postures, Uria could read a wide range of emotions and attitudes in the human throng. Where he looked to be standing idly in back of Carlton Tephros, he was studying the humans thoroughly. To one as adept as Uria in interpreting non-verbal signals, there was little that the humans concealed from him.

He perceived that many were cowards at heart, in spite of the brooding demeanors they exhibited. They were gathered there out of fear, whether of others stronger, or of being separated from the things now transpiring.

The timorous ones showed a propensity for being unable to meet any direct gazes, either with Uria, or with each other. The An-Ki leader paid little heed to the ones he identified as craven, for such individuals were not prone to initiative of their own accord.

Others were of a more brutal inner nature, filled with malice, an odious toxin bubbling at the surface of their eyes and expressions. This was a type that could be dealt with in a primal way, and as such Uria held little concern about them either. In a contest of strengths, the An-Ki feared no humans.

A few had cold, calculating looks about them, and the faces of such individuals Uria committed determinedly to memory. These humans were of a more formidable breed, and would have to be respected, as they were capable of corralling the energies of both the fearful and the barbarous to their purposes.

Some others were little different than how Uria saw himself, exuding a sense of strength and pride, while carrying the air of a survivor. He fathomed that these few could be provoked, but were not prone to being insidious or needlessly cruel.

He could tell that there was little true cohesion in the capacious room. The shifty gazes, glares, and furtive glances betrayed the suspicions and mistrusts that these humans had for each other. While not all of them were like the sentient filth he and Zeyya had encountered, and killed, at the human dwelling they had taken over, he felt little regard for their lives.

They were not a clan, though in some ways the assemblage was like a conglomeration of small clans, just as Carlton had described to Uria before. It was not difficult to tell the various allegiances, or the leaders, several of which were the ones with the icier, more scheming looks.

Uria and Zeyya flanked Carlton as he moved forward, stepping to the center of a raised platform situated at the front of the long, rectangular room. The others of Uria's clan formed a compact line a few paces in back of them.

He could see what Carlton was doing, as the An-Ki, in their third forms, were plainly intimidating to the humans. It was an open show of strength, meant to bolster the words that Carlton Tephros delivered.

Some coughs and whispers drifted about the room, but everything quieted down, for the most part, as Carlton's eyes scanned the crowd at a measured pace. A host of eyes were fixed back on him, and Uria read all manner of doubt, resentments, and curiosities in the varied gazes. It was not a group of humans much inclined toward cooperation, and Uria believed that Carlton had a very large challenge lying before him.

"My friends, I thank all of you for gathering here, during such uncertain times as we face now," Carlton began, in a strong voice that was amplified louder by another invention of human ingenuity. "We have reached an impasse in the history of this country. We can all see the direction we are being taken in.

"With Living ID, how do we hope to conduct our business? Are we to be shackled like the rest in this country, monitored and regulated in our every move? How are we to purchase our influence, with every transaction recorded?"

Carlton paused, while a low murmur filled the room. There were many nods of assent, and shared glances. Uria could see that the man had the attention of all in the room, no matter what smaller group they represented.

"In time, we may return to the way that things were," Carlton continued. "Fighting amongst each other, protecting territories, and establishing our influence with those who govern the populace ... but now is not that time. This is a time for union, and cooperation, for the best interests of all of us. Separately, we lose everything. Together, we have the manpower, and the guns, to take control of much of this city.

"The feds will have to reckon with us, and we will negotiate from a position of strength. In one way or another, we have had the police, judges, and all manner of city, province, and national officials in our pockets. We need only to join forces and assert ourselves now, while they are reeling from the instability pervading this nation. We must strike before they can become rooted, as they seek what is unacceptable to all of us.

"The wealthy can keep their control of the government, but we must retake our hold of the streets!"

A loud cheer erupted, as the emissaries of the numerous, disparate groups lent their voices to vigorous acclaim for Carlton Tephros' words. Uria could see the eagerness blooming in the teeming faces before him. There was a palpable hunger in the undercurrents flowing all about the room.

What Uria sensed in the humans was much more uniform now, no matter what nature rested inside them. It was not far removed from what he had perceived in the men that he and Zeyya had come upon, the night they discovered the human dwelling.

These humans thrived on violence, and fed earnestly on the promise of it. Understanding their expressions and tones, there was not one in the room that Uria would have any reservations about killing.

That was a good thing, Uria thought, as Carlton turned and gave a slight nod to him. Uria understood that he and the An-Ki might be called upon to kill any number of the humans in the room, at some point in the future. He could not allow bonds to form with any of them.

Carlton spoke low, as he used the words of the An-Ki. "Look about you, Uria. Do you perceive any that are innocent?"

"No, I do not," Uria responded, staring past Carlton at the throng.

Carlton smiled. "See, I have not deceived you."

He turned back towards the crowd, holding his hands up to regain their attention. They quieted down, and again listened fastidiously to his every word.

"There are many details to work out, but I see that we understand the need for common cause at this time. I shall be in communication with all of your organizations. There is a way we can work together, to take hold of all Troy, to our mutual benefit."

Uria heard Carlton's annunciation of each word clearly, and understood enough of them to know that he was indeed seeking to draw all of the human clans together. Again, it was clear that he had not misled Uria regarding his purposes. Carlton had certainly achieved cohesion amongst the humans, at least as far as things appeared.

The assembly mercifully drew to a close, and Uria kept back with the other An-Ki, close to the doorway they had first entered through. Carlton mingled for a short time with a few of the humans that, to Uria's perspective, seemed to be leaders of the various groups.

Many furtive glances were cast in the direction of Uria and his clan members, but nobody approached the An-Ki. Uria preferred it that way and quickly grew impatient to leave the place.

He was immensely relieved when Carlton broke away from the humans and nodded towards Uria, striding directly towards him. Away from the humans, he shifted back into the An-Ki language.

"You have all been here long enough. I thank all of you for doing this," Carlton said, looking pointedly at Zeyya, who was glaring hotly back at him. "It is one step towards a larger goal. And I must remind you that it will achieve a better, stronger position for your clan."

"I have had enough of the stench here. I want to leave this place," Zeyya stated rigidly. Her eyes then gave off a dangerous flare, as she added in a low, pitiless voice, "Or you will be picking up the pieces of these living piles of dung."

"We can go now," Carlton replied evenly, nodding to her.

Uria watched Zeyya closely, knowing her words were not an

understatement. Her ire was at the breaking point, and he knew without having to ask that the humans giving her lascivious gazes were prodding her dangerously close to a reaction they could not possibly imagine.

Without waiting a moment longer, Carlton led the An-Ki out from the chamber. They made their way to the outside of the building, where the cluster of wheeled vehicles they had arrived in rested idly. The other humans allied to Carlton, who had driven the vehicles, were standing attentively by the gleaming black objects.

Uria found the men and women interesting, as they all carried a trace of something that shared a common aspect with the essence he perceived in Carlton. They were fully human; of that he had no doubts. But they all harbored a distinctive whiff of the Messenger's core essence. It was like a marking of a sort, as far as Uria could tell, and he determined to give close scrutiny to any other humans bearing the peculiar tang.

Ducking and squeezing into the vehicle, and taking a seat behind Carlton, Uria dreaded the coming ride. His nerves were rattled severely as they rode back in the human vehicles, which were definitely not fashioned for those with the stature of the An-Ki.

The ordeal of riding in the vehicle seemed to last forever, filled with unfamiliar sensations that Uria knew would take considerable time to get used to. He loathed the feeling of being confined, which was made eminently worse by the tightly cramped space within the vehicle.

He was overwhelmed from the sights he took in as the short column of vehicles passed through the midst of the human city. Strange noises resounded in the streets, from the growl of other vehicles, to strident blares, and muffled, rhythmic whumps, which Uria finally realized came from inside a few of the other vehicles occupying the streets.

The humans of the modern age had progressed tremendously, as their constructs seemed to go on forever, no matter where he turned his eyes. The edifices reached to unbelievably great heights, as tall as cliffs, and fashioned with shiny facings.

The human numbers were astounding, exponentially greater than they had been in Uria's former age. They were everywhere he looked, including the places where they congregated together on the other side of clear facings on some of the human constructions. He could only begin to imagine the totality of their numbers, contained in the multitudes of structures.

Peering up at the constructs soaring high above them, he was reinforced further in his decision to join with Carlton. A human society that could build such immense things, in such abundance, was not one that Uria could afford to breach.

He needed every possible insight he could get about their ways, and was beginning to understand the importance of the An-Ki third form, in terms of blending in with the human world. The great forest of human constructs was a wilderness in its own right, containing more pitfalls and perils than any natural environment Uria had ever traversed.

The column had to stop briefly at the cusp of a bridge spanning a broad river, where a man carrying a weapon Uria now understood to be called a gun came up to the side window by Carlton. The man was not the only one with such a weapon, as several others attired similarly to him, and holding weapons, were in clear view.

At first, the man had a hardened look about him, but he quickly became complaisant in demeanor after a few words from Carlton. It was readily apparent that the man regarded Carlton as having a superior status; in a similar way to an An-Ki clan member recognizing Uria's authoritative position as a chieftain.

The weapon-bearing humans allowed the vehicles through without further impediment, and the column proceeded out of the city. The rest of the journey out to the dwelling they resided in passed without incident, but Uria felt a great sense of relief when the column finally arrived at their destination.

It felt wonderful to stand up straight again, and stretch his cramped body back up to its full height. He looked around the grounds, as he made his way to the back of the house, feeling his body limbering up with every stride.

The sound of the wind, and the birds chirping in the branches of trees, were comforts to his ears after the raw assault of unfamiliar noises within the city. The scents of the natural woodland air were pleasantly fresh, after the noxious aromas he gleaned within the air pervading the forest of human-made structures.

"Let us shed these false skins," Zeyya remarked sharply, as she walked up behind him. "I can bear them on my body no longer."

Uria looked over to her, and saw that she was already stripping off the human clothing, casting it disdainfully into a lumped pile off to the side. Her ice-blue eyes gazed back to him, as a tendril of wind buffeted several locks of silvery hair. Her body glistened with a light sheen, which highlighted the tones of her shapely muscles.

Uria peeled off his own clothing, welcoming the gentle touch of the air against his skin. Everything about the human world seemed so unnatural, from what they put on their bodies, to the places where they gathered in great numbers.

"Join me … let us forget the humans. I want to run in the light of the moon, and hunt," Zeyya said, giving Uria one more hardened glance, before striding across the grass towards the trees.

The shadows were lengthening, and it would soon be night. Zeyya's form vanished into the trees, as Uria walked after her, feeling the cool grass underfoot.

He could not think of anything else he would rather do at that moment than run by her side. The thrill of the hunt beckoned, as it did within the hearts of all true An-Ki. The rush of energy in the pursuit of prey was like nothing else in the world.

Not a thing would be lost in going forth with Zeyya into the depths of the woods. The world of humans would still be there when he returned, as it dominated the new age he was struggling to assimilate with.

He cast the discomforting thoughts aside as he stepped into the woods, feeling the first tingles in his body as he set his mind to transformation. The burdens of worry gave way to the primal, bestowing a purity of focus as he underwent the painful shifts from the third form into a four-legged one.

# GREGORY-THE COMPOUND

The federal troops were effectively pinned down, but a stalemate was brewing that did not favor the insurgents. A few had fallen on both sides, and the crackle of gunfire periodically broke the stillness, as snipers ensconced in both forces took selective shots at each other.

Gregory chafed with frustration, knowing that time was not his ally. A few enemy drones had come and gone, levying death with every sweep of the area.

His forces were helpless against the lethal aircraft, and he could do nothing more than grit his teeth, hoping that the drones ran out of missiles before his troops incurred too many casualties. The only relief was that the enemy was sending a limited number of sorties, indicating more widespread troubles on their side.

There would be no trouble from the airfield, as Dante's group had managed to reach it, setting off explosives that rendered the military helicopters resting there unusable. Gregory did not want to think of the predicament he would now be in, had the enemy's helicopters been able to fly. He had seen what they could unleash often enough in the blistering heat and sands of the Central East.

The rebels kept to small, scattered groups just as planned, concealing themselves as best as possible in the densely wooded terrain. Despite their lower numbers, they were able to sustain enough of a cordon that no federals within the compound had been able to escape.

Gregory turned his eyes towards the main road leading up to the compound, the air shimmering in the heat of the midday sun. He expected to hear the rumble of armored vehicles at any moment, heralding a specter that would compel him to sound an immediate retreat to his own forces.

Some smaller attacks had been launched elsewhere in the region as diversions. Brief radio messages had indicated the operations had been executed successfully.

A barrage of crude rockets into a supply depot in one area, an explosion of a power station in another, the various strikes were designed to create some damage, and give the impression that more might be coming.

Perhaps the quick blows would distract the enemy, and buy the main assault a little more time, but they would not hold off the federal response forever. The arrival of overpowering force in support of the federal forces was only a matter of time, and the insurgents had to maintain constant alertness.

Gregory wished that he could press the main attack on the compound, but the open ground before the double line of barbwire fences would rapidly become a killing field if he was foolish enough to do so. The enemy troopers were dug in solidly, and they had machine guns, assault rifles, and likely a deep supply of ammunition at their behest.

The hills reverberated with an outburst of shots from several assault rifles, as federal troops hunkered down within the compound opened fire. Listening to the clattering guns of the federals, Gregory hoped that their bullets had found no targets; and it was likely that they had not.

The federals had shown an increasing tendency to loose bullets towards any area where they guessed a sniper to be nestled within. Such sprays of bullets rarely found victims, sounding far more formidable than they ever were effective.

The fire betrayed a rising anxiety in the federal ranks, and they had good cause for concern. Gregory's forces, though small, had many excellent shots arrayed all around the detainment compound.

Gregory looked through the scope of his rifle, and slowly panned from left to right. He had only been able to take out two federal troops so far, as they had been extremely diligent about keeping out of sight. He wished that he had a dedicated spotter assisting him, but knew that he would have to rely on his own efforts for the time being.

The optics did not reveal any inviting targets on his first pass. Without pause, he slowly began another sweep of the compound.

There was no sign of the throngs of detainees either, and Gregory was glad that they were keeping to the barracks-like housing units. They were not entirely safe, as stray bullets could easily punch through the walls of the long, rectangular buildings.

The day began to drag onward, with no major tilts in the combat. About two hours later, Gregory added a third federal to his tally, when he focused on a spot where he had seen a muzzle flash.

Patience and scrutiny paid off, as the trooper who had fired made the ill-fated mistake of coming up for another shot. One trigger squeeze from Gregory, and the enemy gun was silenced permanently.

In the afternoon, a low, growling noise sounded abruptly to Gregory's ears, coming from the vicinity of the road. His heart sank, as he set his rifle aside and whipped his binoculars up.

The command to retreat perched on his lips, poised for conveyance to Chuck, so the dutiful operator could disseminate Gregory's mandate through the radio gear. The worst of his fears was about to be realized, as his forces had no solution for armored vehicles.

The main road leading to the detainment camp was being watched over tightly by the federals farther out. There was no doubt that anything coming down the road, in force, was to the relief of the troopers guarding the mass detainment facility.

Like swelling waves of thunder, the sounds of whatever was approaching continued to grow. The deep, throaty resonance increased with every second, and Gregory steeled himself, knowing that something was about to come into view.

Yet the low-pitched, reverberating tones did not sound like any armored vehicles that he was familiar with. On nothing other than gut instincts, he refrained from giving the order to pull back.

He stayed riveted to the line of the road where a low undulation in the terrain masked the farther distance. His heartbeat was steady, if a little quickened, and his breaths measured, as the sonorous din continued to wrap itself around the wooded hills.

The stillness of the horizon was broken with movement at last. Gregory's eyes widened in surprise at what he saw through the binoculars.

A flag whipping defiantly in the winds, from a short shaft mounted to the rear, a lone rider on a motorcycle manifested abruptly into sight. Two other motorcycles broke into view a second later, as they crested the small rise behind the first.

Gregory's eyes widened further, as a row of four motorcycles rolled into view, followed by rank after rumbling rank. The air shook with the guttural roaring of the bikes, whose chrome gleamed resplendently in the sunlight. The unbroken column pouring over the crest was an incredible sight, a procession like nothing he had ever witnessed in all his years.

Flags flew from the backs of many bikes, mounted in similar fashion to that of the figure leading the bold, proud cavalcade. Gregory could see they were tri-colored UCAS flags, as he continued to stare in amazement towards the steadily lengthening column.

Many clad in black, studded leather, and wearing a variety of helmets, the bikers were a tough, hardened-looking lot. Burly, bearded figures with bandanas wrapped around their heads, and women with long locks flying wild and free in the winds, were just some of the figures Gregory observed amongst hundreds upon hundreds thundering down the roadway. Rifles could be seen strapped to the backs of a great majority of the riders, and many of the bikes were carrying a second passenger.

The hills were now shaking with the resonance of well over two thousand engines, at the very least. A determined river of steel flowed ever closer, glittering spectacularly in the light of day.

The lead figure finally slowed down, and drew to a halt, bringing the entire column to a stop. Turning, the rider gestured to those behind him, and some sort of command was relayed on down the line.

They stopped just clear of the effective range of a standard assault rifle. Someone within their ranks knew what they were doing.

As the riders dismounted their bikes, they streamed towards the front, gathering into a large throng in minutes. Those with rifles slung over their shoulders took them from their backs and into their hands.

Gregory began to wonder what their intentions were, as they began to mill around. The only thing he was pretty certain of was that they were not federals.

"I've got someone here on the radio … claims to be with the bikers," Chuck called excitedly, gesturing for Gregory to come over.

Gregory leaped up to his feet, and strode briskly over towards Chuck. He took the headset from the anxious-looking operator, and put it on his own head.

"Gregory Andreas speaking," he said firmly.

"Figured you boys and girls could use a little help," replied the gruff, southern-accented voice on the other end.

"I'm assuming you are involved with the very prominent display of bikes I'm seeing down on the road right now," Gregory stated.

"Yessir, I am. And we brought ya over three thousand men and women that don't much like what's happenin' to their country," growled the other man. "It's been enough to bring together a bunch of us that didn't always get along so well before. Lots of different groups found in this column, and more'n a few lone wolves, but I promise you we're united about this."

"How did you know about this?" Gregory asked. "The attack on the compound we're carrying out?"

"We've got more than a few eyes out, and we've been scanning radio channels constantly. Yer boys have been broadcastin' quite a bit lately. Ham radios come in handy in times like this, don't they?" the other man responded, with a trace of levity.

"Yes they do, and thanks for responding, then," Gregory replied, still more than a little baffled at the unusual, but very welcome, development.

"That damnable camp grates on me every moment it stands. We wanna get that eyesore removed right away. So how can we help ya? We've got plenty of guys and gals with military experience. Lots of veterans, myself included. Hundred and first airborne, I was.

"We hear you're a marine too. Got a few of your brothers in this bunch … Oh, and we've got plenty of guns, and a few surprises we've kept around over the years, for a rainy day like this."

"Let me come down and meet with you all, and we'll work out a way to cooperate," Gregory said. "Not enough time to put things into the order you and I have dealt with before in the military. But we can come up with something workable, to bring some quick pressure to those bastards dug in at the camp. We've got to move quick, as you understand they've summoned help long before now."

"Sounds fine and good to me," the other man replied. "So as we can bring some heat on those government bastards quick, like you say."

"We will. I know you are keeping out of their range right now, but you don't want to stay out in the open, they've got some drones," Gregory warned. "And they've got some pretty good shots in their ranks. We've lost a few of ours already."

"We'll spread out into the trees and hills then," the man replied.

"Tell me one thing though. How did you get down the road?" Gregory asked, unable to hold back his curiosity.

Since they had begun talking, Gregory had wondered how the column had made it unscathed through the federal checkpoints. The bikers were undoubtedly tough individuals, and many were probably very capable soldiers in their pasts, but the roadblocks were under military control.

"We were prepared to fight our way through, as best we could, if we needed to, but it was entirely clear, all the way up here," the man answered. "Kinda surprised me, but I'm not complainin' about it. We got here a lot quicker with it bein' open."

The news stunned Gregory, and he could not figure out why the federals would leave the road to the compound wide open. There was much more to the story, but he did not have the time to investigate.

"So what's your name?" Gregory asked.

"Jack Morgan," responded the other man. "Of the Iron Grizzlies, and proud to be at your service. You've been doin' a good thing."

Gregory grinned, shaking his head, and could not believe he was talking to a leader of one of the toughest, most notorious bike gangs in the entire UCAS. They were not the kind of individuals it was advisable to cross, and the domestic enemy had clearly provoked the Iron Grizzlies out from their den of hibernation.

"Great to meet you Jack," Gregory replied. "Fighting back is the only response I could have to all this. I'll be down in a few moments. Just get your guys and gals under tree cover, while I'm on my way."

"Will get right to it, Gregory," Jack replied, with a vigorous lilt.

Gregory handed the headset back to Chuck. "I'm pretty sure I'll have a few new instructions for you to relay soon! Keep ready for me."

"I will! Looks like we got some help!" Chuck said excitedly, his right hand twitching as he looked back to Gregory.

"Looks like we did, Chuck," Gregory confirmed, with a broad smile.

# DAGIAN

Dagian eyed the lifeless body atop the bed. Jibade's sightless eyes were dull, entirely devoid of the spark of life.

His death had not been a natural one. She was certain about that. His face was contorted into an expression of terror, and she wondered at the cause of it.

She had known that something had occurred when she woke up from a dreamless sleep, with a burning sensation all over her body. At first the feeling alarmed her, but she quickly sensed that no harm was coming to her.

She did not fathom the purpose of the sensations until she discovered Jibade's death. Then, understanding came to her.

The special blessings given to Jibade and Dagian in Set's realm had definite purposes tied to them. With the departure of Jibade from the mortal world, the power lent to him from Apep had transferred over to Dagian.

She had never felt stronger, and could never have imagined the heights she was reaching when she first began to seek out the powers shrouded in the darkness during her sixteenth year. Her revulsion towards her parents' fundamentalist idiocies had spurred her forward in the earliest stages of her path. But now that she was steeped in the mystical arts of the Shining One, her motivations were much different; and far more purer.

Dagian lay down on her back, next to the corpse of Jibade, feeling no discomfort at the thoughts of being next to a dead body. It was just a husk, as the spirit had fled to whatever reward or torment had been determined for Jibade in the Ten-Fold Kingdom.

At first, she allowed herself to slip into the trance-like state that brought her vision to a level that could perceive the things unseen in the material world. The inner sight opened up, and her perception was filled with movements.

Dark wraiths drifted and glided around her. The sight brought her instant comfort, as the small, black entities were always close in attendance to her.

A few larger ones floated a short distance away, somewhat slower in their movements. The familiar pair of demonic spirits, who often helped exercise her will in the occult arts, gazed upon her quietly, maintaining an upright position.

Knowing she was warded, she allowed her body to relax, easing into a deeper state with every long, slow breath that she drew in. Dagian closed her eyes, and centered her focus on the increased power within her.

She imagined it localizing where Anat had touched the flaming spear to the skin of her forehead. Deeper and deeper she felt herself sinking, as if she were falling into herself.

Her ears were gradually filled with a load roaring sound, like a great wind rushing by her. Sight came back to her quickly, as she floated upward, and detached from her physical body.

Orienting herself more upright, she looked about the room. A few things looked a little larger or smaller than before, and there was no sign of the wraiths and servile entities from the depths of the Abyss.

Her spirit was on another plane of existence, one that reflected the material world very closely. With a nudge of the will, she slowly drifted out of the room, continuing through hallways and walls until she found herself in the bountiful gardens of her lavish estate.

She knew that she was not looking upon the actual foliage, but rather a close reflection of it. Trees, flowers, and well-manicured grounds surrounded her, but there were differences in hues and shapes, a few being slightly abstract in form.

Easing downward, Dagian touched upon the ground, and began walking forward. She had all of her faculties, including memories, and savored the lucid state as she made her way toward some hedges that were carefully maintained on her grounds.

Turning the corner of one of the high growths, she stopped in her tracks. Confronted by an unexpected sight a short distance ahead of her, Dagian found that she was not alone.

A black, frog-like creature of great size, with a gaping mouth, bulbous body, and long, skinny limbs, sent up a throaty call as it took notice of her. Misshapen, jagged teeth lined its mouth, and it displayed an aggressive posture, half-jumping, half-trotting towards her.

The obsidian depths of its protruding eyes showed no sign of keen intelligence. It was a brutish, witless creature, one of the common kinds found within the astral wilderness.

Dagian did not try to take flight, or avoid its approach. Though it was large enough to swallow her whole, she calmly leveled her gaze at it, incensed that it dared to menace her.

"Attend to me," Dagian called sibilantly, invoking the powers of the darker realms.

The two larger denizens of the deep Abyss she had painstakingly cultivated into her dedicated service manifested like short columns of smoke, rising up to either side of Dagian. Silent and swift, they fell upon the abomination without delay, as the astral creature sent up a flurry of guttural cries.

Latching onto the creature, the dark entities bore it upward, carrying the astral beast higher into the sky, as if it weighed nothing. It flailed helplessly at them, as its croaking, angered cries faded with the distance.

She did not care what her spectral attendants did with the feeble-minded creature, only that they removed it from her presence. The encounter proved to be a welcome revelation, and one that she had theorized was possible. Dagian was emboldened by the idea that she could summon the abyssal spirits onto the astral plane, to come to her aid.

Abruptly, she was distracted by an inner, tugging sensation. She looked all around her, but saw nothing to indicate the source of the feeling.

Bringing her eyes upward, she peered into the underbelly of the astral sky. Like a great inverted whirlpool, the clouds immediately above her were circling around a dark hole.

She knew from extensive study that the presence of doorways and portals indicated a means of going between the myriad levels of the non-physical realms. What she saw above her was undoubtedly a gateway to something else, but she did not think it led merely to an adjacent plane of existence, whether comprised of lighter, higher energies, or denser, lower ones.

As she gazed into the core of the swirling mass, she felt a strong compulsion to go through the huge portal. She trusted to her instincts on the matter. Leaving the ground, she ascended towards the core of the upside-down funnel, heading for the circle of darkness calling out to her.

The edges of the cloud-funnel were a blur as she passed through the portal, attaining a great speed. Suddenly, she broke through the far end of it, her perspective shifting at once, finding herself in the heights of a placid, night sky.

A barren vista was spread all around her. The sands of an immense desert, the boundaries of which could not be seen, extended to all horizons in a tremendous sea of rolling dunes.

Coming down out of the sky, Dagian angled for the top of one of the larger ridges of sand, alighting upon its summit. Waves of heat drifted over her, thick with a sulfuric pungency.

A magnificent, starry sky twinkled in the heights, presenting hosts of constellations that were utterly foreign to her own world. Dagian knew where she was, as she took in the sights, recognizing the nature of the place with little difficulty.

Sensing movement, she looked down, and saw a lone figure approaching her with measured stride across the top of the ridge. The headdress and long snout on its inhuman visage immediately identified the figure as a priest of Set. It carried one of the distinctive-looking staffs that she had seen during her first visit to Set's night-cloaked dominion.

The Setian priest gazed down on Dagian as it halted, looming high over her.

"Child of the Shining One, Great Anat bid you here, and you have found your way," the priest addressed her, in a deep-pitched, resonant voice.

Dagian lowered her head respectfully at the name of the Dark Avatar, even as she caught a hint of approval in the priest's words.

"The other who was graced by the lord of our realm, and Great Apep, now burns as a light in the Sky of Enduring Midnight," the Setian priest continued. "His suffering will not cease until Set's anger at his failure abates."

Dagian said nothing, but the words were a sobering reminder of the delicate line between tremendous reward and hellish torment. She had seen her own fortunes swing greatly in a short amount of time, and could only determine that when her moment came to take her place in the Nether Kingdom, she would enter in a state of favor.

"The Walker testified to what happened to him, before he was severed from the mortal realm," the priest continued. "Great Anat bid me to bring you knowledge of his fate, and to warn you."

"I am most grateful," Dagian replied, bowing her head again.

"You have gained the power that was bestowed on the Walker, but beware … the Enemy has one like the Walker amongst them. A woman."

The priest gazed into her eyes, and an image of a tall, blond-haired woman formed within Dagian's mind. The woman's blue eyes carried a great intensity in them, and her jaw was set firmly, in an expression of grim determination. In her hands was an unusual-looking, ebony blade, which was wreathed in vigorously burning flames, blazing from the tip down to the top of the short black hilt.

"She could not have used that weapon without the help of an Avatar," the priest said. "It is one used by lesser spirits, that enables them to use the force of their souls to empower fires that can cause harm to the substance of spirit.

"That woman is a warrior of the Enemy, and she used that weapon to sever the line that connects the spirit to a body of flesh and blood. It is not known what Avatar gave her help, but Great Anat wanted you to be forewarned."

"I am thankful, and will heed this warning," Dagian replied, with yet another bow of her head.

"A similar weapon can be provided for any such as the Walker, or the warrior of the Enemy, but it is one that cannot be taken into your world. It can only be brought to one who is in spirit, once they have entered these realms, and separated from the physical body," the priest informed her.

"I will do whatever I must to help find this woman in our world," she declared. "I am not as she, and am at a disadvantage, but I will employ every art that I can to stop her."

"Your path is not finished," the priest replied, with a cryptic undertone. "You will grow in your abilities."

"And I will use any new art that I master, in the service of the Shining One," Dagian promised the priest.

"You will have the Walkers of the Setian Path at your disposal, as it was one of their greatest who was slain by the enemy warrior," the priest announced. "Even now, they hasten across continents and seas. Soon you will leave the city of Troy, and go meet them to the north of the city of Yorvik.

"There you all will combine your arts to defend against this enemy warrior, hunt her down, and destroy her. There is One carrying the favor the Risen Throne who must be protected at all costs, One who will soon be made known to you."

"I will always do as commanded by the Lords of the Abyss," Dagian responded solemnly.

In her heart, she felt a great eagerness to learn the identity of the figure being referred to. She took the news regarding leaving Troy for Yorvik in stride, knowing that something of tremendous importance was taking place. She felt a surging pride that she was being made a part of it, and took it as another sign that her tarnished state in the eyes of the abyssal lords was being redeemed.

"Be vigilant in all things, and know that the gifts of no less than the Great Lord Apep, our own Lord Set, and Great Anat lie within you," the Setian priest said. "Continue on your path of discovery, and remember now the body that you yet inhabit."

The words of the priest triggered thoughts of the physical world, and the raiment of flesh she inhabited. Bringing to mind her slumbering body, Dagian's sight became fuzzy, and then darkened, as the sensations of movement at tremendous speeds overtook her. The feeling lasted only a moment, before everything became still and quiet.

Her eyes fluttered open, and she sat up slowly, finding herself back in the dim bedroom next to the corpse of Jibade. She smiled as she recalled every thing that had happened to her in the out-of-body state, with perfect clarity. From the encounter with the astral denizen to the audience with the Setian priest, she looked back on the experience as if it were just another part of her waking world.

The smile grew further when, well over an hour later, she found that not one detail of her out-of-body sojourn had been lost to her. She did not miss the implications, as a great step in her mystical evolution lay right before her.

# GREGORY

Buoyed by over three thousand new fighters, the ring around the enemy encampment became a chokehold within a few short hours. With the detainment camp fully enclosed by rebel forces, all observations indicated that the enemy had to spread their modest numbers thinner around their perimeter, to keep a defensive posture facing all sides. Despite proceeding carefully, they lost a few more troopers during the shifts and adjustments of their positions.

Fortune continued to favor Gregory, as no drones appeared in the sky following the arrival of the huge motorcycle column. Their conspicuous absence struck Gregory as very odd, as the enemy's aircraft were uncontested, able to come and go at will in the skies over the battlefield.

Jack Morgan had not been kidding about the bikers coming with a range of arms. Gregory had always expected that the more established bike gangs harbored arsenals, and his conjectures were soon confirmed beyond a shadow of a doubt.

There were many fully automatic assault rifles, a few machine guns, and even some rocket-propelled grenade launchers brought along with the bikers, accompanied by plenty of ammunition. Even a fair quantity of hand grenades was available to the rebel force.

A shoulder-fired, anti-aircraft missile launcher was in the possession of the newcomers as well. It was not too old of vintage either, and Gregory knew it would be effective against a helicopter, or other low flying aircraft. As it was of UCAS manufacture, he wondered how the bikers had gotten their hands on it. It was a story he would have to probe later, as time was precious.

A few more ham radio operators were sprinkled in amongst the new, hastily-formed contingents, so that when the order for all-out attack was made at six o'clock, all groups were engaged from the outset. It was more of a bludgeoning assault than a surgical one, but a crushing fist ended a fight just as well as a crisp chop to a nerve point.

A storm of lead rained down upon the areas where the federals were entrenched, as blasts from a flock of rocket-propelled grenades reverberated throughout the hills. Crackles, rattles, and booms created a hellish cacophony, as the sorely outnumbered federals were visited with a hurricane of righteous fury.

The compound was designed well enough to corral a large number of detainees, but it was not intended to withstand a comprehensive assault. The areas where the federal troopers took cover were easy enough to concentrate on, and the enemy was kept down and suppressed, as rebels charged in from all sides.

The bikers made good use of the hand grenades and other implements with them, tearing the outer lines of fencing to shreds, and creating channels that they rushed through to penetrate the camp. The enemy troops were rooted out and neutralized wherever they could be found, though several rebels fell in the short, blistering firefights that ensued within the compound.

A few federals acknowledged the stark reality they faced, and threw down their arms, putting their hands up as they surrendered to the incoming rebels. The sounds of gunfire ebbed, and then died down completely, as the rebel forces swarmed over the entire camp.

Before the hour was out, Gregory, Jack, and Benjamin were walking through the shattered front gates, entering a scene of unfettered euphoria. Throngs of people poured out of the residential structures and crowded around, smiling and shouting out to Gregory and his companions, as they marched deeper into the encampment.

Many were crying, with tears that were a mixture of both joy and sorrow. Gregory could sense that several of the detainees had considered themselves doomed, consigned to the whim of the authorities that had taken them into custody.

A little girl of no more than seven ran up suddenly, hugging him tightly about the leg. Gregory chuckled, as he ruffled her long, curly locks of blond hair.

"Thank you sir!" exclaimed a beautiful young woman, who was plainly the girl's mother. "Thank you so much!"

The woman was just the first of hundreds of personal expressions of gratitude that he received, as he worked his way through the masses of liberated citizens. Gregory smiled as he took in their joyous celebrations.

"A real war of liberation this time," Gregory remarked to Benjamin, who was walking along at his side.

"And I'm really proud to be here with you for it," Benjamin replied, looking out over the spreading revelry. His brother's eyes sparked with delight, and he shouted out, "Hey! Panos!"

Benjamin shouldered his way to a tall, middle-aged man and gave him a big hug. Gregory did not know the man, but his brother had many friends in the community that he was unaware of.

The scene was to be repeated a few times more, as Benjamin and others among the rebel force came across friends and loved ones in the multitude they had just freed. The outpouring of gratitude was immensely rewarding, as Gregory felt an immediate, intimate connection in the core of his spirit with the oath he had taken as a UCAS soldier. The liberation of the camp fulfilled the intentions of that oath, to a degree like he had never before experienced.

The only mar on his gladness was the sight of a cluster of federal troopers recently taken prisoner. Keeping their eyes averted from the celebratory activities swirling around them, the brooding soldiers showed no sign of remorse.

Their glares and sullen expressions told Gregory all he needed to know about them. They were hardened men and women, not foolhardy enough to fling their lives away, but not the kind that could be absorbed into the rebel forces. He respected the federal troopers as fighters, but knew he could not reach out to them.

Gregory made his way up to Jack Morgan, who was looking out towards the empty railroad tracks. About Gregory's height, Jack looked to be chiseled out of stone, thick of chest with brawny arms.

The shape of his nose, and scars on his leathery skin, spoke of many previous fights. Gregory had no doubt that the opponents of the robust man had more than a few marks of their own to show for such physical contests.

Jack's gray eyes matched his dense, silver goatee, and his head was shaved bare. Judging by the crow's feet at the corners of his eyes, and the nascent creases on his face, Gregory figured the leader of the Iron Grizzlies to be about fifty years of age.

"Didn't think I'd be doin' anything like this," he remarked, shaking his head, as he looked towards Gregory.

"Neither did I," Gregory admitted.

"You know we'll have to keep an eye on that," Jack said, indicating the railway. "Maybe we should just blow up the tracks."

"Might be a good idea," Gregory concurred.

"Part of me always figured it would come down to this," Jack said, his face growing somber. "Nobody was doin' a damn thing when it was clear we were all being undermined."

Gregory concurred. "It was like this whole country was just sleep walking."

"They aren't sleep walkin' no more," Jack said, with an edge. "Where do you think this is all headed?'

"Don't really know. I take things day to day now," Gregory said. "Sad thing is, a lot of people will not want to fight back, or might even see us as the bad guys."

"If they believe the Living ID is a good thing, then they're just hopeless, and they deserve what they're gonna get," Jack growled.

"Most people are really, really stupid," Gregory said, with a rueful chuckle.

"I'll agree with you on that," Jack said. "We're not perfect, but we're not so dense we can't see the obvious."

Gregory looked to Jack. "There's going to be some really hard fighting ahead. We could use some help, if some of you want to stay."

Jack smiled. "We're all in this now. Not much chance of backing away, after today."

"No, I guess there's not ... but today was a good day," Gregory replied, with a satisfied grin, as he called to mind the mass of freed detainees behind him.

# BENEDICT

Benedict groaned, opening his eyes slowly as the door to his cell slid aside. A TTDF trooper entered the room, coming into greater focus as his bleary vision cleared.

The trooper was a tall, broad-shouldered man, with a narrow forehead and angular chin. The stern-faced individual walked towards Benedict's cot, stopping a couple steps away.

"Benedict Darwin," the figure addressed him.

"My name hasn't changed since yesterday," Benedict retorted with sarcasm, relieved that he had not yet lost his spark of defiance. It told him that he had not yet been beaten, despite all he had suffered and witnessed in the bowels of the horrific prison.

"Get up, and come with me," the trooper replied humorlessly.

Benedict did not want to invite the guard's ire so soon after awakening. He rolled over and sat upright, acutely feeling the aches riddling his body. At least he was already dressed, being clothed in the jumpsuit he had worn since they had taken his own clothes from him after his arrest and incarceration.

"And what wonderful new machinations will you be treating me to today?" he asked the guard, casually.

"Put your hands together behind your back and turn around," the guard instructed him curtly, completely ignoring his caustic inquiry.

Benedict shrugged, and turned around, knowing that he was saving himself further abuse by cooperating. He felt the guard's strong hands slip a plastic tie over his wrists, hearing the zipping sound as the strip of plastic was pulled tight, biting into his skin.

The guard grabbed him firmly about the upper arm, and led him out from the cell. Benedict squinted in the brightness of the corridor outside, as the guard nudged him forward.

Benedict's step was unsteady, but he managed to trudge down the length of the passage. They passed by many doorways, but whether they were other cells, or had some other kind of use, Benedict did not know.

After a modest distance, the guard tugged Benedict to a halt before an elevator door. He pressed a series of buttons in a keypad to the side, and they waited for about a minute until the doorway before them slid noiselessly open.

The guard stepped into the elevator, punching in a floor number on the keypad inside as he held firmly onto Benedict. The elevator ascended at speed, and for the first time since he had arrived, many floors were traversed.

The entire episode was a deepening mystery, as Benedict glanced toward the lone guard. Normally they came for him in pairs, or even trios.

After drugs, physical pain, and being made a helpless bystander at abhorrent, gut-wrenching cruelties, Benedict could not fathom what new tactic his enemies were about to employ. A part of him was filling with dread, as he knew that pressures escalated in the process of an interrogation, and did not ease.

The elevator cab slowed smoothly to a halt, and the door slid open. The shining corridors Benedict was used to on the lower levels were replaced by the sensation of immense space, as metallic and electronic noises echoed within the shadow-strewn vastness of steel and lights meeting his eyes.

The guard escorted Benedict from the elevator down an iron-wrought walkway lining a huge, square-shaped shaft. Only a waist-high set of rails separated them from a dizzying drop.

Taking a couple sets of stairs, they made their way up to the lip of the yawning shaft, were Benedict set his eyes on a sprawling scene contained under an immense roof. As they proceeded across the ground, and were stopped periodically by security personnel, it became apparent that Benedict's guard was an officer of high authority.

A batch of armored vehicles was arrayed in a few short rows off to the right, and the guard led Benedict directly towards them. Like the opening to an enormous hangar, the entrance to the base loomed before them.

It was the first time in several days, or perhaps even weeks, that Benedict had set his eyes on daylight. He did not have a firm grasp on how long he had been underground. With no repeating regimen, and often drifting through the hours in a substance-induced stupor, he had no way of calculating the days.

After nothing but florescent lighting over the extended period of incarceration, the natural daylight was a welcome, soothing sight. He longed to gulp in some fresh air, and feel the raw wind against his face, after breathing the antiseptic, chilly air pumped into his holding cell through the base's ventilation system.

Benedict doubted he would have much of an opportunity, guessing that he was about to be transported from one detainment facility to another. He concentrated on his steps as they continued across the open ground, still feeling some instability after the extended confinement.

He had been jostled roughly and half-dragged to the overwhelming majority of the nightmarish sessions with his captors, and was not used to having his legs fully under him for an extended period. Having his arms secured behind his back only added to his difficulties.

Benedict pushed the awareness of his bodily aches deeper into the recesses of his mind, knowing that dwelling upon every feeling of soreness and abrupt spasm would do him no good. He had to press forward as best as he could, striving to keep pace with the long strides of the tall guard.

They finally drew close to the cluster of armored vehicles, where the guard paused to look upon them. Starting forward again, he led Benedict up to one in particular.

"Don't try to get away here," the guard instructed him, as Benedict felt the ties on his hands being cut. He winced a little as he brought his arms forward.

The guard helped Benedict get into the back of one of the Inter-Service Tactical Vehicles, one that had plainly been designed for the transport of prisoners. The interior had no manual locking mechanism, and a layer of glass, undoubtedly bulletproof, separated Benedict's compartment from the front where the driver was located.

Benedict took a deep breath, as the door to his section of the vehicle was shut. The guard got behind the wheel, and started up the engine, which rumbled with a steady cadence. The vehicle rolled forward, moving slowly as they made their way through the hive of activity.

The guard had no trouble passing through the main checkpoint set at the entrance to the base. He was quickly waved through, further convincing Benedict of the man's status, and making him wonder why he was taking Benedict alone outside of the base.

The vehicle picked up speed as they continued down an open road cleaving through a stark, rocky terrain. There was little elevation to speak of in the land surrounding them, which was dotted with tufts of hardy growths suited for an arid environment. The miles flowed by without event, as Benedict stared out the thick glass of the window to his side.

Benedict's heart sank as the vehicle suddenly drew to a halt in the middle of nowhere. Nothing but barren wilderness surrounded them, and only the empty roadway indicated any sign of civilization.

The landscape dismayed him, as he knew they were far removed from Venorterra. He wondered which of the western provinces of the UCAS they were in, even as he pondered what was going to happen to him.

He heard a lock click on the door next to him. It swung open in the grip of the guard.

"This is where you get off," the guard announced firmly.

There was something about the guard's voice that had changed, giving Benedict a start. It had taken on layers of tones, a quality that no human voice could assume.

The guard turned his head to look at Benedict. He did a double take, as he looked into the red, flaming eyes of his uniform-clad driver.

"You are … an Avatar?" Benedict asked, with a timbre of disbelief, even though he knew the answer.

"An Avatar seeking a way home … even if it is an impossibility," the figure replied dourly. "Now get out here. We cannot remain in the open. I will lead them astray."

Benedict kept his eyes on his unexpected benefactor as he opened the door wider, and got out of the armored vehicle. Before the Avatar closed the door, Benedict said, "Thank you, whatever your purpose is."

The being nodded to him, but said nothing. The Avatar got back into the driver's seat, shut the door, and then pulled off down the road.

Benedict stood on the gravel at the side of the road, and quietly watched the vehicle dwindle into the distance. A lonely breeze brushed against his face, filled with the chill of the early evening air.

With a crunching step, the sound of which was instantly swallowed up by the gaping desert silence, Benedict began walking.

# GREGORY

"I will go to them," Gregory replied curtly, his jaws taut with the considerable tensions coiling within. "There's no sense in ignoring them. I learned long ago you can't avoid reality. You just deal with it."

After coming so far, and receiving the miraculous support of the bikers, everything was unraveling fast. He had no doubts that the reports he had received were no exaggeration. Gregory knew the accounts were sober, meticulous assessments, which made things all the worse.

A million thoughts swam in his head as he departed the recently-liberated compound, which was now being utilized as a temporary base camp for the rebel fighters. He was greatly relieved he had expedited the return of as many of the detainees as possible to their homes.

Gregory had wasted no time in beginning the reunions of the detainees with their families and communities, as he knew the unavoidable counter-response by the federals would be harsh and powerful. He just had no idea how immense that response was, until his eyes gained their first look upon the massive force approaching the detainment camp.

The column undoubtedly stretched for miles. If it came out of Fort Lincoln, then Gregory had a pretty good idea what he was facing. It would contain second generation Lafayette tanks, not to mention Devers Armored Fighting Vehicles. At least two companies of tanks, two companies of mechanized infantry, and a self-propelled artillery battery were stationed at the base.

One tank would represent an enormous problem for Gregory and his fighters. Over thirty modern tanks spelled out something Gregory did not want to contemplate.

Accompanied by Dante, Consuela, and Benjamin, Gregory got out of the black SUV, and walked with a steady, robust gait towards the tip of the column. His instincts compelled a cool, level-headed demeanor, even though the display of martial force was overwhelming.

A tall, dark-skinned man stood patiently at the head of the column, flanked by two others in military garb. As Gregory strode towards him, he took note of the man's impressive height and build. He was every bit of six foot five, with wide shoulders, and a thickset frame that exuded strength.

Old instincts died hard, and Gregory extended the man a formal salute as he drew close, instantly noting his general's markings. He also recognized the colonel and command sergeant major insignia on the other two men, which hinted at brigade strength within the winding column stretching behind them.

Gregory's salute was returned promptly by the grim-faced general. Hard, calculating eyes latched onto him, showing neither anger nor friendliness. The man had the consummate air of a professional imbued with lengthy command experience.

"Let us speak at ease," the general stated, in a deep, gravely voice. "I am General Robert Jackson, of the UCAS Army. I assume you are the leader of the insurgents who recently took over the detainment camp."

Gregory locked his eyes with General Jackson, and did not blink. He was not going to apologize for his actions, and felt no shame in leading attacks on powers that had so brazenly violated the Grand Charter of the nation.

"I am Gregory Andreas, a former UCAS marine, and proud leader of a force that is defending this country," he declared, in a staunch tone of voice. "It is no insurgency, sir.

"The ones among my force with military backgrounds pledged to defend this country against all enemies, foreign and domestic. The ones who occupied that encampment prior to our intervention are domestic enemies. I am living up to the oath that I took when I became a UCAS marine."

Gregory fell into silence, and stared into the other man's eyes without wavering. His chin was slanted up, as he felt a fierce, burning pride in the choices he had made. Standing before the deadly array of military force, he awaited the general's verdict on his statement.

"Then why have you come here?" General Jackson asked, with a stony expression. "Look behind me. Surely you, as a marine, recognize the kind of assets I have with me."

Gregory could see the unending line of tanks, armored vehicles, and trucks behind General Jackson. A line of huge Lafayette tanks spearheaded the column, and they were not being carried on flatbeds.

He knew plenty enough about the tanks. Monsters of the battlefield, their composite armor shielded them from virtually anything that could be hurled at them. Their 120mm smoothbore main guns could loose a range of projectiles with mind-boggling accuracy.

Each was provided with no less than three machine guns, and the tanks were all equipped with exceptional sensors and night vision. There was little in the entire world that could stand a chance of contending with them.

"I am aware of the assets you have in that column, General," Gregory said, flatly.

"I have set up a large encampment not far from here," General Jackson said. "It is well-supplied, enough for a sustained campaign."

"And you have come reclaim the detainment camp, and keep honest people imprisoned," Gregory replied with a steel-edge, feeling a defiant heat rising within him. "Then why delay with me when you know you can push right through and take it?"

The other man did not so much as flinch at Gregory's abrasive flare, and his tone did not change, as he responded, "I have come to help you and the others who liberated that vile abomination. I salute your conviction, Gregory Andreas, and your good judgement in the service of your country, which is under all-out assault from within. You are correct. They are domestic enemies that have wormed their way to the heart of power."

455

Gregory said nothing for a few moments, blindsided by the general's words. He had expected to face the overwhelming might brought by the general with dignity, but had never thought for a moment that kind of military strength would be committed to the resistance. He could not find the right words to respond, but the general continued before he could speak.

"I have brought along some air defense assets, and we do have some aircraft available. Attack choppers, and a handful of various fighters that have come over to us, defecting from a couple of air force bases in the region. I have not coordinated with you and your forces, but I took the liberty of keeping drones away from the vicinity of the detainment camp later yesterday," General Jackson said, with the hint of a grin. "And it would be very nice to begin making some use of that airfield by the camp."

"What … why have you done all of this?" Gregory asked, wrestling with the stunning revelations.

"I saw the footage of the camp that was aired by the group they are calling terrorists. I knew the truth of it right away. It has been hard to live with myself the last few weeks. I cannot turn guns on the people of my own community, and the province I have called home all my life," General Jackson replied firmly. "Whatever may happen, I must stand with the people of this country, not against them. I gave the same oath as you did. I will honor that oath."

"And you were able to order a full brigade to follow you?" Gregory asked, in unabashed amazement.

"What I have behind me is brigade strength, but we have more than that being organized. We gave every man and woman the freedom to examine their own conscience, and to think about the oath they all took when they became soldiers," General Jackson replied.

"And so many remained?" Gregory asked.

"Not all, but a great many," General Jackson replied. "Enough to bring a solid force of armor this way. I don't think those TTDF boys and girls will want to stand in front of what I brought for very long."

Suddenly, Gregory realized why the bikers had been able to travel right up to the detainment camp without incident. The army was probably the branch charged with operating and manning the checkpoints, whereas the detainment camp was staffed by the TTDF. With a mass defection occurring in the army, the checkpoints had been abandoned.

"I suppose this indicates secession is in order?" Gregory asked.

"I think you could safely say that," General Jackson replied. "The momentum is certainly there, if it has not yet happened officially."

"Is this happening everywhere?" Gregory asked, unable to stifle his curiosity.

"In some places, but far from all. We've got a hard fight ahead of us," the general replied somberly. "But the trends are clear, when it comes to many military bases, and the province-level politicians.

"Looks like provinces across the south, and much of the midwest, are coming together to defend what this country once stood for. It looks like provinces in the north, northeast, and west coast remain firmly in the hands of the regime in the capital."

Gregory took the news calmly, knowing that civil war loomed. He had studied enough history to know how bloody the last one in the UCAS was, but he also knew that there was no other way to confront the alien malignancy seeking to assert itself over every last individual. It wielded brute force with impunity, and like a bully it had to be resisted with boldness.

The choice was to uphold his soldier's oath, and defend the Grand Charter, or to betray that oath, supporting something that was eviscerating the enshrined protections that had made the UCAS unique in the world's history. Where the rights in other countries derived from the power of humans, the rights in the UCAS were natural rights, whose source was above and beyond the ken of men and women.

Knowing that, Gregory knew that his fight was of a far greater nature than just a conflict between people. The choice could not have been more clear, or defined.

"Then how can we coordinate?" Gregory asked the general.

"With those barracks and the airfield, that detainment camp would make for a good base of operations," the general replied. "The regime is going to hit back hard. Make no mistake about that."

"I expect that," Gregory replied. He then added somberly, "And that's what I first thought your force represented, the first major counterattack."

"I am pleased to say that is not so," the general stated. "The regime is coming as sure as the sun rises, but we will have some time. Once they know they will now be going up against missiles, armor, and aircraft, they'll be a little more cautious."

"Maybe we will get lucky, and the military will defect fully," Gregory said, with the hint of grin.

"Don't count on it," the general said. "The White Pyramid houses more than a few that are devising ways to crush all of us, right as we speak."

"I'm not counting on it, as I have always tended to plan for the worst," Gregory replied. "Just tell me how we can help."

"Every man and woman you've got will be needed in the days and weeks to come."

"They've got good morale, don't worry about that," Gregory said. "Plenty of fire in their bellies."

General Jackson nodded. "That's good, but that morale is going to be tested severely. You and I, and some others, have really angered more than a few in the capital."

"Good, because if we are making them mad, then we are doing the right thing," Gregory stated.

"Then let's make them even madder," the general replied, with a ring of determination to his words. "Let us go ahead together, so that you can tell your forces what is happening."

"Which would be a good thing, as looking up and seeing a line of Lafayette tanks rolling towards them would not make their day," Gregory said, with a chuckle.

"No, I imagine it would not," the general agreed, with a bemused grin.

Following some brief introductions with the others, the general walked back with Gregory towards the SUV. Behind them, the colonel and command sergeant major hurried back, to get the huge convoy rumbling forward again.

# IAN

Ian drove his pickup truck unobstructed through Godwinton. Several cases filled with equipment were loaded in the covered back, and an aura of purpose encompassed him.

A smile rested on his face, as he saw men on A-frame ladders removing surveillance cameras from the light poles. He laughed aloud as he saw one of them hurl a camera down into the concrete, relishing the sounds of the impact through his open driver's side window.

For the moment, an invigorating air of freedom was rushing into Godwinton, and coursing throughout the surrounding area. The prison that was being made of general society had been thoroughly shattered, and its infrastructure was crumbling fast at the hands of a populace stifled for too long.

There were no checkpoints, no surveillance apparatus, no security towers, or any of the eyesores representing the cancerous police state imposed by the federals, and their lackeys at the province and local levels. The stranglehold of martial law had been unceremoniously thrown out by the will of the people, just as things should always have worked.

Ian knew that the momentum would carry further in the days to come. People could once again board an airplane without being made to feel like criminals, presumed guilty in all things as they were invasively scanned and patted down.

Ian now felt truly safe, with the genuine threats of unchecked federal authority disintegrated. Not all of the terrorists in the world gathered together could have done the harm to personal freedom that the enemy within had accomplished.

Terrorists could commit spectacular acts of violence, but they could not impose their will on the populace. The erosions of freedom in the UCAS had been facilitated at the hands of political elites, working in close concert with economic giants harboring no fondness for truly free business climates.

Finally, all of that malignance could be swept away. Self-determination, a return to personal responsibility, and the sanctity of private property could be welcomed once again into the heart of society

Possibilities and potential beckoned invitingly, from every angle. There would no longer be burdensome mountains of regulations and bureaucracy to stifle invention and innovation.

Freedom was never without its warts and rough edges. Ian knew there were no guarantees in a free society and individual efforts could not be safeguarded from failure. A great deal of work lay ahead to rebuild things, but a far better climate would emerge from the ashes of the monstrosity that wielded fear and empty promises to hold a nation spellbound.

The news of the fall of the prison compound and the incredible reports of army units joining the resistance in the immediate aftermath had elated Ian. The summons to come out to the compound and work on some electrical repairs had arrived about two days after the battle to liberate the detainment camp had taken place.

Never before had Ian been so eager to go to work. Before he had departed in the morning, he had to force himself to stop and take inventory of the gear he had loaded onto his vehicle, just to be certain he was bringing along everything he needed.

He was so giddy about the turn of events that it was not easy to concentrate. He had hugged Peyton and Allyson tightly to him, and given Alena an impassioned kiss, before setting off.

He had blocked out every thought of how the federals would respond. He was not naïve, in that he knew their hunger for control would drive them to assert themselves once more, even if every last person in the area wanted nothing to do with their failed, corrupted schemes. Every day that passed in liberation proved that life could go on, and even thrive, without them.

Ian's existence was now a very sobered one, living in the moment rather than looking far ahead. If the precious time he was experiencing proved to be ephemeral, then he determined that every moment of it would be cherished.

A short while later, Ian drove up towards the open gate of the former detainment compound. It was being guarded by a couple of soldiers, who checked Ian's name against a list they possessed. The gates were opened, and he was allowed access.

He gawked at the huge tanks resting a short distance inside the compound. A few tracked armored vehicles within view were only marginally less intimidating than the hulking tanks.

Several military helicopters could be seen in the distance at the airfield, and Ian had already espied a pair of fighter jets streaking through the skies overhead. The presence of friendly aircraft was reassuring, as it meant that warnings would be sounded long in advance of the counterattacks that Ian and everyone else expected.

All of the military hardware in view encouraged Ian greatly. The resistance was not just a hodgepodge of civilians and former military men with light weapons. It had the capability to resist weaponry that the guerrilla fighters were helpless against.

Getting out of the truck, his eyes fell upon a pock-marked, craggy face, a visage that was one of the best looking sights he had seen in a long, long time.

"Chris!" Ian exclaimed, breaking into a trot, despite the dull pain in his knees.

"My, my, what an unexpected visit," Chris replied jubilantly.

He was wearing his sheriff's uniform, including the wide brimmed hat shading his face from the bright sun. His gun rested in the holster attached to the belt around his waist. To all appearances, Chris looked as if it was just another day on the job.

"Looks like we got our sheriff back in town," Ian said, laughing.

"Didn't think it was gonna be this soon," Chris replied. "So how's my hometown doing?"

"Everyone's so happy ... people are just thrilled that everything is back under local control. Things were chaotic for a few minutes, but everyone came together quickly," Ian said, chuckling. He grinned, as he thought about the reunions that had recently taken place in droves all around Godwinton. "And I'm pretty sure all those who were imprisoned here have made it to their homes by now."

"Let me guess, you are a part of all this now?" Chris asked, with a raised eyebrow. "As in an official part of this resistance? There's something different in the air about you. You can't hide that from me, Ian. I've known you too long."

"Is there any other choice? I've got some skills that I can bring to the table," Ian replied, with a laugh. "Might not be a soldier, but I can sure keep generators under repair, and it looks like they have quite a few needs for my services out here."

"Who got you into this big fracas?" Chris asked, with a smile.

"Sam and Ollie," Ian replied. "Paid a little visit to me one night, and I liked what they had to say. Couldn't see a reason not to join."

"You know our cause is right, when the owner of a hamburger stand is reaching out to a commercial electrician to join a rebellion," Chris said, laughing heartily. "I'll say, it does have echoes of the founding revolution in this fine country of ours."

"You know ... it actually does," Ian agreed, laughing as he thought about Chris' observation.

"Then again, it's not so much of a rebellion, as it is resisting an enemy," Chris said, a little more somberly.

"That's the way I see it too," Ian concurred.

"So why are there so many people still around here?" Ian asked, glancing beyond Chris at all of the clearly non-military people milling about the grounds.

"Turns out they shipped quite a few detainees in, from other regions," Chris said. "Probably have quite an overflow at detainment camps near the big cities.

"The locals incarcerated here have all been helped, but we have no way of getting many of these other people back to their homes. At least not just yet. For the time being, they are going to have to stay here. Of course, they aren't being confined … They are free to go anytime they want. It's a new day."

"I don't even want to think what's been done to the people in the bigger cities," Ian said grimly.

"Hey, let's just control what we can control, and see where things go," Chris said. He looked around. "Well, come on, let's get you to your job."

Ian and Chris started walking through the camp, as he began to get an idea of the layout. It was orderly enough, with rows of barrack-style structures, and a small complex of buildings located at the forefront of the grounds.

The sight of soldiers doing maintenance on equipment and weapons everywhere was a vivid reminder of the tenuous position they were all in. Others not in military garb were attending to rifles and handguns, and these individuals Ian figured to be other civilian members of the resistance. A great many looked to be biker-types, confirming the rumors Ian had heard of a big column of bikes that had broken a stalemate in the fighting for the camp.

The raucous sounds of an altercation breaking out drew Ian's attention abruptly. Chris quickened his stride, and Ian fell in alongside his friend, as they hurried towards the sounds of the scuffle.

A huge, long-bearded figure was slapping a slender, narrow-faced man across the face, open handed, over and over. A spreading wet stain in the smaller man's crotch area more than testified to the imbalance of the conflict. It was as lopsided as it could possibly get, as the thin man could do nothing to stop the onslaught.

Ian guessed the much larger man to be one of the bikers, with his rougher appearance, and the emblems stitched to the studded leather jacket he wore over a t-shirt displaying a popular motorcycle company's logo. The man had an angry scowl on his face as he administered the beating.

"Ya happy now, you damn, no-good talking head? Think we're all just stupid now 'cuz we don't have one of yer fancy degrees," the biker roared at the disheveled-looking man, who yelped, struggling to cover up as he got smacked around again.

Chris trotted up swiftly, with Ian close in his wake.

"Hey man! What's this all about?" Chris called out forcibly to the biker as they neared, causing the other man to hold his next blow.

The biker glared up at Chris, eyeing him with iron-hard eyes. Ian thought for a moment that he would have to throw himself at the biker.

Chris was a tough man, but the biker looked like a human wrecking ball. Ian could hold his own, and had accounted well enough for himself during brawls in earlier years, but he doubted that even his assistance could help Chris counter the primal force clad in a leather jacket before them.

"I'll tell ya what's up," the biker said gruffly. "Recognized this squirrelly bastard, who's been locked up with everyone else ... 'prolly the only one in this whole godforsaken place that deserved to get imprisoned.

"I tell ya, I always wanted to get my hands on this little, devious rat. And just like I always thought he would, this candy-ass pissed himself right away."

Ian looked closer at the frightened man, and finally recognized him. He was one of the television pundits that had constantly infuriated him on news shows, and was one of the great many media personalities possessing northeastern university pedigrees that apparently brought along a sense of elite entitlement along with the degrees. Like others of his seedy ilk, he had always seemed to be focused on tearing apart anyone trying to bring real transformation, or reform, from outside the beltway of the capital.

"You spent yer days making fun of anyone speaking plainly, calling 'em extreme, or unelectable, or just calling 'em names. Well, see what your side got you? Look around you, you dimwit punk. How's that big degree suitin' you now?" the biker lambasted the man, in sharp tones of condemnation. "Think yer invincible? Here, just incase ya forgot, let me show you again how yer not ..."

The air cracked with another hard smack across the man's reddened face, as he flailed helplessly against the overpowering strength of the biker. The huge man pinned him down with little effort, and quickly backhanded him on the other cheek, eliciting a high-pitched shriek.

"Feelin' elite enough now?" the biker mocked. "Sound like a man, at least. You sound like some damned bird!"

"That's enough, my friend," Chris stated firmly to the biker, but not in an overly confrontational manner. "I know who he is. I can't stand that guy either, but we gotta keep things in order here. Help me out here."

"This little punk deserves a lot more. He and his kind got everyone ridiculin' folks who might have tried to do something to stop all this," the biker replied, continuing to glower at the cowering, former television news figure. "Don't worry, I'm not doin' any permanent damage to him. I ain't gonna give him the honor of a closed fist. His bitch-ass just deserves to get slapped around, like the pansy ass he's always been."

"You've slapped him around pretty good now," Chris said evenly, stepping in a little closer. "I think he's had plenty enough."

Ian could not tell what Chris intended to do, but his friend was not going to allow the man to continue being beaten, no matter how loathsome the caustic pundit was. Chris Howard was the sheriff once again, now that he was no longer confined in the federal prison camp. He could not allow a vigilante climate to fester.

The biker stared down at the quivering man for a long moment, and finally a big, toothy smile broke through his thick gray and black beard. "Yeah, yer right, Sheriff. I've given him a pretty good smack down, haven't I? Nice and thorough...."

As if to put an exclamation point on the session, the biker grabbed the man up by the scruff of his neck, giving him a solid kick in the butt with his black boot, launching the slender man forward a few feet. The man squealed, and looked far different than the haughty, beltway political commentator whose barbs against good people Ian had railed against time and again.

"Go on, wimp! Get out of here! ... Not feelin' so elite now, are ya?" the biker yelled out, laughing, and plainly enjoying the other man's misery.

The man scrabbled feverishly to get his feet under him, whimpering, and ran away as fast as he could. He disappeared around the end of one of the barracks-like residential buildings.

The biker looked up to Chris and Ian, and his mood seemed to change in an instant. The tone of his next words was relaxed, devoid of the teeming hostility that had been present just seconds before. "Haven't met you two boys just yet, but I've seen you around in here, Sheriff. Sorry you had to see me venting like that. I've been told I get carried away sometimes. Rumble Dog's the name."

The biker extended his large, meaty hand towards Chris and Ian, who doubted that the biker's parents had been the one to bestow that particular name on him. The moniker fit the man well, though. Ian felt the great strength in the other's grip, and was glad that he and Chris had not been compelled to physically intervene.

"So yer the sheriff? I'm usually tryin' to avoid yer kind, but seems we're all on the same side now," Rumble Dog said. He appeared to straighten up a little, and pride reflected in his voice as he added, "I'm one of those that stormed this damn place."

"I thank you for that, and we're going to need everyone … it's going to be a long road ahead," Chris stated.

"I'm used to travelin' long roads," Rumble Dog replied, with a low chuckle. "So what are you two boys about in here?"

"Just getting things back to order, which is why you need to avoid doing things like you just did," Chris said. "I can't let that kind of thing happen again. No matter how much we all would have liked to smack that guy a few times."

The two men held each other's eyes for a few moments, and neither one blinked. The warning underneath Chris' words were clearly understood by the biker. Ian could see that the two men had a respect for each other, even if there was no sign of backing down in the biker.

"Straight talk … I like your kind," the big biker said finally, nodding his head with a low-pitched chuckle. "But admit it, you think he deserved a little smackdown."

"He was guilty of having a part to play in the things that got us all into this mess. I don't deny that," Chris said.

"Well, can't say I won't give out beat-downs to those that ask for them, Sheriff, but I know where things will stand between you and me. You'll have to do what you gotta do then," the biker said. "I don't fault you for that. But I can't change what I am."

"Let's just try to work together, as much as we can," Chris said.

"I'm good with that," Rumble Dog said. He turned towards Ian. "So what are you doin' here? I know you ain't a sheriff."

"No, thankfully I'm not," Ian replied, with a laugh. "Just an electrician. Gonna be repairing some of the wiring that got damaged in the fighting, and work on some generator maintenance, since they're planning to use this place for the near future."

"Ya know, I was a certified electrician … and did more'n a bit of construction work … before I decided to take to the open road," Rumble Dog replied.

Ian grinned, finding that he was surprised by very little anymore. "You still remember everything pretty well?"

"Sure do. I've tinkered quite a lot since then. Helped a few bars out now and again," Rumble Dog said. "Found it got me all the beers I could drink, and that's more'n a couple."

The big man laughed heartily, and Ian did not doubt his boast.

"If you feel up to it, I could sure use some help," Ian ventured, on a whim.

Rumble Dog nodded. "Be glad to. Even if ya don't got any beers. If I stay busy, serves to reason I won't need to vent at the candy-asses I come across."

Ian laughed. "I have to admit, I did enjoy seeing that little bastard get smacked."

"See what I mean?" Rumble Dog said, glancing towards Chris, laughing.

"And thanks for working with me, and not pushing things any farther there," Chris said.

"Sheriff, now's not the time for cops and robbers. Don't worry, we'll get back to playin' sheriff and outlaw when we get this country back in order," Rumble Dog replied to Chris, with a wink and a grin. "At least I'll be able to get a fairer day in court if you get me."

"It's a deal," Chris responded, laughing warmly as he shook his head. Ian could sense that his friend was taking a bit of a liking to the bombastic biker.

"And just wait until you meet my woman, she's twice the tempest I am," Rumble Dog countered, grinning.

"Then I will have to deputize a few more men and women of my own, thanks for the warning," Chris replied in good humor.

Ian tried to envision what kind of woman would pair up with Rumble Dog. The first imaginings manifesting within his mind were somewhat disturbing.

"Don't mention it. Everyone needs a warning with that wildcat of mine," Rumble Dog said. He looked back to Ian. "So whaddaya say? Load me up with some tools, and let's go see how I can help ya."

"Sounds like a plan," Ian said. He looked over to Chris. "They said I needed to check in with Ollie Pryor, to get the specific list of things that are highest priority."

"He'll be in that building over there," Chris said, pointing to the last structure in the nearest row of barracks. "It's being used as a kind of headquarters for those in the resistance. I'll take you over there right now."

The three men started for the building, with Chris and Ian walking together, and his giant new assistant striding close behind.

"Feels like a great new day, doesn't it?" Chris asked him.

"Sure does," Ian said. "Don't have a functioning government, or know what's going to be used as money, or about a million other little details, but I tell you, I've never felt better."

"Did we ever have a functioning government before?" Chris riposted, with a grin.

"We'll do much better now that we're free of that dysfunctional nightmare. That's one thing I'm certain about," Ian said.

"It's going to be great to see people being allowed to live their own lives again," Chris said. "That's what I'm looking forward to most."

"That's all I've ever wanted," Ian said. "Just let me live, and raise my family like I want. Let me keep what I earn. And I'll promise to stay out of your business. Is it really that complicated?"

"You'd think so, the way they ran things," Chris replied.

A vicious struggle lay ahead, but Ian and all the others in the resistance were fighting for a clear purpose. It was nothing more than centering the principles outlined in the Grand Charter, restoring what had been lost, ignored, and twisted over the years.

Like Chris had said, it was not really a rebellion that was occurring, but rather a war against an enemy that had finally become unmasked, enough for everyone to see the beast for what it truly was. The great mistake was that it had been tolerated, enabled, and compromised with, for far too long.

Nevertheless, it was better late than never that everything would be set to rights, once again.

Ian glanced over at Chris, and smiled. "Well, it'll be a little less complicated now ... the people are running things again."

# UCAS

In all of the provinces awash with outbreaks of insurgency, the implementation of Living ID was cast aside. All efforts were made to disseminate the stocks of vaccine available, the supplies of which had been confiscated swiftly by insurgent forces.

In the provinces of the northern regions and the west coast, where federal authority remained entrenched, Living ID began to be distributed, right alongside the vaccine. People lined up willingly, in great lines that lasted hours on end, to receive the nanoscale implant and the promised protection against the virus.

Claiming that the widespread upheaval in the UCAS had disrupted supply, the vaccine's distribution slowed markedly across the face of the world. Curious to many, the absence of the vaccine was most noted within the poorer, more overpopulated parts of the world.

Abundant Harvest continued to exact its grim toll on humanity, sending countless thousands more to a torturous fate that only death abrogated. The outrage in the neglected countries spawned riots and violence that merely accelerated the global culling.

Military force ran roughshod everywhere, with little to rein its ferocity in. Authorities, especially those involved with the Convergence, were evacuated to safer havens, while the fires of violence swept through country after country.

It was truly a world in deep turmoil, with financial markets crippled, global-level institutions ineffective, and endemic violence. Natural disasters were compounded by the absence of coordinated relief efforts. Riots and mass demonstrations were as commonplace as the harsh crackdowns that followed in their wake.

People everywhere were crying out for a savior, one who might at least bring some sense of order back into daily life. A desperate world starved for order began to look for a leader.

# JOVAN

Throughout many rooms, and indeed in many bedchambers, higher level members of the Society of the Red Shield and the Order of the Temple were engaged in a celebratory, indulgent mood. The night was still very young, and rivers of exquisite wines coursed from the generous bounty provided by Jovan.

Other substances used to enhance moods were available in abundance, and the atmosphere was one of extreme regalement. Nothing was off limits for the privileged, wealthy attendees. As it had been before all the tumult, they operated under a set of rules much different than the broader populace.

Jovan nodded and smiled, as the head of one of Yorvik's largest banks sauntered past, winking back at him with a knowing smile. The sixty-year old man was arm-in-arm with two voluptuous beauties, each comfortably over six feet tall in their silver-strapped high heels. Their silken-smooth attire hugged their bodily contours alluringly, with snug mini-skirts culminating a few scant inches above their shapely knees.

While a salacious aspect imbued much of the ongoing activity, there was a decided levity to the air. Jovan found it all very strange, given that so much was shaking right underneath their feet.

It looked as if a true uprising in the UCAS had begun, which definitely compounded matters. It was not entirely coordinated yet, but the outbreaks were extensive across the south and midwest.

At the least, the implementation of Living ID was proceeding in the provinces firmly held by government forces. It would be an invaluable way to delineate friend from foe in due time, but it would be long-delayed in the turbulent regions.

The markets were as tumultuous as always, and Jovan's own wealth swayed back and forth on paper, with the plunges and spikes that had become so commonplace he rarely felt unease at massive shifts. Juliana had done an artful job in keeping close track of Jovan's holdings, though the reports she rendered to him on a regular basis were more often negative than positive. Jovan had engaged in few transactions, choosing instead to hunker down and wait for the storms to pass.

The only favorable thing happening at the moment was that Kaira was having a press conference concerning her succession to David Sorath's position in a couple of days. She was not on the premises at the moment, having told Jovan that she needed to make some preparations for her first initiatives as the head of the Peace Commission.

He missed her presence, as she would have been a welcome oasis in the surrounding debauchery. His desire was admittedly selfish, as he knew that she had always avoided such nights, showing no inclination for carnal appetites. Kaira always showed a propensity for moderation, and Jovan had never seen her take anything to excess.

Jovan wended his way through the revelry, until he was in the quiet refuge of his own bedchamber. There would be no scintillating adventures of the flesh this evening, as there had not been for quite some time.

The more that he had become attuned to Kaira and her career progression, the less of a hold his flesh had over him. He had not minded the change, as it always seemed that the fires of lust put the powerful in compromising positions, of the kind often utilized by others to secure their cooperation. Jovan was beholden to nobody, and that was the way he liked it.

A chill graced him as he entered the bedroom, and he turned his head towards the right, where the shadowy outlines of three female figures billowed slowly. The ghostly apparitions smiled as he looked to them, becoming more distinctive in form in seconds.

"Well done, Jovan," Lilith praised him, from where she stood in the center of the spectral trio.

"Well done? I haven't done anything, other than try to keep my own ship from sinking," he replied, with an irritable edge, thinking that there was some mockery in the other's words.

"You have been a friend and refuge for Kaira," Naamah stated.

"She has become my dearest friend, and I would do anything she asked of me," Jovan replied, without hesitation. Thinking on the words that had just left his lips, he knew them to be unshakably true.

"She is of the utmost importance to the Convergence," Agrat bat Mahlat said.

"Lilith has made me well aware of that," Jovan replied.

"You must dedicate yourself to supporting her approaching work at the Peace Commission," Lilith said. "It must be advanced swiftly."

"If she asks me for anything, you know I will not refuse her," Jovan said firmly.

The three woman-spirits smiled again, and seemed to be very pleased with his response. Yet it was no difficult admission to make. Kaira had become the only light to him in the midst of the raging tempests besetting the world.

In some ways, he wished that she had the credentials to take leadership of the World Summit, as she was exhibiting the kind of fortitude and level-head necessary for unprecedented situations. That kind of leadership had been sorely absent in nations and at the World Summit, which was filled with men and women that were of thin substance.

"So the Convergence is almost complete, I take it?" Jovan queried, with an edge of hope in his tone.

"Yes, and everything will be made new," Lilith replied, with an exuberant lilt to her voice.

"I just want to get past that point, so the world can be brought to order again," Jovan said. "It hasn't been very pleasant recently."

"And it will be, Jovan, an order like you have never witnessed, or even read about," Naamah said, and for a moment, her dark eyes appeared to glitter. "I am a mother to many, and those I have brought to life will take their rightful place in the forthcoming age."

Jovan wondered what kind of offspring such a being could give birth to, but he refrained from voicing his curiosities.

"And we will still the hearts of those who will not be suitable for this age, while they are still slumbering in the womb," Lilith said, with a hissing edge that made Jovan's blood run cold.

A distant part of him wondered what such an age would be like, where the undesirable would be determined, and eliminated, before birth. The speck of concern was washed away in a moment, as the overwhelming desire to see order brought to the global chaos flooded him.

"The world will be very different, Jovan, but if you remain loyal, you will flourish," Agrat bat Mahlat said, with the air of a promise.

"All I know is the world can't stay as it is," Jovan said. "It is falling apart at the seams, and it is all we can do to execute the most basic of things."

"Which is why you must support Kaira's efforts, and facilitate whatever support and resources she may need," Lilith said. "The men and women indulging in their hungers this very night under your hospitality are but a fraction of the power that you can draw together."

Lilith had stated the obvious. Banking and finance magnates were profligate on the grounds of his estate, at the moment, but he could pull together political, military, and business leaders in no time at all. The reaches of the Society of the Red Shield, and their allies in the Order of the Temple, went very far, having been extended and entrenched over the course of centuries.

Still, as he had indicated, it was difficult to do things that would have been afterthoughts just months before. Logistics were beset from all angles when markets were disrupted, and fighting was breaking out everywhere one looked.

Every day it felt as if he was stepping slowly along cracking ice, just an instant away from plunging into freezing depths.

"New help is about to be brought to you," Lilith proceeded. "Of a kind that your order has never had available before."

"What kind of help?" Jovan asked her.

"It will be revealed to you soon," Lilith replied.

"Apparently, I'm the only one who sees how precarious everything is," Jovan snapped, thinking of the people in his house and the seeming lack of urgency in the spirits before him.

"Only a world at the brink of collapse can see clearly the One that will bring them into a new Light," Lilith said.

"You play a very dangerous game," Jovan said.

"The stakes could not be higher," Lilith replied firmly. "Which is why you must do everything you can to assist Kaira."

"And I suppose you still can't tell me what is so important about her work," Jovan said, feeling more agitated with every evasive answer.

"All will be made clear, very soon," Lilith said. Abruptly, she looked away from Jovan, as if hearing some distant call.

Jovan stood awestruck, as the dark, billowing forms began to radiate a great light. He had never seen such a manifestation in them before.

It was as if their forms were unfurling, exposing a deeper light that had been cloaked by the swirling, dark substance of their exteriors. The three female spirits looked to be in a rapturous state, their faces filled with ecstasy.

"Do everything you can for her," Lilith said, in the voice of a command, as the forms of the three spirits began to dissipate.

"Where are you going?" Jovan asked.

"We are summoned," Naamah answered, in a voice like a song of joy, as the three spirits faded from view. "The Shining One calls to us…"

As her voice trailed off, Jovan stared at the now-empty space where they had been. Their admonition to help Kaira had not been necessary, as Jovan would do anything she asked. But Lilith's persistent counsel to him, as well as her presence at the hospital the night David Sorath died, underscored the great importance they gave to Kaira's new work.

Loosing a deep breath, knowing that the answers would not be given to him that night, he slipped off his shoes. At a bare minimum, he was determined to get a few hours of good rest.

# XAVIER

Simmering with anger, Xavier tromped down the bright corridor at Station Central. His mind swarmed with the tasks spiraling before him.

His world was increasingly like the nature of a mythical hydra. When one problem was subdued, several others rose up in its place.

The fires of rebellion had to be doused all across the south and midwest. It seemed that more insurgent flames broke out with every hour that passed.

Government forces were facing no mere rabble. A disturbing trend had unfolded, as defections occurred all across the military. The mushrooming conflict would soon be pitting full divisions and brigades of the UCAS against each other, both sides equipped with advanced weaponry.

The breakdown of the UCAS military, with air force squadrons, tank brigades, and more splintering off to join the resistance was dismaying. The only comfort was that the government forces still retained overall superiority in numbers and equipment.

A comprehensive strategy to deal with the insurgency had yet to be fully crafted. War planners at the Defense Ministry, which was still located in the White Pyramid at the capital, were diligently working to come up with a way to break the back of the insurgency before all its elements could coordinate effectively.

Adding to Xavier's immediate concerns, Benedict Darwin had somehow managed to get out of his cell, ascend all the way to the surface of the vast complex, and exit the front gates of the base; without so much as one person taking note of the man.

Not one man or woman in Station Central could describe Benedict, and none of the surveillance cameras had turned up anything to indicate who had assisted him. Something far beyond Xavier's ken was involved, and he had gone to Aaliyah swiftly.

Aaliyah had been enraged at the news, though she also sensed something deeper at work in Benedict's escape. Erkorenen were being loosed in the vicinity of Station Central, in considerable numbers, at her direct command.

According to her, they were like hounds that could pick up a trail that nothing else of flesh or technology was capable of sensing. Xavier had to staff special TTDF troopers, all Initiates of the Faith, in the rooms where radar signals and other sensors trained on the air and ground around the base were monitored. No alarm was sounded as large flying shapes glided in the skies over the barren landscape.

Xavier was looking forward to using the Erkorenen in the coming operations to suppress the rebellion. They were multiplying quickly in number deep within the base, and grew rapidly, offering Xavier a most unusual weapon to wield in the coming months.

Several had been deployed near Godwinton, all of them flying varieties, including the dragon that had carried Xavier through the ancient storm to bring the surviving Erkorenen through the gate. A group of TTDF troopers had nonetheless been wiped out by an unknown force before the creatures could respond.

The perpetrators, some manner of beasts serving the enemy, had eluded the Erkorenen in the aftermath. Apparently, they were the same kind of creatures that had attacked the Erkorenen during the first use of the latter, in the Frontiersman National Forest in Venorterra.

Aaliyah, much to Xavier's irritation, was not forthcoming, even though he could tell she knew more about the enigmatic assailants. Whatever they were, the enemy creatures were extremely formidable, and Xavier resented Aaliyah's reluctance, as it left his forces more vulnerable during their operations.

Another group of TTDF troopers had been ripped to shreds on a bridge leading into Troy. The tales of giant wolf-men had poured from the eyewitnesses of the brazen attack.

The assault had opened the bridge to a group that had commandeered a downtown television station, to allow a former high-ranking Babylon

Technologies employee to make an address that had been broadcast nationwide. The media was working overtime now to paint the claims as outlandish, but great damage had been done, as more than a few high level military authorities had evidently been swayed by the statements.

Xavier paused to address the electronic panel governing the door into the chamber beyond, before proceeding through the entrance. The terrible stench that always clung to the air in the chamber slammed into his senses as he strode across the floor, his heavy boot steps echoing in the capacious cell.

The remains of a grisly meal were piled off to one side, a high mound of broken bones, both human and animal.

The appetites of the giants among the Erkorenen were astounding. It was highly fortunate that they were not great in number, as merely feeding a greater number would have been an onerous task requiring resources Xavier could not afford to spare.

"Helel!" shouted Xavier.

A resonant groan filled the chamber, as the giant rolled over, and roused himself from his slumber. The massive creature got to his feet ponderously, towering high over Xavier.

"Commander Xavier!" Helel's voice boomed in the chamber. The giant's eyes were like glistening saucers as he stared down at Xavier. The giant was learning Xavier's language rapidly, to the latter's great satisfaction.

"You will go to another place soon. You, and others like you, will begin your work. You will guard a special place. You will kill anything that tries to go near this place," Xavier said, trying to keep his words as basic as possible.

To his pleasure, the giant nodded immediately, with a look of understanding. Jovan ignored the pungency that engulfed him in the giant's presence, as the creature would be in the open air soon enough.

Xavier had been tasked with the security of a very prominent individual, whose identity had not yet been made known to him. All he knew was that he was taking no chances with the strange enemy creatures that could kill Erkorenen, and who could tear through a force of TTDF troopers equipped with modern weapons without difficulty.

The giants, in his estimation, were the strongest of the Erkorenen, and he would have to commit his best available assets into his charge of establishing security at a wooded compound just north of Yorvik.

Some TTDF units, Initiates of the Faith, would be employed in the assignment, with all manner of sensory equipment. But if the enemy sent their own formidable creatures to penetrate the compound, or threaten the unnamed individual to be protected, Xavier intended to counter them with the titans like Helel.

"I will kill enemy," Helel thundered, giving the only response that Xavier wanted to hear.

# THE MIDDLE LANDS

A number of Sentinels were gathered at the location where Enki, Inanna, and the others had finally ended their long journey up from the depths of the Abyss. As before, Enki took care to avoid rousing unnecessary alarm amongst those warding the upper realms, guiding them first to the Grey Lands, and finally across the span of darkness reaching to the edge of the Middle Lands.

The extensive journey back took place without incident, but whether or not Erishkegal's realm had been put at risk was not known. Kur, and a throng of dragons, like the head of a great lance, had speared through the darkness until they were far from the outskirts of the underworld realm.

It was a fortunate thing that the dragons formed the vanguard, as several times teeming clouds of Galla were blasted through with withering fire. It was as if their initial passage through the Abyss had attracted vast swarms of the demonic creatures, and Friedrich understood a little more clearly why the Anunnaki Tribunal had been so reticent at first in allowing them to leave.

Enki and Inanna used their powers to cloak the Exiles, Gryphons, and Peris as best as they could when they separated from the dragon escort. As they ascended upward, Friedrich thought long about Kur and the flying brood of underworld guardians, hoping with all his heart that the disturbance had not been great enough to attract the focused attention of the Shining One.

The Vortex was thoroughly avoided on their return journey, and did not even come into view as a pin-prick of distant light. Friedrich was profoundly relieved, as he did not want to set his eyes upon that maelstrom of wickedness ever again.

They had wasted no time in the Grey Lands, proceeding immediately to their destination in the Middle Lands. It was all the better, as Friedrich had little desire to see the shadow-filled, dismal landscape.

With jerky, fast-shifting movements, one of the Saltic had come forward from the other Sentinels when Enki, Inanna, and the others landed on the surface of the Middle Lands. The nimble creature came to an abrupt halt a short distance before the two Avatars.

"Great Enki … Great Inanna, welcome back," the eight-legged Aracha greeted them, its front end lowering in the equivalent of a slight bow. The creature had beautiful coloration, an aesthetic mixture of deep blacks and cobalt blues.

"Yezdegal, the journey has been long, but we have brought nothing in our wake," Enki declared.

"We will yet maintain vigilance," Yezdegal replied solemnly.

"As the Sentinels always have," Enki said, in the tone of a compliment.

Confirming Yezdegal's statement, a giant, thick-bodied Theraph moved out from the band of Sentinels, and strode slowly towards the border. Friedrich looked up at the huge Aracha's underbelly, which was carried well above him. Vibrant yellows could be seen on its underside, as Theraphs exhibited a considerable range of hues and patterns.

Several Aran followed the Theraph. The Aran were masters of web weaving, and Friedrich knew that they would labor to erect additional obstructions, both for warning and defense, in the instance that any creature of the pit had somehow eluded the detection of the Avatars.

"What can you tell me of the Grey lands, Great Enki?" Yezdegal asked.

"Those lands have fallen further under shadow," Enki answered the Aracha, gravely.

"We will strengthen our guardian forces there," Yezdegal replied.

"We must all beseech Adonai Most High to reach the hearts of the spirits that dwell there, as they are being swayed towards the darkness," Enki said, with a melancholic edge. "It is a place teeming with dark wraiths of the pit."

The Saltic grew quiet for a moment, its multiple, glittering eyes looking back to Enki. Finally, it said, "We will resist, until we are in the

Void, or the End of Days comes."

"As will every spirit loyal to Adonai," Enki said. "May the Grace of Adonai be upon you, Yezdegal."

"And with you, Great Enki, and Great Inanna, and all of your companions," Yezdegal replied, its set of eyes taking in all of the others with the Avatars.

With quick, bounding movements, the Saltic headed for the stark edge of the Middle Lands, as the rest of the fascinating race of Aracha followed in its wake. There was urgency to their motion, and Friedrich knew the dedicated creatures assumed nothing when it came to the possible threats from below.

Enki turned to face the Exiles. "The Gryphons will bear you to a safer place in the Middle Lands, but Inanna and I must go to Mikael. He must be counseled of the things witnessed in the realm of Ares. I must also seek understanding of the mysteries occurring within Erishkegal's realm.

"You all have my deepest gratitude for what you risked on my behalf. You are all true friends … Exiles, Gryphons, and Peris. I could hope for no better, anywhere within the infinite realms."

Enki turned to regard the small band of Peris, and Friedrich saw the looks of joy sparking on their faces as the Avatar commended the little spirits. Asa'an smiled radiantly, beaming bright, and he knew that the Avatar's words would be a comfort against the enduring sorrows she carried deeper within.

"And all of you have my gratitude," Inanna said, in a beautiful voice, one that transformed the utterance of words into the essence of melodious song. "Peris, Exiles, take heart, your road will lead to the gates of the White City and Beyond.

"Stay true to the path you are all taking. Your choices to go with Enki testify that you are rightly guided. One day you will all walk in His Pure Light, each and every one of you. This I solemnly assure you."

The words flowed with consolation, and encouragement, and Friedrich could see the first of many lambent tears streaking down the face of Asa'an, as she began to weep. All of the Peris shook with powerful emotions, as one of Adonai's great Avatars gave open voice to their dearest hope and desire.

The power rested within the truth that Inanna's words were not spoken idly. They pulsed with the promise of realization, and Friedrich knew that she was extending a special mercy to the brave Peris, speaking in full harmony with Adonai, as a portion of their dark, inner scars were washed away in an instant.

Though both Avatars were in their blazing, multi-winged forms, Friedrich could feel the joy emanating from them, as they gazed upon the Peris, and then looked back to the Exiles and Gryphons. They turned with wings gracefully spreading outward, lifting up from the surface and climbing smoothly into the air. Flying side by side into the east, the celestial pair ascended swiftly towards the rainbow-hued skies.

Friedrich stared after the Avatars, well after they were gone from sight. He was jolted from his reverie by the action of the Gryphons taking flight, as the one he was astride launched itself upward.

In a loose cluster, the Gryphons carried the Exiles deeper into the Middle Lands. Friedrich was gladdened by the splendor all around him. His perspective had matured significantly with the journey into the darkness.

The Grey Lands, the Vortex, the horrific realm of Ares, and even the shadowy dominion of Erishkegal prompted him to savor and appreciate the Middle Lands like he had never before. Every ray of light appeared to dance, and every surface sparkled to his eyes, as they glided across hills, streams, fields, lakes, and a particularly wondrous forest, where the leaves were of shining gold, and the trunks and branches of gleaming silver.

After covering a great distance, the Gryphons descended and alighted in the midst of a swathe of lightly glowing, silvery grasses. The Gryphons then lowered themselves to the ground, as Friedrich and the others dismounted their steeds.

He turned towards the noble creature that had carried him into the Abyss, even into the hell of Ares' realm, and back safely. The golden sheen of its folded wings was richly lustrous, in the light from the dazzling skies overhead.

"Thank you," Friedrich said to the Gryphon, looking straight into its piercing gaze. "I would be in the dreamless sleep of the Void were it not for you. I owe you more than I can ever hope to repay."

The strange, interior voice of the Gryphon sounded within him. 'You owe nothing, where something was freely given. It was an honor to carry a soul so courageous. If you should ever need me again, I will come to you.'

"I am the one who is honored," Friedrich said, in a low voice, with a feeling of deep humility.

The Gryphon looked upon him for a moment longer, before turning around slowly, and taking to the skies with its other brethren. Friedrich recognized the presence of a new bond in that moment, as he gazed upon the cluster soaring upward, one that had been forged between him and the Gryphons.

He would never look upon the Gryphons in the way that he had before, as mere guardian creatures. For that matter, he would not look at any of the creatures that warded the Middle Lands with the same eyes. His respect and gratitude towards them were more heartfelt than ever before.

"Well, we made it back," Maroboduus exclaimed, slapping Friedrich vigorously on the back, as the Exiles started walking across the shimmering glade.

"Yes, my friend, we did, thank Adonai," Friedrich replied, with a smile.

It felt so good just walking under the luminous, chromatic richness of the Middle Land's skies. The longing for the White City was still burning inside of him, as that fire never abated, but there was a distinct sense of coming a little closer to home.

A bright, petite form darted into view from the right. A gleeful, and somewhat mischievous, look was on the winged spirit's face.

"And you didn't want to go visit the other Peris?" Friedrich greeted Asa'an, grinning. "You felt the urge to keep pestering me, did you?"

"You forget that I've known them since the beginning of time," Asa'an replied, in a chiding tone.

"Well, it always gladdens me to see you," Friedrich said. He then added with a wink, after a pause, "At least until you've thoroughly worn out your welcome."

"I can say I am happier now than I've ever been," Asa'an declared, with a resplendent smile. Friedrich had to admit that he had never seen her so exuberant.

"Then that is one of my greatest rewards from this rather dangerous journey we took," Friedrich said, feeling a surging wave of emotion inside.

The audience he, Asa'an, and the Gryphon had with Erishkegal, following their arrival at Egalkurzagin, had revealed the extent of the burden the little Peri carried within her. Friedrich had never fully appreciated just how painful the guilt was for Asa'an to bear. His spirit reveled hearing the Peri speak of her unprecedented happiness.

"And it looks like I am not the only one abounding with joy," Asa'an said, looking away, and then flitting upwards with a laugh.

Peering ahead, Friedrich saw a large, two-headed form bounding swiftly towards him through the grasses. He smiled, bracing himself a moment before he was vigorously tackled by an ebullient Seele.

The Orthun's two heads licked him simultaneously, on each side of the face, smothering him as he struggled to speak. The creature's eager eyes gazed into his own, warm with affection.

He cherished the look, so very different from the frightened, crazed eyes that Friedrich had beheld when he had come across the stranded, wounded Orthun following the battle against Beleth's legions. A sustaining light had been kindled in the creature's spirit, which had dwelt in darkness and fear for a long age.

"So, you actually missed me, Seele," Friedrich managed to get out, laughing merrily as broad tongues brushed his face again. "Well, I'm back, and glad to say none the worse for wear."

The Orthun barked excitedly, pulling away suddenly from Friedrich. He looked upward, seeing the sprite form of Asa'an as she leaped nimbly from one of Seele's heads to the other. Her merry laughter swirled around them.

Seele reared up abruptly, balancing on his haunches as he brought his paws together, catching Asa'an squarely in mid-air. The Orthun's grasp on the Peri was firm, but gentle, and it raked one of its tongues the entire length of her body.

Her wings and body quivered within the big paws as she endured the Orthun's attention. Friedrich laughed heartily at the face she made as Seele's tongue completed its trek atop her head.

"Got you good, little one!" Valaris called out, guffawing at the sight.

"Quite a predicament you are in, noble Peri," added Dietrich, as the others in Friedrich's group joined in the merriment.

"And that's what you get for teasing him, Asa'an. Be careful, he's getting better with your antics," Friedrich remarked, with a grin.

"Or I'm getting worse," Asa'an managed to get out, giggling as she was licked again by the Orthun's other head.

"Alright Seele, you can let her down now, the little nuisance has learned her lesson for the day," Friedrich said, winking at Asa'an, as she made another face of mock-annoyance at him.

481

"Nuisance? So you say," she replied in a tone of mild defiance, though she was smiling warmly as Seele loosed his grip on her.

The Peri stretched her wings and fluttered higher into the air. Friedrich got to his feet and rubbed the Orthun's left flank, as Seele playfully eyed the hovering Peri. Both heads barked at her, as if inviting her to come down just a little lower.

"He knew you were back," interjected a female voice.

Friedrich looked down, and saw Gisela striding across the open field towards them. He gave her a wide smile, looking into her glittering blue eyes. Her lengthy brown tresses shined richly as they fell over her shoulders, covering the top of the bright blue dress she had manifested for outer attire.

"Gisela … Wonderful to see you! And it looks like you took very good care of Seele," Friedrich said.

"It is great to see all of you," she replied, her eyes taking in Friedrich and his companions, who were milling around behind him.

"I could not keep up with him, when he sensed your return," she said, with a grin. "He could have kept up with a High Avatar, I believe."

"Thank you for looking after him while we were gone," Friedrich replied, in a lower, serious tone. "Seele means so much to me."

"It was no burden, and it was the least I could do for someone so courageous," she replied. Her gaze shifted, and her smile broadened. "Hello Silas. Welcome back to the Middle Lands."

"Hi Gisela," he replied, and Friedrich caught a hint of shyness in the younger soul's voice. He added, after a brief hesitation, "I am very, very glad to be back."

He knew that Silas was unmarried in his mortal life, as was Gisela, and both of them came from the same generation. It was amusing to see the young soul exhibiting nervousness with a female who was essentially his peer.

Friedrich kept his thoughts confined to himself as he watched the two interacting.

"And I am glad to see all of you back," Gisela said.

"That's the only thing I hoped for," Silas told her. "I've never been eager to go on adventures, but I couldn't just stay here when they left."

"I'm sure you have a lot to tell," Gisela said. "Me, not so much. I played with Seele, and took him along with me, to explore a couple of areas in the Middle Lands I hadn't been to yet. But that's about it."

"I would love to tell you all about our journey," Silas said, with a clear trace of eagerness.

Friedrich paused, taking note that Gisela was well-aware of Silas' shift in mood. To his further surprise, she seemed to be warming to it. He had the distinct impression that she was flirting with him.

"Then I want you to tell me of your adventures," Gisela said.

Silas came about as close to blushing as a non-physical being could. He smiled and there was a spark of excitement to his eyes.

"If Friedrich looses me from my charge," Gisela said, with a grin.

"Yes, yes, Gisela, I will take care of Seele from here," Friedrich said. "Go on, Silas."

Silas cast him a boyish grin as he stepped forward, and walked onward with Gisela at his side. Friedrich watched the two strolling off together, as he felt a sturdy pat on his back. Glancing over, he saw Maroboduus grinning broadly.

"He's a hero now, and a hero deserves a good gal at the end of a dangerous journey," the big spirit chuckled. "At least that's the way I see it. That's the way the best stories always went too."

Friedrich turned, and looked at the faces of Maroboduus and his other companions. "And I want thank all of you for keeping an eye on Silas. I have a hunch you are each a little part of the reason he's still here with us now."

"He was not a soldier in his mortal life, but he proved himself well enough down there," Dietrich stated. "He's a soldier, by all rights. Does not need to prove anything more. Survived the battle here, and made it through a journey into the Abyss."

"The lad smacked his share of the uglies," Valaris said, his thick beard shaking with his boisterous laughter. "You should have seen him when he saw you were separated from us. He was a storm! Whacked one of the beasties, then another, and then another!"

"Silas?" Friedrich asked, grinning, and finding it hard to believe the mild-mannered spirit becoming some sort of afterworld berzerker.

"Valaris speaks truly, there were just too many of the ugly bastards, or we would have routed them," Heinrich said.

"Adonai's Grace was with us for sure," Friedrich said, remembering the lethal swarms that pursued them in the blackness. He could hear their shrill, inhuman cries in his head, and his spirit shuddered momentarily.

"Look, Friedrich!" Ulrich exclaimed suddenly, from his right.

At first it looked like a sprawling firestorm was descending out of the sky, but Friedrich recognized the magnificent presence of a High Avatar immediately. It was an awe-inspiring vision to behold, as the great being swooped down towards the surface.

Like a soaring column of fire, the gigantic Avatar approached the recent arrivals with huge, flaming strides. Friedrich and the others just stood riveted in place, and he felt Seele pressing close against his side.

The presence of the celestial being was overwhelming to Friedrich's senses, pulsing with might. All of the Exiles nodded their heads respectfully towards the oncoming, enormous figure. Friedrich knew he had nothing to fear, but the powerful presence cast by the being was encompassing.

"Behold Haniel, seventh of the Ten Eminencies of Adonai Most High," Asa'an explained in the lightest whisper, where she was crouched down on Friedrich's right shoulder. He could feel her lips at his ear, and the nervousness in her voice. "It is said He once took a wise man in body directly from the mortal world into the infinite realms."

Friedrich had seen Metaraon before, conducting sojourns of child-spirits through the Middle Lands. Though giant in stature, Friedrich had known that Metaraon had not assumed his elemental form on those forays.

Never before had Friedrich set his gaze upon the prime form of one of the ten greatest Avatars loyal to Adonai. Though there was no presence of hostility, Haniel was fearsome to witness.

Haniel's great head angled downward, orienting upon Friedrich and his companions. Friedrich was frozen with inaction, not knowing what to do or say.

"Do not be afraid, Exiles," Haniel thundered, in a deafening voice. "Look to me, as I have brought a message unto you."

The words did little to mitigate the feelings inside, as Friedrich forced his gaze upward. His eyes traveled up a tremendous span filled with blazing fire, forming the contours of an immense body clad in long, flowing garments. His visual trek finally drew to a halt as he peered far up into the huge, fiery pools that were the High Avatar's eyes. He was transfixed as he looked into that ancient, burning gaze, reflecting a purity and strength far beyond his comprehension.

"As I have taken humans in body into the infinite realms, so I am empowered by Adonai to take two from Purgatarion into a mortal realm," Haniel boomed. "You have shown great courage, Precious Souls, and a task from the Great Throne is to be given to two of you."

"Which … two … do you wish?" Friedrich finally asked, after an uncomfortable silence had passed. His voice sounded tiny and thin in the aftermath of the other's sonorous words.

"You shall be one, as it was you that was first to approach Enki, to help seek out Erishkegal," Haniel declared. "Your spirit is strong, and it must be for the task that lies ahead of you. Choose one companion."

Friedrich pulled his gaze away from the High Avatar, and looked to his friends. He knew that all of them would be willing to go on another quest, no matter how perilous.

As he did not know what kind of task he would be given, Friedrich hesitated. Pensively, he turned back towards Haniel, and looked upwards.

"I do not know the task, so I do not know what I would be asking of them, or who would be best suited to go with me," he said, peering up at the blazing visage of the enormous being. "If you have this knowledge, who would you send, if you would counsel me?"

"One who would not find the world his own, but one who would not find the world too strange to his eyes," Haniel replied.

Friedrich had a strong sense that Haniel was referring to a particular Exile, but knew that the choice would be his own. He again looked at his friends.

He could rule out one of his main companions. It was obvious the Avatar was cautioning him against choosing Silas, who was quietly watching the proceedings at a distance, where he had come to a halt with Gisela.

Valaris, Maroboduus, Ulrich, and Heinrich would find a modern world entirely bizarre. Likely, so would Dietrich, had been removed from the world's timeline by nearly a century and a half.

That left the sixth and seventh of his companions, Hans and Stefan. The lives of both had been embroiled in horrific, worldwide wars, and neither man was too far removed from the modern age.

A few who still lived in the world had been alive at Hans' time. Further, a sizeable number of souls from Stefan's own generation yet lived.

Friedrich had spoken to both men often about their experiences, and knew that the technological marvels emerging during Hans' time had come into a greater fullness during Stefan's. "Stefan, I think you best fit this description," Friedrich pronounced, with conviction.

Stefan stepped forward, nodded to Friedrich, and then gave a low bow towards Haniel. "You know I would be honored to go with you."

Friedrich turned back to Haniel. "It will be the two of us, then."

"I will return for the two of you, when it is time to depart," Haniel replied.

With a swirl of fire, the Avatar turned away from the Exiles. Haniel's vast wings spread outward as the Avatar launched up towards the sky.

An enormous wave of heat passed over Friedrich and the others, as the fires of the High Avatar's body surged brighter. The Avatar picked up speed, gaining altitude swiftly.

Friedrich felt both anxious and excited as the gargantuan entity flew to the eastern horizon. He had thought that his period of quests was over, at least for some time; but evidently, another was beckoning.

# FATHER BRUNNER

Father Brunner stood quietly at the edge of the steps leading down from the thick bronze doors set in the front façade of St. Bosco. A cold night breeze flowed over him, causing him to shiver, even though he was wearing a long, black cassock. High overhead, clouds dark with the promise of rain glided steadily, pushed forward by the winds that lashed without warning against the stone blocks of the main church building.

Not everyone in the church community had chosen to go, as Father Brunner had anticipated. Over half of them had refused to leave, despite Father Brunner's many entreaties. He had stayed behind with Father Rader, resolved to attend to those who remained in the city.

Athanasius pushed his broad head against Father Brunner's hand, prompting the priest to scratch the mastiff between the ears. The dog stared outward with a stoic countenance, as if mirroring the unflappable mood of the burly priest.

Father Brunner was determined to his course, come whatever may. He was not immune from fear, as he knew that remaining in Troy was the equivalent of being stranded in a den of waking lions.

A ravenous, demonic hunger would soon overtake the city, and good souls would be among the first to be preyed upon. Nothing was more delectable to the things of darkness.

At least the recent operation had gone exceedingly well. Paladin's Light had been thoroughly evacuated, even as the strike force held the bridge open for Juan Delgado, and those with him, to reach the downtown television station.

The images paraded through his mind. A long, winding column of vehicles stretched into the distance, as Father Brunner watched the beleaguered inhabitants of Paladin's Light heading to a better refuge. The sight of their departure was a precious comfort that he returned to often, in the rickety days since everything had transpired.

Many church members had gone, wisely heeding Father Brunner's advice. He had hugged many of the men and women as they said goodbye, not knowing if he would ever see them again, at least in the physical world.

Father Rader had given him full permission to go onward with the departing church members, and many of those had pleaded with him to accompany the group, but he had given his word. His heart still ached, as he watched the vehicles pulling away from the gates of Paladin's Light.

The last to part from him were Hank and Zhang, who were with a group from the Order bringing up the rear of the column. The priest had wished them well, and given both men a blessing, but had not missed the sadness in their eyes before they parted ways.

It was the forlorn kind of look where he suspected they felt they were seeing him for the very last time. He could not blame them, as he did not feel much different about the predicament facing him.

Precarious did not even begin to describe the condition of the ground underfoot. Father Brunner could not peer beyond the physical world, at least not with an act of will, but he imagined that a most terrifying sight would meet him if he could.

He could feel a dark presence pervading just about everything around him, gathering in strength. It teemed with venom, coiling to strike.

A brooding, tense atmosphere reigned over the city. The sense of evil pervading the streets was palpable, as if demonic figures leered from every shadow, nook, and crevice in the labyrinth of buildings.

The church would soon be like a fortress under siege. He knew that Living ID would be forced upon the population of Troy, and his own position was irreconcilable with the merciless reality that was coming fast.

The remaining church family might have ignored his pleas to leave the city, but they could not afford to dismiss his warnings about Living ID. At least Juan Delgado's message had been broadcast, illuminating the true nature of Living ID. He hoped that Juan's story would help sway the more stubborn minds he would be appealing to.

He would continue imploring his church community to avoid Living ID at all costs, putting him in a very undesirable position. Father Brunner would be openly, and adamantly, counseling his church members to break the law. He doubted that the authorities would be tolerant of his presence at the church for long.

There was no other choice. The mortal life was a passing one, and his concern was for an everlasting state of existence. When it came to a truly diabolical thing such as Living ID, there was no viable option for a priest other than refusal, and resistance.

Nonetheless, he had a heavy heart, and wished that the cup of the approaching trial could be passed from him. He would not run from it, and knew that he would somehow find the strength to endure, as Another had accepted a brutal trial long ago, which was far, far worse in nature than what he was being faced with.

Glancing upward, he took solace from the sight of the Rising Dawn finial, dark against the parade of storm clouds farther above. It did not sway, no matter how brisk the gusts of winds buffeting against its surface. It would not flinch when lightning rippled, thunder boomed, and rains fell in torrents. It would be there, immutable, when the sun rose again.

He knew he would have to be just as steadfast, when he became a pariah to the powers governing Troy, and the UCAS. An ancient rage would be focused on him soon, as it would be on anyone that defied its authority. The priest would have to be unshakable when the hellish winds began to lash against him; as they inevitably would.

The barricades were about to collapse, and when they did, the streets would become a place of terror. The most primal, basest instincts in the human heart would be given hell's license to gorge upon the weaker and more vulnerable. Such was the way of the demoniac spirit, but it would encounter unyielding opposition at the doors of St. Bosco as long as Father Brunner still breathed.

"Come on, Athanasius," he said gently. "We've been out here long enough, and you've been very patient with this brooding priest. Let's go back inside, and see if I can find you a few good morsels."

The priest turned slowly, and strode towards the doors of the rectory building, as the big mastiff padded alongside.

# JOVAN

"I accept this solemn duty, with the firm conviction that the goals of the Peace Commission will be achieved in their entirety," Kaira stated resolutely, as camera flashes went off in a vibrant cascade all around her.

Her voice resonated with strong confidence through the speakers, and it seemed as if her smooth skin gleamed in the glittering parade of lights. Jovan stood to the side of the platform, with his hands folded in front of him, watching the proceedings.

For the moment, he had blocked out all his latest worries caused by the eruption of insurgency throughout the south and midwest of the UCAS. The center of his world was focused on the beautiful figure in the middle of the dais before him. She was manifesting into her wholeness before his very eyes.

Though it was a later press conference, with the announcement made at seven o'clock, the room was filled with members of the national media. The channels would soon be dominated with the news of Kaira's appointment to the top of the Peace Commission, as it was a story of governmental initiative being taken to address the extreme crisis facing the world.

"I accept this duty during a time of great upheaval in my own country, a nation being torn apart by the malignancy of rebellion," Kaira continued, in a firm tone. "My commitment to all nations is the seeking of peace. Peace is achieved through order, and order must be achieved on a comprehensive, global scale, if we have any hope of ending all wars.

"I have many new initiatives to introduce for consideration by the main body of the World Summit. They are ideas that I would ask no country to consider, if I were not willing to enact them within my own country.

"Some will find my new initiatives bold, but they are designed to achieve order, through which a lasting, encompassing peace may be achieved. I will fulfill the labors of many great individuals, who have gone before me, working without respite over so many long years. This, I solemnly assure you."

She closed out her prepared statement, and turned the podium over to a spokesman for the Peace Commission. A flurry of questions jostled against each other for attention, as the crisp-looking spokesperson chose the first of the eager throng.

Kaira turned towards Jovan as she strode across the low dais. She exuded confidence, and he could see no blemish in her, or flaw in what had just taken place. To his eyes it seemed as if a shining aura flowed about her, as she smiled radiantly at him.

There was no one better for the position leading the Peace Commission, especially at the critical juncture the world was in. Strength and boldness were what was required in a leader, and Kaira was showing that she had both in abundance.

His faith in her had never been greater than it was in that moment. She was the vision of a goddess, ascending to a gilded throne in her appointed hour.


# ARES

Power gushed in abundance, channeling down the massive, shifting column of light spanning from the roiling skies to the huge, bone-white altar. Deep grooves in the stone flowed thickly with blood, running from the area where the spectral light touched the altar's surface, and continuing down into great crimson pools set to either side.

The broad pools were the headwaters of two demoniac rivers, coursing outward from the altar, and cutting across the barren terrain surrounding the grand shrine to war. From high above, the dense flows looked like lengthy gashes, rending the skin of a diseased body.

Unceasing since the dawn of history, the currents of elemental power were fed by the purest essences of war and violence, irrespective of sides, intents, or causes. Wars in the non-physical realms generated useful energies just as much as did those in the material realms.

Ares had triumphed in harnessing the pure energies within the heart of wars and conflict. His realm gained strength derived from all sides engaged in any kind of martial strife.

No side in a battle could feign innocence, as wickedness found succor deep in the hearts of many comprising the ranks of opposing armies. Soldiers across all time performed acts they would otherwise have deemed unfathomable, if their minds were illuminated with the light of the Enemy.

The sons and daughters of parents in all nations were offered up on the insatiable altar dedicated to the Lord of War. Conceptions of duty and patriotism fed the voracious appetite of the sacrificial altar with the flesh and blood of loved ones. It gorged upon anxiety, sorrow, fear, and mourning, yet generation after generation served Ares purpose without fail, often with thunderous cheers and passion, as they sent rank after rank of sons and daughters into the fetid maw of war.

The fathers and mothers could slow the channel of power to a mere trickle, any moment they chose to do so, but they did not possess the willpower. Instead, they repeated the folly of previous generations, one after the other, increasing the currents of power to Ares' realm many-fold over the ages.

In every victory hailed by a nation, the seeds of future bloodshed were sown within fertile soil. As the Sons of Ares had sprouted wherever the teeth of Ismenios had been scattered, so did new wars erupt all across the mortal world. Violence sired violence, the most egregious affronts to the Enemy being most fruitful, and swiftly multiplying.

Fighting in the mortal realms was unceasing. Ares' might accumulated without pause, making his realm one of the strongest in Diabolos' abyssal kingdom. Ares' dominion served as the outer ramparts of the Ten-Kingdom, the first line of defense, and a staging ground for the great assault that Diabolos would eventually hurl against the reviled White City.

Gazing into the frothing skies, like drifting seas of volcanic ash, Ares basked in the potent energies raining down upon the deathly altar. Anger, bloodlust, hatred, and many other emotions that drove a great portion of violence were intertwined with the icy dispassion that could witness a million beings put to death without hesitation, or regrets of any kind.

Of the two, emotion-driven versus dispassion, the latter was a far more powerful source for the infernal column empowering Ares' domain. Unemotional violence involved the calculated, uncluttered exercise of free will, and was also resistant to the sways that inner emotions could invoke.

Bringing Ares to the heights of ecstasy was the suffering and destruction of the innocent caught up within wars. Whenever the blameless were torn and slain by the storms of war, it was yet another sign that the Enemy's Way did not preside over the world. Any death of innocents was a stark sign that the Enemy could be defied with boldness.

The brilliant fires of Ares' celestial body flared even brighter, as the sweet taste of a wedding destroyed by a flying war machine in the mortal realm suddenly graced him. Including young children, three infants, and a man and woman deeply in love, the joyous gathering had been incinerated just a moment before in a massive explosion.

The hopes and dreams of over thirty souls had screamed out in horror, before abruptly falling into silence. Ares could hear the voice of each one of the dead, savoring the exquisite music of their shock and fear.

The anguished cries and laments rising up in the aftermath from survivors molded a delightful chorus. It was a particular music that Ares relished, each and every time he heard its mellifluous notes.

The usual professions of apology would be made from the side in command of the flying war machines, but the empty words mattered little to the infernal lord. The truth could not evade Ares, as it was the pure source for feeding his power.

The order for the attack had come from men with cool, level-heads, and the one executing it had not flinched even a bit when loosing the hellish missiles. They would all go to sleep that night without pangs of conscience. Their actions were precisely the kind that bolstered the strength of his realm the most; calmly chosen, and impassively carried out.

Ares looked downward, and espied a huge, dark cloud approaching the massive shrine from the distance. It streaked across the barren lands at great velocity.

The cloud was not one of the flocks of Birds of Ares that roamed the tremendous expanse of his realm. Thousands upon thousands of large ravens comprised the dark, amorphous mass, though, as it approached, a distinctive shape began to form out of the avian multitude. A head, six enormous wings, arms, legs, and a torso emerged as the hordes of ravens condensed into a solid-looking form.

At that instant, a flying war machine, in another part of the mortal world, brought eleven more souls to the end of their physical lives. Under the hallowed sanction of an international body, one wicked regime would be replaced with another, one whose deceits would be decidedly more subtle in nature.

While he knew it was all part of the ongoing Convergence in the mortal realm, the conflict presented no concerns to the Lord of War. Ares could not lose, no matter which side prevailed, and the nectar of more immolated souls invigorated his own spirit, as he focused his attentions towards the oncoming figure.

Pulling himself away from the abounding channel of power, Ares moved around the altar. He stopped in front of the wide edifice, quietly awaiting the arrival of the other Avatar; one who was much greater than himself.

The prominent being slowed, fully formed, and glided to a halt before him. Ares, the exalted general of Diabolos, was small in comparison to the Avatar wreathed in a layer of darkness before him. Of the Ten Eminencies serving Diabolos, which reflected ten performing a similar function for the Enemy, Herab-Serap was the seventh.

Each had been provided a glorious throne in the heart of the great Vortex, though each was fully dependent on the preeminent throne of them all, the Risen Throne of Diabolos. They were each possessed of immense power, beyond all Avatars within the Nether Kingdom, but they were also the most closely guided by Diabolos' will.

The personal presence of Herab-Serap in Ares' realm was no casual visit. Ares was very conscious of that fact as he silently regarded the other being.

"Strength beyond strength, the power that you gather pleases Him greatly," thundered the celestial titan.

"All is tribute to His Glory, the Bearer of the True Light," Ares rumbled, deferentially, and reverently.

"The Sons of Ares are a most wondrous gift to His Kingdom," Herab-Serap stated, his sonorous voice encompassing Ares.

"May they help tear the ramparts of the White City down, when He gives us the command," Ares replied.

"A glorious day it will be, when those walls are laid low, and the legions of the Kingdom flood into the Enemy's dominion," Herab-Serap boomed, his voice swelling in volume. "The Shining One has made it known to me that I will join with you here, as the hour draws closer for the great assault. I will commit all my strength and power to your final preparations."

"An honor, to have one of the Ten at my side," Ares replied, extending a slight bow towards the magnificent Avatar.

"You are bestowed with a grace from the Risen Throne, this very day," Herab-Serap announced. "An appointed hour has arrived. A throne is raised in the mortal world. You are called to bear witness, with the greatest of the Ten-Fold Kingdom. Come with me, and stand before the Risen Throne in an hour of triumph."

Like a living storm, rippling with power, Herab-Serap turned and took to the skies. Ares followed in other's wake, as they headed through the churning skies of his realm and continued outward.

Tiny, sparkling lights, the flaming essence of condemned souls raining into the Vortex, cascaded around the multi-winged forms of the Avatars as they plunged downward. They hurtled down the midst of the vast, circling, spectral coils of the Vortex, heading towards the distant, center-most point beckoning with a rapidly surging light.

Other Avatars, all of the highest ranks of their kind, were flying in from every direction. Some emerged from various levels within the concentric rings of light, while others came from the darkness above the Vortex, speeding in from wherever they received the summons.

Ares could already feel the energies swarming within the deepest depths of the Vortex. They called seductively, filled with whispers of an extraordinary order to come. The feeling was exhilarating, permeating him with visions of a dawning new age.

No longer would the Nether Kingdom be confined to the bottomless Abyss. The authority of Diabolos would take hold of all realms, both of spirit and flesh.

At the heart of darkness, Diabolos reigned with unyielding pride, and unrelenting defiance. Ares swept downward, finally reaching the core of the Vortex as he joined the extensive ranks of High Avatars arrayed in splendor before the Risen Throne.

Herab-Serap continued ahead to one of the thrones situated along the outer perimeter of the infernal court. The Risen Throne at its center, the ten thrones of the court were now occupied with the most powerful of the Nether Kingdom; Thaumiel, Chaigidiel, Sathariel, Gamchicoth, Golab, Togarini, Herab-Serap, Sammael, Gamaliel, and Lilith.

All who were present to witness the sacred occasion reflected the Shining One's glory. Each one of them represented vast hordes in the Abyss, strength beyond strength gathering for the moment the thundering rage of Diabolos would be unleashed against the White City.

Only a few layers of the impenetrable darkness flowing around the form of the infernal ruler had been pulled back, hinting at the dazzling brilliance of the Entity they shrouded. Here was the sentient core of the vast worlds contained with the enlarging Vortex, the indomitable will to which all in the Ten-Fold Kingdom submitted.

Displayed before the assembled ranks of mighty Avatars, in front of the Risen Throne, was the figure that had been fading gradually over the long ages of the mortal realm. Ares was elated as he set his eyes upon the barely visible human shape.

The faintest trace of its form was all but imperceptible to the blazing eyes of the hellish throng. The translucent figure perched on the very cusp of vanishing entirely.

Ares knew what the nearly indistinct figure represented. The hated force that had resisted the grandest of incarnations, and prevented its realization for so unbearably long, was finally about to collapse.

Galvanizing, rapturous waves of joy flooded Ares, as they did all of the Dark Avatars. Final events were being set in motion, signaling the completion of the Convergence on the mortal realm; and the imminence of the final struggle against the Enemy.

A haunting, overpowering chorus rang out, as the swirling, cyclone-like tempests at the far boundaries of the massed gathering increased in speed and intensity. The distant echoes of uncountable sorrowful cries and lamentations were swallowed up within the whirling maelstrom forming the edge of the infernal court. The melodious voices of the fallen beings melded in dark union, sending up an infernal hymn of praise and glorification to the Shining One.

Ares and all the other Avatars were delirious with anticipation. They gazed in wonder upon the expanding brilliance of Diabolos, as He revealed the glory of His original form to them in the triumphant moment.

Swirling, dark layers pulled away, revealing beauty and magnificence unsurpassed by any created being. Though His appearance was familiar to all Avatars who had heeded His call to arms, Diabolos was far beyond the High Avatar that He had been, when He had clashed His flaming blade against that of Mikael.

He now wielded the power of a god, taking power to Himself without rest since the outbreak of the Great War. He commanded the substance of darkness, which was infinite in the bottomless pit, and melded it to His will. In the Nether Kingdom alone, He had fashioned realm after realm, and dominion after dominion, each an entire world, in and of itself.

Without boundary in the uncountable fathoms of the Abyss, He could expand the Ten-Fold Kingdom across the reach of eternity, but vengeance loomed. As Ares and all Avatars in allegiance to the Shining One understood to the depths of their being, one Throne remained to be seized. There could be no rest until it was cast down to ruin.

The Shining One's Voice came to each of them, flowing in grace and power, with the caress of a feather, and the thunder of a hurricane. "Behold, Blood of My Blood, in Whom I am well pleased."

The last hint of the figure disappeared from view as the multitude of voices reached a euphoric crescendo. Ecstasy poured over every mighty lord of the darkness as they exalted their Master, whose immortal champion had finally been unleashed upon the world the Enemy provided for humankind.

Worlds away, full incarnation had taken place, the powers of the Enemy no longer able to resist the diabolic manifestation. The darkest, most abominable of spirits ever to be cradled within the hellish depths was now fully ensconced in the midst of the Enemy's precious, and vulnerable, humanity.

The inexorable march towards the final battle had been signaled.

# APPENDIX

**ABUNDANT HARVEST VIRUS** - developed by Dr. Hadar Tricheur, the virus is known by this name among the people that understand and support its purpose, to effectively decrease the world's population. The virus is eventually named the Thanatos virus in the media and public, to reflect its worldwide manifestation and lethal effect.

**ADONAI** - the only being possessing the power of primary creation, the ability to call existence out of nothingness, Adonai transcends all time and space. Adonai's Presence has a manifestation on the Great Throne, which is within the heavenly realms, and is attended by the orders of Avatars and all manner of other spirits who have made it into the higher realms.

**AISHIM** - a special order of Avatars, the Aishim are spirits that were originally mortals, who have been graced with the gift of being an Avatar in the afterworld. Dark Aishim are their counterparts, wicked and malevolent souls that have gained special favor with Diabolos. Entire legions of warriors are formed on both sides out of the Aishim.

**ANAT** - Anat is a Dark Avatar who is one of the consorts of Set. Great in power, she has exacted brutal vengeance on many who have caused harm to figures of the Ten-Fold Kingdom

**AN-KI** - A shape - shifting race introduced in *The Exodus Gate*, where they take the forms of large, wolfish creatures, able to shift between a 4-legged form and a humanoid, 2-legged form. They were being hunted to extinction in the ancient world, at the time of the Great Flood, by the Nephilim. The Nephilim are referred to by the An-Ki as Night Hunters, due to the latter's tendency to strike unexpectedly out of the darkness.

**ANUNNAKI JUDGES** - There are seven Nephilim judges on the Tribunal established by Erishkegal in Manzazu, and they are tasked with making judgments on all matters taking place within the underworld realm. The Nephilim existing in Manzazu go by the name of Anunnaki.

**ANZU** - Lion-headed and eagle-bodied, the Anzu are a form of Nephilim that Friedrich encounters during his visit to Manzazu.

**APEP** - an exceedingly powerful Dark Avatar, who has few peers in the Ten-Fold Kingdom. Often interacts with Set, who periodically renders tribute to Apep in the form of imprisoned souls.

**ARACHA** - also called the Edge Dwellers, or the Sentinels, the Aracha are giant spider-like creatures that take a variety of forms, such as the huge Theraph or the rapid Saltic. They ward the boundaries of Purgatarion, and those that are capable of web-spinning have fashioned an enormous network that reaches far down into the bottomless pit.

**ARES** - A Dark Avatar of great power who draws strength from the very essence of war and violence. Ares realm serves as the outermost boundary of the Ten-Fold Kingdom in the Abyss. Ares realm features a wide array of beings and figures, from the Birds of Ares to the Makhai, all of whom ward the ramparts of Diabolos' infernal kingdom.

**ASTARTE** – Astarte is a Dark Avatar and consort of Set.

**AVATARS** - beings comprised of flame-like light, who vary in power and abilities and are grouped into a variety of orders. Once united, there are now two great factions of Avatars. Following the rebellion of Diabolos, a great number went into the Abyss and joined with Diabolos in the building of the Ten-Fold Kingdom. These are known as the Fallen Avatars.

**AZAZEL** - A powerful Fallen Avatar who was one of the leaders of the effort to take control of the world before the Great Flood. It was Azazel that guided a number of Fallen Avatars into the world, to take on physical forms, and to mate with humans. The offspring of such unions were the Nephilim. Azazel also had a major influence on the development of humans, teaching those that came under his influence the art of weapons and warfare. In the Abyss, he is attended by great numbers of a special kind of Fallen Avatar, called the Seirim.

**BABYLON TECHNOLOGIES** - A multi-national, hi-tech company with military and civilian divisions, whose headquarters is located in Troy, in the UCAS. The CEO of Babylon Technologies is Dagian Underwood.

**CALLIEL** - an Avatar who becomes involved with Benedict and Arianna in the events of *The Exodus Gate*. He plays a pivotal role in the rescue of the An-Ki, and acts as a guide to both them and the small group of humans that aid them.

**CERBERONS** - huge, three-headed, dog-like beasts that are spawned from the union of the Fallen Avatars Typhon and Echidna.

**CHIMAIRA** - another race of offspring from Typhon and Echidna, they are two headed, with one head like that of a lion, and the other of a goat. Their hindquarters are reptilian, including a snake-like tail. They can breathe short jets of fire.

**THE CONVERGENCE** - a term describing the effort to usher in a new global order, one that will bring about a world-spanning law and economic system. While many groups labor to bring about the Convergence, their visions of it range from purely material perspectives to deeply occult ones. The roots of the Convergence goes back thousands of years, and the process has been meticulously guided by Diabolos and other powerful entities from the Abyss. The manipulation of wars and economies, the creation of crisis, and the response to crisis have been major components of each new step along the road to the achievement of The Convergence.

**THE CRAFT** - the mystic, occult arts aligned with the will of Diabolos. Only a special few who have pledged their entire beings and souls to Diabolos are given access and revelation pertaining to the Ten-Fold Kingdom, and are able to wield spiritual powers derived from the Abyss. Dagian Underwood is one of the most powerful of those who practice the Craft, but with the granting of such power comes the tether of responsibility, and accountability.

**THE CRYSTAL FORESTS OF PURGATARION** - immaculate and breathtaking, the Crystal Forests of Purgatarion are where the Exiles can obtain the material they need to fashion hand-wielded weapons that draw off of their own spirit to empower them. As a spirit in Exile cannot draw forth a weapon from their own essence, like the Avatars do when they pull forth fiery blades or spears from their own forms, the Crystal Forests are vital for those Exiles that choose to help defend Purgatarion.

**DEIMOS** - One of two fearsome Dark Avatars who are like lieutenants to Ares, and dwell in his realm.

**DIABOLOS** - also referred to as the Shining One, the Light Giver, the Morning Star, and other names, Diabolos is the lord of the Ten-Fold Kingdom, the greatest power within the Abyss. Diabolos has grown in might ever since leading the first rebellion that began the Great War, and always hungers to be equivalent to Adonai, the only being in existence greater than Diabolos.

**DJINN** - gargantuan elemental beings that manifest most often as maelstroms of fire. They ward the Void, and take no active part in the Great War. They respond to any disturbance in the Void, such as spirit beings crossing to and from the material planes.

**EGALKURZAGIN** - This is a great palace complex located within and atop a towering plateau in Manzazu. It contains the Sanctum, which is where Erishkegal can most often be found in her underworld realm.

**EMQU** - A serpent-headed Anunnaki, one of the seven judges on the Anunnaki Tribunal.

**ENYO** - One of the several powerful Dark Avatars that dwell in Ares Realm. Enyo is extremely powerful, and is accompanied often by a very fearsome, monstrous demonic entity called Kydoimos.

**ETHON** - giant eagle-like creatures that are the spawn of Typhon and Echidna. Used both for attack, and to ferry the flightless hellspawn to and from the depths of the Abyss.

**EXECUTIVE ORDER 2013** - This is given by UCAS president William Walker, to impose martial law across the country.

**FUSION CENTERS** - Locations housing personnel and technology for multiple security and surveillance organizations that are part of the UCAS government. They are located all across the country, and they share databases and resources.

**GERYON** - brawny and towering in height, the Geryon are offspring of Typhon and Echidna that serve to drive the Orthun into battle, acting like pack-masters. Set upon two thick legs, multiple torsos sprout upward on each Geryon, each torso fitted with powerful arms and a head. The Geryon carry obsidian shields and spear - like weapons that act similar to the crystal weapons carried by the denizens of Purgatarion, in that they draw their force from the spirit of the wielder.

**GODRAL** - the principle lieutenant to Sargor, Godral is a powerful An-

Ki warrior, who is dedicated to his leader and mentor. Godral's Life Mate is Mariassa, and the An-Ki warriors that he is closest to are Kantel and Valia.

**GODWINTON** - This is the town where Ian, Sheriff Howard, and many others live. It becomes quite a focal point in the *Rising Dawn Saga* for the resistance.

**THE GREAT WAR (ALSO KNOWN AT THE FIRST WAR)** - This is the war being fought by Diabolos against Adonai, hearkening back to the initial rebellion when a host of Avatars sided with Diabolos.

**THE GREY LANDS** - A dreary part of the Middle Lands that has broken off, and contains Exiles who are tilting closer and closer to abandoning a path to the White City. It is still warded by Adonai's guardians, but is increasingly infiltrated by the things of the Abyss.

**GRYPHONS** - creatures of legend in the material world, Gryphons populate the Purgatarion, where they help to protect the Exiles. With the head of eagles, and the bodies of lions, they are swift and powerful.

**GULAGAR** - not unlike a living Gargoyle, these creatures are as still as stone wherever they position themselves throughout Purgatarion, mostly keeping to lofty overlooks. Whenever a creature of the Abyss draws near, they come into full consciousness and motion. Tall, winged, and daunting in appearance, they are one of the strongest guardians for the Exiles.

**HERAB-SERAP** - A very powerful Avatar, one of the Ten who attend Diabolos at the Risen Throne.

**THE HUNT** - presided over by the Avatar Arawn, and a penitent, but powerful, human spirit named Mallt, the Hunt consists of a horde of massive hounds that track and pursue anything from the Abyss foolish enough to linger for very long within the boundaries of Purgatarion.

**INITIATES OF THE FAITH** - humans who have willfully committed themselves to Diabolos. They are very involved in the Convergence, and hold or have been placed in many key positions of authority or responsibility. From special units of soldiers, to officers, to administrators and executives, the Initiates of the Faith see to the things that must be done to clear obstacles and advance the Convergence. Unlike many who work for the Convergence, they understand the true source of the effort.

**ISMENIOS** - One of the offspring of Ares, whose physical teeth are used to give rise to a new, powerful group of beings, the Sons of Ares.

**JEQONADIN** - One of the Nephilim, Jeqonadin is the son of the Fallen Avatar Jeqon. Of the Nephilim that share its form, Jeqonadin is the mightiest, and is a relentless hunter of the An-Ki.

**KYDOIMOS** - A huge demonic being that dwells in the realm of Areas, and often accompanies the Dark Avatar Enyo.

**KYKNOS** - One of the offspring of Ares who died when the Great Flood was loosed on the world to destroy the Nephilim. Kyknos always desired to build a temple made out of human skulls, and Ares raised a ghastly temple of skulls in his realm to honor the wish by his son.

**LADON** - the Ladon are titanic, wingless, dragon - like creatures with as many as a hundred heads. Mainly confined to the Ten-Fold Kingdom, they have not been used in war upon the Middle Lands prior to the events of *The Storm Guardians*.

**LIFE MATE** - the An-Ki are monogamous creatures that mate for life. The Life Mate is the special male or female that an An-Ki forms a deep bond with. Only with a Life Mate does an An-Ki engage in Life Unions, which take place during one special time of each year, and results in new life. The bonds and commitments of Life Mates , and the connection of those elements to the generation of new life, resonate at very sacred levels with the An-Ki.

**LILITH** - A Dark Avatar who is one of the Consorts of Sammael. Lilith provides guidance to Jovan Avery, and helps with the progress of the Convergence in the modern age.

**LIVING ID** - Living ID is a nanoscale implant that is part of a comprehensive personal identity system that was developed by Babylon Technologies to help in the final stages of the Convergence. It ties everything together, from financial transactions, to health care, to personal identity, and with full implementation, no individual can function in society without it.

**MADISON**- A town in the province of Venorterra larger than Godwinton, where Seth and others live.

**MAKHAI** - A formidable group of demonic entities that are in service to Ares in his realm. The Makhai are warriors, and are at the forefront of Ares' best legions.

**MANZAZU** - the name of Erishkegal's underworld realm.

**MIKAEL** - the great general of Adonai, Mikael led the legions that hurled Diabolos and his legions out of the heavenly realms following the outbreak of the Great War. It was Mikael that announced the coming of the Deluge to the Fallen Avatars that had become incarnate to give rise to the Nephilim.

**NAMTAR** - Namtar is Erishkegal's vizier, who dwells in Egalkurzagin when not needed at the Anunnaki Tribunal.

**NEMEANS** - massive lion-like spawn of Typhon and Echidna, these creatures from the Abyss are capable of great speed and punishing attacks, and are often deployed in large numbers.

**NEPHILIM** - also referred to as the Erkorenen, the Night Hunters, or the Annunaki, they are the offspring of Fallen Avatars and humans, who came into existence during the age prior to the Great Flood. They have a variety of sizes, shapes, and forms, as the blood of the Fallen Avatars expressed itself in the generation of all manner of monstrosities that serve as the basis for most all of the mythical and legendary creatures, in all cultures across the world.

**NETI** - Neti is the giant Anunnaki that wards the seventh and final gate into Manzazu. Neti is the most formidable and wisest of the gate guardians, and is the final authority on allowing access into Manzazu.

**NINGISHZIDA** - Ningishzida holds the one of the highest levels of martial authority in Manzazu, and commands its defense and issues of security.

**NUMMUS** - This is the monetary unit that is planned to replace the UCAS dollar and other currencies, and will serve as a true global currency, though it will not exist in a physical fashion.

**THE ORDER** – A dedicated order of men that have existed since the Holy Wars, several hundred years ago. They are still called Knights, honoring that legacy, and are involved in active resistance against the forces behind the Convergence.

**ORDER OF THE TEMPLE** - a centuries-old secret society that is one of several that have come together to advance the Convergence. Members of the Order of the Temple have their own system, signs, and practices, but they have come to work closely with other orders sharing the common cause of bringing about a new global order.

**PARZILLU** - The name of one of the Anunnaki judges of the Anunnaki Tribunal. Parzillu has a fierce leonine countenance.

**PEACE COMMISSION (OF THE WORLD SUMMIT)** - A very powerful part of the World Summit tasked with facilitating peace among and within nations.

**PERIS** - a fairy - like race of spirits, who once sided with Diabolos, but have come to reject their ways and seek to gain Adonai's kingdom. They live among the Exiles in the Middle Lands, where they must face their greatest enemies, the bestial Deevs, from time to time. Asa'an, a Peri encountered in *The Exodus Gate*, has a friendship with the Exile Friedrich, and helped him to witness the rare appearance of Quilin within the Middle Lands.

**PHOBOS** - like Deimos, a Dark Avatar who is a lieutenant to Ares, who dwells in his realm.

**PYLONS** - Among the Walkers of the Setian Path, focused groups have formed behind the leadership of powerful priests. These groups, called Pylons, tend to explore or focus upon certain specific aspects of the non-physical, and are named according to their special area of emphasis.

**PURGATARION** - also called the Middle Lands, Purgatarion is where spirits that are not yet pure enough to enter the heavenly realms, but are not wicked enough to fall into the Abyss, take refuge. A variety of guardians have been placed in the Middle Lands to help protect the Exiles, such as Wyverns, Gryphons, the Aracha, the Hunt, the Gulagar, and many more.

**QUERAN** - the An-Ki leader of one of the three clans that exist after the schism of Sargor's original group that came through the gate. She is supported by a great warrior named Gorthaur.

**QUILIN** - fearsomely powerful creatures of the heavenly realms that diligently protect the pure of spirit. They are encountered in *the Exodus Gate*, accompanying a group of child-spirits being guided by the High Avatar Metaraon

**THE REMAKING** - The Remaking is the goal of Diabolos, in which all of creation would be reshaped according to the Shining One's will, following the overthrow of Adonai.

**REMIEL** - One of Adonai's greatest Avatars, one of seven who personally attend the Great Throne.

**THE RISEN THRONE** - the seat of Diabolos at the 10th level, it represents the genesis of the Ten-Fold Kingdom following the fall from the heavenly realms.

**SAMMAEL** - one of the greatest of the Fallen Avatars, Sammael has three consorts, Lilith, Namaah, and Agrat Bat Mahlat. Sammael came into the world to subdue it, and prepare the way for the ascension of Diabolos in the time before the Great Flood.

**SARGOR** - aging leader of the largest faction of An-Ki following the schism in the forest. Sargor is the father of Sarangar, and is supported steadfastly in his leadership by Godral.

**SEIRIM** - goat-like, demonic creatures that serve the Fallen High Avatar Azazel. They walk upon two legs and have a humanoid body, with a goat's head.

**SET** - A High Avatar in service to Diabolos. His realm features extraordinary deserts, pyramids, and obelisks, and a special order of priests, the Priests of Set, have been established to administer Set's realm within the Ten Fold Kingdom.

**SHIELD MAIDENS OF THE RISING DAWN** - Another long-lasting order that has existed for centuries, the Shield Maidens are women who actively fight against the groups involved with the Convergence. Their activities span all spheres, from physical combat, to politics, and economic activity.

**SPHINGON** - another kind of offspring from Typhon and Echidna, these winged creatures have lion-like bodies with the heads of stunningly beautiful human women, only their jaws are lined with an arsenal of long, spiky teeth.

**SOCIETY OF THE RED SHIELD** - one of the age - old secret societies that are working towards the attainment of The Convergence. Jovan Avery is a member of this Society, and after reaching its highest level has been introduced to spiritual entities that have given him greatly useful advice and guidance.

**THE TEN EMINENCIES** - also referred to sometimes as the Grand Council of the 10th Hell, these are Fallen Avatars of great authority, each one empowered by Diabolos over one of the 10 Hells that comprise the Ten-Fold Kingdom.

**THE TEN-FOLD KINGDOM** - the great Vortex, the realm of Diabolos which is ordered into ten general levels, represented by the Ten Eminencies that attend to Diabolos around the Risen Throne. Each of the ten levels are a Hell each and of themselves, containing innumerable environments and lesser realms.

**THANATOS VIRUS** - The public/media-given name for the Abundant Harvest Virus that ravages the world unexpectedly.

**TROY** - the third largest city in the UCAS, where Babylon Technologies is headquartered. Troy is also where Benedict Darwin hosted Sea to Shining Sea, and is also the location of St. Bosco, the Universalist church where Father Brunner and Father Rader are.

**THE VOID** - the Void is the inner space between the material planes and the non-physical realms. It contains the unconscious spirits that have fallen in conflicts and battles across the ages, and is guarded by the great Djinn, gargantuan elemental beings that manifest most often as maelstroms of fire.

**URIA** - leader of the third faction of An-Ki following the schism of the original clan that came through the gate. Uria's clan is the smallest of the three, and contains no elderly or young, but has some of the most physical, dangerous warriors of the surviving An-Ki.

**WALKERS OF THE SETIAN PATH** - A mystical order dedicated to Set. Set has given power and patronage to this order, revealing hidden arts to those he deems worthy. They are organized into groups called Pylons.

**WATCHERS** - two groups of Watchers are portrayed in the *Rising Dawn Saga*. The first were servants of Adonai originally, who were assigned to monitor the world. They were seduced into joining with the Fallen Avatars that took on physical bodies and mated with humans to produce the Nephilim. A new order of Watchers was raised up following the great deluge, huge, multi-winged beings, with many eyes, long, extended bodies with four legs, out of which rises a humanoid torso with arms. They are of four general types; echoing the forms of bulls, eagles, lions, and humans.

**THE WHITE CITY** - a resplendent, pure city with towering ramparts and a great, golden gate that serves as the eastern boundary of Purgatarion. Beyond it are the infinite realms of Adonai, and only a pure soul can approach and pass through the gate. For Exiles, the brightness of it is too dazzling to even gaze upon.

**THE WHITE PYRAMID** - located in the UCAS capital, the White Pyramid houses the Minstry of Defense.

**WORLD SUMMIT** - The World Summit is a member - based world body that the advocates of the Convergence would like to evolve into a true world governing authority.

**WYVERNS** - two-legged, dragon-like creatures, the Wyverns are another race of guardians provided by Adonai to protect the souls dwelling in Purgatarion.

**ZEYYA** - A female An-Ki who is close to Uria. She harbors a deep hatred of humans and the things of their world.

# ABOUT THE AUTHOR

Born in Denver, Colorado, Stephen Zimmer is an award-winning fantasy author and filmmaker based out of Lexington, Kentucky.

Stephen has two series being published through Seventh Star Press. One is the epic fantasy *Fires in Eden Series*, and the other is the epic scale urban fantasy series *The Rising Dawn Saga*. *Crown of Vengeance*, the first book of the *Fires in Eden Series*, garnered Stephen his first literary accolade with a 2010 Pluto Award for Best Novel.

Other published works include the Harvey and Solomon steampunk short stories "In the Mountain Skies" (*Dreams of Steam* anthology, edited by Kimberly Richardson, Kerlak Publishing) and "An Island Sojourn" (*Dreams of Steam II: Of Bolts and Brass*, edited by Kimberly Richardson, Kerlak Publishing).

As a filmmaker, Stephen has credits in fantasy and horror, including the supernatural thriller *Shadows Light* (feature), *The Sirens* (horror short film), and *Swordbearer* (fantasy short film based upon the H. David Blalock novel *Ascendant*)

In addition to his busy writing and filmmaking endeavors, Stephen appears regularly at conventions, bookstores, and a range of other events, maintaining a thorough, year-round personal appearance schedule that is one of the most active in the industry.

Updates and information about Stephen can always be obtained at:
www.stephenzimmer.com.
http://stephenzimmer.blogspot.com
www.facebook.com/sgzimmer
Twitter:www.twitter.com/sgzimmer
And now on Google+

photo courtesy of Patrick Bowling

Check out the following pages to see more from

All Seventh Star Press titles available in print and an array of specially priced eBook formats.

Visit www.seventhstarpress.com for further information.

Connect with Seventh Star Press at:
www.seventhstarpress.com
seventhstarpress.blogspot.com
www.facebook.com/seventhstarpress

Now Available from Seventh Star Press, Michael West's newest
Harmony, Indiana novel, featuring illustrations and cover art by
acclaimed artist Matthew Perry!

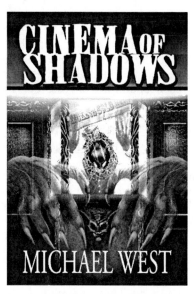

Trade Paperback ISBN: 9780983740209
eBook ISBN: 9780983740216

# Welcome to the Woodfield Movie Palace.

The night the Titanic sank, it opened for business...
and its builder died in his chair.   In the 1950s, there was
a fire; a balcony full of people burned to death.  And years
later, when it became the scene of one of Harmony, Indiana's
most notorious murders, it closed for good.  Abandoned,
sealed, locked up tight...until now.

Tonight, Professor Geoffrey Burke and his
Parapsychology students have come to the Woodfield in
search of evidence, hoping to find irrefutable proof of a
haunting.  Instead, they will discover that, in this theater,
the terrors are not confined to the screen.

**Immerse into epic fantasy and let your imagination soar with two incredible series from the mind of Stephen Zimmer.**

## Epic Fantasy-Fires in Eden Series

Explore the lands, seas, and skies of Ave in this epic fantasy adventure, as eleven individuals from the modern world find themselves in lands both wondrous and dangerous. The enigmatic figure known as The Unifier has unleashed a war to end all wars, but the nature of it is far more insidious than any of the kings and rulers supporting it can possibly imagine. The fate of Ave hangs in the balance, as the eleven exiles discover the reasons for their presence, and the choices that they will have to make in response.

# Book One: Crown of Vengeance
### ISBN: 978-0982565612

"This is definitely a book for people who like character driven stories with gorgeous and detailed descriptions of a fantasy world and their inhabitants mixed with beings who follow devious plans who will face more resistance than expected....."

**-Only the Best SciFi/Fantasy**

"For me to say so many great things about a fantasy book is an accomplishment as these types of books used to be towards the bottom on my list that I was willing to read. This book with the help of Mr. Zimmer has restored my faith that fantasy makes for some thrilling reading."

**-Cheryl's Book Nook**

# Book Two: Dream of Legends
### ISBN: 978-0983108627

"Dream of Legends is a solid installment to the Fires in Eden series and left me hanging on to read book three."

**-Bookworm Blues**

## Epic Urban Fantasy-The Rising Dawn Saga

A shadow falls across the world, and realms beyond, as a war that has raged since the dawn of time itself draws closer to a decisive clash. As groups aligned with a movement called The Convergence speed up their efforts to bring about a global economic and legal order, resistance mounts after the host of a syndicated radio show, Benedict Darwin, discovers the true nature of a virtual reality device that has come into his possession. The Rising Dawn Saga will take you into mythical, supernatural realms as it unfolds, as the most unlikely of individuals rise to confront powers that have existed since before the world began.

## Book One:  The Exodus Gate
### ISBN: 978-0615267470

"With The Exodus Gate author Stephen Zimmer sets the stage for an adventurous new science fiction fantasy series that is sure to entertain the reader from beginning to end. Zimmer has weaved a tale of fantastic realms populated with exotic creatures. Keep a sharp eye out for this new series."
**-Mark Randell, Yellow30 Sci-Fi**

"...a book that Fantasy Book Review recommends for lovers of thoughtful-fantasy. It is also a book with an ending that is near-prophetic, written as it was before the world's economic meltdown."
**-Fantasy Book Review**

## Book Two:  The Storm Guardians
### ISBN: 978-0982565636

"This novel transports me from my bedroom to the edge of an upcoming storm — a battle to be fought by incredible villains and noble heroes of all forms. I love Zimmer's imagination, as each of his creatures play a pivotal role in the bigger picture. Unfortunately, for every auspicious being there is an ominous beast lurking in the shadows. Zimmer's weave of fantasy and religious fables leaves the reader sated"
**-Bitten By Books**

"The scope of The Storm Guardians is massive, opening up and expanding on the conflict only hinted at in The Exodus Gate. The intrigue and action promised in the first book is fully developed and mercilessly exhibited. The Storm Guardians is a non-stop thriller that lives up to the promise of The Exodus Gate and points at an even more amazing denouement in the final book of the series. Once again, Zimmer has used his command of cinematic imagery to give us a spectacular vision of war both heavenly and hellish. Two thumbs up on this one."
**-Pure Reason Book Review**

Now Available from Seventh Star Press, Jackie Gamber's
fantasy novel REDHEART, featuring illustrations and cover art by
fantasy artist Matthew Perry!

Trade Paperback ISBN: 9780983108672
eBook ISBN: 9780983108696

Enter the lands of Leland Province, where dragon and human societies have long dwelled side by side. Superstitions rise sharply, as a severe drought strips the land of its bounty, providing fertile ground for the darker ambitions of Fordon Blackclaw, Dragon Council Leader, who seeks to subdue humans or wipe them off the face of the land.

As the shadow of danger creeps across Leland Province, a young dragon named Kallon Redheart, who has turned his back on dragons and humans alike, comes into an unexpected friendship. Riza Diantus is a young woman whose dreams can no longer be contained by the narrow confines of her village, and when she finds herself in peril, Kallon is the only one with the power to save her. Yet to do so means he must confront his past, and embrace a future he stopped believing in.

A tale of friendship, courage, and ultimate destiny, *Redheart* invites readers to a wondrous journey through the *Leland Dragon Series*.

Now Available from Seventh Star Press, Steven Shrewsbury's hard-hitting, heroic fantasy novel THRALL, featuring illustrations and cover art by fantasy artist Matthew Perry!

Trade Paperback ISBN: 9780983108634
eBook ISBN: 9780983108641

## For Gorias La Gaul…
## Deliverance Will Come

Set in the mists of ancient times, *Thrall* tells the story of Gorias La Gaul, an aging warrior who has lived for centuries battling the monstrosities of legend and lore. It is an age when the Nephilum walk the earth, demonic forces hunger to be unleashed, and dragons still soar through the skies … living and undead. On a journey to find one of his own blood, a young man who is caught in the shadow of necromancy, Gorias' path crosses with familiar enemies, some of whom not even death can hold bound.

*Thrall* is gritty, dark-edged heroic fantasy in the vein of Robert E. Howard and David Gemmell. It is a maelstrom of hard-hitting action and unpredictable imagery, taking place within an incredible antediluvian world. In Gorias La Gaul, *Thrall* introduces an iconic new character to the realms of fantasy literature. Thrall invites the reader to go on a perilous journey where it is not a matter of whether one has the courage to die, but whether one has the courage to live.

All Seventh Star Press titles available in print and an array of specially priced eBook formats. Visit www.seventhstarpress.com for further information.

# Coming Late Fall 2011 from

 SEVENTH STAR PRESS

CPSIA information can be obtained at www.ICGtesting.com
Printed in the USA
LVOW101318180613

339132LV00005B/48/P

9 780983 740247